JUBILEE JIM
AND THE
WIZARD
OF
WALL STREET

JUBILEE JIM

AND THE

WIZARD OF WALL STREET

Donald Porter

DUTTON NEW YORK

DUTTON
Published by the Penguin Group
Penguin Books USA Inc.,
375 Hudson Street, New York, New York, U.S.A. 10014
Penguin Books Ltd,
27 Wrights Lane, London W8 5TZ, England
Penguin Books Australia Ltd,
Ringwood, Victoria, Australia
Penguin Books Canada,
2801 John Street, Markham, Ontario, Canada L3R 1B4
Penguin Books (N.Z.) Ltd.,
182–190 Wairau Road, Auckland 10, New Zealand

Penguin Books Ltd, Registered Offices:
Harmondsworth, Middlesex, England

First published by Dutton,
an imprint of Penguin Books USA Inc.
Published simultaneously in Canada
by Fitzhenry & Whiteside Limited.

First printing, April 1990

1   3   5   7   9   10   8   6   4   2

Library of Congress Cataloging-in-Publication Data

Porter, Donald, 1939–
Jubilee Jim and the wizard of Wall Street / Donald Porter. — 1st ed.
p.   cm.
ISBN 0-525-24841-2
I. Title.
PS3566.064429J83   1990
813'.54—dc20   89-36184
CIP

Printed in the United States of America

Designed by REM Studio

To my wife, Diane

CONTENTS

Part One

THE
FLIGHT
TO
JERSEY

*All the world over, poverty
is a misfortune. In New
York, it is a crime.*

—James McCabe,
   *Lights & Shadows
   of New York Life,* 1882

1

I use the Harlem Central just as though it all belonged to me, and that is the way I shall control every other railroad as long as I control any, as though it all belonged to me.

—Commodore Cornelius Vanderbilt, 1869

The large black carriage pushed its way southward along Broadway, which at midmorning was at the peak of its daily frenzy.

Oxen wagons blocked white public omnibuses, and the liveried drivers of spidery cabriolets lashed at squealing pigs to move them from under their wheels. Battered delivery vans cut off aristocratic victorias. Hanging in the air were street grit, cinders, burnt offal, and fish scrap. Dampened by the cold, raw mist, the driver of the large carriage—a ponderous, hulking victoria—was huddled in his greatcoat to keep the March chill at bay, while he expertly picked a path through the logjam of carriages, carts, wagons, vans, pigs, and goats.

William Henry Vanderbilt, seemingly above the fray, was settled comfortably against the massive victoria's leather cushions. His pasty, middle-aged face gazed through the window glass with dignified amusement, while his intelligent blue eyes followed with sharp interest the progress of the melee. Second-in-command of the mighty New York Central Railroad, he was returning from three weeks of business in Chicago, a large city but a placid village compared with Manhattan's boiling, angry bedlam.

Red-faced drivers argued. Whips cracked. Tempers clashed. William's thick Vanderbilt lips lifted in a slight smile. Impatient passengers leaned from the windows of elegant hansoms and cabriolets and shoved themselves into the arguments. Fashionably dressed ladies as well as gents tossed in well-aimed, sharp remarks at drivers and other passengers. To see better, William lowered the greasy window glass; the stench of sulfur, unlimed privies, horse sweat, and pig droppings assaulted his nose. Broadway appeared more like a smelly dung heap on which elephantine insects battled for fodder than the center of the New World's civilization.

William's victoria lurched forward. A boy's grimy face appeared at the carriage's high window.

"Give me something, mister!" shouted the boy, and his head swayed as he struggled to maintain his balance on the small steel step below the victoria door. William laughed, for he admired a fellow who took a risk for reward, and dug in his pocket.

"Sure, sonny!" Afraid that if he tossed the quarter the boy would miss it and fall beneath his wheels' iron rims, William leaned over and stuck the coin between the boy's rotten teeth. A fast widening of his eyes and a bob of his head were all the thanks the boy gave before he dropped out of sight.

William slid across the cushion and poked his head into the damp and heavy air, afraid he would find the boy sliced in two. Only churning iron rims on cobblestones, no blood or writhing limbs—the boy was gone, swallowed up by the closely packed carriages.

His hand on the windowsill, plump features creased by an amused grin, William stared at the swarm on the far sidewalk. Although he had grown up in New York, the vitality of its bold, restless people still fascinated him.

On the corner stood a tall, lean bank messenger with plump satchels likely full of gold and bonds. That pudgy telegraph boy in the neat brown uniform might well be carrying words hastily scribbled ten minutes ago in California: "BUY 1,000 TONS COTTON AT $400." "SELL 10,000 OUNCES GOLD AT MARKET." The fat, pig-faced man who leaned out of his carriage's window and screamed up at his sullen driver was a steelmaker more important to the fate of his fellows than many kings.

In every face warred the familiar New York struggle, a mixture of hope and cynicism. Every New Yorker possessed a ready eagerness for the main chance along with a jaded look; sharp, alert eyes darted between cheeks and brows grown weary of the city's thousand jangling stimulations.

Twenty minutes later, William stood in the warmth of his father's seventh-floor office.

Cornelius Vanderbilt, founder of the line, stood at the side of his rolltop desk, a white-haired, hawk-nosed, bull of a man in his middle seventies. As usual, William's father conveyed the air of resenting his Maker's great trick in aging him.

"What's going on, Pa?" asked William.

"Going on?" said Cornelius. "Nothing."

Puzzled, William looked around. The largest office in the Central Railroad building, designed by his father when the building was erected, it was twenty feet square with a twelve-foot ceiling. Four three-quarter-length windows opened onto Broadway, four onto Pearl Street. Around the walls mahogany panels came up waist-high, while a six-globe chandelier out of a ship's ballroom was suspended from the plaster ceiling. Nothing really unusual—despite files heaped on the broad worktable and the rolltop desk, visitors' chairs parked helter-skelter—but his father's office felt different, electric with tension.

The amusement William had felt in his carriage dribbled away. He was uneasy, as if three weeks in the milder pace of Chicago had ruined him for the tumult of New York. Stephens, the New York Central's chief clerk, scurried out of Cornelius's office uncharacteristically fast. On William's heels Judge George Barnard crept in. In contrast to the usual mood of the Central's executive offices—the unhurried calm on the bridge of an enormous ocean liner with a solid, experienced captain at its helm—the whole office, acres of clerks and junior executives, possessed the flurried air of a henhouse preparing for the entrance of a particularly vicious terrier. Besides, Pa was avoiding his eye. William nodded toward Barnard, who stupidly bobbed his head in William's direction like a toy cuckoo.

"What's he doing here in the middle of the day?" asked William.

His father and Judge Barnard stood silently in front of him. At forty-three, the portly, raccoon-faced judge wasn't of his father's generation, indeed was a couple years younger than William, yet the two were cronies. They saw each other almost every day, and the judge issued any court order that the Central needed.

"Why are all those police vans downstairs?" William pushed on. "Has there been a train crash?" Barnard's glazed smile tentatively widened. The uneasy tightness in William's shoulders increased. His father's face was redder than usual, his blue eyes bulging, as if some pressure within might cause his head to explode.

"I'm going to put him out of business, son!" shouted Cornelius.

William shook his head and frowned. "Who, Pa?"

"Drew," shouted his father, referring to his old riverboat rival, Daniel Drew, who now ran the Erie Railroad. "He's pulled his last trick, his last swindle." William smiled and swallowed in relief. He dropped his coat onto the broad worktable, on which were heaped stock certificates in a dozen wire baskets.

"Come on, Pa," said William. "What would you two do without each other?" He turned to Barnard. "What's it now, Judge? An injunction to make the Erie's engineers toot their whistles when a Central caboose goes by?"

Barnard's pained grin expanded and he continued to stare at William in a glassy-eyed way. Barnard was giving William the creeps.

"All right, Pa," William tried again. "What's up?"

"Not much."

"Don't 'not much' me," said William. "What is it?"

"He stole our money."

"What did you do to him?" asked William, sighing with the exasperation of a parent forced to unravel a quarrel between children. Indeed, his bull-like father and his old whist-playing crony Daniel Drew were more like William's gawky sons than adults, always wrangling. Barnard's creepy air gave it away. A judge ought to separate them, not egg on two old roosters so his law firm could collect more fat fees.

For a seventy-five-year-old afflicted with gout, arthritis, a bad back and hip, Cornelius spun around quickly. He grabbed a double handful of thick certificates off his desk.

"These, William!" He was practically sputtering. "Look at them!" Confused, William plucked a share certificate from his father's hand. The paper was thick, heavy parchment; the lavish green, black, and gold engraving announced its value.

"Erie stock?" asked William.

"Yes, newly issued," said Cornelius. "Issued *last week*." Barnard cleared his throat.

"The Erie bylaws specifically prohibit the issuance of new shares," Barnard said in his sternest courtroom bass. "Trusting those bylaws, your father bought a substantial amount of the subject shares—" The words wound around William like a cloud of obfuscating smoke.

"How much?" William asked sharply, dreading the answer.

"A few thousand," Cornelius said. The answer was too casual. The stock certificate crackled as William opened it, and the acrid odor of fresh ink hit his nose.

"A few thousand what?" William pressed. The certificate was for a hundred shares. Cornelius's blue glare ignored his son's question and fixed instead on the potbellied judge.

"Write out that warrant, Judge," Cornelius ordered. He picked up the black coat on the back of his chair and made for the door. "Time's wasting."

William stepped forward and blocked his way. "Hold on," he demanded. "A few thousand what?"

His father looked up, sheepish. "Shares," his father answered in a small voice. Uneasiness nibbled at the base of William's spine. He took a deep breath.

"How many thousand shares?"

"Ten thousand," said Cornelius. "At first."

"Ten thou—" William looked at the stock certificate in his hand. On it a gold locomotive chugged over a green-and-black bridge that bravely spanned the gaping chasm of a green mountain. "How many all told?" Under William's coat on the worktable rose piles of similar stock certificates, and now that he examined it, his father's desk didn't hold its customary clutter of newspapers and correspondence, but another dozen baskets of black-and-green certificates.

William turned to the eight windowsills. Four foot-high piles of certificates sat on each. More wire baskets, each with its jumble of crisp certificates, were on the floor along the base of the walls. A flash of memory made William spring to the door, which opened onto the clerk's bull pen. On the desks of the five clerks nearest the entrance were also dozens of wire baskets, each piled with the black, gold, and green of Erie certificates, and on the floor by their desks squatted yet more baskets, each stuffed with plump certificates. Dozens, scores of wire baskets, each crammed with Erie shares! One hand clutching the doorjamb, William turned and gave his father a look of wild demand.

"Two hundred thousand," said Cornelius softly.

William advanced toward his father. "At forty dollars a share! My God, Pa—that's—that's eight million dollars. What do you want to do, take over the Erie? Oh, no—you didn't try—" Stunned, he dropped into a visitor's chair and stared at his father. "You bought new stock, right? And it's all watered, worthless?"

Judge Barnard leaned over him, his tricky eyes narrowed. "That's right, watered stock. It's fraud, that's what it is. And fraud is still illegal in New York State." The Judge rattled the blue-backed set of legal-looking papers in his hand. "I'm signing a warrant right now for Mr. Drew's arrest."

"Arrest? You're going to arrest Uncle Dan'l?" In his youth William had once worked for him and like most on Wall Street called him "Uncle Dan'l" behind his back. Barnard raised a stern forefinger.

"I will keep him in the Ludlow Street Jail till he buys back these worthless shares," he said. It was unsettling to picture Uncle Dan'l—near eighty and far more frail than William's father—in jail. A few weeks in filth and dampness would kill the old miser. Cornelius cleared his throat.

"And you'll hold everyone on his board of directors."

Barnard nodded eagerly. "Of course."

All the amusement William had felt a half hour earlier was gone. This was a vast loss. It was as if a large hole had been blown in the hull of a mammoth ocean steamer below the waterline; those on the bridge didn't know whether the ship would go to the bottom or not, but they knew they had sustained a serious blow, an injury they must attend to speedily. Eight million dollars!—why, such a fabulous sum lost, once word hit Wall Street, would start a panic in New York Central stock that—for all its massive strength—would bankrupt William and his father. William's mouth was dry. For a moment his father's red face, the stacks and stacks of stock certificates, and Barnard's gray flesh wavered before his eyes.

"Pa, you've been a damn fool!" said William.

"Son, I own this railroad," Cornelius threw back. William sat up straight.

"Not for long if you keep up this craziness."

"Are you calling your father crazy?" shouted Cornelius.

"When he acts like a senile old fool—yes, I will." For a few seconds father and son glared at each other. With a growl of exasperation, William shoved himself up out of the visitor's chair. "So what are we going to do?" he asked.

"We've got police vans downstairs as well as vans of our own detectives," said Cornelius. "I'm going to serve this damn warrant myself."

"I can't even go to Chicago for a couple of weeks without all hell breaking loose," said William. He picked up his coat, which caused a foot-high stack of Erie certificates to slide to the floor. God knew what fresh trouble his father would start this morning. "I'm coming with you."

Broadway at midday was like a mighty river jammed with logs and debris; nothing moved. Ineptly holding his fury in check, Cornelius Vanderbilt clutched Barnard's warrant in his left hand while his right clung to the black leather strap by the carriage's window. The carriage occasionally lurched forward, moving freely only a few moments at a time. He had hoped to settle this business with Daniel before William came home; instead his son sat across from him, occasionally shaking his head in a sour way.

"Hurry, Henry, will you?" Cornelius bellowed up the speaking hole to his driver, but there was little Henry could do but shout at other drivers, provoking only curses in response.

Unable to sit still, Cornelius twisted about helplessly on the leather cushions. His home for all his seventy-five years, New York had become nearly too large and overpopulated for even his titanic strength. Like a cancer gone wild, the city might eat him. When he was a young man, New York was no more than a large English-Dutch town, not buildings towering five and six stories high, mashed against each other like fat sausages in a butcher's box. Back then it was green, full of shade trees on slow, quiet streets. Greenwich Village was simply that, a green village to the north of New York, not another district of a smoky, dingy metropolis. Back then there were no smelly, gabble-voiced hordes of Irish, French, Italians, Poles, Jews, Greeks, and Chinese. In the street you heard little but calm, solid English and Dutch. Back then the sidewalks weren't blocked with rouged prostitutes, darting-eyed thieves, filthy beggars, wild homeless children, and pickpockets with fast hands. Back then the sky wasn't full of humming copper wires on lopsided poles carrying urgent messages to buy and sell.

Over the eight years since 1860, during the Civil War and the three boom years following, New York had become a powerful metropolis of immense opulence, grandeur, and elegance as measured by the block-large department stores and stone mansions that crowded smugly along Fifth Avenue. At the same time other districts of the city had decomposed into stinking bogs, narrow, rat-filled streets where dingy alleys and dank courtyards overflowed with shiftless immigrants, half-naked children, and barrels of putrid garbage. In grimy areas called Five Points, Hell's Kitchen, and the Lower East Side, ten to twenty sullen immigrants lived crammed together into one basement room. Cornelius had come to loathe as well as love the city in which he had lived his entire life.

Finally Cornelius's heavy carriage turned off Broadway into West Street. It had hardly pulled to a stop before the Erie headquarters when Cornelius, to make sure William understood who led this expedition, pushed his son out of the way and jumped to the cobbled sidewalk, the warrant for his rival's arrest thrust before him like a sword.

As he clattered up the first flight of wooden stairs, his gouty right toe stabbed him with pain. Cornelius closed his mind to it and pushed upward. Sweat broke out on his forehead, neck, and cheeks.

The warrant clenched before him in his fist, he lunged through the gold-lettered double glass doors into the Erie's main offices.

9

Into a large silent room filled with forty empty desks.

Empty desks!

Cornelius skidded to an abrupt halt and peered around the vast, deserted bull pen, silent except for his own labored breathing.

Empty desks!—on an ordinary Thursday? Behind Cornelius, William and the police clattered in through the double doors.

"Where are they?" asked William in a hoarse whisper, as if afraid someone would hear.

Still huffing, Cornelius couldn't answer. His heart knocked against his ribs and shook his stout frame like an engine with a loose rod. It didn't make sense. Their competitor's main office deserted on an ordinary workday! Struck dumb, Cornelius swung around looking for an explanation.

"My God, Pa," asked William, "what's happened?"

Cornelius shook his head. "I don't know, damn it," he said. "Let's find out."

He dashed forward to find Drew's office, where the money would be. A brass plate on a door read *Treasurer*, and he plunged in. The iron walk-in safe there stood open, its yawning metal mouth empty of the bonds, ledgers, and cash of a healthy business.

Cornelius's stomach lurched as it once had on the docks when a workhorse was gutted belly to haunch by a wild loading boom. For a weak and sick moment his breakfast rebelled. This empty safe meant Drew had moved the money to a hiding place, probably to some Wall Street brokerage. Cornelius spun and strode back into the bull pen. With William trailing, he toured the whole floor. In the entire headquarters of the Erie Railroad, the sixth largest rail line in the country, the second largest in New York, a bustling enterprise with 30,000 employees, there was but one person, a telegraph clerk. Impossible!

"Where's Daniel Drew?" bellowed Cornelius at the frightened clerk, who was held in front of him by the police. After forty years Cornelius knew his old crony well and didn't trust him at all. A millionaire several times over, tall, stringy, and cheap, Daniel Drew made a great whining show of piety and churchgoing. He was a crafty, pious crook masquerading as a frail old man, a ruthless creature who tied his rivals in a thousand knots when they misjudged his wily strength. For forty years Drew had fought with Cornelius, won and lost, and come whining back afterward claiming friendship. For decades Cornelius sourly played pinochle with him and listened, trying to pierce his rival's hypocritical platitudes and meowing complaints to see what greedy scheme Drew's crafty old brain planned next.

"Gone, sir," said the clerk in a heavy Irish brogue.

"I see that, but where?" Cornelius lashed back. He tapped the clerk's cheek with the warrant. The boy flinched, but said nothing.

"Where's the ledgers, the cash, the bonds?" the owner of the Central roared, "all what was in the safe?"

"Taken it with them."

"Those are ours," shouted William.

Cornelius's face was reacquiring its customary reddish glow. "How about Mr. Gould and Mr. Fisk?" he asked, referring to the line's president and managing director. "Where are they?"

"Gone, too, sir," said the clerk with a smirk.

Cornelius studied the blond youth. From his thick accent, this one had only recently come steerage class from Ireland. His smooth-cheeked face looked innocent of guile, but Cornelius didn't trust anybody connected with Daniel Drew. From his smirk and the dancing light in his blue eyes, this pup thought his masters had gotten the best of the Lion of the Rails. Cornelius slapped the youth hard across the cheek, snapping back his head.

"Hey, no call for that!" said the clerk, his teeth bared.

"Then don't get fresh," said Cornelius.

William grabbed Cornelius's arm. "Pa, don't hit him!"

Cornelius knocked away his son's restraining hand as he turned back to the clerk.

"Now, where's your bosses?" he demanded.

"They gone 'cross the river to Jersey City. Left half hour ago."

"Across the river!" exclaimed Cornelius, throwing himself toward the clerk. His eyes large with terror, the clerk lunged uselessly against the Dutch detectives' restraining grip. Cornelius's face was three inches from the clerk's. "He can't have!" In the clerk's quivering face was the vision of Cornelius's gloating rival, Daniel Drew, sitting on a pile of steamer trunks as he sailed over the state line that the Hudson River represented, forever out of the reach of Cornelius.

William yanked the clerk's chin toward him. "He took everything from the safe with him?"

"Yes, sir," said the clerk. "They settin' up our headquarters there."

"Headquarters!" said Cornelius as scenes of a stock market panic shot into his mind.

"To Jersey for good!" cried William. "Pa, we'll never get the money back!" Cornelius shook the crumpled warrant.

"We'll arrest them no matter where they run," said Cornelius.

"Barnard's warrant is no good in Jersey," said William. "No city judge's warrant is." Cornelius's solid breakfast of bread and fish gave way. He felt dizzy, light-headed, seasick, but he must chase Drew.

"Which dock?" Cornelius demanded.

"Canal Street," said the clerk.

Cornelius gripped his son's arm. "The ferry hasn't left," he said. "Let's go get him." They clattered down the stairs and scrambled into carriages. No matter how often and hard Cornelius rattled his fist against the car's ceiling, Henry couldn't make speed against Manhattan's midday traffic. As they rolled up to the dock the salty odors of rotting fish, hull tar, and coal smoke blew into the cab, and it possessed the empty mournfulness of all piers after a ferry had pulled out.

"Left a quarter hour ago, sir," said the plump, ruddy-faced dockmaster, who as an employee of the Vanderbilt Ferry Lines stood at attention. Cornelius drew himself up to his full imperial majesty.

"Was Drew on it?" he asked. "An old man bent up with age?" The dockmaster bobbed his head vigorously, eager to be of help.

"Yes, sir, an old gent was," he said. "With maybe twenty young fellers and a dozen real heavy trunks." Cornelius recoiled as if struck.

"A dozen trunks!" he said. He turned to William. "That's what was in the safe."

"Right particular about them, they was," said the dockmaster. "They was glad when the ferry pulled out, put up a little cheer." He squinted around at the ring of policemen and Central detectives. "Them fellers do something wrong, sir?" Cornelius stuck his face in the dockmaster's.

"Stole some money," he said. "Was a fat young man with them?"

"One with a cavalry mustache?" asked the master.

"That's him!"

"He was, him and a thin, little feller with a big, black beard—but now, Commodore, they didn't go."

"Didn't go!" said Cornelius. The dockmaster shook his head firmly.

"No, sir. After the ferry left, them two tooken a hack back into the city.

"Who the hell are they?" asked William. A sprout of hope pushed tendrils through the crust of Cornelius's anger.

"Fisk and Gould," muttered Cornelius. "Drew's cat's-paws. Idiots that he's made managing director and president. They will do to grab. Not only is Daniel too old to run the line, but he'll wither in Jersey all by his lonesome."

"They said they'd join him later," said the dockmaster. "Sounded like tonight after they done their business in the city."

Cornelius would have to hurry. "Pervault! Voorsted!" he shouted as if they weren't standing four feet away. "Gather your men." To William he said, "If he wants war, he'll get war."

"War?" said William. "Come on, Pa."

Drew would be so helpless without his cat's-paws that he would be forced to negotiate; certainly Cornelius exerted more leverage over the pair if they were in jail rather than loose in Jersey.

"War," he bellowed. Around him gathered city policemen and Central detectives. He raised the tattered warrant and shook it. "The criminal has escaped," he shouted. "Two of these crooks are still at large, here in the city. I don't care how many men it takes, Voorsted—500 if necessary—but get those two—today. Do you hear me?—*today!* I'll pay the men who bring me these thieves two thousand dollars for each one. Will that do it?"

Underneath their bushy mustaches the police sergeants and the Central detectives grinned craftily at each other. Their nods, mutters, and pleased faces agreed with the big detective Voorsted when he said, "Commodore, it damn sure will."

"I want every train depot, stable, pier, hack stand, ferry station, and dock watched," Cornelius ordered. "Keep them bottled up in Manhattan and we'll have them by nightfall. Bring them straight to my office when you catch them."

2

At ten o'clock a group of Erie officers dashed from the Erie office to the ferry, looking more like a frightened gang of thieves, disturbed in the division of their plunder, than like the wealthy representatives of a great corporation.

—Charles Francis Adams, *North American Review*, 1869

"Where is he?" asked Jay Gould of his eldest son.

"Up at the far end," said George.

Jay nodded gravely, and father and son walked through the stable. He felt relaxed, relieved—wonderful. Now that he had put Daniel Drew and the Commodore's money on the Jersey ferry, he could let go and really enjoy buying his twelve-year-old son his first horse. Saddler's Stable was a warm, cozy place to do it on such a raw March day. From the stalls came the hollow stamp of hooves against the wood floor and the soothing odors of horse sweat and molasses-soaked oats. Jay and George had been visiting stables for three hours, and with the prickly hay dust and earthy scents of each new one, Jay relaxed more. It was over! He and his partners had beat the Commodore!

George stopped before a stall. "Here," he said reverently.

The horse stuck his head over the half door. Reddish-brown with a bold blaze down the center, the head was well shaped.

"He likes me, Pa," George said. The small New Forest horse and Jay's lean, muscular son appeared wonderfully suited to each other. Jay smiled again. Raised on a farm in upstate New York by a widower who felt what a boy needed to become a man was hard work, toughening, and the discipline of the switch, Jay as a parent veered in the opposite direction, toward persuasion, reason, and kindness with his four children.

"I think you like him, too," Jay said.

"Oh, I *love* him," said the boy. Jay nodded, pretending more graveness than he felt, drawing out the moment. Over the last few hectic months there hadn't been enough such delicious moments. For months now as president of the Erie, he had smelled fresh ink and fear instead of such ordinary smells as straw and oats; he had heard shouts, oaths, and the riffle of ledger pages and stock certificates instead of the soft voices of his four children practicing their reading; and he had spent from seven in the morning until eleven at night combating Vanderbilt's vicious raids against the Erie instead of taking placid rides with George through Central Park and along Bloomingdale Road. It had been a hell of a fight, but finally he and his two partners had soundly beaten the old boar.

"Let's have a look at his legs," Jay said to his son.

Moving slowly so as not to alarm the stallion, they entered the stall. One hand on the horse's thick-muscled shoulder to reassure him, Jay lifted a front leg. He and George peered down. No tears or gaps where the nails went in, no reddening in the tender inner flesh from misriding.

"His withers aren't so flat your saddle will slip," said Jay. "His neck's a good bit longer on top than bottom, so his head will balance." He ran his hand over the horse's shoulders, chest, and loins, then around his legs in a search for small, round, bare patches. "No ringworm." He pressed his palm gently against the animal's stomach, and when the horse didn't start, he pushed harder. "No colic, either."

"What do you think?" whispered George.

"Do you want him?" asked Jay. George's struggle to be dignified and manly was lost in a childlike smile of delight.

"Oh, yes!"

George's excitement kindled Jay's own. Although he tried to suppress it and keep a manly countenance, he couldn't. A grin encircled his face.

"Let's buy him," Jay said. "Today's a great day for the Goulds."

"Oh, Pa! Can we, really and truly? That's wonderful!"

Jay eased himself out of the stall, but George didn't follow. His son talked softly to the horse and stroked his neck. The horse seemed to sense a change in his destiny; he turned and investigated George's ribs and back with his muzzle. George looked up at Jay and giggled with delight.

A rough hand fell on Jay's shoulder and spun him around. Startled, he jerked backward, sliding on the slippery floor.

"What!" he shouted, for he hadn't heard anyone.

Before Jay stood a large ruffian in a filthy, torn overcoat. On his huge body sat a beefy, unshaven face with a rotten hole for a mouth. He looked like a layabout from the Five Points or a member of a Hell's Kitchen gang. The rough fellow leaned forward in the dim light to peer at Jay's face, his breath stinking of stale beer and onions.

"Ain't you Gould?"

Alarmed, Jay stepped backward against the oily pine stable post, his feet slipping on the slick straw on the oak floor.

The rough face twisted into a knowing scowl. "You Gould, ain't you?" The fellow's huge presence was blocking them from the stable's front door. Could this be one of Vanderbilt's men? No—they couldn't find him this fast. Keep calm now. Act dumb and pray George doesn't give us away. Smile.

"No, I'm Methodist," replied Jay. He held out his hand to George. "Come on, son. Let's go downtown." George's face fell in disappointment.

"But, Pa, aren't we going to—"

Putting all the urgency he could muster into his voice, Jay said, "We'll do it later, son." He moved to the left, but the big fellow shifted to block their way.

"You is Gould."

Holding his son's thin hand, Jay glanced to his left. The back door was closed. This cozy stable was a trap. Jay's body tightened, ready to run. With an effort he held himself still and shook his head no. The knowing scowl returned to the man's beefy face.

"Harry said you was back here with your boy. That there's the boy."

"No, I'm not—"

Frightened, George moved against him. "Pa, what does he want?" asked George.

No, Vanderbilt couldn't have found them this early. This was a robbery.

"Well, well, now!" came a hearty, booming voice from the daylight at the stable's far end. "What have we here, Ox, my man?" Ox's head jerked backward. The tall, dark newcomer was framed by such bright light that hard as Jay strained, he couldn't see him clearly.

"Mr. Voorsted!" said Ox.

The newcomer came into view. His broad, stolid face sported the long muttonchops and bushy mustaches Dutchmen favored. He was large in the shoulders, and his full paunch strained his worn gray trousers and vest. Jay recognized the look of the man—a Central detective, probably an inspector—and despaired of shaking off the two of them.

Voorsted leaned toward Jay and smiled. "I see one two-thousand-dollar prize," he said. "The Commodore's waiting for you."

"Let my boy go," said Jay. "This has nothing to do with him."

"Ox, help me tie them up and get the hack," said Voorsted. "It's at the corner by Whitlow's."

"I'll have you in court," Jay said to Voorsted. With expansive gestures, the Central inspector took out a large cigar from a worn leather pocketcase.

"No, sir," said Voorsted heartily. "The Commodore will have you in court—Judge Barnard's to be exact."

"I'll have you arrested for kidnapping," said Jay. Voorsted struck a kitchen match and drew deeply on the thick cigar.

"No, sir," said Voorsted again, clipping off the hard flat words with enjoyment. "You are the criminal and I am performing the court's work. If I understand Judge Barnard's intentions, you'll be in jail for thirty to sixty days. Bail will be denied because you've already shown your propensity to flee his jurisdiction."

A quarter of an hour later, Jay and George were on the gummy floor of a battered public hack. Ox and Voorsted faced each other on the two narrow seats. As Jay pulled himself out from under Ox's foot into a half-sitting position, his nagging winter cough grabbed his chest, and he fixed his attention on calming the flapping nerve endings in his throat and lungs.

"Some cough," said Voorsted. "You got consumption?" Jay shook his head.

Ox gave him a mild kick. "Tell me where your buddy Fisk is," the beefy fellow asked.

"I don't know," said Jay. Ox kicked him again, this time hard. "Where's Fisk at?"

"I told you I don't know."

Mashed in between the two seats, hands tied behind with thick grass rope, his rib aching, Jay still couldn't breathe easily. The carriage bounced and shook. He squirmed to give himself more room and forced himself to think. They hit a pothole, the jar tearing Jay's sore rib. He yelped in pain. Ox laughed.

As bold and ruthless as a highwayman, Vanderbilt was once more outsmarting Jay with this move. The old river pirate owned the majority of the city's judges, not to speak of a fair sprinkling of New York State's. With Daniel in Jersey City, Vanderbilt would keep him and Jim Fisk in jail the two or three weeks it would take to convince the Wall Street crowd and the public that the Erie's shares were worthless. The Erie's share price would plummet. Jay's margined position would be sold out by brokerages and banks eager to save their financial necks. Vanderbilt would buy up the Erie on the cheap. Jay, Jim, and Daniel Drew would be broken men.

The carriage swayed as it turned a corner, throwing George on top of Jay's legs. Through the open window the dirty gray stones of Trinity Church's spire thrust skyward. The hack must be turning onto Broadway. He wished his partner Jim and a dozen Erie guards were here. They would make short work of these toughs.

The Trinity Church clock struck one. In a few minutes the Erie guards would be finishing their tours, changing clothes and milling about their room at the Erie's South Street Station.

That vision gave him an idea. If he couldn't get Jim and their men here, maybe he could get Voorsted and his crew there. It would be tricky. Voorsted and Ox knew he wanted to escape. George! George must be his motive. Jay tilted his head to Voorsted.

"If I tell you where Mr. Fisk likely is, will you let my son go?" he asked. He would lure Voorsted into the back of the station, where the Erie guards milled about. Voorsted smiled.

"You know where?"

"I think I do. But you've got to let the boy go."

"Let Mr. Fisk alone," cried George. "I'm all right."

"Be quiet, George," said Jay. "I don't want the boy in the Commodore's hands," he said to Voorsted. "It's not his fight. It's between grown men."

George shot him a hurt, dirty scowl that his father would betray his partner. "Aw, no, Pa!"

The boy's disappointment stung, but he would explain later. He insisted that Voorsted stop and let George go before he revealed Jim's whereabouts. But their captor was stubborn—only after they captured Fisk. From Voorsted's crafty wink at Ox, it was clear that he had no intention of letting George go.

Jay took several breaths to calm himself. Let Voorsted think what he liked, for Jim was most likely bedded down with an actress playmate in one of his bolt-holes around town. The important thing was that the jackals who hunted with the Lion of the Rails had taken the bait.

Jay Gould and his son still sat on the gummy, tobacco-splattered wooden floor of Voorsted's hack as it pulled up to the Erie's South Street Station.

"Let's go, all of us," growled Voorsted. "Once we get him, I'll let this cub go. Any funny stuff, and Ox here's got a butcher knife and one of you're going to get cut—bad."

Inside the station's hollow cavern the four, plus the cranelike carriage driver Skinny and his tiny helper Pepper were plunged into a clamorous swirl of rattling handcarts, officious porters, blasts of steam, conductors' shrill cries, and steel wheels grinding against steel track. Passengers, some in rags and some in elegant clothes, streamed by. The six tightly bunched figures, ungainly as a stiff, giant crab, waddled across the vaulted lobby. The aroma of South American coffee and the wet smack of freshly cut lumber jostled with the rotting stench of buffalo hides. No one paid the least mind that four thugs escorted Jay and his son, hands tied behind their backs, across the station floor.

Recognizing Jay, the wide-eyed, elderly guard at the office door sprang to open it. Jay stiffened, asking himself if he should shout now. No, one old guard wasn't enough. Inside the office, several telegraphs clattered and spat out yellow tongues of messages. At the counter two shirtsleeved clerks in neat mustaches, armbands, and eyeshades were helping freight customers; behind them a half-dozen clerks hunched over cluttered desks filled out freight billings. Not here, either, Jay counseled himself.

"Back here," Jay whispered to Ox, moving more quickly than the big thug could think. If only the guards hadn't gone home!

Hands still tied, Jay shouldered past the startled ticket clerk behind the counter's green gate, his eyes fixed on the green slats of the swinging door that led into the guards' dressing room. Suddenly the six were through it, and he, George, and their four captors stood in the middle of eight open-mouthed Erie guards. The long, narrow room was filled with banks of green wooden lockers and a long, troughlike sink, as well as the raw stench of soap, urine, and disinfectant. At the sight of their boss, the guards ceased knotting neckties and combing hair.

"Look sharp now!" shouted a guard. "It's Mr. Gould!"

Move fast! Jay ordered himself. He spun, dropped his shoulder, and with it pushed George against the diminutive Pepper and into the midst of the four guards at the long sink. Pepper hit the floor and broke George's fall. The four guards stepped back and stared goggle-eyed. Jay spun to face the startled Voorsted, Ox, and Skinny.

"Grab those fellows!" Jay said.

The unarmed guards stood frozen. They were large, lumbering fellows used to the easy work of tossing bums off trains and chasing hobos out of baggage cars, not thinking fast in street fights. Voorsted shoved Ox forward. Jay backed away and struggled to free his bound wrists.

"Grab him," shouted Jay. Ox drew the butcher's knife from his sleeve. Looking dazed, George struggled to his knees. Skinny drew a long thin shiv and edged close to Ox. The two groups stared at each other. As if wanting no part of the trouble, the guards edged toward the rear of the room.

George clambered to his feet and backed away. Pepper scampered on his hands and knees to Voorsted's feet. Jay and George stood in the middle of the two groups like soft, uncertain balls in some savage game. Ox slashed about with his butcher's knife as if it were a short sword.

Jay stepped between Ox and George and with his back pushed his son into the unarmed guards. "Protect the boy," he ordered his men.

"Don't nobody help him," said Ox, "or he's going to draw back a sliced gizzard."

For long moments the only sound in the room was the muffled bell and puffing locomotion of a freight leaving the station.

Voorsted stepped up next to Ox. "Quick," he said. "Snatch Gould."

"Come with me, Gould," growled Ox. He advanced toward Jay. "I don't want to cut these here boys."

"No, sir," said Jay. "You get out." Voorsted, edging by the sink, inched toward George. Jay turned to the most senior-looking guard, a heavyset fellow with a face like a slab of loose tallow.

"Stop him, Sergeant," Jay said. Two of the younger Erie guards seemed to wake up. They reached on top of the wooden lockers and pulled down two heavy billy clubs. They moved next to George. Thwarted, Voorsted drew back and stood near Skinny.

"Get behind us, Mr. Gould," said the tallow-faced sergeant.

"Watch those knives," said Jay. The Sergeant slapped his club into his palm.

"Throw down them knives, chumps," the Sergeant ordered Ox and Skinny. He took two steps forward. "Step up, boys. Come help the boss."

Ox skipped to the right and viciously slashed the air with his knife. Voorsted suddenly threw himself forward, and his large hand grabbed Jay by the collar. Jay, hands still bound, was dragged away from his men, but he dug in his boot heel. This action swung him around, and as his other foot came up, he shoved his boot toe forward with all his might and smashed it into Ox's crotch. The effort threw

Jay backward, out of Voorsted's grasp, and he hit the solid wooden floor with a jarring thud. Clutching his crotch, Ox dropped the knife and sank to his knees.

"Awww!" he shouted. Voorsted stooped for the knife. Jay rolled himself over on top of it.

Cursing, Voorsted dropped to his knees and shoved his hand under Jay, scrabbling for the knife. Still unable to free his hands, Jay rolled onto Voorsted's forearm. Voorsted lunged to the other side for the knife, and Jay rolled back against that arm.

"Grab them!" shouted Jay. Voorsted put his palm against Jay's mouth to shut him up. Jay sank his teeth into the inspector's rough index finger, tasting tobacco, grime, and blood as he bit down. Voorsted screamed and his other hand beat Jay's rib cage, but Jay closed his eyes, turned his face to the floor to protect them, and mashed down harder.

Two guards quickly overpowered the groaning Ox. Skinny held out his shiv and backed toward the door, where shirtsleeved clerks were crowded. A younger guard stepped forward and brought his billy club down on Skinny's wrist, and the shiv clattered to the floor.

Pepper was against the wall, his hands up to protect himself. Two guards grabbed him. Three guards pulled Voorsted off Jay and held him. Another guard helped Jay to his feet and untied him. His hands prickled painfully as the blood darted into them, and his rib felt torn. George, arms still bound, rushed to his father, all smiles.

"You really walloped him, Pa!"

Jay put his arm around George and pulled his son's toothy, warm face into his neck. Jay's legs were wobbly; his ribs, forehead, and butt were sore—but they were free!

He grabbed Ox's knife from a guard and cut the hard rope on George's wrists.

"Is Mr. Fisk here?" George asked.

"No, no—that was just a trick."

"Oh, Pa, I was hoping so. What are you going to do to Mr. Vanderbilt?"

Jay snorted. "I don't know. What do you think I ought to do?"

Eyes wild, mouth open, raring for another game, George stepped back and stretched out his long arms in a boxer's pose. "Tie him up and bloody *his* nose. You're going to get him back, right?" From the group of bound captives, Voorsted glared up with the venom of a large gray bull whose four limbs were hobbled together.

"If you know what's good for you," Voorsted growled, "you'll let us go."

Jay laughed. To the tallow-faced senior guard he said, "Keep these thugs here for a couple of hours. If they try to escape, give them a couple of kicks for me." At that, George walked over to the bound Ox and kicked him in the thigh, hard.

"Ooof!" Ox grunted. He glared sullenly at George, who kicked him again. The guards laughed. Jay stepped forward and pulled George back.

"Son!" he said, giving him a wry smile. "Don't kick a man who's tied up."

"He kicked us!" said George.

"Yes, but we're not thugs. Let's go home."

3

DIVORCES cheaply, without publicity;
desertion, incompatibility,
non-support, intemperance, compulsory
marriages; parties any State;
explanatory blanks free; always
successful; consultations free;
confidential.

—*New York World* legal
advertisement, *1871*

Still shaky and trembling, Annabelle Stokes pushed open her kitchen door. She took a deep breath to bring under control the tremor of her hands and the rapid beating of her heart.

All three members of her household—Matilda, her four-year-old daughter, Richard, her eight-year-old son, and Bridget, the last of what had once been a staff of six—looked up, fear and hope in their faces. The empty cupboards begged for food, and the room stank with a cold, damp dread that none of Bridget's obsessive mopping swabbed away.

"No," Annabelle said by way of explaining what had happened at the front door with her leering mortgagee. When they all stared at her speechless, she went on, past evasions, "If I don't raise some money in ten days, we have to get out."

"Where will we go, Mother?" asked Richard tremulously.

Annabelle's stomach sank. "I don't know," she said. As they could no longer afford soap, the room reeked of the cheap vinegar in the scrub bucket. The obvious answer was rented rooms, but landladies demanded the first week or two before you moved in. Right now she couldn't pay more than the first few hours.

"Maybe we can go live with Daddy!" shouted Matilda, her eyes darting from one to the other. The boldness of her question made Matilda's eager face both hopeful and scared.

Richard's face filled with scorn. "I told you a hundred times we can't, dummy," he said. "He doesn't want us."

"Daddy wants me!" Matilda screamed. "I know he does!" Bridget's trim figure stepped between them and she raised her forefinger.

"Richard Stokes," she said, "don't you call your sister a name like that." Annabelle pulled the crying Matilda against her. After the child was soothed, she said, "You children go in the backyard and play. I have to talk to Bridget."

"I want to hear, too, Mother," protested Richard, but a single sharp glance from her convinced him this was no time to argue.

The children ran out. Annabelle took a deep breath to steady herself and sat down on one of the cane-bottomed chairs at the kitchen table.

"I can't ask you to stay, Bridget," she said. "I don't know how I'll ever catch you up." She owed Bridget three months' back wages.

Bridget flushed. "I've got nowhere to go, mum," said the Irish girl. Only nineteen years old, she had come over with her brother two years before. Last year she had lost him in a barge accident. "I'd as soon stay. The children, you—you're like family to me."

"The trouble is, I can't see any way of keeping the house," said Annabelle. "Likely we'll be moving to rooms. Maybe the country. I don't know." Bridget blinked back tears.

"What did he say?"

Annabelle's hands still trembled from this morning's encounter with her swaggering mortgagee. "Boggs? He said get out—or let him move in."

Grown rich from selling overpriced flour to the Union army, Bob Boggs was typical of the newly rich breed that the Civil War had spawned by the thousands. Distributors of foodstuffs, manufacturers of uniforms, and traders of cotton, powder, and metal, they were now eager to triple and quadruple their war-swollen fortunes through any scheme that promised a quick return. To a man stout and plump, done up in frock coats and gaudy-colored satin vests, they waddled through Manhattan's streets bloated from whiskey, rich meals, and arrogance, like hogs grown fat on palace slops.

"Men!" said Bridget sharply, then her voice softened. "Well, some men. We had one like him back in the village. He owned everything that was worth having. If a girl come to work in the house, he took her that way. She get in a family condition and it was good-bye, find her a husband, get another young girl. It wasn't right." Annabelle took the girl's damp, cold hand in her own.

"I feel terrible not having your money for you," she said.

"Something will turn up," said Bridget. "I don't need wages so long as I have a place to sleep and something to eat. As beautiful as you are, a man will turn up. They'd be fools not to. And one much better than that pig or Mr. Stokes." She clapped both hands to her lips and stared in horror as if a frog had leapt out of her mouth.

Annabelle couldn't be angry. She stood and threw her arms around the girl's neck and gave her a long hug.

"It's no more than what I think myself." Between the long-empty sugar bowl and the milk jug was tucked a yellow envelope.

"What's this?" asked Annabelle, picking it up. The telegram crackled in a way that said its news was electric and dangerous.

"Oh, Mother of God," said Bridget. "I forgot."

Annabelle ripped open the envelope. ARRIVE ON NOON TRAIN STOP JENNY STOP.

"Who's it from?" asked Bridget. "Bad news?"

"My sister. She'll be here for lunch."

"Praise God! Will she help?"

The telegram made Annabelle uneasy. "I wrote asking for it. She doesn't say."

"But you're her sister," said Bridget. "She can't say no. And she's married to such a powerful man."

"Maybe," said Annabelle. "Still, she and Ulysses helped us once before. Maybe they will again. What on earth can we serve her for lunch?"

"More tea, Jenny?" Annabelle asked, extending the cracked, everyday teapot in her sister's direction. Three months before she had sold the English tea set.

Jenny's pudgy features smiled. "No, sis," she said. "This is fine." Her left hand on the hot earthenware lid, Annabelle poured herself more weak tea.

Her sister chattered on. A tiny fire, made from scraps of wood that Bridget had ferreted out from the trash in the back alley, jumped feebly in the grate. In the parlor's air hung the faint resin of cloves that only two hours ago had been breathed into it by her tormentor Boggs, chewed to hide the whiskey he had drunk for courage. The Italian marble mantel, cupids flying up and down its sides, and thin maroon stripes of the cream wallpaper testified to the good taste with which Annabelle had decorated the room, but now it was denuded

25

and grim, as if the house's inhabitants were moving out this afternoon. Gone were the oriental rugs, the Belgian sofas, the elegant porcelain vases, the Japanese screens, and the French chairs that Jenny commented on the last time she visited, three years ago right after the War, when Ulysses made his triumphant parade up Broadway. So far Jenny had said not a word about the parlor's drafty bareness or the plea in Annabelle's letter for a loan. Instead Jenny filled in the country meal of eggs, potatoes, and tea with gossip of Logantown and chatter about Ulysses's rising fortunes in national politics. Annabelle hoped that the odor of the cloves didn't make Jenny think she possessed ham she wasn't offering.

It was hard to believe that her dour sister would likely occupy the White House next year with stolid Ulysses. However, Annabelle knew that the Republican party was hopelessly split by the Radicals and the moderates, and desperately needed a savior to bridge the chasm between them.

The Radicals in Congress were demanding that the army occupy the beaten South, convict the impeached, beleaguered President, Andrew Johnson, and seize all the powers of the presidency for Congress itself. They made it seem as if a defiant and disloyal South were planning to revive the Confederacy. Around town Annabelle didn't hear the words *peace, pardon,* and *clemency* as she had two years ago after the War; she heard of armed force, punishment, and retaliation. Alarmed that harsh measures would again threaten the federal government's stability, the party's moderates were insisting on carrying out Lincoln's plan for the South: deny that the southern states had seceded at all, so that they didn't need punishing, and maintain the Presidency as a separate force in government equal to Congress and the judiciary. Annabelle herself believed that Lincoln, now murdered, had grasped a great truth: that the reconstruction of a shattered empire must be approached with wisdom rather than strict justice. The defeated must be helped to their feet and treated more like prodigal sons than convicted felons. Hotheaded, pugnacious, and vituperative, President Johnson was not the man to carry out such a wise policy. And now her brother-in-law Ulysses Grant, the Commander in Chief who three years ago had fought the bloody conflict to a victory for the Union, was seen as the only possible man able to bridge the bitterness that separated both factions.

Even more surprising was Jenny's newfound insight into politics. "Mr. Johnson may be proud of his simple Tennessee ways, of his honesty and courage, but he lacks tact."

"But the papers say his policies are the same as were Mr. Lincoln's," commented Annabelle, pretending ignorance.

"Ulysses knows how to keep his counsel. Mr. Johnson antagonizes people with his foolish speeches."

At last Jenny sat back, made a deep sigh, and said, "Well, I had to come, Annabelle. Despite everything that went on between us as young ladies, you *are* my flesh and blood." Annabelle ignored the reference to their girlhood rivalry and gave her sister a warm smile.

"It is good to see you," Annabelle said. Back on the farm Jenny had been interested in cooking and baking and sewing, while Annabelle worked in the little bank next door to the farmhouse, willing to do Pa's endless bookkeeping chores so long as she didn't have to sweep, darn, wash dishes, stir a pot, and slop the pigs. Their different duties set the two sisters at odds. By the time Annabelle was fourteen and Jenny was twenty, each saw the other as a sorry excuse for a woman.

Jenny now made a point of gazing around the bare parlor, as if taking in for the first time its meager furnishings. Her eyes rested on the portrait of Grandfather Stokes, Annabelle's ex-husband's forebear, that hung over the mantel of elaborately carved Italian marble.

She shot Annabelle a shrewd, questioning look. "And the famous Philadelphia Stokes won't help their grandchildren?"

"They don't have any more use for Ned and me now than Pa has."

"He lost them money, too?" Jenny's voice was dominated by barely suppressed glee and an I-could-have-told-you.

Stiffening under the assault, Annabelle wondered how much sharply vinegared crow she would have to eat to get a loan. "Yes."

Jenny helped herself to more fried potatoes. No use explaining to Jenny how wonderful it once had been with Ned. Back when they were still—well, carefree children with bright, new toys. That was how they had come to New York eight years ago, as a youthful, glittering couple.

Ned had insisted on buying this house just months after their arrival. How much money Annabelle spent fixing it up, and how she wished she had that money now! But it looked so wonderful! Seen from the street at night it glittered and sparkled with such bright, golden warmth that the face of every passerby glowed with the desire to enter. And the parties! During the War the house overflowed with jolly gaiety—titters, giggles, chuckles, roars, and shrieks. The pungent spice of cloves then meant large baked hams, and the scent waltzed about the polished, glittering downstairs with its dancing partners, the rich perfumes of madeira, rum punch, and sherry. Then Annabelle didn't feel rough cotton, but the whispers of silk, velvet, and aersphane. The best-dressed, the fastest comers, and the brightest of Manhattan flocked to Thirty-fifth Street to attend the Stokes's glossy at homes. She and Ned were seen everywhere: at opening nights of the opera and the theater, at the homes of the best hostesses, and at the fashionable hotels along the Jersey shore. Within twelve months of their arrival, not a week passed without a newspaper calling them one of the handsomest couples of New York, he with his yellow waistcoats, confident laughter, and hot, smoky bedroom eyes, and she with her charm for everyone, bold flair for clothes, and daring neckline.

Jenny put down her empty plate with a determined clink. "Papa's not doing at all well," she said in her portentous way.

The accusation in Jenny's voice made Annabelle stiffen. "So Mama writes," she said cautiously. She wondered if Jenny too blamed her for Papa's bankruptcy. She put off for another few minutes asking for the loan. Jenny pulled her practical wool shawl more closely around her shoulders.

"You were always the smart one," the accusation continued. When Annabelle didn't reply, she went on. "Just how *did* you lose so much money?"

Annabelle shook her head in a bewildered way, as if it were beyond the female mind. "I don't know," she said soothingly. "It was Ned's brokerage, not mine."

"But you know business," Jenny pressed. "You were with Papa in the bank from the time you could hold a pencil. He always said you were smarter at banking than he was."

"No, I'm not. I'm a mother now, Jenny, trying to raise two children without a provider, and having a hard time of it."

Jenny gazed around the parlor again, her eye taking in the chased marble mantel and the gilt trim around the edge of the ceiling. "Sell the house. Even without all that gaudy furniture it looks smart."

Annabelle could hardly control her irritation. "Oh, Jenny, there's nothing left to it!"

"What?"

"I mean I've borrowed and borrowed against it," Annabelle said. "The next step is rented rooms, and to tell you the truth, I'm not sure what in the way of rent I can afford." Jenny glowed with the righteousness of the frugal toward the spendthrift come to grief.

"How'd it happen?" she asked. "To you and him, of all people? I thought you two were the smartest there was."

Annabelle suppressed a huff of exasperation. "Ned overdid it, I guess," she said, reluctant to spread out the sordid mess for Jenny's inspection. She recognized, however, that her sister wasn't likely to give any aid unless she could paw over a soiled underslip and pantaloon or two. "We did fine when we first got here. I'm sure Pa showed you the newspaper articles. Every bale of cotton Ned put his hands on he sold to the Union. Back then he could get almost any price for it."

"All the clippings talked about were your parties," said Jenny in a prissy tone. Annabelle hefted the tepid teapot, hoping to distract Jenny.

"Oh, Jenny, it seemed as if all of Papa's rules about saving were turned on their heads. It was so strange in the War; everything was topsy-turvy. The way to get ahead was to spend money, not hoard it like back home. The more we spent on parties and clothes, why, the more we made."

Jenny was aghast. "But all that money—and you didn't save *anything*?" When Annabelle said nothing, Jenny plunged on. "Of course, you could be excused, you had the children to think of."

Annabelle smiled, delighted at a fresh topic. "Pregnancy certainly was a shock," she said. Maybe family feeling would provide a warmer atmosphere in which to ask for money. "I didn't want to get pregnant so early. Then I was sick a lot with Richard and couldn't entertain, and about the time I was feeling better I couldn't fit into my dresses. I wasn't one to parade my big belly around in satin, so I lay low till after he was born."

"Children do change a woman's life," said Jenny, her sober voice implying that such change was all for the better.

Actually Annabelle had been sure for the six months before Richard's birth that children ruined a fashionable lady's life. A hard labor, eighteen hours of sweating, agony, writhing, and gripping rough towels, and a harder birth. The midwife said Annabelle didn't have the hips for it. Afterward she lay in the bleak little birthing room, limp and weepy, feeling sorry for herself. Her body felt pulled apart and only loosely reattached. When the grinning and cooing nurse first brought in the ugly, red-faced dwarf that months earlier she and Ned had agreed to call Richard, she crossed her arms tightly against her breasts and refused to take him.

"You'll feel better after he's drunk a bit," said the nurse, and she pushed forward the roll of white cloth at the end of which was a splotchy, shrunken, misshapen head. Forced to take him, Annabelle hated and was fascinated by the eager mouth pulling at her nipple. He butted and poked as if he wanted to invade her, a cross between some large clinging blind leech and a puppy who would adore her if she treated him kindly.

"I wasn't all that sure I wanted Richard when he was born," Annabelle now admitted to Jenny.

29

"Lots of women feel that way, but it changes as the children grow."

Annabelle smiled, surprised she and Jenny were finding common ground. "Yes, it did."

Having Richard certainly had changed Annabelle, but it wasn't a change she liked. In a four-year span she went from being her father's industrious assistant, to her dashing husband's consort, and then to a nursing mother, never more than four hours away from the hungry dwarf. Her nipples hurt constantly, for he was rough with her. She couldn't stand her own odor, that of curdled milk. Getting up to feed him every four hours at night made her tired all day. The midwife insisted she drink milk and eat, when all Annabelle wanted was to starve and regain her twenty-inch waist. Finally, like the other ladies of her set, she ordered in a wet nurse who slept in the downstairs birthing room with Richard.

An enormous load lifted off her. With vast relief she reimmersed herself in Manhattan's social swirl, frothy waters in which she swam easily. Her milk dried up. In a span of three weeks she planned and gave two dinner parties. She had her hair done three times a week. She bought new shoes, new shawls, new hats, and new gowns at Broadway department stores on outings that took three-quarters of the day. Rewards were the blossoming smiles that thin-eyed bankers, blustering politicians, Wall Street traders, and self-important editors turned in her direction when she entered a room, as well as their wives' dark stabs of envy. Ned loved the attention she received and insisted she dress well, for she was gaining the reputation as the best-dressed lady in New York. Her neckline floated across her breasts; men could hardly tear their glazed eyes away.

Jenny leaned back against the sofa. "What happened after the War?"

"After the War . . ." repeated Annabelle, stalling to discover an answer acceptable to Jenny. "I don't think Ned ever realized it stopped."

"But— What do you mean?"

"Ned figured he would always be able to sell cotton at a higher price than he paid," Annabelle explained. "He kept buying and buying, and prices went down instead of up." The expression on Jenny's face said she wouldn't be satisfied till she had heard every last smidgen.

"Then he just—left you?"

"For a year after the War things were fine," said Annabelle. "Then Ned kept forgetting to leave me money for accounts. Tradespeople started knocking, wanting to get paid—the gas man, Ned's tailor,

Richard's schoolmaster. I would put it to Ned, and he would say that he was temporarily short and to tell them to go to the devil. After a few weeks of this I got so sharp with Ned that he moved out to his club."

Jenny straightened up into her grandest air of matronly dignity. "Moved out!" she said haughtily. "But you and he were man and wife!"

"That was it exactly," Annabelle said, glad to have her feet firmly on yet more common ground with her sister. With this foothold she attempted to take more territory. "I went to his club to make up. We had a terrible fight. He hadn't paid the rent on his office, yet he bought another 10,000 bales of cotton on credit. Afterward the servants there lied, said he was out when he was in." Her laughter was tinged with faint hysteria. "He didn't pay the club, either."

"But *divorce!*" said Jenny. The awful word hung in the chilly room for a long moment. "Annabelle, how could you agree to such a thing!" Annabelle's spirit swooped low; divorce almost made a lady as much an outcast from society as if she had given birth out of wedlock. No gentleman would have her for a wife, and few ladies were comfortable with her as a friend.

"I never agreed to it," Annabelle said hotly. "When my lawyer pieced it together, Ned got some Broadway shyster to file in Rochester, drum up three witnesses to say I had been immoral with another man, and persuade the judge to sign a divorce decree without my ever being notified."

Jenny's hand flew to her opened mouth. "What! Had you?"

"Not you too, sis! How can you think such a thing?"

Jenny dropped her gaze in embarrassment. "Yes, but divorce," she murmured. "My God, Annabelle, I wept when I got the news."

"It's none of it pretty, but it's all true."

"But you were married! Surely, even in New York that counts as something sacred."

Annabelle shrugged. She had plowed this ground many times with her lawyer, as well as in her own mind on a hot pillow at three in the morning.

"My lawyer says it's done every day here."

"But how— That's impossible—isn't it?"

Annabelle smiled ruefully. "I'm not without business and legal skills," she said. "My lawyer and I attacked it vigorously. In a manner of speaking, we won. Ned agreed to give me the house and the bank account, but the house was saddled with two mortgages and the bank account contained no money. And Ned was saddled with nothing, a bachelor again as if he were never married."

"Which was when you wrote me originally."

Annabelle saw the means of edging nearer her request for a loan. "And you were good enough to help us." And Jenny, please, please help us again. But Jenny's smile was bitter, not accommodating.

"It must have taken some nerve for you to write," she said, "with all that's gone on between you and me."

"Yes," Annabelle admitted in a weak voice.

Such a long silence fell between the two sisters that Annabelle began to fear Jenny wouldn't help after all. She smiled in a tentative, kindly fashion at her sister's dour face. Could Jenny have come *only* to push her into groveling? No, she *would* help. Annabelle was her sister. Jenny gathered her skirts.

"Everybody thinks Ulysses and I have lots of money," she said. "The truth is we don't. He receives something from the army, but nothing like what it takes to keep up his position."

Annabelle didn't like the cast of this and rushed in. "I've been grateful for your help in the past," she said. "I wouldn't ask again if I weren't desperate. I made a stupid mistake with Ned, one I regret."

"A man ought to take care of his children," said Jenny. "Richard and Matilda—and you, too—are my family, so I am going to give you some more money—"

"No, Jenny—lend, lend only!"

"*Give*," said Jenny firmly, reaching for her leather-and-cotton handbag. "So it will be the end of this. Understand?"

Annabelle knew enough about her family's logic to understand. If it were lent, the door was open for her to come back. "Given" somehow firmly shut the door on future loans or gifts.

"We have four boys of our own, Annabelle. Ulysses knows nothing of this, and I'd prefer him not to know." She reached into her handbag and took out a long envelope of mustard yellow that her fleshy hands gripped tightly. "I'm going to give this to you," said Jenny. "It's enough to put you on your feet for a month or two, I daresay, but you must make other arrangements." Annabelle stared at the envelope, which looked as plump as an overfed yellow cat. This morning she had been something of a hypocrite with her mortgagee Boggs; she would be a better one with her sister.

"Yes, of course," said Annabelle in a meek voice that she hardly recognized as her own. Jenny raised the yellow envelope and shook it at Annabelle with the stern righteousness of a preacher's finger.

"And on one further condition," said Jenny.

Annabelle made herself look away from the yellow envelope, and with an effort willed herself calm. "Yes?"

"That you go see Papa."

Annabelle stared at her sister's smug face. "Go see Papa!" Annabelle said. "He doesn't want to see me."

"One, he needs you," said Jenny. "This thing has ruined his health. And two, between you maybe you can figure some way out of your misery as well as his. You're the two smartest people I know."

See Papa, after she had caused him so much pain? All Annabelle felt toward the idea was frozen numbness, leaden dread. She wondered if the envelope was thick with singles or fives.

"I'd rather not," breathed Annabelle. "He hasn't answered a one of my letters. We would only have the most awful row."

"True, he has lost his faith in you," said Jenny, her hand gesturing as if she might put the envelope back in her handbag. "I always thought that faith was somewhat overdone. But you're the only one can do him any good."

"I certainly don't have anything else to do, and I shouldn't mind a visit to my own papa." But she did—how she did!

"I never thought the day would come when I insisted you visit him and you resisted," said Jenny.

She handed over the envelope, and Annabelle's eager fingers slid over its rough surface. As she squeezed it, the wad of bank notes yielded in a welcoming fashion to her fingers' pressure.

"Don't forget," said Jenny in a no-nonsense voice. "You must make arrangements to support yourself, leave the city, which is so expensive. Or take a job, maybe as a stenographer. Perhaps in banking, although it would be unusual for a woman. Men wouldn't trust their money to a woman, would they?"

Annabelle's broad smile concealed how tightly her fingers gripped the envelope, as if it might fly away. If only the notes weren't singles! She wanted to rip it open and count them, plunge her nose into the bills and smell their wonderful, filthy reek, but she didn't dare.

"Thank you, Jenny. No, men don't trust women with their money." Warm strength flowed from the envelope's plump thickness into her fingers, up her arms, into her chest. God! Ready cash! How bad could a two-day visit to Gantry be? Her forced smile wavered, and she was afraid she looked like a clumsy marionette. Seeing Papa could be pretty bad. "Thank you, sis," Annabelle said. "Thank you very much. I will go see him."

Jenny smiled as she stood up. "I have to go. I'm meeting Ulysses at city hall."

As she rose to see her sister out, Annabelle stuffed the envelope deep in her dress pocket, but she was unable to push it completely out of sight. "I'm sorry not to see him."

Jenny laughed. "He wanted to see you," said Jenny. "I said no." In her brittle laugh and tone Annabelle heard the old accusations.

"All that was years ago," said Annabelle, "and it was nothing even then." Strange, she thought, that no matter how much she protested, Jenny believed she was the one who chased Ulysses, never willing to recognize it was the other way around. Jenny gave her a sharp-eyed, cagey glance.

"I take the preacher's advice, and I don't tempt the devil."

"Oh, Jenny!"

"For all your problems, you haven't lost your looks, Annabelle. I wouldn't trust Ulysses within twenty feet of you."

Annabelle tittered in order to treat this thrust as a joke, but it was too filled with venom to be a toothless jibe.

4

There are not many first-class houses of ill-fame in the city—probably not over fifty in all—but they are located in the best neighborhoods, and it is said that Fifth Avenue itself is not free from the taint of their presence.

—James McCabe, *Lights & Shadows of New York Life*, 1872

Eight blocks south at this hour, Josie Mansfield yanked the bellpull of a dignified town house west of Fifth Avenue on Twenty-seventh Street. Shivering against the damp cold, she threw anxious glances east and west with the hope no one saw her. The cheap soles of her patent-leather shoes were soaked through by the sidewalk's mud. After the brass tinkle of the doorbell there was nothing but a long, ominous silence. Why didn't the maid hurry?

The wet town house looked as solid and prosperous as the others on this block and along Fifth Avenue. Its brownstone was as well cut, its lace curtains as rich and intricate, and the brass of its railings and knocker as highly polished, but it was the knowledge of the nightly goings-on behind its solid oak door that prompted Josie to scan the street anxiously. Its owner, Sally Woods, was one of the well-known Seven Sisters, once-poor women from the same mill town in New England who had set up shop in similar quiet town houses along this block. Through lending each other money and sharing information on how to keep the heavy-handed police and light-fingered politicians from interfering with business, they had fashioned the finest houses that offered the gentlemen out on the town a woman's most intimate favors. The seven conducted their trade with a Yankee sense of decorum; on Christmas Eve and New Year's no gent was allowed in Sally's unless he wore evening dress and brought flowers.

A sullen, middle-aged Negro maid with a bulldog's face and wattles showed Josie into the empty front parlor on the quiet second floor, an airy room that a banker's wife might have furnished—mahogany paneling to waist level, scroll-backed sofas and chairs covered with maroon velvet, and a brass chandelier whose frosted gas globes hissed softly on this raw, wet day. Although she had never visited after six o'clock, Josie's imagination saw vividly the nighttime scenes. Well-dressed gents whispered into saucy girls' quivering ears. As each couple left or modestly rejoined the company, a titter and a whisper rippled across the elegant crowd.

The door opened and Sally Woods swept in, her hand out and a big smile on her face. On her wrist jangled a gold bracelet from which dangled scores of miniature charms: gold fish, gold canary cages, gold rifles, gold carriage wheels, gold thimbles, gold roosters, gold sewing baskets, gold hymnals. Rumor said each was a solid-gold trophy that Sally demanded from the men who slept with her. Once Josie had heard her shake and rattle the bracelet and trill that as long as she possessed it, she would never be broke. Josie stepped forward and smiled.

"So good to see you again," said Sally. "And my, my, you look wonderful!" She stepped back and eyed Josie's mass of black curls, creamy complexion, gray dress, purple ribbons, cinched, corseted waist, puffed white sleeves, and full bust with such professional scrutiny that Josie flushed. Sally went on. "I don't know why you haven't taken this town's stages by storm." This razor swipe of irony made Josie smile uneasily.

"It's not for want of trying," said Josie. "I make the rounds every day." Sally waved her into a plush chair and sat nearby.

"I asked you over because I have a little job you might like," Sally said, always one to come straight to the point. "I also thought you might pay me back some of the money you borrowed."

The wings of Josie's heart missed several beats and swooped low. This was exactly what she had feared when she received Sally's note. She had been in New York two years. In the past six months she had borrowed a total of five hundred dollars and received a dozen introductions to prominent strutters when the two went to the theater or had tea together at the Hoffman House or the Fifth Avenue Hotel.

"Oh, Sally, I'm sorry!" said Josie. "I don't have any money." She lowered her voice as if someone else were in the room. "In fact, I was hoping you would be good enough to make me another small loan."

"But aren't things going well with Jim?" Sally asked, her innocence as bold as an actress's stage paint. "I hear the two of you are *all* over town." Sally had introduced her to Jim Fisk, a big shot with the Erie. Stout Jim. His easy, warm, rich laugh. The diamonds sparkling on his starched chest, dazzling and blinding her. Sometimes if she only glanced in a store window he would buy her the dress. Josie squirmed about.

"Yes, we are," she said. "But I can't ask him for money."

"Why not?" asked Sally with the jocular casualness of an experienced butcher arranging a chicken's head on the block. "Whatever else are men for?"

"I've only known him two months," Josie said. "Of course he gives me presents—jewelry, and the occasional dress, but not money."

"I want you to help me put on a little party," said Sally. "Gloria's gone to Chicago and Marie is laid up after a visit to Madame Restaille's."

Josie reacted as if a cold knife sliced her insides. The Fifth Avenue abortionist. Strolling along Fifth Avenue with Jim, Josie had seen her once, a thin woman with no lips and not much expression. Jim joked that her face was like a rusty razor.

"A party?" Josie asked, stalling. She wasn't that kind of girl, but she didn't want to hurt her friend's feelings by saying no.

"You know, a little *soirée dansante*," explained Sally, using fancy talk for the cancan and other bold dances. "You have those wonderful legs, and somebody said you once showed her how to do a butterfly kick. The Mayor of Boston is bringing his city-council chums for his annual outing."

A slippery eel of disgust slithered through Josie. She saw through the fancy talk. It meant sleeping with fat, wrinkled old men off on a toot, away from their wives. She couldn't do that.

"There's a hundred dollars in it," said Sally. "Since you're short, I'll give you half in cash and put the rest against your loan."

"A hundred dollars!" exclaimed Josie. She could live on fifty dollars for a month. It was a fortune when you were down to three greasy quarters and twelve worn one-dollar bills. "But I can't," she said, phrasing her refusal carefully. "Jim might find out."

Sally laughed. "No, Ma'am. I always have some girls in masks."

"Masks?"

"Some married girls like to work a party like this every now and then," explained Sally. "It's not that easy to get a hundred dollars out of the bluejays they married."

Josie saw a dozen girls wearing only dark body corsets and red masks, the white flesh of their breasts and buttocks swelling out against black lace. Half-naked girls sitting on the laps of plump middle-aged politicians, whose pudgy fingers stroked their delicate flesh. Despite the nearby fire's warmth, a shiver rippled up the back of her neck.

"Couldn't you simply make me another loan?" asked Josie in a voice as small as a child's.

"Look," said Sally briskly, "I need you. I don't have a good dancer. You're the kind of girl they expect me to have—long legs, full figure, knows how to have fun."

"But I'm an actress, not a—" She caught herself before the word came out, but the damage was done.

Sally's face went from mobile jocularity to the hard density of stone. She shook her head, rattled her charm bracelet, and stood up.

"Come on. I'll walk you out." Sally's voice was sharp, brittle, and cold, devoid of interest in Josie. She sailed out the parlor door.

Josie had to hurry to catch up. "Sally, don't be upset with me."

Sally threw her a glance as sharp as broken glass. "Why shouldn't I be? Didn't I help you out? Now I need help, and you won't come through." She sped down the stairs, and Josie raced behind breathlessly.

"But this is my big chance," said Josie. "Jim thinks the world of me. He's going to build a big theater and put me onstage. He's going to make me a star. I couldn't do 'that' with anybody but him."

They came downstairs into the long, well-appointed entrance hallway, where everything was as lush, well ordered, and quiet as the mansion of a millionaire. Sally turned and faced Josie, her green eyes magnetically drawing the younger woman to her.

"If you don't have work and no capital to invest and won't ask Jim for money—pray, how do you live, child?" asked Sally. Warmth shot into Josie's cheeks and ears at the insult of *child*, but she couldn't contradict those hard, green, adult eyes.

"I've sold a few things he's given me."

"Maybe you'd better get him to marry you."

"That's just it, Sally. He already has a wife."

"Do tell, precious."

"Sally, you're making fun of me," said Josie in a low, meek voice. Those hazel-flecked green eyes saw every corner inside Josie, searched out every pretense and half-truth, and made her shrivel like a plucked violet under the furnace of August's sun. She said, "I know I haven't been in New York as long as you, but we're in love. Really and truly, we are."

"Love's fine," said Sally, her hard tone contradicting her words.

"But in my experience it doesn't last. Is he going to divorce her and all those children for you?"

"But he only sees her once a month, and then for only a few days," said Josie. "I'm his New York wife, he says."

Those green eyes wouldn't turn Josie loose. They knew men—the ones that counted, the ones with money—and what they would pay down to the last quarter. "Josie, wise up," said Sally, her voice gentler. "You're not an actress, and Jim Fisk will never put you on-stage."

"I am and he will!"

"How long have you been in New York?"

"Two years."

"How many parts have you had?" Like a dentist's steel pick Sally was probing where it really hurt.

"A . . . few," Josie lied.

"And in addition to you, Jim Fisk has an arrangement with Helen Tomlinson and I wouldn't be at all surprised if he still stops in to see Susanna Cummins and God knows who all else." Josie's stomach shifted as if a small rodent that had been squatting on one side chose this moment to scamper to the other.

"Stops in?" repeated Josie, covering her confusion. Jim hadn't come right out and said he wasn't seeing anybody else, but they had silently agreed.

Sally explained, "Stops in—gooses, stuffs, humps, tickles, whatever you want to call it."

It wasn't true. It couldn't be. Josie felt country stupid, as if Jim was having a city joke at her expense. Or was Sally making this up to get her to work the party? She made up her mind to trust Jim.

"Jim loves me," she insisted.

"Jim Fisk is a man of large appetites," said Sally.

"I'm enough for him."

"You're young," said Sally. "Younger than I realized. Go your way. If you smarten up before you lose that wonderful figure, come back. I have buckets of discreet fellows who'll make sure you won't need to borrow money. Okay?"

All Josie could do was nod.

"And figure out some way of paying me back," said Sally, opening the door. "I won't press too hard, but at some point I'm going to mention it to Jim and see if he'll bail me out of a bad investment in the theater." Her smile wasn't cruel, yet there was little kindness in it, either. On hearing this, Jim would think that Josie had worked for Sally.

"No, Sally!" she pleaded. "Don't do that!"

39

Sally opened the front door. Outside was a dark gray wall of raw mist. "Then *you* get it from him," said Sally.

Josie stepped forward into the wet gray cloud. "Yes, Sally. Yes, yes, I will."

By this hour much of Cornelius Vanderbilt's Canal Street confidence had shriveled into restless, nagging anger. Standing alone in the window of his large paneled office at the Central, he stared out at Broadway. The gathering fog obscured the ox carts, clerks, fruit and vegetable peddlers, and full-skirted shopgirls hurrying home. Fisk and Gould also must have slipped across the Hudson, and yet his men swore that no one resembling the pair had boarded a ferry or been spotted at a pier all day. Nor were they at their homes or offices.

Vanderbilt's finger joints and ankles ached from arthritis. His loose back teeth throbbed as if miniature demons with tiny mallets and chisels hammered on them. His gouty right toe was so swollen that he could not wear his right shoe and limped about the office in stocking feet. Tonight it took a gigantic effort of will to push back the orchestra of pain that blared throughout his body.

He took out his handkerchief, gray from a single day's use in Manhattan's sooty air, and mopped the sweat off his flushed face. At the corner the skinny lamplighter set his satchel on the curb, propped his ladder on the lamppost, and scampered up to light the gas lamp. This afternoon his son William had called him a stupid old fool, and declared that when this news hit Wall Street every sharp trader would sell their stock short and drive the price down, down, down to make a whopping profit at the Vanderbilts' expense.

The lamp now lit, the Broadway lamplighter clambered down the pole, picked up his ladder and satchel, and with a whistle swaggered into the mist. Two drunken young clerks lurched out of the fog, singing a bawdy limerick. A quick stab of envy for their youth and freedom pierced Cornelius. Despite being seven stories above, he possessed a sudden urge to throw himself headlong through the window's glass to join them. He pressed his hot forehead against the cool, dark pane. Underneath his feet, all around him in the headquarters building, lay his company, the one he had built, the New York Central. It was the largest rail line in America, forty years of work and accumulation—2,000 miles of track, 40,000 employees, 100 locomotives, 700 passenger and freight cars. It was a mighty octopus with a thousand arms and ten thousand eyes and ears, and the headquarters under Cornelius's stocking feet was the heart that pumped millions of dollars as blood to every toe and fingertip. He, Cornelius, was its brain and soul—and if Drew and Gould and Fisk were to have their way, it was all to be ripped away from him by this single clever theft.

A chorus of "Jeanie with the Light Brown Hair" floated upward. Remembering his strength as a young captain on New York's harbor, Cornelius longed to trade places with one of these larky, singing clerks. How much simpler life had been back then! How full of himself he was in his teens! The son of a Staten Island farmer, he had started with nothing and put aside every penny. By the age of sixteen Cornelius had steadily saved enough—a hundred dollars—to buy his first periauger, a flat-bottomed boat with two masts, with which he ferried passengers five times a day between Staten Island and Manhattan.

What a thrill it was that gusty June day to first put his hand on the bucking tiller of his own boat! So long ago, he thought. Blue skies, fluffy clouds, waves lifting him like giant, gentle fingers. It must have been the summer of 1810. Rapidly sketched and resketched by a master hand, fluffy clouds scudded playfully across a canvas of vivid blue. Cheerful gulls wheeled overhead, and with the light boat under him Cornelius felt he, too, was flying. All that first day the waves crested gently under the bow of the periauger, the water's easy heft and lift raising him and the boat with the strength of an infinite power lifting and driving him through life. Several times that day, his hand gripping the rough wood of the whippy tiller, he burst out laughing in wide, rich joy.

The two singing clerks disappeared southward into the mist. A light March rain rattled the windowpanes. Cornelius gently pressed his gouty toe, but it was no better. The fog was so thick that the corner gas lamp was little more than a pale yellow glow. Yet, in what he reckoned was the last and most painful decade of his life, Cornelius saw one thing clearly: that bright June day's thrill had never been matched by all the triumphs of his bulging life, eventful as it was. That day wasn't matched five years later when he was the proud owner of five more periaugers. Nor fifty years later when he broke the back of the cheaters in the vicious Harlem Rail corner and made two million in as many months. Nor when he set up steamship routes to Europe, nor when he personally drove his sailors and laborers across the steaming isthmus of Nicaragua in his vain attempt to cut a canal across Central America. And not even when he triumphantly toured the capitals of Europe as American royalty in the *North Star*, the 2,500-ton steamer he built for the voyage at a cost of $500,000.

Then the Civil War. While it had been good for the steamers, it established for the first time that railroads were their equal, if not their superior, in transport. During the War, track had been laid at a furious rate, enabling the War Department to shuttle troops and artillery from one point of the Northeast to another, an advantage

41

the less industrial South could not match. The War over, the tracks remained in place, ready for commerce.

The Erie shared in this boom, for the South of course closed the Mississippi to the North's barge and steamer traffic. All the great trunk lines such as the Central and the Erie found themselves transporting huge cargoes that taxed their capacity but sent their earnings soaring. Before the War, Erie stock sold for $8, but by 1862 it had risen to $65. The following year it hit $122, driven by booming earnings. It established a gigantic new terminal at Jersey City, and with its two western terminals at Dunkirk and Buffalo, it became a formidable competitor of Cornelius's New York Central in carrying freight between the seaboard and the Great Lakes.

And now, Cornelius thought, dragging himself back into the present, to give his empire the business that it needed to survive, that it needed to live on after he was gone, he needed to cripple Daniel Drew's Erie before his opponent crippled him. For years the two roads had been bitter rivals in hauling through freight, and a rate war last year had increased the rivalry. Just as a military commander felt obliged to acquire an additional base in order to better protect the one he already had—and so on endlessly—so did Cornelius decide that the simplest way to end the Erie's competition was to obtain control of the road. After all, Cornelius reasoned, it was a much shakier line than his Central, weakened by a decade of tricky financial maneuvering by Drew, its treasurer.

Crippling Drew meant finding Fisk and Gould, his cat's-paws, before they escaped Manhattan, for even though they were new aboard the Erie, they were his aged rival's eyes, ears, hands, and feet.

Outside, the streetlamps along Broadway were only a string of fog-dimmed halos. The glow of Cornelius's hopes was shrinking with the arrival of night and mist. If his men couldn't find Jim Fisk and Jay Gould in the daylight, they would never find them in this fog-shrouded dark.

Never find them! In his mind's eye Cornelius saw a stock market panic, a crash, and his Central stock—the cornerstone of his empire—driven down till it was worthless. If the trading on the Exchange tomorrow lurched the wrong way, this might be one of his last nights on earth as the richest man in America, Commodore Cornelius Vanderbilt.

Josie Mansfield trudged the eight fog-gloomed blocks toward her boardinghouse. The damp fog clung stickily to her fox fur, her sleeves, her hair, and her face. She hadn't got the loan she wanted, and Sally had rattled her, but she resolved not to let Sally's brass contempt drag her down. And Sally was her friend! Her back teeth ground against the rocky bone of her anger.

In addition to paying Sally back, she must pay Mrs. Gascoyne the March rent and Madame Rumplemeyer's overdue dress bill. Not to speak of the rent that would come up again in April and all those shoes she had charged at Stewart's. She took a deep, bracing breath— the main thing was to be in bubbling good spirits for Jim's visit. She clomped up the three flights of stairs to her two rooms and closet of a kitchen.

With a bang and a shout Jim arrived ten minutes later. His diamond smile, ruddy face, broad shoulders, and sandy cavalry mustaches filled her door and blew away her mean spirits. She flew into his stout arms, and their warm squeeze made her worries sizzle away. He swept her off her feet, dangled a bottle of champagne in her face, and carried her into the bedroom.

She half pleaded, half giggled, "Jim! *Jiiiim!*" She resisted a little, which inflamed him further. A cloud of bay rum and talc, splashed and dusted on each morning by his hotel barber, rose off him like church incense. Something exciting had happened since yesterday, for he charged her with the energy of a bull exploring a new herd of cows.

After they made love, Jim wilted like a pricked balloon. He mumbled something about having to go to Jersey as soon as he got up, then started snoring. Josie wanted to talk, but instead she curled herself around his large bare back—her cheek against his wing bone, her hands on his fleshy sides—and drifted into sleep, lulled by the regular rhythm of his light snores.

Pay Dirt, California. Life in that half tent, half log cabin. No real floor, just tamped-down dirt. A privy out back, go to the well for water. Hot in summer, gray dust everywhere; miserably cold and damp all winter. Mud knee-deep in the streets, mud on the sidewalk, on your clothes, in your grit-filled fried beans, on your bread—everywhere.

Over the years, a parade of hard-muscled miners with Mama. Gold pickers with mud on their cheeks. Blond men with dust on their smiles. Cocky sluice men in greasy pants. One or two a year came to live with them, sometimes liking to say they were her stepdaddy. Although Josie couldn't remember her father, she didn't much like the newcomers, but Mama insisted that she kid along with her "stepfathers." After all, they brought dimes, quarters, and half-dollars into the house. At thirteen, under her probing, amazed fingers, her breasts blossomed. Suddenly every man in the tent city had his eye on her. To her surprise, she gained a new power; with only a glance she could make men approach or retreat. When she was sixteen she brought Dave Malobar close with her eyes, but then he wouldn't back off. Handsome as the head of Satan, he was the only one of Mama's boyfriends she let touch her. It didn't take much to make him suggest that they escape Pay Dirt for San Francisco.

There was a sudden snort, and the stout bull beside Josie sat bolt upright. Startled, she opened her eyes. Her pink bedroom. New York. She pulled the pink sheet over her bare breasts. It was Jim who was in bed with her, dear, dear Jim. She wasn't back in California with Dave and Mama. Jim's large hands repaired the damage that sleep and their lovemaking had done to the waxed tips of his mustaches.

"What time is it?" he asked. Mama's ever-boiling washpot and her passive, cow luck with miners. Josie saw the truth and faced Jim.

"You're leaving me, aren't you, Jim?" she asked. As soon as she said it, she regretted opening her mouth.

Jim shot her a quizzical glance. He appeared as strong and rumpled and innocent as one of those enormous buffaloes that Josie had seen from the train when she came east with her ex-husband. Jim shook himself to throw sleep off his large head and shoulders.

"Now what gives you that idea, kitten?" he asked. She took a deep breath.

"Because you said you were going to Jersey," she said.

"So?"

She faced him. "Where in Jersey?"

"I'm not all that sure," he said slyly. Her temper boiled, and she put her hands on her hips, arms akimbo.

"You're going to Jersey and you don't know where you're going?" she said. "Come on!" He wouldn't give her a straight answer. Sally was right.

"I think it's stupid, too, but Jay swore me to secrecy," said Jim, adding amusement to his boyish smirk. Oh, he looked all smiles and sunshine, but every man sounded the most convincing right before he took off.

"Jim, take me with you."

"Aw, sugar, I told you I can't. I'll probably be back Sunday night to take you to dinner at Del's."

"Sunday! But that's not but—three days!"

"That's all, kitten," he said in such a sober fashion that she almost believed him.

Sally was wrong about Jim. He wasn't like those limps she had known till now; he was a bull of a man, his blond mustaches his horns. Whenever she hit him in one of their playful tussles, it was

44

like slapping a large rock. Little bothered him. He grinned at every insult and often he exaggerated the jibe so that none of it was the truth. This time it was different. He wasn't a treacherous Dave or a weak Peter.

"Oh, Jim, I'm sorry," she said. "I get so worried when I think you might not see me." He reached across the bed for her arm.

"Have you forgotten all the things we're going to do?" he asked. Warm bubbles of pleasure welled up. She snuggled against the heat of his body.

"A trip to Paris and Rome?" she said.

"We'll see every show in both towns," he said. She pictured the two of them in European capitals. A rich, handsome couple dawdling in outdoor cafés, lingering over bittersweet coffee and tart pastries, and watching the pursuit of elegant furbelows by rakish dandies. Living with Josie for weeks would make him see how much more fun she was than any other woman. Every night they would visit a different theater and take notes on what she should do when she was a leading lady onstage.

"You're going to build a theater?" she asked.

"The biggest in New York," he said. "You'll strut the boards every evening with star billing."

"I'll make you proud," she said. "I played Lady Macbeth in St. Louis. I was wonderful." Even if the boos and catcalls of those hicks had forced her off the stage.

"Every man in New York will buy a ticket to see you," said Jim. "Why, even now when we walk into the Broadway Central or the Hoffman, every eye turns to you." Josie giggled and hugged him. She liked this part the best. The spikes of his mustaches waggled with hot excitement. "They all *want* you, but they know only I *have* you," he said in a breathy voice. "They'll stare at you from the stalls with adoration shining in their eyes."

"And our house?" asked Josie. Her own house! Then Sally Woods would see that what she possessed with Jim was special, that she wasn't some casual thing like Helen Tomlinson or Susanna whatever.

"The snuggest little house on Fifth Avenue."

Josie saw frosted glass in the front door's side windows, a little brass bell, and portraits of snooty ancestors. "I'll cook you little suppers after the show," she said. She felt calm and wonderful; Sally Woods had been calloused by too many rough men's hard uses to know real love. "I'll be the best hostess there ever was for your friends and clients. I'll make sure your coats are properly pressed. How will we get around town?"

"Something special," said Jim. "One of Poinsettia's carriages.

Black with silver trim—real elegant. Naturally we'll need a driver."

To show Jim how practical she was, she said, "He can double as our butler. He'll serve us late-night supper by the fire when we discuss how our busy day went." His deep sigh reeked with satisfaction.

"We'll have it all," he said.

She squeezed his chest. "I'll make you happier than any woman has ever made a man," she said. "That's a promise." He pulled her face around and gave her a long intense kiss.

She fell an enormous distance into a warm, sweet darkness with no prospect of hitting bottom. She opened her legs slightly, expecting his hand to move between her thighs—

Jim broke away and snatched his gold watch off the nightstand. "Oh, no," he shouted. "I've missed Jay!"

"You're not going to Jersey?" she asked. His forehead creased with worry, he swung his legs over the edge of the bed, snorted, and reached for his pants.

"We got to. We done yanked the cat's tail and he's chasing us."

"Jim!" she said. "You could stay here."

One leg in his pants, he turned to her. "Stay here?"

"Yes! I'll get us champagne. I'll cook, or run over to Delmonico's for meals." She ran her hand over his bare shoulder in a caress. "I can promise you more fun here in a week than a whole year of New Jersey." Jim lowered his half-panted leg to the floor.

"Hummm," he said. For a long moment they stared at each other, and she didn't breathe. His ruddy face brightened. "It might work. Nobody seen me come in here. All we need is four or five days till the Commodore calms down and sees there ain't nothing he can do but dicker with us." He grimaced. "Damn, though! I got to meet Jay at Del's. I promised to meet him an hour ago. His old tin oven's burning up, I bet." He thrust on his pants and stood. "Tell you what, though. Let me go see Jay and tell him to go over alone, and I'll pick up dinner for us on the way back."

Josie threw herself on him and gave him an excited kiss. Sally was wrong! Wrong! Wrong!

5

Yes, indeed! We often give dinners that cost $100 a head. Why, sometimes the flowers cost $20 for each diner, and I have paid as high as $20 for each and every menu card. It doesn't take long to run up to $100 that way.

—Lorenzo Delmonico, 1868

As Jay Gould crossed Broad Street, a large carriage came tearing out of the fog and almost ran him down. Delmonico's loomed up, a four-story brick building with windows as yellow and cheery as a farmhouse's. The carriage that almost ran him down drew up in front of the restaurant. Against Delmonico's merry, gaslit windows, the plump figure of his partner Jim Fisk swaggered out of the heavy carriage. Swinging his cane, Jim shouted a loud good-bye to the cabbie. He turned and danced a little jig, his large cape billowing around him. Jay hurried forward.

Jim shouted his usual hearty greeting to the doorman. "How's your old tin oven, Barney?" Coming up from behind, Jay grabbed Jim's fleshy arm.

"For God's sake, Jim," said Jay. "Keep it down! We've got to get out of town." Jim spun, his face flushed with pleasure in the bronze glow of Delmonico's gas lamps. The sharp points of his Napoleon III mustaches waggled with delight.

"Jay!" he shouted. "How's *your* old tin oven?" His ruddy heartiness overpowered the fog, his plump face a jovial sun amid the thick mist. Jay shook his head in annoyance. Jim's checked suit and gaudy cape begged for attention. Two businessmen, entering Delmonico's, stopped and stared, and Jim shot them a little glance of pleasure. Jay put his finger to his lips.

"They're everywhere," Jay whispered. "Every stable, depot, pier, and ferry dock." Jim turned to him, puzzled.

"Who's everywhere?" his impish baritone asked.

"The Commodore's men, damn it," Jay said urgently. "Who else?"

Jim swung the tip of his cane in a careless circle. "So what?" he said. "I've got the *Providence* coming." This was the lead steamer of Jim's steamship company. Relief spread through Jay. Suddenly Jim didn't look like a simpleminded Broadway fool.

"Thank God!" said Jay. "Let's grab a hack and get to it."

"But it won't dock till eight."

"Eight!"

"Sure." Jim rolled his eyes toward Delmonico's hot, sunny lights. "Let's get us a bite before we go into exile." Jay stared at him openmouthed.

"Not till eight!" said Jay. He told the story of his capture and escape this afternoon, and said that even when he arrived back at his Twenty-eighth Street brownstone, black police and Central vans were crowded hard by the front and back entrances. He and George then tried to cross to Jersey from three different piers, only to find each swarming with Central agents.

"Take it easy, Jaybo," said Jim. "Is he looking for us in dining rooms—or depots?" However, the white-eyed glance Jay shot at the lace-curtained windows was as full of fear as a horse's at a burning house.

"I'm not going in there," said Jay. "We'll be in plain sight."

Jim pulled him under the shelter of his large arm in a conspiratorial manner. "Do you see any railroad dicks around here?" he argued. Jay's reluctant feet were drawn toward the front stoop, where Barney's plump face and red nose beamed a welcome.

"But only if we take a table upstairs or in a private room," said Jay.

Barney pulled open one of the frosted glass doors, and Jay entered behind Jim's broad back. The cozy, wood-paneled front hall greeted him with a hundred cheerful fragrances. Woody bayleaf vied with fried Maryland oysters, while sweet rosemary flirted with a dozen aromatic gravies. Jay's stomach clenched like a fist. He didn't want to eat, he wanted to get across the river.

Keeping his cane and cape, Jim entered the main dining room, called the Long Room, and paused. Jay stood slightly behind him. The vast space contained a couple hundred feet of white tablecloths, mouth-watering aromas, spangling crystal, and white-bibbed, dark-suited diners that stretched the entire block from Broad to New Street. Because its hall formed a shortcut between the two streets for hurrying Wall Street clerks, the downtown restaurant was never empty during business hours.

Lorenzo Delmonico, the tall, large-girthed, middle-aged owner, gave a dignified whoop and raced forward. Three plump fellows rose from their table and headed in Jim's direction. Jay recognized them, prosperous stockbrokers, one of whom, Walter Kidder, owned his own firm. Jay pinched Jim's elbow to say they should nip on upstairs, but Jim stretched out his large hand to greet the four.

"We're going upstairs to a little nook by ourselves," said Jim in a low, conspiratorial growl. "Me and Jaybo here gonna hold hands."

The three brokers hooted with laughter. Jay forced a smile through his black beard. He was small and quiet, no taller than the average man's chin. His dark, conservative suit was a bit shabby and out-of-date for Delmonico's and for a man who was the President of a major railroad, as if he were too insecure in his position to spring for fashionable suits. The truth was, he had little use for show. As usual, with Jim among backslappers he felt like a stiff idiot. If his partner often presented himself as a harmless clown—even at times as a buffoon—there was something almost too quiet about Jay, something furtive, that didn't inspire trust. To others he held himself aloof and superior, but to him the space between himself and them seemed vast, an abyss, best not braved out of the terror of failing to reach the other side and falling. His was a shyness of reticence and caution that often came across as sinister and calculating.

Lorenzo Delmonico poked his head into the circle around Jim and Jay. "Your table's ready, gents. I'm sending over two bottles of our best champagne, on the house. You've done the city right today. Somebody ought to have kicked that old walrus in the crotch long before now."

Jim rubbed his hands in appreciation. "Champagne!" he exclaimed. He dashed forward and followed Lorenzo across the crowded dining room. His hat and his coat on his arm, Jay raced after his partner.

While he always disliked crowds, particularly half-drunk, boisterous mobs, tonight the money-dark stares of these Wall Street jaybirds struck Jay as particularly ominous. Any one could be a Vanderbilt spy. Lorenzo led Jim across the thick carpet toward the Long Room's most conspicuous table, one right in the center of the white-dickeyed horde. Jim sat facing the other diners, and Jay threw himself into the chair next to him.

"Damn it," shouted Jay, "this isn't a private room—not by a long shot!" Jim waved his arm at the crowd, and the three diamonds on his white shirtfront winked obscenely.

Followed by a half-dozen brokers, Walter Kidder strutted up to their table. "Say, Jim, how the hell did you and Jay here get the Walrus to bite off all those new shares?" Jim shot him a glance of exaggerated delight.

"The Walrus?" asked Jim, artfully suspending the moment.

"His Majesty King Vanderbilt," replied Kidder.

"How do you get a walrus to take anything?" Jim asked. The showman in him let the moment hang before he capped it with "We just tucked them shares in dead fish and tossed 'em to him!"

The brokers guffawed along with him. As usual, Jim was the center of attention, even in a room so vast. He struck many who first met him, especially those who considered themselves socially superior to him, as of no consequence—a hearty clown, vulgar but harmless—but a quarter hour with him almost always changed that first impression. His loudly checked suit, which seemed at first fit for Van Amberg's circus, became jolly and unpretentious. Those who wore conservative getups felt themselves to be hypocrites in expensive black wool, hiding passions that were sinister, whereas everything Jim felt shot across his face and tumbled from his lips. His jokes and rolling eyes made everybody around him feel included, as well as wise, smart, rich, pretty—whatever it was you wanted to be, around Jim in some mysterious fashion you gained it.

Jay recognized the fleshy, florid mugs of the men who hung over their table, although he didn't like them. They were typical of the post–Civil War crowd who swaggered nightly into Delmonico's to pay absurd prices for dinner to prove to themselves and their drinking companions how smart they were. The square-jawed lamppole now arguing with Jim was Marshall Roberts, who had greatly increased his fortune by chartering freighters to the Union navy at exorbitant rates. His *Empire City*, bought for $12,000, returned him better than a million dollars in wartime charter contracts. The snuff-stained blubber lip was John Baskins, who was indicted for manufacturing and selling defective black powder to the Union Army, but whose six law-twiddlers got him off with a $1,000 fine.

The noise in the restaurant subsided to a loud, dull rumble. Jay pulled Jim's head down to his to make himself heard.

"Jim," he shouted, "let's get the hell out of here."

But Jim shot to his feet and shouted over the crowd's head to a waiter, "Henry, Henry, Henry—come over here and take my order!" An enormous white-aproned penguin with slicked-back hair shouldered his way through the flock around the table. Even at such close range, Jim was forced to shout to reach his target. "I want two dozen oysters, Henry. A thick cut of your best roast beef. Red wine, something with a bite to it. Put me a decent lobster on the plate, and give me a bowl of Frank's pan-roast potatoes." He dropped back into his chair and Jay grabbed his arm.

"Damn it, Jim," he said. "We're sitting ducks in here!"

"These are our friends," said Jim, yanking his arm free.

"A hundred screaming friends—and likely one Judas."

Jim shook his head with the weary exasperation of a parent dealing with a child's night fears. "Then, you run down to the pier and wait," said Jim with mock seriousness. "I'll be along shortly."

"I told you—Vanderbilt's men are all over the piers."

One of Henry's boys set a platter of raw oysters in front of Jim. Employing a dinner fork, Jim speared the oysters two at a time and stuffed them in his mouth. Jay leaned back, again searching for faces who would report their whereabouts to Vanderbilt. The gas sconces along the elegant walls peered at him like a row of malicious yellow eyes. Everywhere he looked, red-splotched, fleshy fellows slurped oysters, carved duck, loaded forks with beef, swilled champagne—and glanced over at them.

Couldn't Jim see? Delmonico's bright elegance was only a giant lamp spotlighting them. In short, they were boxed in here precisely as he and George had been boxed in this afternoon at Saddler's Stable. Was Jim too blind to see that they were sitting in a perfect trap?

At that hour Cornelius Vanderbilt and Judge George Barnard sat in Cornelius's large office at the top of the New York Central Railroad building. Outside the rain lashed and rattled the dark windows in long, ropy waves.

"How the hell could they have gotten away?" Cornelius asked for the eighth time. Both men needed shaves and looked gray in the light given off by the mahogany room's large gas chandelier. Judge Barnard's pleasant raccoon face smiled agreeably, as always.

"They haven't," he said in a soothing tenor. "Your men will turn them up."

"My damn toe is killing me." Ever the sympathetic listener, Judge Barnard scrunched up his raccoon eyes and nodded. Cornelius had come to hate all wet weather, for it made his arthritis swell his ankles and his old hip injury ache. "I can't let William and Sophie know about it," he said, "or they'll be yelling again for me to retire. One little limp, and they want to rush me into my grave." Judge Barnard beamed in appreciation of the joke.

"You been in tough spots before. It'll come out all right."

Cornelius glanced at his desktop at a gray-and-black daguerreotype. In it stood an erect young man in the smart dress gray of West Point. It was his son, George Washington Vanderbilt, dead five years. George's cocky cadet's smile grinned at his father, wavering no more than it ever had during the ten years since that graduation day.

"Now, if George was here, we would have had the Erie a year ago," said Cornelius. "He would have figured out how to find these two rogues in a flash. He would have understood what these young rascals were up to."

"He was a charming scamp, that one," said Judge Barnard. Staring at his dead son's firm, bony jaw, Cornelius shook his head sadly.

"He was a young wizard," he said. "He possessed guts and brains as well as charm. He would never have wanted his old dad to retire."

"Your William is all right," said Barnard. From the daguerreotype Cornelius heard the rattle of drums and felt the crispness of the Point, everything done in such a splendid, sharp-edged style.

"William doesn't have the feel for it," Cornelius said. "Most fellows would give an arm to inherit the Central. Not William. I had to beg him to come to Manhattan after George died. Said he didn't want to be in my shadow. Said he was happy farming on Staten Island. I had to give him a whole block of stock to get him over here. But who else could I trust?" George's bold face continued to stare at him. Cornelius never tired of looking at the confident jaw, the uplifted eyes, and the trace of ironic smile on the fleshy Vanderbilt lips.

"That damn war!" said Cornelius. "The rebels couldn't put a bullet in George, so it had to be the damn malaria. I sent the lad to the south of France to recover like the doctors told me. I would have sent him to the moon if it would have helped." The moon. Now George was farther away than even the moon. "Wasn't any of us with him, Judge, not a single family member, to comfort him, when he died out there—" Cornelius stopped, unwilling to spill more grief. On the desk, George looked as ready as ever to step out of his gray-and-black square of pasteboard to help his father. Died, died, died, Cornelius thought, my own flesh I loved died before his time and prime. Died!—even after five years he had trouble believing that George was gone.

Judge Barnard stood up and walked to the window, where he stared politely at the crystal-black rain. Cornelius blinked back unseemly tears and shook his head from side to side to throw off this resurgence of grief. He would have been more than glad—eager—to take George's place.

After he recovered, he said to Barnard's back, "I'll tell you this— I'm going to eat Drew's heart and liver over this one."

There was a knock at the door and William stuck his night-pale face in.

"Pa, there's a man out here that says he knows where Gould and Fisk are. He won't talk to anybody but you." Cornelius swung his painful foot off the visitor's chair, hoping William hadn't noticed it propped there.

"What?" he shouted. His spirits blossomed as rapidly as a fire given kerosene. "Get him in here!"

It was Higgens, the shifty little lawyer who handled suits for injured railway passengers. In his collar, jaunty black cravat, and lady's-pink vest, he swaggered in, cutting a legalistic smirk. Cornelius scowled at this old adversary, for Higgens often arrived at Central train wrecks before ambulances.

"So where are they?" demanded Cornelius.

"What's the reward, governor?" asked Higgens in his snotty, high-pitched tenor. His shifty eyes took in Judge Barnard, before whom he often appeared, and his smirk cringed into servility. Sick of failure and delay, Cornelius stalked toward Higgens, who held up two manicured hands to stop him.

"I was in the bar at Delmonico's," Higgens said quickly. "Mr. Gould and Mr. Fisk are eating there. They were bragging that they were eating off your losses, Commodore. Feasting off them, to judge from the size of their steaks. Broke my heart to see it, man of your stature. Mr. Fisk was making big jokes about it. A lot of the Wall Street crowd thought it was quite the laugh."

"Are they still there?"

"They were ten minutes ago."

That night a different Negro serving girl, young and buxom, admitted Josie Mansfield into Sally Wood's richly furnished town house. She showed Josie to a well-appointed receiving room off the front hall.

Josie was too agitated to sit. Icy thumbs of panic pressed against her stomach as she paced up and down on the maroon-and-cream oriental carpet. Maybe Jim hadn't lied this evening. He hadn't returned, but had written her a hurried note that said he would need to go to Jersey after all. He enclosed a fifty-dollar bill, a vile, greasy bank note that told her the truth—that he had only been toying with her this evening. She was simply another dolly on his string. He figured she could be settled with for fifty dollars.

She hated him. She hated all men. No week of cozy breakfasts in bed, no friendly tussles beneath pink satin sheets, no firelit *tête-à-têtes* with nose-pricking champagne and icy oysters. No snug little house on Fifth Avenue. No cometlike career onstage, plotted and executed with the man she loved. No glorious trips to Paris and Rome.

The door to the drawing room slid back. Male laughter, warm gaslight, and the tinkle of crystal stemware surged in with Sally.

Tonight Sally wore a daring, slender tube of spring-green silk. Her only jewelry was her heavy charm bracelet that jangled with the savagery of an untamed gold pet with a hundred writhing arms, legs, and mouths. Her red hair swirled up and back into a bold bun at the rear of her head. This afternoon's freckles had faded into creamy, unblemished cheek.

"Josie!" said Sally. "You look awful! What's happened?" Josie lowered her eyes in shame.

"I've been a fool," said Josie. "Don't laugh at me, Sally."

"No laughter, just tears." The hazel-orange flecks in her eyes added and subtracted, multiplied and divided. "You'll party with His Honor?"

"Yes," said Josie, unable to raise her head. "Can I have an advance?"

For a few moments silence separated them. As if a door opened and closed in another part of the house, the tinkle of a piano, a man's money-rich bass laugh, and the shriek of female gabble rose and fell.

"I shouldn't ask what happened?"

Josie took out the handkerchief balled up in her pocket. "He's left me."

"Aw, Josie!" said Sally. In her swooping tone Josie heard the convincing thump of shared pain. "Come 'round tomorrow for some money."

"Thank you. I'll go now."

"Fine," said Sally. "Unless you want to meet some of the fellows?"

"No, thank you," said Josie. "I wouldn't be good company tonight."

In Delmonico's, his shirt sticky with sweat, Jay Gould loosened his collar to give himself room to breathe. At his side Jim crammed overloaded pitchforks of pink-and-white lobster into his fat, oily cheeks. Jay felt more and more woozy, as if he might throw up.

Several dozen brokers, customers' men, and other Wall Street hangers-on were still jammed against their table. For the third time tonight Jim was regaling this admiring horde with his and Jay's methods of selling Commodore Vanderbilt newly issued Erie stock.

"Hell, the Old Walrus wanted our Erie shares, the brokers told us, and he wanted them the worst way," Jim bellowed. He waved about his forkful of lobster with the zest of a high-spirited orchestra conductor. The eyes of the plump crowd were rapt. Jim clapped Jay on the shoulder. "Jaybo here had all the ideas, like always. I'm too dumb to think up this stuff. So like he told me, I went down to the basement to our printin' press. I run off convertible bonds representing 50,000 shares, took them to the office, converted them into stock, and tossed them into the Street. They was gone in three days!"

An admiring "Ahhh!" rose from the crowd. Spurning his fork as inadequate, Jim dug out the lobster's tail from its shell with his fingers, dragged it through butter sauce, and jammed it in his mouth.

"I said to myself, Jim, these-here certificates are costing you two cents apiece for ink and paper, and here's the Commodore paying you forty dollars each for them—hell, this kind of business I'll do all year long!"

The crowd guffawed and poked each other in the ribs. Jay wanted to slide under the table. How stupid I was, he thought, to take a partner like this!

"So I printed me up another batch of 50,000," Jim continued. "He took them, too—just like a walrus slurping down a tasty salmon. I said to myself, Jim, this is some business you got yourself here! And gents"—here Jim paused to bestow an admiring glance on Jay— "before we followed our wizard Mr. Gould's advice and shipped it off to New Jersey, we had eight million of the Commodore's money laying on our table in cash, bonds, and certified checks!"

Jay occupied himself by calculating ways of forcing Jim off the Erie's board of directors. If he was ruined by this lard-mountain blabbermouth, he decided, he had only himself to blame. He put down his napkin and stood up, ready to bolt through the mob.

Pushing through the crowd was Frank Renhofer, Delmonico's head chef, bearing aloft Jim's bucket-sized chocolate soufflé. Eyes and lips contorted by lust, Jim lifted his thick arm toward the quivering mountain of chocolate.

"Ahhhh!" he roared, "the reward of success! Frank, eating this is almost as much fun as snatching money from the Walrus. Don't forget, now—send the bill to the Commodore!"

In the middle of the hoots this provoked, a crash exploded in the entrance hallway, the din of a dozen angry bulls smashing through Delmonico's front doors.

In an instant, as if a heavy blanket were thrown over every table from Broad to New Street, the clatter and babble hushed. Then chairs thudded on the thick carpets as every diner stood, the better to run or protect himself. Jim shot to his feet.

Through the Long Room's entrance burst a dozen hefty men— blue-suited policemen with billies and hunky railroad detectives with pistols poking in the air—headed by the seventy-five-year-old Commodore Vanderbilt himself, his lampblack cape billowing behind him. The Commodore's angry red face, bulging eyes, and winglike, white muttonchops made him look as vengeful as a fiend from Hell raiding a whorehouse. He stopped near the entrance to cut off escape.

"All right," he shouted. "I know they're here. Where the hell are they?"

Cornelius Vanderbilt pushed his way past Lorenzo Delmonico's protests into the Long Room. Hundreds of white-dickeyed diners were on their feet staring at him. For a moment Cornelius's vision went a bit giddy. He thrust his confusion behind him and demanded the thieves' whereabouts, yet not one man admitted having seen Fisk or Gould.

Waving about Judge Barnard's tattered "Warrant for Arrest," followed by William and a dozen policemen, Cornelius raced through the private rooms on the restaurant's upper floors. Despite a thorough search, he discovered no cowering Fisk or Gould.

"Damn it," he roared to William, "they're here! I feel it in my bones."

Cornelius raced downstairs and into the steamy kitchen. The cooks and waiters insisted they hadn't seen either Gould or Fisk. Finally he bullied out of them that the pair, on their hands and knees, had escaped through the scullery into the back alley.

He ran out the back, followed by his men. From a shivering driver at the public hack stand he learned that they had taken a cab to the Central Street docks.

Again they had eluded him. But he was getting closer. No time now to hold back.

"Come on!" ordered Cornelius, waving his men toward their carriages.

With a youth's energy, he pulled himself up onto the open box next to his driver. His carriage tore up Broadway, followed by William's and three police vans. Pedestrians, dogs, ragged children, and gaudy, lip-rouged hookers—any soul out on this eerie, misty night—lurched out of the path as they sped northward.

Cornelius's blood pounded in his throat. Now he had the upper hand. That dumb pair would try to hire a boat and pilot to cross the river, but no harbor captain would put his hull into the Hudson's tricky currents on such a fog-bound night.

Standing, craning about from his eight-foot-high perch, he began his search at the south end of the Canal Street piers, a wide expanse of wet wood planking that extended northward for fifteen blocks.

In their berths four-masted schooners rocked gently in the river's waves, their windows lit by the yellow glow of lanterns. Cornelius's hands and face were hot from excitement and cold from stinging whips of mist. A harmonica's hum wove a lacy pattern in the watery night air. The five carriages bumped slowly northward. Facing the docks were cheery windows lit by cobalt-blue or scarlet lamp globes. On them neat white lettering spelled out women's names, *Julie*, *Lena*, *Rose*, or *The Flower of the Rhine*, the sure sign of waterfront whores. Cornelius yelled questions at the sailors loitering around the ships' gangplanks, but no one had seen the fat thief and his small, thin sidekick.

At the north end of the docks the haze hung in the air like suspended clumps of rain. Down by the end of the pier swung a yellow halo. Cornelius leaned foward. A plump silhouette holding an oil lantern was daintily lowering itself off the dock, very likely into a rowboat.

Plump? Dainty?

"Ahhh!" Cornelius bellowed. "Fisk!" He turned to the rear and yelled for his men to follow. His driver seemed befuddled. Cornelius snatched the wet reins and whip from the fool and lashed the four horses. They shot forward, the carriage's iron rims roaring and clattering on the slippery dock planks. His driver grabbed the seat rail with both hands and held on. Cornelius lashed the horses again and turned his head to scream backward, "Come on, damn it! Come on!"

Illuminated by a raised lantern, two pale ovals, like pink balloons on a dark fence, rose over the edge of the pier. Spying the carriage, they ducked down.

When his team was twenty feet from the end of the pier Cornelius reined them in. Night, fog, and Fisk's lantern had combined to blind the lead horses, who didn't see the black water rushing up. Cornelius pulled harder on the reins, and next to him his driver yanked back the brake handle with the entire weight of his body. With a tearing scrape, the iron-rimmed wheels slid sideways on the slippery planks.

Pawing the air, the four horses arced off the planks of the dock, for a moment defying gravity. The carriage, driver, and Cornelius followed. The entire rig shot off the edge of the dock and over the upturned, startled faces of the pair in the rowboat. Suddenly everything went quiet in Cornelius's ears. Suspended. A calm, weightless sail through rushing night air. In one motion Cornelius stood and pushed himself up and clear of the carriage. The last thing he saw before he hit the stinging water was Gould holding up a lantern, the fat Fisk frantically pulling the oars of the rowboat. Then Cornelius hit the water and everything turned cold, wet, and black.

Damn all! Trapped under dozens of cold, black blankets, Cornelius thrashed about for air. He burst above the surface.

The rowboat was pulling away. Cornelius's own men, like ninnies, stood on the dock, their lanterns raised, and watched helplessly as the two thieves rowed into the wall of fog.

"Get them!" he roared from the water. "And get me out of here, damn it!" shouted Cornelius. "I'm freezing."

The detectives and police hurried to obey. Tied to the sinking carriage, the horses in the river still screamed in fear and thrashed about loudly. On the pier, Cornelius scrambled to his feet, water squishing out of his single remaining shoe.

"Shoot the horses," he ordered, "so I can hear those criminals."

At the fog-muffled pop of the first shot, the lantern from the rowboat arced out as Gould threw it overboard. Half a dozen more pops finished off the screaming horses. The gray shadow of the rowboat vanished into night and the solid, murky fogbank. In the near silence, the clank of oars from the rowboat's locks was swallowed up by the heavy mist.

"Let's go to the Battery and get out a couple of ferries," Cornelius said to William, who draped his topcoat around his father's shoulders.

"In this weather?" William said. "We can't take a ferry out."

"Like hell we can't."

"You need dry clothes, Papa."

Cornelius pulled the edges of the dry coat around him. "Like hell I do," he roared. "Those two don't know the currents out there. I was *born* on this river. They'll spin around in circles all night. We'll pick them up easy. Or run the bastards right down into the water."

Part Two

WRESTLING WITH THE DEVIL

I avoid bad luck by being patient. Whenever I'm obliged to get into a fight, I always wait and let the other fellow get tired first.

—Jay Gould, *The New York Times*, 1892

6

It takes more skill to cross Broadway
than to cross the Atlantic in a clamboat.

—J. H. Warren,
The Crying Shame of Cities, 1875

Jim Fisk strained at the oars of the
rowboat. Utter darkness, as black as being under a blanket in the
closet of a haunted house on a moonless night.

"Weren't no water in this boat when we started, was there?" he
asked Jay. A knock and a thud came from the other end of the skiff.

"Water?" Jay answered, his voice sharp with alarm.

"There is now," said Jim. "See if you can find a pail under the
seat." Damp blackness lay in front, toward Manhattan; more damp
blackness lay behind, toward what he hoped was Jersey; and the black
and filthy Hudson surged and fell under him. A foul paste of salty
fish, tannery scraps, sewage, and rotting offal coated his tongue.

A thumping about from the prow. "No pail," reported Jay.

A wet icicle of fear slithered through Jim's gut. "We must have
sprung a leak. The water's now over the top of my shoe."

"Mine, too. I'll use my hat."

Aroused by his vigorous pulls, the lobster that Jim had eaten for
dinner chose this moment to dig its way out of prison. The ripping
and tearing of these claws against the floor of his stomach awakened
the iced oysters that several hours ago had happily tumbled down
his gullet. Intending to be first through any tunnel, they scooted back
and forth under the crustaceans' prickly bellies.

"You row for a while," whispered Jim. Even though they maneuvered carefully past each other, the skiff almost turned over. But

five minutes of rowing made Jay's cough kick up so bad that Jim was forced to take the oars again.

A half hour later Jay's steady bailing paused. "Do you know which direction you're rowing in?" he asked.

Jim pulled a slimy rope off the handle of the right oar that he hoped was seaweed but that came apart in his fingers like rotting steer guts. "Direction?" he asked. "To Jersey—I damn sure hope."

Distantly came the hammer of a steam engine. Jim paused and listened. Jay stopped bailing. A foghorn blasted. Relief as hot as the cozy little fire back in his Hoffman House suite flooded Jim.

"Hurray! We're saved!" shouted Jim. "A ferry!" No more rowing, and a boiling bumper of rum by the captain's potbellied stove!

"Quiet!" hissed Jay.

"They could see us more easy if you hadn't thrown that lamp overboard," Jim went on. "We'll have to shout loud." Jay's small hand pressed his shoulder.

"Quiet!" said Jay. "It's probably Vanderbilt's."

Jim turned toward Jay, but all he saw was darkness. "Vanderbilt's?"

"Out looking for us," whispered Jay. "Who else would be out in this fog?" Jim's eyes strained to see through the dark.

"Yeah," said Jim, "but better we get picked up. We're liable to get swept out to sea."

"No," said Jay, his low voice as stiff as the oar raised in Jim's hand. "Keep quiet and they won't see us."

"Won't see us? You know as well as I do what the Atlantic is like."

"We can make it across," came the same stiff, hard voice.

Jim opened his yap to argue, but the butter wouldn't come out. Jay's tone, as unyielding as engineer's brick, had thrown his speech box into confusion. Jim knew this starched tone of Jay's; it meant that Jay was set, rigid with purpose. Once he heard it, Jim only rarely managed to budge Jay. Jim pulled the oars into the skiff. His mind raced over possibilities. His partner didn't weigh more than 140 pounds, and his stomach and lungs were frail, but inside that small frame was a will as hard and straight as a heavy length of steel rail. How the hell to get him to change his mind?

"Jay, I'm going to tell you the truth," said Jim, injecting his voice with all the urgency he could muster. "I'm turned around. I don't have any idea which way I'm rowing."

"If we don't get across tonight," said Jay, "we'll spot the shore in the morning."

Maybe Jay had quietly slipped his marbles overboard while Jim was doing all that heavy pulling. "By morning we could be five miles out to sea, partner, probably tipped over," said Jim. "We won't know whether we're pulling to Cuba, England, or the North Pole."

"I had enough of his Hell's Kitchen toughs today," Jay said. "Who knows what 'accident' will happen to us on that ferry?"

The throb of the ship's engine grew into a steady, comforting thunka-thunka-thunk. The watery rush of the ship's wake was such solace that Jim chuckled. Dry clothes. He might even be in Josie's warm arms by dawn.

"Jay, come on," pleaded Jim. "Be sensible. Let's call out. Let's give it up for the night."

"We can make it across," insisted Jay's whisper.

"Make it across!" said Jim. Damn it, he was having as much trouble with Jay as back in the office. Jay always needed to have his way. And his way was never the goddamn obvious answer, always some tricky scheme you had to puzzle your way through. "You stay, then," said Jim. "I'll get picked up."

"I'll stay—and *you'll* get picked up?" scoffed Jay. "You alone? Now, just how do we make *that* little deal with the Commodore's toughs?"

Jim's wet feet ached from the past hour in the cold water sloshing in the bottom of the skiff. So the Commodore put him in jail or ruined him—he had been ruined twice before. It was a damn sight easier on a fellow than drowning.

A monstrous, humming sea dragon bore down on the rowboat. The running lights of a lumbering ferry broke through the fog. Toward them sailed portholes as bright as a row of yellow dragon's eyes. At the railing, hunky shooters bearing rifles and sailors with lanterns peered into the foggy murk. Behind those warm lights was a potbellied stove, tots of spicy rum, and a firm deck. Careful not to capsize the skiff, Jim stood up and shouted.

"Over here!"

Jay's hand firmly grasped Jim's hip; after a moment's pause it pushed him sharply and hard. The skiff yawed, and Jim toppled backward into thin air. Arms flailing, he fell through a grave-crust of cold water. He struck out frantically. *I'll drown! Which way is up?*

His hands thunked onto something solid, and he grasped the boat eye of the skiff. He pulled himself up and opened his mouth to bellow at the ferry, the yellow portholes of which were abreast of them, but Jay's palm clamped over his mouth.

"Say one word and I'll drown you," hissed Jay. His other hand sat firmly on top of Jim's head. A dozen icy tongues of freezing water licked Jim's cheeks. Crystal-sharp teeth bit into his legs, arms, and crotch. Hanging here on the edge of the world, Jim didn't dare move, much less shout.

In seconds it was over. The yellow-eyed sea dragon lumbered and throbbed by, and they were left bobbing on a rotten woodchip in lonely blackness. With elaborate care not to upset the skiff, Jay helped Jim up and in. Grateful to be out of the freezing water, Jim clutched the wooden seat and gasped for breath. The ferry's wake savagely pitched the skiff about. Jim pushed himself up, making the skiff yaw dangerously in the rough waves.

"What did you do that for?" demanded Jim.

"I told you not to yell," said Jay.

"You damn fool!" shouted Jim, half rising. "I ought to throw *you* overboard."

"Don't move!" ordered Jay. "You'll turn us over."

"Why not?" shouted Jim. "You'll see what it's like in there!" He began to shiver all over.

"I'm sorry," said Jay, "but I couldn't let you holler out. Here, take my topcoat." Fumbling in the darkness, Jim took it and draped it, still warm from Jay's body heat, across his shoulders.

"You son of a bitch! I'll need more than your 'sorry' and your coat—I'll freeze out here."

"Then row," said Jay. "It'll keep you warm. I'll give you my scarf, too."

"What's the use?" said Jim. "Which way? Certainly we're turned around now."

"If we assume they were heading up the channel from Vanderbilt's Battery slips, then we ought to pull at a right angle to their path."

That sounded like the smartest, brightest piece of thinking that Jim had ever heard. "Hey, you're right! The worst that would happen is that they're going *down* the channel and we'll wind up back in New York."

"Exactly," said Jay in that dry tone that didn't understand why everybody didn't have a hundred clerks in his head figuring out everything down to the last halfpenny.

"I got to hand it to you, Jay. That's pretty smart."

Twice more they were almost run down by Vanderbilt's ferry, and twice more they used the ferry's direction to reset their course, for the current of the Hudson kept turning them toward the open sea.

Still no land. Jim rowed and rowed. Gurgle, drip, splash. Jim's throat and mouth tasted biliously sour and bitter with vomit. Twice he pissed through his half-frozen, scrunched-up johnny into the sloshing puddle between his feet. Thunks of oars. Needles of rain. His trousers were sodden and crusted against his cold legs. A sharp horn of pain was permanently lodged in his arm socket. All thirty-four years of Jim's life had been a short, merry preparation for agonizing decades of rowing. He figured that he had drowned back when Jay threw him overboard and he was now in Hell. For 10,000 years he had been pulling like a galley slave, and he must row on for another million years until the deafening brass trump of Judgment Day.

"Son," his father called.

"Sir?" answered Jim.

It was the day they buried Ma. A gray rain had steadily beaten down for two days. The aged sexton was thudding the last mud clumps of dirt on Ma's grave. Pa's face was scrunched up.

"Sir?" Jim asked respectfully, and he stepped closer and put his arm around the thin, shivering blades of his father's shoulders. At fifteen, even though he towered over his father, it felt peculiar to comfort him.

"Is your ma getting wet, Jim?" asked Pa. Startled and confused, Jim shot a look at Pa.

"I don't think so," said Jim. "It's a good snug box." Pa's unshaven face looked up with eyes rubbed raw as radishes from crying.

"What have you done to her, Jim?"

"I didn't do nothing to her," he protested. "She's resting. She's fine. Let's go back to the inn."

In those days Pa ran the Revere Inn, which was on the main street of Brattleboro, Vermont. That night the place was deserted of guests and help, for Pa hadn't been able to run it with Ma sick. Outside it kept raining, turning into a real November blow out of Canada. Jim built up the fire in the parlor, fixed him and the old man a supper of beans and cold johnnycake, and brought them hot whiskey toddies. He set Pa by the popping fire with a buffalo robe around his knees. They chatted about getting an older woman in to boss the staff so the place could reopen.

When the mantel clock struck ten Jim reckoned they ought to go to bed. Pa cocked his head and gave him a shrewd look.

"Better go get your ma, Jim," said the old man as casual as anything.

The hairs on Jim's neck spiked up and a cold finger slithered down his spine. He couldn't say or do anything but stare across the hearth at his father's white-stubbled, worn gray face and innocent, watery eyes. The gust of rain that blew against the windowpanes threatened to bust in. Pa nodded twice.

"She's out there, ain't she, Jim?" Pa asked, the shrewd canny of his voice refusing to be lied to.

Jim nodded. Outside, lightning flared and thunder crashed. They were the only living souls in the forty-room inn, and the front parlor was the only room with a fire and candles.

"Ain't right to leave her out in this rain, Jim," his father gently reproached him. His reasonable voice went on, "You go on out there now and get her."

"Pa! She's gone!"

Pa nodded sagely. "I know that. That's why you got to go get her."

Jim went out. The wild rain beating on him felt safer than the spookiness of his father and the deserted inn. At Reverend Marston's house, it wasn't easy to get the cantankerous farmer turned preacher out on such a wet night, but this was more than Jim's fifteen years could handle.

Back at the inn Marston shouted at Pa as if the old man couldn't hear good. "James, where's Betsy?"

"Outside."

"Where's Phil?" Marston went on, referring to Jim's younger brother who had died last year.

"Upstairs," said Pa. "He done gone to bed." Jim watched dully. Ma had died of grief for Phil, wasting away in her bed upstairs. Was Pa to follow?

That night as the storm crashed outside all three men slept in chairs before the hotel parlor's fire.

Two days later Marston said his father was "tetched" by grief, which didn't add anything to what Jim already knew. He would get over it, Marston said. Jim was left alone with his father.

When they were in the kitchen, Pa said Ma was upstairs with the maids. Of course, there were no maids. At the table, both extra places set but empty, Pa said Phil was in the stable; if he and Pa were in the stable, Phil was in the house eating.

"Folks just won't sit down and eat together like they used to," the old man muttered. Although he kept quiet in order not to encourage this stuff, Jim didn't have what it took to argue with Pa.

"Pa, I won't leave you," Jim said. "I'll always be here for you. I'll take care of Ma and Phil too, Pa. Don't you worry none. I swear it—"

"Jim! Jim! Wake up!" A rough hand on his shoulder shook him awake.

"Huh?" said Jim. Oars in his stiff, numb fingers. "Pa?" His wet face and aching neck were cold, and everything was black. "Where are—" He remembered. He was on the wet, black Hudson with Jay. "What's the matter?" God, his hands and shoulders hurt.

Jay said, "You started yelling about your pa."

"I was thinking about him. What'd I say?"

"You weren't thinking, you were sleeping."

"Sleeping!"

"Snoring."

"Why didn't you wake me?"

"You were still rowing," said Jay. "I figured, let you get what rest you could."

At dawn's first gray light Jim couldn't believe it. A sandy, deserted beach lay two hundred yards off their prow. He turned, and through the thinning mist were the faint spires and high buildings of Manhattan. With powerful oar strokes he pulled them to what must have been the Jersey shore.

Firm earth never felt so good. As he dropped to his knees in his stiff, slime-crusted trousers, it felt as if his joints were of hardened plaster that was cracking. He leaned forward onto his hands and kissed the gritty sand, which seemed to pitch and yaw.

"Mama Earth, I *love* you!" he shouted. His joints creaking, he pulled himself to his feet. Firm ground was so strange that he felt woozy.

"Ha! Look here, Jay," he said. He stuck out his chest, on which three diamonds still blazed. "I didn't even lose my studs in all that tumbling around!"

Barely glancing in his direction, Jay nodded morosely. Jim gave him a big smile to cheer him up; after all, they had come out all right. This morning Jay's slight frame looked even smaller. His bulbous forehead was paler and more prominent, his shoulders a bit more stooped, and his black suit and white shirt filthy. But his strongest feature, his dark eyes, blazed as intensely as ever. Jim grinned and shook his head with respect. The little fellow, driven as he was to make a big success out of the Erie, to make it the country's first transcontinental line, had been right, after all. As last night had showed, Jay was one hard cuss to beat. Plenty of times his partner's earnest grimness was funny to Jim, and his lack of ease in getting along with the jolly gang on the Street perplexing, but this morning Jim saw clearly how much gravel his diminutive partner had in his craw.

No house or building was in sight, only a long shoreline of tan beach, dull gray sky, and the lapping of small waves. Sunrise might come soon. Jay turned and trudged up the sand dune, heading vaguely northward. Sore and chilled, Jim followed, figuring that Jay was setting out for Taylor's Inn in Jersey City, where Uncle Dan'l had set up the Erie's new headquarters.

For a few minutes they walked Indian file through the dunes. Dry grass, salty air, scrub bushes, and stunted, naked trees. The wind blew strongly, whipping dark masses of clouds across the sky. The only sound was rolling grains of sand and the crunch of their shoes. They had barely walked ten minutes when Jay spoke up without looking back.

"I been thinking, Jim."

Jim chuckled. "And when wasn't you thinking, partner?"

Jay stopped, turned, and fixed Jim with his hard gaze. Jim pulled up short to keep from toppling into Jay. "Don't call me partner," Jay said. "I won't take any more of last night's shenanigans."

A chill blew over Jim. "Shenanigans?" he asked.

They stood on top of a dune. Light flecks of sand were whipped against them by the wind. The growing light behind the scurrying, dappled clouds promised full daylight shortly. Off to Jim's right the ocean or river or whatever surged about, as listless, heavy, and dirty as a tub of day-old wash water.

As usual, Jim had a hard time looking directly into Jay's strong gaze. Jay's luminous black eyes were what you first noticed about him, not his dark beard, pale, prominent forehead, or short height. Unlike most folks' eyes, his didn't blink or waver when he looked at you or thought out a problem. If eyes were the windows into a fellow, Jim reckoned that Jay Gould had a soul as straight and forceful as a bullet. Jim averted his gaze, grinned awkwardly, and backed up a step.

"You were late to meet me by two hours," said Jay. "We should never have exposed ourselves in Delmonico's like that. And where was—" Jim's hand went up to stop Jay.

"Hey, Jay, you're a hundred percent right," said Jim, bringing out the soft soap to smooth things over. "I was excited. It ain't every day you get eight million off the Walrus." Jay's gaze didn't waver in its attempt to bore two holes in Jim's face.

"Where was the steamer you ordered to be at Canal Street at eight?"

"Damned if I know," said Jim, his grin making light of his steamboat's failure. "But I'm going to wring that captain's neck when I get aholt of him." Often between them it was like a taciturn man and his fat, jolly wife. She chattered, he was mum. She gossiped, he silently listened. She proposed and proposed, he rejected. Her voice had range, sweep, warmth, and indignation; his was a constricted bass of a single hard tone. Except for crises, Jay said little; but when action was needed he spat out sharp, quick orders that said the brain behind these intense black eyes had been working furiously. Now Jay shook his head in disgust.

"You blab our business to every two-bit hustler in Delmonico's—"

Jim interrupted him, "I never said—"

"Then in the middle of the river you want to give us up," Jay pushed on. Jim went to answer, but the scorn in Jay's voice and eyes withered his tongue. "That was the last straw. I don't need a partner like you—I have enough enemies. Let's call it quits."

Grains of sand stung Jim's cheek. He felt stiff and sore. He wanted a hot bath something awful, but he needed to have this out with Jay before it festered into a poisonous boil. You couldn't keep a fifteen-room house in Boston, a suite at the Hoffman House, and entertain big shots without a roost like the one he held with the Erie.

"Hold on there, fellow!" said Jim. "What's wrong with your old tin oven? I thought we was partners?" For the first time Jay glanced away, as if acknowledging that he and Jim were more than business associates. When he spoke, however, his voice was firm.

"No more we aren't," said Jay.

Jim popped his fingers scornfully. "Ain't you the feller said I was special because you'd never had a buddy?"

Jay's thin shoulders hunched forward. The wind made a faraway whistle. Jay suddenly appeared tiny against the enormous background of tan dune and gray horizon.

"You—were."

Alarmed, Jim pounced. "Were? Just like that—*were?*" If he weren't on the inside of the Erie, he wouldn't be able to trade its stock, the lack of profits from which would mean fewer champagne parties, fewer hot-blooded actresses, fewer giddy trips to the track, and fewer nighttime frolics to Broadway theaters. He couldn't give up actresses—he loved them too much, the way they moved, their hoarse playful voices, the easy way they lived.

Jay nodded stolidly and said, "Were."

"We're different, Mr. Gould—ice and fire, didn't you put it?" said Jim, his voice full of scorn. "Hand and glove, horse and wagon. That's what makes us a strong team." Jay half turned, as if restless to move on.

"Jim, business is business."

"Well, no wonder you ain't had no buddies," said Jim. "A few little things upset you."

Jay's dark eyes flinched. A month back, one night when they were hanging around the office, Jay had told him how much it hurt when a boyhood friend broke off because he felt Jay betrayed him. Even though Jim was certain he had struck home, Jay still looked as rigid as a beetle.

"You leave the Erie and I'll buy your shares at the market price."

"The Erie is just as much my company as yours," said Jim. "I don't *want* to leave it." But he also didn't want Jay as an enemy, for he had often seen from the inside how Jay fought. Unlike Jim, Jay wasn't impulsive in battle. Jim was like an angry rooster, pecking furiously and blowing off his anger, forgiving five minutes later. Jay was more like a boa constrictor, unobtrusively sliding around his opponent, silently wrapping his coils around the other, fastening him with a secure grip, and tightening it every time the other released a breath. Before his opponent could wriggle out, scarcely understanding what was happening, he had choked to death.

Jay asked quietly, "You want me to *force* you out?"

"Force *me*? You force *me*?"

"I'll bet you didn't meet me on time yesterday because you were goosing one of those damn actresses," said Jay.

Jim opened his mouth to protest, but he couldn't bring it off. His grin was more sheepish than he intended.

"It's all over your face," said Jay. As the breeze riffled his neatly trimmed black beard, his hard smile mocked Jim. "I might lose everything I've built in the last ten years because some hot-eyed actress wiggles her rump at you."

He turned and walked briskly down the dune. The abrupt end of their argument caught Jim short. He shouted down the hill at Jay's retreating back.

"Just don't think I'm a dumb dog that's going to roll over and play dead."

As if he wasn't listening, Jay was trudging up the next dune. Jim shouted across the little valley between them.

"You can't fire me, Jay Gould! I'll get the votes to stop you!"

Jay's back never wavered in his steady march. He reached the top of the next little sandy hill and went over.

"You son of a bitch!" shouted Jim. "I'll have *you* fired."

His shouts produced no effect on Jay's straight back, which disappeared down the other side. Jim broke into a trot to catch up.

With a loud "Ooof!" Jim went sprawling, tripping over a tangle of dead roots. He pulled himself to a seated position. The gray roots looked remarkably like a hollow mask that was laughing at him.

"Nooo!" he shouted at the leering tangle of dead root. "I'm down but I ain't out." He scrambled to his feet. "And Jay Gould be damned."

With renewed energy he capered down the hill toward Jay's marching back. Jim had tasted those parts of life that he relished most, and he wasn't giving them up just because Jay had got himself a little miffed. "Mr. Jay Gould will simply have to swallow his bile," he said, but not so loud that his voice carried forward as far as Jay, "no matter how sharp it sticks in his tight little craw."

7

Her very earliest observations and intuitions teach her this fact, that Beauty's path through life is a sort of rose-bordered one, a royal progress; for to Beauty the world, big and little, high and low, pays homage. As the girl ripens into the woman, every experience in life teaches her that her share of its successes and pleasures will be in proportion to her own ability to win favor, to please, and that the first and foremost influence is physical beauty.

—Ella Adelia Fletcher, *The Woman Beautiful*, 1901

In that same cold dawn, across the Hudson River in Manhattan, Annabelle Stokes boarded the Erie train that ran west of Philadelphia. As she had promised her sister Jenny, she was on her way to visit their papa.

Six hours later the train squealed into Gantry, named ninety years ago after Mama's grandfather. In the dazzling sunlight of late morning, the village's dozen one- and two-story buildings squatted in the dust, unpainted, country-aged, and feeble.

Not her father but her mother, looking ten years older than her midfifties, came to meet her in the canvas-roofed buckboard. Annabelle wondered where Papa was, but was afraid to ask. Her mother's face looked unnaturally faded, as pale as a country woman's print dress bleached out after too many washings. The train stamped out, and the village grew still smaller and quieted down. The old dog who had banged its tail in the excitement of the train's arrival settled back to sleep.

Annabelle drove, the reins of hot leather pleasant to hold. They left the station, passed through Gantry's slow, dusty main street, and hit the road to the farm. As she made small talk about the train ride and the children, she asked herself over and over where Papa was. Before Ned went bust he and she had brought the children down every few months. The ride from the station back to the farm was always merry, with Papa telling the children funny stories about how Burl the pony had taken to eating at the kitchen table with him and Gran'ma.

After a half mile Annabelle could no longer stand her mother's skirting the obvious question. "How is he, Mama?"

Her mother's lips drew away from her teeth and she made a sharp, hissing intake of air. "He said for me to give you a message."

"A message?" she asked, startled.

Her mother's face quivered. The words came out in bursts and jerks. "Not—to come in—the room—to see him."

Annabelle gasped. "Not come in the room!"

"He hasn't left it in weeks," said her mother.

Oh, God, much worse than she thought. "He hasn't gone to the bank?"

The harsh expression her mother shot her way contrasted oddly with her drained color. "It's closed."

"Closed!"

"Daresay it'll never open again," said her mother in a sullen tone.

The spring sun was dazzlingly white. The clopping horse entered the dark tunnel of the covered bridge over the River Gantry. Inside the hot, dark, confining shell, the wheels clattered hollowly over the loose planks. Annabelle's temples throbbed. *Closed*—the word's echo was garishly scrambled by the wheels' clatter. She couldn't absorb the news. The Gantry Bank & Trust Company might be only one room in which she and Papa had worked at a large partners' desk, yet there she spent some of her happiest days. Keeping neat ledgers for Papa. Listening to the excitement in male voices eager for loans. Hearing Papa's soothing assurances that deposits would be safely cared for. And when she was older, fifteen and sixteen, analyzing with him whether a pig farmer, corn merchant, or storekeeper possessed the character and the wherewithal to pay back his loan. She had started as her father's clerk and became his equal before she left Gantry with Ned for Manhattan. Her mother clutched Annabelle's arm.

"Oh, Annabelle," she cried, her sullen tone gone. "I'm so worried.

Lord knows, if you can't stir him, nobody can. Oh, Annabelle, help me! I'm afraid he's lain down to die!"

No sooner had Annabelle set down her traveling cases than she gathered her green skirts and marched into the small sitting room. Sitting in the armchair by a tiny spring fire was a shrunken elf-like creature with a thin, lifeless face. She scarcely recognized her father.

"Papa!" she gasped, immediately wanting to take back her shock. The planes of his slack face were sunk like those of a person near death. His skin hung on his jaws and neck. He must have lost forty pounds. His otherworld frailty derailed her angry stride.

His blue eyes glanced up at her and back to the fire. *Such dead eyes. They can't be Papa's.*

"Hello, Papa," she said softly. When he didn't answer she went on. She forced a bright, gentle tone, but her voice shook. "You haven't answered my letters."

He turned his head away as if from a foul odor. She lowered herself to perch on the arm of the chair opposite him.

"Papa," she said and held out her hand. He turned his head farther away. "I'm sorry, Papa," she said. "It looked like Ned was doing well. He was, for a while."

Her father's only response was to swallow. The parlor possessed a musty, rancid odor, like meat gone bad. Uncharacteristically, he hadn't shaved for days. His wrinkled neck and its scraggly, diseased stubble disgusted her, and in turn her disgust rankled her about herself. She should love her father no matter how scraggly his neck looked.

"Times changed, Papa," she said gently. "What worked so well in the War didn't work afterwards. Ned wasn't smart enough to see it."

Still no response from his stiff face.

"Aren't you going to talk to me, Papa?"

He swallowed again, his hard Adam's apple bobbing under aged, flabby skin as wrinkled and disgusting as a turkey's wattles. Annabelle wanted to shake a response out of him.

"Papa!"

Nothing.

"Papa, talk to me!" she shouted as if he were deaf. "Aren't I still your daughter? Don't do this! I love you!"

He stirred slightly.

"This hurts, Papa—hurts, hurts, hurts!"

Finally his eyes turned to her. Throughout her entire life all that had shone for her in those pale blue eyes was warmth and respect.

He had possessed endless patience with her every fault and mistake; she could count on that. For eight years—from her ninth year till she was seventeen—the two of them sat across the partners' desk, alone together all day when she wasn't in school, and talked about everything under the sun—and the moon and the stars—while they worked on the bank's accounts. She hadn't been that intimate even with Ned. Now only a wild, vicious anger spun in his eyes, anger that pierced her with such force that she shrank back.

Still he said nothing, only fixed her with his furious pale-blue gaze. A scream rose, but she held it in.

She wrenched herself away and walked to the window. Through the dust-haze on the panes were the outlines of the dead bank. It was moments before she could speak.

"Papa, I know you . . . lost money," she said, faltering. She heard herself making his bankruptcy sound like a temporary setback. She turned to him. She laughed nervously, then stifled it. "But I've lost everything, too. Ned's gone. Sometimes I don't have enough for the children." She paused to let this sink in, but not even the mention of his grandchildren broke through the hard blue shell of his angry gaze. "Jenny's done what she can, but she and Ulysses don't have much. I can't find Ned to even ask for money, which he won't give me. I got a divorce."

While his face didn't move, the word *divorce* seemed to spread contempt across it more thickly. She turned away from his accusing eyes.

"Papa, please don't look at me like that," she went on. "Please! I didn't know he was going broke, honestly I didn't. New York is different from here." The pressure of a sob rose, but she squashed it—he hated tears in a woman, despising them as manipulation by the weak—and she heaved a great, broken sigh.

Papa's head turned toward the tiny fire as if he hadn't heard her. She lowered herself onto the chair arm opposite. For a long time they faced each other in silence. Twenty years ago, she thought, when she was seven or eight, she lay on the rug and read out loud as Papa corrected her pronunciation. It was hard to believe such perfect, innocent joy was lost forever. She wouldn't say any more. If it took all day she would sit here and wait him out. That had been one of his lessons. Use your silence to make the other fellow talk.

An eternity passed of averted glances, hard swallows, and silence.

"You and him were crooks," Papa finally announced in a high crippled voice. The hobble in his voice startled her as much as what he said.

"Crooks? No, Papa!"

"Stole my money," he said, voice cracking with self-pity. "My own daughter. My *own* daughter!"

"No, Papa. No, no."

"Borrowing only a little to get started with me, right?" he said, his voice rising in an indignant whine. "Then paying me back quick— even early—and borrowing a little more and then a little bit more— till it was a lot, a whole lot." He rocked back and forth in the armchair, making it creak, the way a child in a corner comforted himself by rocking and crooning. "Oldest trick on a banker I know. And my own *daughter* did it to me!"

"But it was Ned!"

"You were there. I trained you. I trusted you. You know a shaky business as well as I. Don't lie, don't tell me you didn't see it."

Annabelle opened her mouth to protest. Her face was flushed, heated, near scalding tears, but nothing came. Given what had passed between them for years, her training at his knee, he would never see it differently. But she had stayed home, given birth to the babies, run the house, and been the hostess of Ned's lavish entertainments. True, a number of Ned's stories didn't dovetail properly, but she hadn't worked at Ned's brokerage, hadn't seen the firm's books, and hadn't promised to pay back what the firm borrowed.

"Papa, it was no trick," she said. "I know you lost a lot—"

"Lost a lot?" he shouted. "Ruined! You're looking at the laughingstock of Gantry. Can't go out. Can't go to church. I held people to their loans all my life. Now they laugh at me because you and him took me for everything. Go away! Just let me die, and let them bury me. Go away. They'll soon enough stop laughing once I'm out of sight under the ground."

Toward noon Jim Fisk and Jay Gould came bouncing, rattling, and sliding over a hill in the farmer's wagon on which they had begged a ride to Taylor's Inn, the Erie's temporary headquarters.

They were greeted by two dozen reporters, as drunk on a big out-of-town story as they were off Ben Taylor's stone jugs of corn hootch. While Jim clapped his Broadway buddies on the back and admired the headlines their nighttime flight had provoked, Jay shot off upstairs to the telegraph in the makeshift office, eager as always to run his fingers up and down the wires to check Erie operations from Buffalo to Philadelphia. So startling had the city's two dozen dailies found the story—that two of the city's youngest businessmen had bested the aged monarch of the rails—that news of the Johnson impeachment trial and the Grant campaign had been pushed to the bottom of the front page.

"Hey," Jim asked the reporters, "anyplace around here that a fellow can get some eggs and a snort?" They laughed and pointed the way.

Jim strode into the inn's dark interior and was shown by the befuddled Mrs. Taylor into the bar, a long, dim room that reeked of last night's whiskey and cigar smoke. Jim gave a little roar; he felt at home. He was followed by the crowd of reporters; hoots, yells, booming laughter, and the scrape of chairs filled the room. He shouted to the old man behind the bar to serve up a round of his best whiskey. A cheer rose.

Six fried eggs, a dozen rashers of bacon, and a platter of fried potatoes were plunked in front of him by the old geezer, who turned out to be Taylor himself. Jim gave him a few friendly words and asked for a pint of brandy, which he poured into the gray-enameled coffeepot. As he wolfed down the breakfast, he slurped cup after cup of spiked coffee. Three or four reporters were present whom he didn't know, so he called them over and introduced himself. Gradually his paunch, grown slack from lack of food, filled as plumply as a mainsail before a stiff breeze.

Chirky now, he laughed and bantered with the boisterous scribblers. Manhattan reporters were his kind of people—a bit raffish, but a damn sight warmer than Jay Gould's ice block of a personality. He called old man Taylor over for a whispered chat. No, the old fellow said, it wasn't no trouble to put all this on the Erie bill. Jim laughed and bought a third round, which produced another loud cheer. The lunch-breakfast took on the lively, tangled air of a Park Row party. The drinks, laughter, and banter pushed away Jay's threats to kick him off the Erie board.

From three reporters Jim heard scuttlebutt that Vanderbilt intended to raid the inn. The Walrus's thugs were to drag the three Erie directors back to the "justice" of the city courts presided over by Vanderbilt's crooked judges. The morning editions quoted the Commodore as calling him, Jay, and their partner, Daniel Drew, "common thieves." The *Herald* stood up and called for quiet.

"Now tell us—are you a 'common thief,' Jim?" he asked in a loud, sarcastic voice. The voices of many quieted to hear Jim's answer. His face darkened, a cross between a legitimate scowl and a stage glower. Half a dozen reporters laughed.

Jim pushed back his table with a loud scrape and stood up. A shaft of sunlight hit his chest, where set off by his soot-stained, crumpled shirtfront, the three large diamond studs still sparkled. He raised both hands.

"I want everybody to hear this," he bellowed. His hands came down and twisted the corners of his Napoleon III mustaches to restore their points. "I'm going to give you the inside story of last night." At the bar, one of the reporters drunkenly called for a cigar. "Quincy, damn you," shouted Jim, "get out your pencil. I'm going through this only once." Long pads came up, and over them hovered pencils.

Jim described Jay's and his son's brush with kidnappers. "His Majesty, the Lion of the Rails, needed to kidnap a twelve-year-old boy to keep his empire together." He painted a vivid picture of how he and Jay were run down on the pier, as well as the dangers they faced in rowing the Hudson on a lightless night, a risk he didn't need to embellish. That the Commodore's toughs had shot at them from the pier, that his ferries had tried to run them down, showed clearly, his ringing voice declared, that Vanderbilt was a bully who would do anything, legal or criminal, to complete his rail monopoly in and out of New York City. For emphasis, Jim snapped his head back, squared his shoulders, brought his finger up, and raised himself on his tiptoes.

"Commodore Vanderbilt *owns* New York," he shouted. "He *owns* the Stock Exchange. He *owns* the courts. He *owns* New York's streets and most of its railways. We are poor but ambitious young men. Me and Jay saw he had left us no chance to expand in the city, so we come over here to Jersey to grow up with the country." The reporters guffawed. Jim beamed at his own oratory.

"Tell your readers that the Great Monopolizer wants to raise the price of their eggs and bacon," he cried. Two dozen pencils scraped across the reporters' pads with the scratchiness of insects hurrying across dry leaves. As he continued, the reporters' heads swayed to the periods and rhythms of his oratory. Behind the whiskey-dark wood of the battered counter, the thin face of old man Taylor stared with a slack grin and a rapt blue eye, as if nothing so exciting had ever broken his country inn's placid quiet. "Not to speak of their cotton and hides, lumber and pig iron," Jim thundered on. "Me and Jay and the Deacon, we been poor. We want to keep the Erie out of his hands for the little man. We may be exiles from our homes, driven from them by a rich man's greed, but we won't give up the fight just because the Walrus rears up and tells us to play dead!"

8

His mind has been as weak as his body and he now seems more like a child than like Jay. He has been very nervous, so much so that we have been very careful about doing anything or saying anything that would in the least excite him. It would make him tremble sometimes just having the Doctor come in unexpectedly.

—Polly Gould, letter on her brother's illness, 1854

Three afternoons later in the Senate chamber in Washington, D.C., Ben Butler and Thaddeus Stevens were exhausting every device, appealing to every prejudice and passion, to ride roughshod over legal obstacles in their ruthless attempt to convict President Andrew Johnson of "high crimes and misdemeanors" for his opposition to the Senate Radicals' plans to occupy the South and make the President a puppet under the rule of Congress. In the South, military commanders under Johnson's command were directing 20,000 troops in efforts to maintain order and supervise the subdued region's new political structure, which was producing Negro voting majorities in Alabama, Florida, Louisiana, Mississippi, and South Carolina. Out west, the Sioux under Red Cloud, the Indians' foremost military strategist, Sitting Bull, their political leader, and Crazy Horse, the brilliant military tactician, were rousting out the bluecoats from the northern Great Plains, reclaiming their hunting grounds and homelands.

And at Taylor's Inn, on this lazy afternoon in March, Jim Fisk was trying to sleep with a pillow over his head. However, the past few days' excitement had charged him up too much; his thoughts raced like burning demons.

Till now—despite his successes—he had been on the outside of Wall Street looking in, struggling to figure out how to shove himself into the center of the melee for the really big potatoes. Early on as a boy and a young man, he had got to where he wanted by being a jolly leader. He had led his gang back in Brattleboro, Vermont, on raids and adventures through his enthusiasm and boldness; and he had sold millions of dollars' worth of blankets and cotton in the War by making Washington generals and paymasters into buddies during nightlong bouts of drinking and wenching. This worked only partially well on Wall Street, for there not only did you need the inside word, but you needed to puzzle out what all the numbers and close print of contracts, stock plans, and financial statements really meant. The success of taking on the Commodore himself—the Street's most powerful operator—and knocking him to the ground in a one-two punch had gone through Jim to the core of his being. It said to him that he was now, finally, fully a man, ready to take his place with players of any size, strong enough to wrestle with alligators and grizzlies if need be to get ahold of those twelve-pound potatoes the big boys raked in.

And little bitty Jay Gould, no bigger and sassier than a nettlesome flea, was threatening to snatch it all away, bounce him off the platform that gave him the spot from which to exert his leverage, the board of the Erie. Damned if Jim would allow it. Besides wanting to work with Jay, who was smart enough to figure out all the fine print that Jim couldn't be bothered reading, he loved everything about the train business. Unlike Jay, who mostly wanted to expand the Erie to the West Coast, Jim was in the train business for the money and the fun of it. Except for the theater, it was the most exciting enterprise he could imagine. Not only did he relish his position as Managing Director and Chief of Staff—which meant that thousands of employees, investors, and passengers looked to him as the Erie's spokesman—but he loved the muscles, blood, and guts of railroads. The rumble of freight cars clickity-clacking lickety-split. The rat-a-tat-tat of copper telegraph keys rattling urgent messages at electric speed. The blazing growth of track westward. The haggling over rights-of-way, and the sale of stock issues for sums in the millions. The whizzing rushes of trains, the ringing of their brassy bells, and the blare of their horns. Nothing was more modern and up-to-date than railroads! With their fresh, daring technology and iron-heavy power, they were the very marrow of the future.

To stop this torrent of thought, Jim held the pillow against his eyes with his fists. Too often he had seen Jay's single-minded resolve. His little partner ran the Erie like the engineer of a crack express determined to make every stop on time. If Jay declared that he was going to kick Jim out of the locomotive's cab, then despite the little engineer's size, Jim was in for the fight of his life.

This wasn't the only reason he felt low. He liked Jay. Despite their quarrel, he still wanted the smart little fellow as his buddy. But Jay stumped him. How could your buddy break with you over one day's troubles, and them not all that bad? What kind of cold fish was he?

About three o'clock in the afternoon Jim dressed in a boldly checked suit and strolled outside. He wanted to keep out of Jay's sight for a day or two in the wan hope that Jay's fury would cool off, so he was avoiding the Erie's temporary offices on the third floor.

Since all the reporters had taken the noon ferry to Manhattan to write up their stories, he had the wide veranda to himself. Before him the smooth green lawn flowed down to the pier. A bit dizzy from the tumult of the past few days, Jim picked his way down the wooden steps.

He circled Taylor's. The springy grass under the soles of his boots soothed his sore feet. Ducks waddled out of his way. Any romance of the countryside was lost on Jim. These wide-open spaces sure weren't Broadway. No Sally Woods and her saucy, dignified girls to cheer up a fellow. After he had walked around the inn twice, he strolled down to the worn gray pier.

What he saw alarmed him. With but twenty men the Walrus could launch an attack from the pier, race up the hill, break through the inn's flimsy doors, and drag the three Erie chiefs down to his waiting packet boats, which would rendezvous with his ferry in mid-river. The whole thing wouldn't take five minutes. In Jim's ears rang the loud blare of brassy trumpets.

He took at once to the idea of himself as a beleaguered general. He pressed old man Taylor into driving him to the Erie terminal in Jersey City, where he recruited three dozen Erie guards and clerks as frontline marines. Back at Camp Taylor with his wide-eyed troops, using the ever-eager old innkeeper as supply sergeant, Jim outfitted them with shotguns filled with rock salt—so they wouldn't kill any-body—box lunches from the inn's kitchens, whiskey jugs from the bar, and a half-dozen rowboats. Freed from such mundane chores as selling tickets and storing passengers' luggage, Admiral Fisk's ma-rines were enthusiastic over their new duties. He ordered them to patrol up and down the Hudson in front of the inn's pier, shotguns at the ready.

All evening long as they patrolled the inn's half-mile frontage, their lanterns glowed like giant, low-flying fireflies, and their drawn-out halloos to each other echoed across the water.

That night in the crowded saloon bar at O'Malley's Theater, Josie Mansfield met a man who particularly appealed to her—a thirty-year-old fellow named Ned Stokes, who was from Philadelphia, and obviously—to judge by his subdued blue suit, yellow silk waist-coat, elegant manners, and smooth speech—from a grand family there.

It was intermission. The jostling, buzzing crowd pushed Josie against the red crushed-velvet wallpaper. Ned Stokes's resinous co-logne was strong enough to shove aside the competing odors of the brandies he bought for them, the sweat of unwashed bodies, and nearby ladies' flowery perfumes.

She let it slip that she was an actresss. Ned's face lit up, for like many men he probably thought it meant she was loose in her be-havior. She snapped her dark eyes twice and took a deep breath, which pushed the tops of her exposed breasts higher.

"I'm a serious actress, Mr. Stokes," she said, a touch of petulance in her voice to make sure he was set right at once. "Not a dance hall girl. The theater is an art form, and I intend to realize its most intense tragic implications." The glow from the saloon's gas chandelier warmed his glossy black hair, lean, aristocratic face, sharp widow's peak, and the large dimple under his full lips. As if it had seen every-thing, his face radiated upper-class tolerance and amusement.

"Yes," he murmured. Because of the crowd's pressure, he stood so close that his dove-gray eyes looked right down her gown's low-cut neckline. She decided to pull her shawl over the bare tops of her breasts, yet for a few moments her hands refused to move, for his lazy stare, piercing her right between her breasts, kicked up such a peculiar stir of excitement that she was choked and flushed. The awkward moment passed.

"And what do you do with your days, Mr. Stokes?" she stam-mered. In her experience the second-best use men had for women was to brag about themselves. He shrugged with the careless grace of a prince.

"Well, I used to own a brokerage," he said.

Ummm, she thought. Didn't that always mean money? "And now?"

"I sold it." His unguarded smile and the easy wave of his hand said businesses were to be bought and sold like horses. "I'm looking around for an investment." Better and better. She judged him to be a sapling sprung from one of America's oldest and sturdiest oaks.

"Perhaps the theater would interest you. As an investment." She put forward a well-calculated, bold expression to say that such an investment would amuse a sophisticate like him.

"If I could invest in *your* success onstage," he murmured, "I'm sure I would recoup my investment many, many times." Did he murmur everything? The bell rang for the *opéra bouffe* to resume.

She pressed his arm with her hand and gave him a warm chuckle that was designed to say that he was a rogue as well as a sweet man, interesting because he was powerful, and that he might, if he played his cards right, have his way with her.

"What's that?" asked Jay Gould. The aged country doctor stared at the large, greasy cow horn in his hand, his breath a loud, rattling wheeze.

"My chest horn," said the stooped Dr. Weatherby. Sitting on his bed on the third floor of Taylor's Inn, Jay paused in the act of unbuttoning his white shirt. The noon bells began to clang.

"What's it for?" asked Jay. He eyed the waxy-looking horn apprehensively, for country doctors often possessed farfetched ideas. Dr. Weatherby's graying, mottled head reared back in an arrogant toss.

"I took care of nothing but folks with bad chests before I retired, young squirt," said Dr. Weatherby. "I had my own sanitorium, Weatherby's New England Asylum, before I sold out. I've listened to more bad chests the past twenty years than the average cutpurse hears in a hundred lifetimes." Still apprehensive, Jay stalled with another question, for a cow horn belonged more to Indian superstition than modern science. "Why don't you use a stethoscope?"

"Because this works a whole lot better," said the old man.

"It's only a cracked rib," said Jay. "All I want is a plaster."

"First, some questions," said Dr. Weatherby. He drew a grubby notebook and a pencil stub from his black frock coat. "Your pa living?"

Jay sighed with exasperation. "No."

"Died of what?"

"Lung trouble."

The doctor's hand shot out and turned Jay's jaw sharply to the left and to the right, holding up his chin to examine the neck glands. His hand dropped away.

"Your ma?"

Jay's exasperation boiled over. "What's this got to do with bandaging my chest?"

"A patient's history has everything to do with his chest," insisted the country doctor.

"My ma's dead, too."

"From what?" the doctor asked sharply.

From what? A cold memory stirred in Jay. *She died of death, that's what.* Ma's pale, worn face on the pillow. Pa stony-faced, his older sisters standing around weeping. Ma had clasped Jay's hand, her fingers feeble and as cold as bony icicles, her black eyes struggling to shout, her mouth whispering. She insisted he kiss her. Her lips were cold, cold, already cold, as if she were turning into a block of ice. He wanted to scream, but didn't want to scare her away. For a long time, from then till he was eight, Heaven was where you hugged your warm mother tightly and never let go.

"She died of consumption," Jay said softly, and he was pushed to admit that his sisters Nancy and Polly also died of the same disease. "Pa called it the old Gould disease 'cause so many of us die from it."

"Describe your illnesses."

"My own lungs haven't ever been strong," said Jay. "I almost died three times when I was eighteen—typhoid, bowel inflammation, pneumonia."

His sister Polly had nursed him through all three bouts, sitting next to his bed for weeks, refusing to sleep and insisting that Ann and Elizabeth bring in fresh clothes and meals. Her presence, her strength—they were what saved him. She spooned him cool water, boiled buttermilk, and the broth off trout, soups made of shadows. She read to him, her melodic voice weaving in and out of the awful nightmares in which he was lost in a scrubby, godforsaken wilderness, condemned to run through it for a thousand years. Polly comforted him, nursed him back from the cold lip of the grave, and three months later she herself raced off to Heaven on the back of galloping consumption. That summer's grief for Polly laid Jay so low he was unfit for anything the next fall and winter.

After the examination, the doctor pulled up a chair and sat before him, his face as hoary and worn as an ancient tombstone, his yellow-flecked gray eyes a contradiction of cruelty and kindness.

"I suppose you know you got it, too," the doctor said softly.

A numb shock hammered through Jay. *Got it, too,* meant only one thing. Consumption, tuberculosis, the spitting disease, death.

"I—" Jay couldn't go on. Nancy's flushed cheeks. Polly's hacking cough and the blood on her handkerchiefs. His mother's cold lips. Pa's stooped, gray emaciation. The worm that slithered about in his own chest, tickling whenever he took a deep breath. A numb, involuntary tremor shook him. The doctor's warm, rough hands clasped both of his.

"You don't seem too surprised," said Dr. Weatherby, the worn husk of his face a mix of amusement and gravity, the struggle of a longtime preacher not to laugh over one of God's excellent perverse jokes.

Jay turned his eyes away, toward the window. "I am . . . a bit."

"It don't have to be bad, you take care of yourself," said Dr. Weatherby in a voice softer than he had used up to now. "That's what I done for thirty years, taken care of folks with it. Hear my wheeze? Don't think I've escaped it. You got to take it easy. Maybe get yourself south in the harshest weather."

Jay pointed at the cow horn. "Did you hear it with that?" he whispered. The doctor nodded. "How long do I have?" asked Jay. "I've got a family, young children, babies. They . . ." His voice trailed off.

"You can go another ten years, maybe twenty," Dr. Weatherby said, "if you're not foolish. You got scars from those earlier bouts. Depends on whether it breaks out of them scar pockets. Some folks make it twenty-five or thirty years, but given your puny lungs, I wouldn't put my money on that."

"But I'm not going to die soon?" asked Jay. The doctor laughed.

"Depends on what you mean by soon. Some folks think ten or twenty years is soon—to others, it's a lifetime."

A half an hour later Jay was walking through the sunny hayfields surrounding Taylor's Inn. He seemed to reel, as if he walked the deck of a swaying boat. The sky was empty of clouds, the river serene. Except for the snap of insects and the flutter of tiny wings, the countryside was silent and empty.

All his life he had been small, weak, and thin, never as robust as Roxbury's other farm boys. He now felt plunged back into the harshness of life after his mother died, that period of his life between the time he was four and seventeen, when he left home to work as a surveyor, when he had taken charge of his life. As he was the only son after so many girls, his mother and the girls doted on him. He remembered her holding him, her singing to him, the flowers she gave him to play with. It was an idyllic time, his early years, a paradise filled with the scent of grass, the humming of bees, the coziness of the fire in winter.

The bewilderment of her three-month illness. Galloping consumption, it was called, as if the victim were tied to a horse charging out of this world. Four years old, he had been puzzled but not afraid by her remaining in bed. At dawn he would creep in on all fours and sleep on the rug by her bed, keeping silent if she was awake so she wouldn't send him out, reaching up to grasp her cool, limp fingers if she were asleep, anything to maintain touch with her. He took at face value what his sisters and Pa said, that she would be all right shortly.

A change in the atmosphere. Urgency. The doctor came and went every day. Whispered conversations by the doctor's buggy with Pa. Jay had the sense that something terrible was about to happen, but nobody would tell him anything.

The afternoon when everybody gathered by Ma's bed. Her feebleness. The growing sense that something was wrong, that events were galloping away from him, that he couldn't hold on. Polly, nine years old, drew him outside the sickroom door, and hugged him. "Mama's going on a long trip," she whispered, tears in her eyes.

He brightened. "When will she come back?" he asked, remembering the trip to Hobart last year when she had stayed overnight.

"A long, long time," she said, wiping her eyes with her apron. "We—may not see her till we—go visit her."

He couldn't figure this out. Ma was as much a part of the house as the hearth, the kettles in the kitchen, the flowers in the boxes in the windows, the buzzing of insects.

"You want me to be brave, don't you?" he asked, taking Polly's hand and pressing it to his chest. "Not to cry."

"Oh, Jay!" she gasped, pulling him to her and holding him tight, "she'll be gone!"

He was puzzled. She would be gone, but not for long. Ma would never leave them for long.

Later, back at Ma's bedside, it was nice for everybody to be together in the afternoon instead of at night, but in spite of the June afternoon's heat, the room felt cold and Jay shivered. Polly, Ann, Nancy, Elizabeth, Pa stood around looking at Mama, all with anxious frowns. Pa was gloomy and even more quiet. They would hold Ma's hand in turn and cry.

When it was Jay's turn he asked, "When are you coming back, Mama?" and behind him the sobs all rose together. She pulled Jay to her and she was crying, too.

"Kiss me, son," was all she said.

Happily he kissed her on the lips. Not warm as usual, but cold, cold, cold. As cold as a tombstone in the churchyard in June. As cold as a brook in summer. And when he touched her fingers, they were cold, too.

Burial. Mama's gone. Numbness, shock, grief, puzzlement. Mama's in Heaven, she's happy, she's watching over us. But for all his sisters' words of comfort, Ma wasn't in the kitchen. She wasn't there to put your head in her lap, making you feel warm and cozy. Days that summer he lay in the grass and peered up at the clouds to see her, yet she never raised her face over the edge of a one.

A year later Pa insisted that Jay work with him in the barn. At first it was fun, being with Pa and out of the house. After that he led the mule in the hayfield while Pa loaded hay. When he wanted to go back to the house, tired of cutting his feet on hay stubble, Pa wouldn't let him, even threatened to use his belt on him if he didn't work on. Pa said he was going to leave the farm to him, but that Jay had to work to earn it, that Jay mustn't think he could sit around the house all day like a girl and get the farm. Jay worked on, driven by the urgency of his father, but was puzzled, for he didn't want the farm or the work, but he sensed it wouldn't be wise to say so.

Taking deep breaths to throw off this terrible numbing sensation of being five again and powerless, Jay circled Taylor's Inn, keeping it at a distance. And now he had Ma's disease, and Pa's and Polly's. He would take care of himself. Weatherby himself had said it; he could live a long time. It was foolish to be frightened. He willed his mind to focus. As if he had sensed all along that he didn't have much time, he had been working furiously since he left home at seventeen, conquering one business goal and then the next, till they led to his life's work, building this rail line to be the best in the country, the one to establish a transcontinental link.

Last year Jay had chosen the battered Erie for his ambitions, as it was large enough to carry them out. Incorporated in New York State in 1832, the New York and Erie Railroad embodied the most sublime of visions: a ribbon of steel to link the Atlantic Ocean to the Great Lakes, to bind the port of New York to the vast lands of the Trans-Allegheny west. When founded, the line had promised to guarantee forever to the port of New York the commerce of the huge hinterland that the city had first secured for itself by means of the Erie Canal.

During the boom years of the War the line expanded. It ran 445 miles between Piermont, on the Hudson 25 miles north of New York, and Dunkirk on Lake Erie, and it shot yet more track westward into Pennsylvania. What made the line ripe for destabilizing speculation was the large number of shares actively traded on the Exchange, making it easy for bears such as Daniel Drew to borrow the stock to sell it short. Till Jay took over there was no strong hand at the line's helm, so that for years the company's fortunes had oscillated between shimmering hopes and tangible disasters, producing the wide fluctuations dear to a speculator's heart.

And now the country was exhibiting remarkable prosperity, whereas during the War the wisest heads had declared that the war boom presaged a depression afterward. However, coal and iron still arrived on bulging cars from mines, along with mountains of grain from the Midwest, shiploads of cotton from the South, and rivers of gold from the West. To Jay the country seemed to have an insatiable appetite for more: more land, more tracks, more towns and cities, more profits from grain—and more buffalo coats, more silk gowns, and more cigars and champagne. To his dismay, the Stock Exchange had become as delirious as a child with a fever, and as dangerous as that same child with a loaded pistol. Credit was easy, hopes ebullient, and speculators could choose from gold mines, steel mills, Broadway emporiums, New York City lots, raw land, silver, and any of the grains.

Central to all these ambitions were the railroads, for Jay knew that without swift, easy, and cheap transport few of these dreams could be realized. If this boom lasted long enough for him to consolidate his hold on the Erie, and long enough for him to transform it from the Scarlet Woman of Wall Street into a respectable lady of means, he could make his mark on the world. I do have time, he said to himself, I do. Time to toss off Vanderbilt's dead hand on the company, time to throw a set of rails to San Francisco, and time to leave his affairs so after him Helen and the children would not want.

To his left the Hudson flowed on serenely, and around him came the snaps and flutters of delirious insects. Willing his fear to be smaller, more compressed, colder, he clamped his mind down on it and stalked back to Taylor's. He was determined to do what he could with what he had.

Jim Fisk was cheerful now that he had set a plan in motion.

The first thing the next morning he called at the local armory, where he presented a case of Wild Turkey to the grateful commander, Lieutenant Major Charles Thompson. The Major had lost an arm at Gettysburg, but the undimmed blue eyes that peered at Jim showed no loss of vigor.

"Sir," said the Major, "it would be an outrage for a Manhattan gang to carry off three fine new citizens of New Jersey." Jim chuckled in appreciation.

By midafternoon a half-dozen of New Jersey's howitzers were squatting on the pier, manned by a company of fifteen cannoneers as intoxicated with Jim's buoyant holiday air as the clerk-marines patrolling and hallooing on the river. Jim kept them generously fortified with box lunches from the inn's kitchen and an unending supply of jugs from Taylor's cellar. Occasionally, with a loud boom, the cannoneers practiced shooting into the river. Everyone cheered. Except for the third floor of the hotel, the eighteen rooms of which Jay and his headquarters clerks occupied as the Erie's temporary headquarters, Taylor's Inn took on the air of a military camp.

Every two hours that day and the next, Jim toured the stations of his troops to keep up morale. In his head fifes piped and snare drums rattled. Thoughts of what Jay was doubtless even now plotting against him were pushed aside. Jim was never more fully himself than when organizing and promoting a project. As a boy he had been a genius at deploying his gang to evade Crabapple Conners's shotgun so they could grab apples out of the old man's orchard, and several dozen campaigns since had increased his talent for inspiring troops.

By the afternoon of the second day, General Fisk was being followed by a gabbling, cackling retinue of twenty reporters, whose own holiday spirits were kept constantly buoyed with Taylor's best whiskey, as well as cigars and delicacies ferried over from Manhattan. As if the trailing reporters were also part of his gang, Jim used the intervals between reviewing the outposts of Fort Taylor to declaim the evils of the Walrus's attempts at rail monopoly and the merits of the Erie Exiles' efforts to promote cheap transportation for the good citizens of the republic.

The next morning's editions told him, from the space and the slant they gave the "Great Erie War" on their front pages, that New York's reporters and editors had joined his fight, for even the impeachment trial had been shoved to page two along with news of the imminent formation of a National Prohibition party. Central shares had plunged on the Exchange and were wavering. The Erie's share price, on the other hand, had bounded upward and now held.

That afternoon the *Mirror* asked Jim how the cannoneers would aim if the inn sustained a night attack. Over a festive dinner with Lieutenant Major Thompson and his aides, Jim arranged for the State Guard to plant rockets on the hotel's roof. Standing with Jim on the giddy heights of the widow's walk the next morning, the thin, mustachioed rocketmaster assured him that within seconds of the alarm he would light up the inn and its grounds for a half mile about as bright as day.

"Particularly, sir," the rocketmaster went on, "if me and my men are as well provisioned as them cannoneers down at the dock." His eye, still bloodshot from last night's elaborate dinner, gave Jim a wink. General Fisk winked back. No problems with provisions for gallant troops!

That night Jim entertained the curious mayor, five aldermen, and the Police Chief of Jersey City at the best dinner Ben Taylor could provide. By setting Daniel Drew as his cat's-paw, Jim even prised a grumpy Jay Gould out of the line's upstairs offices for the occasion. Jay too saw the advantage of getting in thick with the locals, but as usual he left it to Jim to entertain their guests.

Jim started the jokes, bonhomie, and laughter with the arrival of his first guest. Drinking almost nothing himself, he slopped whiskey generously into the Aldermen's tumblers. During the first course, a lobster bisque he and Mrs. Taylor had seasoned together, he circled the table as often as the serving girls and splashed sparkling white wine into the balloon-shaped glasses brought over especially from Manhattan.

Back at the head of the table, he spun out over twenty hilarious minutes the story of how once during the War he had hidden all night in a shallow ditch not ten feet from a rebel encampment, its punch line how by midnight he had been forced to dirty his trousers. After another four or five stories, he drew out the Mayor, who told the story of his first and most disastrous election. Jim led the laughter, twice asking His Honor to repeat the punch line.

By the time the roasted clams were served, the entire company, including the pinched Drew but excluding the sour Jay, felt as witty as Puck. The roast suckling pig was brought in, along with six bottles of tangy madeira. Jim carved the pig and called on the Mayor to pour the wine. During the main course he told a half-dozen Wall Street tales, in most of which he turned out to be the butt of the humor.

A port that Jim announced had been liberated by Napoleon Bonaparte was served with heaping bowls of sherry fool. By midnight the britches of each guest were straining at the seams. Holding his heavy paunch as if it might slide off his lap, the Mayor allowed that he had cackled so long that he was as weak as a hen who had laid too many eggs.

In return for the Erie's promise to build its new headquarters in Jersey City, the town fathers agreed to furnish fifteen policemen to ring the inn on a twenty-four-hour basis. It was a few minutes before one o'clock when Jim, a fresh cigar in his plump hand, helped them into their carriages.

As he stood on the veranda and waved good night, he glowed with the accomplishment of a job well done. But to the extent that he had succeeded with the Jersey officials, he had utterly failed with Jay Gould. As if nothing tonight possessed any significance in running a railroad, all evening long Jay had said little, picked at his food, toyed with his wineglass, watched Jim's antics bleakly, and put forth weak smiles at the jokes. He hardly ever looked directly at Jim, who sensed that in his partner's eyes all this generaling and admiraling was only Jim, once more, acting the role of clownish boy.

9

As for Madame, she must have money. The husband may not be able to furnish it, and there may be a limit to even the pawnbrokers' generosity; but money she must have. She sells her honor for filthy lucre.

—James McCabe, *New York by Gaslight*, 1882

Annabelle Stokes was edgy. From the roguish glances and attentiveness that Jim Fisk bestowed on her, it was clear he found her attractive.

"The Rawlings acres?" he asked in comic disbelief as exaggerated as a clown's. "You want us to buy right-of-way land from you? Now?"

"Yes," she said, covering her disappointment. The rocky acres were her last property of value, little more than a hillside of scrubby bushes that no one but the Erie could use.

Fisk let out a laugh, a large, rich guffaw that rocked him so hard that it might have split the seams of his bold hound's-tooth suit.

His features sobered up. "How's Ned doing?" he asked.

A dry wind of anger kicked through her. How dare this buffoon bring up her divorce? "You know Ned?" she asked sharply. Her certainty that this Jersey hotel room had been a bedroom before being converted into an office added to her uneasiness. Being alone with a man in a hotel bedroom of any sort was no place for a lady who wanted to maintain her reputation, much less reestablish one. He shrugged.

"Sure, everybody in the cotton business knew Ned," he answered. "I sold him cotton in the War."

At least the room's two doors were open. From the adjoining room bustled in the metallic clack of telegraph keys and the laughing banter of shirtsleeved clerks. From the door to the hall came the bark of rapid orders and the quick steps of messengers.

Annabelle couldn't make up her mind about Jim Fisk, the only officer of the Erie at Taylor's Inn who would see her. On the one hand, he possessed every swaggering barnyard quality she had come to despise in postwar men—loudness, youth, overconfidence, too much enthusiasm, and the general air that a speedy brain and a flapping tongue were a man's best virtues. In short, a roguish pig with a dashing cavalry mustache. Yet in spite of herself she was amused by his puckish manner and the way his stout form, encased in a boldly checked suit, bounded about the makeshift office.

"Is the General going to run for the presidency?" Fisk asked.

She hadn't seen much of her sister Jenny and her husband over the last eight years. Accustomed to speaking the truth, she opened her mouth to say so, then instinctively shut it. If this elfish pig knew Ned, and knew that Ulysses Grant was her brother-in-law, then he was shrewder than she had reckoned. Although she possessed no more idea of Ulysses's plans than what the newspapers printed, she gave Fisk a paragraph on Ulysses's prospects that he could read in any month-old magazine.

"About buying my acres," she said. "I'm offering them at a good price, and you'll need them for your Pittsburgh tracks."

He shook his head. "You'll have to see Mr. Gould. Expansion's his department. And just now, expansion's the fartherest thing from his mind."

She forced herself to be pushier than a lady was supposed to be. "Still, if I may, I'd like to discuss it with him."

After Fisk left to ask his partner to see her, she tugged at her corset to readjust the thorn of a broken stay that dug painfully into her waist. Everything was against her. She was a woman in a man's world, a seller in a buyer's market, and a simpleton among thieves.

Fisk came back with the news that Mr. Gould would see her. She followed him. At the far end of the hall the atmosphere was quieter, less noisy, more concentrated. They entered another hotel bedroom converted into a makeshift office.

"Jay," called out Fisk in a deferential tone. A small, neatly bearded man, also in his early thirties, briskly swiveled around from his desk and stood to greet her. "Mrs. Stokes."

As Fisk introduced them, she was startled by the difference between the two Erie officers. She had been prepared for another Fisk— someone plump and loud. Instead Jay Gould was thin, quiet, and radiated calm. His prominent forehead was as pale as if sculpted from bleached bone. He was short, too, two inches shorter than she was. Unlike the Broadway dandy's up-to-the-minute outfit that Fisk wore, Gould was dressed in an ordinary black suit so out of date it might have been tailored before the War.

He invited her to sit. As if Gould's calm radiated out to include the adjoining bedroom-office, through the open door subdued clerks industriously scribbled in large red-and-black ledgers. A furious rat-a-tat-tat came from the three telegraph keys on the table before two clerks in green eyeshades.

"I sent Mr. Pinrose before," explained Annabelle, "but he can't speak for me as well as I can speak for myself."

On hearing her voice Gould's luminous black eyes regarded her with new interest. Some of her diluted courage renewed itself. Her father had trained her to speak with the crisp decisiveness that businessmen valued. Like him, she couldn't stand female, calflike helplessness.

"I must sell that land," she went on. "I know that puts me in a bad position from which to negotiate, but I've had some reverses and must obtain cash for those acres." She paused, but Gould said nothing. Like a blind crab, his right hand picked its way along the rolltop desk till it found the edge of a newspaper. His delicate fingers ripped off a corner and rolled it into a little ball. "You're likely to give me a better price than some casual buyer," she went on, "and when you expand your road you'll need those acres. At that time you'll pay three times as much to the speculator who buys them off me." A second tiny ball of newspaper was added to the first, and with an almost inaudible rasp the deft fingers clawed off another scrap.

For a long moment none of the three spoke. Despite the hammering loudness of the room's hush, Annabelle held a tight rein on her tongue. There would be no negotiation without both sides talking. The thornlike end of her corset's broken stay again pinched her waist. Finally Gould cleared his throat and broke the silence.

"Surely you've seen the newspapers, Mrs. Stokes," he said. "You must know the awkward situation we find ourselves in."

"Yes," she countered, "but I'm equally sure that clever businessmen such as yourselves are interested in a bargain."

Gould nodded. "How much do you have in mind for this land?"

She mentioned a sum just under Pinrose's last figure. Gould shook his head. They jockeyed awhile, with Fisk merely watching.

She was on the edge of her chair, about to rise and take her leave, when it struck her that busy people with no interest in her land would not have allowed her to stay so long. She sat back. Again the broken stay dug into her flesh. She toughened her stand. Gould wanted the acres, recognized he could get a bargain, and was wrestling with her to obtain them. A tense joy welled up—she had a chance! she could make this sale!—but she clamped a curbing hand on it. Cockiness might destroy her bargaining poise.

Fisk, who had left the room, returned and gave Gould a nod.

Gould took the signal. "Will you have lunch with us?" he asked, rising. "Mrs. Taylor sets a fine table."

Lunch? A lady in a hotel dining room with two men unrelated to her? It felt daring. Yet, as Papa would say, if you're still talking to them, they haven't said no. As gracefully as the broken stay allowed, she stood.

"Yes, I'd love lunch," she said with a trill.

Gould smiled and offered her his arm. "Good! Let's postpone business till afterwards."

They were shown to a reserved table at the end of a surprisingly bright dining room. Annabelle's excitement, the cool morning, and her hunger combined to make her highly alert.

With a start, she realized she was famished. A plain country girl in a smudged apron served a good codfish soup and poured white wine, followed by a watery grilled sole. Taylor's Inn seemed both seedy and comfortable.

Fisk told a couple of stories about Ned's wartime coups. "What a pity Ned's firm went under," he said. "Back in the War, I must have sold him a million bales of cotton."

What was going on? She knew men often made small talk, engaged in the most meandering of conversations before knuckling down to business. It was their way of getting a better grasp on those with whom they dealt, a facet of business life about which it irritated her to be awkward, as if you had to master tumbling off a log.

More jokes, more stories. Purposely she did not direct the conversation. He father had trained her to be alert in negotiations, during which, he maintained, nothing was said accidentally. All of Annabelle's nerves quivered as she took a lady's tiny bites of fish. These men wanted something, and her conviction swelled that it was neither her land nor the intimate favors her mortgagee Boggs maneuvered for.

The conversation drifted toward national topics. Jay Gould's views of the War's aftermath were typical of those she heard in town. John Wilkes Booth had not only killed a great and good president, he had given life to the very forces of hate and vengeance that Lincoln was trying to kill. Had Lincoln lived, surely his magnanimous policy toward the South would have prevailed, for even after his death it almost went through despite furious opposition from the Republican Radicals. Jim Fisk thought it said a lot for how the South should be treated that almost every civil and military leader of the beaten section had expressed regret over the murder of Lincoln.

"Yes, but I'm afraid the South is winning the peace," said Annabelle. "It is preserving the essence of slavery—a pool of cheap, subservient Negro labor." The other two looked surprised at her comment—as if ladies weren't supposed to have such sharp political opinions—and nodded. Gould said that at least the South had quickly accepted the War's verdict. Had this been Europe there would have been a Confederate government-in-exile, guerrilla operations.

The watery sole was followed by dark slabs of roast beef, salty and overcooked. Beneath her calm, cheerful demeanor she watched the two Erie officers with the attention of a poor relation, all the while despising her neediness. Along with this vigilance she felt a nearly hidden happiness—a joy she scarcely acknowledged, it was so unfeminine—because she was rubbing shoulders with businessmen as if she were their equal. It was the first time she had ever done so without her father's or her husband's mantle of protection, and she liked this freedom from male constraint.

To show the two of them that she wasn't completely dependent on the sale of her land, she described the Fifth Avenue dressmaking shop she hoped to open—the finest seamstresses, the most exact fittings, the best satins, laces, and silks—leaving out how impossible it was for her to finance.

Twice the conversation circled around to her brother-in-law, Ulysses S. Grant, hero of the Civil War, about whose politics Jay Gould asked a half-dozen casual questions. When Ulysses's name came up for the third time, the reason for this lunch sparked across her mind like a Roman candle through a night sky. Fisk and Gould didn't want her rocky hillside; they wanted to know more about Ulysses Grant because he was a shoo-in for the Republican nomination. Her hopes wilted.

"I'd like to meet General Grant," said Gould straight out. His fingers blindly crept over the cloth to toy with one of the breadballs they had absently fashioned. "Mr. Fisk and I have large plans for the Erie. This raid of the Commodore's is diverting us from those plans."

Still wilted, she mechanically drew him out. "Plans, Mr. Gould?"

"I want to link the two coasts together by rail," he said.

His matter-of-factness startled her. "Link the two coasts together by rail!" She had heard such talk before, but never in this sober fashion, said as if he planned to cross the street. "That's quite an ambition. You have several mountain ranges and thousands of miles of wilderness to cross with track. And will the Indians allow the trains to pass?"

Gould's smile was as faint as a cat's. "You sound a little like my associate here," he said. "He doesn't think it's possible either."

Fisk waved a cigar about, his grin as blatant as a circus clown's. "The financing of such a long line," said Fisk, "along with the costs of its upkeep, could never be borne by its meager traffic. But Mr. Gould is a practical man in day-to-day operations, so we allow him his pipe dreams."

It was the sharpest sally Fisk had made in Gould's direction. A wavelet of anger flickered across Gould's bone-white face, and the harsh glance made Fisk start.

"Farmers in California will ship their grain to Europe," said Gould heatedly; "they can't now." The ardent gleam in his black eyes pinned Annabelle and Fisk to their chairs. "Merchants in Denver will import factory products cheaply from the East Coast—they bring them in on stagecoach now." His voice was urgent, racing a little, as if this plan had lain like a coiled spring impatient to jump out. "Miners will ship coal and iron to eastern refineries. Cattlemen will ship steers from Iowa to Boston, rather than first walk them to death to St. Louis and Chicago. Bankers will ride from Philadelphia to Salt Lake to inspect building sites, rather than withhold their loans."

Annabelle put down her fork to listen. His hard, rapid speech described the great plains west of Kansas and Nebraska, the high plains, and the Rocky Mountains region as uninhabited by white men except for the mining towns of Colorado and Nevada and the Mormon settlements in Utah. These lands were ripe for settlement. Mail coaches of the Overland State Line required at least five days to carry passengers and mail from the Missouri River to Denver. Silver ore extracted in Nevada had to be freighted by wagon to San Francisco, and from there transported around Cape Horn to the refineries on the East Coast and in Great Britain. His voice flicked about, as sharp and flexible as a rapier. His hand hadn't touched the little pile of breadballs. Finding she was holding her breath, Annabelle covertly released it.

Transportation was the key to developing America, he went on, and rails were the new heart of transportation. Track had more than doubled during the War, to 35,000 miles. Activists in Congress were arguing, and rightly, that land grants to railroad companies would do for the West what the Virginia Company of 1612 and the Ohio Company of 1785 had done for their regions. He made her see that railroading could easily become the biggest business of a booming era, and that railroad builders like Jay Gould and Cornelius Vanderbilt were of the mettle that in Europe made Von Moltkes and Napoleons.

In the next breath Gould called railroads the magician's wand that had woken up the sleeping energies of the New World's land and water. "Steam has freed the country from its waterways," he said. The task of railroads was to lay a steel web of track across the rest of the country, for wherever track ran, civilization, profits, and jobs quickly followed.

"This country will never achieve its strength," he went on, "truly prosper—grow into its real manhood—until it's linked together by a complete rail system. Today we're only a collection of scattered colonial cities, moons stumbling around the sun of Europe. Using a rail system to bind these moons into a single planetary system is the only way to escape the dreadful magnetic pull of our motherland's economic domination."

Despite the hot sunlight that poured across the table, a shiver spidered up Annabelle's spine. Fisk's broad face smiled in a mocking way, as if he had watched Gould ride this hobbyhorse many times. In her rose a sharp jet of anger toward the fat man. She admired enormously such a continent-wide vision—the sweep of great plans, the ability to envision the larger scope of affairs. As if a cold, wet broom had brushed through her, the urgency of his vision had swept away the cobweb of her worries. It had been years since she had listened to a man who was larger than his own greed. She was more aroused and alert than she had been in days, weeks, even, as if for months without being aware of it she had been sleepwalking.

Over a final cup of the inn's bitter coffee, Gould murmured, "Mrs. Stokes, we might be able to buy your acres. Perhaps at even a higher price than you've mentioned. But there's something you must do for us. Will you introduce us to General Grant?"

Higher price! Too stunned to speak, Annabelle stared from one to the other. Gould leaned forward as if the three were conspirators.

"Someplace casual," he said, his fingers groping for the breadballs the serving girl had removed. "Perhaps a little gathering in your house where we could talk quietly." Her astonished silence pushed Gould to speak further. "We need a friendly relationship with the next president," he said. "The Erie needs friends in high places if we're to keep predators like Commodore Vanderbilt at bay."

Meet Ulysses! Still too dazed to give a sensible reply, Annabelle nodded. Nothing should be easier than introducing your brother-in-law to a friend. But it was impossible, because her sister Jenny wouldn't let her within a mile of Ulysses.

She told herself to keep silent and to keep nodding. She must get away and think.

On the way upstairs, Annabelle excused herself to freshen up. She needed a chance to regain her wits. In the small ladies' room off the second-floor hallway, amid the rattle of dishwashing and the pig-slop reek that floated up through wide gaps in the floorplanks, she sat in front of the vanity mirror and stared at the pale, bleak version of herself that stared back.

"Jenny," she said into the mirror, as if rehearsing, but the disapproving frown of her matronlike sister that glared back forced her to jump up and turn away. Hemmed in by the room's tiny size, she threw herself back onto the seat. Mechanically noticing how white her face was, she took out her rouge and gave her cheeks a properly faint touch of color.

The memory of her sister's bitterness was stuck in her with the sharpness of that damn stray whalebone that pierced her side. Hoping to calm herself with the familiar, repetitive action, Annabelle pulled her comb through her hair.

Plain Jenny had always resented her, Annabelle, their father's favorite. Jenny had been "Little Mother" at home, while Annabelle was "Little Father" in the tiny bank beside the farmhouse. Each sister thought what the other did was ridiculous for a woman. Jenny spent her girlhood learning how to churn butter without turning it into buttermilk and how to roast a turkey without drying it out. Annabelle spent hers learning how to write up bank deposits, make out statements, persuade depositors to invest more with the bank, draft loan agreements, and compute interest.

The first time Jenny spoke to her about Ulysses was in front of their own vanity mirror, Annabelle recalled. Nine years ago! She pulled the comb through her hair. She had been in her teens. The two unmarried sisters shared a good-size bedroom on the second floor of the farmhouse as well as the dressing room made over from a large closet.

"Oh, Annabelle, do me this one favor," Jenny pleaded. "I want him. I want him so bad."

"Him" was Captain Ulysses S. Grant, stationed at nearby Fort Webster. Several weeks before, Ulysses had met the sisters at the church's covered-dish supper, and since then, along with whatever other beaus were in favor, he had been a regular at the Lawsons' midday Sunday dinners. Captain Grant—it was hard to call a man twenty years older by his first name—was far quieter and calmer than the boys who courted them. He had a wheatfield-thick beard where the boys had facial hair as ragged as garden weeds. Solidly fashioned for burdens, his broad shoulders were always squared; the local youths slouched about on the front porch. While Captain Grant was polite to his younger rivals, his impassive eyes regarded them as unimportant as second lieutenants. Annabelle's quick mind found him as dull as churning butter or roasting a turkey.

"Jenny," Annabelle explained, "Ulysses isn't my cup of tea. Here, would you comb this out?"

Anxious to please, Jenny slid onto the bench next to her sister and went at the knot. "Then how come last Sunday after dinner you walked to the well with him?" Jenny asked.

"Because he asked me," Annabelle said. "I had to listen to an entrancing lecture on how artillery was deployed at Waterloo." Jenny stopped combing and glared at Annabelle in the mirror.

"Will you stop?" Jenny screamed. Annabelle jumped. Pain twisted Jenny's face as if it were a mirror shattered by a hammer's blow. "Please! You're so beautiful. I know I'm plain. I'll never get married till after you do. They come over here to see me and get stuck on you." Annabelle was stung to the quick by her sister's pain, for she didn't recognize herself as any such thief. She pulled Jenny to her in an embrace.

"Oh, sis—don't say that! You are pretty."

"No, I'm not," said Jenny over Annabelle's shoulder. "I don't know how to be. I just know I want him." Annabelle pushed her to arm's length. Jenny was crying.

"I don't chase your fellows," Annabelle said. Jenny applied a handkerchief to her raw, exposed eyes.

"You say that, but somehow they all get stuck on you."

"Well, I'll make sure Ulysses doesn't get stuck," said Annabelle. She dried Jenny's tears. A middle-aged, stodgy army captain was certainly not the man Annabelle wanted for a husband. In a way carefully calculated to spare his feelings, she made this clear that Sunday afternoon on another windy, autumnal stroll to the well.

"I'd like to call on you some more," he stiffly objected.

The situation was delicate. If she told him not to call and he stayed away, Jenny wouldn't see him. If she said it was all right, he would receive the wrong idea. "You know how much the entire family enjoys your company," she put it, "so I can hardly refuse your offer to visit. But you must understand that I've said no." In fact Papa liked Ulysses so much that he several times had urged him to come to Sunday dinner every weekend, "whether these featherheaded girls think to ask you or not."

Ulysses said, "I'd like you to come to know me better." She put her hand on his arm and shook her head.

"You're making this difficult," she said.

Over the following weeks the captain of artillery, as if he had encounted a particularly difficult fort, laid weekly siege against Annabelle's heart. He fired cannonballs of pralines and chocolate-covered cherries against the palisades, peppered her battlements with gold-filled trinkets, and scrambled up to the embrasures on ladders woven from colored ribbons and dried damask roses. She supposed that his sudden, consuming interest in the mechanics of Papa's bank was his version of the Trojan horse. Ulysses was polite, considerate, stubborn—and still tedious.

Nothing Annabelle said dissuaded him from his winter siege. Predictably, Jenny was upset. No matter how much she tried, Annabelle could not convince her sister that she hadn't set out to steal the first man that Jenny really, really wanted.

For the first time since she was eight, Jenny burned pots of vegetables and pans of bread. The entire season's apple butter needed to be thrown out because she added salt instead of sugar. Uncharacteristically, she couldn't cut a pattern without wasting yards of fabric. And when Annabelle was in her presence, Jenny sulked. The strain between the sisters grew till they didn't speak. It took three winter months of Ulysses's eating Sunday dinners to convince him that Annabelle would never have him.

For the next eight weeks Ulysses didn't come to Gantry to church or to the house afterward for dinner. Jenny went from sulking to crying. Gloom blighted what once had been a cheery home. As obtuse over such things as he was sharp at banking, Papa continued to ask about the captain, for he liked Ulysses's solid inner strength.

When with spring Ulysses returned to the Lawsons', he ignored Annabelle and right away asked Jenny to marry him. Surprised, hurt because it was obvious that she was second best in his eyes, Jenny delayed her answer, but only for two days. At last she said yes.

Annabelle felt embarrassment and pity for her sister. Clearly Jenny possessed no sense of what such a beginning would mean to her marriage. Ulysses would never value her the way a man ought to value his wife. It made Annabelle shudder to watch her sister strolling to the well arm in arm with Ulysses. At the same time, her hands were full then with a certain Ned Stokes, whose especially frisky pair of bays trotted him over every weekend to see her.

Certainly Ned was Annabelle's cup of tea—dashing, handsome,

from one of the great old families of Philadelphia, and full of exciting political and financial plans for a future in New York that included her. He wore the new mode of tight trousers that daringly showed off his strong legs and the bulge between them. With winks in Annabelle's direction, he made oblique jokes about the thickheadedness of the army, which appeared to go over Ulysses's head. For Jenny's sake, Annabelle didn't entirely approve of them, but still it was all in fun and Ulysses's stolid, mulelike slowness irritated her.

Everything was fun to Ned. Nobody as gorgeous as he was could be bad. If the country beaus surrounding the two girls were like crickets—thin angular legs and arms, awkwardly sprawled about on the porch—and if Ulysses was like a large bearded carpenter ant sitting stolidly among them, then Ned was a daddy longlegs, prancing over the sprawled country bodies in a dandy's blue coat, gray trousers, and yellow cravat. Tousled back curls. A widow's peak. Delicate skin that women envied.

Two April weekends after Jenny accepted Ulysses, Ned asked Annabelle to marry him. He proposed that they move to New York, where he would establish a cotton brokerage.

Ned and New York! She lost no time saying yes. Their father proposed a double ceremony, humorously declaring that he could afford a much more lavish celebration if he married both girls at once. With some misgivings, not wanting to hurt Papa's feelings, the daughters agreed.

The memory of her wedding day faded in the vanity mirror of Taylor's Inn, and the rattling of dishes and ripe stench of pig slop reasserted themselves. The ladies' room was hot and suffocating. Annabelle's hands were trembling.

Now Jay Gould wanted her to entertain Ulysses Grant—which meant Ulysses *and* Jenny, for Jenny would never allow Ulysses to call on her divorced sister alone. Oh, God, Annabelle groaned. A groundwork would have to be laid. That meant warm letters, visits, fake cordiality, and scheming. Despite Jenny's lending a brief hand in her hour of terrible need, it meant struggling to patch a relationship that had probably been shattered forever.

Did she want to do it?

No, just as she hadn't wanted to visit Pa.

Did she have to do it?

She sighed and reckoned yes.

Added to that yes was the prospect of working with Jay Gould. She dismissed Jim Fisk as a clownish lightweight like her former husband, but Jay Gould was a different story. He was a young man going places. He reminded her of the father of her youth—sober, reflective, yet well prepared to carry out bold plans. A man who knew what he wanted and worked to get it. An intense man with a vision and the courage to act—the sort of man who thrilled Annabelle and who she wanted as a partner for life.

On her return to Jay Gould's makeshift office at the quiet end of the third floor, she was glad Fisk was not there. Fearful that it would weaken her value to him, she didn't mention how things stood between her and Jenny.

"I'd be delighted to introduce you to Ulysses," she said. "But to properly entertain the 'great man' that Ulysses has become, I need some ready cash."

"We'll advance what you need against the sale of your land," he said.

The arrangement was set. When Gould returned to New York, they would finish negotiations for the ultimate price and terms.

Fisk popped in. "Can our clerk Morosini ride to town with you?"

She said graciously, "I'd be pleased to oblige."

Half an hour later, Morosini, a small, neat man in a black suit and starched collar, and with a carefully trimmed black mustache, perched birdlike across from her on the carriage seat as if afraid to relax in her presence.

The weather was cold and clear, a brisk, sunny March afternoon that lifted her spirits. As the hired carriage bounced along to the ferry, Annabelle pictured herself as the wife of a man like Jay Gould. It would be like being married to Ned, except on a surer, more mature footing. He would know all the bigwigs of New York, many of the people she and Ned had known before but who ignored her now.

She was acquainted with hundreds of New York City men, but no one like Jay Gould. To a snout the others were only interested in what they could root for themselves out of the city's rich compost heap. The only people with Jay's calm, intense vision were the editorial writers she and Ned had sometimes invited over, public men with broad vision but without the means or energy to make it real.

But a man with vision—and the drive and the means to carry it off! A warm glow spread through her.

She dwelled on the details of their meeting, the times at lunch when she had caught the gleam of his eyes fixed on her. Was something besides Ulysses and her land on his mind? She had come with the hope of selling a few acres, but what more might be here? She would not deny that the youthful president of the Erie interested her.

Soon her carriage was aboard the ferry. They pushed off for Manhattan. Fluffy white clouds raced along the tops of the faraway church spires. The life and slide of the ferry further buoyed her spirits. In a mental shift, an opening of perception, she suddenly viewed her life as the passage of a boat on open water, much like this ferry on the Hudson. Under her as the ferry slid about was the liquid sensation of maneuverability. Morosini was still perched on his seat, his eyes carefully averted from hers. Here was an opportunity to learn more about her new partner.

"A family?" repeated Morosini to her question. "Oh, yes indeed, Mr. Gould has a family. You'll never find a more devoted family man. Four children. Even when we work late at the office he has his carriage take him home to dinner. Afterwards he might well come all the way back downtown, but he won't miss his evening time with them. His eldest, George, says he reads to them every night. . . ."

As he chattered on about Gould's devotion to his children, she was reminded of her own broken marriage, and her spirits sank. The choppy waves and fleecy clouds still kicked about through the carriage's window, but the bright spring day mocked her. Jay Gould married, happily married! What a fool she was to imagine more than a business partnership. She scolded herself for building cloud castles. Besides, she was no dummy about men. If Jay Gould were free, he would want a virginal twenty-year-old girl, not a divorcee near thirty with two children.

The ferry docked. Her hired carriage passed from downtown, full of top hats and swallowtail coats, to upper Broadway, decorated with the soft pastels of ladies under parasols out for their afternoon stroll.

She needed to lay her plans carefully. If Ulysses were unmarried and she wrote, he would come. But if she directly wrote to the married Ulysses, Jenny would block the visit. Better to write Jenny first, forge what friendship she could, and assume that sooner or later Ulysses would show up with her. Yes, that was the way.

The sight of her town house, her trim, dignified castle of brownstone blocks, strengthened her determination not to give it up. She paid the driver his three dollars and reluctantly parted with a fifty-cent tip.

She entered the bare, ugly hall, shorn of last year's gilt sconces, fringed banners, and small oriental rugs that had made it glow. A square, empty gap on the wallpaper indicated where the gold-framed mirror had hung. Annabelle wanted them all back. She needed to write a series of brilliantly friendly and chatty letters to her sister, ones so engaging that they would induce General and Mrs. Grant to stay at her house during all their stopovers in New York City.

10

It is impossible to regard Vanderbilt's methods or aims without recognizing the magnitude of the man's ideas and conceding his abilities. He voluntarily excites feelings of admiration for himself and alarm for the public. His ambition is a great one. It seems to be nothing less than to make himself master in his own right of the great channels of communication which connect the city of New York with the interior of the continent, and to control them as his private property.

—Charles Francis Adams, Jr., 1869

A day later William ushered into Cornelius's seventh-floor office Kerry O'Brian, the New York chief of Pinkerton's. A large, pear-shaped fellow whose sandy hair was almost gone, he had hurriedly scraped up information on Fisk and Gould, about whom the Vanderbilts knew almost nothing.

To Cornelius's surprise, Gould wasn't one of those clever Jews, but a country fellow, Protestant, and only in his early thirties. He had left home at seventeen, O'Brian reported, to work as a land surveyor. At twenty, he founded and ran a tannery in the wilds of Pennsylvania. He had always been sickly, and his lungs had been further corrupted by the fumes from the lead salts and mercury used in tanning. Since being in the city, he had been a dabbler in rail stocks.

"Isn't this enough, William?" asked Cornelius, figuring they would have heard more about this Gould if he were important. Cornelius still suffered from the head and chest cold his dunking in the

Hudson had inflicted on him. His lungs felt as squishy as the rotten timbers of an old barge, and just as likely to collapse and let him drown.

But William wanted to hear about Fisk, too. To their amazement, Fisk had been a barker with Van Amberg's traveling circus, and after that, a peddler of tinware and fabrics across New England. "Had his traveling wagons painted up to look like circus wagons," O'Brian reported, "all red, white, and gold, the horses with silver harnesses and them stiff red brushes on their heads."

Cornelius snorted. "These aren't dangerous people," he said to William. "They're small fry—dabblers and penny-ante hustlers. Drew's own sons won't work with him—he's too cheap—so he's picked up these nincompoops. A sickly runt and a circus barker. The first real pressure and the Erie will collapse like a rotten egg under a boot heel."

But this news didn't cheer his son. In a much better mood himself, at midmorning Cornelius led his son onto the floor of the Stock Exchange, where his staunch and energetic buying amid a blizzard of sell orders kept the stock of their outfit, the New York Central, from selling off too much.

Two afternoons later the market crisis had let up enough so that Cornelius was able to leave the Exchange floor to go to the funeral of his boyhood friend Vincent Walloon. As the plain pine coffin was carried from the Broadway church into the cemetery out back, he and Judge Barnard trudged behind it. Cornelius sneezed again. Barnard peered up with the friendliness of a raccoon after table scraps.

"I hear it's been rough at the Exchange," the Judge said.

"I'm going to eat his liver, George," said Cornelius. Barnard nodded quickly, for Cornelius didn't have to explain that he meant Daniel Drew.

The spring sunlight behind the church was cold. In the pine box on the trestles rested the Staten Island boy who had been his playmate sixty-five years ago. Cornelius shook his head in bewilderment, for none of it seemed real—the sunlight, the bird whistles, his chest cold, the droning voice of the preacher, the five bold daffodils by the Morris tombstone, the restless old men standing in a quiet circle, the ache in his joints. What kind of Maker played such a trick on you as palsied old age and death? A man no sooner figured out how to make a go of things than he was yanked away.

The pine box was lowered into the damp earth amid the flowering green and the shrill calls of birds. Cornelius decided not to go to any more funerals. At forty and fifty years of age he had understood perfectly well that only through dying did the old make way for the young. If a tree's leaves didn't die, new leaves couldn't sprout. Now at seventy-five, watching the gravediggers drop spadefuls of earth on his chum, he knew much less, only that death shoveled six feet of dirt on top of you. He didn't want to suffocate under a blanket of black, airless mud.

Shovels of dirt clumped onto the coffin lid, the hollow, muffled booms of a drum that beat as much for Cornelius as for his dead chum. Sixty years ago Cornelius had manned his single periauger on the bay and possessed infinite riches—his youth, more valuable and mightier than all his present wealth. In those days his little boat danced merrily through the waves as it dashed across the sun-struck bay, and he never suspected how enormously rich he was.

It had been a long road from that periauger to the railroad business. It was in the forties that Cornelius first saw the peaceful valleys of the Hudson scarified by the chugging, snorting, screeching monsters of iron with jutting cowcatchers and bulbous funnels. From the vantage of his steamships Cornelius saw a fever of railroad construction rage from Boston to New Orleans, matched on the stock exchanges by fits of speculation. He and Drew and other steamboat owners watched with disdain these early railroads, with their need for a corporate structure, a state charter, and huge sums of money. The earliest lines were but five and ten miles long, small links between small towns, established by men not so much interested in the transport these lines would produce as enthralled by the banging, clanging excitement of the ride. Then in the fifties shrewder fellows bought up and stitched these short lines together, selling stock to finance the purchases, adding track where needed to connect them, so that a series of a dozen lines could connect Albany to Rochester.

After that men of larger vision saw that these lines could yet again be spliced together, repeating the process of organization on a larger scale. If a line from Rochester to Albany could successfully sell stock, why not one from Buffalo to New York? From Philadelphia to Baltimore? All it took was imagination and the confidence of large banks and Wall Street, which Cornelius had enjoyed for years. Men were going to get rich from railroads, and Cornelius came to see that he wasn't in the steamship business, but in the business of transportation. He bought into rail lines defensively—enabling his customers to transship between his steamers on rail lines controlled by him—and he kept buying till the small lines he had obtained became the New York Central, the mightiest rail line of the country.

And now the Erie lay before him. A line with great prospects ruined by years of Drew's financial manipulations. Still, tens of thousands of trained employees worked for it, and it owned hundreds of miles of track, which when added to the Central would give Cornelius a solid foundation for forging farther west. Now that the War was over and no depression or panic had ensued, now that the South had been brought back into the Union, now that the tonnage hauled of grain, cotton, ores, and ingots was surging upward month after month—the man who controlled the nation's rails would shape its destiny, and become yet more rich in the bargain. Cornelius would be that man. And to think that two pipsqueaks and a frail humbug stood in his way!

Cornelius clapped on his top hat. "Come back to my house, Judge," he said. "I need some help." Barnard's worried face brightened.

"Anything I can do for you," said the Judge, "you know I will."

Barnard's cheery tune changed when Cornelius explained what the help was that he wanted.

"But you know who I got in there," said Barnard, referring to the prisoners in his Ludlow Street jail. "They're the roughest trash in the city."

Cornelius's scheme was to send the meanest roustabouts he could put his hands on to Taylor's Inn to bring back the three fugitives. Now Barnard was trying to wiggle out of his promise to help.

He and Judge Barnard sat in Cornelius's private office, the one he had fixed up in the stables behind his house. In this rough but cozy snuggery, Cornelius conducted his personal business, for he owned mortgages, stocks, farms, stables, steamship companies, and other railroads—all the wealth he had earlier this week pledged in order to purchase millions more of Central stock—that it wasn't politic to run out of the Central's offices. A kettle of peppermint tea softly bubbled on the top of a cheery potbellied stove. Through the half-open window floated the snorts of horses, murmur of servants' voices, and frisky stamp of hooves as his grooms rubbed down his mounts.

"Well, Bully Morrison's in there," said Barnard. "And Spitting William. You don't want such as them." The Judge leaned forward, his mug of peppermint tea tipping dangerously toward the floor. "That whole lot comes from Hell's Kitchen." Barnard leaned back, his averted eyes announcing that this surely dismissed the matter.

Cornelius considered this. Hell's Kitchen was the tenement-crowded blocks from Fourteenth to Forty-second, Hudson River to Ninth Avenue. The breeding ground of the Nineteenth Street Gang, the Forty Little Thieves, the Whyos, and the Tenth Avenue Gang, a sprawling zoo of pimps, thugs, looters, gangsters, burglars, thieves, and brawlers. Cornelius's own Central Railway yards were the private hunting preserve of these gangs. Policemen didn't like to venture into Hell's Kitchen in troops of fewer than four.

Cornelius refilled his mug with peppermint tea. "They've been paid plenty by the Central," he said, referring to their many thefts from Central yards. "Now let them earn their keep."

"Bully was written up in the papers last year when he came before me."

Cornelius struggled to be patient. "I don't like the papers." He asked, "So what?"

"He's a big, red-bearded Orangeman, must be seven foot tall," said Barnard. "Mean as a wildcat with the red ass, especially when he has a load on. He tore a lamppost out of the sidewalk and used it like a club against the heads of the Catholics."

Cornelius chuckled. "Just the man we want."

"There's Battle Annie," said Barnard. "She's an Orangeman, so she'd get along with Bully. I don't have any of her gang—"

Cornelius sneered. "A woman with a gang?"

"The Lady Gophers, sort of the Ladies Auxiliary of Bully's outfit."

"This is no job for women," said Cornelius. "Fisk and Gould have guards onshore and in the water."

Barnard snickered nervously. "This is a she-bear who sits in Mallet Murphy's bar brooding till she works up enough bile to chase those she fancies have wronged her. She comes out the family entrance and gives a yell that for a block or two drives the rats out the trash heaps. She'll round up twenty to thirty amazons, valkyries in tatters, who run through the streets looking for her enemies." The small fat man giggled, as if afraid she might hear him. "Lord help those they catch. She's taught them how to knee a groin, stave in ribs, gouge out an eye. The gang busted three strikes last year."

Cornelius grimaced. "I don't want them permanently hurt," he said. "Only roughed up a little and stuck in your jail."

"C'neal, you got to be responsible," said Barnard in a brave tone.

"Responsible?"

Barnard squirmed. "If any of them run away. Don't come back to jail."

Cornelius grinned and poured more hot tea. "So, let's send along a few policemen to make sure Bouncing Bully and his chums follow orders."

"I can't. It's not their jurisdiction."

Cornelius leaned over and gripped Barnard's arm in a tight squeeze. "I want those three in jail."

Barnard sighed. "All right. I'll tell Bully I'll take three months off the sentence of every man who helps out."

Cornelius's blue eyes gleamed. "That's the stuff! Let's do it to-morrow night."

Barnard started. "No, no, that's way too fast. This is a delicate matter. A few people have to be 'spoke to' the right way."

Cornelius stood up. "You know, this tea has cleared my head something wonderful." He gave a little roar to test his chest; it wasn't clogged. "Spend what you have to, Judge. The faster the better. The sooner I eat Drew's liver, the tastier it'll be. Now, excuse me. I'm going to take my horses out for a trot. I swear I feel a hundred percent better."

On the first gorgeous spring afternoon of the year, Josie Mansfield presided over a starched white tablecloth in the elegant tea salon of the Hoffman House. Across from her sat Ned Stokes.

On the platform at the far end of the long salon, a violin and oboe quartet sobbed a solemn measure that Josie couldn't name but that sounded refined and classy. Light, amused chatter tinkled delicately in the air. The aromatic bouquet of pungent coffee, musty tea, and the fruity tartness of raspberry, fig, and molasses pastries from the triple-tiered silver trolley made the tea salon a perfumed garden. Josie wished the afternoon would never end, but already shadows were drawing on the buildings across the avenue.

"Another pastry, Mrs. Mansfield?" Ned asked. "Perhaps a fig *tart?*"

"Please, a *raspberry* tart. I've always said the Hoffman House served *uncommonly* good pastries." There! Let him know she was used to coming here. And let him know she could drawl words as fashionably as did his Main Line accent.

"You're quite the prettiest *lady* here," he drawled back. She ducked her eyes under the brim of her yellow hat, which was held onto her dark, curly hair by a wide ribbon of white organdy. He had been flirting with her with this sort of aristocratic froohaha for the past hour. She hoped he was too ignorant of ladies' fashions to recognize that her lemon-yellow dress of satin crepe, with a high collar of ruffled white lace, was two years old.

"Mr. Stokes!" she exclaimed from behind her fan. "You really *must* stop." Across the room skinny Flowers Crawford, one of Jim's broker cronies, stared at her. Well, she thought, Jim would learn that two could play his game.

He poured her more China tea with the aplomb of a leading actor elongating a pregnant moment with a deft bit of stage business. She loved his long fingers and elegant movements. His patrician features might have been a girl's, they were so delicate and sensual. His skin was as clear as the petals of a cream-colored tulip, and his arched eyebrows luxuriantly black and glossy. The pouting fullness of his lips was made to be crushed. The only other men with such casual beauty and lanky elegance were actors who played leads, men almost too handsome for the ordinary professions of law and business. Ned raised his eyes. Their cloudy ice pierced her, causing her chest to swell with heat and confusion.

"But I find you so *uncommonly* pretty," he murmured. She smiled, basking in the warmth and urbanity of the salon, a hungry, freezing cat finally before a roaring fire with a plate of hot milk. She had been born to spend her afternoons sipping tea in grand salons while lordly princes slathered her with compliments.

"Don't *say* such things in public," she answered in a throaty growl that begged him to continue. Rich violin notes sobbed on. Her bosom, which she had accented by sitting on the front edge of her chair, was thrown even farther forward by her tight corset. His gray eyes lifted lazily to the ornate ceiling.

"We might adjourn to where it's private."

Puzzled, she too glanced up. "What—" Then she understood. The hotel suites above, the heavy furniture set just so in the afternoon sunlight, the large bed turned down by a discreet maid. Ned's strong arms lifted and carried her to it. She blushed.

"*Please*, Mr. Stokes, you're being entirely too forward." He was, yet he got away with it. He was a master at conveying a serious comment while making it sound like frivolous repartee.

It was certainly different here with Ned instead of Jim. Ned didn't shout, no one had come up and sat down without being invited, and Ned had focused on Josie the whole hour. He had real class. She could do herself a lot worse, an awful lot worse. Still, Jim was lots and lots of fun. God, she had missed him.

"We've known each other long enough," he said.

"Now I *must* go," she said. Actually, she wanted to stay in this gilded room forever.

With cultured, amused lethargy, Ned pulled himself to his feet. His very posture was maddeningly insulting and paradoxically attractive. She wished her manners were as aristocratic as his.

"I want to see you again," he said. She hid her excitement. She wanted to see him, too.

"Perhaps you shall," she said in her best throaty voice.

Then she left, grateful that he hadn't offered to run her home in his carriage, for she didn't want him to know yet that she lived in rented rooms. She had eaten half a dozen cucumber sandwiches and two raspberry tarts and washed it all down with four scalding cups of China tea. She could have eaten three times as much, for she hadn't eaten yesterday or today, but gentlemen didn't like to see a lady eat much, and she had already crossed the limit of good breeding.

At home, a letter from Jim had been slipped under Josie's door. A candle by her side, her heart tripping, she sat on the window seat and slid her long nail under the envelope's flap. As if it were a thief lurking about outside, a soft breeze made the leafless lindens sway in the streetlamp's yellow gleam.

It's lonely over here, wrote Jim. *Jay's burned up with me, and the Deacon ain't much company. I see George of the* Herald *and Spencer from the* Mirror *but all we do is play cards. I miss you something awful and the times we have on Broadway. I wish tonight I was taking you to Del's for canvasbacks and champagne, and afterwards we could snuggle up in your pink cloud of a bedroom!*

In his pen strokes were the nakedness of his need and openheartedness of his feelings. Desire for him grew hot inside her. Oh, Jim! Tears burned her eyes. She missed him, too. Ned struck her as only one more dandy wanting a roll in the sheets. She was sick of Manhattan and its treacherous people. She missed the impish smile of Jim's plump, confident face.

Her mantel clock chimed midnight. This was their time of night, at Delmonico's for a little supper, where dozens of tony gents and their sweetcakes sauntered up to their table. After all, Jim was the most popular gent in New York. From the open, bighearted way he strutted about, everybody saw that he was going to be the greatest impresario in the theater's history. She would be the city's greatest actress. Together he and Josie, impresario and star, would triumph over Manhattan. They went together, she and Jim, like iced oysters and bubbling champagne.

She woke up early the next morning feeling trapped and angry. Her two small rooms seemed especially shabby, her pink-and-white wallpaper altogether too feminine and weak. She felt dispirited, sure that she was drifting into a Manhattan life little different from that of her cow of a mother back in the California mining camp.

She felt pulled in two directions. She wanted to see Ned again. A delicious tingle ran through her whenever she pictured his languid bedroom eyes and the dimple under his full lips. Yet, remembering the good times she had with Jim and the chance for a career onstage, she still wanted to be with him. She must settle this. It was impossible to keep two beans on the string in such a tiny place as Manhattan. She had been seen in public with Ned three times. Already someone might have reported this to Jim.

She realized with a shock that she could simply go see Jim. Why, he was only across the river! And shouldn't a woman be with her man when he was in trouble? Jim's letters from Jersey City said he loved her and that he missed her a lot. Well, she *would* be with him. She would stand by him, do more than even his wife. At the same time, if she played her cards right, she could borrow what she needed to repay Sally Woods.

With this decision, her trapped sense fell away. She was suddenly full of more energy than she had been since the evening Jim walked out, promising to return in an hour with supper from Delmonico's.

With a light heart, she pulled four of her cases off the shelf of her closet and started packing her best outfits.

11

A onetime peddler of silks, poplins, and velvets by the yard, Fisk is almost as broad as he is high, and so round that he rolls rather than walks. But his nervous energy is stimulated rather than deadened by his fat, which gives, indeed, a momentum to his mental movement and his personal influence.

—Samuel Bowles, *Springfield Republican*, 1868

At this same hour Jim Fisk, standing in the doorway of the dining room of Taylor's Inn, peered around anxiously. The sun-drenched tables had yet to fill up with the lunch crowd of Erie employees and Manhattan reporters.

There he was! Daniel Drew, the aged treasurer of the Erie, sat alone at the edge of the room and spooned a plate of soup. Jim hurried over and plopped into the chair next to the thin old man. As if afraid Jim might steal it, Drew pulled his furled umbrella, greenish-black with age, closer to his side.

"I want to go home, bub," opened Drew in a querulous, whining voice.

"Home, Uncle Dan'l!" boomed Jim, hoping to infuse some life into the hunched-over, tight-lipped old stock trader. "We only got here a few days ago!" Drew's withered, liver-spotted hand paused in the act of shoving in a spoonful of carrot-potato soup.

"Shhhh!" said the Erie treasurer. His undertaker's eyes scrutinized the serving girls and scattered diners as if they were Vanderbilt spies. "I don't like it over here." Everything about Drew slanted down—narrow shoulders, hollow cheeks, tight lips, shifty eyes, long nose. His ancient black suit reeked of musty wool, decaying old man, foul breath, and meanness.

Now that General Fisk's army and navy had secured the perimeter of Fort Taylor, Jim could concentrate his attention on the feud with his commander in chief. As the paymaster of this outfit—and the line's largest shareholder—Jim needed the treasurer. If he could enlist Drew as his ally in his fight with Jay to keep his Erie position, he would have won half the battle. The old galoot liked and trusted Jim, who had helped make him a bundle in the wartime cotton market. With any luck, the cautious, shifty-eyed treasurer would promise Jim the support of his thousands of Erie shares.

The important thing was to approach the old miser the right way, for as Jim well knew from their years together, every appeal to his mentor's generosity had first to run the gauntlet of his boyhood poverty.

Seventy-eight years ago Daniel Drew was the eighth arrival of eleven children, born to the long-suffering wife of a drunken cobbler in Putnam County. In good years the cobbler rarely opened his shop more than three days a week; what money he took in that Daniel's ma didn't grab, he stretched out over three or four woozy days of drinking.

To Ma Drew fell the labor of making sure her gang got fed. Her brood regularly ate twopenny-pound scraps from the butcher, half-rotted vegetables the greengrocer tossed away, and three-day-old bread.

Daniel's earliest memory was of trying to keep his balance on a rickety crate while he watched his older brothers and sisters eat. Unpoliced by Ma, shares of food were determined by size and strength. It was a satisfaction of sorts to the sharp pains of a rumbling stomach to see someone else chew food. From the raids on the pig troughs, Daniel received the leftovers that the older ones wouldn't eat; what he couldn't eat he passed on to the three younger and weaker children. To the older ones he was fawningly grateful for their largesse; toward the younger, he showed thin-skinned annoyance at their existence. His chief differences from the other ten children was his cunning tendency to hide part of his share in his pocket and store it in back of a few loose bricks in the chimney behind the shack. He learned the bitter way that fresh food such as tomatoes and scraps of meat didn't keep; his stash grew till it held nearly four pounds of hidden comfort.

One chilly November morning his youngest brother Boots saw him at his stash and tattled to Ma, who promptly made two dinners of it for the clan. Through both meals everybody ate heartily and poked fun at the sullen Daniel. He wasn't foolish enough to neglect eating his share, but he glowered at his jeering family. It taught him an important lesson—never let anybody know about your stash. When a year later Boots died of something wasting, lengthy, and painful, Daniel felt no remorse, only quiet triumph.

Not even seventy years later would he admit that he was worth any money, particularly not to his wife Jane and the boys. In a day when rich men wore silk hats and sported gold-headed canes, Daniel Drew went about in a beat-up drover's hat and with the same aged, greenish-black umbrella, rain or shine. To Jim the pathetic old fellow seemed to resent having to know that he was rich, as if terrified that the knowledge might awaken a sharp-toothed inner demon who would spend his millions in a drunken spree and toss him back onto the dungheap of poverty.

Now, in Taylor's dining room, Jim peered at his Wall Street mentor closely; cadaverous, lean, and pale, he looked five years older than his seventy-eight years, as if his millions were an affliction sucking the life out of him. Jim flapped his starched napkin open and stuffed a corner in his collar.

"Hell, I don't like it over here, either," he said. He signaled the pretty little brown-haired serving girl to bring him a plate of soup like Uncle Dan'l's. "It ain't a bit like Broadway. But we got to stand firm in the trenches. If we run back now, the Walrus is going to bash our heads in." Uncle Dan'l avoided Jim's eye and slurped carrots and potatoes.

"C'neal?" scoffed Drew. "Naw!"

Jim didn't like the way his Street buddy avoided his eye, and so he pressed. "Didn't he chase me and Jay across the river?"

"But he won't do that to *me*," said Drew in his bold whine. "We go back a long way, me and C'neal. When we was on the river—"

"*Whoa!*" said Jim. Alarmed at Drew's thickheadedness, Jim poured it on heavy. "This here ain't no steamboat race, Dan'l. This here's *war*."

"I got to pass the plate on Sunday," said the old man. "I ain't missed a Sunday in eight years."

Pass the plate! Jim exclaimed to himself. Fat chance of much left in it but nickels and dimes when it got to the back of the church! For all his zealous churchgoing, Uncle Dan'l's greed—as cunning as a Philadelphia lawyer's and as bold as a Mississippi riverboat gambler's—was feared by every Wall Street trader. He had started in business as a cattle drover, driving herds to Astor's market. The story went that he fed the cattle nothing but salt the last two days of the drive so they would drink barrel-bellies of water before Astor's men weighed them, a story Jim had no trouble believing. Indeed, the stock market term *watered stock* was said to have come from this trick of Uncle Dan'l's.

He had spent years as a steamboat owner. Jim knew that Drew, like other steamer men of his day, had initially sneered at railroads, while admitting they were spreading like "measles at a boarding school." The steamship owners said that trains would never catch on with the public; they were too dirty, too noisy, too small, and too dangerous. The steamer was leisurely, not cramping its passengers into small quarters on hard wooden benches. From the decks of Uncle Dan'l's graceful steamer a passenger could view the stately banks of the Hudson River, that Rhine of America. What could you see out of the smudged windows of a train? Did a steamboat bump and jolt its passengers? Water came from Heaven, and transport on it was ordained by God himself; the passage of a train, with its infernal soot and smoke and earsplitting rumbling and screeching was a visitation from Hell.

But trains had made progress despite Uncle Dan'l's whines. Steamboats went only where there were deep rivers. Ice didn't stop trains, neither did mountains or deserts. A train could rattle into a station, pick up its passengers and freight, and be gone before a steamboat had passed from the harbor entrance to the dock. Uncle Dan'l, along with other steamer men like Cornelius Vanderbilt, discovered he was being put out of business. Like his competitors, he bought railroad stocks.

The sunny dining room began to fill. The old man whined on about how much he missed his church. Jim listened with a patient, frozen smile. He might have been given more favors and intimacy by the old galoot than Drew gave his own sons, but he knew and feared Drew's greed. It surged like a powerful underground river through his partner, and Jim was certain that the old buzzard himself didn't know when and where it would erupt in treachery. Drew was entirely capable of ignoring the promises he had made to his two partners before they left Manhattan. He could make a secret arrangement with Vanderbilt and sell his Erie position to the Central in a deal that gave him millions in profits. Such a sale would leave Jim and Jay stranded over here at the mercy of their opponent's wrath. If they were to hang on to the Erie, Drew must be convinced that going back to Manhattan was dangerous—as it damn well was.

"You can go to church over here," suggested Jim. The watery blue eyes of the old miser wobbled about sadly.

"It ain't the same," whined the old man. As if to make sure no one snatched it, he pulled his moth-eaten umbrella onto his lap and looked sharply at Jim. "What's going on between you and Jay?"

Jim started. As usual the old man was keener than he let on. "Nothing."

"He says we got to fire you. That you're pissing away our assets."

Jim waved a hand about airily. "You know Jay. He sometimes gets hot under the collar." He leaned forward. "What'd you say?"

"That we're in enough trouble without the two of you squabbling." Drew's morose expression was that of an undertaker at a friend's funeral; it was hard to tell if the grief was real or professional. "You know our deal. As President, he runs the line. As Chief of Staff, you supposed to make sure the employees and shareholders are happy with us. I handle the finances. We all agreed."

"I get along with him," Jim insisted.

"Can you run the Erie?" Drew asked point-blank. "I mean day-to-day, make sure everything happens the way it's supposed to? Move the trains on time? Order out the right number of pay packets at the right depots? Draw up the freight rates to cover our expenses? Have repair schedules written up and maintained, not too many porters and trackmen but enough to do the job?" Uncle Dan'l appeared feeble, but his thin, pointed nose had lost none of its ability to stick itself into the heart of the matter.

"No," Jim had to admit. The business end of Drew's umbrella poked up from beneath the edge of the table to emphasize his next point.

"Neither can I," said Drew. "The Erie needs Jay Gould more than it needs you or me, bub." Jim squirmed. He didn't like the way this conversation was going, not at all. The serving girl set a plate of soup in front of Jim. When Jim thanked her, she gave him back such a sunny smile that despite the pressure from Drew, he winked. He liked the saucy way she tossed her brown hair as she left.

"No, I got to get back to New York," the old man whined. "If you two done fell out, we'll never make it over here."

"We ain't done fell out," Jim protested. "We only got into a little disagreement." A smile as thin as the edge of a dollar bill raised the old man's lips.

"Now that more'n a week's gone by," he said with shrewd cunning, "I ought to sit down with C'neal and see if he wants to sell that stock." At the edge of his mouth was a white crust of spittle. "Of course, not at persackly the same price he paid for it."

Jim's spoon fell back into his soup, splattering potato and carrot on his napkin. Persackly what he was afraid of.

"There won't be no sittin' down nice and polite this time," insisted Jim. "This time 'C'neal' wants revenge." Jim's voice dropped into a growling exclamation. "This time is like with Roper and Sanders."

Drew's head jerked up from its plate of soup. Fear swam in his weak blue eyes, and his head shook in a palsied tremor. Five years ago, while Vanderbilt was out west for a couple of months, minor partners of his, Roper and Sanders, had tried to steal one of the railroad king's smaller lines. On his return he penned them a simple note, well reported in the newspapers:

Gentlemen:

You have undertaken to cheat me. I won't sue you, for the law is too slow. I will ruin you.

Yours truly, Cornelius Vanderbilt

No one knew where Sanders was now, while two years ago Roper had thrown himself into the East River. Sensing that he had Uncle Dan'l on the run, Jim said, "It's a damn sight better here than in the Ludlow Street Jail."

"Jail!"

"Unc', he swore out a warrant for our arrest, didn't he?" demanded Jim. "You know as well as I do that that damn Barnard is his lapdog."

"C'neal put me in jail?"

"Jail," said Jim firmly. Like an aged, emaciated hound huddling against his master for warmth, Uncle Dan'l scraped his chair and edged closer to Jim.

"The line needs both of you," said Drew. The filthy end of that damn umbrella poked into Jim's ribs.

"That's persackly right," said Jim, resisting the urge to edge away.

"But it's got to have Jay," said Drew. "I want you two boys to get along. If he won't work with you, sooner or later I got to make a deal with C'neal. I'm not spending my life over here."

Jim opened his mouth to go back over his arguments, but the old man gave him another poke with the umbrella and pushed back his chair with a rumble. Before Jim could say anything, he lurched away.

119

*   *   *

Late that morning Josie Mansfield, dressed in a severe traveling outfit of yellow-and-brown plaid, was driven up the graveled road of Taylor's Inn.

Her heart thudding, she minded her manners and quietly asked the old man behind the desk for Jim. A shuffling, elderly bellman escorted her into a deserted bar in the rear of the hotel, a dark, smelly cave in which overturned chairs were piled on the tables. The stench of stale beer, acrid cigar smoke, spilt whiskey, and misspat plugs of chewing tobacco pawed her, leaving the sticky grime of a thousand miners' hands. She removed the bolero of her dress, exposing its low neckline, which she adjusted to give Jim a fuller view of what he had missed the two weeks.

The door opened and she spun toward it. Jim's large head poked in. She started to yell his name, but he held a stiff forefinger to his lips. She froze. He jumped inside, hastily closed the door, and strode in.

She opened her arms, and he clasped her. She held him tight, and the weight of his massive, solid body flooded her with relief. He squeezed her and lifted her off the floor. His long kiss, the tickle of his mustaches, and the maleness of his bay rum cologne intoxicated her. They swayed together. His chest made a deep humming, as if holding her satisfied something deep and primitive. How could she have doubted his stout love? He was no pouting youth like Ned Stokes. He dropped her to the floor.

"How I've missed you, dovey!" said Jim.

"Oh, how I've missed you!" she answered. She tilted up her face, and they kissed again. Josie slipped down an inky well of soft bliss. She wished this bar had a bed. Jim suddenly pushed her away.

"But you shouldn't have come," he said.

Josie jerked back a quarter step. "I what!" she exclaimed.

He glanced at the door with the wildness of a three-card-monte player spotting the police. "Reporters," he said. "Nothing but reporters over here. We've got to get you out before they recognize you and write it up. It could ruin us." Confused, she didn't know what to do.

"Ruin you?" she asked, stalling. Jim looked bloated. His suit was too tight and his hair disheveled. His mustaches weren't well tended, probably because he wasn't seeing Andy, his barber at the Hoffman House.

"Me and Jay and the Deacon are on the side of Right," he said. "The Commodore now, he's in league with the Devil. Me being married and all, I can't be seen with a single woman, an actress, in a hotel. It would make me look in the Wrong."

"But we've been in every hotel dining room in Manhattan!" she said. "We've been to the theater together dozens of times. How many times has that fat fellow George Whosit from the *Herald* had dinner with us?"

Jim rubbed his hands together with the uncertainty of a prosperous shopkeeper anxious to please a difficult customer. "Everything's changed," he said. "We have to present ourselves the right way now."

"I'll take a separate room," she said, injecting hurt into her voice. "*Maybe* we can see each other from time to time, if you're not too afraid."

"Just promise that in public you'll act like you don't know me," he said with his old grin. "In the lobby and the dining room. A word of us in the papers and I'm ruined. You see that, don't you?"

She pulled his head down and brushed his ear whorls with her lips. "I'll act any way you want," she whispered. She rubbed her breasts against his starched shirt.

He pushed her to arm's length, his face creased in a wild, distracted scowl. "God, don't," he said. "I can't stand it." Delighting in her power, she laughed. He squeezed her hands and went on, "And if any reporters ask what you're doing here, say you're passing through."

"Fine, Jim. Any way you want it."

However, the room that Jim obtained for Josie—under the eaves, narrow, and low-ceilinged—grew smaller and smaller over the next two days.

On the second afternoon, desperately restless in her cramped prison, she dressed demurely and went downstairs. The tiny lobby was quiet, almost deserted of city dandies in gaudy neckties. The old man behind the desk gave her a merry blue wink, which she ignored. From the scraps she overheard, she gathered that Jim was out with the flock of reporters surveying the guards and boats that defended the hotel.

At loose ends, she strolled up to the second floor, where Jim had a suite. She decided to see what his rooms were like. Doubtless a hell of a lot more comfortable than a maid's room on the fourth floor.

She knocked softly. No one answered. She tried the knob. Her heart beat with excitement. The door swung open to reveal a spacious, sunny sitting room with cheerful white wicker and plump, green cushions edged with white piping. What a difference from the closet he had put her in! In its country way it looked comfortable. She stepped in and closed the door behind her.

The door to the right must be the bedroom. What would Jim say when he came back to find her in bed, her head and all snuggled up under the covers, no clothes on, and ready for a little fun? Her neck and face flushed, and her legs tingled.

She opened the bedroom door. A large bed stood against the far wall, and in it a startled girl. Straight hair. Open mouth. Long, pitted face. For a moment the two stared at each other, till Josie realized that she was staring at the girl's naked breasts.

"What are you doing here?" Josie said.

The girl, her red face cratered by pox scars, only stared at Josie, as if struck dumb or paralyzed. Josie's anger drove her forward. The girl's hands scrabbled for the quilt. Josie stopped at the edge of the bed, her whole body trembling with anger. At her feet lay the girl's country clothes—faded dress, stained apron, filthy shoes, grimy slip, gray drawers. Josie snatched away the quilt that the speechless girl had half pulled over her chest. Her naked haunches as sickly white as a chicken that had dropped its feathers, the girl hopped out of bed. She ran to the corner and backed herself into its crack, one hand over her crotch, the other over her droopy, dangling breasts.

"Get out!" shouted Josie. "Get out of this room right now!" The girl cowered before Josie's anger and struggled to squeeze herself farther into the corner's crack.

"Gimme my things," the girl said in a tinny squeak.

She wasn't even pretty. She was thin, her face and hands country raw. Jim wanted some country stick like this! Josie reached down to pick up the slut's filthy clothes and throw them at her. Their reek of gamy sweat, sour mud, and hog slop made Josie gag. She straightened.

"No," Josie said. "Let them lay there. What are you doing here?"

The scrawny girl only stared at her, the blush from her face creeping down her gaunt neck and across her bony shoulders.

"Cat got your tongue?" asked Josie. "I'll throw your damn stinking clothes out the window if you don't talk."

The girl blurted, "Just waitin'."

"For who?"

The girl's head bobbed crazily. "For—for Mr. Fist."

Josie wanted to drag the wretched creature across the two rooms and toss her bare-ass naked into the hall. Instead, she backed off and ordered the girl to dress. The girl hurriedly drew on her clothes. Josie stood over her, arms folded, fingers tapping out the rapid measure of her fury. Head bowed, weeping softly, the girl left.

"What a fool I am," Josie scolded herself out loud. "I'll believe anything a man tells me. Oh, damn you, Jim!—you're throwing away more love than any other woman will ever have for you."

Furious, she decided to pack and leave the hotel at once. As she opened the door to the hall, she halted, her hand on the glass knob. She recalled Jim standing in the bar in a bull-like stance of pleading and belligerence. Her leaving was exactly what he wanted.

"A wife in Boston, an actress in New York, and a scullery maid in New Jersey," she said to the dim, empty hallway. Not to speak of any number of other women wherever he hung his hat. She turned back into the room and slammed the door shut. She stalked to the sitting room window.

The green lawn of Taylor's stretched down to the wooden pier, and across the broad sweep of the Hudson was Manhattan's busy skyline. She longed to change the course of her life in one bold stroke. She was sick of being at everyone else's mercy—sick of theatrical agents, sick of the contemptuous looks of so-called decent women, sick of sports' bold glances, sick of Sally Woods, and sick of Jim Fisk. Ned Stokes was probably one more hot sport looking for a tumble in the hay.

She saw a way to change things. At the same time she would find out once and for all where she stood with Jim. A little notoriety might even do her career a lot of good. As things now stood, she had seen casting agents for more than a year without success. Even Jim's influence had accomplished precious little. If her picture was plastered over the front pages with Jim's, it might very well draw a crowd into a daring manager's theater to see the scarlet woman. It would also teach Jim Fisk a lesson about two-timing.

She marched upstairs and repacked her four cases. Fueled by her anger, in four bumpy trips she lugged them down herself. She didn't want Jim to have any warning from the hotel help, as he would have spread around enough money to buy loyalty. She unpacked in his commodious bedroom, and shoving his things to one side, she hung her dresses in his closet and piled her lacy underthings in his drawers.

With her unpacking done, she closely inspected the double bed to make sure the scullery slut had left no lice, and remade it. She undressed, put on her bottle-green silk robe, slid in, and with a battered *Harper's Weekly* propped before her, settled down for Jim's return.

12

The excitement of the situation was rather enjoyed by Mr. Fisk, who now bustled about with a most determined visage, mounted his guard, issued orders, puffed away at his cigar, kept up a constant discharge of puns, and vowed he would never be taken alive.

—*New York World* on the Siege of Fort Taylor, 1868

It was a tense moment. The pot in the center of the poker table was over a thousand dollars, enough money to pay a reporter's salary for three months.

Deadpan, Jim Fisk peeked at his two hole cards, a pair of tens. With one ten showing, he had a good chance of picking up this pot, which he needed, for in three hours of play he was down eight hundred dollars. It was a few minutes past midnight, three nights after his big and futile fight to oust Josie from his bedroom. The spring air was thick with the fragrant blue smoke of the Cuban cigars ferried over from Adams, Jim's Manhattan tobacconist.

The *Mirror*, who was dealing, spoke up. "The bet's to you, Jim."

Jim pushed a stack of twenty red chips into the pot. "Raise a hundred." The dozen onlookers, reporters not in the game and standing in a circle around the table, noisily sucked in their breaths.

Over the last three days, fearful that Josie was a 120-pound bomb that would explode in his bed at any moment, Jim had tiptoed about the inn on eggshells. There was a chance that if he kept up the right appearances, he could squeak her presence in his suite right by his newspaper cronies. Surely in another few days the Erie Exiles would be back in Manhattan and this country gallivanting would be over.

After all, not one of these Broadway galoots personally saw anything wrong in what he was doing. To a man they hopped into bed with a Josie every chance they got. And if they did suspect she was sleeping in his second-floor suite—well, writing stories that condemned his "loose morals" would only carve up the gander who laid the golden eggs—the easy days and the nighttime card parties, the surefire stories on page one, and the respite from working under the noses of bossy editors who assumed they were always squandering the paper's time.

Over the last three days Jim had been all the more jovial and openhanded with the mob of scribblers who accompanied him on inspection tours of his marines, his rowboat navy, and his roof-mounted rocket corps. He bought more whiskey than ever, and he made sure that Mrs. Taylor served the best of everything at the buffet lunches and evening dinners paid for by the Erie, insisting she make up the shortfalls of Jersey provisions by ordering delicacies from Manhattan.

Things held. If any reporter had discovered something morally disgraceful about his and Josie's living arrangements, he hadn't said so to Jim, or more important, hadn't written a word of it. After all, camping out with a jolly railway officer was a damn sight more fun than covering yet another droning city-council hearing or yet another dedication of a public building by William Tweed, the powerful Tammany Hall leader.

"Well, what are you going to do?" asked the *Mirror* of the *Journal*.

"I'm going to raise another fifty dollars," said the other.

This drew more sharp intakes of breath and a couple of scrapes of chairs. Jim smiled inwardly. This would push the pot over thirteen hundred dollars, the largest since they had come to Taylor's.

The bet was again to Jim, and he casually shoved extra chips into the pot. He wanted to win, but he didn't mind losing. Reporters who put his money in their pockets weren't apt to push to discover precisely what was what between him and Josie. Dishrag in hand, Ben Taylor stood frozen, as if he had never seen such a large pot. None of the onlookers dared say a word, sip brandy, or pull on a cigar.

The other players studied their hands. Jim leaned back, took a puff on his fat cigar, and reflected what good fellows were these city reporters. They knew Manhattan from the slums of Hell's Kitchen to the mansions of Fifth Avenue. They had seen and forgiven everything. They witnessed man's sins and victories as God might, with an even eye—the sins as wayward blindness, the victories as yet another step in man's constant search for means to prop up his vanity. When it came down to it, Jim liked the company of actors and reporters a lot. Both professions saw too much of the various roles a fellow played to get stuck in any one point of view the way a blacksmith or a bank teller did.

Through the open window came a shout and a heavy thud. The inn shook, and the glasses and brandy bottles on the sideboard rattled.

Finally the *Herald* asked, "What the hell was that?"

Jim jumped up, knocking over his chair, and shouted, "An attack!" Pointing a stubby finger at the pot, he shouted at the *Mirror*, "Ruddy, stick the money in your coat pocket!"

The *Journal* sprang up. "And don't you dare take none of it out!"

Jim ran up the stairs to the second-floor landing, where he had rigged a grass-rope bellpull to the rocketmaster on the hotel's roof. The first rocket shot up fifteen seconds after he yanked. He rushed back downstairs. He snatched up the oak cudgel he had stashed in the front hall's umbrella stand and barged out onto the inn's veranda.

The cool spring night was illuminated by an eerie yellow glare. Jim looked up. Three parachute flares floated gracefully in the wide, dark sky, their glow the sulfurous yellow of an open furnace door of Hell. He rushed to the veranda's corner post. Across the long yard every bush, fence post, blade of grass, and rock gleamed a blackish, diseased yellow. The sharp stench of burnt rocket sulfur mingled strangely with the delicate spring air. More rushes and soft pops exploded overhead as another set of flares arced up. Jim struggled to adjust his eyes. The sickly glare intensified, turning more cool night into feverish day. The yellow faces of a dozen policemen, standing around the yard in twos and threes, were tilted toward the rockets' sulfurous paths.

Far away, faint shouts punctured the bittersweet night air. Jim leaned off the veranda, keeping himself from falling by hanging on to the post. Down at the pier, yellow stick figures lifted clubs and brought them down. Raiders!

"Down to the pier!" Jim shouted at the policemen. "Quick! Push them back into their boats!"

Startled, the helmeted policemen looked at each other in bewilderment. Irritated by their slow-wittedness, Jim shouted more orders. Half a dozen policemen set off down the hill in a fast, jerky walk that imitated speed without achieving it. The veranda's screen door screeched and slammed as reporters rushed out to stand around Jim. Overhead, another round of mortar tubes popped, and five flares shot from the roof toward the pier.

"Must be fifty blokes down there tearing off each other's heads," said the *Times*'s man. Jim pushed his way back onto the porch. He slapped the knotty end of his cudgel into his other hand.

At Jim's elbow, his buddy from the *Trib* asked in a mocking tone, "Ain't you going down?" Jim turned to give him a wink and a knowing look.

"A good general takes the high ground and keeps his eye on the whole field," he said. The knot of reporters laughed.

From inside the inn came a long clatter that sounded like somebody falling down a flight of stairs. Jim pushed through the reporters to peer through the window into the lobby. The gas lamps weren't lit; shadows glided about holding candles and lanterns. A high-pitched scream cut the night and froze Jim's marrow.

He pushed through the dark clot of reporters and ran into the inn. He commandeered a lantern from a shade and charged up the stairs to Uncle Dan'l's third-floor room.

The door was open, lock busted, mattress half off the bed, room empty—exactly what he had been afraid of! The raiders had snatched Uncle Dan'l!

Jim raced downstairs, full of sick dread, and barged back out onto the veranda. Halfway down the hill six or eight thugs were carrying Uncle Dan'l aloft, his white nightshirt flapping behind him, a giant centipede struggling along under an inadequate sheet.

"Dan'l!" Jim shouted.

"Help!" came the old miser's thin, feeble shout. He flailed about in the hellish glare with the helplessness of an overturned turtle borne aloft by a half-dozen hungry gulls.

"Oh, Lord, no!" shouted Jim. When Dan'l's captors joined their chums, they would all retreat into skiffs. Out on the river just beyond sight doubtless lay one of the Walrus's ferries, its lights extinguished.

Jim's last hope for hanging on to the Erie slithered out of him. Without Uncle Dan'l, he and Jay were without the votes to stop Vanderbilt's takeover of the line.

"Ain't you gonna rescue your partner?" the *Mirror* asked.

"Yeah," said the *Herald*. "A good general ought to show his boys how to do it." In the darkness a dozen reporters laughed.

Jim winced with embarrassment. Still held aloft by thugs, Uncle Dan'l was now halfway down the hill.

"He's scared," said an anonymous reporter behind Jim. "Like all big shots, send the troops in, but don't go yourself."

The other reporters guffawed. In a flash Jim pictured tomorrow's headline:

ERIE HERO TURNS COWARD

AGED DIRECTOR KIDNAPPED
UNDER NOSE OF WINDBAG PARTNER

Shouts and thuds, like a dozen laborers whacking plump sacks of grain, came up the hill. Jim winced again. He was one of the people these thugs had come over to snatch. It would be stupid to put himself where they could drag him into the rowboats. Yet if he didn't, he would be the laughingstock of Broadway.

Jim swung his cudgel against the porch post with a loud whack. He gave a ringing halloo, and was off the veranda in a broad jump. He hit the ground running. From the porch rose laughter and ragged cheers.

He ran down the hill toward the pier, bellowing at the top of his lungs and swinging the oak cudgel around and around his head. He was a goner, for there looked to be twice as many attackers as Erie troops, and they were doubtless rougher than office clerks and country policemen. He kept running and shouting. Since he was good as knocked out and dragged into the rowboats, he figured to put on a good show for the scribblers, who would at least give him a hell of a write-up.

The dark centipede carrying the flipped turtle reached the knot of fighters at the edge of the pier. Jim was a dozen feet behind. He entered the fight with his head high and his oak cudgel swinging. With two great strokes he whacked four of the centipede's legs, and two thugs fell screaming to the ground.

"Ha, haaaa!" Jim shouted. Uncle Dan'l slid off the shoulders of the others and fell to the earth with a hollow plop. Jim struck one of the startled thugs across the back with his stick.

"Run, Unc', run!" shouted Jim. The aged millionaire, on his hands and knees, cowered and pulled his nightshirt over his head, exposing withered legs and thighs. Three manic thugs turned on Jim, who held his stick over his head like a broadsword and danced away. He shouted for Captain Boyd and Sidney to come help.

A large, heavy woman, her face as rapacious as a witch from Hell, lunged at him, an ax handle raised above her head. Jim froze—a skirt with a club! A moment before she struck, he dropped to his hands and knees like Unc' Dan'l. The force of the female pirate's rush threw her over his body. He turned and jumped on her. Underneath him, she fought like a large, fat cat, all claws, teeth, legs, and blubber. He grabbed at her hands, confused by her sex, afraid of hurting her, when his rage at Josie welled up. He walloped the amazon across the jaw with the heel of his hand, stunning her.

Jim tore a long strip off her skirt and tied her fleshy wrists behind her. He picked up his oak cudgel and stood up. Immediately four raiders rushed toward him. He danced away, circling around them. A body like a monkey's flew into his back, and he dragged the fellow who was choking him to the water and tossed him in the Hudson.

Huffing, Jim drew himself up and looked around. He was at the edge of the pier, and all around clubs lifted and fell. He spotted the heavyset commander of the Jersey police on the little knoll in front of the pier.

"Captain Boyd!" Jim shouted. "Whistle for your men. We'll group around Mr. Drew here." Jim strode toward the little knoll on which huddled Uncle Dan'l's white form. Boyd's high-pitched whistle piped.

"Stop, men!" he shouted. For a moment the struggle continued, then many stopped. Boyd's stout voice ordered, "All you Jersey men come here!"

"Come here, you Erie men!" shouted Jim.

In seconds they were surrounded by two dozen of their fighters, policemen in ripped uniforms, clerks whose small faces were smeared with blood.

"Let's make sure the Deacon ain't hurt no more," shouted Jim. "Kick these New York scum back into the river they climbed out of."

Their enemy regrouped on the pier, two dozen thugs, amazons, and brawlers in the tattered rags of Hell's Kitchen. In the infernal yellow glare, one raider stood on a peg leg; the faces of the others were scarred and twisted, fiendish as demons released from Hell. Their leader, a seven-foot-tall monster, had a fierce red beard and a head the size of a small horse.

"Give us the fat one and the old gooze," shouted the pirate chief. "Them's the ones we come at."

Jim raised his stout club. Down at the far end of the pier, more thugs clambered up from rowboats, shotguns stretched before them. Shotguns! Jim groaned inwardly. They couldn't fight shotguns. To keep his men from being seriously hurt, he decided to go quietly.

The four thugs with shotguns scrambled to their feet and ran forward up the weathered planks—but they were four of Jim's clerks, fellows who had been on rowboat patrol! Jim grinned. Although their shotguns were loaded with fairly harmless rock salt, these rogues wouldn't know that.

"Larry! Murry!" he hallooed. "Up here! Shoot these fellows with the shotguns!"

The word *shotgun* spun Red Beard around, as it did his two dozen thugs. On the pier one of the clerk-marines raised his double muzzle and pointed it toward the raiders. Boom! it sounded, its muzzle flashing white, followed by another boom and flash. Rock salt rained around them, and the raiders jerked about as if being splattered with real lead pellets.

"Charge," Jim shouted. His shout and the approaching shotguns gave his troops courage, and they shouldered forward, but his four armed clerk-marines stood cautiously at the near end of the pier, double-barreled shotguns tentatively at the ready.

"Bring those guns around here," ordered Jim in a loud voice. "This crew is leaving and we want to make sure they do."

The four Erie clerks with shotguns hesitantly crept forward, their muzzles pointed timidly toward the thugs. Jim itched for them to hurry, for he saw in their faces that if one of the raiders shouted "Boo!" his artillery would drop their cannons and run.

"Boyd!" Jim yelled, striding toward the frightened clerks. "Come here." Jim took a shotgun from the timid clutch of a clerk, and so did Captain Boyd. The two trained the shotguns firmly on the pirates.

"Into the boats, or into a Jersey jail," commanded Jim.

Silently the raiders trooped down the pier and into a dozen rowboats. Jim stuck his shotgun into the air and fired one barrel.

"Hurray!" he shouted. A cheer went up. Red Beard, his orange face twisted in sweaty pain, glared up from his rowboat. Jim put his shotgun on the leader. "Pull them oars!" Jim ordered. "Get it moving!"

Boyd's shotgun went off, too. Several raiders cringed, and oars were pulled. Far away, out on the middle of the river, floated the red eye of a lantern.

"There's your momma," Jim said to the rowboats. "Pull for her before I blow a hole in your pants."

Laughter rose from Jim's team. The rowboats pulled away. He turned to his men and raised the shotgun like a triumphant king's battle sword.

"To the bar!" he shouted. "After a good fight a fellow needs to wet his throat!" A chorus of eager cheers agreed.

Jim ordered two husky constables to carry Uncle Daniel up the hill. They all boiled into the front bar of the hotel, and the old man was eased into a chair. Jim sat on one side and draped his arm over the thin, bony shoulders, while Phyllis, the buxom barmaid, sat on the other side. A noisy shout from a police sergeant standing on the bar demanded that Jim accept a toast. In a short speech Jim announced that "Fort Taylor stands," and he praised his men for their "night's labors." The inn shook with cheers, shouts, and whistles.

Jim turned. Jay Gould stood in the doorway of the bar, dressed in only an open-necked shirt, the trousers to his black workday suit, and a scowl. He looked disapproving and grouchy, as if he resented being dragged out of bed. Uncle Dan'l's gaze followed Jim's.

"He's done it," said Uncle Dan'l to Jay, whose scowl twisted into a blacker knot.

"Done what?" asked Jay, his voice sharp with irritation.

"Saved the Erie," said Dan'l. "Beat off C'neal's men." In a few words the old miser summed up the kidnapping, the stout defense put up by Jim's militia, and his own escape through Jim's heroic actions. Jim's chest ballooned with pride, yet he bowed his head modestly. "He's a hero, Jay," the old man's high whine concluded. "He's the goddamnedest hero the Erie has ever had." Things were working out wonderfully. Jim not only had the old miser in his corner, but unbidden, he was persuading Jay to join him.

"That's all a little thick," said Jim in a further display of humility. He gave Jay the sunshine of his best smile to show that he held no hard feelings. "How about a celebratory drink, partner?"

But to judge by his persimmon-sour expression and the hard fast shake of his head, Jay was having none of it. Jay spun on his heel and walked out—probably, Jim reckoned with a sigh of vexation, to march right back upstairs to bed.

The burst of rockets and the never-ending clatter of boots on the stairs shook Jay Gould out of his sleep at a little past midnight. After dressing amid shouts, rocket flashes, and the acrid stench of sulfur, he went downstairs. Slipping unseen among the reporters on the veranda, he watched the dockside hand-to-hand struggle and Jim and his mob hallooing in triumph as they bore Daniel Drew back up the hill.

When he left the roaring mob in the bar, he was stiff with displeasure. The scene wasn't a triumph, but a disaster. He had called a board meeting for next week, when he expected to force Jim to give up active management and resign from the board. All this gallumphing around in the night made it that much harder to force Jim out.

Back in his narrow bed on the third floor, the drunken shouts, bawdy hoots, roars of laughter, and raucous songs kept Jay awake.

He turned on his side and put a pillow over his ear to block the din. Despite his fourteen-hour days of actually running the rail line, because of Jim's partying with reporters and his filling them with tall tales, in the eyes of the press, the shareholders, and the train-riding public, Jim Fisk *was* the Erie. Asking most shareholders if Jim Fisk ought to be fired was like asking the Erie to give away its locomotives.

The hot pillow didn't keep out the earsplitting songs from the bar. *". . . and tossed her right over the wall!"* Jay turned over on his other side and arranged the pillow on his left ear, but he couldn't get comfortable. *"Bring back, bring back, oh, bring back . . ."*

In plain fact, Jim baffled Jay. In his small dark bedroom, the flushed, gleeful face of his partner, celebrating downstairs, floated before him like a flesh-colored balloon. The hoarse laughter and the gruff lyrics surged to a new rowdy height. Although he did his best not to show it, he didn't like his partner's constant nighttime partying, cardplaying, drinking, and wenching. Jim was rarely around when Jay needed him, refusing to keep normal business hours. Everybody in the world owned a bit of Jim, and thus nobody had much of him, least of all the Erie. Jay got out of bed, intending to go back to the bar and ask Jim to hold it down, but no sooner had he put on his dressing gown and slippers than the singing fell off.

As he stood by the door of his dark, lonely room, the boisterous party sounded like the very life of the Erie, much as a baby's cry marked life at its most robust. He couldn't bring himself to open the door and go downstairs. While a part of him was drawn to the jolly laughter and backslapping camaraderie, if he went downstairs he would only want to escape. He hated mobs. Drunks would bray at him. Jim would shout, give him drunken hugs, and slosh liquor on him. Tomorrow morning Jay would be too tired to work well.

He crawled back into bed. As he twisted about on his pillow, his disapproval of Jim sounded an awful lot like his stern father's voice eternally commanding him and his sisters to be quiet. With the help of his impressed clerks and local constables, Jim had won the Erie a great victory, for if Drew had been kidnapped they would have lost the line. Rather than rejoicing in their—and his—victory, Jay had reacted by wanting to kill the celebration, just as his father often ground under his boot heel the exuberance of Jay and his sisters.

Jay threw himself to his other side. And now that damn sloe-eyed actress was in Jim's suite.

Yesterday her presence had alarmed Jay the minute he set eyes on her from the dining room's entrance. Seated alone, she was eating quietly at a small table on the far side of the room, away from the Erie crowd. At first Jay didn't understand his alarm, but he recognized that this yard of Broadway silk didn't belong in the country air of Taylor's. Her clothes were too fashionably cut and daring, made from high-quality velvet and lace, and her brunette ringlets were curled in the tight style that had yet to reach the country. As well, she didn't eat in the dainty, picky way of ladies, but with large bites and sure, eager movements. She glanced around the dining room with alert intelligence; a proper lady averted her eyes from men's bold glances. All in all, a female with appetites she was used to indulging.

His brow knit with thought, Jay headed for his own table, where Daniel Drew sat. Quality in dress and roguishness of gaze, he mused. Her glance snuck toward Jim at the press table. In turn Jim gave her a sly wink. The truth struck Jay like a miniature lightning bolt. This was the actress Jim had talked about back in town, Josie Mansfield! The reporters at Jim's table eyed her and made comments to each other behind cupped hands.

At their table Jay asked Daniel, "Who's she?"

The old man glanced over. "Jim's friend," he croaked.

"What's she doing over here?"

Daniel rolled his ancient eyes. "What do you think?"

"She's not in his room?"

"Where else?"

"Oh, God."

"I talked to her, Jay. She's a nice lady."

Jay sat up in bed and plumped up his two pillows. He straightened his sheet and the light blanket. All Jim's work in getting the newspapers on their side, in foiling Vanderbilt's thugs, was wasted effort. Jay not only had Vanderbilt to fight, but Jim's stupidity, too. Any morning now, righteous editorials would thunder down wrath on "the Erie Exiles" for "living in sin" instead of "holding themselves aloof from temptation till they returned to the bosom of their families." Vanderbilt would be "a far better steward of the public interest" than "loose-living scoundrels." The three would lose the Erie to a fury of public indignation, a fury all the more rabid for Jim's having hoodwinked them days earlier.

Jay's pessimistic thoughts were interrupted by giggles, bumps, and clunks from the room over his. Next came low growls and more laughter. The bed above began the rhythmic thumping of sex. Flashes of naked breasts, buttocks, and limbs shot across his eyes, and he almost burst out laughing at the sorry spectacle of himself—alone in a dark cell while around him bubbled a bright, blooming celebration. Naked flesh—hot, naked, female flesh. He pictured himself with his wife Helen, then with Annabelle.

Annabelle Stokes.

A naked Annabelle Stokes.

Small high breasts.

A waist he could put his hands around.

133

An alert face, alert expression, and eyes as large, black, and alert as his dead sister Polly's.

Smooth thighs.

A hard passionate mouth.

"Annabelle!" he said out loud, and the plaintiveness of his own cry startled him.

He was hot and damp. He condemned Jim so easily—yet he wanted Annabelle as much as Jim wanted his actress. In the deepest part of himself he envied Jim's easy ability to cut a wide swath through perky chorus girls, knowing that he didn't have the courage to do the same. The squeak of the springs and the knocking of the bed above him grew louder, more forceful.

Since Annabelle Stokes's visit more than a week ago, several times a day Jay had envisioned her long, lean face, high cheekbones, and slender neck. A flowery, musky fragrance had floated off her that day at lunch, its intimacy confusing his thoughts. The silken rustle of her clothes whispered mysterious, liquid delights. He had even briefly considered risking Vanderbilt's prison by sneaking into town to meet with her over the stupid acres she wanted to sell.

The bed above his head knocked so loudly that he thought it might work its way through the thin floorboards and fall on him. He didn't care who she was up there, Jay wanted her, he wanted to be rocking and thrusting and holding her tight. Amid the bed clatter, gruntlike voices floated down.

The clatter mounted to a crescendo that abruptly stopped. He cocked his ears. Silence. Peace. No conversation, no one leaving the bed. He seemed to float. The damp night air and the sound of crickets drifted through the open window. What a difference between the two women, he thought. Helen plump, even heavy; Annabelle as lean and graceful as Polly. Helen moved in a slow march through Jay's and the children's lives, even speaking slow, careful syllables; Annabelle was all speed, poise, and dexterity. The solid Helen had expected from her father and then from Jay stolid, middle-class comfort; Annabelle was a fast thoroughbred who had fallen onto hard times, one who only needed a little cleaning to shine like a showhorse. The man who lived with her would never feel stolid. Jay owed the solid Helen everything he gave her; she had worked faithfully for it. But Annabelle he wanted to give to the way one put a first-quality emerald in a fine gold setting, a master's drawing in a Van Wallis frame, and white orchids in a French vase of cobalt blue. He was attracted to Annabelle the way he had been attracted to his dead sister Polly, for her lightness and quickness of spirit.

Annabelle's mysterious aloofness dared him to approach. The

alert haughtiness in her manner, her face, promised him everything and nothing. She seemed aware of him in a way nobody had since Polly's death. Her glances toward him—which only flared for moments and disappeared before he could confirm them—imperiously singled him out and confronted him with an intolerable choice. It was as if, for two or three moments scattered throughout that sun-drenched lunch, the two of them stood outside the multitudes through which they moved, the horde of New York, and she was offering a silent communication that ignored everything, everyone else, outside themselves. It was as if since Polly, no one else had been aware of him, truly aware of him, as if for the first time in fifteen years he was truly being seen, truly being recognized, and truly coming alive.

Such thoughts betrayed Helen. Helen!—the most wonderful woman in the world. She ran the household and tended the children, but she possessed almost too much faith in Jay. Her plump, familiar body held no cavern of mystery, no nervous promise of extravagant pleasures. Helen had little feeling for the difficulties of Jay's struggle, no interest in such projects as forging a railroad to span the continent. But Annabelle!—in those few brief glances her dark eyes penetrated him and absorbed his every thought and feeling. Annabelle knew he was daring the impossible and thrilled to it.

For the first time he understood how Jim and the hearty idiots he hung around with could risk their businesses and their positions in society for a woman other than their wives. Jay had only felt such headiness during the weeks before his marriage, before and after the birth of his oldest son, George, and the three times he had engineered enormous coups in business, coups that netted sums only dreamed of before.

So for all his righteousness, how much difference was there between his nature and Jim's?

Damn little.

No matter how much he hated it, he was as much a rogue.

Sometime before cockcrow he fell into a fitful sleep glutted with alarms and sulfurous rockets, fights up and down the dark stairs of Taylor's. In one highly charged dream fragment, a naked Annabelle, lying on the floor, pulled him over the edge of his hotel bed into sexual ecstasy, but Helen arrived at Taylor's in the nick of time to stop their coupling. For the rest of the night, dodging a Helen puzzled by his running from her, Jay followed an elusive Annabelle up and down a dozen labyrinthine staircases throughout the hotel, never touching her again.

13

Daniel says up—Erie goes up.
Daniel says down—Erie goes down.
Daniel says wiggle-waggle—it bobs both
ways.

—Popular Wall Street jingle, 1860s

No matter how much coffee and soda water Jim downed the next morning in his room, his throat was as parched and scratchy as a dirt road in August. While he worked through the stack of morning papers, his head thudded as if a rugged little demon swung a steel mallet against the back of his skull.

The *Tribune* shouted, ERIE EXILES REPULSE ATTACK, while the *Mirror* announced, NEW YORK CENTRAL'S MARINES THROWN BACK. Jim decided to order a late breakfast to his suite; he and Josie could have a quiet meal by the sitting room's cheerful windows. When he opened the front door to whistle up the hall maid, there stood Jay. Jim jumped backward.

"Jay!" he shouted. His partner had never come to his rooms before.

Jay scarcely looked like himself. His thin shoulders were slumped, his protruding forehead was bumpy, his expression sheepish. His frame appeared smaller than usual, as if worn down. His face held dark spots, bruises on his cheeks and under his eyes, the color of a ripened pear where it had been pinched by the hard, suspicious fingers of shoppers.

"May I come in?" Jay asked. Jim's eyes darted to the left—Josie was in the bedroom and might come out at any minute—if Jay saw her, he would have a fit.

"Naw," said Jim, "why don't we go up to the office?"

A resigned wave blew over Jay's poker face. "I know she's in here."

"Oh." Jim moved to one side, gave a wide-gestured, mocking bow, and waved him in. "Well, please enter, Mr. Gould."

Jay perched on one of the wicker sofas. Jim ducked his head in the bedroom and told Josie not to come out. He raised the shades, and the harsh sunlight blinded him and increased the throbbing against his skull. The lazy clucking of chickens and the noontime heat of spring, scented by cut grass, drifted in the windows.

"You don't look so hot, pard," said Jim with his usual good humor.

"I've come to a conclusion."

"What's that?"

Jay squirmed about and the sofa creaked. "That you're a hell of an asset to the Erie," he said, his tone dull and forced. Jim leaned back against the squeaking wicker.

"Ain't that a novel goddamn idea on your part!" said Jim, jamming sarcasm into his voice. Jay's hands fidgeted together in his lap, two pale, delicate crabs taking weak swabs at each other.

With a look of weary defeat, Jay said, "Instead of asking the board to fire you, I'm going to ask for a commendation."

Jim stared openmouthed. "Commendation!" Jay nodded dourly, and Jim pictured a gold medal, three times the size of a silver dollar and festooned with red, white, and blue ribbons. A dignified little ceremony at the next board meeting. Handshakes and warm smiles all around. Afterward, a gay champagne lunch at Delmonico's. He would rise, strike a water glass with his knife, and make a generous toast to his "Jersey marines." Jim chuckled and rubbed his hands together. "Ah, Jay, together you and me'll show 'em how to run a railroad!"

A cloud of doubt shadowed Jay's face and he said, "We have a couple of immediate problems, however."

Jim could only beam. How he loved this little cuss! He didn't know if it was Jay's business smarts or something as simple as the precise way he held himself, his catlike alertness, but he cared as much for Jay as he had for his own dead brother, Phil.

"You tell me what it is, pard," said Jim, "and I'll take care of it." He wanted to sit down next to Jay, throw his arm over those thin, bony shoulders, and give him a big squeeze, but Jay didn't like such things. His diminutive partner was at once the boldest and the shyest skate Jim had ever met. He was much smarter than anyone else Jim had ever worked with. Thinking, thinking, always thinking, that was Jay. In a pickle Jay could come up with the most unexpected idea, rapidly sketch out a plan, and at once devise the steps needed to put it into action. Yet, confronted by a group of harmless brokers knocking back a few snorts and spinning a couple of spicy stories, he was as much fun as a clam with the lockjaw. Jay's eyes went to the closed bedroom door.

"Mrs. Mansfield," Jay whispered.

Jim hid his wince. "Mrs. Mansfield?"

"Staying here in your rooms."

Jim shook his head violently. "Not really. She's got her own—"

"She hasn't," said Jay, "and I'm surprised those Park Row vultures haven't made a big thing out of it."

The denial that Jim was puffing up collapsed before he could float it out. He expelled a great sigh. Josie was thumping about in the bedroom, probably putting away clothes and wondering how long she had to remain cooped up. It *was* a miracle that none of this had popped up in the papers, due more than likely to no editor wanting to be the first to publish "filth" in his family newspaper. However, all it would take was the mention of it in one rag for the others to play follow the leader; with a whoosh the kerosene would be on the fire. Overnight all the support Jim had built on Newspaper Row would burst, explode in a fiery orgy of editorial righteousness.

"I'll find some way to deal with it," Jim said in a small voice.

Jay rose to leave. "Would you talk to Uncle Dan'l, too? Even after those toughs roughed him up last night, he came to me whining that he ought to go back to Manhattan. He listens to you better than to me."

"Oh, damn him!" said Jim. Keeping the Deacon's backbone stiff was like propping up a scarecrow without a broomstick.

With Jay gone and Josie next door, the sitting room felt close and uncomfortable. Jim's mood swooped low; he didn't want to deal with Josie, damn her. Again his headache beat against his skull. Josie knocked softly on the bedroom door. Jim hurried to open it. Josie's curious face peered around the empty sitting room. Jim drew her to him and gave her a squeeze.

"Say, Josie—how would you like to have a house?" Her face tilted up, its brown eyes large. "Your very own town house in Manhattan."

She backed away several steps and frowned as if he had gone mad. "What's all this about?" she asked. He cast about for a way to justify it.

"Me and Jay done made up," he said. "That's what we was talking about. We're going to run the damnedest railroad this country's ever saw."

She frowned. "You only want to get rid of me."

"No, no," he said. "I want you to have it ready when I get back to town." From her scowl she wasn't buying it, but inspiration hit. "It needs to be ready so I can entertain private parties. I need you to be my hostess." Her brow smoothed and a tentative smile played around her lips.

"Will you help me furnish it?" she asked, moving close to him and rubbing her breasts against his starched shirtfront.

"Hey, of course I will."

She rubbed his nose with hers. "There's just one thing," she said. His johnny was stirring. A bit of slide-and-tumble might ease his hangover.

"Anything, my little sugarplum."

Her eyes skidded away from his. "I need five hundred dollars to pay some debts."

"Will you leave today and first thing tomorrow start looking for the house?" he asked.

"Oh, yes, Jim! Yes, yes!"

He waved his hand airily. "Then the money's yours."

She kissed him again, hard. His johnny was at attention now, a flagpole demanding a flag. He felt as frisky as a stallion ready to dash to a mountaintop. He swept her up and carried her back into the bedroom to celebrate their common victories.

Vanderbilt, father and son, sat in the younger's office, a small, plain room down the hall from the father's. In contrast to Cornelius's, William's held no mementos of the sea, only of railroads—pictures of old-timey locomotives with funnel stacks, framed menus from the Central's first nonstop run to Chicago, two brass bells from early trains, and a vast map that displayed the rail lines of the Northeast.

"Papa," he said, "let's call off this war."

"What?" Several times over the past three days William had urged him to sit down with "the three," as he called them, to see if a deal couldn't be worked out. Each time Cornelius turned aside the boy's notion by bringing up something else that needed to be done. Typical of his children, and William the best of the lot! Not even he understood that business was *war*, and that the other side would gut you if it sniffed the least weakness.

"You're acting as if it's you and Drew back on the river in the old days," William pushed on. "Times have changed. You owned your own boats then. Today we have shareholders to think of, and share prices—"

"All right," said Cornelius, injecting browbeaten capitulation into his voice. If only his first son George Washington Vanderbilt hadn't died. With that son by his side, he could have taken on the whole world and won. "I'll talk to Drew. He's the key to this."

William's features lit up. "You will? Drew?"

"Nobody will know who you are. Go up the line to Thornton and come in on the stagecoach in a drummer's getup. Arrive after dinner, go up to Drew's room before he drinks himself to sleep."

A subtle smile hovered about William's lips. "They wouldn't expect anyone from New York to come from upstate. It might work."

"Tell that shriveled-up old apple I'll buy all his Erie stock at next Friday's closing price plus some extra a share," said Cornelius.

William sat back and folded his soft hands over his small paunch, his face studying the plan. "Let's keep in mind that he's still treasurer," his son said. "We better insist that the cash you bought those watered shares with be in the Erie's treasury."

"Let's just get the whining bastard over here. Once he's in Manhattan I can deal with him—particularly once I get him away from his dogs, Fisk and Gould. Once we've dealt with him—then we'll see about those two."

Cornelius basked in the admiring look on William's face. The boy saw that he couldn't yet outthink his old pa.

The closed carriage, its black curtains tightly drawn, was as humid, warm, and dark as the inside of a freshly baked loaf of bread.

Mopping his brow with his sweat-damp handkerchief, Jim Fisk peered out through a tiny slit in the gathered curtains. In contrast to his usual ruddy, casual expression, one that broke easily into clowning, this morning his brow was furrowed, his jowls stern, and his jaw clinched. Across Washington Place stood Cornelius Vanderbilt's four-story brick house, an imposing heap of Dutch-style granite and brickwork characteristic of the turn of the century.

Behind Jim the carriage door opened. He jerked around, expecting to see Vanderbilt's beefy anger come to get him. Instead, an eager smile on his rugged face, his regular driver Rufus was hoisting himself up. Jim pulled his driver on in and hurriedly shut the door.

"You scared the bejesus out of me," whispered Jim.

"They're in place," Rufus whispered, referring to the two Erie guards that Jim had directed him to post at Vanderbilt's back door. Tall and skinny, Rufus possessed the awestruck air of a lanky hill farmer recently arrived in the city. Like Jim, he was a Vermont Green Mountain Boy, which six months ago had gained him a job as Jim's driver five minutes after he introduced himself and asked for work. Jim turned back to peer through the slit in the black curtain.

"That old man really going to sell you out, Jim?"

Jim hissed into the curtain, "What the hell else has he snuck in there for?" He ran the edge of his wet handkerchief around the inside of his stiff shirt collar. "When he said he was coming over, I told him Cornelius would have him tossed in the jug, but he says, 'No, it's Sunday. I only want to see Jane and the boys and go to church.' "

"Church!" said Rufus. "He come off that ferry in a right big hurry for a old geezer, grabbed the hack at the head of the line, come straight here."

The shades and curtains of Vanderbilt's sturdy red house were drawn. Its brick face looked dull and sleepy, as if no one was stirring at ten o'clock on Sunday morning, although some lazy smoke drifted from the kitchen chimney. In front of it stood the public hack Drew had hired, its driver bent over and half asleep in the warm sunlight.

Over the next half hour Jim and Rufus took turns watching the house. As the sun mounted, it heated the roof of the black carriage something fierce. Although a light April breeze swayed the little linden and mulberry trees, no fresh air penetrated the cab's moist heat.

From the window Rufus suddenly hissed, "It's him! He's coming out!"

Jim pushed Rufus aside and thrust his sweaty face into the slit. The door of Vanderbilt's house stood open and framed two white-haired figures, one stout and vigorous, the other an aged, twisted stick. Cornelius Vanderbilt was on the left, wide-shouldered and expansive in shirtsleeves, casual cherry-red suspenders, and black trousers. His flushed face was framed by white whiskers and floated over a thick paunch.

"He looks like the very Devil, don't he?" whispered Jim.

Beside Vanderbilt stood Uncle Dan'l, as dry, scratchy, and frail as an oak sapling after a harsh winter. Jim muttered, "There was a crooked man and he walked a crooked mile. . . ."

"What they been up to?" whispered Rufus.

"Drew's been telling him every little trick and game we been playing," said Jim. "Offering all his Erie stock if he can make a big profit from it. Slinging me and Jay to the Devil for a few more dollars."

Drew finally hobbled down the stone steps, waved good-bye in a sprightly way, and climbed into the waiting hack. From the sour expression on Vanderbilt's face, and the perfunctory manner in which he waved good-bye, he wasn't smacking his lips over the saccharine bait on Daniel's hook.

"You want to follow him?" asked Rufus.

"No, I'm sorry to say I know enough," said Jim. "He promised fifty times he'd never sell me out. Some good Samaritan ought to poke him down a privy hole where he belongs. Take me back to the ferry."

"The ferry? Back to Jersey City?"

Jim straightened up. "Yeah, Morosini is checking the Erie's books. If our 'stalwart' treasurer is cutting a deal with the Walrus, God knows what he's done with our money." Wilted from the damp heat, bloated with disgust, Jim dropped onto the cushions. He slapped the cracked leather with his palm. "Rufus, can you believe that for years I've treated that old man like my father, and that he's acted like I was his son?"

Rufus shook his head in sympathy. "A terrible thing," he said. As if he were saluting the flag, he placed his right hand over his heart. "I can feel it right here."

"Yeah, me too. Let it be a lesson to you what a skunk will do for money."

At the downstairs front desk, despite his boiling fury Jim jollied Drew's key and a carbide lantern off Ben Taylor's boy. He and Jay crept back upstairs and down the hall to Drew's room, their shadows lurching like monsters on the hallway walls.

The flimsy door creaked open. Jay thrust his candlestick forward and Jim raised high the carbide lamp. Drew's softly snoring form was curled in the narrow bed. The chilly room stank of sour, diseased breath, the acrid stench of unwashed long johns, briny whiskey from the unstoppered stone jug by the bed, and rancid piss from the chipped porcelain chamber pot. Jim held the light directly in front of Drew's sleeping face. Across the old man's cheeks and thin, wrinkled neck, a scrofulous fuzz grew like a whitish, cancerous mold.

"You have sold us out, Daniel!" Jim shouted.

The gray figure shot up in bed, floppy nightcap skewed sideways. He looked like a large scrawny chicken in a filthy nightshirt, a chicken with molted feathers. With a bang Drew threw himself back against the brass headboard, his tendons standing out against the loose skin of his neck.

Jim picked up the heavy, stinking chamber pot. He held it over Drew's head, where it wavered. A few drops of urine sloshed over the edge onto Drew's brow, which jerked upward. Jim turned to Jay, his face a query.

"It would serve him right," said Jay, "but don't."

"Piss sure would make him smell better."

Drew quivered against the headboard, his hands scrabbling for the covers. "Don't take me!"

Jim laughed and said to Jay, "He ain't woke up good. He thinks we're Vanderbilt's men." To Drew, "Hey, you sneaky thief, this is *Jim.*" With his free hand he gently slapped Drew's face, the soft bristles feeling as sticky and filthy as a spider's aged web. "You're dreaming."

Blinded by the lantern, Drew peered around it. He pushed the hissing light aside. "Jim! Jay! How come you boys woke me up? Has C'neal attacked again?"

"You've sold us out, you lump of shit," said Jim.

"No!"

"Jim saw you at Vanderbilt's," said Jay. Drew's fearful gaze swung back and forth between the two angry voices.

"Saw . . . me?" In his mad eyes Jim read fear and a calculating slipperiness. Four years as Uncle Dan'l's broker had instructed Jim in a lifetime of deviousness. Confused by shock and the late hour, Drew was struggling to gather his wits in order to sidestep their attack. "What is this, boys?" he screeched. "You ain't at hurting old Daniel, are you?"

"No more'n you're at hurting us," said Jim.

The old buzzard whined, "I done know C'neal for forty years."

"So what?" said Jim.

"Many times we played whist together all through the night."

"So what?"

"We scrap, then settle things," said Drew. "It don't hurt none to talk."

Drew's helplessness reminded Jim of his own father in the asylum, also as old, thin, and pathetic. At such a plea from Pa, Jim would have swept him into his arms and comforted him. It took an effort to remember that Jay was here and that Drew was doing everything he could to sell them out.

"While I'm up in Albany," said Jay, "working fifteen hours a day to keep Vanderbilt from gutting us, you're down here undermining everything I do." He shoved the thick, crackling sheets of the court order against Drew's pointed nose, jamming the back of the old man's skull against the bed's brass bars. The carbide lantern in Jim's hand wavered. It was a good thing Jay was here, he reflected. Jay was more flint-hearted. Jim reckoned his own trouble was he trusted people too much.

Drew's rheumy eyes bulged at the sight of the three crimson wax seals, in two of which were stuck fancy red ribbons. "What's this all about?" he asked.

"That is a court order freezing your money," said Jay.

"What! My money's—" Drew stopped, clearly afraid to reveal any more. His watery blue eyes were wild.

"—in the Plainfield Bank and Trust Company," Jim finished for him. "And all froze up." He was particularly proud of this sharp piece of maneuvering, on which Jay had complimented him several times.

"Frozen solid as ice until you let go of the Erie's money," said Jay. Drew's neck was yet leaner and more stringy, as if Jim held his head, Jay his feet, and between them they were stretching his emaciated body.

"Nooooo!" wailed Drew. He threw back the covers, jumped to the floor, and lurched at Jim in a move surprisingly fast for such a scrawny old bird. "You ain't! Let it go, Jim!" His bony fingers clutched Jim's wrist, which Jim jerked away. Drew turned to Jay. "It ain't right. Not my money. It will—"

The old man's torn, gray face appeared diseased in the carbide flame's harsh white light. His face rapidly turned from one to the other, but it found no sympathy. "No, no, no," he moaned, a voice in the farthest regions of grief. His eyes rolled back in his head with the violence of man about to have a fit. His bony fingers, as awkward as dry twigs blown by the wind, fumbled across Jim's vest to his lapels. "Jim, please! Remove this judge's hands off my money!"

Jim pulled the fingers off him, their touch as crumbly and dirty as bones that had lain for years in a crypt.

Jay said in a suspiciously mild voice, "Maybe we can come to an understanding."

Drew turned to him, hope desperate in his face. "Yes?"

"We'll set *your* money free if you set *ours* free," said Jay. "Appoint me treasurer. Give up power over the Erie's finances."

The old man drew himself close to Jay, cunning threading its way through the hope shining in his eyes. "All I wanted was to feel out C'neal. I'll tell you, he's still plenty sore, Jay, but he wants an end to this." His voice deepened and wavered, the throbbing moan of a heavy-handed violinist drenching a tune in self-pity.

They left. On the stairs Jim asked, "What do you think?"

"Of course he won't keep his word," Jay snapped. "He has a higher duty than to stick with his partners, a duty to his pocketbook. If he hasn't already, he's on the verge of making a deal with the Commodore—at our expense."

Jim grunted. "Then let's keep his money froze—and him locked up—till we get the deal we want from both old buzzards."

Jay stopped and faced him. "We can't keep it frozen long, and we can't we keep him locked up more than a night or two. What we have is a little time, a few days of his fear, in which to maneuver with Vanderbilt ourselves."

"That's all?"

"I don't see any more. Do you?"

"Damn!"

"Yes, damn. The old fellows have the power, Jim, the money and the power. When they act together, they can stomp us. The best we can do is blunt the damage."

14

If there ever was a man who has made his way in the world, it is Mr. Cornelius Vanderbilt, who is like those old German barons who, from their eyries along the Rhine, swooped down upon the commerce of the noble river, and wrung terrible tribute from every passenger that floated by.

—Editorial in *The New York Times* on the practices of Commodore Vanderbilt's steamship company, 1858

What Jay Gould feared came to pass. Daniel Drew and Cornelius Vanderbilt teamed up to rescue Drew's money and pass control of the Erie Railroad to Cornelius. Still, the headquarters of the Erie was in Jersey City, along with its books, records, and treasury, and most of its track and all of its rolling stock also remained out of Judge Barnard's jurisdiction. Seeing that negotiation with the "pipsqueak upstarts" was likely to be quicker and less costly than uncertain litigation in fifteen separate states, Cornelius invited the pair to his Washington Place mansion for a Sunday morning negotiation.

They met in the old tackle room, reeking with the sweet odor of peppermint tea, behind the house, which Cornelius had fixed up as an office for his personal affairs. With Jim supporting him, Jay argued strenuously that Cornelius should sell out to *them*. Nothing doing, said Cornelius, and he made a lengthy counterproposal to buy them out at a third of what Jim and Jay figured their Erie shares were worth. Jay adamantly refused to sell.

So it went for two hours, each side pushing for control of the Erie, each repulsed by the other. Each grasped enough control of the line to possess a say-so in it, but neither owned enough to knock out the other. The two sides were like two grunting, powerful wrestlers locked in a strained embrace, each unable to shove the other onto his back. Twice the old man stood, hobbled to the potbellied stove, and prepared a new pot of peppermint tea.

Near noon Vanderbilt, noisily slurping a fresh mug, glared at them. From the courtyard came the casual shouts of stablehands and the snorts of horses. A look as sly as a cat sneaking into a pantry slid across his ruddy features.

"Suppose I paid you two extra to leave?" Cornelius asked.

"No," said Jim promptly.

Jay leaned forward. "But suppose we paid you extra to buy you out?" he proposed. Jim turned and goggled at him as if he couldn't understand how they might afford such a large sum.

"You buy me out!" exclaimed Cornelius.

His poker face uncharacteristically infused with eagerness, Jay named a price for Cornelius's Erie stock that was higher than the market price. Cornelius's features lifted in surprise. Jay hurried on.

"We'll pay you in cash what's left of your money in our treasury," said Jay. "But we want Daniel Drew's stock, too."

"You don't have enough money."

Jay sat forward again. "We'll give you a note for the rest," he said. "With interest—better than market interest." Cornelius peered at him warily.

"A note," he sneered. "Backed by what?"

"The stock."

"And when will I collect on it?"

Jay's heart was pounding, his face controlled, his voice fumbling. "Five years."

"And if you don't meet the payments?"

"You get the stock back, the Erie itself," said Jay. "If we can't run it, you get the Erie—*no fuss, no muss, no fight.*"

Cornelius's blue eyes calculated. "Suppose it was *one* year, Mr. Gould." Cornelius rocked back, his face intrigued. "Suppose it was not only what you sold me that was behind the deal. Suppose you two put up everything you have in the Erie—as well as everything that you and your plump friend here own." Excitement fluttered through Jay, but he stilled it.

"Sign personally?" asked Jim. "Put up our houses, carriages, horses, furniture?"

147

Cornelius cackled with mirth. "Wives and children, too, if they're worth anything."

"No," said Jim. "I won't never sign personal. Not after them other times."

Vanderbilt's features broke into a wider grin. "Yes, sir," he said. "Spoken like a gent as been under the yoke of bankruptcy." His voice lowered into a purring growl. "Do you want the Erie or not? Or you boy-wizards can get in your trickly little skiff and paddle back across the river."

Jim and Jay stared at each other. Jay nodded. Jim frowned and nodded less vigorously.

Cornelius said, "And time-of-the-essence, boyos."

"No," said Jay.

Cornelius seemed to expand, as if his plump flesh were becoming more solid. "Yes, sir," said Cornelius. "Time-of-the-essence. If you want this deal you're going to have to stick right with it. I'm betting you can't run this line with any such load of debt." He rared back and grinned with satisfaction. "I aim to pick me up a railroad here."

"What's time-of-the-essence?" asked Jim fearfully.

Jay's throat tightened. "It means no excuse for failure to pay," he explained. "If we miss one payment—miss it by even one day— he gets the Erie."

Cornelius held up his index finger as if it were the stock of a whip. "And houses, carriages, and children's toy wagons," he said. "Payments will be due at sunrise on the first of every month."

The next two weeks were a nightmare of lawyers' battles, hasty meetings, midnight struggles to slip out of legal tangles, mortgage-payout schedules, certified checks for large sums drawn to the Commodore, lists of assets that ran into scores of pages, and monstrously elaborate documents.

The morning after they had signed the papers, sitting by the sunniest window of his Hoffman House parlor, Jim loudly munched toast and regarded with an unperturbed blue eye the sheet of bond that Jay laid in front of him summarizing the Erie's withered finances. Although the heavy silver service offered up Jim's usual morning feast—enough scrambled eggs, toast, honey-nut rolls, coffee, slabs of ham, and potatoes for three—Jay sipped only a cup of tea.

"We must be careful how we run the line," Jay said. "I reckon lay off a couple thousand workers. Forget expansion. In four or five years—if there are no bad times—we may be back to solid health."

The sitting room was lush with plants, cheery with a dozen canaries singing in brass cages, and comfortable with velvet-cushioned chairs on squat legs. Jay was tired. As usual, unable to sleep during times of stress, he hadn't dozed off till after the three o'clock chimes. Jim solemnly finished chewing a large forkful of ham and egg and waved his loaded fork.

"We're famous now," Jim said. "People really like us. While you was home with your family last night, I strolled up Broadway. I can't tell you how many people come up and said they was rooting for us. I went into Delmonico's—I was mobbed. I went into Webster's Theater—I was applauded. In the Broadway Central bar I was cheered."

Jay smiled weakly, keeping to himself his distaste for such a childish love of celebrity.

"We'll sell a lot of rail tickets to those folks," continued Jim. "They're not going to be eager to ride with the Commodore." Jim pursed his oily lips, patted them with an end of the starched napkin, grimaced shrewdly, and asked, "Why don't we float a stock issue— bring in some cash?"

Jay laughed. "A stock issue?" With an urgent finger he tapped the Erie's informal balance sheet. "We're too close to bankruptcy. God help us if we have a bad two months."

"I'm telling you we can." Jim leaned over and rapped Jay's knee with his thick knuckle. A cloud rich in rum cologne and ham cloves rose from him. "The Commodore wants our line, right?"

Jay sat back. "Right enough."

Jim waved his silver fork as triumphantly as a baton. "So the public figures we got our hands on something real valuable, right?"

Jay pointed at the balance sheet. "But when they read our financial statement, they won't buy our stock."

The baton pointed egg at Jay. "Right! But they won't read it."

"Won't read it?"

"No, sir," said Jim. "The public goes on what it believes, what it reads in the papers, not what it studies out."

"I wouldn't buy stock even in a gold mine as close to the edge of ruin as we are."

"I'm not going to ask *you* to," said Jim. "I'm going to ask you to *sell* stock in such a company."

"You are, are you?"

"Yep." The sterling-silver fork conducted an exultant march. "You get our law hounds together and draw up the papers—do it in a hurry, while folks still remember that the Commodore wants what Jay Gould and Jim Fisk have got—and I'll go up and down Broadway, if necessary to Boston and Philadelphia, and I'll move that paper."

"You will," said Jay, his pitch questioning and ironic.

Jim's answer was as low and solid as the granite in a Vermont wall. "I will."

The June sun sparkled on the water glass, the gold-and-rose china, the silver coffeepot, and the starched white matte of tablecloth. A delicious shiver ran up Jay's back. Time stopped and the moment stretched to infinity. His pleasure had to do with having someone else to work and think with him, a partner who really put his back into the business, one who brought him pleasant surprises. Jay couldn't have come up with this idea. Working with the right partner was like discovering you possessed an extra pair of arms or an eye in the back of your head, a hidden strength. All the more amazing was that this idea hadn't come from hard, solitary thought in an office late at night, but from wandering through Broadway on a carouse. And yet it was possible. Daring, bold, likely to fail—yet damn well worth trying. Jay's laugh was tinged with giddiness, and he reined himself in. Jim's ruddy face lifted and he beamed.

"Like it, huh?"

"Very much. You're okay, Jim."

"Hey! We're partners."

"Give me a couple of weeks to mull over the best way to set it up."

Jim's eyebrows lifted and his forehead wrinkled into impish fun. "You just gimme something to sell!"

Morosini came to the door of Jay's office and said, "Sir, she's here." Jay stood up abruptly and put on a calm face that didn't match his excitement.

"Mr. Fisk is just leaving," Jay said. "Give us a couple of minutes, and show her in when he leaves." It was a week later, they were back in the Erie's old West Street offices, and business had nearly settled back to normal. They were discussing the stock offer, which would take place a month later in July. Jim snorted in surprise.

"I'm leaving, am I? Who's this?"

Jay quickly shoved the papers strewn over his desk into neat piles. "Mrs. Stokes," he said. "To discuss that Pennsylvania right-of-way." Jim laughed heartily.

"Annabelle!" bellowed Jim. "Beauti*fool* Anna*bool!* No wonder you're excited. You haven't wasted any time, have you?"

Jay flushed. "Shhhh! It's nothing like that."

"Why not?" asked Jim. "She's something."

"I don't—you know, Helen and all."

Jim peered up from the visitor's chair with a shrewd gaze. "Now that I think of it, you been jumpy all morning." His large blue eyes were liquid with steamy knowledge. "And I haven't ever seen you in such a bright waistcoat, although that black tie is all wrong." One of Jay's hands shot to his neck, the other to the maroon-and-gold silk at his waist.

Jim stood and with one easy gesture untied the floppy maroon silk at his own throat and held it out. "Change ties with me," he said. "Here, I'll knot it for you." He came around the desk, and his warm fingers scrabbled at Jay's collar.

"Jim, no, I—"

"Hey, take it easy." His bright blue eye, a few inches away, winked. "Things will go great." His knuckles scraped Jay's Adam's apple. "A feller never know, now do he?" he said, echoing the tag line of a popular minstrel show. He stood back and beamed at his handiwork. "There! Right handsome, I'd say." His voice dropped into a conspiratorial growl. "I'll send her right in."

He was gone before Jay could tell him not to leer or wink at her. Jay sat down, picked up a report, and pretended to read, but his eyes wouldn't rest on the paper. His ears strained to hear her footsteps.

This morning when he dressed before daybreak he had put on a gleaming white shirt, spotted a frayed fringe on the cuff, and changed it. He put on his newest blue broadcloth suit and this damn jaunty waistcoat that was like some flat gold-and-maroon snake around his middle. He arrived at the office at eight, but for the last three hours he had done almost no work. Twice he went out to give Morosini instructions, but when he arrived at his chief clerk's desk, he couldn't remember what they were. Time lost its usual pace; minutes crept by, but the hour between nine and ten o'clock swept by in seconds.

She would think he was too short and slight, a comic figure. He was losing his hair. These West Street offices were too plain, downright shabby. And Jim! What was he saying to her right now? His heavy-handed antics would put her off. She probably thought the railroad business was too new, too slick, too unstable for a real gentleman.

Where was she? It would be like Jim to stop and "palaver" with her. He heard rustling and soft laughter. He wondered if he should stand now or wait till she entered. Here he was, a man who knew the schedules of a hundred daily freight trains, and he couldn't remember what to do in such a circumstance. In his confusion he half stood, thought he appeared too eager, and sat again.

Annabelle swept in, all rustle and breeze of fuchsia-colored silk, white lace, gleaming smile, black curls, and poise.

"Mr. Gould!" she said, extending her hand. He awkwardly rose and touched soft fingers. She wasn't quite as he remembered, but taller and more assured. Her black eyes were alive with intelligence and awareness, her high cheekbones and attenuated creamy skin full of quick arrogance. Even through the white gauze of her veil her eyes reminded him of his long-dead sister's, Polly's.

"Mrs. Stokes," he murmured and waved her into the visitor's chair. Inwardly he kicked himself because he hadn't gone out to greet her or come around the desk to seat her. Her cool fingertips still burned his own. He sat.

"Certainly hot, isn't it?" he said. She lifted her gauzy veil. Her dress fitted snugly across her bosom and waist, but flared below. As she settled herself her skirts shimmered as if the half-dozen rustling petticoats were delicately wrestling with each other.

"Have you been to the shore?" Her mocking lips said small talk was childish. Jim's necktie was choking his throat.

"Not yet, but we hope to," he said hurriedly. He was making a bigger fool of himself by not looking at her.

Unable to think of anything intelligent to say, he launched into the business at hand. He handed her a copy of the proposed sales contract he had dictated to Morosini and brought up the first problem.

"The easement into the property," he murmured. Underneath that rustling fuchsia silk was a slender torso of white skin with faint blue veins, perfumed by limes, soap, sachet, and musk. Unbidden, his mind imagined a suitor easing into the liquid flame of this woman's eager body. Her index finger held her place as her dark eyes looked up.

"Yes, I spoke to our neighbor," she said. "You may have it. You'll be able to come and go as you will."

"That's good," he murmured. He lowered his eyes to the looped scrawls of ink, wondering what it would be like to come and go upon such graceful limbs. "I suggest a balloon payment in ten years," he went on. Balloons of breasts, balloons of buttocks swelling against gentle, probing fingers.

"Five," she said. Her gaze was bolder than most ladies', frank without being aggressive. He should have waited till she turned him down before marrying anyone else.

"Seven and a half," he countered. With the terror of a runner in a nightmare, a trickle of sweat rolled along the inside of his thigh.

She said, "Done and done."

Together they continued to read the sales agreement, sentence by sentence. *All that certain plot, piece, or parcel of land, with the buildings and improvements thereon erected, situate lying and being . . .*

Except for her, the pale June light had washed all the color out of his office. Luminous energy danced around the lace at her throat, bounced off her black curls, caressed her smooth cheeks. Her fingers moved over the inky words like a high-stepping horse across mud, careful not to sully its hooves. Her throat was the most refined and pure throat God ever made, as if only a pedestal of creamy porcelain was fit to hold that proud head. He forced himself to concentrate on the contract—normally as easy as reading the morning paper—but it was too much.

He flattened the document on the scarred desktop. The exculpatory clauses reminded him that it was impossible to erase the guilt of adultery. *All right, title, and interest* made him wonder at the wonder of possessing all right, title, and interest to a woman. In *roads abutting*, his trunk and limbs butted hers. *Thereon erected* a man thrust upon a woman.

By noon they had negotiated all the items of the contract, and the back and underarms of Jay's shirt were soaked with sweat. They initialed the changes and signed the two copies. Where his left palm held it down, his copy was as damp and crinkled as a soiled bedsheet.

She, on the contrary, still sat silkily poised in the visitor's chair. Her bright smile, as cool as it had been the moment she came in, appeared ironic, as if it amused her to use flashing eyes, rustling undergarments, and creamy skin to write a more advantageous contract. Her smile said she knew everything he felt, and that he was a foolish schoolboy.

"Perhaps you would come to tea in two weeks and meet the Grants," she said.

Bewildered, he said, "Tea—Grants. Oh, yes, yes—I'd like that." The other part of their bargain had slipped his mind.

A question hung on his lips, but he couldn't utter it. He wanted to take her to lunch, but Manhattan was too small. It would make talk that would get back to Helen, his lunching with a divorced woman. Besides, she might refuse.

It took her several moments to put away the contract, and several more for her slender fingers to lower her veil. Still, she didn't rise to go. She murmured a few observations about the difficulties of the railroad business, from which it was clear she had followed closely the newspaper accounts of his clash with Vanderbilt.

His thumbs hooked into his vest pockets. He explained a couple of subtleties that the daily papers hadn't got right. She understood them easily, grasping more quickly than even Jim what Vanderbilt had been up to in his last maneuvers at the bargaining table. In fact, damn few high-priced brokers could follow such fine points. Her eyes gleamed with interest.

"Yes," she said, "a sympathetic president can help you." If he was going to ask her to lunch, he better do it now.

"Your brother-in-law's prospects look better every day," he said.

She rose to leave. "Ulysses loves to travel. He must come through New York to get to New England, not to speak of business here in the city. If I offer him a place in New York that doesn't charge, he'll visit regularly."

He opened his mouth to ask her to lunch, but what came out was, "For the chance to become well acquainted with him, Mrs. Stokes, my partner and I would be very grateful." He was on his feet, his wobbling feet, commanded by a light head.

Concentrating on his movements, he walked her through the rows of clerks' desks to the double glass doors of the outer office. Many of the clerks were out to lunch. She stopped, faced him once more, held out her hand. Again he briefly touched her fingers, cool as soft lips, but not so briefly that he didn't feel their cold fire all the way back across the room.

Morosini rose to stop him with a question, but Jay shook him off and shot into his office. He slammed the door and threw himself into his chair. Never had his office seemed so insignificant, so bare, such a closet; never had his life seemed so impoverished, so threadbare, so paltry. The piles of reports and contracts on both sides of his desk were so much mashed tree pulp and boiled lampblack. My God, she was a creature from another world, a world finer than this one. He sat up straight and sniffed. A faint resin of perfume remained on the air, a wisp of fineness in this pigpen.

The door to his office was flung open. Jim stood there. His elephantine grin was as suggestive as one of his enormous leering winks.

"*Wellllll?*" Jim's quivering treble asked.

Jay couldn't stand his filthy insinuations. Annabelle wasn't one of his easy Broadway tarts. Jay could hardly breathe, the office was so small and suffocating. He rose and headed for the door, directly at Jim.

"I have to go out," he said.

Jim stepped back to avoid being struck by the small body sailing in his direction. "What happened?"

"Nothing," Jay said. —*Everything.*

Jim trailed after as Jay shot through the rows of clerks' desks, heading for the double glass doors. "Are we buying her land?"

"I suppose," Jay shouted over his shoulder. He went out, and the doors banged shut behind him. His footsteps raised a clatter as he flew down the stairs.

Outside, the mobbed sidewalk, full of elbows and hard bodies, was as confining as his cramped office. He needed to get away from people, for he would shove the next braying clerk who bumped him into the gutter. He pushed west, away from the downtown hordes. The sun's heat scorched his back and neck. He drank great gulps of the hot noon air, but his lungs couldn't suck in enough.

His feet took him toward the piers through streets as crooked and tangled as old string. He wondered what a boy or girl of his and Annabelle's would be like. His and Annabelle's child! His head swam. No such marvelous creature would ever live.

The Hudson River swept into view, its openness reminding him what a restricted life he had fashioned for himself. Along the piers a row of giant, masted ships swayed in their slips. His dark blue broadcloth suit was scratchy and suffocating. He wanted to rip it off and run free of clothes. Instead, he loosened Jim's maroon tie, stuffed it in his pocket, and walked southward along the splintery wooden planks. He unbuttoned the gaudy waistcoat and let it hang like a loosened girdle. Foreign travel had scarred the wooden hull of each ship with white salt rust, scratches and scrapes, smears of tar, and the gray smudge of sea water. These whalelike boat creatures weren't afraid to crash through new seas and nose into exotic foreign ports. His limbs felt constricted, tied. He wanted to throw off the giant who was holding him, but there wasn't one. In business when he needed to be bold, to act, he did so at once, but here he couldn't. The inability to ask her to lunch—it was the same inability that would keep him from pursuing her, a combination of fear and lack of confidence. A sudden urge possessed him to board one of these strange, bold ships and go away, sail off anywhere, escape his usual round of home and office, office and home. Yet what he wanted was to be with her, come to know her, touch her, listen to her, caress her—make love to her.

He walked twenty, thirty blocks along the wooden pier. The exercise and sea air, as well as thoughts of the dangers to him if he made advances to Annabelle, calmed him only somewhat. The scandal could ruin him, for the leader of a great rail line, especially one with ambitious plans, must be above reproach in the eyes of directors, shareholders, passengers, and bankers.

The black, liquid surface of the Hudson shimmered. Gulls wheeled through the bare masts of ships. He wanted her. If this torture was love, it was nothing like the glorious experience poets wrote about. This was disruptive, threatening to tear apart his life; yet he only wanted to be with her, to cause her to love him. At the same time he was certain that she would find him dull and inadequate, a bumpkin—him, the President of a major rail line.

If this was love, he didn't want any part of it. If only it would go away.

Several weeks later Cornelius Vanderbilt, acting against his son William's advice, decided to embarrass the new owners of the Erie while the company was still struggling to overcome the depletion of its treasury following the ten-million-dollar settlement with him. The established rate for carrying cattle from Buffalo to New York City was $125 a carload. Cornelius cut the New York Central's price to $100. Jay Gould countered with a cut to $75 a carload. Then both roads slashed their price to $25. In exasperation Vanderbilt finally reduced the Central's price to $1. He had deep pockets; he could afford a few weeks' loss that would enable him to pick up his chief competitor in a bankruptcy sale.

Tensed, sure he was now about to lose the Erie in a rate war, Jay could sleep only a couple of hours a night. The papers were full of it, and until it was over, there was no use attempting to float a new stock offering. Days, a numbing dread pervaded his body, as feverish and physically disabling as a hard case of the flu. For the time being Annabelle was forgotten, but his chronic cough returned, his rib again ached, and he remembered Dr. Weatherby's injunctions not to overstrain his frail system. His dreams were nightmares of his early days at the Pennsylvania tannery. His father's dairy farm seemed mingled with the tannery; and once more a boy, Jay was forced to drive filthy cows around steaming vats of arsenic and formaldehyde. In the midst of this nighttime Pennsylvania wilderness he felt as isolated as a traveler lost in a vast desert. All night long he hurried everywhere, his clothes stinking of mud, hides, and sour milk.

Three weeks after the start of what the newspapers were trumpeting as "the Great Cattle Car War," the Erie suddenly restored its $125 rate. At once the Central's cattle cars bulged with cows, and the Erie's were empty. Cornelius gloated, believing Gould had finally been licked. The Erie depended on the cattle business, and when the line shortly went bust, he and Willaim would pick up its pieces in bankruptcy receivership.

A few weeks later Cornelius learned that he had been celebrating a false victory. Jay Gould had bought every head of cattle his agents could find west of Buffalo and were shipping them via Cornelius's New York Central at $1 a carload, taking a sizable profit at Cornelius's expense. Cornelius nearly lost his reason on learning how he had been tricked and immediately restored the Central's high rates.

The next day the *World* carried the banner headline:

CATTLE CAR WAR OVER

ERIE TROUNCES NEW YORK CENTRAL

and every other daily struck a similar brassy note.

"Fisk!" Cornelius shouted to William. Fisk held those damn ragamuffin reporters in the palm of one hand, while with the other he poured whiskey down their throats. This morning Cornelius would have the Devil's time of it on the Exchange as speculators again shorted and drove down the price of Central stock. While such trickiness as Gould had used to defeat him in the rate war was bad enough, he had never parried a sword of the sort that Fisk wielded. This fighting in the papers was damn unfair.

If only I had a pair of sons as full of fight as them! he thought, glaring at William. For his part, William didn't reprove his father or engage in I-told-you-so admonishments.

Cornelius decided that his next attack on the Erie must be something especially bold and clever—cleverness, skillfully planned cleverness, as boldly and ruthlessly executed as Sherman's march through Georgia, was the only strategy that would destroy Jay Gould. Such an attack must come within the next few months, while the Erie was still weak from the deal Cornelius had forced on it.

Scarcely articulated was the whisper, "And while I'm still strong enough to wrestle them."

Part Three

THE SEDUCTION OF ULYSSES GRANT

If we are about to perform a dishonest act, the warnings of conscience exert their utmost influence to persuade us that it is wrong and we should not do it; and, after we have performed the act this faithful agent upbraids us for it; this voice of conscience is not the voice of thunder; but a voice gentle and impressive; it does not force us to comply with its requests; while at the same time it reasons with us, and brings forth arguments in favor of right.

      —Jay Gould, school essay, 1850

15

The scenery and the legs are everything. Girls—nothing but a wilderness of girls, dressed with a meagerness that would make a parasol blush.

—Mark Twain on *The Black Crook*, a popular musical, 1868

In the fall of the year that Jay Gould and Jim Fisk captured the Erie, 1868, Ulysses Grant was elected president of the republic.

The excited, expectant mood of the country on Grant's election resembled opening night at one of Broadway's newfangled comic operas, or *opéras bouffes*, as the farcical productions were called in France and Italy. The North, and especially New York, prepared for four even more prosperous years of postwar boom. After all, with bulldog tenacity Ulysses Grant had resolved the Civil war, the Union's worst crisis. Surely having the gallant rescuer at its helm instead of the lackluster Andrew Johnson, the martyred Lincoln's vice-president, meant yet more abundant prosperity.

Jay Gould had been pleased and relieved at President Johnson's May victory at the end of the Senate trial to convict the president of "high crimes and misdemeanors." While no lover of the pugnacious president, he felt the nation needed a rest from divisive crises. The Republican Radicals were rabid on the subject of curbing the Chief Executive, of making him their creature, yet all Jay's experience in business told him that an executive needed to act, often swiftly and without fetters. Yet, contradicting the Constitution, Congress had called itself into session last year and virtually deprived the president of command of the army, as well as preventing him from appointing new Supreme Court judges. It was clear to Jay and other hardheaded businessmen that if these Radical senators captured the presidency, the Supreme Court would be their next target. Luckily, however, Chief Justice Chase presided over the Senate trial, and his insistence on proper legal procedure maintained the semblance of nonpartisanship. The Senate voted thirty-five for conviction, nineteen for acquittal, short by only one vote of the two-thirds necessary to convict.

Meanwhile, in the South Reconstruction continued. There Yankee troops and hated political satraps such as General Dan Sickles in South Carolina stayed foreclosures on property, made the wages of farm laborers a first lien on crops, prohibited the manufacture of whiskey, and forbade discrimination against Negro citizens. The troops were mostly confined in forts, army posts, and barracks; they were not quartered at the expense of the people in traditional army-of-occupation fashion, and were not called out except to supervise elections and quell disorder.

During the months after the November election and before the March 1869 inauguration, the nation's businessmen ratified Grant's term by sloshing more money into machinery, ships, stores, and factories. Employment rose. Profits blossomed. Houses went up. Like those from the homemade instruments of a rural orchestra, loud were the sounds of anvils being struck, lathes and shop wheels whirring, freight locomotives chugging, presses hammering, auctioneers barking, and sewing machines spinning. Employers groused about uppity help. Salesmen sold more in months than they had dreamed of selling in years. The nation was thriving, it was united, and with all the country out west that could be filled up—double, triple what had already been settled—it could expand for another century, and surely there was nothing like expansion to bring in ever-larger profits.

Meanwhile, Manhattan expanded northward; the Civil War, vast migrations from Europe, and the rapid increase in factory jobs brought thousands into the city. This growth was not without growing pains. The city's population swelled to 800,000; one quarter were recent Irish immigrants, another quarter Germans. Nearly all arrived penniless.

All remnants of New York's turn-of-the-century country charm vanished. Fifth Avenue thrust northward, crammed with more millionaires' mansions. Streets of the West Side were invaded by more jerry-built tenements, grogshops, slaughterhouses, and warehouses.

By the spring of 1869, the postwar boom had reached every city of the republic, except the beaten South. To their chagrin, Manhattan husbands discovered they had bragged so about how business was surging that they couldn't deny their wives expensive lengths of silk. A certain type of hand-sewn lace, *petit Sainte-Etienne*, crocheted by only a hundred peasant women in the north of France, became so popular in New York and Philadelphia that a shipment was sold out months before it was unloaded on Fourteenth Street. A dinner at Delmonico's cost Jim Fisk what a laborer earned in a week; refurbishing Josie Mansfield's new town house cost him a sum equal to what his father had earned over his entire lifetime. At elaborate balls shunned by the old guard, young ladies sported dresses and jewelry the expense of which defied even the most mathematically astute to calculate how such extravagances were bought on a husband's annual salary of $2,000, especially since the couple paid that sum as yearly rent on their fashionable town house.

If life was prosperous for the nation, it was bounteous for Jim Fisk. He had lived all his life by jumping fully into whatever enterprise curtsied to him. While others held back till they saw whether getting tangled in a new set of skirts would profit them, Jim said little but yes. He trusted his new mate to look out for his interests, just as he looked out for hers. In boom times, no other attitude worked as well. It worked so well that many times he felt he was the star of one of these modish musical comedies that he and Josie attended several times a week. The glittering stars—greasepaint enhanced by the newfangled, glaring limelights—persevered when events crashed against them, led others through hard times, kept their spirits high no matter how towering the obstacles, and in the end always triumphed. In private moments of searching reflection, Jim thought the philosophy expressed in these entertainments was deep. Whenever the star applied his energy and resourcefulness, he figured out how to come out on top by the end of the play. That was Jim's experience of life, too.

Never mind that the Erie Railroad groaned under the overwhelming load of debt that it owed Commodore Vanderbilt. Jim would save the day. With the ease of a traveling peddler hitching his sack into place, he hefted the multi-million-dollar stock issue that Jay Gould had spent months crafting. Using all his skills as salesman and barker, he carried shares of stock onto the floor of the Stock Exchange and to the thirsty reporters with whom he nightly caroused; and he hauled them into the teeming hotels along Broadway, and up and down the mobbed streets and jammed restaurants of the financial district. To everyone he met he touted the shares.

Af if he were the star of a popular musical comedy inviting you up onstage to sing along, it took a special act of will to refuse his expansive wave and deep, rich warmth. He painted a glowing picture of how the old firm, the Scarlet Woman of Wall Street, was being made respectable by marriage to a couple of solid fellows like Jim Fisk and Jay Gould. As he pulled you up onto the stage, Jim grinned, winked, and rolled his eyes to show you that over the hot footlights was a large audience. In a private box barely out of sight was the author who had of course written a happy ending to the drama.

After all, he would argue—declaiming his lines—wasn't this the railroad that the villain, Old Walrus, using his most knavish tricks, had scrambled to snatch? Weren't he and Jay its heroes, the stalwart stewards of its trust? Never mind all this debt that the line owed; that was the purpose of this stock offering: to pay back some of that money so the line wouldn't have the villain breathing down its neck. Why, this-here new stock allowed everyone, bootblack to the mightiest financier, to participate in the fastest-growing railroad in America, the one the mighty Central longed to add to its constellation but couldn't because of the strength of the Erie's present captains. And weren't these two captains, Jay Gould and Jim Fisk, the best navigators in the country to guide this bright star's destiny?

The public applauded and shouted yes to Jim's sales pitch, producing a resounding rattle in the Erie's cash register. In weeks Jim sold out the new stock and took his bows before Jay and the public. While he and his slight partner hadn't raised enough money to pay Vanderbilt back entirely, the danger of their bow being shot apart by another of Cornelius's rate cannons was greatly lessened.

As for Jay Gould during this time, he consolidated the Erie's gains. He threw around little money and continued his calm, methodical habits. He indulged his family in only one purchase, a new brownstone at the corner of Fifth and Twenty-seventh. For the first time each child had a separate bedroom. The backyard of the house was surrounded by its own stable, servants' quarters, and a small greenhouse, for with the margin of safety brought by Jim's sales of Erie stock, Jay now possessed enough leisure and money to raise the orchids he had wanted to from his first days in New York. The new house was a refuge, with a large library to accommodate the hundreds of books of philosophy, horticulture, poetry, and science he had bought over the years.

Jim's position as steward of one of the nation's fastest-growing businesses demanded that he dress more soberly than checked suits with red-and-yellow silk linings, but even his restrained black coats, subdued striped trousers, and sedate waistcoats were cut flamboyantly. His shirtfront's three modest diamonds grew to six two-carat stones through the addition of one to his cravat and two to his starched cuffs. His cavalry mustaches, trimmed, shaped, and waxed daily by his Hoffman House barber, flew upward in ever-sharper points. To the citywide despair of hundreds of dandies, no barber could command the wings above their lips to fly like his.

His partnership with Jay Gould, who Jim touted as the smartest businessman in America, solidified. The stock offering that Jay wrote was something Jim couldn't have put together. Its sale—and at such a good price—was a job Jay couldn't have managed. Jim allowed no opportunity to pass to let the Street know that he only saw himself as a part of the team, the outside man to Jay's inside work. He handled customers, shippers, the press, and the shareholders; the inside man was a genius who managed the road, ran the trains on time, planned expansion, and kept the books.

"Where's your little partner, Jim?" a stockjobber would ask at midnight as Jim bellied his way through the horde at the Broadway Central bar.

Jim would give a big whoop and a laugh, throw his arm around the jobber's scrawny neck and hug him, and bellow in his ear. "He runs the Erie during the day, and I run it at night!" To hear Jim tell it, he was only the thickheaded bloke who carried out the subtle, daring coups that Jay Gould dreamed up. As different as Jim was from Jay Gould, still they went together like a belt and its buckle, a pot and its spoon, a lock and its key. A wink and a nod told his audience that the sky was the limit to how far these two sound, bold fellows would soar. "Come along for the ride, partner!"

As if he were suspended in a hot-air balloon on a cloudless May day, Jim could see for miles and miles around himself. The air up here was fresh and clean, filled with the sweet odors of spring grass and flowers' nectar. From below rose up only faint shouts to catch his attention. The breeze was brisk and pleasant against his cheeks. Far below shone the world of toy houses, ant-sized roads, and model cities, bright and wonderful. Before him was spread an ocean of sparkling life that was all his to sail through, all his to enjoy.

And yet one joy was missing. A dark little cloud, no larger than a brandy Christmas pudding, lay several hundred yards in front of Jim's balloon.

Jim experienced all the family life he could bear when he visited Lucy and the children in Boston once or twice a month; he had all the fillies and then some that a hot, amorous nature could enjoy; he possessed more influence—not to speak of fame—than a thirty-six-year-old Brattleboro, Vermont, native felt he had any right to; with only a little effort he managed to put his hands on enough money to pay the bills for a dandy's wardrobe and Josie Mansfield's whims and extravagances; and yet one joy was not his.

"You say you will buy a theater," Josie put it early one Sunday morning in May 1869, as they were lounging about the parlor of her new town house in their silk morning robes, "but are you ever going to *do* anything about it?" Well, Jim had heard this a hundred times already, and enough was enough.

"Of course I am," he replied with just enough irritation to quiet her. "Nobody in the city knows better than me how to put on a show. Don't we go to all the opening nights? Don't we discuss the actresses and how the play is writ and how loud they played the music?" When the producers pushed their way through the red curtains to thank the opening night audience, Jim saw himself standing there. Coming out like that, warming up the crowd, reminded him of the year he was ringmaster in Van Amberg's circus, maybe the best job he had ever had. "We're learning everything we can about this business, you and me. You don't put up a house in a day."

Raising his voice made her full lips pout. She sidled over, sat on his lap, and trailed her sharp fingernails through the fur on his chest. Josie had filled out and become sleeker over the last year. Her hair and nails were done professionally, and she had taken acting, dancing, and voice lessons that added to her poise.

"I know that," she said, "but we've talked about it so much. I'm sick of talk. I want to feel the lights on me." His robe fell open, and the nail on her index finger traced a circle around his bare stomach. He imagined those hard-edged nails digging into his fishbelly-white paunch in anger, and a shiver tumbled down his spine. "I want to feel their eyes on me when I come out. I want speeches that make them laugh and cry and beg for more."

Josie's breasts, loose under her bottle-green robe, slid silkily against his cheek. Her nipples were as hard as small corks. Sweat broke out between his legs and under his arms in response to the female heat pressed against him.

"Hell, I'm ready to show this town what a show is," said Jim. "Haven't I made Pike six offers in the last three months? I'm beginning to think the old man doesn't want to sell." Josie's nails traced a cunning arabesque on his chest. One hard nipple poked against his cheek.

To divert the newly prosperous from their toil by day, the number of theaters in Manhattan had doubled from thirty-four to seventy-nine. Every night impresarios paraded popular ballet, comic pantomime, musical farce, melodrama, variety acts, and the scandalous sight of women's legs in tights. Entranced by the theater, Jim and Josie attended at least three performances a week, and many weeks, one a day.

By adding two hundred dancers and music, and spending $40,000 on costumes, painted stage flats, and elaborate stage machinery, the producers of a dale-and-glen melodrama called *The Black Crook* created a sensation. Every night it played to houses packed by those who had heard it denounced from the pulpit the previous Sunday. It had run for nearly five hundred performances and grossed more than a million dollars, a record that fired the imaginations of impresarios and producers from Boston to San Francisco. Over the winter of 1868–69, Jim and Josie attended a dozen performances.

"You're not one of those fellows who promise a girl something just to take advantage of her, are you?" asked Josie, voice hoarse and face in a mock pout. Her nails traced their sharp way around a nipple and raised goosebumps across his chest. "Say you aren't one of those, Jim." He pulled her head down and his lips nuzzled her nose.

"Sure, I am," he teased. "It's worked, hasn't it?"

The next morning on the way to the office Jim had his driver Rufus drive the barouche, its top down so he could enjoy the cool air of May, by Eighth Avenue and Twenty-third Street.

There stood the object of his and Josie's dreams, Pike's Grand Opera House. Grasping a silver handhold, he half stepped out of the fancy carriage to obtain a full view of the five-story, square-shaped, wedding cake of a building, a seventy-five-foot-high cube of white granite. Like candles on the icing of a cake, dozens of brass balls and upward-shooting spikes decorated the balustrade around the edge of the roof.

The barouche shook from the prancing of his four black stallions as Rufus, sequestered by the driver's wooden cab, held the team in check. Jim lost himself in his favorite fantasy. Spangled out in evening dress, he pushed through the heavy curtain of red velvet to welcome the full-dress crowd. A gaping acre of bare bosoms, from which rose an intoxicating cloud of floral scents. The limelights gleamed on his white shirt and diamond studs. An expectant hush. His modest, humorous speech. He was presenting what the starched white shirt-fronts and strapless gowns longed to lose themselves in: glittering costumes; a driving brass band; painted stage flats that made them gasp with amazement; scintillating *bon mots* about love, hate, betrayal, reconciliation, and sex; and gorgeous *danseuses* in daring tights—each grateful to him.

This quarter block of theater, owned by S. N. Pike, was only eight years old, but it had been dark the past two years. Jim lusted after this theater as much as he ever had over a young, bold-eyed actress. He liked its roomy size. Its domed auditorium had six proscenium boxes onstage, and it seated twenty-six hundred. In addition to two floors of offices above the theater, below it were three basements. The lobby downstairs was crowned by a vaulted ceiling three stories high, and in his mind's eye Jim had already repainted it with gilt. As he balanced himself on the small step of his carriage, rocking back and forth in excitement, his eyes feasted on the building as a child's devoured a birthday cake.

Rufus peered around the driver's box, his red face eager. "We going to buy it today?"

"Soon," said Jim, "but you keep real quiet about it."

Jim sighed mightily as he rode downtown and tried to figure out how to buy it—and how to buy it, and how to buy it.

He had spoken confidentially to five bankers, but to a man they told Jim, who had mortgaged his Boston house to buy Erie shares, that he didn't have the resources to back such a purchase. One banker friend said that while he couldn't imagine anybody who could make a theater fly better than Jim, he couldn't take to his executive committee "a business as flighty as dance hall girls shaking their rumps at Wall Street clerks."

Rufus maneuvered the barouche through the West Street traffic to the green Erie building. Jim raced up the dark staircase, his heels beating a sharp clatter on the wood steps. There was one solution to his problem—sharing his theater's success with Jay Gould—but that included drawbacks. Being Jay, he wouldn't want his name on the programs, but he would want a large share of the profits. As Jim neared the top, he blew out a bushel of air. Three-quarters of a loaf was better than no slice at all. All Jay had to do was go in halves on the purchase price and the renovation.

The double doors of frosted glass, lettered with gold leaf, swung open under the exuberant push of his large hands. This morning!— he would see Jay right now! Already he forgave Jay for taking part of the profits. Hell, the two of them were partners, weren't they?

"No," said Jay, shaking his small head.

It was a few minutes later, after Jim had entered Jay's office and quickly presented the suggestion that they buy Pike's together. Standing before his partner's battered desk, Jim staggered a step backward as if a giant's stout hand had shoved him.

"*"No?"* Jim exclaimed. Jay leaned back in his wooden swivel chair and gave Jim one of his self-contained, ironic smiles.

"No," said Jay.

Jim danced from foot to foot. "But how can you say *no?*" Despite the cool of the May morning, sweat popped out under Jim's arms.

"This is the opportunity of a lifetime." Now that they were back on regular hours, the tautness across Jay's brow and cheeks had slackened, and his pale color appeared healthy instead of haggard. The lean, wolf-hungry fire had died in his dark eyes, and he smiled easily, despite his characteristic sober, cautious demeanor.

"Jim, I'm sorry," said Jay. "If you want to buy this place and run it, all right—not that I like it. I'd rather have all of your efforts in the Erie, but I'll accept it since your heart is so set on it. But don't ask me or the Erie to come in with you."

Jim stood upright and gave Jay a smile. He hadn't become the greatest salesman of his time by taking no for an answer. A buffalo could knock down a log cabin if he rubbed against it long enough. However, another quarter hour of useless scratching against Jay's increasingly hostile *no* convinced Jim to leave it for the time being.

He stumbled down the dark, cool stairs in a daze. As he emerged into West Street, the noontime May sun whacked him in the face. He was vexed. Jay was close to his last chance, and he was as squinty-eyed and nearsighted as the bankers who had turned him down. It felt like dealing with his brother Phil all over again. Often as a boy Jim couldn't get him to join his gang's raids. Cautious, sober, responsible, Phil felt keenly that the risks outweighed the benefits of raiding orchards, riding the rental horses at Mullin's without permission, and swimming in Brattleboro's forbidden quarry. Rufus hurried over from a knot of other drivers, his grin as eager as a hound ready to trot with its master.

"Run me around so's I can have a think and catch a little sea breeze." Jim climbed in and settled against the cushions, and Rufus pulled up the canvas top to protect him against the sun. They shot off downtown.

As they passed Murray Street, Jim asked out loud, "Have I been wrong about Jay all this time?"

The open window of the canvas-topped barouche resembled a theater proscenium. The intent passersby on the Broadway sidewalk were the rapt audience of the fast-paced drama he was starring in, one called *The Impresario's Triumph*. This part here, where he was despondently riding downtown in his fancy gig, would be called "The Black Scene," where it appeared as if the future great impresario, who later amazed all of New York with the brilliant spectacles he mounted, would fail. Sunk back in his seat, arms flopping about in wide gestures, he presented his case to the audience. "Didn't I offer half? Did I hold back any advantage for myself because I found the theater? Or because I've haggled with fatheaded old Pike all these months?"

The next day they had to feed the Continental Grain crowd at Hanrahan's. After those boys left, Jim slapped down on the crumb-scattered tablecloth a bushel-load of statistics and pro formas, all of which proved how great a profit the renovated Pike's would make. Why, even if you suffered four flops before you had the first hit show, it still paid—

"No, Jim," said Jay, rising and throwing down his napkin. Without looking back, he stalked out of the restaurant. He is a tough one, Jim said to himself. Just come at him again.

After their staff meeting on Wednesday, Jim cornered Jay before he could rise and leave the conference room. "Stay behind a minute." He softly plunked down a thick cardboard folder on the smooth, bare table.

"I saw this yesterday," said Jay, his voice testy.

"Please, Jay," said Jim, "you owe me a look-see."

Jay sighed dutifully and opened the bulky folder. As he picked up the second clipping, one about *The Doctor Alcantara*, Jim described how much money it had made and how many performances were mounted. Jim's eyes were full of hot lights, his mustaches waggled with glee, and his arms were as busy as a conductor's on opening night. He had the facts and figures on *A Night in Rome*, *The Daughter of the Regiment*, and *Wanted, 1000 Milliners*. Jay looked up with a baleful stare. Jim hurriedly explained that the double bill of *Cinderella* and *Aladdin* had run for almost a year.

Jay shuffled the dozens of clippings together and closed the cardboard folder on them. He pushed his chair back.

"No, no, and no, Jim," Jay said in a voice of gentle sadness. "You have to find somebody else to go in with you—other theater owners."

"I'll talk to you tomorrow," said Jim.

Jay stood, and his pale features were as solidly set as one of those low granite fences back in Vermont. "No," said Jay. "No more talk. We've hashed this out. I don't want to spend any more time on it." He strode out before Jim could get in another word.

The next morning Jim popped his head in Jay's closet of an office. He asked if Jay and Helen would have dinner with him tomorrow evening. Jay's face lifted from the heaps of reports, files, and baskets of papers that habitually surrounded him. Behind Jim dozens of clerks were hunched over their desks, cogs in the giant machinery of the Erie. Jay's eyes narrowed and he frowned.

"What's the occasion?" asked Jay.

"None," said Jim. "I haven't seen Helen in a while. I'll pick you two up at six-thirty." He was gone before Jay could object to the early hour.

Jim now understood the game. Winning Jay over was precisely like winning over a coy, reluctant chorine. The more reluctant she was—the more trinkets you bought her, the more orchids you sent her, the more intimate little dinners you shared with her—the sweeter was the pleasure of her eventual capitulation. Jim had to press Jay, woo him.

The next evening as Jay and Helen settled against the leather cushions of Jim's fancy hired victoria, he handed them each a box supper from Delmonico's, festooned with red ribbons into which was stuck a green theater ticket.

"Change of plans—if you approve," Jim said. "I was able to get three tickets to *The Black Crook*, orchestra and center. This here's a little snack to munch on the way to the theater."

Jay's eyes glared at him, but not Helen's. Her plump, bland features happy, she leaned forward and clasped Jim's hand.

"Oh, Jim, you're always so sweet!" she trilled. "Jay, isn't this wonderful! I love doing things on the spur of the moment!" Jay angrily flicked the green ticket with his index finger.

"This play's a little raw," he said. *The New York Times* had damned the play as "trashy," but then hastily added, "No similar exhibition has been made in an American theater that we remember, certainly none where such a combination of youth, grace, beauty, and *élan* was found. This is decidedly the event of this spectacular age." Helen's matronly face filled with alarm that Jay's puritan restraint would derail the evening.

"But everybody's gone," she protested. "I'm dying to see it."

"I've also arranged a little supper afterwards," said Jim. "The three of us and the stars from the show at Delmonico's."

"No," said Jay, with a look of stern warning.

"But Jay!" said Helen. Her full lips pouted, and her brow creased. She took her husband's hand and caressed it. "Where's the harm?"

Glaring at Jim as he spoke, Jay said, "My answer to *you* is still *no*."

Jim's hand fluttered in an airy fashion. "Forget all that," he said. "Allow yourself to have a good time."

Jim had seen *The Black Crook* a dozen times, but still a shiver bristled the hairs on his neck when the Archfiend Zamiel again induced Hertzog, the Black Crook, to deliver a human soul into his power each twelfth month on New Year's Eve just before midnight. Hertzog's fat comic valet, Von Puffengruntz, provoked gales of laughter by fainting into his wife's arms, having his wig unexpectedly lifted, and receiving a drubbing from his mistress. All through the first act Helen sat forward in her seat, as entranced as a child. Jay sulked during it and the opening of the second.

Once more Count Wolfenstein imprisoned the noble painter, Rudolf, and again Jim's sense of fair play was outraged. An evil leer on his face, Hertzog arranged for Rudolf's escape and promised to lead him to a cache of gold. The grateful Rudolf accepted, not understanding the nature of the Devil's bargain he was making. For the thirteenth time in as many viewings, Jim restrained the urge to race down the aisle and warn him.

With the "Grand Ballet of the Gems," Jay's eyes, too, lit up. In the second act, when the hurricanes of swirling gauze blew through the Harz Mountains and cascading nymphs tumbled through the wild glens, a peek told Jim that Jay was as enchanted as Helen.

At the end of the act, in the eerie locale suggested by the Wolf's Glen in *Der Freischutz*, an elaborate ritual of incantation hurtled to a climax in a startling *pas de demons*. Not such a sourpuss after all, Jay turned to Jim and laughed and shook his head, even slapping his partner on the knee. And yet the best was still to come. Scenting victory, keeping any smirk of triumph off his face, Jim leaned back to drink in the superb Second Transformation Scene.

One by one curtains of mist, painted flats, and mountains ascended and drifted away. The horns launched long, haunting notes. The violins scraped sobs off their woeful strings, and the muted drums crept by on tiptoe. Silver couches, on which fairies lolled in negligent grace, descended in a silver rain. From the clouds dropped gilded chariots and the white forms of angels. Jim sighed with pleasure. It was the most beautiful moment ever achieved in the theater, the standard as an impresario that he had to beat.

On his way to the deadly gold cache, Rudolf saved the life of a dove. To the astonishment of everyone who like Helen and Jay wasn't in the know, the dove turned out to be Stalacta, Queen of the Golden Realm. Recognizing Rudolf's nobility, she alerted him to the danger. As the play drew to a close, she saw to it that he won the hand of his beloved Amina. A collective breath of relief swept the theater.

When Hertzog discovered that his evil had proved fruitless, he declaimed his famous speech, "Foiled, tricked, crossed in the hour of my victory!" After it, shouts, cheers, and applause not only stopped the action for five minutes, but insisted he repeat the oration.

At the end of the play Jay laughed and clapped as exuberantly as Jim and the rest of the audience. Jim grinned. It was nice to see Old Vinegar enjoying himself.

When the three arrived at Delmonico's, still under the spell of the play, their spirits bubbled over. They were escorted by Lorenzo Delmonico himself through hundreds of chattering diners to a petal-strewn table for eight. At the moment they were seated, fifteen musicians—horns, violins, and reeds—sprang out from behind potted shrubs and released like a flock of startled doves the sprightly theme from *The Black Crook*. It was as if a net had snatched them back into Niblo's Garden Theater, as if the three had never left the enchanted Harz Mountains.

Out of the kitchen strutted the five stars of the show, their voices trilling high in song. As the three actors and two actresses reached the large table, they fanned out around Jim, Jay, and Helen and sang two verses and the villagers' chorus from the show's most well-known song, the one sung and hummed all day up and down Broadway:

> *Hark, hark, hark, hark,*
> *The birds with tuneful voices*
> *Vocal for our lady fair*
> *And the lips of op'ning flowers*
> *Breathe their incense in the air.*

The entire restaurant stood, cheered, and applauded as the singers turned and took bows, and it was as if Jim, Jay, and Helen were stars, as if they, too, stood onstage with the cast to take bows.

Jim waved the glittering stage personalities into seats around the table. The musicians formed a group under two nearby potted trees and struck up more of the show's sprightly music. Lorenzo's white-jacketed minions trooped in with large platters of oysters, shrimps, and lobsters. Others scurried to place buckets of ice and uncork champagne.

During the merry supper Jim said nothing about investing in the theater. He didn't have to. In *The Impresario's Triumph*—that gay portrayal of his life—this scene would be the high point of the first act, "The Partner's Enchantment."

When Jim arrived at the Erie's office the next day, the eighth of an acre of clerks had been bent to their scribbling for three hours.

He strode at once to Jay's office, and for a minute through the open door gazed at his partner, who was also hunched forward in his effort to write something. Jim's jovial baritone sang,

> *"Hark, hark, hark, hark,*
> *The birds with tuneful voices . . ."*

Jay gave him a stare as sour and baleful as that of a boy who has wolfed down a peck of green apples. All smiles, Jim strutted in and threw himself into the visitor's chair.

"Admit you and Helen had a wonderful time," said Jim.

Jay's face was as sober as a stone, and his sharp voice cut Jim off. "I don't know anything about the theater, and I never will. I'm a railroad man—it's all I am, and it's all I'll ever be."

Jim scooted his chair toward the desk and leaned forward. "You seen last night how much fun it is." Jim lowered his voice. "And women, Jay—more women than you've ever dreamed of! Don't tell me you don't think about women."

"What the hell would John Clavel and George Masters say to 'the Erie Opera House?' " Jay asked, referring to their lead bankers. "We'd be the laughingstock of Wall Street."

Jim fluttered an airy set of fingers. "We'll get other bankers."

"What about Ulysses Grant?" Jay said. "We want to convince him we're sound businessmen. The government might shore up the country's transportation system, but it's not going to come to the aid of the cancan."

"Don't he like women and music, too?" said Jim with a big grin.

Jay shook his head in dismay. "The Old Walrus isn't through with us," he said, using Jim's pet name for Vanderbilt. "This lull is only a quiet moment in a long war. Can't you see that?"

Jim didn't answer, only shook his head and widened his grin to show his disdain for Jay's fear.

"I can feel him out there," said Jay about Vanderbilt. "We're fish he intends to spear. I buy a thousand shares of Erie stock, and I feel him tickle their underbellies. I toss in two or three thousand shares, and I feel him and Drew look it over before buying it. They're constantly testing us, poking, prodding, goosing us—don't you know that?"

"You worry too damn much," said Jim. "What about enjoying life? What about having fun? Why don't you chase that divorcee you been panting for?" Jay flushed, but Jim didn't stop. "You aim to come back in your next life and live it up? Sure, the old fogies will tell you railroads and opera don't mix, because they ain't never done it. Twenty, thirty years ago, when they come along, there *wasn't* no railroads or opera. It's all new, and we got to invent it as we go along."

Jay unfolded his arms and swung his swivel chair forward so that he sat flat. "We see things different, Jim."

"Times are good."

"It's all a kind of false prosperity," said Jay.

"With real money."

"Look at the last hundred years," said Jay. "You get a boom like this, a crash follows. The bigger the boom, the bigger the crash. Good times are the most dangerous. Businesses expand, then overexpand. We need to build solidly so that when the crash comes, it doesn't blow us away like a house of cards." Jim was disgusted.

" 'Good times are the most dangerous,' " Jim mocked. "I just ain't scared of the world like you."

Jay's mouth tightened. "Don't say things you don't mean. I'm telling you it's not smart for the Erie to run an opera house."

"But we're partners, remember? We agreed?"

"In the railroad," said Jay with a big sigh. "*Only* in the railroad. There's lots of things you enjoy that I can't stand."

Jim stalked out, feeling low. As a boy he had always been more generous than his older brother Phil. If he got a nickel, he would round up his brother or another friend, go to the general store, and buy a feast of candy for the two of them. Phil, now, if he got a nickel he might buy candy too, but he would buy it alone and savor it alone on the Connecticut River with a fishing pole. Not much in life was fun if not enjoyed with someone; it baffled him how a miser could suck pleasure out of secret gloating. He ordered Rufus to run him down Broadway to the Battery.

"He can't do this to me," shouted the impresario out of his carriage window to the audience unseen against the blinding limelights. "Who does he think I am—a clerk in the office? Partners go in with each other!"

He wanted to smash the carriage's china vase with its sporty yellow carnation, and he wanted to whack the twin glass-and-silver lamps with his gold-headed walking stick. If he didn't find some way to get up the money to buy Pike's, *The Impresario's Triumph* wasn't going to survive its first act, let alone a long run. To judge from the inattention of passersby, none of the audience cared. Eyes focused intently on the urgent missions toward which they careened, fellow New Yorkers rushed by. Why should they care? He was in a mediocre play with no stars, no sprites, no hero, no music, and no painted flats.

"Damn Jay Gould!" he said loudly. Several alert pedestrians were startled into turning to stare at his troubled moon face.

"No! No! No!" he shouted at them. "I won't give it up!"

16

It's peculiar that Jay never wanted praise or to be noticed if he had accomplished what older boys could not. His satisfaction was in the fact that he had overcome a difficulty.

—Anna Gould Hough, "Reminiscences," on her brother Jay

That afternoon Jay Gould, feeling somewhat edgy without Jim to lubricate the conversation, rode alone in a public hack to Annabelle Stokes's for his second chance to meet with the newly installed President Grant. She had arranged for an afternoon reception to which she had invited a dozen local editors and political bigwigs.

Let Jim stew in his disappointment, Jay told himself; he would attend the reception without the big blowhard. The Erie Opera House indeed! Editorial writers and cartoonists would depict Erie locomotives onstage, and dancing girls in pink tights pirouetting along the tops of cattle cars.

As useful as Jim was in selling stock to the public, his partner baffled Jay. Jim's openhandedness was bizarre, making as much sense to Jay as a fellow standing on the corner of Broadway and Wall handing out roast potatoes in order to obtain a well-cooked steak. That Jim pulled off this trick, over and over, amazed Jay. Of course, he knew that to Jim it was magical that Jay could work alone at his desk for hours, writing a prospectus, fixing schedules, penetrating the hidden structure of a mortgage or the purchase of stock. As different as a mule and a wagon, the partners could nevertheless do things together that separately neither could. Jay simply had to keep a wary eye on a fellow who thought spangles, painted stage flats, and grease-paint were sound investments.

In front of Annabelle's town house stood a half-dozen black police vans and three large official coaches. He wasn't looking forward to the reception's small talk, but it was the job of a railroad president to keep in with officialdom, particularly a railroad president who wanted to throw track across western territories controlled by the federal government. He would far rather spend another hour or two redoing those pesky Boston schedules.

The large second-floor parlor contained three clumps of dark-suited, bearded men, plumper and more self-important than the two stiff Pinkertons at the entrance. The double doors between the parlor and the dining room were thrown open, so that the joined rooms were the length of the house. Muted scents of tea and afternoon whiskey melded with the murmurs of cultivated bass voices.

Annabelle floated toward him on a cloud of bright yellow silk. He smiled, a shy twist of lips that felt as stiff as cardboard. As usual she held herself as straight-backed and dignified as a queen. He was dazzled by her smile, while her large black eyes faintly mocked his confusion.

The wingback chair in which Grant sat was surrounded by a dozen guests, all standing respectfully around him, most of whom Jay recognized—politicians, judges, financiers, and newspaper editors of the major dailies and weeklies. Up close President Grant was a broad man of medium height with sad eyes, a salt-and-pepper beard, muddy hair, and erect military bearing. Although his eyes were a clear blue, his fixed, mournful features were those of a once-scrappy bulldog in one too many fights, content now to watch other dogs war over bones. After Grant wordlessly shook Jay's hand—a meaty clasp with little pressure—Annabelle melted away.

Jay shook the suspicious, inquiring, and obsequious hands of the dozen stuffed shirts crowded around the President. Horace Greeley, editor of the *Tribune*. William Cullen Bryant, the tall and grave editor of the *Evening Post*. Bill Tweed, whom he saw every other week, for as a new director of the Erie, Jay kept him abreast of the firm's affairs. Judges Albert Cardozo and John NcCunn. Russell Sage, the lanky, elderly financier. Jay stood among them quietly, his throat dry, shyly aware that his arrival had produced an awkward lull in the conversation.

As always in groups of men, he felt uneasy. It took an act of will not to shuffle his feet. Assuming that something about himself was deformed, freakish, he made friendships with difficulty. As the only son after five daughters, and living in the country, he had possessed little opportunity to play with schoolmates. After school he had to rush home to milk the cows, slop the hogs, and haul water and firewood. Runtish and sickly throughout his boyhood, he was never much good at stick-and-hoop after church. He was the last in any foot race. As it was no sport to best him, no one would wrestle him. Those things he was interested in—Latin, math, stories in books, science—his chums viewed as dull or perverse. He was often derided as being the teacher's pet.

The discussion before the President had to do with the boom that the United States was enjoying. Half the editors felt that the steam engine, which was increasingly used for manufacturing as well as for trains, would add to the boom; the others felt the boom was getting out of hand. Advances fed on each other, said the *World*'s editor, a plump fellow whose paunch was as full as a sail in a stiff breeze. The textile industry was almost freed from dependency on water power, he declared, the same way the railroads had freed the placement of towns from rivers. The demand for steel rails had increased that for anthracite coal, which again increased the need for rails. Advances in refining iron ores and the heavy rolling of steel allowed track to be manufactured faster and more cheaply. "But I don't have to tell you any of this, do I, Mr. Gould?"

Jay nodded. One eye firmly fixed on General Grant, who wasn't looking his way, the plump editor plowed on. He had lately been on a tour of New England and Pennsylvania, where he had seen rolling off production lines plows, threshing machines, harvesters, revolving pistols, stoves, clocks, sewing machines, a miracle produced by making the parts of these products interchangeable. It was the rails that carried these new products to the corners of the country, not barges. Steam was surpassing water power as the continent's prime source of industrial energy, and rail carried raw materials to its new factories and finished goods to its markets. And what products they were! he exclaimed. Gatling had perfected a machine gun, Pullman a sleeping car, and Lowe a compression ice machine. Bullock had invented a press that printed a roll of paper on both sides at once, rather than on sheets one side at a time. It was the dawn of progress, the first rays of an era that would infinitely ease man's work-laden journey through this vale of tears.

Seemingly unaffected by this gale of conversation, which seemed to blow itself out on the cliff of his silence, Ulysses Grant sat placidly and pulled on his cigar much as if he were alone in his library. Greeley, a shambling, quaintly dressed man in spectacles, broke the silence by asking, "Sir, don't you think the gold price has fallen much too low?"

Without saying anything, Grant looked up and cocked his eye at the newsman. This economical gesture launched Greeley into a busy-body's harangue. He argued that the low price of gold was a plot by Europeans to steal American grain. Jay shifted his weight from foot to foot, hoping his woodenness wasn't noticed.

A harsh sarcastic laugh jerked his attention back to the group. Russell Sage, the moneylender, said Greeley's view was horse hockey. "The price of gold is none of the government's business," said Sage. Jay smiled and nodded in what felt like stiff agreement.

"Sir!" protested Greeley in a huffy manner that declared that Sage was offensive. The financier seemed only amused.

"Gold is the most useless material possible to a businessman," Sage drawled. "It can't be made into railroad track or engines, nor can it draw interest, nor be planted and harvested."

"But it's the government's duty to help American citizens, par-ticularly the farmer, the backbone of the nation's economics," said Bryant. Sage smiled and a twinkle flashed in his eye.

"Trust a newspaper editor," said Sage, "to urge the government to support a substance inert and basically useless." Jay smiled and nodded. From his chair, Grant gave Bryant a blue fish-eye.

"That's commerce, sir," said Grant. "The government governs."

Jay agreed and considered saying so, but he didn't want to appear to be Grant's toady. Itching for something to do with his hands, he pulled out his gold railroad watch, which he consulted and wound. As if imitating him, Grant snaked out his own watch by its heavy gold chain. Its fob was a squashed lead bullet, anchored in a gold finding, with which his stubby fingers meditatively played. For long moments of conspiratorial silence, Jay stood in the quiet, stodgy cir-cle, fingering the stem of his watch while the President toyed with the mashed bullet. Jay supposed it was a lucky piece, a stray bit of shrapnel caught by the Bible in the pocket of his field jacket.

The floodgates were open on the controversial gold question. Every stuffed shirt surrounding the President brayed an involved opinion. Some were for running the price up, others for letting it drift with market forces. To Jay's mind, all these opinions were ill-informed sawdust, but he kept quiet, reckoning any opinion he might advance would only be more sawdust.

It was a shame Jim wasn't here. If this palaver was sawdust, Jim would make a mountain of the stuff and get everybody to laugh at it. Bryant hee-hawed on. Jay felt called on to speak, to be a man with something incisive to say, but the combined presence of newspaper bigwigs, the President, and Annabelle had clammed him up.

The group was deferentially hushed. Grant's bland bulldog features glanced around the circle of faces as if he recognized that he must comment.

"I've told my cabinet to keep its hands off commerce," said the President in a calm, even tone. "The markets will sort everything out."

Jay smiled and murmured agreement. While Horace Greeley argued on with Grant, Jay stole a glance at Annabelle, who was across the room with another knot of black-suited men.

At that moment she was laughing, her head thrown back in careless abandon. The long, pale curve of her throat and neck plunged into the yellow top of her dress. He pressed his fingers, twitching with the desire to soothe themselves on the coolness of her skin, against the broadcloth of his coat's skirt. The parlor's lemony walls and white ceiling lurched briefly and made him dizzy, then the tremor passed.

The rest of the evening came little easier, although later he made small talk about the financial markets with Russell Sage, who clucked derisively over the advice that the editors had given the President as "the blind pointing the way to the halt."

As he was driven home, Jay was stiff and grim-faced, quietly furious with himself. Outside the rattling carriage a light spring rain fell, cooling the city and glazing the dark cobblestones. Shafts of rich, golden yellow from streetlamps and the windows of shops reflected sharply off the shiny black stones. Even though Jim hadn't come, Jay had expected to chat with the President in such an engaging way as to make him favorably aware of the Erie and its president. Yet far from dominating the conversation, he had been out of his element, a cat at a conference of barking dogs. Far from making a friendly alliance with the nation's chief executive, he had made no impression at all.

Far from being the hero of his own life, the man who could handle every situation, he had put himself to an easily performed, almost paltry test—and failed.

About midmorning the next day, Jay entered Jim's corner office, hoping to patch up their quarrel, but the large room was empty.

Jay shook his head in exasperation. What a place to do business! Jim's polished mahogany desktop and table were bare of papers, and a chaise longue in sleek leather lolled about in the June sun. On top of a cabinet, looking like portly soldiers on parade, stood fat whiskey decanters and heavy crystal glasses. Sprightly whiffs of bay rum, bourbon, cigar, talc—and possibly perfume—sprang about the room. Jim's warm, easy laugh seemed permanently trapped by the four walls, the flutter tinkling the crystal leaves of the chandelier. This office was a clubby place to lounge in, not one in which to work.

Behind Jay there was a knock at the open door, and he turned. Morosini poked his neat features in.

"You have visitors, sir."

"Visitors?" asked Jay. He supposed they were upstate village fathers wanting the Erie to stop in their hamlet, or steel salesmen. "Can't you handle them?"

"They say they're from your hometown."

Jay followed him out. In the reception area barred off from the clerks' large bull pen stood seven rough country fellows in Sunday-go-to-meeting clothes. As soon as they caught his eye, two grinned and waved. With a shock Jay recognized them as Billy and Frank, his brothers-in-law from Roxbury. Jay hadn't seen them in four years. With their ill-fitting suits and hair hacked into shape by their wives, the gawky Roxbury farmers looked as out of place in a modern office as seven cows.

Jay rushed through the maze of clerks' desks. Billy Compton, who had married his sister Sarah, clasped his hand eagerly.

"I told them you wouldn't forget us!" said Billy. His stout frame had grown an enormous paunch. Jay grinned.

Next to him was Frank, long and loose-jointed, who had married his sister Mary. Raring back proudly, he pumped Jay's hand. Alongside his left eye his cheek jerked in a tic. His face creased by a grin, Jay clasped Frank's elbow along with his hand.

"Here's Sebastian," said Billy, pointing to a third. "Our old clown and Latin scholar. And Morris, who you used to help with sums, remember?" As they shook hands, the calluses on their plow-roughened fingers dug into Jay's soft palms and brought back his bittersweet rural life of twenty years ago.

Morris Ruthers had a cast that turned his left eye outward, would till the day he died. It hurt to look at him, for he was Jay's age and yet appeared near fifty, a rag doll with the stuffing battered out of him. Here was Sam and Ken and Aaron, all scruffy grown bulls now instead of frisky yearlings. Jay shook their hands, too. The seven weather-roughened farmers were all between thirty and forty, Jay's age, yet every face looked ten years older. Life in the city might be hard, but to judge by the ragged maps of these weathered faces, the country was harder. Jay wondered how he appeared to them.

Their clomping footsteps followed him to his small office, where they sat awkwardly around his desk in the straight chairs that Morosini ferried in. No, they didn't want tea, but allowed with smirks that they would take "something stronger." The grinning Morosini fetched the decanter of bourbon and heavy crystal glasses from Jim's deserted office.

Jay asked questions of Frank and Billy. They gave him firsthand accounts of the Gould clan's births, marriages, and deaths. Then the eight joshed each other about old girlfriends and midnight country rambles. For each visitor, this was his first journey to New York. Yet for all the air of jocularity in the small office, Jay felt uneasy. As a boy he hadn't fit in well with these fellows, walled off from them by his runtiness, his cleverness at school, and the necessity of his doing so much work at home. These were the fellows who had looked down on him, who thought him freakish because he was good at Latin and math. Nor did it seem to him that his success with the Erie had changed the essential way they viewed him. He was still freakish, still the outsider, still the stranger. His prosperity, his advantages of brains and will, were unfair to men who wrestled their daily bread out of rocky fields.

"Well, what brings you fellows down here?" Jay asked fat Billy, affecting an easygoing jocularity. "I suppose you're all down on a toot?"

Billy sat forward. "You, Jay," said Billy eagerly. "We come to see you."

"To see me!" Jay exclaimed with astonishment. "What for?"

"This," said Billy, and from a paper sack he thrust a three-quart glass jar at Jay. It was heavy, made of wavery, bluish glass with rough seams, and full of wheat. Jay's small face frowned.

"A jar of wheat?" Jay asked. "For me?" They were too practical to suppose two quarts of wheat worth grinding.

Billy's puffy face was covered with sweat. "Look at it good, bro."

"Real good," said Frank. The other five muttered agreement. Jay drew it near his face, and his country experience flooded back. Good wheat was plump, smooth, and free of dust; these grains were dusty and small. Withered even. Diseased.

"This doesn't look like anything I'd want to grind," Jay said setting the jar on his blotter. "Not much rain last year, right?"

"Hardly none," said Billy, "and we ain't having enough this year either." Jay handed the heavy whiskey decanter to Aaron, who sat to his right, and indicated he was to pour his own and pass it along.

"It's been terrible for two years," said Frank. The heat and whiskey had flushed his brother-in-law's rough face. "Billy and Aaron here are going to lose their farms for sure. The rest of us might."

"My God, what's going on?" asked Jay.

"When we haul our wheat into town the warehouse says the gold won't let him buy it."

"The what?" asked Jay. The tic in Frank's cheek continued, as if the blade of a tiny hidden plow were turning over his flesh.

"The gold won't let him buy our wheat," repeated Billy. "He explained about it, but all I caught was that when the price of gold is low, the folks in Europe won't pay us for our wheat."

Jay started, recalling the discussion that had swirled around the President last night. The city's editors had complained to the President that the price of gold was at a ten-year low. The Erie had shipped less grain from west to east last month than in any other May for—the past ten years! Jay squirmed in his swivel chair and thought, *I'm supposed to be smart in finance—and I haven't seen this!* No wonder the Erie's profits were down. If farmers and grain operators, north and west, couldn't get decent prices for grain, they couldn't afford to ship it, by rail, east to port. *How stupid I've been!* The low price of gold affected him and the Erie as much as it did these farmers.

"This is terrible," Jay said. "But why have you come to me?"

"We wanted to talk to the governor, the President, and the Supreme Court," said Frank. "Maybe the folks in Congress. We going broke, Jay." The others' grave, bovine faces nodded.

"My folks have always farmed them rocks," said Sebastian. "I'm like a man hanging over a cliff on a rope. I can't let go, but I can't hold on no more. I owe everybody, and I feel terrible about that. I wouldn't ask for no help if it was just me, but I got Jenny and the five children that need a place to live on and something to eat."

Jay squirmed in his chair. "But I don't know how I can help."

"We need somebody to talk to the President for us," said Billy.

Jay exclaimed, "Talk to the President!" He swung around to stare at every face, lean, hard, beaten faces that stared back intently.

"Maybe he'll help," said Frank with bright hope. "The way Mr. Doggims at the warehouse said it, if the President was to pump up the price of gold, why then the price of wheat we sell to France and England would go up and Mr. Doggims could buy from us and ship to them."

Last night Grant had shown no more interest in the price of gold than an Olympian god showed in the plight of a mouse turned out of his burrow by a plow.

"I was with the President last night—" began Jay.

"See!" exploded Frank. He turned to grin wildly at the others. "See! See! I told you he was the right one to come to!"

The right one! Last night he and Grant had hardly passed a dozen words. His face stern, Jay held up his hand to quiet their excited gabble.

"I don't have any influence with the President."

"But you can sit down with him!" shouted Frank. "He'll *see* you. He ain't going to listen to such as us. We ain't even going to get *in* to see him, even if we go to Washington, D.C., itself."

Jay opened his mouth to say again that he possessed no influence with the President. The words wouldn't come out of his mouth. The President was at the top of a mountain, and they were at its bottom. From where they stood, halfway up was near the top. His brothers-in-law and old chums were too desperate, too impressed with his position, to hear him say that he had no influence. They had racked their brains for an answer, and he was that answer.

After another twenty minutes of disparaging his influence, Jay said, "All right. I'll do what I can, but I can't promise much."

To do something—anything—for them, Jay took the seven to Hanrahan's for a grand New York lunch. They stared about at the stout, self-assured waiters as if they were lords. Their downcast faces were pepped up by the self-important rumble and babble of the well-garbed, plump brokers, traders, merchants, and lawyers, who swarmed about excitedly as if Hanrahan's were an extension of the Exchange.

The farmers shunned the lobsters, oysters, and rack of lamb and ordered plain thick steaks, roast potatoes, grilled tomatoes, and butter beans. After discovering that Hanrahan's fancy rolls were free, each appeared to eat an entire basket. What of the second and third baskets they didn't eat, they slyly slipped in their pockets "for later on," with winks and a countryman's smart laugh for putting one over on city slickers. From an overheard comment, Jay realized that the rolls were to serve as wondrous presents from the big city for their children. He winced as he imagined coming home, seeing Nellie or Edwin's hungry eyes, and not being able to feed them. Far from wanting to be one of these men, he was desperately thankful that he had escaped the rural Hell they were condemned to.

The louder and the more drunk they became, the more raucous fun they had and the more miserable Jay felt, but he kept a painful smile plastered across his pale face. Before the three-hour lunch was over, Jay had promised five more times to speak to the President on their behalf.

As glad as Jay was to see them, when in midafternoon he and the drunken seven spilled out of Hanrahan's into Broadway, he was as glad to see they were ready to catch their train back upstate. Jay had grown up with these farmers, but he was no longer one of them.

When Morosini saw that their visitors weren't coming back, he bustled in and out of Jay's office removing the chairs.

Without his country cousins, the office felt as barren and sad as a dusty loft emptied of summer hay. Jay's boyhood hadn't been all pain, hard work, and the darkness of feeling freakish. Dozens of times Jay and Frank and Aaron and Morris had gone swimming in the bend of Moss Creek: loud, cheerful Saturday afternoons in which time and the world stretched before them like an enormous meadow of bright pleasure. In the fall they often tramped across the fire-leaved countryside hunting deer and turkeys. Winters they sat around potbellied stoves in barns, coughed on new pipes, and argued over which girls "did" and which ones they might marry. In the spring, restless, they rambled around the countryside on slow draft horses and on foot, searching for an unnameable something that they never found. Sometimes they acquired a jug of liquor with which to taste manhood, and sat on soft spring evenings and joked over what it was their restless natures were hunting.

"What about this wheat?" asked the clerk. As he picked up the large jar, a cloud of dust rose in it.

"Do you know what that is?" asked Jay.

Morosini's dark eyes gave it a hard stare. "Wheat, and by the look of it not very good wheat."

Jay took the jar and set it in the middle of his blotter. Inside it the dust storm swirled about like a storm of gray, filthy snow.

"That's bankrupt farmers," said Jay. "Every grain is a busted farmer from Maine to California." Jay pointed to the three remaining straight chairs. "Every man who sat here will be bankrupt in six months. Those seven—and another 70,000 like them—will lose farms they've sweated over for thirty to forty years, since they were five and six years old. I sat last night as close to the President as you are from me right now. He as much as said that their losing their farms was only commerce, not something the government had any business meddling with." Jay abruptly nodded in the direction of the bull pen outside his office door. "How many clerks are out there?"

"Clerks?" Morosini's brows squeezed together as he counted. "Forty. Smitty's mother died and he didn't come in—"

"If the price of gold doesn't go up," Jay plunged on, "those farmers won't be able to ship their crops to New York or Chicago. We'll have to let Smitty and half our clerks go, half our engineers, half our laborers, half our brakemen."

Morisini's thin cheeks and lips pinched together. In a hushed voice, he asked, "You see a crash coming?"

A crash was disastrous enough to whisper about. Once every five or ten years, sometimes mildly but often severely, panic charged through boom time's plenty and gored thousands, tens of thousands, on its bloody horns.

"Worse than a crash," said Jay. "We're too used to boom times. We're riding too high. This wartime boom has gone on much longer than the usual good times. Every businessman has borrowed too much."

Morosini, his face paler than usual, his dark eyes round with terror, eased himself onto the edge of a straight chair.

"Banks are going to go under, maybe all of them," Jay continued. "Without the sale of grain, we'll get no gold from Europe. Without gold, our paper money will become more and more worthless. Without paper money to lubricate the wheels of commerce, banks, and a rail system, every cog of business will grind to a halt."

And Jim wanted to finance a goddamn music hall! Jay picked up the jar of wheat and rattled it. Again an ugly dust rose from the diseased grains, which lay scattered about in sickly patterns of plague and famine. The future loomed.

"First, farm failures, then civil war," said Jay. "The last war was fought over principles. The next will be over scraps of bread." The desperate hungry would massacre those with crusts. The blood of this civil war would make that of the last a puddle.

Crouched forward, Morosini whispered, "You make it sound like '57 all over again."

"Worse, worse," Jay answered. "The whole country's like a balloon that's soared up on warm gases. We've gone too high on hot air. Mr. Grant's our captain. If he doesn't see the mountain peak ahead, the basket of passengers will be smashed against it."

Morosini clasped his hands together. "Surely a man who's seen the blood he has won't allow such a thing to happen."

"He didn't listen last night," said Jay. "I didn't see it myself till Billy and Frank were in here." He picked up the jar of wheat and shook it again. He stared at the filthy, swirling dust. "Put this on the sideboard there as a reminder. I'm going to talk to Mr. Fisk about our supporting the price of gold."

"Our buying gold?" asked Morosini.

Jay smiled thinly. "I doubt if we'll need to go that far, but if it takes our buying a bit, yes."

* * *

"No, sir," said Jim on Monday morning, echoing the prissiness of the phrases Jay had used about buying Pike's Grand Opera House, "a sound railroad like the Erie has no business buying gold like a two-penny speculator."

"Not buying—supporting the price of gold," Jay explained for the fifth time. It was a hot June morning and they were bouncing over Manhattan's cobbles. Jim smirked and waggled his head.

"A frivolous business, if you ask me," said Jim. "A most frivolous business." He hummed a jaunty Broadway tune.

Jay winced and did his best to hide it. Jim still held a childish grudge over their not buying the opera house, and without Jim's support it would be hard to persuade the Erie board to let them operate freely in the gold market, needed if Jay was to hedge their falling grain revenues. Jay silently ground Jim's complacent stupidity between his molars.

That afternoon, the June heat warming their offices as if a furnace roared in every room, Jay carried the jar of wheat into Jim's spacious corner office, sat it on his desk, and insisted he listen to the story behind it.

"So what if them dumb farmers filled a jar with piss-poor wheat?" said Jim. "What's that got to do with me?"

"Damn it," Jay exploded. "I just explained!"

Jim's twin index fingers pointed at Jay like small, stubby cannons. "And damn you, too," shouted Jim. "Don't you have the turkey brains to know the best business deal that ever fell in your lap?"

Jay stalked out of the blubberball's office. He had nothing to say to a walnut-brained barker who equated setting up a bawdy opera house with the survival of not only the Erie but the entire country.

Over the next week Jay read the *Tribune* and fumed. Every morning the market page announced that the prices of wheat, rye, oats, barley—and gold—were sliding downward. The paper's editorials pleaded with the government to shore up the price of gold.

For another two days Jay tried not to read the papers, to concentrate only on running the railroad well, but he was no ostrich, he couldn't keep his head in the sand. His stomach cramps attacked again. At night his cough returned, keeping him from sleeping well. His healed rib felt as if it was cracking again, and the pain, recalling Dr. Weatherby, made him imagine the hidden jaws and teeth of consumption eating at his lungs. The Erie would go bankrupt. Meanwhile Jim bellowed around the office, when he was in at all, like a particularly frisky bull. Blinded by his childish, petulant anger, Jim didn't see it. He and Jay could lose the Erie in months.

At the June meeting of the Erie board of directors, two weeks after the visit of Jay's brothers-in-law and boyhood friends, Jim brought in the preacher from St. Stephens Church to address the eleven directors, for he had recently become aware of the plight of the Plains Indians, much discussed in the newspapers. While his fellow directors appeared uncomfortable at allowing charity at the table with a business discussion, Jim introduced the preacher by quoting the new Indian Commissioner: "Every year's advance of our frontier takes in a territory as large as some of the kingdoms of Europe. We are richer by hundreds of millions, while the Indian is poorer by a large part of the little that he has. This growth is bringing imperial greatness to the nation; to the Indian it brings wretchedness, destitution, beggary."

The thin preacher, with a sharp nose and gold-rimmed spectacles, opened by telling the board that while progress in the form of the railroad was opening the West, at the same time it was contributing to the demise of the Indian, "our savage brother, but still our brother." While the directors all shifted awkwardly, none squirmed more than Jay, who wanted this preacher out of here so he could sell the board on his plans for the gold market, but he judged that it would be politic to allow Jim his hobbyhorse before introducing his own strange topic for a railroad directors' meeting.

Between Canada and Mexico roamed fifty million buffalo, the Episcopalian preacher went on, in three great migrating herds. These served not only as the principal larder for the Plains Indians, but as the source for half their worldly goods. The buffalo's horns made their drinking cups, the tendons made bow strings, the hides became robes and teepees, and the skull and bones were reverently shaped into crude religious altars directed at the Great Spirit, "not unlike our own worship of the single Deity." That the attention of the white government in Washington had lately been concentrated on the Civil War, that the West was sparsely populated by whites, and that tribes such as the Apache, Sioux, and Kiowa fought fiercely to keep out the whites had largely kept the Plains for the Plains Indians. However, with the coming of the railroad after the War, ranchers could ship not only beef but buffalo hides and tongues to Chicago, and from there onward to the East Coast and Europe. White men with Sharps rifles were shooting entire herds of the thick-witted beasts at water holes, leaving thousands of carcasses after they had stripped off the hides and cut out the tongues. These mountains of carcasses appalled every Indian as a violation, a desecration of nature, a horrific affront to the Great Spirit. At this rate the Indians' larder would be empty in three or four years.

Recently General Phil Sheridan, hearing that the Texas state legislature was drawing up a bill to save the surviving buffalo herds, had left his regional headquarters at San Antonio and rushed to address a joint assembly of the House and Senate at Austin. During his speech—widely quoted in New York from outraged pulpits and in liberal newspapers—Sheridan declared, "Instead of stopping the buffalo hunters you ought to give them a hearty, unanimous vote of thanks, and appropriate a sufficient sum of money to strike and present to each one a medal of bronze, with a dead buffalo on one side and a discouraged Indian on the other. These men have done in the last two years, and will do in the next year, more to settle the vexed Indian question than the entire regular army has done in the past thirty years. They are destroying the Indians' commissary; and it is a well-known fact that an army losing its base of supplies is placed at a great disadvantage. Send them powder and lead, if you will; but for the sake of lasting peace, let them kill, skin, and sell until the buffaloes are exterminated. Then your prairies can be covered with speckled cattle and the festive cowboy, who follows the hunter as a second forerunner of an advanced civilization."

"Few care, gentlemen," the preacher went on to the impatient directors. His eyes shone hotly and his Adam's apple bobbed nervously. "But I ask you, I implore you, that when you plan your routes west, to set aside some land for the buffalo, and for the Indian, so that this appalling misery that we are visiting on God's innocents may stop."

As a way of shuffling him out, the board showered him with thanks and made sure the secretary noted where they might send donations. The preacher left smiling, and Jay called the subdued, baleful meeting back to order, in the process taking care to thank Jim for his civic interests.

Then he laid out his reasoning and argued for the line's hedging its operations in the gold market. The Erie board of directors was composed of Jim's and Jay's appointees: Judge George Barnard, Bill Tweed, brokers Jay had known over the years, one of the fellows from the Boston crowd, and other businessmen they could trust. As they listened, the members waggled their mustaches, pulled thoughtfully on their beards, pursed their lips, frowned, and said little.

When Jay had finished, Judge Barnard reared back, his eyes spitting fire, and announced that he would put the French consul general in the jug for a few days. Bill Tweed said it ought to help if the state legislature passed a law saying it was illegal to sell gold for less than $150 an ounce. At the other end of the table Jim sat in a stolid posture, his arms crossed in opposition as unyielding as a wooden Indian's.

Finally Bill Tweed asked, "Exactly what do you mean by hedging our operations, Jay?" At the other end of the conference room, Jim's meaty hand slapped loudly against the long table.

"*Buy gold*," said Jim, his loud honk filled with venom. The board's faces whipped toward Jim.

"Get the government to stop selling gold at its monthly auctions," said Jay, making the dozen bearded faces swivel in his direction, "which drives down the price."

"He means *buy gold*," said Jim. His lordly air declared that he didn't have to say more, that the stupidity of Jay's position spoke for itself.

Startled by the opposition between the two partners, the board members glanced at one another in confusion. Barnard and Tweed whispered together, their faces crosshatched with bewilderment.

Jay spent a quarter hour describing the desperate situation the country and the Erie were drifting into. As usual when he argued, he buttressed his contentions with facts, tonnages, and dates. Gradually he forced the board to see that if there was a serious crash, it was wiser to own gold instead of a rocky government's scrip and paper notes.

"*Ha!*" said Jim. For ten minutes he described gold as "an out-moded relic of a bygone era." He said that the extent of the current boom—the fact that there hadn't been the usual postwar crash after the Civil War—proved that the business cycle of boom-and-bust, bust-and-boom, was broken. Driven by western expansion, the country was in for a long, steady spell of prosperity, one possibly lasting a century. Sure, there might be small dips, but nothing like the crashes of '57 or '37. If the Erie's money was tied up in gold, the line couldn't expand. And if it didn't expand, why, the competition was going to smash it as if it were a peanut on an express track. Mr. Gould here, brainy as he was in many respects, was espousing notions true fifty, twenty, even ten years ago, but outmoded in this enlightened, modern time.

Jim's eloquence pulled the board in the other direction and left them disconcerted. Jay could hardly believe that such a bowlful of jolly pudding could sway real businessmen. Himself, he was steel, hard and unyielding, serious. The board, accustomed to rubber-stamping whatever Jay and Jim wanted and confused by their disagreement, stalled.

"You two are the Erie," Tweed summed it up, glancing back and forth between Jim and Jay. "It bothers me that you're at each other's throats. I speak for everyone when I say you two got to get together, make up, decide what's right, and come back to us."

Judge Barnard beamed at this wisdom and nodded. The others murmured assent. Jim and Jay glared at each other down the length of polished table.

As the middle of June approached, Jay felt boxed into a dangerous corner. Prancing around the Erie's offices and mugging it up as if this impasse were a simple form of you-scratch-my-back-and-I'll-scratch-yours, Jim vaingloriously offered to swap support for Jay's gold operations in exchange for the Erie's help in buying Pike's Grand Opera House.

Jim's pettiness made Jay so furious he hardly spoke civilly to him. He wasn't dragging the Erie into *that* steamy swamp. After all, Jay was in the right. He was trying to save Jim's neck as well as his own, not to speak of the necks of all those in with them—farmers, rail workers, anybody who depended on the prosperity of the country. In short, everybody. But even though he broached the subject five times and pleaded with him to be reasonable, Jim wouldn't approve of their buying gold. Time was growing short. They had only a few more weeks, maybe two months, before their losses would be so large that they could kiss their ownership of the Erie good-bye forever.

17

The tenderness and whiteness of the celery are produced by carefully excluding the plant while growing from the rays of light. Women make themselves white and tender by a similar process.

—*Harper's Bazaar*, 1898

Annabelle Stokes carefully measured out seven drops from the tiny bottle of amber perfume, Nuits de Montmartre, into the hot bathwater. A thick incense of oriental musk, spices, resins, and citrus rose from the porcelain tub.

She gingerly stepped in. Gradually her naked calves and thighs grew accustomed to the heat. She lowered herself. Despite the heat of June, only a bath would truly freshen her. With a sigh she settled against the tub's hard backrest and closed her eyes. Her breasts floated. A vast, snug, dark peace descended over her, and the soothing water lapped against her tingling skin. The perfume's heavy fumes wound through her chest, as sensuously intoxicating as laudanum. Worries over how to pay the grocer, the dressmaker, and her son Richard's school receded.

Echoing through the empty house, the bronze tones of the front hall's grandfather clock self-importantly chimed twice—three-thirty. She had plenty of time; Jay wouldn't arrive till four-thirty. That she had good news for him made her glowing pleasure yet more intense. Bridget had Richard and Matilda out with strict orders not to return before seven. The dark, the heat, the cleansing water, and the intoxicating perfume coiled more deeply into her.

Her mind's eye was thrown back to her marriage. She and Ned, racing up and down stairs through the town house's deserted rooms. All the servants were off. Giggles and screams. Her feet were bare, slapping against the cold wood floors, and she wore nothing but a cotton nightshift. He wore only a shirt. He grabbed her, made love to her in whatever room, on chairs, the cold floor, the maid's narrow bed, wherever she allowed him to catch her—

Another image rose. The hard, black pupils of Jay Gould's eyes stared boldly. Warm bath water lapped against her chest, and a shiver rippled over her glowing skin. For weeks now, during their business *tête à têtes*, his intense dark eyes had fixed on her. Yet, unlike any other man she had ever known with such a hard, direct gaze, he never uttered a word of desire or touched her. He wouldn't. He was different, single-minded. He only wanted Annabelle for her ability to supply Ulysses.

You would think a man could take a hint. But not Jay Gould.

As she predicted, Jay was pleased that Jenny and Ulysses, for the first time, would spend the night at her house on their way to Boston.

He drank the China tea, ate a slice of lemon cake, and read and reread Jenny's letter of acceptance on White House stationery, his intelligent face creased by a smile. He kept his eyes averted from her new off-the-shoulder gown of blue-green taffeta, which floated loosely around her breasts and hips, for she had daringly decided against wearing her corset and cumbersome hoopskirt.

The warm desire for him that had ballooned in the bath began to deflate. His eyes might be hot and bright, but he didn't leer, he didn't make sly jokes with a second, winking message, and he didn't casually encroach his way across a sofa till his leg touched hers. No fiery hand brushed hers when she handed him a document. A half-dozen times he had come to tea and they did precisely what they had come together to do—they planned strategy and they worked. Occasionally his glance was so sharp and penetrating that she thought there must be more behind it than business, and he wiped his palms often, as if nervous, but never had a word crossed the line of proper conduct.

"I need time alone with Ulysses," said Jay. "We have to expand west, and we need his influence. I've acquired a large block of stock in the Wabash, which handles freight between Chicago and St. Louis and Kansas City. I'd like to link it up with the Lake Shore Line between Buffalo, the Great Lakes, and Chicago. Of course, Vanderbilt is opposing us by buying up all he can of the Lake Shore." She leaned forward for her tea in such a way that a hint of breast showed against the blue-green silk. She was certain that the perfume she had bathed in wafted across the table.

"Why don't I have a little dinner?" she offered. "Only you, the President, and his family." He frowned and looked confused, tapping Jenny's letter against his thumbnail. He was business, all business, despite the ardor in his eyes.

"I need more than just an evening with him."

"After dinner, you and he will stay at the table and drink port," she said. "I'll take the ladies into the parlor." She wanted to cross the narrow space between them, sit next to him, take his small, precise fingers in her hand.

"He's going to the Boston Jubilee on the Central line," he said. "What I need to convey to him is complex—particularly complex to a field commander not trained in business." He paused and fixed her with a dark stare. "How can I get the President to ride on the Erie to Boston instead of the Central?"

"Boston? Jubilee?"

He squirmed, half smiling in his ironic way. "The Boston Peace Jubilee," he said. "Celebrating four years of peace since the War."

"And you want him to travel there on the Erie?" Then her head gave a little jerk as she saw it. "Yes—it would give you an excellent chance to talk to him!"

He leaned forward, his eyes alive with purpose. "I'll travel up with him—to make sure the President is properly served by the line," he said. He laughed softly and sat back. "That's perfectly natural, and it'll give me hours alone with him." He chuckled. "The President will be trapped into listening to something he thinks is tedious."

"Ulysses is cheap, you know," she said.

An impish grin met hers. "So I hear."

"You might offer him a free car," said Annabelle. "A fancy private car. Maybe one for him and another for his staff. He grumbled about the cost when he came through on his way to Saratoga. It's not cheap, all the traveling he likes to do and all those servants and freeloaders."

Jay jumped to his feet. He strode toward the French windows and then whipped back as sharply as an animal on a leash.

"Wonderful!" he said. "Not just a special car—we'll give him his own train and call it the *Jubilee Special!*"

"His own train!" she exclaimed.

"Sure!"

"Ulysses should love that." Her mind raced as she considered how to arrange it.

His lips were compressed in a tight smile, his eyes bright. He nodded vigorously. "If I can get him off, away, on my own ground—for an entire ride to Boston—I'm sure I can make him see the wisdom of pushing up the gold market." His sallow face was caught up in his plans, his eyes focused with the faraway stare of an explorer at the peak of one mountaintop preparing himself for the next. "This is wonderful! Just wonderful!"

Two days later Annabelle took a basket of beribboned fruit preserves to her friend Louise to thank her for having Richard and Matilda over during the afternoons she had entertained Jay.

"Oh, I should thank you," said Louise, a smartly turned-out, thirty-year-old brunette with a hare lip but almost no lisp. If she was a good enough friend to guess what was going on, she was too good a friend to pry. "Our children play so well together. It's so hot. Come for a drive."

Despite the heat, Annabelle felt good, and it had to do with her relationship with Jay. She didn't know where it would take her, only that she was moving and the journey felt exciting. Of course Jay was married, but she sensed that possibilities lay before her. Despite his small size and runty health, there was something larger than life about Jay that strongly appealed to her own need to be involved in the plans of a general with a great vision.

Louise's husband owned six general stores in the city, four of them in Brooklyn. She had the use of a maroon brougham with gold pinstripes, two sorrel mares, and a coachman.

At the corner of Fifth Avenue, two moving vans were being filled with furniture by a half-dozen boisterous laborers who shouted in Greek. Nodding toward the house, Louise clucked her tongue and shook her head and said her friends Natalie and Jerry had just gone bankrupt.

"You see people at parties, then they're gone," Louise went on. "They vanish in an instant—and some of them have been in society quite a while. You meet them at some brilliant ball in the evening, and pass their house the next day and see tacked to the front door a sheriff's bill announcing the early sale of the mansion and furniture."

The description brought a knot to Annabelle's stomach. "I've seen plenty of it."

"Thank God I can trust Arthur," said Louise. "But some of these skates these girls marry! They'd as soon sell their wife and babies up the spout as pop in the saloon for a snort. I'm just glad I've got my Arthur."

Annabelle gave her friend's arm a squeeze. "I am, too, Louise. I could use one of my own."

Louise's fingers went to her lips. "Oh, no! Have I put my foot in my fat mouth again?" she said, her face open with innocent distress. "I'm such a bigmouth."

"No, no, don't apologize."

Louise laid her hand on Annabelle's arm. "You'll find another fellow," said Louise. "I know you will. Men are fools if they don't see what *you* have to offer."

"Thank you."

"Come on. I'll take you to tea at the Fifth Avenue Hotel. That lovely music will distract us from this awful heat."

Brow knit, Annabelle wondered if Louise had guessed why her children were sometimes sent over in the late afternoon. Maybe this talk about men was Louise's oblique way of warning her. After all, Jay might be no more reliable than Ned. Underneath her good feelings about him was another layer, one of jumpy, nervous feelings, that told her to have nothing to do with him or the Erie or Ulysses, that it would all end up badly. No more than a three-year-old could play with a hearth fire could she toy with the ordinary rules and come out unsinged.

Yet Annabelle decided that over tea she would ask when Louise could keep the children once more.

Two weeks later Annabelle sat with Jay in her parlor, once again over late afternoon teacups. Twice more Jay had come for tea, but still he hadn't responded to her coy signals of dress, perfume, and smile.

Again Bridget had shepherded away the children, first to the park, then to Louise's for a children's dinner. It was as hot as a swamp in August. For three days no breeze had stirred the humid air and the tannery reek that made the city a bog sink. The muggy stench had smothered all hints of her female coyness. Her usual strategy to freshen herself, a warm bath on even the hottest day, backfired; her skin felt as rough and scaly as a cheap wool blanket.

"I'm sorry," she blurted out. "I've failed. Colonel Porter insists Ulysses and their party ride the Central."

Jay grimaced in protest. "But we're giving him a whole train," he said. "Not just one car." Annabelle picked up her French fan, a flimsy construction of pink paper and white cardboard, and stirred the damp air around her face and neck.

"From what I read between the lines," she said, "the White House doesn't want to offend the Central."

"Vanderbilt," he said, the word spat as vigorously as unexpectedly bad fruit. He sprang to his feet and nervously paced about.

196

She nodded, knowing how anything to do with Vanderbilt upset him. "Why don't you simply go to the White House?" she asked.

He came to a halt and faced her. "The Erie has a lobbyist in Washington," he said. "He's approached your colonel five times for an appointment. When Colonel Porter hears what it's about, he says the President has heard enough on the gold question." Jay's head was cocked stiffly to one side, his black beard jammed against his collar, giving him the appearance of an angry black rooster about to peck an encroaching beetle. "Write again," he said in a tone more like an order than a request.

"I've written three times," she said. She resented his ordering her as if she were an employee. She picked up the fan. He was bound to be upset that she couldn't get what he wanted. "All I can obtain from Colonel Porter is an hour after dinner early in July." Jay's hollow features looked startled.

"An hour!" he exclaimed, his voice in pain. "I *have* to get across how close we are to civil war," he said. "Remember the Draft Riots?" During the Civil War hundreds had died in pitched battles in New York protesting Lincoln's draft. "This time thousands of lives will be lost."

"Why?"

"This time it won't be the *possibility* of battlefield death," he said, "but actual *hunger*. Their hunger, and their children's hunger."

She wondered if he was an alarmist, but his face was too intense to admit the question. "Maybe if you interest him enough in that hour he'll stay up and listen."

"Stay up?"

"Ulysses goes to bed early," she explained. "Come ten at night he can hardly keep his head up. That's why Colonel Porter doesn't schedule anything past nine-thirty."

Jay groaned. "Worse and worse. This is important," he said, his tone irritated that she didn't follow the obvious. She forced her clenched jaw muscles to relax.

"I know that." It came out more sarcastically than she intended.

He threw himself back onto the sofa and snapped, "Then why haven't you figured out some other way for me to see him?"

"That's not fair," she snapped back. "I've done all I can." She didn't want to spell it out, that in acting so boldly for the Erie she was risking what little social standing she still possessed as a lady, not to speak of her connection with Jenny and Ulysses. "More than your own lobbyist—who hasn't even gotten you an hour."

"It's not enough. Especially after I've paid for"—his hand swept about to include the parlor's furniture—"all this."

Her blood hammered in her throat. It wasn't fair. Her breaths came rapidly, her chest heaved. He had her boxed in, and he knew it; the Erie was to make more payments for her land, payments that wouldn't be made, she supposed, if he was displeased.

His voice was hard, full of sarcastic venom, and sounded as if far away. "It's abstract economics—the relationship between gold and wheat. Events that will make the markets crash in four to six months. Of course he'll go to sleep." Jay was half thrown against the back cushions of the sofa, as if the spring that wound up his body were run down. He sat up, his weary face searching for a new source of energy. "But since it's better than nothing," he went on in a firm voice, "I'll be here."

"Will you bring Jim Fisk?" she asked. He shot her a wild look, the glance of a dog startled by a strange noise, which gave her a sadistic joy.

"No. Why?"

"Ulysses has asked about him several times," she said in a starched tone.

"Jim and I are on the outs. He wants me to finance some stupid theater."

"A theater?"

"A cancan palace on Twenty-third Street. He can be so damn childish. I can't talk gold to him if the Erie doesn't help him buy his idiotic theater."

"Patch things up with him," she said. "*He's* the Erie director to get Ulysses' attention." His dark eyes flinched as if she had stuck a pin in his flesh. She pushed it in deeper.

"If you want to save the Erie, if you want to save your boyhood chums and the country, maybe you should go along with him. A theater doesn't sound as bad as a civil war."

His teeth bared. "My railroad company won't finance a dance hall."

"It doesn't sound as if there'll be an Erie to worry about," she said. His scowl deepened and he sprang to his feet. She stood. Why couldn't she keep her mouth shut?

"Thank you," he said, his tone one of mock appreciation. He added in a level, businesslike tone, "I'm sure you've done your best, but I expected more."

In seconds his boots clattered down the stairs, over the wide planks of the downstairs hall, and he was out the front door. She followed, and as the slam of the door reverberated through the house, she pressed her hands against the closed door's lukewarm wood. Her body was wilted, the dress on her back as hot and wet as a dishrag. She turned.

Bridget and the children were still out, and the long downstairs hallway was empty and quiet. The town house felt hollow, a strange, foreign, staring shell of bricks and boards and stairs that resented her. She didn't belong in rattling, rushing, crashing New York, she didn't belong back in country-slow, aw-pshaw Gantry, she didn't belong in a rat-filthy tenement in Five Points—she didn't belong anywhere. She was lost. Lost in a wide, raw continent in which it was every man for himself, dog eat dog, and if you died, drag out your own corpse.

Hardly able to breathe air as thick and foul as slop, she trudged back upstairs. On the parlor's low table the dirty teacups, crusts of sandwiches, and soiled plates were hateful to her eyes.

Her damp cotton dress was hot and sticky, confining; she unbuttoned it and stepped out of it and her two petticoats, letting them fall to the carpet. In her white bloomers, she sank onto the sofa. She put her face in her hands and gave herself permission to cry, but no matter how hard she squeezed the sides of her face, tears wouldn't come.

She knew why. She didn't deserve tears. Not only was she no more than a bloodsucking poor relation of Jenny and Ulysses, but she had failed the only man in the world she now wanted to please.

18

*At night the vehicles along Broadway
consist almost entirely of carriages and
omnibuses, each with its lamps of
different colors. They go dancing down
the long vista like so many fire-flies. The
shop-windows are brightly lighted, and
the monster hotels pour out a flood of
radiance from their myriads of lamps.
Those who are out now are mostly bent
on pleasure, and the street resounds
with cheerful voices and merry laughter,
over which occasionally rises a drunken
howl. Strains of music or bursts of
applause float out on the night air from
places of amusement, not all of which
are reputable.*

—James McCabe, *Lights & Shadows
of New York Life*, 1872

The dinner table at the Gould house
was quiet, for Helen made sure that Papa, who worked so hard, wasn't
disturbed by the children's chatter. Bearing platters, the servants
glided about, unobtrusive as ghosts.

After a brief nap, Jay's spirits revived. He sat in the parlor and
looked over George's and Nellie's troublesome school compositions.
Afterward, with the three older children sprawled on the oriental
carpet, he positioned himself under the center chandelier and read
out loud the next chapter from *Great Expectations*. Glasses perched
on her nose, Helen sewed a new dress for Nellie. Jay tucked the
younger children in, and the tenderness of their small arms hugging

him aroused a savage resolution. No matter what, they must be protected. Back downstairs, too stirred up for sleep, he went out for a walk down Broadway.

From Twenty-seventh Street to Union Square on Fourteenth the great avenue blazed with light, the gas globes atop lampposts snaking away like two shining strings of beads. He pushed his way through the evening crowds.

As a resident of Manhattan for thirteen years, Jay knew this horde well. Their faces possessed a phantasmagorical cast, as if they were demons pouring endlessly out of Hell to prance through the night streets. A party of six well-to-do young bloods strutted through the swarm, out for a lark, their starched chests puffed up. They shouted arrogantly back and forth to one another, drawing to themselves the eye of the stout, red-faced policeman at the corner of Twenty-third Street. A group of nine shopgirls passed Jay, arms linked in a human chain, all shrill giggles and darting eyes. A proud father swaggered by, his aromatic cigar creating balloons of blue smoke, the mother close to him, trailing six big-eyed children. They had seen these sights a hundred times and never found them dull.

As usual on Jay's nighttime rambles, he considered, he thought, and he worried. The Erie's western grain business had not improved. Daily the gold market sank lower. Invisibly, a financial noose was tightening around his neck, scratching his throat when he wasn't absorbed by the minute-by-minute details of the railroad. Along with his fears about the rail business, the savage power roused by the awkward, hot touch of his children's hands rode him like a fever. In a couple of months, the grass rope of cataclysmic failure would be drawn so hard against his Adam's apple that no power on earth could prize it off. The trapdoor would spring open; along with everyone else, he would fall through the gallows drop.

As a result, in the deepest, most profound regions of himself, into which he peered infrequently, the weather had become wild and stormy. When Ma had died thirty years before, as if for all time heat and warmth had dropped out of his life. Indeed, all his boyhood he had felt slightly cool, isolated, as if with Ma's death the fire of life had faded; with young manhood he only dimly envisioned how to regain what he had lost. In the regions of himself hidden to his own view he had come to believe he could regain the fire, the warmth, and the gentle breezes of his lost paradise by becoming a man as great as Cyrus Field, Columbus, Jay Cooke, Washington, Rothschild, even Vanderbilt—by accomplishing a deed that earned him fabulous sums and the gratitude of the nation. Then what had flowed easily to him from his mother would flow as easily from the entire world.

201

Life would cease to be a struggle. All angers toward him would fade away, and he would live in the center of harmony. He would take his rightful place in the community, valued as he had been when he happily ran in and out of his mother's kitchen.

But now all this was in danger. If the Erie went bankrupt, so would he. All the advantages accumulated over fifteen years of cunning, cautious, and paradoxically bold moves would be destroyed overnight. His feeble chest let him know with wheezes and pains that he couldn't start over; the energy and hustle of his youth—which most men retained in their early thirties—was lost to him. If he was to succeed before the worm in his chest finished him off, he had to hold on to what power he had accumulated, or all his dreams were over. All these ideas were only dimly visible, but their influence was so powerful that they gave him the sense of living at the bottom of the sea, under enormous pressure.

Finally the theaters released their hungry and thirsty audiences. Stimulated by the brisk air, more New Yorkers—rich and poor, men and women, young and old—mobbed the sidewalks, spilled into the streets, and dodged the spinning wheels of carriages. Jay pushed through the crowd, jostled by it, but not a member of it. Vendors hawked homemade candies, ices, and hot corn fritters, dripping grease and molasses, which were bolted down by those with pennies to spare.

It all made Jay's head swim, for New York was a monument to paradox and contradiction, a place full of opportunities to accomplish his dreams and traps designed to destroy him. A number of flashily dressed women, their lips and cheeks painted red, slid rapidly through the throng, eyeing it for prospects. Though young, they weren't attractive. Avoiding their stares, he didn't take them for respectable women, nor did they intend him to. They didn't dare stop to talk to a man, or the buck-toothed policeman lounging on the corner would tell them to move on. Their prey weren't the dandies and skates familiar with Broadway, but eager, awkward strangers. The savvy New York blade knew that the next step with one of these gaudy pusses was going for a drink in a smoky, noisy dive below ground, where bad or drugged liquor led to losing your wallet and maybe your life.

Their sharp faces reminded him of Annabelle, who in turn reminded him of his dead sister Polly, who in his deepest self reminded him of Ma, only thirty-five when she died—about his age. In addition to desperately wanting to make himself—through willpower alone—into a great man, he wanted Annabelle sexually, and the desire terrified him. Up from his own murky depths came the fear of what

Helen would say, how hurt she would be, as well as his father's censoring voice. Chasing, capturing Annabelle seemed betrayal of a terrible sort, second only to taking a knife to Helen.

A young woman, her lips and cheeks painted blood-red, placed her hand on his shirtfront and stared in his face. Jay was frozen, unable to speak. Her face was lean, its features a caricature of lasciviousness and hunger, as if she were starved for something he possessed. She took his immobility as a sign of acquiescence and chuckled throatily. Her clawlike hand hooked his arm and pulled him toward the darkness of Seventeenth Street.

He shook himself free and dodged into the crowd. Behind him came a jeer.

Around him not one of these revelers saw that the ship on which he danced was sinking, that the deck thumping under his banging shoes was drawing close to the water's edge. By the time the waves lapped across the deck and he became alarmed, it would be too late. The orchestra would abruptly cease playing. Uselessly flinging their instruments ahead of them as life preservers, the musicians would throw themselves into the sea. Mad with fear, the waiters would scramble over the backs of women and children in a dash for the lifeboats. Those who didn't drown when they jumped into the sea would be sucked under by the giant whirlpool created by the ship as it plunged beneath the waves to its underwater grave.

His head swimming with fatigue and fear, Jay was at his desk at seven-thirty the next morning. He had to make sure that George, and Helen, little Nellie, Edwin, and Howard, weren't sucked under by the sinking of the Union ship, thrown up like debris on filthy streets.

By eight-thirty he had read the mail and marked it up for Morosini to answer. When Jim came in at midmorning, Jay went straight to his elaborate office. His partner's door was open, and Jim sat at his wide rosewood desk, writing. Jay stepped in.

Jim looked up, and when he saw who it was his smile hardened into a stolid grimace. Although Jim didn't ask him to sit, Jay dropped into a visitor's chair. At that moment Jay felt the light-bodied breathiness of a man sailing out into space with nothing under him but the hopeful conviction that he could fly. Jim continued to stare at him over his immobile steel pen, his face a mask of quizzical indifference.

"What would this theater of yours cost?" opened Jay. The coughs of clerks and the scratchy whispers of steel nibs skating across green-ruled ledgers drifted through the open door. Morosini's voice rose as he scolded a clerk for misadding a page of figures. For a moment Jim's broad face didn't change expression, then he stuck his fat pen

203

into the brass inkstand and leaned back. His mahogany swivel chair squeaked.

"Why?" asked Jim.

Jay smiled. "I thought maybe you and I could come to some . . . arrangement."

"An arrangement?" Jim's hands went behind his head, the gesture of a fellow waiting for an offer. "What sort of arrangement, Mr. Gould?"

"Suppose we bought this theater."

"*We?*"

"The Erie. You and me."

"Suppose we did," said Jim, his face still suspicious.

"Then suppose we leased it to your theater company," said Jay.

Jim made one cautious nod.

"As a real-estate investment," said Jay. "The Erie could use the upper floors for offices. We need more room anyway."

"The upper floors," mused Jim in a drawl. His large hands came down from behind his head and his chair made a snap as he leaned forward. "The third floor would make us *wonderful* offices," he said loudly. "But what do you want? I know you. You don't never give up something without wanting something back."

"I'm not as bad as that," said Jay, an impish grin of recognition tugging his features.

"You're as good as that!" In the warmth and eagerness of Jim's response Jay heard a deal struck. He knew that click in another's voice; he had trained himself to listen for it and heard it a thousand times.

"I want your help with this gold business," said Jay. "I want your help with Grant. Maybe you can even talk up gold with those buddies of yours at Delmonico's." Jim shrugged. His face softened into its more usual plasticity, as if it were a ruddy leather sack and excited thoughts were bumping around in it.

"Sure, I could do that," said Jim. "What do you want the President to do, though?"

"Why, stop selling gold." Jay said this as if it were the most obvious thing in the world, but as the words flew out, he recognized that few of his countrymen saw the connection between the piece of gold and the actions of the Treasury.

Jim frowned. "But the government ain't in the gold business."

"Yes, they are," said Jay. "They sell thousands of ounces every month at auction."

"Where do they get it from?" asked Jim.

"Lots of places. They take it in trade out west. If the Treasury takes in English pounds or French francs, it swaps them for gold. The South Americans have to pay their notes in gold. Sometimes the Treasury gets it in from California and Alaska."

"And the President can stop the sales?" asked Jim.

"Sure. Certainly for two or three months."

"The President! I wouldn't mind getting to know the old war horse better." Amused pleasure rippled across Jim's ruddy cheeks. "And just where do we find him?"

"At Annabelle's."

Jim's face lit up. "Ah, now it's *Annabelle*, is it?" He leaned back again, his eyes laughing and his mouth making a silent *ho, ho, ho*.

Jay's lips tightened. "Stop it, Jim. It's nothing like that."

"Well, why not?" boomed Jim's voice. "Ain't she something, though? Her skin's so creamy, her dresses so fine, all that black hair. She looks so strong-willed and devilish, too. You just *know* there's fire in *that* furnace. And divorced—knows all the ropes, if you get what I mean." His broad wink made Jay wince.

"Please—she's a lady and a friend of mine."

In a parody of disbelief, Jim opened his mouth and leaned forward. "A lady and a friend of yours. Okay." He turned his head and gave Jay an amused sideways glance. "But don't ladies do it, too, Jaybo?"

"Damn it, don't call me Jaybo." Irritated by the snippiness in his voice, Jay reined himself in. "Please don't joke about her. She's not some tart masquerading as an actresss."

Jim's face became mock-serious as he said, "Right." His face broke into curves of mirth as he added, "But just because you're prissy about it don't forget that sometimes good friends jump into bed together."

"Jim, you're going too far."

Jim spread his palms out in a conciliatory gesture. "All right— but I thought I'd tell you in case you didn't know. Sometimes you know—and don't know—the damnedest things, Jay Gould." In his voice was frank admiration and perplexity.

For a few moments they stared at each other and didn't speak. From the bull pen came the soft slams of ledgers as lunch-bound clerks shut them, and the slide and scrape of chairs being shoved under desks.

"I want to buy some gold, Jim."

Jim blinked. "Why're you telling me?"

"Well, I'm talking about with Erie money. Like yours, most of mine's tied up in the Erie."

"Buy gold with Erie money," Jim mused. His stare was long and shrewd. "You really think it's that good a thing?"

"Yes," said Jay. "It can't go much lower, especially if some of us start buying it. The market is so dead that purchases by half a dozen houses the size of ours will shoot it up. Plus, if we get Grant's ear, he'll stop selling Treasury gold."

"What makes you think that?"

"Because the logic is clear as water," said Jay. "Nobody's ever explained it to him right." Jim's blue eyes narrowed and his thick lips pursed, thrusting the tips of his waxed mustache backward.

"We'll sell out our position once the government starts selling again, won't we?"

"Of course."

"I mean for more than we paid, right?" asked Jim.

"I'm not setting us up as martyrs. I expect to make a profit on every operation."

Jim's face was wreathed in a smile so broad and warm that it pushed out of the office any remaining coolness between them.

"So I get me my theater—and we make us some money, keep the Erie's business up, and give the country a boost?"

"That's about it," Jay agreed. There was nothing slow about Jim, and if he, Jay, hadn't been so stubborn, this could have been done weeks ago.

"Did anybody ever tell you you was one smart fellow?"

Jay's smile was sheepish. "Sometimes I try to tell myself that," said Jay, "but often something happens the very next day to show me how wrong I am. Let's see how cheaply we can buy this pile of granite you want to get hold of."

"All right!" said Jim, rubbing his hands together briskly. "Now *this* is my partner talking!"

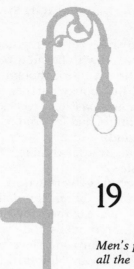

19

*Men's passions are unduly stimulated
all the time by woman's attire.*

—Elizabeth Cady Stanton, 1856

"The President, Jim?" repeated Josie Mansfield absently.

Despite her busy Japanese fan, which only blew more July heat against her cheeks, Josie's attention was riveted on the buxom clothes model who whirled about on the tiny dais in front of them. Jim had promised to buy Josie a new dress for the gala opening night of the Grand Opera House, and she wanted it to be extra special.

"The one and only," Jim said, his voice arch with pride.

"That's nice," she said. Madame Rumplemeyer had locked the door to her jewel box of a Fifth Avenue shop and was putting on a fashion show for only the two of them. They sat side by side on matching straight chairs, and over the last half hour three models had paraded a dozen evening gowns. Jim's attention was also fixed on the model, but if Josie knew Jim, he was ogling Marie's firm flesh, not the cobalt-blue silk that swaddled her busty charms.

The damp, warm air of the small shop was larded with perfume, the musk of sweating clothes models, and the excited whiffs of starched cotton, crisp lace, slick silk. Josie was rarely happier than when buying clothes, and it added to this morning's pleasure that Madame Rumplemeyer's tiny, exclusive shop was simply the best in New York, maybe in all the world, except of course for a few in London and Paris. It was particularly nice to buy clothes when someone else paid for them, especially when it was Jim and he felt loving and generous, as he did this morning to an extraordinary degree.

She gave Jim's large hand a squeeze of gratitude. His manly odors

of bay rum and talc, robust talismans of his regular morning visit to
the Hoffman House barber, warred with her new perfume's oakmoss,
citrus, and cedar. Without giving it much thought, she put his high
spirits down to having talked his mousy partner into going in with
him on the opera house. Over the past few weeks, an army of Erie
carpenters, plasterers, and painters had labored to put on a new roof
and repair the rain-damaged auditorium.

"Me and him talked last night after dinner," Jim continued.

"Oh, good, Jim," said Josie.

Liselotte emerged from the blue velvet curtain in an evening dress
of pink silk, starched lace, and red ribbon. Her waist was cinched so
tightly that Josie was abruptly aware of the bone and strings pressing
into her own middle. The German model's body was thrown into an
exaggerated S shape, breasts forward, derriere thrust out behind.
Three-inch heels intensified the bosom's forward jut, while a bustle
enlarged the rear. In her excitement Josie forgot the heat. In this
dress no man could help but stare at her with longing. She clutched
Jim's arm.

"What do you think?" she hissed. He nodded in Liselotte's direction. He was breathing shallowly through his open mouth.

"Do you want it?" he asked. Sweat had broken out on his flushed
face. Josie glanced down. The apex of his beige trousers bulged. Madame Rumplemeyer's gaze was obscured by Josie's open fan; with
her long fingernail Josie gave his inner thigh a light stroke. A shiver
rippled up his leg and stomach, and he turned to her and grinned.

She knew what had gotten into Jim, and she was making sure
that he knew that she knew. He loved silk, bows, stays, corsets, ribbons, garters, and lace; the rustle of women's underclothes; the sweet,
talcky fragrance of face powders; the flash of naked limbs; the chatter
and complaints of models—any boudoirlike room that reeked of wom-
en's preparations. But then Jim loved everything more than any man.
Josie several times had thought Jim bought Pike's just so he could
wander through the actresses' dressing rooms.

"I'd love to have it," she said.

To Madame Rumplemeyer Jim said, "We'll take that one." To
Josie, "He's going with me to Boston on the *Providence*."

"Ummm, that's good," said Josie.

"I'm personally conducting him to the Peace Jubilee," said Jim.
"In Boston."

"Who, Jim?" asked Josie, an edge to her voice at this incessant
nattering when she was trying to concentrate on gowns.

"Listen," he said in stern tones. "I am personally conducting our
nation's president to the Peace Jubilee. On my very own ship the

Providence.'' He cocked a merry blue eye at Madame Rumplemeyer, whose open mouth registered that this was important news.

It finally hit her. Josie jumped to her feet, her fan and handbag clattering to the floor. *"The* President—on *your* boat!" she said. Her own Jim and President Ulysses Grant, both in white tie and tails, sitting together in that huge dining room, puffing away on giant cigars!

"All the way to Boston," he said, his pride now modest. Josie's arms pumped up and down in excitement.

"Jim, Jim—the big celebration in all the papers!"

He gave her his wickedest grin. "You're finally getting it, lamb chop." Mad, dancing lights spun in his eyes, the lights that gleamed whenever he was clambering up another half-dozen rungs on the ladder of success. "I'm seeing him again tonight. We'll leave on the tenth, he'll dine with me on board that night, and we pull into Boston the next morning." His thumbs and forefingers came up to twist the twin waxed tips of his mustaches. He said in a mock-casual manner, "I suppose I'll be going with him to the Jubilee itself."

She threw herself into the chair next to his and hugged his thick arm in excitement. Her brain whirled with possibilities. First Jim had swung the deal for Pike's, now the President!

"Oh, Jim, this is wonderful!"

"Imagine an old Brattleboro boy like me giving General Ulysses a ride!"

Liselotte swept into the room wearing a full-length gown of scarlet moiré satin with a white silk border, the ruffled skirt of which she whipped about in smart flourishes. Its neckline was suspended across the milky tops of her bosom in a way that miraculously defied gravity.

Josie instantly imagined herself on board the *Providence* in this scarlet dress. The milky tops of her bosom, contrasting with the red satin, attracted every eye. A long table covered with starched white linen and sparkling crystal. Handsome gentlemen in dress clothes perched stiffly on either side of her. Waiters hovered mothlike behind her. She shivered in anticipation. Eyeing her appreciatively, the President drew meditatively on a plump cigar, the fumes of which circled his grizzled face with ropy, bluish-white wreaths. Before dinner, important men had sidled up to feather compliments into her ear, for each of which she rewarded its author with a warm smile and a merry twinkle. Their wives glanced down their jealous noses, telling each other in waspish snippets that Josie was an actress and vulgar. In answer, Josie swung her head and let her eyes glide over their lumpy shapes.

Coming out of her reverie, she followed Jim's gaze, which was fixed on the pearl-white tops of Liselotte's breasts floating above the daring scarlet satin.

"Do you think that dress is too much for dinner that night?" she asked Jim.

"Dinner that night?" he asked.

"With President Grant," she said loudly enough so that Madame Rumplemeyer would know what august company she would be keeping. Jim's mustaches jerked about, their pointed tips waggling back and forth like confused oars.

"President Grant?" he asked. She took his right hand in both of hers and fondled it as though it were a small dog.

"Yes," Josie said. "I wouldn't want to embarrass you, even though I know you like me to look—dashing," she said, meaning "sexually alluring."

"It's the President," said Jim. "I can't do it. I can't take you."

Josie tried to rise but her legs wouldn't lift her. But something in her face must have alarmed him, for Jim was on his feet and moving back, away from her. She stood and advanced on Jim.

"What do you think?" she shouted. "That I'll embarrass you? That I don't know how to act?" He was backing away, his head shaking from side to side, his lips silently mouthing nooo, nooo, nooo. "I'm a lady," she said. "I'm somebody, Jim Fisk. I can travel where I want." He was backed against the wall, his palms extended toward her.

"Hey, Josie," he said. "Sure you can." Sweat streamed down his flushed cheeks, and the whites of his eyes glared at her.

"I can?" Her voice softened. "I can come, then?"

His face broke into a dark scowl. "Josie, Josie, Josie."

"Don't 'Josie-Josie' me."

"It's the President."

She held her ground and forced her voice to soften more. "I don't have to stay in your cabin."

Jim blew out a gust of foul breath. His smile was ghastly, a gambler trying to cover his losses with no more than a fake grin. His hands were still up in that palms-out gesture of warding her off.

"I can't let you come," said Jim. "Too much is riding on it."

She had to go—her life was riding on it. Everybody in the world would know what a terrific actress she was if she rode around with the President. "What do you mean you *can't*?"

"Me and Jay got to talk to him, make a deal," said Jim. "It's big-time, and it's serious."

"And I'm going to sit here in hot, stinking New York," she said, "while you sail around the cool Atlantic having a merry old time?"

"I'll make it up to you."

"I've heard that before," she said.

"I will, I promise."

If she couldn't go, then she knew what she wanted more than anything else. "How about the first lead at the opera house?"

"Yes, yes, the first lead," he said.

"The night it opens," she pressed.

His open mouth and wide eyes stared at her. Opening night was in less than a week. "Look, Josie, we got to get into the black first," he said. He was backtracking, taking away the first lead after this very moment promising it. "We're spending a fortune down there in materials. We haven't even opened and Jay's all over me about costs."

From behind the velvet curtain came the low-pitched jabbering of Madame and her models, the squeak of rats in a wall. The air was raw and sticky, and Josie was flushed and prickly with sweat. Smiling to show she had forgiven him, Josie tiptoed up to kiss him on his sweaty left cheek. At the touch of her lips, he flinched.

"What was that for?" he whispered in a weak, suspicious voice.

"Let's not fight."

"Good!" His shoulders slumped, and he smiled a weak grin of relief. She pushed her breasts against his starched chest.

"Hold me," she said. Hesitantly, he put his massive arms around her. "Squeeze me tight." His strength pulled her against his large frame. "Tighter," she said. He squeezed her. "Tighter still." It was hard to breathe and her back and ribs felt crushed by his power, but it felt good. Often Jim couldn't say no when he was holding her.

A few silent moments passed. No air stirred in the closed shop, and they were both drenched with sweat. Their hearts beat against each other in a wild, irregular rhythm, while the odors of bay rum, sexual heat, perfume, and talc tumbled together in mad confusion.

When he finally released her, she fixed his eyes with hers and said softly, "I'll be as good as I was in Jersey City. Remember? I didn't embarrass you over there."

It took his eyes a second to blink and register that it wasn't all over, that she still intended to go. Jim shook his head in a violent shudder, a ghastly grin exposing yellowish teeth. "No, no, I can't let you."

"Ho, ho!" she said, throwing as much haughty contempt as she could heap up into her voice. "You can't stop me! Not when I march down to the ticket office and buy my own passage."

"No!"

"Yes!"

"Josie, don't do this. Don't. I'm telling you this is serious." He paused and wet his lips. Flecks of white foam were caught in the corners of his mouth. So much of the whites of his eyes showed that he looked like one of those bulls they said went crazy and stabbed everybody with his long horns. Abruptly she was frightened, for the first time around Jim. "I don't want to stop you," he said, "but I'll have my sailors bar you from boarding."

"You wouldn't dare!"

"It's my boat. I will, I swear it."

"I hate you." She swung her handbag in a wide arc and caught him in the ribs, which pushed an "oouff" from him. She spun and marched to the front door, shouting over her shoulder, "I *hate* you."

His hands against his ribs, he pleaded, "I'll make it up to you."

She was at the front door, which she unlocked. She stood in the doorway, hand on the knob, making sure she had the last word.

"You won't have to," she shouted. "I'll make it up to myself."

With that she turned, snatched her skirts and hoops through the narrow opening, and slammed the door behind her.

20

*Happiness consists not so much in
indulgence as in self-denial.*

—Jay Gould to his teenage friend
James Oliver, 1853

Restless and overstimulated, Jay
Gould shifted from foot to foot, his patent-leather dress shoes restless
on the maroon, cream, and blue flowers that luxuriated in the carpet
of Annabelle Stokes's second-floor parlor.

All the other guests had left or were in the hall downstairs leaving.
The parlor was deserted, a jewel box empty and naked without the
filigree and gems of its self-important guests. The President and Mrs.
Grant had gone upstairs to bed a half hour ago. Jay's fingers snaked
out his large railroad timepiece—near midnight. He really ought
to go.

Through the open French windows drifted in the cool air of a
sweet July night. In the street, plump, well-satisfied burghers jovially
tossed good-nights to each other. Carriage doors slammed. In an absent, studious fashion, Jay moved among the florid, curved backs of
the chairs and sofas, on which carved wreaths, shells, fruit, and flowers fought for space. Inside he was electric with excitement.

Ulysses Grant had sat right here, the cup of coffee balanced on
his knee almost turning over from spasms of laughter during Jim's
tall tale of being treed in Tennessee by a bear. That warm laughter
promised that the dour, taciturn Grant would listen tomorrow night
on the steamer trip to Boston when Jay presented his case for the
Treasury's supporting the price of gold.

Tonight Jay had talked excitedly to Russell Sage, the financier,
about John Muir and John Wesley Powell, explorers and surveyors

of the West. Jay's first job, at seventeen, was surveying the county. In retrospect the job had a wonderful glow to it. He thrilled to Muir's feat of walking a thousand miles from Indianapolis to the Gulf of Mexico. Powell, who had lost an arm at Shiloh, was planning to lead a nine-hundred-mile descent of the Colorado River in boats through the Grand Canyon. These were adventures Jay wanted to take, on which he would have liked to take George, but the Erie was a mistress who wouldn't allow him even a few weeks away.

When Annabelle came back upstairs, Jay's breath caught at the sight of her beauty. To him women were divine creatures who mitigated the cruelty of life's struggle. Annabelle, who again reminded him of his long-dead sister Polly, seemed all this and more. Her ability to deal with Ulysses Grant was as valuable and mysterious as Polly's to intercede with his father. Dressed in a double-skirted deep-blue evening dress, at the waist of which were attached wide, white ribbons and bows like bellpulls, she stood just inside the double doors and surveyed the parlor.

"I thought it went rather well," she said with exultant satisfaction. Above the white lace across her bosom rose her bare, pale shoulders. Jay stared, but then to mask his fascination, he averted his gaze.

"It was Jim," he said, crossing to her. "He has a way with everybody. Two weeks ago he went to Pennsylvania to stop striking trackmen from rioting—when he arrived, before he opened his mouth, they cheered him." She laughed and the blue dress rustled as she drifted toward a sofa. The candles in the wall sconces fluttered gaily in the night air, radiating cozy splendor, and the chandelier's globes beamed as jovially as Jim's smile.

"I think Ulysses is a little in awe of you and Jim," she mused as she gracefully slid onto the sofa. He eased himself onto the sofa across from it.

"In awe?" Grant had gazed about with sad, taciturn eyes, as if he had seen so much blood in the War that he was reluctant to speak up about anything.

"Because you have done so well, he probably thinks you and Jim are frightfully clever, much more so than he," she said. "Remember, only nine years ago Ulysses made fifty dollars a month in his brothers' store, the only job he could find. He's quiet so as not to appear stupid."

Jay chuckled softly, expansively pleased that she thought he was clever. "Nine years—from store clerk to president," he said. "It hardly seems possible."

"Getting Ulysses to sail on his boat was a brilliant stroke on Jim's part," she said. "Does he know what a pinchpenny Ulysses is?"

He threw his arms across the back of the sofa. "Jim has a kind of genius for getting people to go along with him," said Jay.

Her smile radiated admiration and respect. "And you do the thinking," she said.

"The planning," he admitted.

"I saw it often when I worked in Papa's bank," she said, "the same partnership. One stayed in, managed the business, while the other went out selling clients and customers." Her smile was rueful. "When they weren't at each other's throats, it worked well."

"We have our share of that."

"Jim admires you tremendously. When you're around he always looks to see how you're reacting to what he's saying."

Any talk about himself—praise or blame—made Jay uncomfortable, left him exposed, and he smiled awkwardly.

"To me Jim's always doing something outrageous," he said. "I remind myself every day that he isn't me, that we don't think alike."

"You're fond of him, aren't you?"

He hesitated; he had never thought about Jim in the same breath as *fond*. "Yes, I suppose I am."

She smiled. "He's so unlike you."

"He's—sometimes I think I'd like to do what Jim does," said Jay. "Speak without thinking. Be everybody's friend. Stay up all night, play cards, booze it up with anybody who wants to have a party . . ." His voice trailed off. Cat-quiet, Bridget padded in with two snifters on a tray and murmured that she was off to bed. Annabelle nodded good-night.

Balancing the snifters of brandy on their knees, they sat silently. Aroused by this talk about him, other home truths stirred in his depths. How his drive to make the Erie into a great enterprise left him too little time and energy for Helen and the children; indeed, he often kept his son George at his side at the office in order to combine his need to be with the boy, run the line, and have a successor. But at other times he was afraid that his attention smothered George, crowded the boy's personality, so that its roots didn't have the room to stretch and grow.

Jay squirmed about, because for all his brilliance at seeing into the heart of business problems, for all his fearlessness in acknowledging the truth of whatever financial position he was in, it was painfully difficult to face squarely the truth about himself and his relationships with family and friends. He preferred to ignore these truths, for when he examined them, he heard his father calling him selfish. At best he considered himself to be a rolling stone, on which

215

the moss of friendship didn't grow easily. At worst, a selfish monster who lived only for himself. The brightest face he put on this distance between himself and others was to call it "heroic strength," but even to him this sounded hollow. To live this "heroic" life, which would magically restore the paradise Ma had taken with her back to Heaven all those years ago, he was often forced to murder the pleasures of ordinary daily life, the simple ones shared with friends and family.

The French mantel clock of gold and glass struck midnight with tinny, brass quavers, and it was followed by the deep chimes of the grandfather clock in the downstairs hall. A shiver scampered up Jay's back, the claw-scrabble of a mouse scratching across a polished floor at midnight. Her eyes darted everywhere except at him. What was *she* thinking? He wanted to get up, cross the room, take her in his arms, but he couldn't move. With a tremendous effort he kept himself from checking his railroad engineer's watch, afraid it would draw the late hour to her attention and cause her to send him home.

The parlor's warm, cozy splendor was strangely thickening into an underwater sluggishness, as if the late hour were curdling the yellow light from the guttering candles and gas globes into sinister black clots. He ought to go, yet his feet seemed rooted into the intricate patterns of the oriental rug. They hadn't said a word since the clocks struck—and although the mantel clock said that was only five minutes ago, it felt like hours.

A boy's wild shout came from the street. She lifted her brandy snifter, and the soft gulp of her swallow sounded loudly. Her movements were as sluggish as an underwater frond waving in the soft currents of night. The air was so thick now that he could swim, float, in it. He had to leave. They would float around the room, her long, black hair flying slowly upward, like fronds from an underwater fern—

"Do you want another brandy?" she asked, the question as abrupt as a slap. He pulled himself together.

"It's late."

"I know," she said, her voice warm and gentle, "but I won't see you till you come back from Boston."

He didn't know what she meant. Jim would know. He heard Jim's throaty growl, "Hey, boyo—if she lets you stay after everybody's gone, you're in."

He pulled himself to his feet, and it was still like being underwater. He moved through the thick air toward the parlor door. They drifted downstairs. The hall was lit by a single gas sconce whose jet threw ominous shadows off the antlers of the large hat rack onto the patterned wallpaper. She took his black felt hat from the hat tree.

Her dark eyes looked past him as she handed it to him, as if she didn't want to focus on his face. The hat felt large and clumsy, a bit of outlandish gear. He should have left with everyone else. The Erie's paying for an evening's entertainment didn't give him the right to impose.

As he put on the stiff hat, he said, "On goes my frog."

She giggled and her eyes met his. "Your what?"

He doffed it. "My big black frog."

"What on earth do you mean?"

He didn't know why he had said it. When he played with the children on weekends, he often said such silly things, the first thing that popped in his head. A fountain in Central Park was a troll's bath. Red licorice was a pig's tail. Marble statues were people frozen by Jack Frost last winter. Autumn leaves were the summer's tears.

He held the preposterous hat out at arm's length, studied it, then with his eyes rolling up to watch it, he slowly placed it on his head as he might have for the children.

"Then it isn't a frog?" he asked in comic innocence.

"Why not a cow?" she asked eagerly. "Or a turtle? A black, hump-backed turtle!"

He doffed it again and studied it with mock seriousness. "All right, I'm putting on my Erie turtle." He clapped it back on in the exaggerated manner of a comic policeman putting on a bell helmet.

She shook with suppressed laughter, and he started laughing, too. Half bent over, he hopped about the hallway.

"Shhhhh!" she warned, her elbows digging into her sides, her lips clamped to stop her cackles. "We'll wake Ulysses, Bridget." Her hand grabbed his arm and her head jerked toward the kitchen.

He put his hand on top of hers. Its heat was startling, as if he touched ice and found it hot. Instinctively he yanked it away, but she grabbed it back. Through the closed front door came the jingling of carriage harness and hoof clops. For a second or two, her soft, moist fingers enveloped his. Her eyes were full of tears. He pulled his hand, but the desperate strength with which she held on was even more startling.

"Jay!" she whispered. "I wish it—we—were different."

"Yes," he answered, the word coming from a stranger within him.

Her fingers were behind his neck, and she pulled his head to hers and went to kiss him on the cheek along the line of his beard. Awkwardly his mouth turned and met hers.

They kissed. Frightened, he pulled back, but she held on. He stopped resisting. His hands were around her back, holding her blue dress where the stiff stays and gathering of elastic were joined. His senses sharpened to perceive the moment in microscopic detail. The world fell away. Kissing had always been a blurred pleasure, a mashing together of pulpy flesh. With Annabelle he felt the exact conformation of their lips, the minuscule changes in pressure as they settled into place, the smooth, blue material of her dress grazing his arm, and the erratic measures of her breath, which tasted suprisingly tart, like brandy lemon icing. The unhurried delicacy of the kiss aroused him as no other ever had, and a force like a torrent of underground water breaking through rock rushed up and overwhelmed him. It broke through years of patient, methodical work, months of distress over betraying Helen, weeks of mooning over Annabelle, and days of tension over Grant and the gold market. Released, he seemed to fall, as lost as if he were in a dream, and yet the tangible, warm, sweet, breathing creature in his hands was more real and desirable than anything he had ever touched in his life. They broke away, gasping.

"Please go," she said, her expression startled and fierce.

"I'm sorry," he said. "I didn't want to hurt you."

"You haven't hurt me," she said. Her eyes darted in fear up the stairs where her sister and Ulysses Grant slept. "It's just—don't you know? I want you. I can't stand working with you and not having you. Now leave. Please, before they hear. You must go."

He was outside, halfway down her stone stoop. The dull clack-clack of crickets. Damp night air nuzzled him. His lips still felt hers. Shaky fingers examined his lips, which felt bruised and numb. The air—a wave of night dew, damp earth, and sea breeze—flooded him. He shivered.

He turned, his leather soles sliding loudly on the stone's grit, to stare at the house. The wooden door was closed as if it had never been open, its brass knocker barely gleaming in the weak yellow light of the faraway corner lamp.

An upstairs window was open—those French windows to the second-floor parlor—and he willed himself to rise and fly into them. For a dizzy moment he was lifted up a foot or so, then he forced himself back to reality, and walked toward the streetlamp at Fifth Avenue.

The hard ridges of bone and elastic at the waist of her blue dress still ground into his palms. In the dark of the street, her pale breasts heaved and fell above the gown's neckline. He felt deliciously dizzy and confused. Her pearl-white neck rose from the blue velvet bud of her dress, a pallid stem holding her face, an exotic white orchid.

Thirty-fifth Street was deserted, the yellow light from the gas lamp on Fifth Avenue glimmering eerily through the leaves of the linden trees. The air was cold, liquid, otherworldly, and dark. The night was cold lips pressing against him, making shivers ripple over him from crown to toe. Yet home was the last place he wanted to go. He wasn't the least bit sleepy. He wanted to walk, to walk and walk. He closed his eyes, and happily blinded, strode along the sidewalk. Her mouth again conformed to his. Her fingers once more pressed the back of his neck with a light, burning touch. Her hair, the flowery scent of herbs and lemon. Her touch, trill of voice, scents, heat—Annabellessence. And she wanted him! There was no doubt about that. But he wasn't sure what to do, for unlike Jim, he hadn't possessed another woman since he was married thirteen years ago.

Paradise! Warmth, thawing his frigid soul, surged through him. He wanted to do great things, greater things than ever, to amaze and delight her. He laughed, and realized how little he had laughed recently. Inside he was light and free, open and happy. As if a stone casing around his heart had burst open, his chest felt as if it were expanding like a hot-air balloon. He was ready to soar skyward.

He turned downtown, strolling an inch or so above Fifth Avenue's cobblestones. And walked and walked, although he couldn't have said how far or where. The city—lights, bars, carriages, gas lamps, clopping horses, prostitutes calling—spun through him with the sharp flicker of a nightmare.

In the excitement of the night, his dead sister Polly was closer than she had been in years, as if her spirit rode the cold, dark air that licked his sweaty neck and cheeks. Polly, Polly, Polly—who had clung to his hand while he hovered over a huge doorway into darkness infinitely larger than the daylight world. That had been so long ago, and yet tonight she was so near. At her funeral, unable to bear her delicate sweetness under the ground, he had to force himself not to jump into the grave to clasp her coffin. She wasn't dead. Nobody who had been so alive could die. Somewhere she still lived, and in the night breeze her warm lips nuzzled his neck and cheeks. Paradise was no more than inches away.

He was at the Battery, as far south as he could go in Manhattan. Before him, unseen, the dark, hidden sea thrashed about like an enormous whale disturbed by monstrous dreams. It must be near daybreak. He must get home, snatch an hour's rest before the big day tomorrow.

The eyes of Henry Smith darted about Jay's West Street office, rarely resting on Jay's face. The ferretlike broker leaned across the desk to whisper.

"Are you sure, Jay?" Above Henry's long, pointed face, his brown hair was slicked back and held down by something as stiff and gummy as axle grease. His long nose wrinkled and sniffed about like the night animal he resembled.

It was one o'clock the next afternoon. Jay had to leave the office in a few minutes to reach the *Providence* in time for the two-thirty sailing, and he was hurrying Henry along.

"You don't have to whisper," Jay told him. Annabelle's teeth still bruised his lower lip. "I said keep it a secret, Henry, but not from me." A pleasurable laugh bubbled up.

Henry smiled at the joke, glanced around the office, and sat back. The broker's forefinger tapped his notes for the huge order of gold bullion that Jay had given him.

"I can see you feel real good about this," said Henry. By using money borrowed from Henry's brokerage firm in what was called a margin account, Jay was buying ten times as much gold as his dollars otherwise might have allowed. The huge purchases pushed the Erie to the limit of its credit, but now that he and Jim had the President's ear, gold wasn't going anyplace but up. "I've handled a lot of stock jobs for you, but never gold. I don't know anybody who's ever bought so much gold. What I . . ."

Henry droned on. Annabelle's lips and tongue had tasted richly of coffee, rum cake, brandy—and the secret, sharp, languid taste of *her*. Her thin body still pressed against his. The slick silk or satin or whatever of her blue dress, underneath which were those female, springy bone stays and elastic, mashed again against his palms.

Helen was wrong for him. She was too pedestrian. He had chosen her because she was quiet and protective. It was as if an eagle in its late adolescence had taken as a mate a motherly goose. When the eagle reached full maturity, he wanted to fly with another eagle, mate with her, make a nest on a high, rocky crag, and raise other bold, daring eagles. But now he was stuck. He was like an eagle with clipped wings, prevented by the gooselike Helen from soaring where he truly belonged.

Henry leaned across the desk again, his eyes fixed on Jay's, to whisper, "I haven't said a word to anybody, but I know something's going on. Can I buy some gold?"

"Can you?" asked Jay in surprise. "Who's stopping you?" His starched collar scratched his neck, and his three-piece broadcloth suit was as hot as wool against his chest and legs. The July heat was made worse because the windows were closed against New York's grainy haze of horse droppings, factory grime, and carriage dust. He looked forward to this afternoon's cool Atlantic breezes.

"I mean, you wouldn't think it was amiss of me?" asked the broker.

"Henry, buy anything you like," said Jay sharply, "after you've executed my orders. Simply keep my name out of it." Her hand was as small and warm and delicate as the petal of a hothouse flower, and as easily bruised. Henry licked his lips and peered around as furtively as a guest bent on slipping a teaspoon into his pocket.

"I value your business," Henry whispered. "I don't want to do the wrong thing by you. Can I put my other customers into gold?" His V-shaped ferret's face twisted into a question mark and bobbed as if to induce Jay to say yes.

"What's all this about?" said Jay in a voice loud enough to dispel Henry's silly furtiveness. "Will you stop whispering?"

"I thought at first you was just taking a flyer," said Henry. "But you're smart and these orders are big. I suspect these ain't the only orders you're placing. Some say you're the smartest skate on the Street. You must know something or you wouldn't buy so much."

Henry was shrewd. The other four brokers that Jay had given orders to might have thought of this, but they hadn't asked. Jay smiled faintly and said nothing. If Henry only knew how much he had really bought! His palms rasped again from the squirm of her stays and elastic. Over several days of quiet buying, using all the margin he could scrape together for himself and the Erie, Jay had placed what he reckoned was the largest order ever made for gold in America—very likely the largest ever made in the world. While they didn't know about each other, Henry Smith and the other four brokers wouldn't keep his secret, any more than ants with a pot of honey in their anthill could keep a secret. If brokers didn't talk, their traders would; and if traders didn't, clerks would. It was only a matter of time before Jay's enormous positions became public. What was important was to keep them secret till he had made all his purchases at the market's current low price.

"Buy me my gold," Jay said. "I don't know of any reason gold will go up. I only know that for the good of the country it *ought* to go up."

"*Ought* to go up," Henry said with stiff intensity. "Yes, sir." Jay smiled as her light fingers glided across the back of his neck. The lemony, herbal scent of her hair was tangy, sweet, intoxicating.

"After you've bought what I want," said Jay, "without using my name, you may say a customer has made large purchases and put whomever you want into gold."

Henry shot to his feet. "Whoever I want," he said. He left abruptly, as if Jay had given him something valuable that he might snatch back. Jay hoped he did put others into gold, lots of others with lots of money. That would help drive the price up.

Now that he was done with Henry, Jay had bought all the gold he dared to. The massive purchases, his lack of sleep, and the desire for Annabelle had stretched his nerves till they rustled like onionskin, thin and brittle. And yet he felt confident. He and Jim would make Grant see the advantage of halting the Treasury's sale of gold for three or four months, till after the fall harvest. With this support of gold by the government, even more of Henry's clients, and other companies like the Erie, would step into the Gold Room and buy. The price of gold would rise. A month or two from now the Erie would sell out, having made enough money on gold to further buffer itself against Vanderbilt's attacks. The country's illness would abate without the patient's ever knowing how near collapse he had been. Jay felt quiet pride. He didn't expect anyone—except Annabelle—to know what he had done. He didn't make a spectacle of himself like Jim; he conceived plans and quietly executed them. As well as a solid profit for a more stable Erie, his reward was knowing that those at home he cared about, and others like them, would be spared the horrors of a devastating panic. His sister Mary and her husband Frank, his sister Sarah and her paunchy Billy, all his farmer neighbors back in Roxbury—and those like them across the country—would sell their corn, wheat, cotton, oats, and rye to Europe at fair prices. With harvest shipping to count on, he and Jim could hire back the five hundred rail employees they had been forced to lay off over the last three weeks.

Jay trotted down the Erie's stairs, his heels clattering in a merry tattoo. While the plan ought to work, still the thousands of ounces of gold that he had bought wobbled on his back like a quarter-ton load on a runty donkey. Ahead lay a long, narrow, rocky path across a steep mountain. He had committed the Erie to such large purchases, on so little margin, that if the overloaded donkey missed its footing it would fall thousands of feet to its death. He emerged from the dark stairwell into West Street, the sunlight dazzling him. He turned right.

The next narrow defile on the mountain path came tonight on Jim's steamer. After dinner he and Jim would try to convince the President that supporting the price of gold was as patriotic as winning the Civil War.

At the Hudson River he turned toward the piers. He couldn't wait to get to sea. His boots clacked against the cobbles with the quick springiness of a mountain goat's hooves, not those of an overloaded, cautious donkey. As he clattered toward the docks, his upper lip rubbed his lower, making the sweet bruise there again ache pleasurably.

21

Mr. Fisk has refurbished the Providence
*with new carpets, plush upholstery, gilt
decoration, bronze statues, and brass
spittoons. He has purchased 250
canaries, installing a bird in each
stateroom, naming many of them after
friends and national figures—Jay Gould,
William Tweed, Jeff Davis, President
Ulysses Grant, and others. A lover of
sounding brasses, he has furnished the
ship with a brass band, an innovation
regarded by many as sensational.*

—*New York Tribune, 1869*

The *Providence* cut through the At-
lantic with ease. The sun was low in the sky, turning the afternoon's
deep marine blue into a fiery celebration of carmine purples, salmon
pinks, and orange magentas. Treasury Secretary Boutwell, President
Grant, his aides, and Mrs. Grant were being served a lavish shipboard
tea on the broad fantail by a half-dozen white-jacketed waiters. Jay
stood at the rail with Jim, out of the President's earshot.

"Do you think now's the time?" Jay asked. He was afraid that
all the drinking, eating, and entertainment that Jim planned wouldn't
leave an opportunity to discuss the main reason for the trip—the low
price of gold and the harm it did the country.

"You'll get your shot tonight," said Jim. "Leave it to me. You're
going to go at him *after* dinner, *after* we've got him softened up good."
Reluctantly, Jay nodded. It was hard not to cross the twenty feet, sit
down next to the President, and discuss Treasury sales, but Jim's
tactics appeared to be working.

When Jim rose at dinner to introduce the two German sopranos, like his male guests he was dressed in a white tie and tails. Barrel-chested, his ruddy face glowing from excitement and the bronze glare of the gas globes, he further aroused the party to a delightful evening. Accompanied by four French horns and two trumpets, the highly trained sopranos' rich voices sang a series of melancholy Viennese songs of lost love. Terrapin consommé was served. Jay relished the hot, sherried essence of turtle, his nerves stretched as tautly as the strings on the violins.

The entire party sat at one large, T-shaped table, with Grant in the center at the place of honor. Jim sat on one side of the President and his wife Jenny, and Jay sat next to Jenny. For each three guests one black-suited waiter hovered nearby or glided about, pouring champagne or presenting, with a flourish, an ice-covered platter of cleverly arranged iced lobsters, shrimp, and oysters. Secretary Boutwell sat across from Jay, and Jay succeeded in drawing him out with small talk. His pride quietly ballooned. He wished Ma, Pa, and Polly could see him now. Pa would have to realize that being a man wasn't all hard farm work, the ability to withstand cold and heat. Ma and Polly would be quietly proud, knowing that their Jay was as smart as the best of them.

A raised eyebrow, the waggle of a finger, and his pursed lips were all Jim needed to command the dozens of servants who flew about. While Jay would have preferred stewed fruit and poached eggs on toast, he picked at the seafood and nibbled the dry biscuits. The stuffy, well-educated voices of aides and officials loosened, and laughter blossomed to fill the polished space. The *Providence* was so wide and well bottomed that the floor swayed only slightly from its movement through the rolling Atlantic. A sense of power welled in Jay, the confidence that on the Atlantic, as in the gold market, he rode an enormous, elemental wave that thrust him forward.

Wineglass in hand, mustache tips flying, Jim rose again. The laughter and excited chatter hushed, but then the amusement bursting through his ruddy cheeks made laughter ripple across the thirty diners. Jay beamed. His partner was a wonderful person, a comic actor able to command an audience without a word, able with a glance to say that he too found himself hilarious and joined their laughter.

"I have to tell you ladies and gents that an old dirtboy from Brattleboro like me," Jim began, "didn't never think he would stand on the deck of his own ship, raise his glass to the President of this glorious country, and shout, 'Hail to the Chief!' "

A chorus of "Hear! Hear!" rang out. Jay's glass raised with the others. Jim toasted every official, giving each a witty tag.

225

"Here's to Tres'ry Secretary Boutwell, the man who makes sure no cutpurse grabs our country's loot!"

Like the others, Jay laughed at the toasts, many of which made Jim the butt of their wit. As the comic toasts continued, Jay fingered the bruise on his lower lip, a pleased smile peering furtively through his neatly trimmed beard. With his two fingertips there, he felt Annabelle's lips again crush his. Her fingers again held the back of his neck. The ridges of her dress pressed into his palms. The lemony scent of her hair flew around him, and the rich taste of her mouth mingled with his.

Still on his feet, Jim said to the President, "I have big news, sir. The Grand Opera House is opening two nights after we arrive back in New York. If Your Worship will accept, I would take it as a great honor if you and Mrs. Grant would accompany me to its opening night."

As the table applauded, Grant gave the slightest of nods, a cautious acceptance. His chest puffed up yet more, Jim sat.

Jay studied the President closely. Tonight, more so than the other times they had met, Grant's rough features appeared soft and at ease. He was of middle height, of a spare, strong build. His eyes were a clear blue, his forehead high, nose aquiline, and jaw squarely set, but not sensual. Though Grant was reported to hate evening clothes, his barrel chest filled out his starched white shirt splendidly. Across his broad front was the red sash of some military order, while his left breast gleamed with multicolored rows of campaign ribbons.

Jay sat back and reflected. It was hard to believe this august official had been an ordinary tanner's clerk ten years back. "His schoolmates called him 'Useless,' " Annabelle had told Jay several nights ago, filling in the gaps of his knowledge of the President. "His brothers told me that as a boy he didn't have any friends, and was cautious and mediocre," she went on. "Beyond a knack for managing horses, he had no abilities. Neither 'Useless' nor his family expected him to pass the West Point entrance exams, but somehow he did. He didn't much like the military, but he liked the free education. He graduated twenty-first out of thirty-nine in the class of '43, which I constantly hear is the sorriest class West Point ever turned out. As a married captain, he resigned from the army and tried his hand at farming. Almost every crop he planted failed. One year he was reduced to pawning his watch to buy Jenny and the boys Christmas presents. The next year they moved to Illinois, where he stood behind the counter in his brothers' leather store for fifty dollars a month."

Jay had asked Annabelle, "How did such a failure ever get to be a general, much less top general?"

Annabelle laughed, a shrill edge of malice in her voice. "By default—and yet, to be fair, some skill. During the War, Captain Grant proved to be a surprisingly able head banger. He brought every unit under his thumb into a fast state of readiness. He became brigadier general when he was the only colonel from his Illinois district who was also a professional military man. The one-star general emerged a hero—to a Union thirsty for them—after he captured Forts Henry and Donelson."

"When he first used the phrase *unconditional surrender*," remarked Jay.

"Right," she said. "Mr. Lincoln had found a general who could win."

"A leader who fought rather than talked," said Jay.

Annabelle's hand had waved airily. "The rest is history."

Four rolling carts now wheeled in four enormous sides of roast beef. Four European wines were uncorked—a fruity Italian and a dry French red, a sweet hock and an icy Sauterne. President Grant accepted a glass of the French red, and several guests tried all four. Silver serving platters of roast potatoes, turnip puree, and glazed carrots were borne around twice. When the company was full to bursting, they were further tempted by five flavors of ices and twelve platters of artfully arranged Italian, French, and German pastries. These were followed by a savory, an anchovy in the shape of a J, for the Jubilee, on thin, crisp toast. Even though he refused two-thirds of the offered dishes, Jay felt bloated.

The conversation rose in a rich, warm gabble. The President and his party were stimulated by the crisp, clear night, the bracing sea air, the massive jubilee toward which the ship plowed, the lavish service, and the comic flash of Jim's admiralcy. It was as if the solid *Providence*'s brightly lit voyage was a respite from everyday shore cares.

When the dinner was over, the women withdrew to the Petite Saloon. Jim invited the dozen men of the President's party to take coffee, brandy, and cigars on the fantail. Here it was, the big moment. Jay restrained his eager patent-leather shoes from skipping outside. As plump as penguins, the men strolled onto the windy deck, the cool air a welcome tonic. The horsefaced Colonel Hugh Porter, Grant's chief aide, remarked to another aide how surprised he was at the President's high spirits. Jay's strained nerves sang.

On the wide, polished planks of the fantail, comfortable wooden deck chairs and pillows had been gathered into a semicircle facing the ship's rushing wake. The wind tugged at coats and ties, and it ran slippery fingers through Jay's beard. He felt tremendously excited, as if a thousand hornets whined in his chest and strained for release. Like an amused balloon bobbling along behind them, the full moon beamed down, its smile as rich as a clown's. The roaring flames of twenty hurricane lanterns, almost blown out by the stiff breeze, illuminated the rear deck with an eerie, fluttering light.

Grant sat down first. With the waggle of a finger Jim motioned Jay to take the chair facing Grant's. Jim settled himself into the one next to the President. As one official after another sat, a servant came forward to tuck a blanket under his legs. Small cups of hot black coffee were set on side tables next to each man, and French brandy was liberally splashed into balloon snifters. Fat Cuban cigars were passed around. The bracing coolness of the salty wind perfectly balanced the soporific effects of the large dinner, various wines, and snug blankets. This entire voyage, gangplank to cigars, had been orchestrated as carefully as a theatrical production, and Jay felt its power bearing him on to his mission's successful conclusion.

A servant went from deck chair to deck chair with a squeaky, covered tin lantern, into which each lounger poked his cigar for a light. While Jay never smoked—his stomach rebelled against far milder stimulants than cigar smoke—in order to blend in he accepted a cigar. The smoke that rasped his mouth was harsher than he expected.

Jay had agreed to allow Jim to open the discussion. For a few breezy moments, no one spoke. The moon spread a white glare over the dark Atlantic; the foamy rush of their wake slithered behind like a mile-long, Chinese dragon. The wind whipped them, picking at the loose ends of blankets. Cigar tips glowed briefly. Smoke streamed from noses and mouths. Occasionally the shouts of servants and the clink of dishes floated back from the kitchen. For a few brief moments time stood still, or in some mysterious way the powerful thrust of the steamer's hull through the ocean's bottomless black waters canceled time's passage. Then for five minutes they made small talk, Jim casually but sure-handedly maneuvering and selecting topics.

With a little wave to a servant, Jim made sure Grant had a topped-up brandy glass and a lit cigar. His face tilted expectantly, he turned to his partner. "Jay, you were telling me t'other afternoon about some fellers that come to see you," Jim said. As if the strong breeze were a servant of his, Jim raised his hand and flicked cigar ash into the windstream, which carried it over the stern. "Farmers, you said, worried about their wheat crops. What was that all about?"

With Jim drawing him out, Jay told the story of his boyhood

friends' visit. From there he launched into his vision of the financial future of the United States, briefly describing its strengths and weaknesses. Well aware how boring most people, and particularly Grant, found economics, he focused on the hard conditions that farmers of the Northeast, West, and South were facing after two years of poor crops.

"As you know, sir," said Jay, "here at home we transact business in greenbacks, but foreign merchants won't take them, will take only gold in payment. So an exporter in Philadelphia has to buy wheat with greenbacks and sell it for gold, and our importers must do the reverse. It takes a few weeks to complete these transactions, and if in the meantime the price of gold goes up or down much, it can wipe those traders out."

"How do they keep from losing their shirts, Jay?" asked Jim in an innocent voice.

"They pay to borrow gold," said Jay, "and sell that borrowed gold for the greenbacks they need to make their purchases. This is the function of the Gold Room, to grease the wheels of commerce, to allow the exporters and importers to sell today the gold they're going to get in three weeks, or buy today the gold they're going to need then."

Jay sensed he was losing his audience, and inwardly cast around for a less complex, less detailed, means of describing the market.

"A sharp rise in gold causes merchants to put up more greenbacks on the Gold Exchange against what gold they have borrowed," said Jay. "Our farmer gets the same greenbacks per ton, the foreigner gets more corn. Thus with the price of gold high, in the European market we can beat out the growers from the Mediterranean."

"The farmer gets the same price," said Grant in a puzzled tone, "but the fellow in London gets twice as much corn?"

Jay nodded. Simplify, simplify, simplify, he shouted to himself.

He plunged in again, hammering his main point—the high price of gold meant prosperity for the nation, its low price meant hard times. Once he was caught up in his argument, Jay made his points well. In fact, halfway through, the President's own chief aide, Colonel Porter, took Jim's place in asking questions. He drew Jay out as if he particularly wanted the President to hear this line of argument.

Recognizing from Colonel Porter's questions how little understanding he and Grant had of grain and gold markets, Jay went back over their mechanisms in simplified detail, leaving out the effects of short selling, the availability of letters of credit, and seasonal fluctuations. Now that Jay's cannons had found their targets, he pounded in shot after shot. Weakness in the gold market caused weakness in the wheat market. Indeed, last week the price of gold had fallen to 131 and wheat prices declined 20 percent, a steep enough decline, if it lasted into the fall, to bust every American wheat farmer. The nation's farmers had suffered poor harvests for two years; they couldn't stand another bad year. This very week grain traders refused to buy, and wheat receipts at ports had dropped sharply. It was up to America—particularly its leaders—to protect Americans' interests.

The steamer plowed on through the Atlantic's dark waters. Grant gave only an occasional grunt or a murmured yes.

In a calm, reasonable voice, Jay insisted that the government must support the price of gold or face dire consequences this winter: riotous strikes, factories' production halted, massive unemployment, deserted farms, trains rusting in yards, hunger, maybe famine, and yet more civil war. When Colonel Porter asked what the Grant administration might do to prevent this, Jay was forceful in his answer. "Halt the sale of the government's gold stocks until the first of the year."

With a glance at Grant, as if he wanted to make sure that the President grasped this point, Colonel Porter asked, "You're referring to the several thousand ounces the Treasury sells every month?"

"Yes."

"That doesn't seem much to do," said the aide.

"It's not," said Jay. "It will give the government the most effect for the least cost. It's like the rudder of a ship—not much in comparison to the bulk of the vessel, but mighty in steering it."

Grant spoke up. "But we'll lose all the income from gold sales."

With a thin smile of apology in Jay's direction for his chief's financial obtuseness, Colonel Porter said, "No, sir. We'll still have the gold we haven't sold, and with the price up, we'll recoup that through gradual sales after the first of the year."

"He's right, sir," said Jay. "It's a costless move. Just allow gold to rise. It will give our farmers a strong chance of selling their crops abroad."

There, thought Jay; after some initial confusion, he had made his points well, and he had asked for what he wanted. No other businessman—not even Jim himself—could have done better. Grant continued to puff silently on his cigar as if deep in thought.

After four or five presidential puffs, Colonel Porter asked, "And your interest here, Mr. Gould, as owner of the Erie, is in shipping these farmers' grain and turning a profit?" Jay hid a wince of embarrassment.

"Of course we stand to profit," said Jay more tartly than he meant to. He was troubled at this sliding by of his own purchases of gold. The thousands of yellow ounces he must now own, bought by Henry Smith and the Erie's other brokers, rose in his mind like a yellow mountain, but he wasn't arguing here for only himself and the Erie. "My main interest, Colonel, is to keep my countrymen solvent so we can continue as a republic. Remember the extremists in France. Prosperous men are not anarchists." Every civilized man shuddered at the bloody excess of the French Revolution, brought about because royalists ignored the people's basic needs.

"No offense, sir," said Porter.

"And none received," said Jim, stepping in. In his rich, warm voice was the peacemaker, the benevolent sage who would draw dissenting views into a satisfying close. "Gents, it's no secret that railroads such as the Erie are an important part of this nation's commerce. This winter, though, if the ugly picture my partner paints comes to pass, even a rich hugamug like Commodore Vanderbilt will feel Jack Frost bite his butt."

Dry and talked out, Jay was grateful to Jim, who knew how to ease over rough spots. Grant's cigar glowed a long time as he took a deep draw. The moon above the steamer no longer resembled a jovial face but a cool metallic disk. The long, white wake was only dissipating froth on a thousand fathoms of cold, black water.

"If our rails are tore apart," Jim went on, "it'll set this country back years."

"Maybe decades," said Jay. With no word or gesture had Grant indicated what he thought of their views. Except for the movements of his cigar to his mouth, he sat as stone-still as a statue, not playing with his mashed bullet watch fob, or scratching his beard, or licking his tongue over his teeth. Jay pressed on. "If our government doesn't support our farmers by keeping gold off the market, we'll see war before the first snow hits Washington."

Blue smoke streamed from Grant's mouth over the fantail rail. "But war, sir?" asked the President, his tone biting and skeptical.

"Civil war," said Jay. He had made it as plain as that inch-thick weed in his mouth, and still the old fool couldn't see it. "The collapse of gold will cause the collapse of agriculture, which will cause the collapse of our merchants and transport systems, rail and barge. Stockyards will be full of thin cows at giveaway prices. In our large cities able-bodied men will scrounge through trash for crusts. Farmers will march on towns. Hysterical depositors will make runs on banks. The frightened militia will be called out to protect merchants from food riots. Shots will be fired, blood will stain the snow. Children will go hungry, and honest men will be out of work as in the panics of '19, '37, and '57. Mobs will march on the offices of our mayors, governors—perhaps even on your own office."

These bold words hung over the fantail only an instant before the breeze scattered them across the moonlight. No one of the President's party said a word, as if the gala evening, the night's smooth, white-jacketed service, the bountifulness of the plump, hot roasts, the balm of rich wines, and the enchantment of the moonlit sea rendered such a bleak vision impossible. Yet these stout lizards stretched out beside Jay, swathed in white tie and tails, were skating over the Atlantic's vast, hungry depths. Let a boiler explode and they would find out how near they were to a thousand fathoms of horror.

All eyes watched the President. Grant stolidly pulled on his second cigar and stared off the fantail at the frothy, moonlit wake as if he had no response. Jay wanted to rise, shout at him, shake him.

"Sir," said Jim to the President, "if I may be so bold, what do you make of this future Mr. Gould has painted?"

Grant drank off his remaining brandy, threw back his blanket, and leaned forward as if to rise. Colonel Porter and several of his aides quickly stood, while those cabinet members still seated came to attention. Grant paused in the act of rising, freezing the company.

"It's late," he said. "It's been a fine evening, Mr. Fisk. It's time for me to retire." He glanced about, not looking anybody in the eye, before he continued. "I'd allow there's a certain fictitiousness about the prosperity of the country." He stopped, and his eyes darted about as if searching for words. "I don't know much about business. I'm a soldier. But I expect the bubble has to burst sometime, and it might as well burst one way as another."

"*Burst!*" cried Jay. A dozen moon-pale faces stared at him. As Grant rose, Jay and Jim and the entire crowd of officials stood.

"Yes, sir," said the President. "What expands like a balloon must deflate or burst." Jay's pallid face was startled, afraid.

"But, sir—*burst?*" asked Jay, his voice high and a little hysterical. "Is that wise?" Grant nodded in the stolid way of a stone man.

"And if it's burst we must have," he said, "better sooner than later." In face and voice he was the general overruling a youthful aide horrified by the number of casualties they would take in battle. "The explosion will be less severe. Good night, gentlemen." With a soldier's swift strides, the President marched off, followed by four aides and two servants. Horrified, unbelieving, Jay lurched forward two steps.

For a moment, the wind tugging at their dress tails, the remaining men shuffled awkwardly and said nothing. Then Colonel Porter spoke.

"The picture you paint has its alarming points, Mr. Gould. But if I may offer some insight as to how the President reasons, he doesn't believe the government should interfere with the natural course of the nation's business."

When Jay opened his mouth to argue, Colonel Porter held up his well-manicured hand.

"My opinion is that what you say may well be true. I'm only giving you the President's predisposition."

It was two o'clock in the morning on the rear deck of the *Providence*.

Shivering despite his change into a three-piece broadcloth suit, Jay hung over the rail. The ship's engines throbbed, and its screws propelled water before him in a loud, powerful rush. The steamer's wake was a faint whitish outline, ghostly dim now that the moon was sliding off to the other side of the earth.

"What are you doing out here?" came a voice behind Jay.

Jay jumped and spun around. A large dark figure. "Jim?"

"Yeah."

"You startled me."

Jim's bulk edged next to him along the rail. "Couldn't sleep?" asked Jim. The sleeve of Jim's velvet robe brushed Jay's hand. The breeze pulled his beard and made his trouser legs flap against his ankles and calves.

"I woke up," said Jay. "I had a terrible dream. I was in the bottom of a ship and water was rushing in. I was trying to save George and Helen and Nellie and the other children, but every time I grabbed their hands they slid away from me. Their fingers were slippery, greased or something. They were swept away through a hole in the hull. Pleading and crying for me. It was awful."

There was more, but he couldn't say it to Jim. Inwardly he recognized that he wasn't a great man after all, that all his recent thoughts of what he would accomplish were hokum. He had been the victim of his own pride, his own gilded flattery of himself. Always he liked to think of himself as a practical man first, a visionary second. Yet he had made the most elementary of practical mistakes: assuming that Grant was as intelligent and reasonable as the average person, and placing a large bet on the assumption. Stupid! He was little better than Wall Street's penny speculators, whose reckless handling of money Jay despised.

Jim grunted sympathetically. "I couldn't sleep at all." The dark fantail was bare of deck chairs, brandy cart, and warm blankets. The hammering vibrations of the steamer's engines were transmitted to

Jay's arms through the thick railing. The ship plowed steadily on through the dark Atlantic as if nothing untoward had happened on board this evening.

"What are we going to do?" asked Jim.

"I don't know," said Jay.

"We got to get out of all that gold."

The deck surged upward and fell in slow, regular waves. Jay's stomach swayed from side to side. *Burst!*—the word hung in the air like a large black sword, invisible in the night, threatening to slice off their heads. He liked to think he was on his way to becoming a great man—a great financier like Jay Cooke, a great industrialist like Cyrus Field, a great developer like Samuel Morse. He was no more than a mangy, runtish rat in a trap. Again his shoulders shivered.

"Yes," said Jay, "but it's not so easy."

"Suppose I have the Captain pull in someplace for water tomorrow morning," said Jim, craftiness larding his voice, "and you wire them brokers in New York to sell our position?"

"I've thought about that," said Jay. He had been in the brokerage business nine years to Jim's three. "What happens in the Gold Room tomorrow?" In the dark Jim shifted about as he turned this over.

"Well—we sell out—so much gold hits the floor—oh, God! I suppose the market will collapse, right?"

"Yes," said Jay. "And suppose I wire just one broker, ease out of a part of our holdings, what will happen then?"

Jim groaned. "Some telegraph operator or clerk or trader will figure out that a wire from the President's party to sell gold means him and his buddies should all sell gold."

"Right," said Jay. "So there's panic selling all day tomorrow. We get a huge margin call." A margin call was a trumpet blast from your broker demanding more money for your losing position, or he would sell you out. Given the size of their holdings, their not meeting a margin call with cash would cause their position, indeed the entire gold market, to collapse with the speed of a matchstick dollhouse under an elephant's foot.

"God, a margin call!" said Jim. "Let's don't put any more money in this damn market."

For a few minutes they were silent. The breeze was cold and dark. Jay pressed his shivering arms close to his ribs, but he didn't want a coat. Let the cold wake him up, make him shiver, punish him for making such a crack-brained mistake. He had been blind, arrogant, stupid.

"I kept wondering why the market didn't go up while you was doing all that buying," said Jim.

"Grant didn't listen to a word I said."

"We done all we could, Jay."

"I should have left well enough alone!" said Jay. "We've got to be careful. If we sell too fast, it'll push the market still lower." The varnished wood rail was cold and real to his moist palms, yet less real than the thousands of ounces of gold pressing against his shoulders. The firm rail kept him from falling off the throbbing deck, yet the gold on his shoulders pressed on him, trying to push him through the rail down into the Atlantic's black depths.

"You done what you thought best, partner," said Jim. He put his heavy arm around Jay, and for a moment Jay leaned into his partner's solid warmth. Then he shook him off.

"I feel terrible," Jay said. "I mean, I've done this to you as well as to myself and my family."

"The man that don't make mistakes ain't doing nothing," said Jim. "We'll work it out."

"Success, Jim," cried Jay. "Success is what's done this."

"*What?*"

"Beating Vanderbilt the way we did—our sales of stock, the Cattle Car War, the eight-million-dollar shellacking we gave him—made me cocky," said Jay, his voice high and shaky. "All my life I've worked hard, never expecting things to come easy. I've always worn plain black suits, nothing ever fancy, and wore them till they wore out. I don't spend on myself, really—no cigars, wine, trips to the racetrack, women, fancy horses—any sort of luxurious living—"

Jim put a restraining hand on Jay's arm. "Easy, partner, easy," his voice soothed. "Don't get yourself so worked up."

"What I wanted first was to be free," said Jay, his voice rising and shaking. "Free of my father, free of that damn farm, free of the tannery, free of my first partners Pratt and Leupp, free of Vanderbilt." He paused. "Now it's all about to be swept overboard."

"Hey, we been in rough spots before," said Jim in a warm, soothing tone. "We'll work together, work out of it. We bought the yellow stuff—it's worth something—we'll unbuy it." When Jay said nothing, Jim asked in a less confident tone, "Do you think we'll take much of a loss?"

Jay turned to Jim. In the dark, little of his partner's face was visible, but the shaky distress in the word *loss* was clear. The donkey on which the two of them were making their way over the mountain had slipped. One quivering, frightened hoof was stuck out over the precipice, and the overburdened donkey was tottering in its struggle to regain its balance. The least shove would send him over. The Erie hadn't earned a profit for three months, and not much of one over the past year and a half, so focused had they been on fighting Vanderbilt. All the money they had gathered from the sale of stock was now in margined gold. Their shipments of wheat, oats, and corn from the west were down. As a result of Grant's stupidity, these shipments would be off right through the harvest season. He and Jim faced heavy losses from their rail operations, and trading losses on top of these were even more disastrous. You could bluff your way through some bad times, but too many and your donkey couldn't find its footing and tumbled over the edge into the mountain's rocky gorge, carrying you with him.

Jay said, "I don't see how to avoid a large loss."

"Maybe we can still change Grant's mind," said Jim.

"He's too stupid to change his mind," said Jay. "Just pray none of those imbeciles around him understood what was said tonight and lets the cat out of the bag."

"Cat out of the bag?"

"To some reporter or gold trader."

"My God!" said Jim. "If they spill the beans to some smart trader, the market will collapse. We'll be ruined."

"That's the size of it," said Jay's dull voice.

"I don't see how that old war horse can act like this," said Jim. "There's nothing in the papers these days but editorials saying the same things you did. Maybe other investors will see it like we do and buy—force the market up no matter what he does."

"Yes," Jay answered, "and maybe bullfrogs will sprout wings and start singing like canaries."

The next morning the *Providence* looked huge and splendid easing into its slip at Boston harbor. On board a brass band played a sprightly march. Around Lucy Fisk, Jim's wife, hundreds of Bostonians, the well-to-do as well as ordinary workers, were dressed in their Sunday best even though it was Thursday. Flags waved. Bunting flapped gaily against the faces of wharfside stores. Yesterday's fluffy clouds were swept away; the sky was as blue and wide as a deep sea.

Lucy felt so excited she couldn't stand still—Jim bringing the President to Boston on his own ship! Under her voluminous skirts she bounced from foot to foot. A dozen sailors shouted at each other in their scramble to set up the gangplank. Where was Jim?

Several score policemen pushed Lucy and the other onlookers back. At the rail of the ship two dozen stern-faced men appeared, all dressed in black. Finally, there was Jim! Dressed in a morning coat, his brilliant diamond stickpins flashing like miniature suns, her Jim strutted among the shipboard officials. Led by three grim-faced Pinkertons, the officials filed down the gangplank. Jim was in their middle, his jovial face creased by a grin. With his air of easy command, her husband was the handsomest man there. When he saw her, his face lit up still more and he waved. Joy like fire flamed within her. The crowd clapped and shouted approval. Jim waved more vigorously to Lucy and the crowd. Such a look of delight proved how much he loved her.

From pictures in the newspapers, Lucy recognized the stout man with the blue eyes and salt-and-pepper beard as the President.

As the officials spilled off the gangplank onto the pier, she edged out of the crowd and around a policeman to run to Jim. He gave her a quick, hard embrace, and waved off a grim-faced Pinkerton. After he nuzzled her face, he took her arm and introduced her to the President. Grant's stubby fingers touched hers with the strength of a child or an old man, feebly, and he mumbled, "Pleased to meet you," while his blue eyes remained on something over her shoulder.

The Mayor and a self-important Pinkerton guided the President and his plain-faced wife to a large black brougham.

"What's going on, Jim?" she whispered.

"We're going to the Peace Jubilee," he said. "At the Coliseum." The new building, as magnificent as a cathedral, that rose on the north side. It had been two years in the building.

Lucy frowned. "We are?"

"Yes, indeed," said Jim, "you and me—in the President's party."

"Oh, my goodness!" It was hard to believe, but Lucy had almost given up marveling over Jim's surprising accomplishments.

In their carriage she was introduced to Jim's partner, Jay Gould, a small, balding man with a thick black beard. He smiled and said he had heard an awful lot about her from Jim, and that it was a pleasure. His eyes were the most intense she had ever seen, black eyes that lit on hers for several long seconds, that seemed to drive into her like long, thin knitting needles, then flitted on. Both Jim and the newspapers said he was smart, maybe the smartest man in New York, but as he stared at the passing street scene, he only looked distracted and sad.

In fact Mr. Gould didn't speak or look at her the entire way into the city. She thought he was the most nervous man she had ever seen. He stared out the window with the air of seeing little. He tapped his foot continually, drummed his fingers on his knee, and jumped at every shout or sharp noise. Like Jim, he was dressed in a morning coat, but unlike Jim it didn't look well on him, as if his tailor hadn't taken any pains, or as if he had lost a lot of weight after it was made. Still, she liked him. There was nothing fancy about Gould, but an air of solidity lay close to him, as if he was a man she could trust.

The closer the half-dozen carriages of the President's procession came to the Coliseum, the larger grew the crowds of pastel sunbonnets and dark felt hats that lined the streets. The crowd clapped. Jim leaned out the window and waved, and at his attention the crowd waved back frantically.

The Coliseum was an enormous structure—six stories high, several acres large—of granite, steel, and glass that had been built to house trade shows, fairs, and exhibitions. When they had pulled up behind the main hall, Jay Gould muttered something about sending some wires and opened the carriage door.

Jim restrained him with a hand on his arm. "You're not coming in with us?"

"Certainly not."

"But the ceremony!" said Jim. "With the President!"

"I can't spend another minute with that moron," he said angrily, and he spun away to disappear into the crowd.

"Goodness!" said Lucy. "What was that all about?"

"Things don't always work out the way you want," said Jim in a vague tone.

At the rear of the building she and Jim gathered with the President's party. They were introduced to the Mayor of Boston and the Governor of Massachusetts, who were puffed up at being in the presence of the President. Back here the hot air stunk of trash, rotting food, and the construction privies that still squatted nearby. A ring of several dozen policemen in the field that surrounded the building kept the curious at bay.

"Isn't this great?" whispered Jim.

Lucy nodded uncertainly. After a fidgety wait of five minutes under the hot sun, aides opened the back doors and announced that the hall was ready for the President. Lucy, Jim, and the officials—a shuffling knot of thirty people—entered and strode in a slow procession through a long passageway. They emerged into the main space of the new Coliseum.

Lucy had never been inside it. No cathedral had such a large indoor space. The ceiling arched upward so high it hurt the neck to look at its flying steel struts. And the people! There were thousands and thousands standing in front of chairs and on bleachers. It was more people than she had ever seen in one place, all clotted black on bleachers like flies thick on butchers' offal. Cheers and whistles rang against the overhead steel beams and echoed, hurting her ears. The roar of the people was as loud as Niagara the time she and Jim visited the falls.

The President's party made its slow way up the main aisle. Hot faces with wild eyes pushed toward Lucy, then were gone, pale scraps in a great flow. All over again she realized what a great service General Grant had done for his country. He had beaten the rebels and brought peace and saved the Union, and these thousands and thousands had gathered here to thank him.

Stolid, impassive to the applause, President Grant marched at the head of the little troop behind half a dozen Pinkertons. The staunch way he carried himself made a little thrill shoot up her spine; how lucky the country was to have such a solid man at its helm. Still, she felt awkward under the glare of so many thousand eyes. The eager faces on both sides appeared ready to surge forward and crush her. She could never be in the limelight. She maneuvered herself into the middle of the President's party, out of sight. Of course, Jim was just the opposite. He stepped to the outer edge of their group and gave a little bow and wave, then scampered back to the other side to repeat the performance. She smiled. How different were the two of them!

Against one wall was an eight-foot-high platform constructed of raw planks, which they approached. A row of thirty wooden straight chairs were lined up behind a pulpit, where the officials would speak. Huge American flags were draped above the platform and along the other three walls. Four twenty-foot-high portraits of Grant hung on the four walls, each festooned with red, white, and blue bunting.

Lucy's feet dragged when she was expected to climb the stairs onto the platform with the President. In front of all these people! But Jim didn't give her much chance to draw back. He grabbed her elbow and marched her up the wooden steps. The President sat down beside his wife and the Governor. Lucy sat and faced the cheering horde, which covered the bleachers and seats like a vast clustering of loud, angry insects.

Next to her was an empty chair. She looked around for Jim. He stood alone, to the right of the pulpit, out front at the edge of the platform. The eyes of the crowd were on him. He was taking bow after bow, as if it were him and not the President whom the crowd had come to see. Lucy started and her muscles tightened to rise.

"Jim! *Jim!*" she called, wanting to tell him he was making a fool of himself, but her call was lost in the roaring ocean of cheers, applause, and whistles. There must be a hundred thousand people out there.

Jim gave the crowd a final wave, then stepped backward as if to take his seat. She was relieved, but the cheers and applause rose, as if protesting his sitting down, a sound yet more deafening. With a self-deprecating wave and a reluctant shake of his head—as if the crowd was forcing him to acknowledge this new outburst—Jim turned and walked back to the edge of the platform. The cheers rose in appreciation, and as he bowed to the left, more cheers came in response. He bowed to the right, and from there they became louder, too.

"Jim!" Lucy shouted, but still he couldn't hear. At such a distance much of the crowd probably thought he was President Grant. Glancing to her right and left, she saw that the President, the Mayor, the Governor, and everyone else in the row of straight chairs was as shocked and frozen as she. From their startled looks, no one knew what to do.

Lucy's cheeks burned and she felt flushed. If it were her son Robert, she would have marched over and dragged him to his seat by his ear. But what could she do with a grown-up child who was, moreover, her husband? In the loudest shout she could muster, she said, "Jim, come sit down! This is not for you!"

But Jim, reared back, prancing and strutting about, again stepped to the edge of the platform and gave another series of bows to the right, left, and center—light, airy, adroit bows for such a plump, heavy figure. They were bows that thanked the audience for its generosity and at the same time modestly effaced the man who made them. The audience denied this effacement by applauding still more. Jim opened his hands in a final gesture that combined gratitude with a denial that he was worth so much praise, gave a final bow, and without turning his rear to the audience, backed up to plop down next to Lucy, his face a hot beacon of delight.

Lucy wished she could sink through the heavy planks so that nobody would associate her with the buffoon who had pranced before the crowd.

Part Four

BLACK FRIDAY

He that sells what isn't his'n
Must buy it back, or go to prison.
—Popular Wall Street jingle on short selling, attributed to Daniel Drew

22

*If we take hold of roads running all the
way to Chicago, we might as well go to
San Francisco and to China.*

—Cornelius Vanderbilt to William,
1869

Seated in his swivel chair, Cornelius Vanderbilt shoved himself away from the rolltop desk in his Central Railroad office and held up the twenty-dollar gold coin between thumb and forefinger. He cocked his eye at his son William.

"This gold piece is his calling card?" Cornelius asked, his voice incredulous. William's plump face was amused.

"His calling card," confirmed his son. "Yours to keep if you hear him out. If you don't have time to see him, he's going to call on Daniel Drew or Jay Cooke with his business." The bond merchant Jay Cooke was probably the richest man on Wall Street.

At the mention of his rivals in wealth, Cornelius snorted. He peered at the shiny gold coin, a Liberty Double Eagle with the date 1849 stamped on one side, the head of Liberty on the other. July morning sunlight flashed off the coin's shiny surface. What was this all about? he wondered. Perched atop the sixth floor of the large Central building, Cornelius felt through the floorboards the tremble and throb of his weblike empire across the continent: clerks inking figures in outsized ledgers, flushed messengers arriving with freight orders, the clatter of information flooding into telegraph rooms, the careful disbursement and collection of money by his finance managers. The Liberty Eagle looked real enough, and new, as if it had been packed in cotton for twenty years waiting for this moment. He gave the coin a little bite, and it had gold's sweet, metallic tang. His teeth left little bite marks on its surface, which meant it wasn't alloyed from some harder and baser metal.

"For a twenty-dollar gold piece, I'll hear the fool out," said Cornelius. "Show him in."

"You mind if I listen in?" asked his son, his grin announcing that the meeting would be great sport.

"Why not?" said Cornelius, wheeling about to face the door. He smirked. "Maybe we can get him to give you a calling card, too."

When his son had gone to fetch Mr. Gold Piece, Cornelius examined the yellow coin again. A Double Eagle held nearly an ounce of the precious stuff, and nobody passed them around like Elevated tickets. Back in the War it would have been worth $150 in "shinplasters," Mr. Lincoln's nearly worthless greenbacks, but today, with the price of gold dropping, it was worth about $75.

In the months since the Cattle Car War, Cornelius and William had devoted themselves to expanding the Central. If just yet they couldn't possess the Erie, and give themselves a shipping monopoly along the eastern side of the Central's network, then they would develop one on its western side and pick up the Erie after those fools dropped it.

Three strong rail lines in a series—as perfect as three pearls on a string around the neck of the Great Lakes—now served the Buffalo-Chicago route: the Buffalo & Erie went from Buffalo to Erie, the Lake Shore connected Erie with Toledo, and the Michigan Southern & North Indiana connected on west, Toledo to Chicago. They were such sound companies, and priced so high by Wall Street, that not even the Lion of the Rails and his son possessed the wherewithal to buy them.

Then several months ago Cornelius had discovered that Gould was trying to establish exclusive contracts with the three lines. Such a clever arrangement would supply the Erie with eastbound traffic in exchange for an Erie promise to ship them its westbound traffic. It showed Cornelius that he couldn't take his eye for a second off his alert, nimble opponent. In the normal course of business, Cornelius's Central exchanged a lot of traffic with the three lakeshore pearls. If they slid onto Gould's string, the Central would lose millions in revenues. On the other hand, if Cornelius could hook them up permanently to his operations—perhaps swapping some Central stock for theirs to cement the deal—he would create a powerful east-west rail system. Such a system might destroy the Erie, strangle it, by denying Fisk and Gould almost all of the long-haul east-west business that their line needed to grow. It would also begin the Central's domination of the eventual New York–San Francisco route.

A thin sharpie with a slight stoop and greased-back hair entered his office, followed by William. Cornelius regarded him closely. He had a cocky spring to his step, and he wore the black coat and striped trousers of a broker. The thin, V shape of his face made him look like one of those furtive night animals with long skinny bodies that burrowed, mole or ferret, but his eyes were those of a New Yorker—bright, cunning, sly. In some mysterious way his fast eyes danced over the whole room, saw everything, and fastened earnestly on Cornelius's face all at the same time.

In response to the wave of Cornelius's hand, he sat in the visitor's straight chair a few feet in front of Cornelius's own. Ready to enjoy the show, William settled his stout bulk on the horsehide sofa against the side wall.

"My name's Henry Smith, Commodore. And I come here with that Double Eagle as a sample of the profits I want to make for you."

"I own two brokerage firms," said Cornelius. "I ain't going to give you business 'cause you come in and give me a twenty-dollar gold piece." Smith leaned closer. More slick, cocky grin.

"I know that," said the sprightly voice. "I only brought that along to show you what's up."

Cornelius edged his chair back an inch. Gingerly he fingered the slippery gold coin, turning it over and over to stare at Miss Liberty and the Double Eagle as if searching for a flaw.

"All right, what's this all about?" Cornelius demanded. Clinging to Smith as closely as his slick hair oil was the gleeful air of his harboring a great secret about to explode.

"Some friends of yours are buying gold," said Henry, his voice smarmy. "I figured you might want to sell them some."

"Gold!" snorted Cornelius. "I don't deal in gold, I deal in railroads. Get out of here, Smith." The cocky broker inched forward, his straight-backed chair scraping along the oak floor.

"I didn't say you had to own any to sell them some, Commodore."

"Smith, you're talking riddles," Cornelius said. "I buy and manage assets that make me an income, not inert metal. I have all my life. I buy track and engines and steamers that bring in money. What I own makes me twenty-five cents a year on the dollar." Cornelius held up the gold piece and waved it in Smith's face, throwing a coin of yellow sunlight across the other's cheeks and nose. "I own this slippery, dumb stuff and it don't make me a dime. Just lays there and winks at me. Fool's gold, that's what I call it, and no thank you."

Smith's oily grin grew bigger. He turned to William, whose face was plastered with smug amusement, and shook his head in a pantomime of vast admiration. "Precisely what I've always said, sir. Your father's smarter than all the rest of them."

"Smith," said Cornelius, "you're wearing out my patience."

"Sir," Smith replied, "if I was to show you how to make some dollars in the Gold Room that would lay the Erie weak, would you be interested?" For a moment the atmosphere in the room, the various bumps and knocks from the Central building, the faint shouts of clerks, the din from Broadway—all that went dead, as if a foot-thick blanket of cotton had settled on the world. Cornelius was as stunned as if someone had snuck up behind him and whacked him hard with a solid goose pillow.

"The Erie?" he finally said. "The Erie ain't got nothing to do with gold." His own voice sounded hollow, small and far away.

"There's where you're misinformed," said Smith. Cornelius had heard such cocky, brisk voices before—from gardeners, trackmen, hack drivers who knew that they knew their own trade no matter how much money Cornelius was worth. The hard, bony tip of Smith's finger tapped Cornelius smartly on the knee. "All I ask is your word of honor that if you decide to buy and sell gold as a result of our talk today, I be your lead broker." To keep away from that hard finger, Cornelius swung his knees to the right.

"My word?"

"Yes, sir. On the Street the Commodore's word is as good as a gilt bond."

Cornelius felt exasperated and tricked. Anything that had to do with the Erie, he wanted to know about, but he didn't want to do business with Henry Smith any more than he wanted to buy gold. In his time Cornelius had done his share of speculation, but he had learned that, on balance, speculation didn't work. What did work was twenty-five cents on the dollar, year after year. Compounded annually, your investment doubled every three years, which meant in ten years each dollar became eight, quite fast enough for anybody to become richer. He knew a dozen men who made a fortune every year plunging in rails and gold, but the trouble with making big money easy and fast was that by that method's very nature you could lose your investment just as easy and just as fast.

"I'm going to listen, Smith, but I ain't going to do nothing with gold."

Smith held up his bony index finger with the fast, slippery air of an auctioneer about to stick a bidder with a dubious lot. "But *if* you do, sir," he asked, his voice rising dramatically, "do I have your *word* that you'll make me the lead broker in your arrangements?"

Damn it, he should never have accepted the gold piece, but he had to know what the Erie was up to.

"Since I ain't, okay," said Cornelius in a draggy, grudging tone.

Henry Smith then laid out the pattern of Jay Gould's and the Erie's purchases of gold over the past weeks. Cornelius's brow furrowed, and his stubby fingers rubbed his lips to hide his amazement. He knew, Smith said, of three brokers other than himself whom Gould had used. That a natural railroader like Gould and a railroad itself had bought gold was such bizarre news that Cornelius turned to frown at William, who shook his head in a worried, perplexed way. Cornelius did know that that damn fool Fisk was spending a small fortune renovating a white elephant of a theater on Twenty-third Street. If those two pups were buying this much gold as well, it meant that the Erie had stupidly stretched itself to its limits.

Cornelius again fingered the slippery gold piece and eyed the yellow luster of its finish. So Jay Gould wasn't so shrewd as not to fall under gold's siren charms! Thin tendrils of excitement snaked through his veins. His breath came in little airy puffs. He had to bridle the eagerness that pushed into his chest. He sniffed a coup in the offing, a big coup.

"You're suggesting we short gold?" he said in a cagy tone. In other words, place a bet that the price of gold would go down. Use that clever stock- and gold-market maneuver in which you sold gold before you bought it, with the expectation that you could later buy it back more cheaply. In this case, much more cheaply.

Smith sat back and beamed as if he were a schoolmaster and Cornelius his star pupil. "Yes, sir, exactly."

William's hands were on his knees, his grim face thrust out like a stuffy fellow who thought he had been insulted but wasn't sure. "They would have to be awfully big short positions."

Smith threw him one of his earnest, slick glances. "Of course, but the profits would be big, too."

William shook his head in disgust.

"You wouldn't have to come in alone," said Smith in a hurried way, as if he wanted to get in all the good parts before he left. "That's the beauty of working with me," the broker went on. "I have other customers who would come into a short pool, especially with the Commodore. Some pretty good size customers."

Cornelius nodded. "Me and my son here have to think this over."

Smith looked about and smirked as if the three were conspirators. "Yes, sir," said Smith. He stood. "But was I right to come in to see you?"

To give the Devil his due Cornelius bestowed a smile on him. "Yes, you were."

"Should I call back in a week, sir?"

"No, Henry, don't stay away that long," said Cornelius. "Come in on Friday. Maybe by then we'll have some business for you."

"No, Pa," said William as soon as the door closed behind Smith.

"Why not?" demanded Cornelius. As puffed up with righteousness as a preacher in a saloon, William stood up and paced across the office.

"Because as you always said, short selling is the work of the Devil."

"This is different."

William drove back toward the sofa. "How do you know he's telling the truth, or that his information is correct?"

"Of course we'll look into it first," said Cornelius, adding in an awed, forceful whisper, "We could put them out of business, William."

William answered briskly. "We don't know the gold market. You yourself have said a thousand times that twenty-five percent a year is enough."

"But we have a chance to obtain something of *infinite* value," said Cornelius, his voice purring over the word. "I'm telling you, we would have a lock on the transportation of this country for the next *thousand* years," giving this word a drawn-out growl of relish.

William's huffy laugh dismissed the notion. "You and I won't be around."

"You know what I mean." He meant that they would acquire an empire, a grip on this entire raw continent, that would not only make the name Vanderbilt shine forever but carry their greatest-grandchildren into the farthest, dimmest murk of the future as masters of their own destiny.

Father and son stared at each other. Finally William said, "Pa, you're seventy-six. Leave short campaigns to younger men."

The noise that jumped out of Cornelius's mouth was more a bark than a laugh. His blue eyes danced merrily and his head jerked about in eager movements.

"Son, I only want to look into this. I'm not dead yet."

William opened his mouth to speak, but like a fish spying a hook, he thought better and closed it. Cornelius grinned and went on.

"I'm an old hound, I know that," Cornelius said. "The last thing I want to do is lose anything I've built up so that you have less."

Again William opened his mouth to protest, but Cornelius held up his palm to cut him off. "I may be an old dog, but the musk of rabbit still gets me up off the hearth. I may have chased rabbits hundreds of times, but when the thousand and first jumps up, I jump up, too." He hung his head and shook it slightly, as if it was a minor failing, one that amused him. "A hound's made to chase rabbits. I'm made to run down rascals."

William sighed. "Pa, I want you to live as long as you can. I want you to have all the fun you can chasing rabbits. I don't like any of this gold business, but I won't stand in your way." Cornelius followed up quickly.

"Will you send somebody over to Drew's office and ask him to step up here?"

"Drew!"

"Who knows the Erie better?" said Cornelius. "He wants to make money. And there ain't nobody that knows how to sell short the way Daniel does. If we're going into a bear raid, I want the great bear himself and his money in my pool."

"C'neal," said Daniel Drew, "they was with the Gen'l on their boat for the longest time."

"General?" Cornelius asked, puzzled.

"That war hero in Washington—Grant," said Daniel.

Daniel Drew sat in Cornelius's office, his aged greenish-black topcoat pulled tightly across his chest despite July's heavy, muggy blanket of heat. All the lines of his bewhiskered, cadaverous face and long, lanky body were slanted down, as if some force in the earth was reaching up through the Central building's seven stories to pull him to it. His narrow shoulders, hollow cheeks, tight lips, and shifty blue eyes threw off an aura of caution, timidity, and petty meanness. Daniel had once been struck by lightning, and Cornelius wasn't sure he had ever completely recovered.

"They took the Gen'l up to Boston," said Daniel. "It was in all the papers. Boutwell was with them." Secretary of the Treasury.

Daniel narrated the story, which startled Cornelius although he didn't let his old rival see it. He leaned back in his swivel chair to ponder this news. He was glad William wasn't here. Daniel was right. Gould was no dummy. Very likely he was buying up all this gold because the President had assured him that the Treasury would help drive up the price. The President probably had a secret account at some brokerage that Gould had ties to. The Treasurer was there to seal the bargain. One day the price would shoot up suddenly. All those purchases that Gould had cleverly made in a weak market would be worth a fortune. He would adroitly unload everything onto eager fools.

Cornelius asked, "You think they got his ear? That Grant's in with them?"

"They got something," said Daniel. "That Gould now, he's got a shrewd mind. And he's tough as a bobcat. Bold, tough, and shrewd. I tell you, if he's buying gold, C'neal, I'm tempted to buy some myself." Daniel might appear thinner and more frail than ever, but with the subject millions in profits, his blue eyes glittered with a crazy eagerness.

Cornelius took the Double Eagle out of his vest pocket, and for the twentieth time over the last twenty-four hours, he rubbed it between his thumb and forefinger and scrutinized it. Since Henry's visit yesterday he had carried it about as a lucky piece, but suddenly it didn't appear so talismanic. Its seductive wink was really a bear trap with steel teeth. It would fasten first onto his leg, then his entire purse, and finally drag him down the way it had destroyed thousands of foolish speculators. Thank God he hadn't really listened to Henry Smith.

For several silent moments Cornelius and Daniel eyed each other with the scarred, battle-weary wariness of two aged pit bulldogs.

Finally Daniel said, "C'neal."

"Yeah."

"Do you think Jay Cooke might come in with us on a bear pool?"

"Jay Cooke," mused Cornelius. "In gold?"

"In gold," said Daniel. Over his thin face, stubbled with patches of white whiskers like a poorly cut field of hay, crept a sly expression. "After all, Cooke is General Grant's bond man. The man that raised all the millions it took for him and Mr. Lincoln to win the war. Now, you tell me, what's a rise in the price of gold going to do to Mr. Cooke's bonds—his huge fortune in *margined* bonds?" Cooke's brokerage made a market in U.S. government bonds, which meant he carried hundreds of millions of dollars of them by borrowing ninety-five cents on the dollar. Cornelius grinned as he saw it.

"Bring 'em down in price."

"Way down," said Daniel.

"Maybe bankrupt his firm."

Daniel lifted his scrawny chin to scratch the white stubble there with a clawlike fingernail, the rasp as loud and rough as a dry twig on granite. "We want the price of gold to go down, Gould wants it to go up. What's the natural thing that Jay Cooke is going to do?"

Cornelius said, "Help us drive down the price."

A crafty grin twisted Daniel's thin lips. "That's right."

"He would know what Grant was going to do, wouldn't he?" speculated Cornelius.

"He would," said Daniel. "He would make it his business to know." There was nothing aged in his face now; it looked as merry as a toddler's in his bath. "And if he comes in with us, puts his money up, then we'd know he had the straight gin on Grant, wouldn't we?"

Cornelius said, "He wouldn't come in it without checking with the War Hero." They grinned at each other. "I think you got something, Daniel."

"I think so, too," said Daniel, his grin sly and broken.

"I'll make it my business to talk to him this week."

"I'll come back in Monday," said Daniel, rising to leave. "We might do some selling as early as next week."

23

*Miss Mansfield is of a full, dashing
figure. Her eyes are large, deep and
bright, and inclined to Chinese in type.
Her purple-black hair, worn in massive
coils over a well-shaped head is a
wonder in its luxuriance and native
gloss.*

—*New York World*, 1870

The morning after his triumphant trip to Boston, Jim Fisk charmed his way past Josie's Negro servant Carter and snuck upstairs. Held before him, as a peace offering, was a present wrapped in white tissue and tied with a broad ribbon of red satin. He knocked on the parlor door, and when Josie opened it, he spoke first.

"I'm awful sorry!" he said, his balloon face slumped in apology.

Her features sagged and her shoulders drooped. "Oh Jim, I've been such an awful fool!"

"Josie!" he bellowed, and he charged into the room and swept her off her feet. As he kissed her a dainty shoe clattered to the floor. Her body went slack and spongy under his hands, like an overripe peach in greedy, hungry fingers, and her mouth mashed against his. The taste of her was an exotic compote of wild fruits and liquors— Persian pomegranates, wild California cherries, resinous wine of the Mediterranean. She sobbed. He groaned. Their swaying bodies knocked over a round side table draped with a fringed green cloth. A magpie collection of jade boxes, photographs in silver frames, and bits of old ivory and amber rattled across the oak floorboards.

They cried and moaned and kissed and held each other tightly, and their faces became slippery with kisses and tears. As they finally broke away, he almost laughed out loud at the thunder of the imaginary audience's applause. The lovers were reunited! The impresario had triumphed again!

"I wish I could have taken you," he apologized. He let her feet come to the floor but held her tightly against his chest. "You would have made those old fogies sit up straight, believe me."

"I just hate so to be hidden away, Jim," she said. "Like something you're ashamed of. I want to go everywhere with you."

"I had to be as proper as Peter or blow everything. The President has to be real careful what the papers write about him."

The tissue-wrapped box lay amongst the scattered jade boxes and bits of ivory and amber spilt across the floor. He bent to pick it up.

"Here, looky what I brought you from Boston."

For a long time Jim slept. When he woke up, lengthy shadows were creeping through the wooden Venetian blinds behind the heavy curtains of red-and-gold filigree.

"I got to hop," said Jim, but still under her spell, he didn't move. Sweet French perfumes and rose-scented talcs wrestled with the sour odors of sweaty sex. He kissed her soft, bare shoulder. "Got to get back to the office and get ready for tonight."

As soon as the words popped out, his eyes opened wide. He was fully awake now, aware that he had said the wrong thing. He sat motionless, waiting to see whether the bird was going to fly through the cage door that he hadn't had the God-given sense to leave shut.

Josie sat up in bed, wearing only the moonstone-emerald bracelet and earrings that he had bought her. She made no attempt to cover herself. Not even the girls who worked the cigar-store brothels liked you to see them naked. Sitting straight-backed, not four feet from him, she was voluptuously beautiful. Her breasts, tipped by pink-tender nipples, were firm and high. Her skin glowed with the sumptuous promise of a cream-white bonbon from Pietrello's. The lush, exuberant patch between her legs was as richly tangled as an overgrown blackberry bush.

"Oh, my God," she gushed. "It's tonight!"

He could only grin foolishly and plot some way to entice the bird to hop back into its cage. "Yeeees," he said in a low voice that wasn't definite about anything.

"Whatever am I going to wear?" she mused. "What time will you pick me up, Jim?"

With all the innocence he could muster, he asked, "Pick you up?"

"Tonight."

"Oh—tonight!"

She laughed, but it had a spasmodic, rusty edge to it. "It's only the biggest night of our lives."

"Well, there is a little problem." Thank God for the expensive emerald bracelet and earrings! They had to do double duty now, bail him out of not taking her to Boston and not accompanying him tonight.

"Problem?" Her plump features sharpened.

"The old war horse wants to come, and I just couldn't say no."

"The old—? President Grant!" First her face blossomed with joy at the idea of sharing a box with the President, then darkened. Jim reached for her hand, but her creamy fingers evaded his and jerked the pink sheet up around her torso. "*Nooo*, Jim."

"I'm sorry, Josie. Really, I am." He reached for her in order to comfort her, but she pulled away. She stood, turned her back to him, and wound herself in the folds of the pink sheet. She walked away.

"Can't you see?" he pleaded. "Caesar has to be above suspicion."

"Caesar? What's he got to do with this?"

"Newspaper reporters will be writing about him," he said. She turned, the pink sheet wrapped around her full figure, her face a scramble of planes and lines as if she was about to cry. Why couldn't the curtain come down right when the impresario needed it the most? Women got their feelings hurt so easy. You did everything you could to please them, but it never was enough. When it got down to getting your feelings hurt, there wasn't a feather's worth of difference between Josie here and Lucy in Boston or any other companion he had enjoyed over the past four years. He said, "I'll make it up to you."

"You can't make this up to me," she said. She was bent forward, elbows tight at her ribs to hold the sheet to her, tears overflowing her brown eyes. "This is the only opening night the Grand Opera House will ever have. I won't be there, and everybody will know I'm nothing. They'll know that I'm only the woman you stuff when you want something outside your marriage—"

"Stop it, Josie!" he shouted. "You know I love you."

Arms tight against her ribs, hands clenched into fists, she said, "All I am is your high-priced fancy lady. Give her some jim-cracky jewelry, and every now and then buy her a new dress. She's just a child, happy and carefree whenever she gets a stupid trinket—right?" Her creamy, dark-lined face broke into its component parts and tears once again spurted over their dams. She wailed, "All I am to you is a whore!"

Naked, he got out of bed and came toward her. "Don't touch me," she shouted. "You're just a coward, that's what you are. I'm an actress, an *artist*. Of course they don't want to accept me. I don't live by their stupid rules. I *thought* that was one of the things you *loved* about me."

He lowered his head and thought about it. Decent ordinary folks might allow themselves to be jollied along by "Jubilee Jim," as the papers continued to call him, and he might be able to twist reporters this way and that, but there wasn't no way that decent, ordinary, respectable folks would forgive him for flaunting Josie in a public display with its most august public official.

"Hey," he said. "Cut it out." He raised his hand to get her attention. "You have the best of me, the best there is. You have a good time when you're with me, except when you get your own nose turned out of joint. I give you everything you want, near about—more than any man I know does his wife. I certainly don't shutter you up the way a lot of fellows do them as is married to them. I take you more places than anybody you or I know ever takes his wife. You ain't got it so bad."

"Get out of here!" she shouted. "You make me sick."

The venom in her voice shocked him. This was no time to stick around. Keeping an eye on her, he reached for his clothes. She glared at him as he dressed. The crystal doorknob felt as welcome as a plank to a drowning man. He threw back, "I'll see you tomorrow."

"You'll see me tonight."

Still gripping the knob of the bedroom door, he turned back and said, "Now, Josie—"

"Have somebody leave me two tickets at the box office," she yelled. "And don't you dare tell me I can't go to the theater tonight like you did that boat trip." He had been about to, but thought better of it. Maybe this was a way out.

He cautioned her, "You can't sit in my box, now."

She screamed, "Who *wants* to sit with you and that old White House boozer?"

"Will two be enough?" he asked in a deferential voice.

"Two will be fine. But make it a private box."

"A private box?"

With injured pride, she sniffed back her tears and said, "It's the least you can do. A private box."

At a quarter hour before eight the impresario, ribbon-bespangled chest stuck out proudly, escorted his distinguished party of six—

President Grant and his wife Jenny, Jay Gould and Helen, and Bill Tweed and his wife Mary Jane—under the gilded vault suspended over the lobby of the Grand Opera House.

Up the wide marble stairs, down the narrow hall to the proprietor's private box. Because of the tragedy of Lincoln's final night, dozens of federal troops with rifles were stationed in the hall. Jim and his guests seated themselves in plush chairs. An obsequious servant took orders for wine and coffee. Below, across the large auditorium, the rows of red velvet seats were filling.

The specially printed, gilt-edged programs were handed around. Jim explained to the President, Jenny—as he now called her—and his other guests that tonight's spectacular, *The Twelve Temptations*, was based on the Walpurgis Eve, a popular German legend, and that it would be done in the style of *The Black Crook*. He nodded toward the twenty-five-foot-wide bronze chandelier on which dangled five thousand leaves of Polish crystal.

"How do you like the new light, Mr. President?" Jim asked. The yellowy rays of its two hundred gas jets reflected off the thousands of crystal leaves, and the warm breeze from the hot jets made the leaves tinkle like innumerable tiny bells. Grant's somber eyes regarded the mammoth fixture warily.

"Won't fall, I hope."

Jim laughed heartily, slapping his thigh at the presidential wit. "No, sir, I supervised its installation myself. Up inside the ceiling it's on a chain bolted to four rafters."

The President nodded in agreement, his eye cautiously lingering on it.

Jim sat back, as exultant as a king on a gold throne. Tonight was a fabulous start! Every one of the twenty-six hundred seats was sold. The last two hundred went yesterday afternoon after Jim leaked the news that the President would attend the opening.

The times were a-booming, and Jim was riding at the top. From listening to Jay, he had come to see that the War had profoundly changed the country, given it a real shot of juice. Tested by war, the Union had proved its strength, and with its attitude of forbearance toward the South was exhibiting a maturity few European countries could match. Scarcely realizing it, the thirty-nine million people of the United States had come to exceed the population of every European nation, excepting Germany's forty-one million. Jay claimed that the country was shifting from an agricultural economy to an urban and industrial civilization. Jay followed such things, whereas Jim kept up with what regular folks talked and read about. Jim saw that since the War folks weren't only reading the English books of the day—*Alice's Adventures in Wonderland* and stories by Charles Dickens—but their countryman Bret Harte's stories, too, and Mark Twain's *The Celebrated Jumping Frog of Calaveras County* and *Innocents Abroad*. Two years ago Horatio Alger had published *Ragged Dick*, which had made Jim cry and shout as he read it. It had become a sensation. Louisa May Alcott was charming little American ladies with *Little Women*. In Paris, Offenbach's *La Vie Parisienne* and *La Grande-Duchesse de Gérolstein* might be all the rage, but over here *The Black Crook* was packing them in nightly. Jim figured that pretty soon the Newnited States could take its rightful place next to any nation of the world, and about time. Certainly, he thought as he gazed in deep satisfaction at his chandelier's hundreds of gas jets, in bringing *The Twelve Temptations* to New York, he was doing his part as a citizen of the world.

As the well-dressed crowd strolled to their seats, their heads craned about to take in the broad expanses of red velvet, the walls of intricate gilt, the startling chandelier, the flying nymphs and satyrs, and the occupants of the expensive boxes. Jim thrilled to the start on their faces when they spotted him and the President chatting in his own private box. They openly gawked before swiveling their heads downward, as if abruptly realizing that by staring they announced themselves no more cultivated than country folk. All the while, hands folded across his ample belly, Jim smiled benevolently. It had been a long struggle from muddy Brattleboro to this velvet-lined box, but the audience saw clearly that the Impresario had Triumphed!

Tweed's wife Mary Jane was leading a conversation about New York's schools with the other ladies; Grant, Bill Tweed, and Jay Gould silently studied their programs. Across the theater from his party's box was the two-seat private loge that Jim had reserved for Josie. It was one of the best boxes in the house, one from which she would see the stage well and be seen by everyone. He idly wondered which of her actress friends she would bring. He had made sure her box was too far away for her to call to him, yet close enough so that he could smile and give her a friendly nod. A pair of really first-rate tickets was the least the impresario could do for such a good trouper.

With only minutes to go before the curtain, however, Josie had not arrived. Her pair were about the only two unoccupied seats in the house. Jim fidgeted. Damn her! It hadn't been easy even for him to get such special seats. He was going to be burned up if she didn't use them out of some damn female notion of spite.

A movement in the red velvet at the rear of the empty loge caught his eye. Josie pushed the velvet curtain aside and stepped into the box.

Her new scarlet gown was stunning, daringly suspended across the exposed white tops of her full breasts in a way that challenged gravity. Her dark hair had been swept up and piled on her head in a fashion that made her appear taller, even imposing. Carrying herself upright in a regal manner, she stood above the rows of orchestra seats like a queen before commoners. How lovely! Jim's chest swelled with pride and love.

However, her gaze didn't settle in his direction, although of course she knew exactly where he and the President sat. Jim sighed. He reckoned his regal flower-blossom was still hurt. Sooner or later she would glance over and see him and his important friends, but at the same time Jim was relieved that she was a good enough trouper not to embarrass him.

Confusion and a slight sense of shame crept over him. She had been forced to come by herself. Certainly, if it had been up to him alone, he wanted her by his side tonight of all nights. Propriety ought to be damned. He was a fool to let the small minds of others dictate that he not enjoy the company of such a lovely, independent creature. She openhandedly gave him everything she had, and like some filthy hermit of the swamp who found a white satin pillow, all he did was drag her through the mud and carelessly fling her about his dirty cave.

Tonight at dinner she would have been a whiz at making the stodgy Grant, rockified Bill Tweed, and the worried Jay Gould loosen up, a service she performed with a bold flair whenever he needed a hostess to make a few stiff skates let down their hair. God knew the silent old screech owl needed something to stir up his blood; being around the stolid Grant had convinced Jim that the White House was a boring place and that being president was a boring job. Folks had a lot of respect for it, that was for sure, but did the President need to act like a stuffed hat all the time? Well, if Jim was ever president—and why not?—he wasn't going to act like any stuffed owl, you could bet your last gold nickel on that.

In the box across the way the velvet curtain swayed again. An erect young fellow entered Josie's box wearing a perfectly tailored set of white tie and tails. Well, good for her, Jim thought; she got somebody besides one of her girlfriends to come with her. He understood that. Hell, if he had been in her place he would have done the same thing.

From the crowd below arose a buzz. Jim glanced down. Josie and the slim young fellow's entrance had provoked a stir, for scores of pale, oval faces were turned upward. Chatting together, Grant and Jenny had taken no notice. In fact the President was still staring at his program and stabbing at it with a stubby finger as if only hard, thorough work would make the evening's performance intelligible.

The pale ovals below swiveled to stare at Jim. As the buzz intensified, Jim grasped that the audience—knowing his and Josie's story only too well from New York gossip and what was hinted at in the papers—supposed that the two of them had suffered a falling-out. They would further suppose that she had taken up with this slim young fellow. Jim had seen this dark-haired youth with the long, thin face and sharp widow's peak before—where was it?

With a start that made him wiggle about on his velvet cushion, he recognized the dandy's features—Ned Stokes, Annabelle's former husband! The charming fellow that Jim had sold cotton to at least half a dozen times during the War, the one whose firm had gone broke afterward. Jim glanced uneasily at Jenny—this was the heel who had divorced her sister—and prayed that being in the same theater wouldn't prove so embarrassing that she and the President would have to leave.

Ned must have come into a pot of money lately. Not only did he wear a spanking-bright set of evening clothes, but the gems sparkling on his shirtfront were diamonds. Nothing else winked blues, golds, and pinks like that. Jenny Grant spied Ned, stiffened, and gasped. Ned bowed toward her in a single grave, dignified nod. She made a half wave back with her closed fan, and she leaned over to whisper urgently to the President. He shook his head no.

Relieved, Jim sat back. The orchestra was making the practice honks, scrapes, and drum beats that said the show was nearly ready to start. The giant chandelier's jets dimmed. Ned leaned forward to whisper in Josie's ear. She giggled behind her half-opened fan as if she were a debutante to whom a charming rake had told a naughty but entertaining joke.

While the house lights were dimming, more and more of the audience craned their necks backward to watch Josie and Ned—and at the same time catch Jim's reaction. Jim stared resolutely at the closed stage curtain. Damn it, did all of New York know Josie was his best girl? It was embarrassing to have folks believe that an empty-headed fop like Ned had somehow stolen her from him. Josie didn't realize what her innocent escort was making people think. Sure, this fellow was handsome, but he didn't have any real money. Sure, he came from a fine family in Philadelphia, but that family wasn't going to help him any more after he had busted half a dozen of them in his cotton brokerage. To buoy his own spirits as well as the President's, Jim turned to his guest of honor.

"Now the fun starts!" he said.

The red curtain swept open, and the music dashed forward in a brassy leap. The cleverly painted flats depicting the Ancient Convent were lit up as bright as midday by brilliant limelights. The troupe of coryphées and a full corps of ballet dancers pranced about the Mill of St. Donatus. Red, green, and yellow skirts flashed about actresses' bare thighs. During the First Temptation, smiles and shouts from the stage flew into the audience like flocks of gaily-colored birds. The cast of two hundred entered, danced, sang, and exited, flawlessly meeting their cues.

Yet to Jim this busy spectacle seemed seventy-five miles away, not seventy-five feet. Several afternoons in rehearsal he had watched it with a deep glow of pride and satisfaction; now the actors' shouts rang distant and phony, their costumes were so many yards of brass-flecked cloth, and their lively faces the stale product of a heavy hand with greasepaint. He didn't care whether Ulric, "the Lost Soul," found his spirit, or whether Rudolph, "the Tempter," and Kalig, "the Spirit of Evil assuming many forms," were punished. Who cared who won the Grand Tournament when Ned Stokes was leaning over Josie's shoulder to whisper something wickedly enticing into her cocked ear?

Her saucy fan, spread to its full width, was again up. For the tenth time it hid her expression and any chance of reading what her mischievous lips said in return to Ned's amused, attentive face.

Jim tore his gaze away. He said something he hoped was amusing to Grant, who merely grunted. He made a firm resolve not to look across at their box again tonight. All he was doing was stupidly torturing himself by imagining that she was interested in Ned. Below, a few dozen of the audience were still turned away from the stage's prancing tumult to stare up at him and over at Josie's box. Several nudged their companions and whispered to them, causing them to glance upward, too. Like a man forcing his tongue to leave a rotten tooth alone, Jim stared fixedly at the stage for the next quarter hour, which lasted as long as a year's torture.

Horns blared. The Cataract of Terror by Sunset, even with its cascades of Real Water, only irritated him. The shouts and overly bright colors jarred his brain and gave him a headache. The Grand Triumphant March of Clergy, Knights, Esquires, Banner Bearers, Soldiers of All Nations, the Emperor of Germany, Ulric, and the populace of Flanders, singing "Hail to the Beauteous and Brave," took a hundred years to stream past. As they finally exited and the noise died, a light clatter made Jim turn to his right. Grant's square head had sunk onto his chest, and despite the discomfort of his straight chair, the President was snoozing.

Jenny Grant gave Jim a wry grin. Jim's smile said not to bother the weary statesman as he gained his much-needed rest. He hoped like hell no reporter saw that the play was too boring to keep the President awake.

Every time he could bear the suspense no longer and snuck an offhand glance—a dozen times an hour—the two were as busy as actors onstage. Either Ned was leaning over her, whispering, his eyes plunging down the top of Josie's dress, or she was leaning back, nearly popping out of the silky suspension across her chest, to whisper to him. Their heads were hidden behind the pink-and-white spread of her fan, which had to be the biggest damn one ever made. With it open, only her eyes and the bottom part of her white bosom could be seen. Ned would duck behind it, so that Jim had no idea what he was doing there—kissing her neck, blowing in her ear, or tracing her cheek with a couple of languid fingers. With the dexterity of a stage conjurer presenting birds and silk handkerchiefs, she used that cunning fan to hide as well as reveal giggles, winks, and half a hundred flirty glances.

And Jim, shifting from side to side on his narrow, cushioned chair, could do nothing, although he thought of plenty. Run downstairs, snatch a horsewhip from one of the carriages, and publicly thrash Mr. Stokes. Have a few of his stage roustabouts drag the fop down the marble stairs, his elegant head thumping along the steps, and throw his pretty carcass into Eighth Avenue. Grab one of those stage swords and carve him a new bunghole.

The busted cotton trader was no gentleman. Josie, he understood. She had expected Jim to escort her here tonight, and this was her way of getting even. She was angry and she was hurt. She had started something with Stokes that she probably had no idea how to handle or how to finish. She didn't realize how awful it looked for Jim. But Stokes, he should have been a gent. He was raised to be one. All right, bring her here, sit quietly, and take her home. But to carry on in this shameless way, to force Josie to act as if more was between them than there was, making her appear as cheap as a tramp—this was the act of a cruel heel, no gentleman.

Yet worse than not enjoying his night of triumph and not knowing what was going on behind that fan was the continued curiosity of the audience. To judge by the incessant craning of heads and the whispers that rose like swamp vapors from the orchestra seats, this side drama was provoking as much interest as what was happening onstage.

Yet it dragged on and on. Jim wiggled, and he fidgeted. The heat rose over him from the banks of limelights. The Dungeons of the Inquisition were torture. The Desert and Distant View of the City in

Flames roasted him. The Superb Transformation Scene—with Eight Senses, Five Graces, and the Temple of the Muses in the Golden Palace of Contentment—almost pulled him, roaring, to his feet to release his compressed fury.

So it went for three weary, exhausting hours. Onstage it might have been a good performance, it might not—it was lost on Jim. He spent his life's greatest evening struggling to keep his eye on the brightly lit stage, listening to Grant snore, and straining to keep himself from so much as peeking across the abyss of theater at the playlet between Josie and Ned Stokes. By the time the curtain finally rang down, his shirt and two handkerchiefs were as wet as if they had come out of a hot washtub.

Damn them both, damn Josie and damn Ned Stokes.

The greatest night of his life had been ruined by their making a fool of him in public. Even if she hadn't realized what she was doing, he wasn't going to be quick to forgive her for this.

24

There are few palaces wherein so rich a coup d'oeil could be presented as that of the main offices of the Erie Railway Company. The carved woodwork, the stained and cut glass of the partitions, the gilded balustrades, the splendid gas fixtures, and above all, the artistic frescoes upon the walls and ceilings, create astonishment and admiration at such a blending of the splendid and the practical. Mr. Fisk, who planned and superintended the arrangement, has certainly reason to be proud of the result, there being nowhere in the country or in Europe anything of the kind to compare with these splendid rooms.

—*New York Sun,* 1869

On a blisteringly hot morning late in July, Jay Gould picked through the filthy rubble and construction scaffolding on the third floor of the Opera House looking for Jim Fisk. When completed, this vast floor of plaster dust, open lath work, and grime would be the new corporate headquarters of the Erie Railroad.

Jay found his stout partner, dressed in a workman's blue overalls and a white apron made out of enough canvas for a dozen carpenters, at the southeast corner of the floor. Around Jim's girth was a broad leather belt adorned with carpenter's tools—an awl, two rasps, a hatchet, a miniature crowbar, a keyhole saw, two hammers, and pouches for a half-dozen sizes of nails.

"What's this going to be?" yelled Jay over the din. They stood in the middle of a giant-sized rib cage of two-by-four struts. "The conference room?" Under his broad canvas apron, Jim's proud belly shook with laughter.

"*My* office," he shouted. "Like it?"

Jay's face frowned with displeasure. "It's big enough for five offices," Jay shouted back.

"It ought to be," said Jim. "I ripped out six of the rabbit holes that was in here to make it." The noon whistle blew and the din became silent.

Jay wrinkled his thin, pale face and shook his head at this waste of space. He handed Jim a thick, ivory envelope.

"I want you to go here this afternoon."

With a puzzled look, Jim examined it and said, "Isn't this an at home from Mrs. Stokes?"

"Yes," said Jay, glancing away.

Jim leaned forward and peered at him closely. "Are you all right?"

"I'm fine."

"You don't look so fine." With the rough insistence of a mother scrutinizing a sickly child, Jim's grimy hand tilted Jay's face into the sunlight. "Your eyes are bloodshot, and you got bags under them. Your skin is paler than ever. I swear you've lost weight. You been sleeping—or walking the streets at night?" Jay jerked his head away.

"Jim, I—" His shoulders sagged. "What's the use? Walking. I can't sleep." They owned too much gold: forward contracts for fifty thousand ounces, ironclad agreements that pledged them to a ton and a half of bullion. Over the last two weeks, since they had returned from the Boston Peace Jubilee, stomach cramps, chills, and the shakes had made Jay twist and turn all night long. Almost every midnight he rose and, like some restless ghost or night beetle, walked from the Battery to Central Park, from the East River to the Hudson. Night after night he was forced to exhaust himself to obtain even a few hours of precious sleep. Jim put his thick arm around Jay's bony shoulders.

"We'll work it out, partner," said Jim gently. Normally Jay didn't like being touched, but for a moment he relaxed against Jim's hot, robust strength. "You shouldn't be so hard on yourself." Jay pulled away, his face contorted in a shadowy mask of pain.

"I was so stupid," he said, his voice full of self-loathing. "I was sure Grant would see reason."

"Have you been able to sell much?"

"Every time I even dip my toe in the market, the current nearly rips my foot off."

"What!"

"I'm telling you." Jay's voice possessed an hysterical edge, wavering and uncontrolled. "I sell a thousand ounces, and it's like a riptide starts in the Gold Room. I have to go back in and buy fifteen hundred or two thousand ounces to keep the market up."

"You're not buying more!"

"I've had to, I'm telling you," said Jay. "If I let a panic get started, the whole gold market will collapse."

"Hold on, now." Jim's hand clasped his forearm in a firm grip. "I've never known *you* to panic."

Jay pulled away. "It only gets worse and worse. If I didn't know better, I'd say somebody in the Gold Room is after us." He nodded at the invitation in Jim's hand. "You go this afternoon."

Jim's ruddy, mischievous features sobered, and he regarded Jay with a shrewd gaze. "What's happened?"

"Nothing." Jay tried to make the word neutral, but it came out with a high, screechy note.

"I ain't no employee like Morosini," said Jim. "I ain't going nowhere till I get the real scootch." Jay sighed and turned to stare out the window. Not a whiff of breeze stirred.

"I can't go back," Jay said, unable to face Jim. Roasting in the July sun, Manhattan resembled an elaborate maze of boxlike structures, boxes within boxes, a labyrinth constructed by a careless, cruel giant determined to discover how much pain its diminutive inhabitants could absorb. Married to a drab hen, he was confined to this coop of a city. "We kissed that last night."

"Ha!" said Jim boisterously. "Did she kiss you back?"

"Did—?" asked Jay. He hung his head. "Yes."

Jim maneuvered around to Jay's side. "Hooo!" he exclaimed. "A real smacke*rooo?*"

Jay glanced at him shyly. "I guess so."

Jim's mouth and eyes gaped as he shook his head in mock concern. "Awww! Now ain't this a tough problem!"

Jay turned to face him, but couldn't look him in the eye. "Don't make fun of me," he said. "I feel terrible."

"Must be some good feeling to it," said Jim, "or you wouldn't carry on so. Heh, heh—if you'd kissed a pig you wouldn't feel like this."

"I've never felt like this before."

Jim chuckled. "Like there's a stiff, cold breeze racing through you, cleaning you out in places you didn't even know was dirty."

"Racing—cold—cleansing, yes, all that and more," said Jay, surprised how well Jim understood. He stopped, but Jim nodded and beckoned for him to go on. Tears prickled his eyes. "I've found too late that I—I—" Jay took a deep breath. "I married the wrong person."

Jim laughed softly and clasped his arm with a brotherly squeeze. "All of us do." His voice was gentle, his manner humorously sad. "You can't help *but* marry the wrong person."

Jay shook his head vigorously. "No, no, that's not true."

"Ah, Jay—look at me," said Jim. "I married Lucy when I was a boy. I love her as much as I ever loved my pa and ma and Phil, but I'm not a boy now. I ain't no circus barker or wagon peddler no more. Still and all, I couldn't never leave her, and I don't want to." Jim's glowing face, as broad as an ox's, came closer and swam before Jay's eyes. "What would happen to my children?" Jim went on. "How would Lucy feel? But you know the kind of fellow I am. You know what I enjoy here in New York. Josie fits in with my crowd, Lucy don't. What am I supposed to do? Stay a Vermont hick? All my life I've followed my nose, and here I am. You're the same way. You ain't that same young feller as said 'I do' all them years ago."

Jay shook his head in a vigorous no. "I can't go tonight, Jim, but one of us has to keep in with her. She's the only pipeline the Erie has to the White House, the Treasury. I'll send around a note. She'll understand."

Jim's smile was moony. "I love *both* of mine," he said. "No reason you can't too. Although I have to admit two sugarcakes is three times the trouble of one." He sighed and shook his head. "Sometimes *four* times as much trouble. That night the Opera opened I got so mad at Josie I like to have filled her plump behind with buckshot."

"And now?"

"Oh, we had a wonderful time making up. Lasted all afternoon and the better part of a night."

That night the heat from July's strong sun, still trapped in the city's paving stones, made Jay's feet hot and sore as he tramped Manhattan's streets.

Five Points—beggars sitting in the gutters with stupid stares, tiny open stalls lit by kerosene lamps, rickety wooden buildings, the screeches of arguments, and the foul stench of beer, urine, vomit, and smoke floating up from basement dives. Jim's heartiness had kept up Jay's spirits only till the afternoon trading session. Then, hunched over the new ticker-tape machine in the corner of his office, no matter how cleverly he bought and sold, he could not prevent gold from closing down another half a dollar for the day.

Fifth Avenue—solid stone mansions, the warm glow from drawing room windows, well-muscled horses sedately drawing heavy carriages. It wasn't ten o'clock yet. If he went home now, he would toss and turn for hours.

Jay found himself at Thirty-fifth and Fifth. Annabelle's town house was right down this block. He edged into the empty street, the cobblestones painful to his tender feet. Staying well under the night shade of dark oaks, lindens, and London plane trees, he avoided the gaslight and the glances of passersby.

Annabelle's at home was in full swing. In front of her and the neighbors' houses were ranged six large carriages, their drivers clotted together on the curb, talking in low murmurs. Jay passed by rapidly on the other side of the street. Farther on down, he mounted the five steps of the stoop of a dark house, and lowered himself to sit facing her house.

Annabelle's large French windows glowed a brilliant, warm yellow. The back of Tweed's head and the silhouette of Judge McCoy appeared and moved on.

Sitting alone in the dark, staring at her lighted window made Jay feel peculiar, silly even, like a mooning schoolboy. Now a group of portly male guests were gathered at her window, tiny glasses in their hands, which they waved about as they jabbered. Jay wanted to sit alone on this dark, restful stoop till his frayed nerves repaired themselves—say, for a month or even a year. He reflected bitterly that none of his heroes—Columbus, Washington, Napoleon, Morse— would sit in the dark mooning about.

Near eleven o'clock Jim and the other guests came out. Rich chortles floated across the dark street, along with good-natured "Good-nights!" Carriage doors slammed. Teams of horses' iron-shod hooves, occasionally sparking, clacked off in eight-part rhythms. Bridget bolted the downstairs door, and Annabelle herself pulled in the French windows and bolted the inside shutters of the upstairs parlor, making Jay's heart thump loudly.

The night around him was cool and dark. Jay felt invisible and airy, as if now that the world slept, he could do anything, go anywhere, even move in and out of houses and snoring bedrooms.

The street was deserted. Under the faraway glare of gas street-lamps, the cobblestones rippled light and dark in a fish-scale pattern. He stood and walked to her house. Behind the glass panes of her bedroom window was the white of her drawn shutters. His throat was tight.

From his pocket he took a quarter and tossed it, in a soft arc, at the third-floor window. It clacked against the glass as loudly as a thief breaking a window. His heart beat yet more strongly in his ears, and he told himself to run away. The corner lamp's rays picked out the coin as it fell. He caught it. She probably thought an acorn had struck the pane. Turning east and west to make sure the street was still deserted, he tossed the coin again, and it clacked a second time against the pane.

Scrapes and a clank. The window opened. Her head stuck out. "What is—"

As soon as she saw him she withdrew her head and slammed the window and closed the shutter. Damn. She wanted nothing to do with him. He stared at the blind window, imagining the rumpled bed, her warm fragrance, and what she must now be thinking. As he turned away, the snaps and clicks of the front door startled him, and his cheeks and neck prickled as if a bramblebush unexpectedly grazed them.

The door opened. Annabelle stood framed by the doorway, a lacy white robe clutched at her neck with one hand. In the other was a candle in a shallow holder, its light illuminating her long face, which was shocked, pleased, and drawn.

He went forward. For a moment, three feet apart, he outside, she inside, they stared at each other, their faces lit by the flickering candle. Her large black eyes bored into his.

"What do you want?" she said.

The night air cooled the sweat on the back of his neck. Unsure whether he was unwanted or welcome, he couldn't speak, words wouldn't come—he was frozen. As if daylight's usages had fled, inside he was little more than a strange, foreign whirlwind of incoherent whispers, rotten twigs of desires, hard dry stones of words, and bubbles of fragile hopes. Behind her white robe, in the black, mysterious interior of the town house, he imagined for a brief moment the twisting faces of manic devils, and the hunched-over, hopping forms of nightmarish, grinning dwarves.

The candle in her hand sputtered and popped, showering hot wax across her hand. She jumped back and he came through the doorway. He set the candle on the hall table and grasped her hand.

"You can't stay," she whispered urgently.

"No," he agreed. He wanted to close the open front door, but moving to it would create momentum in the wrong direction. He raised her limp, wax-splattered hand, turned it over, and kissed its soft palm.

"Go," she whispered, her face pinched. "We can't."

"I know," he whispered back. He leaned forward and kissed her lips, which tasted of musky incense and spices. "Hold me for a moment."

He put his arms around her. She hesitated against him, then her soft arms snaked around his neck. Inside the white robe her body was warm, and yet despite her body's soft, feathery heat, she seemed ethereal. For a dizzy moment it seemed as if he were holding his dead sister Polly, and a sob escaped the heave of his lungs and he pressed her more tightly. As he relaxed his grip, she felt as fragile as his daughter: a delicate, small-boned sprite, infinitely fragile, infinitely complex, infinitely untouchable.

She pulled away, gave him a dark glance that was unreadable, and pinched out the candle. He fumbled about and closed the door. She glided in front of him like a white shade. A warm, soft hand took his, and he was pulled forward. Then the stairs were under his feet, creaking and popping, and he was led upward. Prickles of excitement ran up and down his spine, for he was unsure why she had pinched out the candle or where he was being led.

The upstairs parlor landing, as dark as a cave. His heart flopped around in his chest like a strange, frightening animal, one that might turn on him. The outline of a hall window illuminated by the street's faint light. Her hot, light hand pulled him farther along the creaking planks into more delicious mystery. Another set of stairs, more hallway.

Finally, the sweetness of perfume, the violet essence of sachet, and the exotic scent of face powder told him they had entered her bedroom.

Like a man in a dream, he pulled her to him, and in the darkness they kissed again, a long, slow kiss that left him little more than a dark mound of pleasure. Her arms stroked his shoulders and ribs. Her robe had fallen open, and when they kissed the sharp nipples of her small breasts, covered by only a light gown, rubbed against his shirtfront.

She pulled back, and as if she were a blind person, her fingers probed and examined his face and beard. He drew her face to his, and during this kiss all the barriers erected against her toppled. As if his spirit were a river locked into a narrow streambed, he swelled and overran his banks to flow into a wide expanse of sunny meadow and rich orchards.

They fell on the bed. His cautious fingers stole into the top of her silky gown, and she didn't stop him. Her breasts nestled against his palms. His daylight clothes were tied in hard knots that they fumbled together to loosen. Finally they were on the coverlet separated by no more than wisps of cloth. Then it was as if they had become some large new bird, albatross or roc, that had just discovered flight. Flapping four broad wings, pumping powerful muscles, cawing a triumphant cry, they soared over the dark, sleeping city, superior to it.

A long wide flight. The roc's wings spread farther, miles in length and breadth, strong and regular as the ocean's pulsing tide. Higher into black space, a rise to a peak above all worlds.

Explosion. Silence. Peace. Calmness.

Hesitant touch. Whispers. Cool sheets. Cold summer night's air.

The heat of her body, the sleek feel of her flat stomach and slender legs.

She stroked his face and clung to his body. He stroked her belly, breasts, and buttocks and held her tightly. They entwined again.

First light. Jay was instantly, fully awake.

"We can't again," she whispered.

"No."

"This once only, then no more." Their voices were low, hushed, the tone of grief-stricken family members preparing for a burial.

"Yes."

Dawn resembled a mile-high gray sword rising to strike them, a bright, vengeful sword with a blade of daylight and a handle jeweled with the eyes of others, eyes that became larger and more dangerous the longer he stayed.

Her fingers lingered on his body as she pulled on his black socks, slid him into his cotton shirt, and reattached his black suspenders. Not to wake the children or her servant, they tiptoed downstairs.

At the front door, she whispered. "No, no, go out the back."

Before he opened the back door, he turned to her. She stared at him, her large black eyes deep and troubled. He pulled her to him, and they embraced. He hugged her warmth with all his strength, as if putting a lifetime of embraces into this final one.

"Go," she said, half a word and half a sob.

He slipped out into the alley. At the bottom of the wooden steps he turned back, but her face wasn't in the kitchen window, only a brief waggle of the curtain.

Behind him sounded a crash and he jerked about. By an overturned trash barrel, a rib-thin, mangy hound stared up in guilty fear.

Like lidded, sleeping eyes, hundreds of dark windows at the rear of neighboring houses stared down. He had to go. Gray was turning to dawn. Someone might see him.

He scurried away down the back alley.

270

*　　*　　*

"But you can't see him again!" Louise said.

Louise's face was open, gaping with terror. The split in her hare lip was red, and she had pushed the upper half of her body across the center table of the parlor till her gray eyes were inches from Annabelle's.

Annabelle drew back. She had hurried over to her friend Louise at seven-thirty this morning, two hours after Jay's hurried departure, carefully arriving after Louise's husband Arthur had left for Brooklyn to visit his general stores. Louise was still dressed in her morning robe, and her brown hair, not yet combed out, hung in a single loose plait down her back. In absent fashion Annabelle picked up the teapot.

"No, no, of course not," said Annabelle. "May I?" To dilute the intensity of the moment, she poured a couple of spoonfuls of tea, saw the pot had lost its heat, and refilled it from the jug of hot water.

The mahogany sliding doors behind them were tightly shut. For a quarter of an hour Annabelle had filled Louise in, talking in a hushed voice, revealing the affair with Jay. They were both afraid that Louise's maiden aunt, one of her four children, or a servant would overhear them.

During the telling Annabelle's stomach had been terribly queasy. The parlor windows hadn't yet been opened, and the room possessed the mustiness of a bell jar filled with last season's dead flowers. This morning Annabelle wasn't quite sure of who she was. It was as if another creature lived inside her heart and lungs, one who could take her over in a raw fury of hunger and shake her violently. She still felt Jay between her legs—his intensity, his force, as if he wasn't merely desirous of her, but desperate to enter her. Their lovemaking had started out gently enough—delicate kisses, tender fingertips, the brush of aroused limbs—but ended up for both as urgent need. His greed for her was flattering, enjoyable—her own alarming, for she hadn't known such an intense need was crouched, hidden, within her. She could talk strategy with Louise, perhaps obtain some comfort, but she could never admit how desperately she wanted him—she could scarcely even admit it to herself—between her legs, how much that satisfied. Once as a girl she had mistakenly locked her cat Pearly in the bank over the weekend; she wanted Jay the way Pearly had ripped apart the roast chicken thigh on Monday morning.

"My God," breathed Louise, gently laying both her hands over Annabelle's, "what if you're—you know—in a family way?" Trust Louise to get to the nub of it. At thirty, she was nobody's fool, never taken in by the social feefaw of Manhattan that passed for wisdom.

She always wanted to know which one of the couple had the money, in whose name the property was deeded, did they have any children yet, and was he out dodging around town with other women.

The extreme reaction of Louise was making an impact on Annabelle. Till she had arrived at Louise's, she had been caught up in Jay's nighttime visit as a thrilling adventure, one leading on to who knew what? That she was so light-headed and stunned was proof of the power of what had happened. Yet all it would take to turn the adventure into the realest possible nightmare was for her to be pregnant.

"It's just been one night, Louise."

"One night!" exclaimed Louise in a loud whisper. "I get pregnant if I plop down on the same chair Arthur's been sitting on."

Annabelle slipped her hand out of Louise's. To give herself a moment to think, she drank the lukewarm cup of tea. There was always Madame Restaille. Within Annabelle slid a cold knife of fear.

Madame Restaille's large stone mansion stood on a Fifth Avenue corner surrounded by vacant lots no one else would buy. Rumor whispered that inside it was one of the most magnificent of the houses on the avenue, with three immense dining rooms and as many formal parlors, furnished like a palace in rare bronzes, gilt-framed mirrors, ornamental clocks, and imported French furniture. Deep red shades of a gaudy, vulgar pattern, framed by pink satin and creamy lace curtains, blinded its scores of broad-paned windows. No other house in New York possessed such thick shades, nor would any other owner want them.

"Madame R," as she was known, charged five hundred dollars "a case." Not daring to use their own—and recognizable—carriages, heavily veiled mommas shepherded equally heavily veiled daughters, unmarried and in a family way, into the side-street entrance, where in her basement surgery the pair found "the relief" they sought.

"I know what you're thinking," said Louise. "But you couldn't go through with it."

"I—" Annabelle paused. "I don't know." In her chest was the muffled beat of a drum stuffed with cotton. "I couldn't have the child."

Outside in the hall Louise's children screeched like a treeful of birds as they clattered up and down the stairs. Silence hung over the table. Annabelle was so stifled by the mustiness of the parlor that she wanted to jump up, scream, do any outrageous thing to disturb it. Louise gave her the pop-eyed stare of the sane at the daring of the mad.

"Do you love him, then?" asked Louise.

Annabelle sighed and her shoulders slumped. "Love? Maybe I

do. It's happened so fast, I'm not sure what I feel." At this moment an intense craving for him—one she wasn't going to elaborate on with the level-headed Louise—was rubbing itself into her bones. Again she wanted to feel Jay on her, in her, stroking her. As her lips pressed against the china cup, she felt his lips mashing harshly against hers. "I certainly enjoy working with him, planning affairs with him," Annabelle said. "Most men are as dull as bricks. They go at things so clumsily."

Louise frowned. "Can't you just limit your relationship to business—no, I suppose not. Once this starts with a man, it doesn't go back, does it?" Louise's face reddened. "It's funny about you. You're too smart to make a man's mistake, aren't you? But you're making a woman's mistake."

"I'm what?"

"Flinging yourself at him because you feel so strongly, imagining that because you feel so strongly—and maybe he does, too—that the feelings will somehow change the way things are." Annabelle's laugh was sharp, its edge as uncontrollable as a knife wielded by a halfwit. Louise's face was pinched, worried. "You can't expect him to leave her, his wife, can you?"

Annabelle was taken aback. "I don't—no, I don't suppose I can. You keep jumping too far ahead. It's a single night."

Louise's voice rose in puzzled indignation. "And he has children, doesn't he?"

"Yes."

Louise's response was just as flat. "He won't leave them, not a man like him." Annabelle's stomach gave a horrid lurch, as if the chair, floor, and parlor were falling, as if her chair were sinking in quicksand that would suck her into the center of the earth. She gasped a quick, deep breath and recovered herself.

"You're right," said Annabelle. "I won't see him again."

Louise reached across the table and squeezed her hands. "Thank God."

Later that morning Annabelle received a letter from her sister Jenny, who was visiting their parents in Gantry.

"Pa's gone to work clerking in Mr. Tibby's feed store," wrote Jenny. "He and Mama have moved out of the old house and sold it to one of those awful Smather boys, who aren't any better since they used to push worms into the cakes at church picnics." Papa and Mama no longer in their own house! The cozy country house that Jenny and Annabelle had grown up in. Annabelle leaned back in her plush parlor chair. Losing the house was as wrenching as losing a member of the family. "It's hard to believe Pa's just sixty-five," Jenny also wrote. "That's not so old, but he looks ten years older. Mama says he needs something to do other than sell farmers grain, but there's not much around here. Whyever he invested so much money in Ned's brokerage, I don't know. How he can blame you for his losses is beyond me, and I've told him so several times. He won't really listen, just clams up and glares at me as if I, too, am in league with the Devil."

With Jay as her adviser, Annabelle thought, she might figure out a way of repairing first her finances, then Papa's. No, no—as she had agreed with Louise, she had to end it.

That afternoon a slim, balding messenger who resembled an office clerk more than a hired runner brought her a plain white envelope without a return address.

"I'm to wait for a reply," he said, his eyes downcast with modesty. She didn't ask him in, but stepped back into the shadows of the hall to read the note. As it had all day at the least excitement, her heart beat strongly, and the summer air gliding in and out of her lungs made her light-headed.

I must see you tonight. Leave the back door open. She noted how cautious he was. No signature, not even a single initial.

Louise was right. She was making a mistake, a woman's mistake that must stop. She penned back, *No, don't come. Sorry. This must stop.*

Late that afternoon she took another long bath in water she purposely made almost too hot to stand. The heat cleansed her and worked deeply into her, soothing her, body and spirit.

Her thoughts moved sluggishly through her thick brain. She was unsure of her ability to make sound plans. In five years she and Jay would bump into each other at some do and wonder what all the fuss had been about.

That night, after Bridget and the children were in bed, Annabelle sat in the parlor leafing through well-thumbed copies of *Godey's Lady's Book*. On the mantel the eight-day clock ticked as loudly as a snare drummer's thunk-thunk-thunk. When the long notes of nine o'clock began to strike, she shivered as if an icicle were being drawn up her spine. She peered around the empty room. The curved shapes of the chairs and round tables glared with sinister expressions. The chandelier's yellow globes tossed dagger-shaped shadows into the corners, from which the black-on-black arabesques of tricksters' faces twisted about. The cooling house made an abrupt, loud crack as if the roof were opening to the night.

She jumped. *He was going to come tonight.* The hairs on the back of her neck stood straight up. Listening intently, she leaned forward in her chair. The skin along her shoulders prickled into goosebumps. He wouldn't take *no* from her.

When the clock struck ten, a strong urge to unlock the back door swept over her, but she fought it. To break this spell she stood and pulled the thick cotton shawl more closely around her shoulders. All day her blood had felt thick and sluggish, and her mind had moved like clay; now the cool of night raced through her veins as thin and fast as mercury. Her thoughts darted through her brain in rapid flutters. Like soldiers expecting attack, every nerve strained forward in an effort to hear a scrape against the back door or an acorn striking a window.

"No, Jay," she whispered.

They stood in the black-as-ink kitchen, which still reeked of the turnips, corn bread, and pork that Bridget had cooked for supper.

"I haven't thought of anything but you all day," came his dark, urgent reply.

She insisted, "We're not free."

"We need each other," he said, his voice as urgent. She couldn't deny that, but Louise was right. She couldn't afford another night like last night.

"We can't," she said.

His gentle fingers found her cheek, and her skin drank their warmth. Only for a moment, she told herself. His smooth hands slipped around her waist. When he pulled her body, she was powerless to stop him. He kissed her and it was better than last night. There was a place for her, a groove in the harsh world in which her spirit and her body belonged. She sighed and let go. His sure hands went up the back of her neck into her hair. His hungry mouth drank at her cheeks and neck, and his fingers greedily caressed her back.

Upstairs in her dark bedroom she closed and locked the door, praying Bridget hadn't heard their tiptoeing through the dark house. The delicious fresh smell of the earlier cold rain drifted through the open window. A horse's hollow hooves clopped by. By his being in it, her bedroom was transformed into a mysterious, magical cave. He was sitting on the bed next to her, his urgent hands boldly feeling their way around her clothes. The urge to halt his fingers warred with one to lie back and allow them their way. She had come up the stairs, down the hall, into her room as if in a dream. It wasn't too late. She could call it off.

"No, Jay, no."

"Annabelle," he pleaded, "Annabelle, Annabelle," and in his calling her name she heard a plea that, like her own child's, was hard to deny.

Everything was different here in her dark, magical bedroom. The harm of his being here was a daylight reason, that harsh, bright, *small* place far, far away, which she visited sometimes but that wasn't where she really lived. Removing his starched cotton shirt was a thrill. She lay back, and he hovered over her. She grabbed what she could—a leg, a calf, his stomach, his man-thing.

A wave of hunger swept over her; again she wanted him in her, not as a wife wanted a husband, but as a skin ached to have a body inside it, as a starving man wanted to rip apart and devour a live rabbit. His clothes, hair, and fingers smelled richly of ink, paper, wool, and some male lotion of lemons and rum. He came from another world, the real world, a hard planet downtown of bonds, power, ledgers, and cold-brained business deals, and she longed to drink it in by gorging herself on him. His sure fingers on her breasts made her shiver with pleasure. The real her was here and now, in this enormous night kingdom where her feelings could expand, where her powers were as large and potent as a witch's. Here everything was hands and smooth skin and sucking lips and the sure touch of his fingers in her hair and straining to kiss him more deeply than ever before and reaching peaks of passion that she had never scaled with Ned. She went up these dark, slippery slopes with the fervor of a powerful mare racing to their top.

He raced with her. Over the next hours the giant bird that they made together flew even higher on stronger wings.

Early the next morning the sword of day and the specter of a thousand curious eyes again announced that this had to stop.

But over the next week, night and its reasons drew him to her, her to him, again and again.

When she thought about it during daylight hours, she agreed with Louise. Her meetings with Jay frightened her, as if her nighttime self were a sleepwalker endangering her by tramping through the city over bridges, across train trestles, around trolley cars, and in and out of lowlife dives.

But at the end of each day, night crept around her again. The house cooled. She sat in the parlor, the hairs on the back of her neck steadily rising in delicious, shivery anticipation. And when the scratching came at the back door, she rose and quietly raced to the door to let him in.

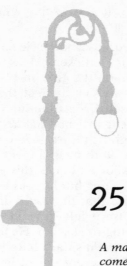

25

A man naturally expects his sons to come into his business, and of course the boys eagerly anticipate that happy day.

—*MacMillan's Magazine*, 1875

By means of long, thick ropes, two stablehands maneuvered a nervous, heaving stallion toward the roan mare held still by other stablehands.

Like four wiggly blackbirds, George Gould and his three school chums, sitting on the split-rail fence of the corral, watched the boss and stablehands attempt to mate the two horses.

For a half hour these stockyard roustabouts had been trying to entice the wild-eyed, reluctant stallion to mount the mare, but despite the strength of a dozen hands and their jeering catcalls, the stallion refused to rear up onto her. Even though it was after school, the four thirteen-year-old boys were still dressed in the black broadcloth suits that Mr. Marks, their headmaster, insisted were the proper dress for his students. As the ropes were once more pulled tight, the stallion whinnied and dug in his front hooves. The long-limbed, gangly boy on the extreme right of the four, Moss, leaned toward the others.

"I don't blame him," said Moss boldly, referring to the balky stallion. "I wouldn't jump up on an old mare like that neither." George and the others snickered. The corral stank of mud, sun-baked rail fencing, and all the odors of horse—sweat, hair, droppings, piss.

Stewart, George's best friend, nudged George in the ribs. "That stallion doesn't know what's good for him," was Stewart's opinion. Small and swarthy, he had lately taken to greasing his hair with dollops of grown-up Macassar oil. "He's a dumb one."

To show he understood, George cackled. He had seen horses coupling—not to speak of goats, pigs, chickens, dogs, and sheep—in the streets. The boy animal jumped on the girl, his pink hickey swollen, and stuck it—George mashed his foot against the splintery second rail of the corral to keep himself from toppling over. Recently his own hickey had swelled when it brushed against his smooth bedclothes, and he fondled it at night till it exploded— The first time he had thought he was going to die. Nothing had ever felt like that before. It had to be bad, nothing was allowed to feel this good. The pleasure mounted. He thought, I ought to stop, but he couldn't, it felt too good; and then when he knew for sure that he would die if he continued, he didn't care if he died because it felt so good. Then it exploded, killing him. Dead, he was drifting to Heaven. He lay in the dark, the blood from the explosion warm on his dark bare belly. But no pain. Just drifting peace. Not dead? He crept out of bed and felt around for the candle and matches. Striking the match carefully so that its burning sulfur head didn't jump off and cling to his bare skin, he looked down to discover the damage. Peering fearfully. No damage. His hickey and everything else was right where it was supposed to be. Just a pearly cream there, which he mopped up.

The spring days that followed were cool and green, and the weather made him dizzy with the desire to share this momentous, exciting discovery with someone, although an inner whisper of caution kept him from saying anything to his best friend Stewart or Pa. And it was smart to have kept quiet. No sooner had he discovered this secret pleasure than he was bombarded by references to it, in talks by the minister about "self-abuse," in cunning jokes by sly-faced men about "tooting your flute" and "Madame Thumb and her four daughters," as well as in his father's medical textbooks, which warned that self-abuse brought blindness, acne, kidney failure, rot of the muscles, and death.

Every morning he peered into the mirror for signs of blindness and pimples. Although every evening he renewed his vow never to touch himself that way again, he couldn't stop his hand at night.

The roustabouts shouted at the stallion. From the low tin sheds behind the four boys rose the insistent chant of the stockyard's auctioneer. With the men pulling the ropes in encouragement, the stallion finally reared up and mounted the mare, and with great lunges and hard gasps of breath did with his large pink hickey what boy dogs, roosters, and pigs did. George and his chums said nothing, only stared.

When it was over, Stewart said, "Hard to believe that that's what your ma and pa did to make you, isn't it?"

"Not my pa!" said George, horrified.

The other three laughed so hard that Stewart and O'Reilly fell off the topmost split rail to the ground, and Moss's hold threatened to pull loose. "What do you think he did?" jeered Moss. "Spit up her!"

The others fell out again, cackling. George threw himself on Moss, knocking him off the fence and into the dirt. With George on top, Moss hit the ground with a loud *oof!* The fall knocked the breath out of Moss, who put up no resistance as George beat him in the sides with his fists. Stewart and O'Reilly grabbed George by the arms and pulled him off.

"He didn't mean nothing!" shouted Stewart in George's ear. Moss dragged himself to his feet. He was breathing hard and holding a handkerchief to his bloody nose.

"You crazy or something, George?" shouted Moss.

George struggled against Stewart and O'Reilly's grip to throw himself back on Moss, but the other two held him tight. "You can't talk about my ma like that!" George shouted.

"You shouldn't have said nothing about his folks," O'Reilly said to Moss. "Tell him you're sorry."

For a few moments, as if he would be damned if he would apologize, Moss's white brow and hurt eyes glared over the bloody handkerchief held to his nose. In a sullen voice he said, "All right, they never did it like that. They never did it at all. Okay?"

When George stuck out his hand to show there were no hard feelings, Stewart and O'Reilly snickered and let him go. Moss grabbed the ends of George's fingers in one disgusted yank and turned toward the auctioneer's loud ranting.

"Come on," said O'Reilly, "let's see if your pa has bought your horse yet." They set off up the dusty alleyway. They didn't understand, George told himself, echoing the stories Mr. Marks read to their class, that a knight of the round table defended the honor of Camelot no matter what.

After George's pa had bought him his horse, the boys and their fathers adjourned to the private bar for George's Horse Party, the celebration of a young fellow's buying his first full-sized horse. The air was blue from cigars and pipes. George and his school chums were struggling to appear as old as their pas. Freed from city tasks over the lunch hour, their pas talked and nodded together.

Hoisting his tankard, secretly spiked with real liquor, Stewart said loudly to George, "As good as fucking, I say." A manic grin rode his lips.

The raw word caught George between laughing and scowling, but he asked Stewart, "Do you think *your* ma and pa do what those horses do?"

Stewart's hard, black eyes stared and a smile glided onto his lips. "Sure they do. Just like your ma and pa." His voice had a mocking lilt, and his tan face assumed that same foreign smarminess as it had lately taken on after church when he exchanged views with Mary Alice Williams over what a fine sermon it had been. Stewart could pretend all he wanted that he was a polite young man who cared about sermons, but George knew full well that the sermon wasn't writ that Stewart gave a hoot about.

"My pa wouldn't do that," said George.

"He sticks it to Mrs. Stokes, that's how kind he is."

The floor tilted like a ship going over a wave and George felt seasick. "He—what?"

Stewart's eyes went in different directions, staring at the floor and George's vest in cross-eyed alarm. He backtracked. "I didn't mean nothing."

George's heat rose. Nobody could malign Pa. "Take it back."

Stewart said, "I ain't taking the truth back."

"My pa doesn't stick it to nobody," said George.

Stewart leaned toward him, a dirty grin on his face and his chin stuck out. "He sticks it to your ma."

George growled, "I beat Moss for saying that."

"You stupid dummy, how do you think you got here?"

That hit George like a slap in the face. He took a half step back. No animal could get born unless the boy animal had stuck it to the girl.

"But it's different with my folks," said George. "My pa wouldn't hurt my ma."

"It doesn't hurt, dummy," said Stewart. "It feels good."

The explosion that wasn't an explosion, the one that made you feel good that you weren't supposed to do. The one that made sticky blood in the dark that turned to salty pearl cream after you lit the candle. George was dazed, and everything spun about—the crowded barroom, the excitement of owning his own stallion, the clamor of his friends' voices, his father's somber presence, the bitter, spiked cider punch, and Stewart's pushiness. He couldn't reply. Stewart drained off the rest of his tankard.

"He sticks it to Mrs. Stokes," said Stewart, "next door to us. He comes in the back door at night, and he leaves in the morning."

"He doesn't!" Heads turned to look at them. Lowering his voice, George hissed, "You saw Moss's bloody nose this afternoon. I'm going to bust you if you don't take that back."

"There ain't nothing to take back." As if this whole matter wasn't really all that important, Stewart said, "Say, if you're not going to drink that, then let me finish it."

Stewart took the spiked tankard from him and emptied it into his own. George felt disoriented. The world he was growing up into was strange. Disheveled drunks tottered out of Eighth Avenue saloons and fell senseless into the muddy gutter. Sonny James's old man gambled away everything their family owned and they had to leave town. Grown men's conversations were little more than a baffling enthusiasm for cards, money, whiskey, horse racing, and shifty cracks about women, none of the subjects that Pa talked about.

Ma and Pa being married made sense—the calm household, the set times for meals, the gentle order of their lives—but it didn't make sense that he, George, would marry some girl and that she would become a ma and he a form of his pa, but of course a lesser form. Dazed, George swayed in front of Stewart. Grown fellows found sticking it to women exciting, although it seemed disgusting rather than a pleasure. Why do what dogs did to bitches, and stallions did to mares, to some girl who was like your sister and dressed in white lace when she went to church on Sunday? No girl he went to Sunday school with would ever stand for that kind of thing the way that mare in the corral had stood still this afternoon.

Stewart's lips twisted and smugness spread over his face. "If you don't believe me, come over one night and see for yourself. They're at it nearly every night." George hated Stewart's dark face.

"They ain't!"

"Come spend the night with me, you'll see," said Stewart. George tried to answer, but nothing came out. A grown-up man would find words to push this away, something smart and brassy that put the whole thing behind him. An ugly leer was stuck across Stewart's face. "Tomorrow night?"

"All right, but he won't come." Something fluttered inside George that wasn't as sure as his voice. Yet his bearded father stood across the room as upright as usual, his face its normal mask of shrewd, calm attention. Yes, he would spend the night with Stewart, and Stewart would see. It would be some other man sneaking into that woman's house. His own father wouldn't visit some woman late at night and stick it in her.

Not his father, not King Arthur.

26

*It is only by making gold high and
scarce that we are enabled to compete in
the London and Liverpool markets.*

—Jay Gould, letter to Treasury Secretary
Boutwell, 1869

The jagged female scream froze Jay
Gould's hand on the brass doorknob.

He was half inside the street door of the Erie Railroad's new
offices, coming to work early on a cool August morning to snatch a
fast start on the day. A wild whoop, followed by another blood-
freezing scream of a woman having her throat sliced open, pierced
the lime and plaster dust that hung in the half-finished lobby.

Cold pinpricks jabbed Jay's neck and shoulders. His head craned
upward, but the sweep of wide marble staircase that arced through
the gloomy three-story-high lobby to the third-floor offices was empty
and silent. Softly, Jay entered and closed the heavy wooden door,
and from a construction trash heap he picked up a two-by-four club.
His feet whispered up the marble staircase. As his head came level
with the third landing, shrieks from two females horrified the air.
Prickles of gooseflesh scampered across his shoulders. Jay crept up
and peered around the corner.

Three young women, dresses fluttering and backs to him, ran
down the hall. They leapt into the air, skirts billowing like half-
attached sails. Jim Fisk, without jacket or waistcoat, meaty arms
akimbo, stood in the double doorway of his office. His ruffled dress
shirt was unbuttoned to the waist, exhibiting a broad turf of curly
chest hair. The three leaping women glided down onto the marble
floor in a long, split-legged slide. One was dressed in an artist's smock

and stage tights; the other two wore loose white garments, little more than dressing gowns, the half-open fronts and billowing bottoms of which flashed uncorseted breasts and naked calves.

"You scared the hell out of me," said Jay. "It's nearly work time. Get them out of here." Jim's head jerked at this irritated tone, his eyes blinking with the double take of a drunk just splashed with ice water.

"What's the matter with *your* tin oven this morning?"

The three girls—all younger than twenty—came squealing and chattering up the hallway.

"Get them off this floor," said Jay sternly, nodding toward the dancers. "Keep them off, too, or so help me I'll move the Erie and sell this cathouse." At his harsh tone the girls were frightened and edged away.

"All right, all right," said Jim. He made a reassuring moue in the girls' direction. "Don't get your tin oven in a boil. Girls, let's call it a good night's fun."

"Please come sit down with me," said Jay. "We need to talk." Jay pushed past him and went into Jim's office.

Made out of six smaller rooms, the newly decorated corner office was spacious enough to satisfy even Jim's elephantine ambitions. Sumptuous red velvet curtains lined the six windows, and a huge French mirror in a gold-and-ebony frame hung on the right-hand wall. The brass chandelier, with two dozen milky globes amid hundreds of tinkling leaves, was suspended like a jeweled crown over the cream-and-blue Brussels carpet.

A woman's red silk scarf was draped over the back of a visitor's chair; on another a whalebone corset stood up as if it held an invisible midsection and bosom; while on a third lay a shawl, a petticoat, and two pairs of white dancer's tights. The air here was thick with stale odors—cigar smoke warred with sweet rosewater perfume; the flat champagne in the long-stemmed glasses vied with the sour stench of animal rutting. Jay felt yet more irritated with Jim: how could real work be done in such a room?

Over the last few days a new kind of fear had squeezed him, a dull, thick apprehensiveness that made every action throughout the day, even washing his hands, seem ominous. Something terrible was going to happen, but what it was and when it would happen, he didn't know. Over the last week Jay had been keenly aware of every breath, every heartbeat, every brush against his skin, much like a criminal waiting to be hanged.

Jim came in and closed the heavy door behind him. "What's up?"

"I need your help in the Gold Room," said Jay. Wordlessly Jim dropped his bulk into the swivel chair behind the Empire desk, his fingers dexterously knotting his maroon silk tie. "On the floor of the Gold Room," Jay went on. "I'll set you up with $100,000 to trade with."

"What's this, now?" asked Jim, face puzzled.

"Yesterday I put in $40,000 and the market went down."

Jim's lower jaw dropped open and his eyes swam with shock. "You bought $40,000 worth of gold in one day—and the market *closed down?* That's impossible." Almost by definition large purchases made a market rise.

"Right," said Jay, his voice as hard and dry as stones. "Now, will you find out what's going on?"

"Hell, I'll find out something today."

The following Tuesday at teatime Jay sat across from Annabelle on a sofa in her large second-floor parlor.

On the low table between them stood a tray of tea things. The odors of China tea, lemon cake, and fear floated on the August heat. Annabelle's open mouth and large black eyes reflected her shock.

"Vanderbilt!" exclaimed Annabelle. Her black eyes were large and bold, as if stimulated with belladonna. "It can't be!"

"Jim is sure," said Jay. "He has a way of pulling these things out of people." He hunched himself forward on the edge of the sofa. While his pale face was as unreadable as usual, his left hand, as tight as a fist, tugged at the bottom of his beard. "He's been on the floor of the Gold Room for four days now."

When a few minutes before he had come in downstairs, distracted by his news, he had forced himself to give her a peck on the cheek. Seeing her in daylight, which he hadn't done in weeks, agitated him. The respectable lady in front of him—back stiff in a sober forest-green dress that rose to encircle her neck with cream lace—couldn't be the gown-clad, sensual enchantress who engulfed him in the depths of night with hands, legs, mouth, and love.

"But Vanderbilt is a railroad man," she said, "not a gold trader." As if she too found his daylight and nighttime selves separate creatures, she had touched him downstairs only once, a brief squeeze on his bony arm.

This afternoon after trading was over, Jim had appeared in Jay's tiny office, flapping his arms with excitement and pacing about rapidly. Not only was Vanderbilt shorting gold, Jim reported, but he led a bear ring of Wall Street financiers that included Daniel Drew and Jay Cooke.

With this news it seemed to Jay as if Manhattan's gravity doubled, tripled. The broadcloth of his suit felt as heavy as lead cloth, his shoulders slumped as if iron sash weights tugged at his arms. His lungs had become bellows made of stiff, aged leather; his head, a thick boulder; and his bones, posts of cement. Toward the end of the day a plan formed, and his spirits lifted. A plan! As long as there was a plan, he could half succeed in shoving aside these leaden feelings. And now it depended on Annabelle.

"Vanderbilt wants to bust the Erie," Jay said to Annabelle.

"My God!" she said. "Bust the Erie—yes, to snatch up the pieces cheaply!"

"Yes." She was fast. He never had to explain much to her.

"But the bond man?" she mused. "Why would Jay Cooke be in with Vanderbilt?"

"His brokerage underwrites almost all the bonds of the U.S. Treasury," said Jay. "He's the man who dreamed up war bonds for Lincoln, the man who raised the hundreds of millions Lincoln needed to whip the rebels." Strange, he thought, how businesslike she was in daylight, as if there were two of her.

She stuck to her point as stubbornly as any businessman. "But why would he sell gold short?"

"Jay Cooke makes a market in bonds," said Jay. "At any one time, he probably has an inventory of fifty to a hundred million dollars. If the price of gold goes up, the price of his bonds goes down. Mr. Cooke could lose several million dollars in as many weeks."

She sipped her tea and nodded thoughtfully as she absorbed this.

Jay said, "Annabelle, I need your help."

Her eyes met his levelly. "It would be useless for me to go to Washington," she said. "I told you that." A week ago he had asked her to visit the President at the White House to find out if the administration was planning heavy or light sales of gold at its next few monthly auctions.

"There's a post at the Treasury office here in New York that's recently become vacant. The fellow who filled it died in the hotel fire on Madison Avenue."

"That was horrible," she said, her voice abstract and bloodless. She poured hot water from the jug into the teapot. "And?"

"I have a friend who would like that appointment," said Jay.

"A friend? Who?"

"General Dan Butterfield."

"General?" she asked.

"The War, Union side. He hasn't had much luck since the conflict."

She slowly ate several bites of cake, her eyes not meeting his but instead fixed on her silver fork. "Ulysses has a soft spot for soldiers who haven't had much luck since the War," she mused.

He took this as a sign that she would help and smiled. "You could go to Washington. We would pay your expenses. And some money besides."

"How much?" she asked.

"Say—three thousand dollars?"

She shook her head no. His voice rose with an edge of panic.

"Let's make it five thousand." Without answering, she jutted her chin forward and stared boldly at him. Then her eyes dropped demurely. Unsure what her silence and hesitation meant, afraid she found his plan morally tainted, he shoved on. "The fellow I'm pushing can do the work. True, he'll let me know what's going on, but these things are done all the time." It was difficult to believe that this hard, angular creature across from him was the dark, soft, receptive woman he had made love to last Thursday night. For a long moment she said nothing, and he waited with anxious hope.

Finally she clasped her hands together as if she had come to a decision and lifted her eyes to gaze directly at him. "What's going to happen to *us*, Jay?"

Caught off guard by this low, throaty shift of subject, he stalled. "*Us?*"

"You and me."

Made uneasy by the question, he opened his mouth to ask what it had to do with Butterfield's appointment, yet he was enough of a negotiator to sense that she was fishing for something. He gave a safe answer.

"I don't know."

"Do we have a future?" He twisted about on the sofa, his left hand gripping his beard in a fist. His insides were a sharp-edged jumble of conflicting answers.

"I—I simply don't know."

"I'll get you the appointment, Jay, but you can't pay me."

She loved him, he reckoned. Knowing of his and the Erie's difficulties, she was offering to work for nothing. "But you must take expense money," said Jay.

"I want you to open me an account," she said. "You still have some influence with the brokerage firm you used to own, don't you?"

Bewildered, he asked, "An account?"

"One in which I can buy gold bonds—on margin." Margin meant buying without paying the full price, having the broker lend you part of the money with which to purchase the bonds. Stunned, he stared at her. He had never heard a woman use a term like *gold bonds on margin*.

She went on, "I want you to buy me two million dollars' worth on full margin."

He gasped. "*Two* million! *Full* margin! That means you wouldn't put any money down."

Calmly she said, "Yes." The steadiness of her nerve further rattled him.

"I—or the Erie—" he fumbled, "would have to guarantee the account."

"I don't doubt that, but I want it to be *my* account."

Jay's poker face slipped. A smile warred with a frown; his left hand fell limply away from his beard. Not a man in a thousand would have come up with such a clever idea. If the gold bonds went down, Jay would have to make good on them. If they went up, she could sell them and profit. It would only take a few dollars' rise in the price of gold to earn her tens of thousands of dollars of risk-free profit. It was damn clever.

As if pushed by his silence, she went on. "Ned lost my father's bank. I'll be in gold a hundred percent with you, my interests the same as yours. If I can make enough profit, I'll set his bank up again and have enough left over to set myself up in business. Papa blames me. He might have been right about Ned, but he was wrong about me. As a member of Grant's family, I don't want to be in your employ—and if I'm not, I don't see why I can't buy and sell all the gold I choose to."

He nodded blandly; however, at the same time his right hand, out of nervousness, found in his pocket a small sheet of notepaper to shred. While the morality of her scheme was as dubious as his desire to staff the Treasury with his own creature, still it was as deft, adroit, and bold as a monkey. Although he was disappointed that she wouldn't simply do him this favor out of regard for him, he recognized the same hardheaded need in her as in himself, to make sure she received *quid* for her *quo*. It would make her a lot of money—or lose Jay yet more. It was the sort of daring, shrewd move that he admired, one that stood to recoup everything in a single brazen stroke that almost no one would see.

"Yes, but I can't afford two million," he said with one of his thinnest smiles, "how about half a million?"

She stifled a laugh. "I knew you'd haggle. One, and it's done." Her calculating smirk stung.

"Then let's call it finished." The additional risk leapt onto his shoulders to squat there as heavily as a brass devil. Her smile deepened, losing its sly trickiness. She stuck out her hand to shake on the deal.

"Then I'll go to Washington the day after tomorrow." It was like touching a limp, white snake to clasp the soft, warm fingers. Only a few nights ago these same fingers, stiff with passion, had clutched his back as he had thrust himself into her. At this moment he wasn't sure who she was—angel or succubus, a creature who would lead him out of this worsening bog into an easier, happier life, or one who was adding to the terrible burdens that were crushing him.

He fished out a handkerchief and patted the sweat off his face and hands. The clock on the mantel showed the time as just before six.

"My God, I've got to run."

Only when his right sole was pressed against the tiny metal step of his carriage did he realize that he hadn't set a night and a time for his return. He eased his foot back onto the paving stone and turned to her house. The shut door and the blank windows gazed at him blindly. Go up and knock, he told himself, but his feet refused to move.

"Sir? Where to?" the hack driver shouted down, impatient. Jay shouted up his home address, pulled himself in, and threw himself against the worn leather seat cushions. How could he have forgotten to ask her? The hack shot down the street. But at least he was cooking now, wasn't he? He had Jim on the floor of the Gold Room and a shot to put Butterfield in the Treasury. His doubts about her were the effect of an exhausted mind. Relief spurted through him, icy slush on a stinging burn. With Butterfield in the Treasury post, he would know what the fatheaded Grant was up to. It would be like having his own telegraph line right into the United States Treasury. Surely none of that could be bad.

The faint lightening of the murky night promised dawn.

George Gould strained to see clearly. Cold air brushed his cheeks, air as cold and damp as that in the chapel when squires and knights stayed up all night, as he and Stewart Adams had done, before setting out on a quest. The two boys were stretched out on Stewart's cot on the sleeping porch cantilevered over the Adams's backyard.

The rear door of the Stokes's house seemed to briefly yawn. Near the door a shadow wavered by the dark trunk of the linden tree. George blinked to clear his eyes. A hat or a dark squirrel slid around the trunk. George pressed his nose harder against the screen's mesh. Leaves from the Adams's backyard oak rustled, and a chilly breeze played across his back.

Then, in the backyard, a white blob of face, the swift outline of a hat, the shape of a black-draped shoulder against the dark bricks.

"There! That's him!" hissed Stewart. The shadowy hat and hunched figure slid along the dark bricks of the alleyway.

"What? That wasn't Pa."

"It was!" said Stewart. "One morning I seen him plain as day!"

Whoever it was, he was gone down the alley. George rolled off the cot. After two night-long vigils with Stewart, he knew no more than he had in Dimsdale's stockyard saloon.

George said, "I'm going in her cellar and wait for him tonight."

"What!"

"I want to know," said George. "It's not right. I'm not going to do what he tells me if he's doing this to Ma and the rest of us."

"Doing what?"

George nodded in the direction of the Stokes's house. "I'll come over late this afternoon," he said, "so we can bust in through the cellar wall like you said." Stewart again regarded him queerly, a squint-eyed look that said George's stupidity pained him.

"No, I'm not going to help you."

"I'm going to find out for sure," said George. "I can't have a man who does something like this for a father."

"What your pa does is his business."

"I'll go after I'm supposed to have left your house for mine—only I'll tell Ma I'm staying over here another night."

Stewart's feet squirmed about. "I won't lie for you," he said. "I'll get in too much trouble."

"All you have to do is show me how to get in her house."

Stewart gripped his arm. "Suppose they catch you?"

"I don't care."

A moan rose from Stewart. "No, George."

"I gotta go home after breakfast," said George. "I'll be back here late this afternoon. You tell your ma to set me a place at dinner."

The witch's cellar was musty and cool. Outside the August sun hadn't set, but here in the cellar it was dark except for the light from the makeshift lantern that George had constructed out of a candle and two tomato paste cans. Behind him Stewart softly cursed.

More spiderwebs. George waved his hand to clear them away. Overhead, floor joists. A feather of sweat tickled his underarms. It wasn't too late to go home.

The lantern hung from George's outstretched hand, peering around like a hot, yellow eye. Busted slats. The glimmer of dusty jars and broken furniture just outside the light's yellow circle. Holding the lantern high, George inched forward, Stewart at his back. The air was so full of dust twice he stifled sneezes. The lantern's yellow light lit on more busted chairs and trunks. A dusty bookcase of jars of pulpy apples, peaches, and green beans. Bottles of home brew that appeared curdled. It reminded George of the East Street Cemetery mausoleum that he and Stewart and Moss had broken into last year: the same musty, rotten odor, as if the ground had given up a stale belch; the same sticky cobwebs; the same hairs raised on the back of his neck as if he were violating a dim-witted, wrathful fiend's cave. If their parents or the coppers didn't grab them, some bony hand from a coffin would.

Clack! Clack-click! Clack! Shoes! Right over their heads! Crossing the upper floor to the cellar stairs!

"Bridget!" whispered Stewart. "She's coming down here!" He blew out the candle. They froze. The *clack-clack* got louder, and softer, then louder and stopped.

Stewart hissed, "Come on, let's get out of here!"

Bridget's *clack-clack* faded as she returned to the kitchen.

"I want to see where those stairs go," whispered George.

"I told you," said Stewart. "Under the stairs in the front hall. Everything in her house goes to the same place as in my house." Good, thought George, for he sure knew his way around Stewart's house.

"I'm going to wait," said George.

"Well, I'm not." A match flared, and Stewart gave George the lamp to hold while he relit the stub of candle. "Come on back upstairs and let's forget it."

"No, I got to find out."

His friend's mouth opened, then closed. He opened it again, as if he had thought of a better argument, then shook his head.

"Then help me back through the hole," said Stewart, "and if the rats and roaches don't eat you for dinner, I'll see you tomorrow."

Boots softly crossing the floor above George woke him again.

Boots, a man's boots! Maybe they were the witch's slippers? No—there, he heard the *slide-slide* of slippers. Two of them. Was that soft thud a door closing? He didn't know how long he had slept. It might be day again, but no light came from the nail hole through which he had seen the orange of the setting sun.

Whispers. Then slide of leather slipping toward the hall stairs near the front door. Then heavy creak of stairs. For a long time the floor over his head was silent to his straining ears.

His heart knocking against his chest, George crept up the cellar stairs and pushed open the door into the witch's downstairs hallway. With the caution of a burglar, he crept up the stairs, stopping to wince at every creak and pop of the floorboards.

On the second-floor landing, he paused. It wasn't cold, but he was shivering. Moans and laughter floated down from upstairs, from the third floor.

He wanted to turn and run back down the black stairs. At any moment the man whose boots he had heard, who could be Pa himself, might come charging out of the witch's bedroom, find him, and kill him. He and the witch would bury him in the cellar. Mama would grieve and mourn. Pa would never say a word. He would keep visiting the witch and mounting her like the stallion-devil he was. Pa was not King Arthur, he was the wicked knight Reinhart masquerading as a stalwart member of the Round Table. George swallowed and lifted his foot. The window at the third-floor landing was open and led onto a roof.

"... hear something?" the witch asked.

"... wind ... curtains," murmured the other.

The night air chilled the sweat on George's face. A faint light came from an open door down the hall. From it came a rustling of bedclothes, which curdled his flesh. He crept forward.

"Ummm, good," said the witch. "*Ooooh . . .*"

Like soldiers on watch in war, every nerve of George's was strained to attention. From the room came loud, rhythmic thuds and grunts. Now by drawing close and pressing his eye against the crack between the quarter-opened door and the jamb he could see into the room.

The witch, pale and naked as a newborn pig, was half on, half off the rear of the bed—on her stomach, her arms and her hair spread out toward the head of the bed, which was at a right angle to the hall door. Behind her, standing on the floor, a white figure leaned over her. The ghost-white, stripped devil was doing what stallions did with mares in Mr. Saddler's corral that made the roustabouts punch each other in the ribs, snicker, and make nasty cracks, except that this was—*Pa!*

Pa!

Pa's hands pressing on the sheets.

Pa's black beard bobbing over the witch's heaving white back, as Pa's white loins drove back and forth against her bare flanks.

Both were as white and naked as the inner bark of a stripped slippery elm. Pa—stripped of warm eyes, gentle hands, soft voice. This was another Pa, the real Pa, stripped naked. This was Pa as raw fury that would destroy any boy, son or not, who got in his devil way.

The pair writhed together like two squirrels skint of fur. They performed some vile, stomach-turning act on each other, an act as disgusting as chewing off and crunching the other's foot.

The large, slimy toad in George's stomach tore its way up through his throat. He clamped his jaws down on its horny, butting head. They would hear. His naked devil-father would chase him down the hall into the cellar, where this devil-stranger would kill him. George's lips stayed clamped shut to keep the toad's butting head in, and he backed down the hall toward the open window. He wanted to race through it, but he couldn't turn his back or the devil-stranger would fly out and grab him.

Out the window. Slick, welcome roofing tin under his palms. Stars against the black sky. Fresh air. A gasp as the toad lunged upward. Down the drainpipe here. Rustle of ivy. Into the back alley. His feet pushed against the ground, but his legs wouldn't hold up. The toad churned about, throwing itself against his belly wall in efforts to burst out. He realized he was crying and pushed away his sobs.

He staggered past crooked houses and dark, staring windows. The toad in his stomach again was clawing to escape. Gasping, he crept into an alley. The toad rose free, and all the chicken and biscuits Stewart's mama had given him at dinner came up in great heaves. After that, tears and sobs; then more heaves, this time only slimy toad bile.

He couldn't go home because Ma would want to know what happened between him and Stewart. He couldn't go to Stewart's because they thought he was at his own house. He would walk the streets and come home after breakfast, as if he had just come from Stewart's.

But he didn't want to go back near Pa. He didn't ever want to be in that evil house again. He wanted to run away to Boston, where he would sign on a ship bound for Africa. He might go out west. There he would become the son of a chief and grow up with the Indians, who lived among clean mountains, rivers, and trees and had nothing to do with the Devil

And leave Ma and Nellie? Leave them under the dominion of Pa's evil? Would a real squire of King Arthur's leave his ma?

No.

No made him dizzy. He gasped.

No, stay and face him.

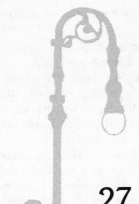

27

*When intensely interested in any matter,
Jay Gould devoted his whole
concentration of thought upon that one
thing, and would seem to lose interest in
things, often of greater pecuniary
importance but of not so much
commercial fascination. He loved the
intricacies and perplexities of financial
problems.*

—Thomas G. Sherman, eminent
nineteenth-century lawyer

The Hanover National Bank presented the most imposing granite façade of any building on Broad Street between the Battery and Maiden Lane.

The bank's seven granite pillars were three feet thick at their base. Inside, its central lobby towered overhead into a three-story-high vaulted arch that made even longtime depositors gasp when they gazed upward.

The bank's working quarters occupied the five stories above this magnificent domed space, while the topmost floor was occupied by the dignified offices of the Hanover National Bank's officers and directors. In the corner of this floor the President of the Hanover possessed a large office, a room with four floor-to-ceiling windows, one was far larger than the Mayor's office and possibly the largest in New York. Mahogany panels, English prints of horses and racing gigs, Persian carpets, and tasteful gas lamps informed the visitor that this hushed commander's post didn't welcome rude laughter or raised voices.

On a hot day in the middle of August 1869, Frank Sibbert, president of the bank, stood behind his desk and stared down at it. There like a holstered paperweight, a long-barreled Navy .44 pistol held down a stack of legal papers. Sibbert's gray face sagged, its flesh having the dirty, loose, dripping aspect of snow that might any moment slide off a roof. He laid his hand on the worn holster. The .44 had seen much service in the Civil War: Shiloh, Vicksburg, Chattanooga.

He had something to do. He was a Harvard man, he was a major in the finest army ever assembled, and he was a Sibbert. He always did what he had to do, and he did it without flinching.

In manly strides Sibbert paced to the mahogany door of his office and locked it, leaving the key in the keyhole. He strode briskly back to his desk. His hands clutched the rear of his swivel chair, his sweaty fingers moistening the worn buffalo leather. Finally, with a sure movement, he pulled the chair back and sat squarely in it.

In his hand the unholstered Navy .44 felt heavy and cumbersome. His other hand explored its cool ridges, hollows, and long barrel with the concentrated intensity of a blind father, returned from a long trip, exploring the face of a favorite child. In addition to his battered steel penknife, pocket New Testament, and wedding ring, the .44 had traveled with him through all three of his War years, from New York to Tennessee, from Broadway to Hell and back. He snapped open the cylinder, and the rear ends of five fat brass cartridges gleamed dully.

The snap of his closing the steel cylinder echoed across the hushed room as loudly as thunder. He cocked the pistol's hammer. Turning the pistol around, he put the barrel into his mouth. The muzzle tasted metallic and bitter, of gun oil and burnt powder. Taking care not to inadvertently fire it, he gingerly worked his fingers into the unaccustomed position of firing the pistol toward himself. It was as awkward as struggling to insert a live crab in your mouth without allowing it to bite you. It took a minute or so—right thumb gently against the trigger, four slippery fingers grasping the wooden grip backward. The trembling muzzle rattled against his teeth, so he steadied his right hand with his left. His noisy breaths down the cold barrel made whistling, hollow notes.

When my thumb squeezes the trigger, he thought, it will all be over; everything will be black and peaceful.

At Frank Sibbert's funeral under the gothic ceiling of Trinity Church, Jay Gould's intense eyes stared at the dead man's grieving family.

Molly Sibbert dabbed her eyes behind her black veil and occasionally broke into mincing, hiccuping sobs. The sweet perfume of lilies, the marble-cool air, and the slight tang of incense seemed to temper displays of emotion. The oldest boy, about fifteen, blinked back tears as if his dead pa wouldn't approve of a display of weakness. The two younger girls clung to their mother's black skirts with a bewildered, lost air. Pale and drained, Sibbert's father and mother kept their eyes cast down on the rail of their pew as if ashamed to meet those of others.

Despite Frank's having shot himself, he was being buried in the churchyard, which Jay figured was sensible. With this inkblot on his soul's copybook, Frank needed all the help he could get. The service was short, which Jay also thought sensible. As a pallbearer, he helped carry the coffin outside.

Afterward Jim Fisk sidled up. Like Jay, Jim was dressed in a frock coat, black vest, white shirt with a stiff wing collar, and a black bow tie.

"Want to walk back to the office?" asked Jim. He sported an ebony walking stick, one topped by a plain brass knob that was tastefully less showy than his usual duck's, lion's, and ram's head canes.

"Sure," said Jay. He had tried hard to push Frank's death away, but it had hit him more strongly than he liked. Like Frank's, Jay's company was hideously overextended. Like Frank, Jay had almost all his net worth wrapped up in his company. It was frightening that such a staunch, muscular fellow would turn against himself, as terrifying and unnatural as a hand taking a knife to boldly slice itself off from its wrist.

They swung up Broadway, refusing half a dozen shouted offers of rides from friends. As usual, the wide avenue was clogged with private carriages, public hacks, dogcarts, whip cracks, yellow dust, and oaths. The street traffic was so thick that they made as much progress walking as did the carriages cursing their way northward.

"I started up a collection for the family," said Jim. "We put in five hundred dollars."

"Good," said Jay. He sucked in and released a deep breath in an effort to dispel the funeral's gloom. "I couldn't sleep last night," he said. "What gets me is that if it can happen to somebody in *his* position, it can happen to anyone."

In fact, he hadn't slept well for more than a month. At first he had tried to lull himself to sleep with warm baths—sometimes two a night—and glasses of warm milk. No good. His brain flapped about the bright candles of his problems like an overstimulated moth. Several nights last week, desperate for sleep, he had taken two tablespoons of laudanum before bed. Each night he slept for six hours, but the opium and alcohol gave him such grotesque dreams and made his head so thick and achy the next day that it wasn't worth it.

In addition to the pressures that their massive position in gold put on the Erie, the Grand Opera House was not selling the tickets that Jim had led Jay to expect. It was draining money from their operations rather than contributing to them at a time when they badly needed extra earnings. Jim blamed its problems on the hot weather. Everybody who bought such tickets was down on the Jersey shore. Fall was the season, he promised Jay.

They both knew some success—in the gold market, on the stage, or with the Erie—some *dramatic* success, had to happen soon, or any day now Jim's and Jay's feet were going to slip. Vanderbilt was going to yank and pull and shove, yell at his team to haul all the harder. With the increased pressures from banks, creditors, and clearing houses, the opera house and the Erie would explode with the force of a steamboat's boiler, its safety valve tied down, in a heated race downriver.

"Now is the time to really push," said Jay, referring to Jim's daily trading in the gold pit, "if we're to get out of our hole."

Jim shot him a worried look. "Push! Jay, I done pushed, but it's like pushing on a harness strap—it don't go." The brass ferrule of his cane clacked against the sidewalk's paving stones. "I tell people gold is the thing to buy and they laugh at me. I don't know who around the President gabbed, but they've all heard about our little fantail chat with the War Hero. If Grant wants gold to go down, why should they bet it's going up?"

Jay nodded. If Jim couldn't turn things around on the floor, they couldn't be turned around. He was a great salesman, perhaps the greatest in New York—a peddler who could sell cow manure to dairy farmers, rags to dressmakers, snow to Buffalo—but he needed a product to sell. It was up to him, Jay, to furnish that product—if Jim's talents were to help them clamber up out of the deep pit Jay had dug them into.

Jay said, "Grant wants gold to go up."

"Come on!" said Jim. "I was out there on the ocean that night."

"He does," said Jay firmly. "He's changed his mind, and I can prove it to you."

"Changed his mind!" Jim grabbed Jay's arm, stopped in the middle of the sidewalk, and pulled Jay to him. *"Prove?"*

"Prove." Jay's hard poker face nodded solemnly, no humor to it. Inwardly he quailed. For the first time he was slipping one over on Jim. While it didn't feel quite right, still it was for the good of both of them. Jay forced a stiff smile. "I haven't kept company with the President's sister-in-law for nothing.

Jim scowled, his lips pursed as he silently mouthed "sister-in-law," and the lancelike tips of his mustaches thrust forward as if to joust with Jay's statement. "Hey, I'm not one of those dumb brokers you deal with."

"I said *prove*," Jay said, voice staunch. "If I can, what can you do?"

"If you *prove* to me that Grant wants the price of gold to go up, what can I do?"

"Yes."

Jim's large bulk bounced with excitement. "It would mean that Jay Cooke, well connected as he is to the government, isn't in it—that all this stuff I hear about him is only a rumor that Vanderbilt's spreading around to make us cut and run." Jim glanced around to make sure no passersby heard him, and like a lumbering bear leaning over to whisper to a fox, placed his head close to Jay's ear.

"It would mean that Grant really did listen to us, or that Colonel Porter got to him afterwards," he went on, his voice animated. "If I really and truly knew that the President of the United States wanted gold to rise—why, Jay, you know what I can do." His meaty hand squeezed Jay's upper arm in a hard grip, his excitement propelling Jay along faster. "I could get every man jack in this country to buy gold. I got friends, Jay, acres of them. They just don't think they can buck the United States Treasury."

With this gust of excitement, Jay felt jerked forward in his plans, as if a second locomotive had joined his to push a laggard train uphill. It might not be quite honest, leading Jim on, but it might get things moving.

"Then I'm going to prove it to you," Jay said, the sober conviction injected into his voice surprising even himself.

"You mean this? You're not just funning your old buddy?"

"I mean it," said Jay. The hard, solid tone of his voice admitted no doubt. Jim straightened, threw his loglike arm over Jay's shoulder, and pulled his partner closer.

"Hey, that's wonderful. *Prove!* We probably don't own *enough* gold! We'll jump out our hole in a stroke, won't we?" His blue eyes, gazing skyward, were lit up by the glare off the fluffy clouds. His fleshy lips were pulled back in a grin, and above them the twin wings of his mustache were ready to beat the air and soar upward. "Gosh, in a single lick we could unload our gold, give Vanderbilt a rap on his old red nose, build up the Erie's reserves, and take off the pressure for the Opry to do well fast."

As he prized Jim's stiff fingers off his shoulder, Jay said, "Well, our war hero wants gold to go up, and I'm going to prove it to you."

*   *   *

The shallow wooden drawer held a .38 pistol, the corner of its dirty bone handle chipped. Its short barrel was no longer blue, but nicked and rusted, as if aged and made ragged by the times and places it had been dragged through.

George Gould hesitantly, furtively pushed the barrel with his finger, and as it spun a quarter turn, the pistol rattled ominously against the bottom of the drawer. Above the drawer, on the top of his father's night table, Pa's alarm clock glared at him and ticked in a loud accusatory whisper, *Tell Pa! Tell Pa! Tell Pa!*

George's brow and upper lip were misted over with sweat, and his palms were clammy. The small bedroom that Pa slept in was cool and quiet at eleven-thirty in the morning, for Pa was downtown at work and Ma was in the kitchen supervising Cook. In fact, now that the maids were finished, nobody was upstairs but George.

In the open drawer the pistol's dull, cold metal dared George to touch it again, for it was death. George dried his wet palms on the forest-green coverlet on the bed. Pa had told him, made him repeat it three times to make sure he understood, that he wasn't ever to touch the pistol. Otherwise Pa would take his hide off. As Pa had never so much as spanked him, it was some threat.

Gingerly his fingers slid around the dry bone handle and he lifted it. It seemed to weigh as much as three pistols, as if made heavy by the seriousness of what it could do. Clasping its bone handle, careful not to touch its trigger or hammer, George raised and aimed it toward the window in the posture of scouts and soldiers in war pictures. It was so heavy that after a few moments its barrel drooped toward the floor.

After a while he swung out the revolver's cylinder and removed the cartridges. The five cases of shiny brass lay as heavily as bright coins on the green coverlet, the copper jackets poking out like fat sassy tongues.

To find out what death was like, he raised the empty gun with both hands toward the window, cocked the hammer, and pulled the trigger. The clean click of the hammer against the strike plate was as loud in the small, quiet bedroom as a thunderclap. George's heart was beating strongly, his hands again sweaty. He dropped the pistol next to the five cartridges. A shiver rattled his spine and whistled through his scalp: if a bullet had been in the gun, if Pa had been in front of him, Pa would be dead.

Mama's downstairs bell tinkled, announcing lunch. He started, expecting to see Mama come through the door. He quickly reloaded the pistol and put it back in Pa's bedside drawer, but he was unsure in what position it had been lying. Would Pa notice that it wasn't lined up exactly as he left it? George repositioned the gun a few times before he gave up and went down to lunch.

The full table downstairs, with Mama and Nellie and Edwin and Howard, was the same. Nellie said grace. Over chops, greens, and biscuits the others chattered together; George only spoke when addressed. For the first time in days he was calm and at ease. He didn't need to talk; he was powerful. Pa had better watch what he did to him and Mama. George now had a thunderbolt upstairs to stop the work of the Devil.

Jay's face was pinched and his shoulders more stooped than usual as he entered the front door.

Some of Annabelle's excitement leaked away and she felt silly in the loose gown, almost naked without the protection of a corset. He hardly glanced her way.

"Was the market down today?" she asked.

"Three dollars," he answered.

She gasped. "What a large drop!" she said. Her fingers pressed his arm in sympathy, and through his black beard he gave her a weary smile. Dark shadows lay under his eyes, and his face was as drained and pale as someone the doctors had bled. He smiled, but it appeared to be an effort.

To cheer him up, she said, "Come and have tea."

"I need something."

She had kept the parlor shutters closed and the shades down against the August heat, and although the room was dark, it was cool. On the low table between the sofas a silver plate of ham and cucumber sandwiches beckoned, and Great-grandfather Pigman's teapot almost glowed with its hot contents. They sat on opposite sofas.

"Any word from Butterfield?" she asked.

"No." He accepted the cup of tea she poured.

He hadn't kissed her on the way in, as if he had forgotten they were lovers. To hide her intense jitteriness, she kept her hands busy with tea plates, pot, cups, and spoons. After all, he had so much on his mind. Sitting in the empty house after Bridget and the children had left for Louise's, waiting for him to arrive, her nerves had vibrated so hard in the anticipation of his touch that she felt she might faint. Now she wanted to run her hands over him, peel away his drab black broadcloth. She wanted to feel his fingers stroking her. He drew papers from his inside coat pocket.

"I've brought your statements," he said. "They're up to date as of today's close." He passed over two sheets of accountant's ruled paper that crackled as if they were alive. She stopped fussing with the tea things to take them. Her account was down $50,000.

"Not what we had hoped," she murmured, masking her despair. He had to bear her losses on top of his others.

"I need more of your help, Annabelle." In his voice was a new note. As if to keep her losses from coming between them, she put the crackling sheets at the far end of the low table. His dark eyes glittered in a manic way. She laughed nervously. He went on, "I need Jim to come into this market."

"Jim? Come in? Does he have the money to make a difference?"

"It's not his money," said Jay. "It's his enthusiasm, his ability to bring others in. If Jim believed, really and truly believed, that gold was going to go up, he's just the promoter to create the market upturn we need." He nodded toward the brokerage statements to emphasize his point. In other words, rather than a $50,000 loss, that statement might be for a $100,000 profit.

"Yes, but can't Jim promote anything?" she asked.

"He promotes best what he believes is true—like any salesman."

"What am I needed for?" She poured herself a cup of tea.

"To convince Jim."

She laughed as she moved an empty sandwich plate back to the tray. "But I can't convince Jim Fisk of anything. I hardly know him."

He glanced toward the French windows as if averting his gaze. "Yes, you can." The forcefulness of his voice made her stiffen. "You're the President's sister-in-law."

The phrase hung in the air, suspended over her abruptly still hands. He had never used it before, had he? The way he said "the President's sister-in-law" made her sound official, like a cabinet officer—miles distant from the soft phrases they whispered in the far-away depths of night. She slowly placed two cucumber triangles on a plate.

"So what?" she asked cautiously.

"I've told Jim you have invested heavily in gold bonds," he said. A form pregnant with meaning loomed before her, a dim shape that she couldn't see clearly.

"Yes," she said, "bonds *you* loaned me."

"I—I didn't mention that," he stammered.

While she couldn't see the cloudy form clearly, his evasiveness made her heavy and numb. This kind of furtive maneuvering violated all her father's teachings. It reminded her of Ned—his use of charm, persuasion, and clever sleight of hand to obtain what he wasn't entitled to.

"Oh? Why not?" Her voice was light, almost airy, but a whining, rapid fear beat inside her lungs.

"There wasn't any need to." The few feet between them had become strained and tense.

"You're not asking me to say that that's Ulysses' money in my account?"

"No, no," he said quickly.

The tension popped, and she laughed nervously. With the dexterous use of a fork and spoon, she put two squares of ham sandwich on his plate. It wasn't what she thought, that he wanted her to drag Ulysses into this.

He went on, "But it wouldn't hurt if you *showed* him that you were invested in the gold market."

"Showed him?"

"Showed him your accounts," said Jay, nodding toward the ruled sheets. "Those statements. I told him you had invested heavily, but I didn't say how heavily." Now the dim form was back, hanging right in front of her so that she had no trouble spotting it. Again she felt tight and squeezed, hemmed in by a Ned-like influence.

"Jim is then supposed to think that through me Ulysses has invested in gold," she said, "knowing full well that the divorcee Stokes doesn't have a million dollars to put into gold." The smothering fear was back, expanding forcefully inside her chest, demanding out.

He hesitated, and his black eyes darted to the front of the room. "Yes."

She sighed. This was as furtive and shabby as two household cats scheming how to snatch the roast off the family dinner table. "No, I can't do that to Ulysses and Jenny," she said. "They've been too decent." He leaned forward, his eyes fixed on hers. His foot was jiggling rapidly.

"I'm not asking you to do anything to Ulysses and Jenny," he said. "Only to help me get Jim fired up."

"She's my sister, Jay."

"I thought you had a father," he said. "A father who wants his bank back. And you have a son, too. One you want to see in private school and in a profession. In a few years Matilda will need a coming-out party, not to speak of a season in Europe and a fancy wedding. You want to buy a business."

Although stunned by his force, she countered, "But I won't lie about Ulysses and Jenny for these things." From her sleeve she drew out her lilac-scented handkerchief and patted the moisture on her upper lip.

301

He went on in a driving voice, "Look at what you're doing to me, Jim, the Erie, your father, your children, yourself—and God knows, maybe even your country." He was nearly shouting. "I don't know where things will go once they become unraveled. I really don't."

"I don't know that I've ever bought your scare talk," she said more loudly and stiffly than she intended. She wanted to push his intensity back; crowding her, it didn't allow her to think. "Panics and civil wars and such."

"Well, you should," he said. "I may be wrong, but I'm nobody's fool. Any idiot who's looked at the past hundred years of history sees nothing but booms and busts. The way the Hanover Bank crashed last week, exactly the sort of disaster that will become an epidemic over the next few months."

She faltered under his onrush of certainty, yet said, "I can't— betray my sister and her husband."

His hand rose. "Don't say 'betray.' All I'm asking you to do is allow one man, Jim Fisk, to believe that Ulysses wants the market to go up. Let him draw his own conclusions. How will that harm your sister?"

Indeed, she saw how to bring it off. She could have Jim over for tea, possibly with a small crowd. She could make sure he remained afterward, preying on his chivalry by resting her hand on his arm, blinking a time or two, softly saying she needed his help. She would casually allow him to see her brokerage statement as she asked a helpless woman's questions about the gold market. She wouldn't say that Ulysses was involved, nor would she have to. Knowing that the bankrupt Ned Stokes's ex-wife couldn't afford a million-dollar brokerage account, Jim would assume that Ulysses Grant was using his wife's sister as a cover. In fact, not saying a word would make Jim believe it all the more firmly.

Jay held his pale hand up again. "Think about what a thirty-point increase in gold could do to that statement, compared to the drop you're looking at."

Thirty points! It meant a fortune, renewed life and breath for her, Papa, Richard, and Matilda. No more fear of having to take rented rooms, no more gowns borrowed off Louise, a business of her own— not having to depend on *anyone*, not even Jay. She took a deep breath to drive away her flutters and fears.

While as the President's sister-in-law she wasn't likely to slip into the ranks of the vagrant, still it would be easy enough for a lady with two children and the scandal of divorce in her past to fall into the position of governess or tutor. Guests to the stuffy household she landed in would murmur how lucky the family was to have such a well-bred servant. Men guests would eye her speculatively; she would modestly drop her eyes and maneuver away from their straying hands. The lady of the house would declare in a soft, patronizing tone, delicately lowered so that she couldn't hear, that Annabelle was "a gem."

Jay's scheme might not be the right thing to do, but it wasn't the wrong thing either if she wanted to survive on her own terms. She had one condition.

"If I help you, will you make sure that Jim doesn't spread around Ulysses' and Jenny's names?"

His face lit up. "Then you'll help!"

She smiled. "If you'll make sure Jenny and Ulysses are kept out of this, that their reputations aren't harmed."

He hesitated, his eyes blinking as he thought it over. "I don't see why anybody but Jim has to think the old war horse is in it. It's really nobody else's business."

"Will you make sure of that?"

"Yes," said Jay. "Yes, of course I will."

28

The loveliness of a rival eats into a girl's heart like corrosion. Every grace of outline is traced like lines of fire on the mind of the plainer one, and reproduced with microscopic fidelity.

—Susan C. Dunning Power, *The Ugly-Girl Papers*, 1875

It was at the Paterson, New Jersey, racetrack on a Saturday in September that Josie Mansfield brought up the possibility of the Erie Railway buying oil from Ned Stokes's refinery. It was as good a moment as she would get these days; Jim had won more than a thousand dollars this afternoon.

All Jim's warm, snuggly-bear generosity vanished. In a sour voice he asked, "And what exactly does that playboy need?" He didn't look at her, but kept his eye on the new trotters coming into the starting gate.

"Only somebody to buy his oil." She tried for the tone of a concerned mother discussing their child's need for tutoring with his tightwad of a father. She was an actress, wasn't she? She placed her hand on top of his, which lay on the splintery wooden railing. "He doesn't have enough customers. You know how little I know about business, but he very much wants to sell oil to the Erie." She blinked her lashes four or five times, frowned slightly to show how confused and uncertain she was over what she was asking, and gave him a shy smile.

"I 'spect he does," he said, "his being in the oil business."

Ned Stokes was one of Jim's few sore subjects, and had been so since the opening night at the Grand Opera House when she played peekaboo with him behind her fan. Probably that had been a mistake, and almost certainly she had overdone it—but then Jim had pushed her too far. Even though she had explained half a dozen times the harmless nature of Ned's escorting her, even though she had never allowed Ned to become intimate, and even though Jim had agreed three times that he had allowed his indignation on this issue to run away with itself—still, he got sullen and pinched-looking whenever Ned's name came up. Like right now. With her request Josie risked ruining more than just a gay Saturday afternoon at the races.

"Don't you buy oil?" she asked, shaking her head to throw the tickle of her straying ostrich plume into the whippy breeze.

She had timed her pitch when Jim was in a mellow mood, hoping he would give in quietly, but it was going to take perseverance. If Ned didn't get the Erie's business, his refinery would go bankrupt in three weeks. It had come as a shock to learn over the past months how little ready cash her handsome, debonair friend had in his thin sealskin wallet. Gone now was his talk of "looking around for the right business to go into." He admitted that the oil refinery he ran for the Philadelphia Stokeses was no more than a meatless bone the family had thrown him. If he made a bust of it, there would be no more help. No help meant no more elegant waistcoats, no more music-drenched teas at the Hoffman House, no more exhilarating afternoons at the racetrack, and no paying Josie back the hundreds in loans she had made to him from the money she had cajoled out of Jim. Worse than all this was the prospect that her new friend might simply bolt New York to avoid the mountain of debts he had run up. She didn't want that. Ned was one of the best things about life in New York.

Josie made herself speak hesitantly. "You do what's best for you."

"Tell him to come up to the Erie office one day," he said. In his strong, confident tone Josie saw his motive: a rival who was dependent on him for oil sales would be a tamer opponent. It would give Jim control over the situation. With a start that she hid, she wondered if success with Jim would make Ned less attentive to her. He might have befriended her solely out of his business needs.

Her voice still meek, she said, "All right, Jim."

"But I'm making no promises."

"No, no, of course you're not."

At dusk three days later, Josie opened the door to her town house. Ned clasped her hands, his face glowing.

"They're going to take five hundred barrels a day!" he said.

"Wonderful!" she said. "I told you Jim was generous."

"To a fault!" said Ned, laughing. "I wouldn't have been so generous to a fellow who hung around my lady friend the way I did that night."

Ned was holding her hands too long, and with a deft movement, one hand slithered down her waist toward her backside. Josie pushed him away.

"Hey!" she said. "Easy!"

Ned just grinned. "He said if the quality of the oil is what I showed him, he might double or triple the orders."

His thin figure turned twice in a little jig, toes and heels rat-a-tat-tatting for joy against the wide hall planks, the tail of his dark blue jacket sailing around him. She folded her arms across her breasts and smiled in pleasure. His powder-blue satin waistcoat and gray trousers set off his trim figure. He always looked handsome, but to-night—gray eyes flashing, black hair falling in locks on the thin skin of his forehead, lips rippling with pleasure—he appeared as dashing as a romantic lead actor.

"And *you* did it for me!" said Ned, pulling her arms apart and again clasping her hands.

"Me?" Josie protested, blinking her eyelashes in mock confusion. Maybe he would elaborate. "All I did was—"

"*You*," he said firmly. "If you hadn't set it up right, it wouldn't have happened." He dropped her right hand and held up a cautionary finger. "Don't think I'm ever going to forget this." The hot gray of his eyes fixed hers. The spot under her breasts caught in that won-derful fluttering that made it hard to breathe, and droplets of sweat prickled her chest. Over the last month Ned's place had grown larger, much larger, in her everyday thoughts and feelings.

As planned, she gave Ned supper. In her dining room, softly lit by the single gas chandelier, her Negro servant Carter deftly served them cold ham, hot roast potatoes, and a salad. Later, Carter spooned out brandied molasses pudding and poured demitasses of coffee. As well as the dining room door, Josie had left open the windows and their indoor shutters, and as they sipped black coffee a soft breeze from the September evening stirred the lace and muslin drapes.

"A fine meal," said Ned as he tossed his napkin with an elegant flourish onto the lace tablecloth. He shot her a wink. "Maybe we should finish it off with a cordial upstairs?" He meant her bedroom.

She shrank back in her chair, which creaked. "Ned, don't. I've asked you not to." His eyes rested on her figure with that bold frank-ness that pictured her in bed and caused a tremor to pass over her.

"All right—but you know how I feel about you."

"Yes," she said. Actually, she wasn't at all sure how he felt toward her. She was useful to him, and he might find her a desirable companion in bed, but whether she had a real chance at something longer-lasting—that she didn't know. Ned was the kind of beau you didn't really know about till you got him to the altar—and maybe not even after you walked out the church doors with him. For a few silent moments they stared at their ponies of sweet, tart wine. Besides, no matter how she felt about a beau, if he didn't have money, she couldn't afford him.

However, an evening in which Ned was grateful was a good time to ask for a favor. Josie said, "There is something you could do for me."

Wary frost crystallized in his gray eyes. "What is it?"

She guessed that he was afraid she would ask for money. He might come from a well-off family, and he might talk extravagantly of large sums won and lost at the races and spent on waistcoats, card games, and parties, but when it came to laying down a dollar, his soft, elegant hand stayed in his well-tailored pocket or else opened palm up for her to put something in it. She rose and shut the dining room door, an intimate gesture that she had never made before when they were alone together.

"I haven't seen Jim much for several weeks," she said. "Not since that week his wife unexpectedly came to town. All I get is a note every other day that the market still has him tied up."

"She was here all right," said Ned. His long, smooth fingers caressed the curved edges of the pony glass. "I read about her visit in the papers. You can't read one without hearing what the sage of Twenty-third Street opines."

"Was she?" asked Josie. "Was she really? You don't know Jim. He and the reporters are thick as thieves. He might have a new flame, and the notices you read were only to throw me off."

Ned sat up straight, the empty pony glass in his hand thrust forward like a baton, his face exploding in mock outrage. "Not another woman!"

His ridicule struck her like a slap. "Yes," she said, her voice level. "Don't play with me, Ned. I didn't play with you about your need for an oil customer." His lips and cheeks filled out with plump disdain.

"You want me to find out who else he's seeing?" Still sprawled in his chair, he made her sound like a fool for being with Jim.

"Yes, if you can."

An expression of amused interest crawled over his face. "Suppose he has some other woman?" he asked. "What would that mean for us?"

"Please," she whispered. "I'm upset enough. I'm asking you to do me a favor, that's all."

"Forgive me," he said, dropping his gaze and rising as if eager now to leave. "Of course I'll help."

Over the next three days Josie received two more notes from Jim. Both called her his "bonbon," and one, his "sugarplum." He would see her when things "broke clear," whatever that meant. Where was Ned?

She was as jumpy as a two-year-old horse who had never felt the saddle. Taking along cousin Virginia, visiting from Boston, she set out on an all-day expedition to the white-marble dry-goods store of Messrs. Lord & Taylor at Broadway and Grand. Five spacious, elegant floors of silks, linens, ribbons, laces, well-mannered clerks, and glass cases. The faint essences of a thousand herbal sachets. Calm spread through Josie like butter through hot toast.

That evening Ned arrived at dusk. The fire in his eyes almost knocked her over.

"That son of a bitch!" he said, charging into the front hall. "That whore!" The small entryway reeked of the whiskey on his breath. His long face was twisted into a hard sneer. Rather than its normal expression of cool appraisal, his face was aflame, as out of control as a theater conflagration she had witnessed in Denver. Frightened, she backed away.

"What's the matter?" called cousin Virginia from the kitchen.

Ned hissed, "Let's go upstairs. You don't want her to hear this."

He led the way to the parlor. Ned had never appeared so purposeful, as if his former languid manner had hidden a volcano of intent.

She slid the double parlor doors shut and asked, "What's happened?" He was panting as if he had been running, and droplets of sweat clung to his brow.

"I did what you asked, right?" said Ned. His face was milkier than usual, and the stubble beneath the skin of his cheeks and chin was a dark shadow, as if his skin had become opaque. "I went by the Hoffman House a couple of times, particularly at noon, figuring the fat oaf would be eating downstairs." He paced around. The stench of whiskey and foul breath had followed him in. All this was said in a dramatic way, chin thrust forward, arms waving about. "Then yesterday afternoon, just before tea, I'm by that stone ledge just outside the building and I hear him give the address of—Annabelle's house."

He stopped pacing and looked askance as if she would surely comment, but it made no sense to her and she stared at him blankly.

"Who?" she asked.

"Annabelle!"

"Who's she?"

"My wife!"

"Your wife? You're divorced."

"My late wife!" he shouted. "The whore!"

"Late?" said Josie, completely bewildered. "You never said she died."

"My *former* wife. I've never said much of her to you."

She struggled to understand. Why was he so upset? Yet, to judge by his stench, the news must have made him bathe in a whiskey barrel. "But—maybe you misheard the address."

"Aha!" Ned shouted, his white face and gray eyes blazing with demonic glee. "That's what I thought. Not that I can afford it, but I grabbed a hack and told the driver to race over there. Told him to rush up Lexington to get there *before* Mr. Fisk." As if it was constraining him, Ned twisted about and struggled out of his close-fitting blue coat. "I went around the corner and pretended to be searching for an address. *His cab draws up.*" As if it were a rope constricting his neck, Ned yanked off his maroon cravat. "The fat rascal prances as bold as you please up to *my* door and *she* greets him like he's her long-lost lover—and *in* he goes."

None of it made sense to Josie. Her head spinning, Josie sat on the edge of a plush chair. "Your former wife."

"That whore."

"From the little you've said, she's not quite the type," she said. "I've never known Jim to go with any woman with money or position." Disliking to put herself in such company, she nonetheless realized that Jim never spent time with any woman who wasn't a shopgirl, an actress, a chambermaid, or some other woman of slender, if any, class or means.

"I have no real claim on her, true enough," he said, his voice still a shout, "but still it *galls*." Josie watched him pace about. In all the months she had known him, he had never been this worked up over anything.

"It really hurts," he went on. "Here I am, selling him his oil, struggling to make sure that it's thin enough for his precious locomotives, and seeing to it that he gets it on time. Sure, I've escorted you to the theater a couple of times, but nothing's gone on between us. You might think he would even thank me for providing you with an escort, mightn't you? But noooo! Every time I'm up to his office he lords it over me by showing me how much richer he is than I am. Brattleboro upstart." Josie knew how much pleasure Jim took in the trappings of his gilded office.

Ned's voice plunged on. "He's always telling me what my refinery can and can't do. Fat hog." Jim, as buyer, would have conditions about the oil he bought. "Now he thinks he can insult me by popping in there any time he wants and goosing *her*. She wants to rub my nose in it. He probably brags about it all over Broadway. They're probably all laughing at me."

To Josie most of this was a preposterous line of reasoning. Still, it didn't appear safe to contradict the entire argument. She limited herself to the important part.

"You don't really think he's—intimate—with her, do you, Ned?"

"What else am I to think?" Ned cried. She pressed her finger to her lips, afraid Virginia or Carter would come upstairs to see what was the matter.

"I think he still owns a brokerage," she said. "Maybe he has business with her."

"Brokerage! She's broke, all right. The sheriff is about to take the house, she told me so herself. Her father got wiped out in the cotton bust. Her in-laws, that dummy in the White House, doesn't own his own chamber pot. Where would Annabelle get any money? —No! The only thing that whore has got that a man wants slides around between her legs."

"Ned Stokes!" she said, taking a step backward in shocked alarm. "I've never heard such."

"I'm steamed up, Josie," he shouted. "I've taken all I can take."

He went back to his feverish pacing. Josie was steamed up, too, but she wanted to think. Now it was clear why at the racetrack Jim had been so reluctant to help Ned. How dare Jim Fisk—if it was true. She could tolerate monthly visits to see his wife, but half a dozen times he had sworn he had given up the others: the lumpy Irish girls in cigar-store brothels, the chambermaids who infested his sheets like bedbugs, and the party girls at Sally Woods's who wanted him for themselves.

Josie sighed. "Ned, we know nothing, really. This could all be your imagination."

He threw his head back with indignant anger. "I'm going to watch him like a hawk tomorrow. I'm going to make sure, absolutely sure, of what that scoundrel is doing to me."

"To us," she said. "Yes, that's good. Let's find out more. Something here doesn't make sense."

In the middle of that night Josie woke up. It was hot and she was suffocating. She threw back the damp top sheet, but that didn't help. She pulled her cotton gown up around her breasts, but so much cloth around her breasts and throat made the sensation of suffocation worse, so she pulled the gown off over her head.

Naked wasn't much better. She lay on the damp bottom sheet and writhed from side to side. The bedroom was stifling, the air stale and as thick as cotton batting. She had an urge to get up and toss everything in the room—chairs, pillows, bottles of perfume, dresses, rugs, lamps—through the window. Her lungs labored, but as if they were undersized balloons, she couldn't draw in enough air.

Overwhelmed and panicked, she sat up on the edge of the bed. To throw off the horrible sense of smothering, she breathed in yet larger gulps of air. Her heavy breasts slapped against her chest. Her belly and thighs were cold and clammy, and the skin on her back was misted over with sweat. In her whole life she had never felt more like the set-upon cow that her mother had been.

As her pounding chest calmed, thoughts galloped through her brain as forcefully as a man's angry sexual thrusts against her. Jim was going to toss her over and take up with Annabelle. Without Josie's connections to Jim, Ned would have nothing more to do with her. Because she had squandered herself by always being available to Jim, Josie would be left with no more than her dress and grocery bills, Carter's wages, the upkeep of the carriage, and the payments on the house and the stable.

Josie could read between the lines: despite Ned's anger and the vague comments he had made over the previous months about Annabelle's lack of funds and intelligence, his ex-wife was nobody's fool in general, and in particular not one about men. She sounded like the calculating sort of doxy who knew just how to sink her hook deeply into a man's jaw and expertly reel him in.

That afternoon Ned showed up at sundown. His face was worn and haggard, his shoulders stooped, and his blue coat streaked with mud. She was drawn and haggard, too. He reeked of whiskey again, and his gray eye shone with a wilder gleam.

"It's definite," said Ned. As if he had been shouting for hours, his voice was a hoarse croak. "He was over there again today. Stayed from three to five o'clock—long enough to stuff her a dozen times. She gives him a warm smile when he leaves. He struts out like the cat who's just lapped up a big dish of cream."

Josie kept her distance. "Did they kiss?" she asked. "Touch each other?" On the verge of snapping, her nerves were wires that had been stretched too tightly.

"I talked to Bridget," he said, his voice calm. "Walked around the neighborhood till I bumped into her."

This oblique answer to her question chilled her. "Who?"

"The little Irish slut who liked Annabelle so much," he said, a smirk coating his hoarse voice. "The only servant who stayed on after I left. I acted like I just happened to run into her."

"Oh?"

"I said, acting like I knew all about it, 'So you got yourself a new mister, a big one with a lot of money.'

"She says, 'A bigger man than you, that's for sure, and has a lot more'n you ever had or will have.'

"I said, 'I don't envy him. That's a cold bed he has to wallow in.'

"She laughs at me in that snotty way she always had and says, 'I 'spect he's not finding it near as cold as you once did.'"

Icy numbness slid over Josie. Her face pinched. This had the solid ring of truth. She felt hollow, brittle. If she let go, she would break into a thousand pieces and her tears would wash her away. She had never been any more than another of his playthings. She should have seen that it was going to come to this. She had lost him to this upper-class priss, someone accepted by all those grandes dames on Fifth Avenue who wouldn't glance Josie's way even though she had her own carriage, good clothes, and driver just like them. It wasn't fair, wasn't fair, wasn't fair.

Ned was standing over her. He drew her to him. Too miserable to resist, Josie allowed herself tears, something she hadn't done in ages and never in front of Ned. It was a relief to give way to the pain. Ned's hot, close body absorbed sob after sob after sob. After a while he drew a crumpled red silk handkerchief from his breast pocket and patted away her tears. A green, fresh shoot poked up through the ashes and slag of her grief. She pressed against Ned's warm, slender body. It would be pleasant to have him next to her in bed—exciting, even.

He pushed her far enough away to lightly kiss her. His lips had a bitter tang, sharper than Jim's mellow taste of cigar. Her throat tightened, and beneath her breasts rose the flutter she often felt around Ned, stronger now, a flutter that warned her to be cautious. Despite her desire for him, she firmly pulled herself from his embrace and walked away, giving herself a chance to cool off.

"Josie, all we have now is each other," he pleaded. "They've betrayed us."

"She's not yours, Ned."

"He's told her I'm with you. Don't you see? He's still angry from that night at the Opera. She's angry because she lost me. They're doing it and laughing at us behind our backs."

Were they? Josie wasn't sure. Ned didn't always get things right.

She needed time to think. She wouldn't allow Ned in her bed tonight. She had nearly been swept away, but if there was one thing about beaus that she knew for sure, you never did your relation with them any harm by putting them off—in a kindly fashion. Most of a woman's problems came from giving in too easily to what men wanted.

Moreover, if all this business about Annabelle and Jim was in Ned's imagination, and if Jim discovered that she had allowed Ned in her bedroom, he would be through with her. In his book Josie was a struggling, sometimes bohemian actress, but not a loose woman.

Jim—warm, fat, generous, funny—through with her! It was like saying you didn't want to see your father or brother again. No, she didn't want that.

She hurriedly excused herself and flew out of the room. Once downstairs she asked Virginia to come up. She and Ned both needed time to cool off. Someone else sitting around the parlor would put the kibosh on any further plans of Ned's tonight and give her a few days to sort out what was in her best interest.

29

The rapid, eager ticking of his gold
Engineer's Special woke Jim Fisk at dawn the following Monday, the
twentieth of September. For a few seconds he lay in bed with a heady,
dizzying sense of excitement. The two plush chairs and the fat armoire's gilt-edged mirror grinned back. With a roar of eagerness, he
flung back his sheet and hopped out of bed.

This was the week Jim was going to deliver the knockout punch
to that damn Vanderbilt. Since he had got the real skinny from Annabelle on Thursday and Friday, he had grown certain that he and Jay
possessed the power to give the Old Walrus a birching he would never
forget.

Dressing up for such a big day, he stuck three diamond studs into the stiff holes of his crisply starched shirt. He pulled on the rich wool of his broker's gray-striped trousers and slipped into the brocaded vest of maroon satin, cut on the diagonal, that his tailor had deliverd only yesterday. He slid the glossy silk stockings on his feet into black ankle boots, and he pushed three gold rings on his plump fingers. He thrust the loudly ticking Engineer's Special into a vest pocket and draped its two gold chains across the broad sweep of his paunch. From the fifteen walking sticks in the elephant-leg urn by the door, he selected his gold billy-goat-headed cane, his favorite, and the horned beast who best represented his mood.

Downstairs at his usual window table in the Hoffman House's grand dining room, he nodded and spoke cheerfully to a dozen other plungers. He hung the grinning billy-goat head of his cane over the edge of the white tablecloth. He breakfasted on hominy grits, two rare slices of grilled calf's liver, four sunny-side-up eggs, six slices of buttered toast slathered with thick-cut black marmalade, two pots of scalding coffee, and his mounting excitement. The gold billy-goat urged him to hurry, its burnished smile eager for the day's work.

As he did every morning, he stopped at the hotel barbershop, a male sanctum of tall mirrors, twenty barber's chairs, and the confident drone of gents' voices. The aromas of talcum, bay rum, and witch hazel aroused his fighting spirit the way whiffs of burnt gunpowder did a seasoned soldier. At the shop's far end, a tall sallow barber, a pair of scissors and a razor poking from the pocket of his white jacket, gave Jim a waxy smile and dusted off his usual chair.

"How's your old tin oven, Andrew?" Jim boomed as he leaned back onto the leather-and-porcelain throne. Andrew snapped out a fresh-smelling towel and wrapped it around Jim's neck.

"Fine, Jim," said the barber with a grin. Andrew's few oily strands of hair were parted way down on the left side of his head and slid, like gray-black streaks of mud, across his shiny, bald dome. His long upper teeth looked as if they had been made of wood and painted white. The barber wrapped the steaming, wet folds of a hot towel around Jim's face. "What's doing? You look fit as a bull fiddle."

"I got a big day," said Jim. He gave Andrew a wink through the folds of towel. He closed his eyes and allowed the damp heat to relax him.

Andrew's long, expert fingers dug into his scalp as the hot towel performed its soothing magic. Jim went along with Andrew's suggestion that the barber put ten dollars for him on Mustard Boots in the third race at Paterson. Jim closed his eyes and relaxed. His excitement was so great that it glowed like an orange ball of power—a small, bright sun—in the darkness of himself. Continuing to chat,

315

he also agreed with Andrew that there wasn't a poor fellow alive, rich or poor, who could predict a female's mood, that women just naturally went from hot to cold without do-damn rhyme or reason. As he shaved and scraped Jim's fleshy chin and ruddy cheeks, making sure every clump and tuft was sliced away, Andrew giggled over Jim's jokes. Toward the end, he laughed softly, for he didn't want his hand to shake as he trimmed the most famous mustache in the city.

After Andrew had twirled its ends into rapier points, he brushed Jim's collar and helped him into his coat. He handed up the gold billy-goat cane and placed Jim's top hat just so on his head. His whisper slithered over Jim's shoulder: "Do you know anything that might help me downtown?"

"Did you sell that Central?" Jim asked in a low voice.

"Yes, indeed, and thank you very much."

"Gold," said Jim over his shoulder, as if leaving, but Andrew grabbed his arm.

"Gold?" clacked Andrew, those funny teeth of his sliding around. "Sell gold?"

"*Buy* gold," insisted Jim.

Andrew's eyes bulged and his eagerness twisted into confusion. "But—"

Coming in close, Jim shushed the barber with a forefinger against his pursed lips. He glanced around the crowded shop. Nobody was looking.

"Not a word to anyone," Jim whispered. "Understand—*not a word.*" Andrew's eyes darted in fear to the thousand receding images of white-coated barbers and reclining gents in the shop's wide mirrors. In a low, urgent voice, Jim went on, "Sell everything else, all your stocks, and buy as much gold as you can stand." Andrew's waxy face puckered with worry.

"But everybody says a big pool is shorting it."

Jim gave him a long, slow wink. "That's right, they are saying that, aren't they?" He lightly touched Andrew's cheek with the left horn of his cane's billy goat. Andrew's eyes widened and he grinned.

"Jim, this can't be right," the barber hissed.

Jim's eyes, cheeks, and lips drooped with hurt. "How often have I steered you wrong?"

Andrew shook his head quickly. "Not often." His speech stumbled. "Just that Overland Shipping."

Jim stared him right in the eye. "Was I responsible for a combine coming in and building another road?"

Andrew shook his head no, but clearly he was still worried. "But *everybody* says short gold."

Jim smiled enigmatically. "Exactly."

He gave Andrew another wink and left, the single hoof of his billy-goat cane clacking confidently against the shop's tiles.

As he hit Broadway for his walk downtown, Jim figured that today alone Andrew ought to spill the beans to thirty sports. With any luck, those thirty would whisper the secret to another sixty greedy buckeroos.

He stopped for coffee at the Fifth Avenue Hotel and the Broadway Central. At three glitzy shoe palaces, he had his ankle boots shined three separate times till they gleamed like the fresh paint on a new black carriage. He dropped into six brokerage offices for hearty visits that lasted no longer than ten minutes.

At these eleven stops he had at least one whispered conversation much like the one with Andrew. These were with plungers—large and small—whom he had known for years, ordinary fellows who were part of his informal trading gang. Over the weekend he had done the same with twenty others. Like Andrew, each had a big mouth and ran into lots of gees who liked to play the markets. Members of his gang regularly made money on his advice. He got them in a stock at the right price, and unlike other advisers, he bullied them out in time to take away profits. Over the years he had built up a following that was large and strong enough to often push a stock up three or four dollars, and sometimes eight or ten—enough for them all to get in, make some money, and get out with no worse than the occasional nipped fingertip.

He was late for the opening of the gold pit, and he hurried down Broadway. What Jim hadn't let on to any of his gang was the news that Annabelle had let slip last Thursday and Friday—that the President himself had laid down his own dollars to take advantage of gold's rise. Skimming along Broad, dodging ladies in bonnets and gents in derbies, his mind's eye lingered on the pleasurable memory of her. Raven-haired, dark-eyed Annabelle Stokes was some beauty, if a bit thin and cool for his taste. Still, if Jay hadn't staked her out, Jim would have made a play for her. Of course, standing there all decked out in blue satin and creamy lace in that fancy parlor of hers, she hadn't come right out and *said* her brother-in-law was in the gold market. Still, any fool could read between the lines of that brokerage statement with the gold-lettered *Morris, Nathan, Kincaid, & Co.* at the top. Any fool would know that she didn't get the jack from that foppish nincompoop Ned Stokes to buy a million dollars' worth of gold bonds.

He waved his billy-goat cane and shouted to several score acquaintances and friends. No, there was only one place that Annabelle's money had come from, her brother-in-law in the White House. Like Jay, she and the President wanted the gold market to go up, but of course she couldn't come right out and say so. And for insurance, she and his clever partner had installed General Butterfield at the New York office of the Treasury.

So, as well as trading the Erie's massive position in gold as per Jay's instructions, last Friday and Saturday Jim had quietly liquidated all his stock positions to raise cash. To raise additional funds in the form of a large loan, he pledged to the bank his Erie stock, his steamship company, his partnership in his brokerage firm, and his house in Boston—in short, everything he owned, down to the three carriages that Rufus drove. This morning, for the first time, he was going to use his own funds to buy gold, not merely the Erie's. By taking advantage of leverage, the ability to buy ten ounces of gold for the price of one, he could multiply every penny he owned five times over the next few weeks.

Jay had begged Jim to form a pool with him, but Jim laughed heartily and declined. Jay was too cautious; Jim would trade his own account. He knew Jay. With his wary partner watching the pool's daily figures, Jim could never buy and then buy again with the pool's profits, and then with those profits buy yet again, doubling, tripling, quadrupling his gold contracts. That was the way to make real money, and unfettered by Jay, he would do it in his personal account.

Jim chuckled as he crossed Wall Street. He would show Jay Gould how to handle the markets. His partner didn't understand how much his own guarded quietness worked against him. After Jim saved the Erie, made it a pile to boot, and created a fat personal reserve for the opera house—all in one fell swoop—Jay would wish he had twenty partners like Jim.

As a result of Vanderbilt's heavy-handed leaning on the market, the gold market was oversold and deeply depressed; when it picked up steam it would roar upward with the speed and power of a crack express train.

Jim grinned as he plunged through the stone doorway of the Exchange. Jay may have designed this track and bought the locomotive; but with his hand on the throttle, Jim was this gold train's engineer and the fireman shoveling coal into the blazing furnace. Let Cornelius Vanderbilt keep his fat rump on the steel rail on which he had so firmly planted it. When he and Jay roared through Vanderbilt Junction they would squash his fat butt flatter than a shiny new penny lying on the tracks.

*   *   *

The two-story-high Gold Room at midmorning resembled the hidden storeroom of a beehive, one in which hundreds of bees had gone mad with greed, each fighting the others to carry off the hive's entire store of honey.

The action in the Gold Room was concentrated in "the pit," not a pit at all but five concentric steps circling a dry fountain in which a boy rode a dolphin. In order to buy and sell, several hundred traders and brokers stood on the concentric steps facing another few hundred who stood on the marble floor. At their feet rustled pink wavelets of discarded trading slips.

Buoyed up with excitement, Jim took his regular spot along the waist-high iron railing surrounding the pit, about thirty feet removed from the mob of traders. The crowd's steady noise sounded like the hollow growl of a large, hungry beast. As he settled against the rail, his hot palms welcoming the coolness of the pipe, the fountain sprang to life. Water squirted up on all sides of the cherubic Cupid riding the leering, blubber-lipped dolphin, and the imp of love squirted his perpetual tinkle.

Jim's eyes coolly searched the agitated crowd for his own traders. In an alcove to Jim's left, twenty frantic clerks at a long wooden table hunched over nests of telegraph keys. They tore off pink trading slips and slapped them into the hands of runners, boys who shot off to find their firm's traders in the packed squabble around the fountain.

Unable to find his men, Jim swung his head around to take in Stumpy Roberts. As usual, his opponent leaned against the stiff iron rail thirty feet opposite Jim. His arms were folded across his solid body, which was as thick as the stump of a stout oak. No more than five feet tall, Stumpy commanded the Commodore's troops. Like Jim, from his post he tried to make the market move his way—which now that he worked for the Commodore was down, the opposite of Jim's need for it to go up. For two weeks Stumpy had leaned against the iron pit railing and had his way, each day selling short massive amounts of gold. Stumpy had driven the price down from 130 to 110 dollars an ounce. This morning the market, edging up another dollar to 111, was finally going against Stumpy.

Yet Stumpy's face was no different in defeat than in victory. Jim often joked that Stumpy's face resembled a cross-section of the same oak his body was hacked from. Although Stumpy never said much— "quiet as a stump," was the room's word for him—it was also said that no one could so much as break wind in the pit without Stumpy knowing it. When he spoke, his croaking honk was the offspring of

319

the marriage of a bullfrog with a foghorn. He communicated in only three- and four-word sentences: "Buy me a hundred." "Get me lunch." "Sell the lot." "Sell me five hundred." The joke had it that he had acquired his wife with the lengthiest market order of his life: "Sell the whores. Buy Molly. Buy me a house. Get me four children."

Jim spied a familiar set of gray curls, and the billy-goat's head of his cane shot out. It snared the arm of a long, thin stoop of a fellow called Weeping Willie, whom he and Jay used for a lot of trading.

"Buy me five hundred ounces to show him what's what."

Following the dart of Jim's eyes, Willie glanced over at Stumpy, whose impassive Scottish eyes stared back as if he could read their lips. Shoving Willie off to the pit with one hand, Jim waved the gold billy-goat's head at his opponent with the other, but as usual Stumpy didn't even nod.

When he wasn't trading or watching Stumpy, like every other plunger Jim kept an eye on the gold arrow that spun in the center of the gilded, circular dial over the entrance, for it told him whether he was winning or losing. Much the way a clock tells time, this gilt arrow announced the price of the last trade in gold. Now it was up another dollar to 112 and holding steady. Jim grinned.

Now to jerk Stumpy's tail. Spotting Willie on the topmost step, Jim used their coded hand signals to ask if he had bought the five hundred ounces.

"Yes," came Willie's hand signals. "One twelve and a quarter."

With Stumpy's eye cocked in his direction, Jim threw him a lofty smirk and signaled for Willie to buy another thousand ounces. Because it was a large order for so early in the day, Willie asked him to repeat it. Thumbing his nose at Stumpy, Jim abandoned his team's private code. The time was ripe to bust Stumpy one in the snout. He repeated it in standard Gold Room sign language: right hand, palm in, pulling to him; left hand opening and closing twice to expose all five fingers.

Around the pit it looked like a tribe of maddened Injun dancers. Trading was done through the method of open outcry, but not trusting voices in the din, traders more often relied on lightning-fast hand signals. Palm out and pushing meant you wanted to sell. If another wanted to buy, he—and others—stepped over and faced you. As if doing a fast, manic war dance, the buyers held their right palms toward themselves and made a pulling motion, while their left hands held up fingers to show the price and how many tens or hundreds of ounces were wanted. In seconds the trade was over. Each scribbled the transaction on a white slip, jammed it into a pocket already crammed with white slips, and stalked his next trade.

On the top step of the pit, Jim spotted Frisky Freyer, a short, plump fellow with a thick shock of brown hair who was always as excitable as a squirrel discovering a new cache of nuts. Holding his cane by its base, Jim waved the billy-goat's head to get Frisky's attention. In fast hand code, Jim signaled him to buy two thousand ounces. Frisky signaled back okay.

To take the pressure off his feet, Jim inched his rump on top of the cool iron rail. When this last order hit the market it ought to put the fear of God, the Devil, Pontius Pilate, and Judas into Stumpy. Jim's goal was to hit 115 this morning. With any luck, at that level the chalkboard lizards hanging around brokers' offices in Boston, San Francisco, Hartford, and Chicago would believe that gold's two-week decline had bottomed. Buying would come in strongly over the alcove's telegraphs, and Jim ought to be well on his way to a victory.

Stumpy must have seen this danger, for he signaled two floor traders he used, McGuffin and Leary, who began to sell as fast as Willie and Frisky bought. Both sides simultaneously piled up massive positions, a situation that Jim had avoided the past two weeks, not wanting to weigh his slender resources in the pan of a scale opposite that in which rested Vanderbilt's and Cooke's vast pool of wealth.

The closing bell clanged, announcing the noon break. Jim reckoned that he had almost got a real nice rally going. At one-thirty the market would reopen for two hours, when Jim could have another try. He signaled "Delmonico's" to tell Frisky, Willie, Bob, and Flowers to meet for lunch and a strategy session. This afternoon Jim would see if he couldn't drive a spike into that wooden face of Stumpy's and split it into kindling.

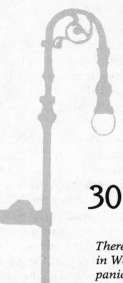

30

*There is no fright as great as the fright
in Wall Street when the bears get
panicky. Burnt brandy won't save 'em,
for the very reason that they have sold
what they have not got.*

—Jim Fisk, 1869

That evening Jim toured the night
spots of lower Manhattan—the Hoffman House bar, O'Malley's, Rien-
hoffer's, the Fifth Avenue Hotel's bar, Hanrahan's, and three of the
four Delmonicos. This afternoon he had succeeded in bulling up the
Gold Room seven points; maybe tomorrow he and Willie and the
other bulls could not only split Stumpy's wooden face into kindling,
but put a match to it.

Every bar was inflamed with stories of Jim's duel with Stumpy,
or rather with Vanderbilt. He hugged, laughed, and joked his way
through noisy, back-slapping crowds. He answered a thousand questions with a dozen quips, and from the fat roll in his pocket he bought
drinks for several hundred traders, brokers, hangers-on, dust merchants, and ounce kickers.

Much the same scene occurred at every bar. He elbowed through
the throng, wound up with his back to the counter, glass in hand, his
head cocked to one side, and an amused grin on his plump, ruddy
features. In addition to touting the rise in gold, he encouraged other
traders to tell their battle stories, and he relished a small trader's
ten-ounce victory with as much fervor as he did a professional's
thousand-ounce win. In detail he described how hard his team had
hit Stumpy and the Commodore today, concluding that "they got to
be hurting, had to have lost $100,000, maybe $200,000." When

pushed—badgered, battered—for more information about what was going on, he held up his billy-goat stick for quiet, and he waited in a dramatic pause while the astute shushed the blabbermouths.

Only when the four or five dozen traders surrounding him were unnaturally quiet did he declare in a soft, uncharacteristically sober voice, "I'm bound not to say any more," while his forefinger lifted like a schoolteacher's. "All I can tell you is that gold's getting ready for a mighty rally, and that's the God's truth."

"A *mighty* rally, Jim?" some soul would ask timidly.

"A *God* Almighty rally."

At this point an eager, hot-eyed reporter was likely to press with "How do you know?" Jim would put his upraised forefinger by the side of his nose, shake his head slowly, and smile enigmatically. What this meant, he had little idea. He had done this at his second stop, Hanrahan's, and reporters had so little trouble interpreting it to mean that he was deeply in the know that he used it all evening long.

Jim had never felt more powerful. In the way that a rudder steered a 500,000-ton ship, or a smidgen of yeast made a lump of leaden dough balloon over the edge of the pan, he was causing the price of gold to rise. If being a barker and ringmaster of Van Amberg's circus was the best job he had ever had, bulling up gold showed him where his talents really lay. All his life he had loved the fast raid, the quick sally. Grab the apples, the new town's loose cash, the spare money in brokers' accounts. Now he and his gang of traders were grabbing Vanderbilt's change, and it was wonderful how easy it was. There was no limit to how much loot enthusiasm could snatch. That was what misers never understood.

At least a hundred galoots—the short, the fat, and the skinny; ounce kickers as well as the slickly dressed; the nervous and elderly skates down at the heels looking for an edge—cornered him, pulled his head to theirs, and whispered into his ear, "Jim! Jim! It's me. What's really going on?"

"Carl, I just can't say."

"Jim, come on! You've let me in before!" Jim drew the ear of the supplicant so close to his own that the other's ear whorls tickled his lips.

"Won't say nothing to nobody else?" Glazed, excited eyes and a fast shake of the head promised anything. "Washington," said Jim. "The Treasury wants gold to go up."

The next morning, Tuesday, the twenty-first of September, showed Jim how valuable he had come to be. Jay himself, eyes glittering, face full of strained feverishness, urged him to deliver the knockout punch to Vanderbilt. Beaming with pride, Jim strutted around the office, assuring the nervous little skate that nothing was going to go amiss, that when he had the chance he would snatch off Vanderbilt's drawers as well as his pants.

Yes, the sky was the limit now. The moon and the stars were his.

This morning Broad Street was more crowded and agitated than usual. Even before the midmorning opening bell, excitement zig-zagged as wild as lightning across the Gold Room. The normal pre-opening hum of voices was a raucous gabble. Some traders stared about vacantly as if gleaming mountains of gold were reflected in their eyes, while the heads of others bobbed in crazy patterns as if listening to the clink-clink-rattle of gold coins. Cupid rode his dolphin over a storm of shouts and mad gestures, for many traders' heads jerked about as if terrified that they might miss a clue to the market's direction. Uncharacteristically late by a quarter of an hour, Stumpy strode onto the floor leading McGuffin and his other two traders as if they had just rushed from a strategy meeting with Vanderbilt him-self.

At the opening bell, gold shot up a dollar to 118, then settled back to 116. It wiggled up to 119, then waggled back to 115. Against whatever Jim and all the bulls threw into the pit, there stood Stumpy, his face dark with its usual impassivity, holding his palms outward as if he didn't care if Jim or anyone else knew his strategy, and sold and sold and sold. Jim loosened his tie and collar, and shortly both his handkerchiefs were soaked through with sweat. Of course, Van-derbilt had hired Stumpy because nothing panicked him; the Gold Room said that his brain was chiseled from a block of ice, his nerves were rigged with piano wire, and his blood ran as cold as the water under a froze-up river.

Even with Jim throwing large orders into the pit, the gold arrow crept toward 119 in an agonizing crawl. Fifteen minutes before the noon bell, as if a strong hand had grabbed it and twisted it down, the gold arrow dropped three points in as many minutes. Jim groaned.

On the way to lunch, Jim muttered to Willie, "What's the Com-modore doing, playing with us? Is he letting us get it up and then coming in to make a quick three-point profit?" The whole tone of the morning's trading bothered him. It had all the zip of a consumptive who ought to be at home in bed.

Tuesday afternoon, the crowd of traders was worn out. The cav-ernlike room stank of stale cigar smoke and the sour reek of wine drunk at lunch. While the noise was still a roar, it sounded dull and wasn't deafening. At his post by the iron railing across from Jim, Stumpy looked much the same: cool, calm, wooden. To change his luck, Jim tried the old trader's trick of turning his gray vest inside out, but even that didn't help. Lifting this market was as hard as pushing a wagonload of rock uphill.

By dint of laborious effort he managed to push the price near 120, when suddenly the same giant hand jammed down the gold arrow. It sank faster and faster as Stumpy sent in sell order after sell order. Finally out of money, Jim watched, openmouthed. A vast moan rose from the traders.

116.

$115\frac{1}{2}$.

$115\frac{1}{4}$. Would it never stop? Jim hopped from foot to foot.

$114\frac{1}{2}$.

114. It would never stop dropping.

$113\frac{1}{2}$. Two whole days' profit had vanished in five minutes, and Jim still wasn't out of the market with his daily trading capital intact.

Around the pit the exhausted traders jerked about as if they were insects—bees, hornets, ants, beetles—being fried in a red-hot skillet.

Willie ran out of the frantic crowd, grabbed Jim's lapels, and shook him. "It may not hold! You got to get out!"

Eyes fixed on the falling gold arrow, Jim nodded. It wasn't holding and he *did* have to get out. He hadn't sold his last 10,000 ounces yet, which he must sell before the close. But like tons of lead dropped on a sinking packet boat, Jim's sales would drive the market down, maybe to under 100. The whole two days of excitement and winning had been no more than a clever bear trap of Vanderbilt's to deliver the knockout punch.

If so, it had succeeded. By tomorrow there wouldn't be an Erie, not if that arrow closed below 110. No Erie—and no opera house, no house in Boston, no suite at the Hoffman House. No account at Del's, no carriage, no Rufus, and no Josie.

On it dropped. At 110 it didn't even pause, but shot from $110\frac{1}{4}$ to 109 in seconds, then fell to 108. Jim couldn't move, was frozen, and yet he must add to this decline by selling his day lots before the market's close.

Without warning, Jay's bearded face was in front of him, twisted in fury. Jim reached out both arms to calm the poor fellow, but Jay danced out of his way. He was shouting—although Jim could only make it out by reading his lips—*"Buy! Buy! Buy!"* Jay's usual poker face was as contorted as the crazy skeets in the asylum that Jim had Pa in, poor wretches who screeched, "Repent, sinner!" Seeing the disaster unfolding on the ticker, Jay had rushed down from the Erie's offices to stop it with his bare hands, like the Dutch boy sticking his finger in the dike.

Jim shouted back, "We're out of money. We've still got to sell off today's positions!" The clamor around them was as tumultuous as a thousand waterfalls.

Jay shouted again, *"No! Buy! Buy!"* His delicate hand waved a bunch of pink trading slips in Jim's face as if somehow they would help. Jim grabbed his arm, intending to drag him off the floor into the anteroom to explain the uselessness of stopping this flood with one miserable finger, for over Jay's bobbing head the price had just skidded to $107\frac{1}{2}$.

Jay knocked Jim's hand away. With a furious motion he pressed one of the trading slips into Willie's hand and made the sign for Willie to buy a thousand ounces. Willie's wide eyes looked at the trading slip, his mouth made an O, and he turned and ran toward the mob surrounding the grinning Cupid. Jay's lips were shouting for Jim to call in all their traders.

"What for?" shouted Jim.

"Damn it, call them," Jay called back. "Not much time!"

Jay shoved one of the pink trading slips into Jim's hand—but it wasn't a trading slip at all. It was a pink bank check, drawn on the Tenth National Bank, said pay to the order of "Bearer" $10,000, and was stamped *CERTIFIED* in bold red letters. Stupefied, Jim let his mouth drop open. This was as valuable, as tradable, as $10,000 in cash. He sought Jay's face for an explanation, but Bob, Frisky, and Flowers were crowding around Jay. He pressed two pink checks into each one's hand with shouted instructions.

In a few minutes Jay gave out a dozen pink checks, each for $10,000. It was five minutes till closing. In the pit the noise had risen from a loud roar to a single long screeching shout. From 107 the needle climbed to 108. It passed 110 and stopped briefly at 112.

To Jim, it was like watching a losing nag at the track sprout wings and fly over the field to take the lead—wonderful, but impossible to believe. As long as that arrow stayed above 110, they weren't bankrupt. Above 114, they weren't in bad shape at all. Jim grinned and gave a loud *wahooo!*

All the while, Jay was signaling their traders, palms in and pulling, *buy, buy, buy.* On the other side of the railing, Stumpy, palms facing out and pushing, was signaling *sell, sell, sell.* Stumpy glanced over at Jim and Jay with nervous little shakes of his head—the most distressed Jim had ever seen him.

At the insistent clang of the three o'clock closing bell—ringing longer than usual to stop traders who maniacally continued to trade—gold was back up to 116; a bellow that was a cross between a cheer and a deep groan rose from the crowd. A broad grin on his face, Jim turned to see how Stumpy was taking the news, but the familiar spot at the iron railing was empty. He leaned back against the railing and laughed and laughed.

All around them traders streamed for the exits. Abruptly the din in the vast hall was gone; he and Jay could hear themselves.

"Old Stumper's gone to tell his master before the news gets to him off the wires," said Jim. "Where the hell did all that money come from?"

The gold arrow was still at 116. Out of the black satchel at his feet Jay took a ten-inch-thick maroon folder and passed it to him. Its cover read *The Tenth National Bank*. Jim vaguely knew the outfit, a small merchant bank so slimly financed that they had never lent any customer more than $50,000. Puzzled, Jim balanced the heavy folder against his paunch and fingered through the sheaves of legal documents.

"It's our new supply of money," said Jay. Jim looked at him sharply. Had Jay become addled?

"We need more money than these folks can give us, son," said Jim.

"We bought it, Jim."

"Bought?"

"I closed on it this afternoon."

"We did what? And with what?"

"Erie stock."

"We did *what*, now?"

Jay grabbed his arm with the enthusiasm of a boy. "Issued stock out of our treasury and swapped it for the bank's stock—all of it!"

Jim had never known Jay to be this misguided. This gold episode had been an enormous strain, and now it had broken him. After all, this runty bank was half busted itself. He put his arm around Jay's bony shoulders, squeezed them, and said in a gentle voice, "But still and all, partner, it ain't *got* that much to loan us."

"I know," said Jay, "but it has unlimited *borrowing* power in the commercial paper market."

"So what?"

"So it's going to borrow money against its new assets—gold."

A cold feather brushed up Jim's back. "Borrow?" He waved his hand over the marble floor, which was littered with six inches of crumpled pink tickets. "It can borrow against whatever we buy for it?" His head was light and dizzy. "You mean we can just write checks against whatever gold we buy?"

"We're a bank, aren't we?"

"*We're a bank*," said Jim, shaking his head. "God, I like the way that sounds: We're a bank. Maybe I been in the wrong business all these years! But how can one tiny little bank—even if it is ours—overcome Vanderbilt's and Drew's and Cooke's and God knows who all else's fortunes?"

"Part of the deal is that nobody is to know we own it," said Jay. "Keep it quiet, *real* quiet, damn it. That's why I haven't said anything to you till now. Keep it as quiet as Grant's part in this."

Jim's finger went to his lips. "Not a word."

"A bank has access to the vast commercial paper market," said Jay, his voice becoming professorial, "as long as the bank officers—the gents who work for *us*—swear that the paper we issue is covered by sound collateral."

Jim's face was ablaze in a grin. "Commercial paper market," he repeated, reverence in his voice. He lifted his eyes into the vast space, which was shot with yellow sunbeams pouring through the quiet gloom from the half-open upper windows. In his mind's eye a flood of greenbacks was pouring down, a Mississippi River fed by a thousand green tributaries.

Jim reached down, lifted Jay up by the shoulders as he might a small child, and held him out before him.

"Sweet pea," Jim asked, "how do you think of these things?"

"Easy," said Jay, wiggling out of Jim's grasp and regaining his feet. "Out of desperation."

After Stumpy Roberts and the broker Henry Smith had been kicked out of his office by Cornelius, there was silence for several long moments.

"Pa," said Willian, his face stiff with anger. "Call it off."

"No, I'm going to beat them. I'm going to see Cooke. He swore Grant wouldn't touch the market."

"You've pissed away a fortune in good money," said William. "Are you going to piss away everything we own?" Cornelius had no direct comeback, for the boy was too close to the mark.

"Son, I've been here a thousand times," said Cornelius, raising his voice. "If you don't finish the race, you lose the route. It's raining, your fantail is busted by lightning, and you ain't got no more coal. Everybody from your first engineer to the mess steward says give it up, it ain't a boat no more but a sinking washtub. I say burn the chairs in the lounge, cut up the railings, chop down the passenger cabin, and feed the Chinese cook to the boiler. I say keep going! That's what made me, son, and I ain't quitting now. I'm going to bust those two if it's the last goddamn thing I do."

His chin jutting out, he stalked out of the office to find his carriage driver himself, a task he normally left to his chief clerk Stephens, but he didn't want any baleful looks from that quarter either.

Cornelius arrived at Jay Cooke's Fifth Avenue granite mansion at six o'clock that night. He was immediately led upstairs.

The financier's wife had decorated the long, quiet halls, spacious banquet room, and three formal parlors in the glorification of the Middle Ages common to the Gothic Revival of the forties and fifties. Suits of armor stood on parade and glared at wallpaper, portraits, and tapestries depicting medieval pageants and jousts. Cornelius shook his head over the expense of so much European geegaw. He was shown into the financier's private study.

Cooke had decorated his large retreat in the more severe style of the early thirties, the so-called American Empire fashion of veneers, heavy handmade pieces, and respectability. Cornelius crossed the high-ceiled room, a thirty-by-forty-foot portrait in mahogany, deep reds, and dull golds, to the small fire, where Cooke stood waiting for him. Tall, handsome in a dark, three-piece suit, and aristocratic with well-brushed white hair and beard, the financier shook his hand and greeted him with a murmured "Cornelius."

"Jay," said Cornelius.

They seated themselves in klismos-style chairs with curved saber legs and concave backs. Cornelius accepted a cigar from the offered humidor with a grunt of pleasure and studied Cooke as the financier stuck a taper in the fire. If the Treasury were to print a ten-thousand-dollar bill, Jay Cooke's smooth patrician face would be the ideal one to grace it. Before them, on the marble-topped table, squatted a decanter of port and two small crystal glasses. It was all too la-di-da for Cornelius's taste, but he couldn't deny that the room was comfortable.

After they had lit cigars, Cornelius laid out in rapid sentences the events of the last two days. On learning the extent of the pool's losses and the havoc in the Gold Room, Cooke shook his head in annoyance. He agreed to talk long and earnestly to the President.

"But his trading gold," protested Cooke, "those are a lot of baseless rumors. Anyway, I'm visiting with him tomorrow."

"Tomorrow!" Relief spread through Cornelius, and he chuckled softly. "Where?"

"At Ogontz," said Cooke, referring to his country estate near Philadelphia. Cornelius knew little about Grant, and hardly wanted to know that, but he did know that while the President was impressed by most men of wealth, he was particularly awed by Jay Cooke. The financier's million-dollar estate was so lavishly outfitted that it contained its own theater, its own conservatory, its own Italian garden, and its own medieval ruins. Ulysses Grant, ever seeking to shave expenses, had vacationed there three times in the six months he had occupied the White House.

The proud, stiff Cooke puffed on his cigar and exuded confidence. "As rich as Jay Cooke" had become a byword in the country during the Civil War, for Cooke's brokerage house, as the U.S. Treasury's chief agent, had taken complete charge of marketing the government's war bonds. It wasn't a business Cornelius understood, but he admired any man who could engineer a business's large success, even if it was done with marching brass bands, miles of red, white, and blue bunting, and a dozen other kinds of ballyhoo. Cooke and his salesmen had marketed over three billion dollars' worth of war bonds in three years to the American people. Any sum with *billion* in it received Cornelius's earnest attention. Along with the mountains of gratitude that the nation had bestowed on him, Cooke had earned a commission on every single bond. His vast wealth had multiplied, spreading into hotels, ranches, coal mines, commercial buildings, rights-of-way, oil lands, railroads, and factories. If anybody did, Cooke knew his way around the maze of Washington politics and would slice off this disaster at its root. Cooke was the kind of heavy frigate to have at your side in a battle.

"Keep your eyes open," cautioned Cornelius. "This Gould is tricky, and he knows something we don't. If the President had a minnow's smidgen of sense, he would have dumped some Treasury gold earlier this week to calm the markets." Just the hint that the Treasury was going to sell gold would cause this market fever to freeze.

Cooke pursed his lips. Cornelius reckoned he was weighing what political capital such a request of the President would cost him. The large losses he was facing won out, for finally he nodded.

"Let's have him sell some gold."

Cornelius felt still better. "Do you think you can persuade him?"

Cooke's fleshy lips took two pulls from the wet end of his cigar with the relish of a child sucking a favorite sweet. "He doesn't think it's the business of the government to affect markets," said Cooke. "But here I think he might make an exception." His smile reflected political depths best left unspoken.

"Will you send me a wire?" asked Cornelius. "One telling me yes or no?"

"Of course."

When he left, prepared to sell yet more gold ounces short in the morning, Cornelius's step had a spring in it. With a little luck here, he still had a good chance to smash those pups in the snout and grab the Erie.

It was the next evening, Wednesday the twenty-second of September, after another hectic day of trading.

Jay Gould entered Jim's elaborate office, where Jim and his four most important traders were relaxing after another victorious day in the Gold Room. His poker face gone for once, wreathed in a wide grin of triumph, Jay stepped from chair to chair, shaking hands and murmuring thanks and words of encouragement to Flowers Crawford, the lanky southerner, Frisky Freyer, the small, speedy trader, Weeping Willie, the sad fellow from Ohio, and Bob Rust, the gracious Pennsylvanian.

For once Jim's office didn't seem too lavish to Jay, but the right size to contain the group's noisy ebullience. Jim was sprawled back in his swivel chair, a tumbler of amber whiskey in his right hand, the cigar in the other waving around like a victory baton. Jay dropped into a seat at the side of Jim's French desk.

"Oh, you should have been down there," Jim growled to Jay. "We knocked their socks, gaiters, and underdrawers off this afternoon, didn't we, fellers?" Their agreement was a cheer. Jim's coat was off, his burgundy satin vest unbuttoned, tie undone, and flowered suspenders looped under his arms. Open whiskey bottles stood on Jim's Empire sideboard, neckties hung untied around Flowers's and Frisky's necks, and the five traders' voices were more like barks than conversation.

The tall, soft-eyed southerner's smile was smug and amused. "I haven't heard so much screaming and hollering since my daddy butchered hogs." His crystal whiskey glass tilting dangerously over the Persian carpet, Flowers hee-heed softly and glanced around to make sure his audience was with him. "I've covered all my losses from the past two weeks and then some," he continued. "In my personal account, I must have made $80,000 off these suckers today." The others murmured how well they had done. "I thought several times a couple of those little boys that run the pink slips around were going to get trampled," he went on. "One poor fellow fell down and I stopped to help him up. I swear he had six heel marks on his shirt-front where people had walked right across him." They tisked, and then Jim began another story.

Jay let the words and tones of victory wash over him. The husky fumes of whiskey and the tall windows restrained the black chill of night. The gas globes of Jim's chandelier hissed softly, the rich, yellow light reflecting delicately off the spangling, inlaid French furniture.

He felt particularly good; not only were they winning, but winning big.

The warm office seemed to be the swaying wicker basket of a large hot-air balloon; the glowing, hissing chandelier, its hot-air burner. As the traders talked on, a shiver of pleasure snuck up Jay's spine. Suspended in the night-dark over this wide ornate wicker basket was an enormous rubber balloon, a mile-wide, swelling gasbag large and powerful enough to transport him and Jim anywhere on earth.

Jay had reassumed his usual poker face, but he was excited, even joyful. He tended to forget how powerful Jim was, how easily his partner could entice thousands of traders, the way the Pied Piper had emptied Hamelin of children. He had been right after all to use a bit of subterfuge to pull Jim into this market. Years from now they would have a good laugh over it.

"I figure the Walrus went to the bank for at least $800,000 last night," said Jim. "Maybe more." Jay grinned at the pleasant idea of Vanderbilt pleading with bankers for money.

"I loved watching that Stump," said Jim, his paunch shaking with laughter. "His behind against that iron pipe, his hands pushing back and pushing back, selling and selling, like he was trying to push back a giant ocean wave falling on top of him." The others guffawed, and to keep from spilling his whiskey, Flowers quickly set his glass on the carpet and calmed his haw-hawing by beating his knee with his open palm.

"It got up there and stayed and stayed," Willie said. "Jay, I been on that floor for twenty years. I seen gold go crazy in the War, and I've seen it lay there sick as a dead dog, but I never seen what I seen today. That market hit 126 and just hung there."

Frisky abruptly became grave and asked, "Wasn't Frank Chambers a sore loser?"

"What do you mean?" asked Jay. Chambers owned his own trading company, no small house.

Frisky said, his voice husky with emotion, "You didn't hear? He *and* his company went bankrupt after the close."

"*Bankrupt!*" exclaimed Jay, frowning. It wasn't only farmers and railroads who stood to lose from the gyrations of gold. For a few moments no one said anything, as if the misfortunes of one of the market's most active and popular brokers would turn the victory celebration into a wake. In the awkward silence Bob Rust and Weeping Willie stared into the amber of their glasses, Frisky got up to close a window, and Flowers went to the sideboard to slop more whiskey into his glass.

"Bankrupt," Frisky said from the window. "He's been short gold for two weeks now. He came up to Jim here after the close and spit right in your face, didn't he, Jim?"

From his reclining position in his swivel chair, Jim nodded and his thick fingers rubbed his left cheek. His brow was furrowed, pensive.

Frisky dropped back into his chair. "Frank just stood there and called Jim every sort of name," Frisky went on. "He said Jim here acted like he was on a—what'd he call it, Jim, a 'glorious lark'?—instead of taking all this serious. I was surprised you stood there and took it. You wasn't responsible for him being short so much gold."

"It's always hard to go bust the first time," said Jim in a hoarse voice. "Frank will be all right."

Jay broke the spell by asking, "How much you reckon the Walrus has shorted?"

"Millions," said Jim, gloating. "Millions and millions and millions. If we play our cards right, all of it's for us. What we got to do is panic that crew of Vanderbilt's and Stumpy's over the next day or so, and that old buzzard is going to *beg* you and me to sit down with him and settle."

Jay grinned. Vanderbilt panicked! This was what they had been working for, the goal for which Jay had scarcely dared to hope: the moment when Vanderbilt recognized that the only way to get out of his shorts was to pay Jay and Jim a bounty for the gold contracts that they owned. In effect, at a huge profit to themselves and the Erie, Vanderbilt would settle his short account with the Gold Exchange by giving it the gold that Jim and Jay had accumulated.

Jim said, "For once and for all he'll be busted. Shit, he'll be begging us to take the Central off his hands." They laughed at that.

"And the Erie will be flush," mused Jay. "We'll lay six sets of track to the West Coast."

There was a knock at the door, and Morosini came in. "Note for you, Mr. Gould," he said. The others were silent as Jay ripped open the small creamy envelope.

It's urgent I see you tonight. I have a letter from my sister.

The writing of the unsigned note was Annabelle's. In the warm, close room, the word *urgent* caused a cool stir of alarm to blow through Jay. If she said it was *urgent* news from Jenny Grant, it was urgent. Yet what news from the President's wife could be urgent? Pocketing the note with a shaky hand, Jay stood.

"I have to hop, myself." Jay shook hands with Flowers and the others. "You fellows have done one hell of a job. Oh, and since I can't get my orders off fast enough from here, till this is over I'm going to work out of my old offices at Morris, Nathan's downtown. Let's meet there tomorrow morning before trading starts." Jay was at the door when Jim called.

"Jay, can I see you a minute?" They conferred in the deserted marble hall, the door to Jim's office shut. "You ain't heard nothing from Butterfield, have you?" Jim whispered, referring to the retired general whom Annabelle had placed in the Treasury office here in New York.

"Not a peep," said Jay.

Jim leaned close. "How will we get word if something pops during market hours?" he asked. "This thing is too slippery to wait long to hear." Jay smiled and laid a hand on Jim's shoulder.

"It's handled," said Jay. "I have a messenger sitting all day long in the Treasury anteroom. If any order comes through from Washington, Butterfield will give him an envelope and he will be in my office five minutes later."

Jim squeezed the hand on his shoulder. "Trust you to think of everything."

As Jay hurried down the long, curving marble staircase to his carriage, he calculated how much time he could spend with Annabelle. He must eat dinner with the family, so probably only half an hour.

He would visit her later, at midnight. He smiled. After all, he and Annabelle had a lot to celebrate after today's market triumph.

31

*Members of the Exchange are held by a
rigid code of laws, but in questions of
morality Wall Street has a code of its
own. Expediency is a prominent
consideration in the dealings of the
street, and men have come to regard as
honest and correct almost anything
short of a regular breach of contract.
They do not spare their own flesh and
blood. Friendships are sacrificed, the
ties of kinship are disregarded, if they
stand in the way of some bold
operation. Everything must give way to
the desire for gain.*

—James McCabe, *Lights & Shadows
of New York Life*, 1872

Beyond the curtains of Jay's car-
riage, the night flew by, full of the clop-clop of horses' iron shoes, the
jingle of trace chain, and the creak of axles begging for grease.

Intoxicated by the night, Jay sucked in the crisp, dark air of fall,
tasting victory, as sweet and electric as the tart juice of the season's
first apple. Sprawled back against the carriage's cushions, he chuckled. They had won!—won!—won!

Annabelle met him at the front door. "Thank God you've come,"
she said. Her hand, smooth and cold, slipped into his, seeking comfort.
"I've been crazy with worry." Her long face was pinched, and in her
intense black eyes he read terror. He gave her a reassuring smile, and
to ease her tension, he slid his arm around her waist and kissed her

cheek. No matter how trained in banking, he told himself, women weren't made for grueling campaigns.

"What's wrong?" he asked.

The hollows under her eyes were dark with the tension of the past days.

Her hand pulled him toward the steps. "Come upstairs."

In her elegant parlor she handed him a lilac envelope on which her name and address were written in a neat, feminine hand.

He hesitated. "I can't read your mail," he said.

She removed the sheets from the envelope and shoved one at him. "Read the last page," she said. He took it. A page of chat ended with the paragraph:

Ulysses is very much annoyed by your gold speculations. You must close them as quickly as you can. The letter was signed *Sis*.

Startled, Jay looked up and met her fear-filled black eyes. He wasn't sure what the paragraph meant, but a cold, dark presence stood nearby.

Her face strained toward him. "He knows," she whispered hoarsely. "He's protecting me by warning me before he does anything."

This whispering in her own empty parlor made a chill blow across him. She lowered herself onto one of the plush sofas, pulling in her elbows and hands with the swift neatness of a crow settling on a branch. He sat down at its other end and wiped his clammy hands with his handkerchief.

"Knows what?" he asked.

"He knows I'm in the gold market," she said. In the yellow light her cheeks looked shiny, rubbery, like the overnight skin on cream. "And he knows he's linked to it."

"He can't know," he insisted, although doubt rippled across his tightened nerves. Could Jim have said things he shouldn't have? She picked up the letter, rattling it for emphasis.

"Don't you see? This is his way of warning me out before he has the Treasury dump gold. You have to get out, too."

"But Butterfield hasn't said anything about government sales," he said cautiously. On the other hand, it would certainly work. The sale of even a few ounces by the government—weeks before the regular auction—would cause this feverish market to cool, probably plummet.

From downstairs a child shrieked—Matilda, by the sound of it. Annabelle started and glanced at the door as if ready to fly away. The cry stopped and she dropped back against the cushion, her face drawn.

"A new man like Butterfield may not discover the plans till the last minute," she said. Jay studied her, his forefinger coiling and uncoiling a shaggy fragment of beard, and admired her shrewdness. Butterfield swore he was in the thick of things, but she might be right.

"Sell me out, Jay. I want my profits, and I must make sure my skirts are clean."

"All right," he agreed, "first thing tomorrow."

She smiled, much of the pinchedness of her expression smoothing out.

"But keep this news quiet," he went on. "A whisper of this, and Jim and I are ruined. Jim has not only jumped in with both feet, he's up to his ears and eyeballs. As the market's gone up, he's taken his profits and bought more gold."

"My God! How much do you two own?"

"Nearing $80 million."

She winced. "On what base?"

"Maybe five to six million," he said. All the millions of difference were leveraged, borrowed, promised.

"And Vanderbilt and Cooke are short the same?"

"More or less."

"Why have you let it get so large?" she whispered urgently.

He twisted his shoulders about in an effort to unknot his cramped muscles. "Each side is riding a tiger," he said, smiling thinly. "Each has to stay mounted, whether he wants to or not. The first to slow down or jump off gets eaten." Her delicate fingers fluttered around her gaping mouth.

She cocked her head toward the letter. "What are you going to do?" she asked.

He followed her glance and grimaced. "Talk this over with Jim."

"But don't you think Jenny's letter means Ulysses is going to sell gold?" she asked.

He smiled and shook his head.

"Maybe you're right," she said. She laughed nervously. "After all, they're not even in the White House, but off on another of Ulysses' vacations."

"Better and better," said Jay, and he grinned triumphantly. "The farther Grant is from Washington, the harder for his aides to keep him informed. Where is the letter posted from?"

She shrugged. "Someplace near Philadelphia called Ogone." She picked up the lilac envelope. "Ogontz."

He jumped as if a whip had struck his naked back and lunged forward. He snatched the envelope and stared at its postmark in horror.

"Ogontz!" he said. "Cooke's place!" From throat to groin his body tightened, as if a slack wire were jerked taut.

"What's the matter?" she asked. "Whose place?"

He staggered to his feet. "Jay Cooke's estate, his fancy compound," he said. The parlor, the whole world seemed to be turning, like a huge ship on a monstrous wave of the ocean, thrown so hard and high it was turning upside down. To steady himself he grasped the back of the sofa. "I've got to find Jim, warn him." He moved toward the door, but she rose and stopped him with a hand on his arm.

"About what?" she asked.

"Don't you see?" he said, his voice almost a shout. He faced the door, only glancing at her. "All this fever in the Gold Room—Grant at Cooke's place! Cooke in the pool with Vanderbilt! Of course, of course, you *are* right—they've persuaded Grant to sell Treasury gold." Trailed by her, he stalked out and flew down the stairs. He would keep the public hack all night if he had to while he searched for Jim through the garish night bowels of Manhattan.

Halfway down the stairs, she called, "Still, you shouldn't say anything to Jim."

"Not warn Jim?" he threw over his shoulder. "Don't be absurd."

"No, wait," she cried. "What you tell him will get around—make the market topple all the sooner." With her on his heels, he reached the front hall and sped toward the hat rack. The door to the kitchen opened. Drawn by the shouts and clattering heels, five-year-old Matilda and the boy Richard appeared there to stare with large, frightened eyes. Jay clapped on his hat.

"I can't wait," he said. It came out as a croak, and he cleared his throat. Tons of gold were poised above their heads, ready to crash, burying Jim and him in a golden avalanche. "Can't you see? It's a disaster." He edged around her toward the door, speaking over his shoulder. "We own so much," he went on. "Jim needs all the time he can get."

His hand was on the brass knob, but she leaned her shoulder against the door to stop his leaving.

"Go back in the kitchen, children," she shouted, but the two in the open doorway didn't move. She looked up at Jay, who appeared wild-eyed enough to bolt right through the door's wood panels. "Then Jim should stay off the floor tomorrow," she went on. "That way the market won't know that you two are selling."

He opened the door. As he passed over the sill, his face lit up with hope. "Yes! We'll even get his brokers—Bob, Flowers—to keep buying to fool the crowd—small amounts, of course. We'll use others to sell . . ."

He was poised on the stone stoop, his eyes on the waiting public hack. His voice trailed off, for as he spoke he saw it wouldn't work.

"What's the matter?" she asked.

"Just his not being on the floor will create suspicion," said Jay. "And without big orders, really big ones, the fellows he trades with will talk, or not buy as much for their own accounts—the game will be up."

He sped down the front steps to the curb. The waiting hack driver picked up the reins. She quickly followed, and placed her hand on his arm to halt his mounting into the carriage.

"Wait," she said. "Then send Jim to the Exchange to *pretend* to buy. You stay in the office and really sell." Worried over who might see them, he removed his arm from her grip.

"Yes, but it's not that easy to pretend to buy," he whispered urgently; "not on Jim's scale. The market sees what he does. His own traders are constantly telling others—through their jokes and swagger—what he's up to." His face was twisted with pain. "Besides, you have to understand how Jim works. He's the best friend of half the world. When Tom and Dick and Harry ask what to do, good-natured as he is, worried over them as he'll be, he'll pull his punches and it won't go over. Better he stays in the office."

"But you already said that will cause the market to crash."

He nodded. If Jim switched, or was thought to have switched, from being a bull—the biggest bull on the floor—to being a bear, as bigmouthed and visible as he was, every trader in the Gold Room would sense it and switch sides. Gold would plunge from $125 to $60 in minutes. Working on thin margins, dozens, hundreds of brokers and banks would be instantly bankrupted, all forced to sell gold. Along with Jay and Jim personally, the Erie Railroad, with its enormous position, would be the last to get through the crowded exit door, as well as the most battered.

The hack driver was peering down, his twisted thin face asking how long before they could get moving. Jay nodded and waved. Passersby, whose scrutiny he wanted to evade, were strolling up and down the street.

"I'll figure something out," he said.

She grasped his arm in a hard grip with both hands. "But don't tell Jim," she said. "At least not tonight, or tomorrow. Wait a day or two—put it off."

Jay looked back at her and groaned. "No, I've got to tell him."

She stamped her foot, and her head shook in rage. "Then the two of you will sink together," she said. "I hope you like being in the poorhouse, because when this market gets through with you, that's where you'll be, along with 'precious' Jim."

"Certainly I'm going to get rid of the Erie's gold."

She laughed in a nervous, almost mad way. "Jay—whatever— don't you see? Don't tell Jim."

"Stop saying that!"

"It's the only thing to do."

"No!"

"You don't have much choice," she said. "Either he goes bankrupt, or you both do." He hoisted himself up, almost into the carriage, then changed his mind and dropped back to the curb. He turned to face her. She was right, but there *had* to be another way.

"Sell out my best friend?" he said. "My own partner?"

"Why should you go broke with him?"

He sighed. Women understood so little of business, how men felt. "Because of loyalty," he said. "He and I are a team. Loyalty's a rare and precious thing, and Jim has been loyal. I can't betray that. We've been through Hell together." He laughed nervously. "God, he and I have been betrayed by the best—Daniel Drew. And before, I was sold out by Leupp, my first partner. When I came to Wall Street I vowed I would never have another partner, a vow I kept for ten years. Then Jim came along—it's been different. I don't have to face every damn thing alone, and neither does he. He knows he doesn't have to worry about the finances, the accounting, the legal, operational aspects of the line—I do that."

Annabelle shook her head, a disgusted look on her face. "Well, I'd rather have a wise enemy than such a stupid friend."

"He's like a brother, the one I never had," said Jay. "He buoys me up, me and my stupid eternal worrying. I can't—play Judas to him." He shuddered. "Imagine, tomorrow morning we'd meet at the office, and I'd have to pretend I didn't know anything, that things are as great as they were"—he sighed and shook his head in anger— "an hour ago. Give him a Judas kiss on the cheek, send him off to the Exchange . . ."

"No, you're right," said Annabelle, sarcasm thick in her voice. "You'll simply tell Nellie when she asks for a new dress that Jim Fisk is wearing it. When George wants to return to that fancy gentleman's school, you'll tell him that this year Jim Fisk is attending it. And Helen, when she wants to know why the marshal is carting off the furniture to auction, you'll tell that you didn't feel right having a house when Jim didn't. Maybe you and Jim's family can get rooms next to each other in Five Points—"

"Stop it!" he said. "I can't double-cross him!" A strolling couple, he in a top hat, she in an evening gown, gave them frankly curious stares.

"Then don't," she said. "Just get *me* out. And see that my name is kept out of the papers, along with Ulysses' and Jenny's." The well-dressed couple were discreetly glancing back.

He lowered his voice, "He's my partner."

"He's a buffoon," she said.

"Save myself and the Erie? Let Jim sink?"

"You've got some time," she went on. "I know Ulysses. He'll give me a couple of days to arrange my affairs. As well, you should have an hour or two between Butterfield's note and the arrival of the Treasury trader at the Gold Room—and knowing how slowly the government acts, perhaps several hours." Her face was as hard and shrewd as a Wall Street trader assessing angles, calculating risks and rewards.

Jay nodded. In a market like this, several hours was a lifetime. "Ulysses should have you running the Treasury," he said.

Her smile was brief and thin. "You could sell off right at the top. Then sell short thousands of ounces and make a profit all the way down."

He felt dizzy. She was right, but it was tricky, as tricky and difficult to execute as any job he had ever done. But it was the only method to escape catastrophe—and maybe, besides, to make money.

"Don't you see?" she said, her voice hard and sure. "If Ulysses is stupid enough to dump Treasury gold, this crazy market will fall no matter what you or Jim or anyone does. Not even God himself can stop the fall."

Her hard-edged blasphemy startled him. Jay blew out a gusty sigh, his face still twisted by pain and confusion.

"But still—it means betraying Jim. I can't."

Annabelle said nothing, only leaned forward. Her vivid black eyes stared at him with a firm, level gaze. It and her contemptuous silence said it all—that he was a fool not to do as she said.

If he told Jim, he was a fool.

But if he didn't, he was no better than that crook Daniel Drew.

32

James Fisk came driving down and turned into Broad Street with two richly attired actresses, one known to fame through her charms as displayed in "Mazeppa" and "The French Spy."

—*New York World*, September 25, 1869

On their way to the Central's conference room the next morning, Thursday, September twenty-third, Cornelius Vanderbilt and his son William paused to confer with Jay Cooke's New York manager, a stocky fellow with the solid expression of a confident young bull.

"What's the news from Ogontz?" asked Cornelius brusquely. The manager was a British type who appeared lordly from the power of the vast fortune he helped manage.

"Nothing," said the young fellow. "So far the President hasn't said yes and he hasn't said no."

In the executive conference room, the nine members of the bear pool were gathered around the long maplewood table. At its foot sat Daniel Drew. Despite the threadbare topcoat he wore and the September sun on his back, he was trembling. Cooke's young manager walked around the table laying in front of each investor a copy of the powder-green, ruled accountant's sheets on which the pool's losses were inked. Last week's round, cheery faces had become this week's weathered tombstones. For a few moments the nine pool members hunched over the green sheets, nine fingernails tumbling down the ruled lines to the bottom where their losses were posted. Brazen fear strutted about the room poking cold, insistent fingers into the investors' stomachs and ribs.

"We talked it over," said Daniel in a high, strained whine, "before you come in." The thin tendons of his scrawny neck sticking out, he glanced around at the other pool members for support. "We're not throwing good money after bad. We all want out." Dry white spittle flecked the corners of his scaly lips. His voice dropped to a low whimper. "It's like the world's coming to an end, the day of judgment is at hand."

"*Out!*" shouted Cornelius. Resting his weight on his two knobby fists, he half lunged at Daniel. "You can't! Imagine what our losses will be!"

"But if we don't get out, no telling how much we may lose," responded Daniel, shaking his head in a lost, bewildered fashion. The other gray-faced men shot cautious glances at one another. This was what investors hated about going short: If you *bought* gold at $100, your worst risk was that it could go to zero, that you could lose your investment. But when you *sold short*, the sky was the limit to your losses—you could short gold at $100 an ounce, and it could go to $200, to $500, or even to $1,000. To go short, you not only had to put up good-faith money, but also your entire net worth, down to your last collar button, to back it up. You could lose your bank account, your land, your business—even the house in which your wife and children lived.

Cornelius pulled out his trump card. "Right now Jay Cooke is conferring with the President on this matter. We expect him to sell gold." Cooke's manager started, pushing himself away from the wall, as if Cornelius wasn't supposed to say this. Daniel's shrewd eye caught the movement.

"Sell gold?" said Daniel. "The President won't allow an ounce to be sold till he's made his *own* money." The flowers of hope on the pool's faces wilted, and their heads nodded in sad agreement.

Cooke's man spoke sharply, "We have no evidence that the President is in this market." Cornelius nodded in vigorous agreement.

"Don't matter," said Daniel forcefully. "The market *believes* he's in it, and if this market *believes* Grant's in it, it's perzackly the same as if he *is* in it." The others nodded. "This Gould is tough and clever," Daniel whined on. "He might *have* pulled the President in. Them boys is acquainted with him, you know. They been to his wife's sister's place here in town to visit with the President any number a times." Daniel paused to catch his breath with several loud wheezes. The other investors' ears were cocked to catch his every rattle. "I tell you,

C'neal, his touch is death. I ain't never going against Gould again."
The others nodded with sober definiteness. "If you was smart, C'neal,
you would take your licking and leave him alone." This was the same
ninny advice that William had tried to sell Cornelius last night at
the dinner table.

"You and your weak sisters get out!" Cornelius said in a voice
packed with all the scorn he could load in it. "Just leave! I got
work to do to figure out how to handle your milksop, yellow-belly
punking."

Heads bowed, the nine investors silently shuffled out.

Cornelius called for Stephens. "Go into the vault and get everything we own," he instructed him. "Odd bonds, all the stocks we've
been keeping there, deeds for all that land in the Poconos—every
piece of paper that is worth a hoot—and pile it up here and inventory
it." Stephens's scrawny face looked as stricken as Daniel's.

"Everything?"

"Yes!"

"But shouldn't we hold something back in case—"

"Not you, too!" shouted Cornelius. "I *said* everything, I *meant*
every-goddamn-thing. Get it ready by midafternoon. I'm going to see
a couple of bankers."

That morning gold opened at 126, and like a crack sailor clambering
expertly to the crow's nest, it rose to 140. All day Thursday Cornelius
worked as busily as the engineer on a steamer when the captain was
racing for the title of the fastest on the Sound. His back aching, he
shoveled in scoop after scoop of coal, shouted at his firemen to shovel
faster, faster; and yet from the bridge all they shouted for was more
speed. Here the furnace was the gold market, and a shovel of coal
was $10,000 in market orders to sell more gold short. He shoveled,
the fire burned hotter, and his eyebrows were singed. His shoulders
ached, his feet slid about on gritty coal pebbles, but still he shoveled
in money—and still he couldn't beat the market down.

What was keeping Cooke? He fired off three wires to Ogontz, but,
ominously, the same exact answer came back three times: NO NEWS
YET STOP DISCUSSIONS CONTINUING STOP COOKE.

Gold spent all day above 140. Like fast yellow rabbits, gold stories
raced about New York. Everybody knew somebody who had never
seen more than $2,000 in his life, yet who had won $40,000 last week
and lost $50,000 yesterday. A broker's arm had become mangled in
the crush after the opening bell. Several traders had lost every shred
of their black frock coats in this morning's melee. Money was scarce;

every silver dollar in the country had tipped itself on its serrated edge, pushed itself off, and rolled into the Gold Room.

In San Francisco, New Orleans, Boston, Philadelphia, and Chicago almost all stock and bond trading had halted. Across the country, anxious, openmouthed sports and gamblers stood before chalkboards waiting for the latest telegraphed quote from the Gold Room, either trading with each other or wiring orders into the New York pit. Several European exchanges had stopped trading in American grain until the price of gold settled.

All day long Cornelius shot off wires and sent runners to and from the Gold Room with orders. Normally the gold pit handled $70 million a day; this Thursday it was $230 million. Despite Cornelius's best efforts, the market closed at 144, up $19 against him. While that was a disaster to Cornelius—it put him and Cooke yet more millions behind—he took comfort that his actions in the wild market had kept gold from crossing above 150.

At the day's close of the Gold Room, every muscle and every inch of Cornelius's gut felt knotted.

The next morning, nerves quivering with excitement, Jim Fisk stuck his head out the front door of his suite at the Hoffman House. In the cool, dim gloom of dawn, the richly carpeted hall was deserted.

"Rufus!" Jim half whispered, half shouted, keeping his baritone voice low so he wouldn't arouse any of the neighboring swells.

Around the corner by the brass elevator gate, a cane-bottomed chair thumped to the floor. Into sight came the raw, grinning face of Jim's driver. It was Friday, September twenty-fourth. Hunched forward, Rufus approached with a friendly, red-faced leer. "D'you have a good time?"

"Great!" whispered Jim.

"What do you want?" asked Rufus. Jim stepped into the hall, dressed in a lounging robe, an ankle-length garment of white silk trimmed in black velvet that he had made up from a picture book about European princes.

"I got to go downtown early this morning." Although Jim hadn't slept all night and his eyes were bloodshot, an air of vigor and excitement swirled around his ruddy face. After all, today was the biggest day of his life, a day as important as was that glorious morning to Hannibal the Carthaginian when he led his thousands over the Alps to conquer Rome. "How about having a car around front in forty-five minutes?"

Rufus's eyes shifted to Jim's right. Jim swiveled to look behind him. Daphne stood in the open doorway of his suite dressed in one of his black wool frock coats—and nothing else. While the flossy actress had buttoned the coat from her belly button down to her crotch, with all the modesty of an alley cat the brunette allowed plenty to show. She giggled.

"Sugar, get dressed," said Jim.

As he pushed her lush, protesting body back into the suite's foyer, another soft belly, hot pair of tits, and delicate hands slid against the silk covering his backside. His fingers still gripping Daphne's warm hip and shoulder, Jim stuck his head back into the hall. Dressed in his green satin smoking jacket, Fanny stood there, giggling, pointing a finger at him.

The door across the hall opened, and General Bulmountin peered out, a craggy profile amid a gray flannel nightshirt, a red nightcap, and a frost-white mustache.

Jim closed the door and stepped over to block the General's view of Fanny. "Good morning, General," he said, saluting as smartly as an ensign.

"Have the rebs attacked, Fisk?" the General asked sternly.

"No, sir," said Jim. "Just one of the maids tripped, sir."

The General nodded sourly and withdrew. Jim grinned and turned, glad to have slipped out of that one so easily. Fanny was dancing down the hall toward the elevator, her plump, delicious bottom waggling below the short hem of the green coat. Rufus stared goggle-eyed.

"Rufus," said Jim, "help me get them in. They're so spiffed they don't know what they're doing." Jim was still a bit spiffed himself. He and the two actresses had gotten in about four this morning with three bottles of iced champagne, and now no more than half a bottle was left.

"*Yes, sir!*" said Rufus. He took off down the hall to grab Daphne, who dashed around the corner with the squeal of a child playing hide-and-seek with her father. As Jim wrestled Fanny back into the suite, from around the corner came shrieks from Daphne and hoarse laughter from Rufus. Backed up against the foyer wall, the blond actress pushed herself against Jim, opening his silk robe with busy fingers. She rubbed her hot naked belly against his. "Come on, Jim," she said. "Show me again what a bull you are." His johnny stirred.

From down by the elevator came Rufus's roar, a loud clank of the brass gate, and girlish laughter. Jim shoved Fanny into the suite's parlor and told her to stay there. Hastily fastening his robe, he rushed back out.

Coming up the hall was a grinning Rufus with a nearly naked Daphne slung backward over his shoulder, her naked butt and hairy, exposed woman's crack cheek by Rufus's flushed jowl. The lock on the door across from Jim's clicked, the door opened, and the General again stuck out his cliffside of a face.

"Good morning again, General Bulmountin, sir," said Jim.

Rufus marched up. Over his shoulder Daphne was giggling and kicking her legs. As she passed the General's stern visage, Daphne lifted her head and wiggled her fingers at the hero of Vicksburg.

"It's my sister, sir," said Jim, with a salute of his fingers to the brim of an imaginary campaign hat. "She's had a high fever of late and sometimes wanders in her sleep."

"Who's that behind you?" roared the General. "Your great-grandmother?" Jim spun around.

Fanny stood in the doorway, hands on her hips, green smoking jacket unbuttoned showing her high tits and yellow bush, her tongue poking out at the stern general. Jim shooed her back into his suite. Without bothering to button up, the two actresses danced around the armchairs near the dawn-gray windows and sang the "Hang the rascal!" chorus from *The French Spy*. Jim sighed. They were too innocent and appealing to scold. "All right," he said, "you girls get gussied up and Rufus will drive you home."

"We want to go with you!" wailed Daphne.

"Yeah!" said Fanny. "We want to trade gold, too."

"Oh, it is fun," said Rufus with a toothy giggle. "Jim here is the world's best trader." His eyes were almost crossed from staring at the two half-naked actresses simultaneously. "Myself, I done made $10,000 with almost no money down by following Jim's advice."

Their shrill cries and pouting lips said it wasn't fair of Jim to deprive them of such an opportunity. They insisted on coming today.

"Trading gold is serious business, ladies," he said in a stern voice, giving Rufus a wink. "The way you scared old General Bulmountin don't give me much confidence in your ability." Daphne piped right up.

"We was just playing, wasn't we, Fanny? We'll sober up fast as church mice if you'll show us how to make $10,000."

"Yeah," said Fanny. "Especially if I get something to eat. I'm so hungry it's making me dizzy."

"Let's all get something to eat," said Jim. "You come, too, Rufus. Go downstairs and ask Pete to bring the barouche around to Broadway. Get us a table in the dining room. Tell Joe to set out triple what I usually order. That ought to be enough for the four of us."

347

*   *   *

An hour later, the four stepped out of the Hoffman House into a glorious September morning, air crisp and dry, sky a gay blue, a brisk morning without the usual acrid stench from the tanneries of Hunts Point.

From the top step of the Hoffman House, Jim gave a little roar and raised his billy-goat cane in a salute to Fritz, the grinning doorman. He felt like doing things, big things, and today was the day for them. The three diamonds on his starched shirtfront gleamed, his frock coat exuded power and wealth, and his top hat was stuck on his head at a rakish angle.

"Lower the hood, Rufus," said Jim. "This morning I want to feel the breeze on my puss."

With Rufus in the driver's box and him in the rear seat of the large barouche with a lollipop girl on either side, Jim set off down Broadway. The sixteen hooves of his new set of reddish-brown Hanoverians clop-clopped against the cobbles in a cheerful rhythm. Although the leaves hadn't begun to turn, fall was in the energetic air. Jim sucked in deep lungfuls. Oh, today was going to be wonderful! Right this minute Hannibal's powerful team was pulling his chariot to the tippy-top of the Alps! In every crisp basketful of air, he sniffed the heady, powerful essence of victory.

Lower down, Broadway was full of straight-backed blokes marching in the same direction as they—clerks in derby hats, brokers in top hats, laborers in cloth caps, and dandies in straw boaters. Every infantryman of this army off to work did a double take as Jim passed, for they made quite a sight: Jim in his broker's silk top hat, on either side the two actresses in bold, low-necked stage dresses, the very frocks they wore last night in their roles as the hero's sister and his mistress in the popular new play *The French Spy*. Because she played the mistress, Fanny wore the dress cut lower, made of yellow satin and dotted with blood-red rosettes. While still strapless, the hero's sister's dress was a more demure purple with gray lace and piping; but still its décolletage displayed Daphne's proud twin charms.

Hannibal the Carthaginian lifted his billy-goat cane in salute. The soldiers tipped their hats back and waved as if they were all going to the same merry party. Daphne and Fanny, hams that they were, fluttered their hankies at these new legions of admirers. If their bare, pale shoulders were cold in the swift, nimble air, they were too much the troupers to show it. A white, horse-drawn omnibus rattled past; male heads snapped about to stare as if the barouche were lit up by limelights. Jim tipped his topper and smiled. The sight of the girls' party dresses, their bare shoulders, and the tops of their pale breasts announced to every man jack that the three of them had been so busy partying that they hadn't had time for sleep.

When they were five blocks from Jim and Jay's temporary headquarters, the office of their chief brokers, Morris, Nathan, Kincaid, & Company, the crush of blokes in the street was so thick that Rufus had to slow the four horses to a walk. Rufus shouted at the sports and galoots who crossed recklessly in front of them, but few were in any hurry to clear out of the way. Open whiskey bottles dangled from the hands of some, while satchels, parcels, and brown paper bags were jammed under the arms of others as if they might be snatched away.

"Does every investor bring his lunch to Wall Street?" asked Daphne.

"Nooo, sweet pea," Jim answered, raising his cane in a jaunty salute to a knot of enthusiastic brokers. "These are my troops, and in those bags is the ammunition for today's big battle—drawn out of mattresses, bank accounts, and jars buried in backyards."

When they were a half block from the offices, Rufus turned back to Jim and said, "I can't get through. You want to walk?"

"Through this herd?" asked Jim. He stood to better view the situation. By his side the conqueror's concubines stood, too. As the troops recognized their general, a festive hurray went up. Cupping his left hand against the sun's glare, he raised his billy-goat broadsword and saluted his army. An ocean of hot, eager eyes rippled before him, the fretting tide of a mighty army that stretched from one side of Broad Street to the other, and as far down its length as the General could see.

"Jim!" came a shout. "What's going to happen today?" The thousand faces spread before him were red-eyed, flushed, and wild, as if they, too, had been up all night waiting impatiently for dawn.

"We're going over the top!" shouted Jim. A mighty cheer rose with a thousand fists. Fanny blew kisses at the audience, who hurrahed each one. Stirred by the enthusiasm, she plucked off the large rosette stuck between her breasts and tossed it out into the sea of outstretched hands.

Not to be outdone, the dark-haired Daphne at Hannibal's left also blew kisses. Slowly, slowly, she pulled the hem of her ankle-length purple gown above her left knee to reveal a forest-green garter sporting its own bright red rosette. Whistles and yells sliced through the hailstorm of applause. With an actress's flair for milking a moment, she waggled her exposed leg from side to side before she inched the garter over knee and calf and off her modest foot. She held up the green-and-red ribbon in the yellow rays of a perfect autumn morning. Shouts went up.

"Here! Here!"

"I want it!"

With the garter raised high in her right hand, Daphne extended her left like a rifle barrel, her two extended fingers the gunsights, to hunt for the right face. A drum roll. Transfixed, the crush of eager, uplifted snouts quieted and waited for her decision. She slowly turned, and the moment stretched. Her left hand found the target it wanted, a seventeen-year-old youth forty feet away. She flung the garter. He caught it, his face perplexed by what to do with it. The garter was snatched out of his thin fingers by a tall, rough-looking pirate with a fierce red beard. Red Beard stuck it under his nose and gave it a long, appreciative, comic sniff that set those around him guffawing.

"They'll let us through now that they see it's me," Jim told Rufus. "Drive on!"

He was right. The carriage inched forward. The captured concubines holding on to his waist, Hannibal stood in his chariot, shook his billy-goat broadsword, and filled the hearts of his troops with courage.

The sea of upturned faces reminded him of how he had picked up Daphne and Fanny. Probably many of these excited fellows had been in the theater audience last night and saw him onstage. When Delacroit was about to be hung during the final scene of the play, *The French Spy*, in response to a thousand-dollar bet from Frisky Freyer, Jim rose from his seat. Swinging his cane, he walked down the aisle, through the stage door, and up the little flight of stairs.

As he did every night, the daring French spy, hands tied, was just shaking off the hangman's black hood when Jim strode out upon the stage to ask in a rich baritone that carried to the back stalls if Fanny and Daphne would like to accompany him to Delmonico's.

The angry face of the French spy glared down from the scaffold, for Jim's loud invitation had interrupted his gallant last words. The limelights burned Jim's cheeks and eyes with the heat of fierce miniature suns. Noose in hand, paralyzed by the intrusion, the black-hooded hangman stared at Jim, while the British redcoats shuffled about in bewilderment.

Out beyond the blinding footlights, the audience, at first thinking this was a part of the play, murmured and squirmed in confusion— it was clear, wasn't it, that after the heroic spy was hanged, the sister and the mistress were, in a grand, teary reconciliation, to become like sisters, not go off with this fat fellow in the checked Broadway suit— Fat! Broadway! Checkered suit! This fellow didn't belong in the play! That was funny old Jim Fisk, the Puck always written up in the newspapers. Every sport in the orchestra punched his neighbor's ribs and snickered. Shouts from the bucks and plungers in the stalls urged the girls to run off with him. On the gallows above, the spy pleaded with Jim to get off the stage so he could finish his speech and be hanged. Applause, whistles, and hoots; shouts, laughter, and delight.

This was how a show ought to end, many in Delmonico's told Jim afterward. Jim grinned, head cocked, spine against the bar, gold billy-goat's head peeking out over his elbow, Fanny and Daphne hanging on either arm.

"It's time somebody yanked the chain of them stuck-up actors," cried Frisky.

Onstage, the real-enough manager and the other actors had ranted plenty at Jim, who raised his hands high in a victory salute to quiet the brawl, hushing the fray long enough to ask the two dazzlers, "Hey, you two beauties want to forget this misery of hanging and come out to Delmonico's for a sure-enough good time?"

"Yes!" chanted the audience for them. "Yes! Yes! Yes!" Daphne held up her hand for quiet.

"Return to your zeat," she said, pointing to him with all the hauteur of the French aristocrat she portrayed. Possibly she feared for her job. "Let us hang zis fellow ze right way and zen we will come out wit' you—okay, Fan?"

In the entire run, the French spy had never been hanged so quickly.

A quarter of an hour later, on the third floor of Morris, Nathan's, a clerk, who couldn't keep his bug-eyed peepers off the upthrust bosoms of the two actresses, ushered the three into a long narrow room nearly filled by a conference table.

Jim's entire team, along with another dozen traders and assorted hangers-on, boiled around the entrance. Jim shook hands and slapped backs all around. Frisky, Bob, Willie, and Flowers boasted that although they had partied all night, they were ready to hunt grizzly this morning.

"How about walrus?" demanded Jim.

"Walrus, too," cried Flowers. A rough hum was in the air, a tense, skipping buzz of energy, as if this crisp morning's electricity longed to zigzag into a target.

Jim turned to the far end of the room. Jay Gould sat at the head of the conference table, his back half turned to the bubbling crowd at the room's entrance. Jay was so quietly and secretively conferring with a frock-coated broker that nothing showed but the back of his head and its pink balding spot, the ragged side of his black beard, and the rear of his broadcloth coat. A lifeless ticker-tape machine squatted on the corner table. The heads of Jay and the broker bobbed together as silently as two secretive, hunchbacked vultures pecking the carcass of a dead rabbit. Jim grinned. Trust Jay not to lose his cool in the middle of merrymaking!

"I don't think there's a store in the city going to open today," said Flowers, grabbing Jim's arm. "They're all going to trade gold." Jim gave Flowers's shoulder a brotherly squeeze.

Frisky shouted, "Not even Gettysburg caused so much excitement!" Yesterday had been the craziest market day in the history of the Gold Room, with the price rising steadily all day long, bankrupting brokerage after brokerage that had sided with Vanderbilt and the bears. Jim rubbed his hands in anticipation.

"They ain't seen nothing yet," he growled.

"According to the papers," said Bob Rust, "all they done in Denver, New Orleans, and San Francisco yesterday was trade gold."

The black-coated broker rose from Jay's side and scurried out the door without looking Jim's way. Jay swiveled around. The sight of his partner's features, etched with anxiety and fear, shocked Jim. To judge by the dark hollows in his cheeks and eye sockets, Jay's slight frame must have lost five to ten pounds over the last few days. Jim shook his head. It was a good thing Jim was with him in this; Jay was made for the levelheaded, even-tempered world of running a railroad, not the boisterous excitement of trading. The poor cuss didn't understand how a bull campaign had to be run.

Jim walked down the length of the room. On the table before Jay were stacked neat ledger books, maroon cardboard files, several pads of accountant's finely ruled paper, the morning news rags, and a half-foot-high pile of those bits of newspaper that Jay tore up whenever he was worried.

"You don't need these," said Jim, and his billy-goat cane drove the trash off the table like snow before a blizzard. "Nothing to worry about. Today's the day we corner the old son of a bitch!" Laughter and catcalls broke out behind Jim. Jay craned his head around Jim and pointed a bony finger at Daphne and Fanny.

"Who're they?" he asked in a hard-edged tenor.

Jim turned. The two actresses were each sitting on a knee of Flowers Crawford. They were stroking his cheeks, rubbing his shirtfront, and cooing to coax him into buying them gold. Flowers made a comic's widened eyes and mouth as he peered down the front of their low-cut dresses. The dozen sports at the end of the room were doubled up with laughter.

Jim chuckled. "Them two's my good-luck charms," he said.

Jay scowled and drummed his fingers on a ledger book. "I suppose that's how you spent your night," he said, his tone irritated.

Jim ignored Jay's attack—the poor fellow's weak constitution couldn't take all this strain—and leaned down, hands on his plump knees, to stare benignly into Jay's dark frown. "And what better way did you spend your'n?" asked Jim. "Walking the empty streets?" Jay's poker face snapped backward as if Jim's remark hit home.

"Get 'em out of here," said Jay. The venom in the words jerked Jim upright, but the pain in Jay's face and the wolfish fever in his eyes kept him from lashing back.

"Yeah, walking the streets again," said Jim, shaking his head in dismay. "That ain't good for the health, Jaybo."

"Get those tarts out," snarled Jay. "I've got responsible brokers coming up here."

"You don't need any more brokers," said Jim in an expansive, benign bass. "I'm going to be on the floor myself." Jay's delicate fingers were tearing off the corner of the *Tribune*, making more paper snowflakes, and his eyes skittered away from Jim's.

"I think you ought to take it easy today," said Jay, "hold back some. There's a near-riot out there. Suppose the state sends troops to clear the streets—shuts down the Exchange?"

Jim snorted in disbelief. "They wouldn't dare," he said. "That would *really* make a riot." He winked. "I'm a jump ahead of you. I seen Tweed last night at Delmonico's. He's promised not to let that fool in Albany send troops, and to keep the Feds out." Jim's face became exaggeratedly serious. "I'm not fooling with Vanderbilt now. He pushed for this showdown. Now he's going to get it." His low growl rolled out of a face flushed with a clown's merriment. "No more feints. No more tricks. Today me and Flowers and Frisky are going to take the gloves off." He rubbed his palms together to show how eager he was to get at them. "It's cannons at twenty paces, Jay, and Stumpy's and Henry Smith's are loaded with cotton puffballs. I'm going to fill their snouts with grapeshot."

Jay looked lost, bewildered. Hands on his knees, Jim leaned down again. He knew how to buck Jay up.

"I get enough loot to run the opera house any way I see fit," he said, his face manic with glee. "We get the Old Walrus off our backs—forever. You get to run your tracks to San Francisco without him cutting off our nuts."

Jay nodded in a tight, constricted manner, but his fingers continued to quickly, cleverly produce tiny snowflakes. "Yes, yes," he said, "that's good." He picked up a folded newspaper, pushed it at Jim, and gave him another frown. "But this. Did you see the *Times?*"

Jim airily brushed it away. "I ain't got time to read no paper!"

Jay angrily shoved it at him, tapping with an insistent finger an editorial on page one headlined, FRENZY IN THE GOLD MARKET.

"Read it, damn it."

Fisk's presence in the gold-room was signalized by the rapid rise in gold. . . . The other engineers of the movement were not idle. . . . They had not only *bulled* gold with a will, but talked freely of the warrant they had from Washington that the government would not interfere with them. The highest official in the land was quoted *as being with them,* and he, of course, controls the action of the Secretary of the Treasury and the New York Assistant Treasurer. Although this must have been known to be false, there were abundant rumors and suspicions insidiously spread around the street to create the belief or fear with good men that the administration would *not* interpose by further sales of gold from the Treasury. . . . Among these rumors was one that the Gould-Fisk party were about to secure the services and influence of Mrs. Annabelle Stokes, sister-in-law of the President.

Jim lowered the paper and said, "So this is what has got you all upsot? Fribble-frabble in this rag?"

"How did they get that stuff about her?" Jay asked sharply. Jim shook his head. In the excitement of the past few days, he had let it slip here and there, but not to no newspaper reporters. He gave Jay an innocent stare.

"Damned if I know!" said Jim.

Jay's foot was jiggling mightily. "Jim—have you said anything about her or Grant?"

"I haven't told a soul," said Jim. Well, it was only a white lie. "On the other hand, it don't matter. This thing's going to be over in a few hours." Jim waved his billy-goat cane about, wondering how to get off the subject. "You haven't heard a peep from Butterfield, have you?"

Jay's hand ripped off the corner of the *Tribune.* "No, not a word."

"You'll send somebody to me if anything breaks, won't you?"

Jay's haunted skull bobbed yes.

"Hey, loosen up," said Jim. "This is the biggest day of our lives. It's going to work out fine. You're letting this rip you apart."

"Jim—" Jay stared at him, his face as torn as that of a wretch about to be dragged to the gallows.

"Yeah?" said Jim.

"Jim—" Jay appeared to be gagging, as if his breakfast would come up.

"Now, you just calm down," said Jim, patting him on the shoulder. "Everything's going to be all right. Take a few deep breaths. I know you don't like to drink and all, but maybe a little brandy in warm milk would soothe you."

Jay nodded dumbly.

Jim shook his head. He had never seen Jay so nervous. When this day was over, the poor fellow was going to have to be carted out of here like one of those busted, ruined brokers hustled off the Exchange floor yesterday.

33

*Business of nearly all kinds became
suddenly stagnant, and all classes and
professions mingled on the sidewalks.*

—*New York Herald*, September 24,
1869

At midmorning Jim, Bob, Flowers,
Frisky, and Willie trooped downstairs to walk the three blocks to the
Gold Room.

A horde of raucous working types, sharpies, well-dressed dudes,
ruffians, and shifty-looking snaps thronged Broad Street, most flushed
and fierce-eyed, hoarse, unshaven, and boisterous. Three times, Jim
and his crew were accosted by insistent street peddlers who tried to
push on them pennants, little whistles, and miniature leather bulls
and bears for their buttonholes. It took them twenty minutes to push
the three blocks to the granite pillars of the Exchange entrance.

The Gold Room was so crowded that Jim couldn't see the gray
squares of floor marble. Runners in green jackets could not run, but
uncharacteristically picked their way through the swarm of hot bodies. Already there was an eager, tumultuous din, like the hollow,
continuous rumble of thunder. Jim's spirits soared on the hot drafts
of this fiery energy, which would surely today swamp Henry Smith
and Stumpy Roberts, and through them, Cornelius Vanderbilt.

"I want to make a bet!" Jim shouted. "I want to make a bet!"
But the crowd, too jammed together to see him, too busy jabbering
to listen, ignored him. Damn! he thought. Fifteen feet to his right
stood Henry Smith, arms folded, hair freshly greased back, and a
sneer on his wide, thin lips. Jim put on his biggest smile.

Silently, clearly, he mouthed, "Stuff yourself, Henry."

Henry shook "the fig" at him, a fist with its thumb poking through its first and second fingers, a graphic return of Jim's curse.

Jim needed to channel all this energy, get this beast to obey the crack of its master's whip. Behind him were the fountain, dolphin, and Cupid, still dry before the opening bell. As a plan came to him, he chuckled with glee. If today was going to go his way, like Hannibal he was going to have to *make* it go there.

He pulled himself up on the pool's brick rim, grasped the cold, leering snout of the dolphin for balance, and climbed up on the top of the five-foot-high iron rail around the fountain. His army was spread out before him like a living carpet of heads. He would lead them over the top.

With the blade of his billy-goat sword, he struck the bronze dolphin's side, making a noise like a large gong: *Claang! Claang! Claang!* Startled, the riotous crowd diminished its roar and five thousand inflamed faces turned toward him. One hand on its snout, Jim continued to bang away at the dolphin's hollow brass flank. When it sank in who was towering above them, like a beast recognizing its true master, the thundering roar from the thousands of roguish traders grew expectantly quiet.

"I'll bet any man in this room $50,000!" bellowed Jim—he paused and waved his sword above his head for emphasis. His blue eyes swept the vast space, taking in every upturned, flushed plunger's face—"that gold goes above $200 today!"

When no one answered, Jim pointed the brass tip of his billy-goat cane at the treacherous Henry Smith, who was staring up with a scowl.

"You, sir!" Jim called. "You snake who betrayed my partner and me by becoming a spy in our camp! Will you take my bet?"

Amid the traders' rumble, Henry held up the fig again and shook his closed fist. Jim's grin grew larger.

"Henry Smith!" bellowed Jim. "In front of all these witnesses, I'll take the whole $50,000 or any part of it!" The crowd roared like a starving beast.

"You'll leave here a ruined man today!" shouted Henry.

"Then, sir," demanded Jim, "will you take $25,000 of my bet?"

Henry folded his arms and shook his head no. Boos, raised fists, and shouts from the traders urged Henry to bet.

"Ten thousand?" demanded Jim, his arms open with stage helplessness.

Henry attempted to escape the taunts from every side with a bold, sneering shake of his head.

"How about a measly $1,000 then?" insisted Jim.

"Bet him!" shouted Henry's side of the crowd. "Do something!"

But Henry turned and pushed through the throng toward the exit. Jim's loud, comic moan and further questions jabbed Henry's back. "Five hundred, Mr. Smith?" Henry kept shoving forward. "How about a hundred, then?" pleaded Jim's rich, comic voice. "Mr. Smith," Jim shouted as Henry reached the door, "will you make a bet with me of just *five* dollars?"

Henry pushed through the door. The traders applauded and cheered. In a broad stage gesture, Jim shook his head as if he couldn't understand a worthy opponent's lack of spunk. The traders cheered and whistled all the louder. He jumped down.

Flowers was the first to reach him. "Jim! Jim!" he cried. "That was brilliant. They all think it'll go over the top."

"It will, Flowers!" said Jim. "I can feel it. By nightfall Commodore Vanderbilt will give us half the Central to get us off his back."

The opening bell clanged, and the golden arrow dashed upward an unprecedented six dollars from last night's close of 144.

Jim shook his billy-goat's head and gave a hurrah that went unnoticed, for the last clangs of the bell were smothered by bedlam. Grinning with delight, he bulled his way through the surging traders toward his usual spot at the outer iron railing.

The journey was like struggling to cross the riptide of a spring river. Once—buoyed up by hot, clamoring bodies on every side—he lost his footing and kicked empty air. Intoxicated by excitement, sleeplessness, liquor, the hope of wealth, and the fear of ruin, rabid traders threw themselves into the crush and were carrying him he knew not where. In alarm, Jim's feet churned. This wasn't funny. He twisted about to make an opening so his body could drop through and his feet hit solid marble, but he couldn't get down. He glanced about in fear. The taut, twisted faces around him all bore the same ferocious grimace: lips dry, teeth bared, white foam at the corners of mouths, eyes glassy and focused on a point in the middle distance. All screamed, "Buy! Buy!" or "Sell! Sell! Sell!"

Jim put his meaty hands on two nearby shoulders and gave a giant shove, making a hole in the sea of flesh that allowed him to drop to the marble floor. Ten minutes later he reached his usual spot by the iron railing, a journey that normally took ten seconds.

To gain an anchor in this wild sea of bodies, Jim pressed his back into the railing. The cold iron pipe was as welcome as a lifeline to a drowning sailor. What had got into these idiots? A thousand backs, elbows, and shoulders scraped his starched shirtfront, while Jim continued to grip the iron pipe tightly. Through storm-tossed breakers of heads, hands, and arms, Flowers, Willie, and his crew were barely visible on the top steps of the pit, but thank God they were at their posts. Behind them the fountain's jets of water playfully rose and fell in a sprightly dance. Astride the smirking dolphin, Cupid urged his mount on faster. Jim was surprised by the power of the mob, for he had only meant to ignite a roaring bonfire, not burn down the house.

Rumors exploded across the jagged swells of the ferocious ocean. Jim cocked his head to listen. A rat-faced fellow whose ear was in Jim's nose shouted to his neighbor that stocks were sinking fast on the Stock Exchange, and that it would shut down before noon. From another side came the shout that the Gold Room wouldn't close for the noon hour. Jim was shoved by a mass of bodies along the railing, his fingers' grip too weak to keep his place. A chap from Kidder's office shouted that stocks had started to rally. No, shouted a runner, the market was closed. No, no, cried another, it was open but falling. The Mayor had wired the Governor to send in the militia to quell the riot on Wall Street. A gent whose pince-nez was twisted into a pretzel shouted to Jim that every official in Washington was long gold. Jim heard three times that Jay Cooke was long gold, and twice "for a fact" that Jay Cooke was short gold.

Hot bodies. Jabbing elbows. Grasping hands. A single apple at the bottom of a basket of apples in a rattly wagon on the way to market couldn't have been more bruised. A spry, elderly dandy, his collar half torn off his neck, said the New York Central had reached a new low minutes before and that Vanderbilt would declare bankruptcy before dark. A broker whose sleeve was ripped off shouted that the rally in gold was a bear trap; Vanderbilt and the bear ring would send the price plummeting when every possible dollar had been sucked into buying gold.

Jim was drenched with sweat. The gilt arrow kept climbing, which was good. He hated this crushing press of bodies, but he had to be on hand in case the tide turned against their huge position. Never well ventilated, the Gold Room was completely unprepared for a boiling, bloodthirsty mob. The heat from the traders was blistering, roasting, scalding, and Jim had turned as bright red as a lobster thrust into a boiling pot. Sweat, panic, and greed had become a biting stench. Jim's shirt sucked against the movements of his body as if a bucket of hot water had been flung over him. Not a hat remained on a head. Urbane brokers stripped off their frock coats and dropped them onto the floor, where they tripped every boot that tangled in them. Once a fellow fell, he had to claw his way back to his feet by pulling himself up on the legs, trousers, arms, and sleeves of those standing, or be trampled to death.

Jim himself worried about falling. His palms were so slick with sweat he could hardly hold the iron railing. Pushed by the frantic mob, he slid back and forth along the pipe as easily as a bead on a string. He couldn't even spy what Henry Smith and Stumpy were doing.

It was downright foolish to remain here—he could be crushed against this iron pipe—but he couldn't leave the Gold Room till things were settled with Vanderbilt. Maybe it would be less jam-packed up there with Willie and Frisky. As fearful as a shipwrecked sailor abandoning a rock at high tide, Jim kicked off from the railing to swim through the flood of traders.

Something soft wriggled under his boot. A young runner's twisted, bleeding face gaped up at him in terror, a boy. Horrified, Jim reached down to grab his hand, which closed around his with the desperation of a drowning child. Before he could get a firm grip, the swirling force of the crowd knocked Jim away. He struggled against the tide to swim back to the boy, but he couldn't find him after minutes of thrashing about. It was useless. He made for the steps of the pit, shoving, pushing to make even slow progress. By the time he arrived he was missing a sleeve and the bottom part of his right trouser leg.

Willie, on the topmost step, gave him the thumbs-up sign. Jim tried to tell Flowers about the boy on the floor, but the trader only leaned close to Jim's ear and shouted, "I'm a millionaire, Jim!"

Following Flowers's pointed finger, Jim looked up. The gold arrow stood proudly at 164, a mark it hadn't reached since the war years. He was shocked, for he had scarcely noticed it since the market opened.

Behind Flowers, a short, dumpy fellow was bent over in the shallow water of the fountain's pond. It was Stumpy Roberts, picking up handfuls of water to splash into the armpits of his black frock coat, as though he were bathing in some country stream on a hot summer day. Stumpy took his order book from his pocket, and as if it were a bar of soap, soaked it in the water and scrubbed his chest, crotch, and the crack of his behind. Two of Stumpy's helpers climbed over the iron rail of the fountain and led him out.

An insistent whisper pressed against Jim's ear, "Make it happen." He turned to see who had said this before realizing that he had said it to himself. He glanced back up at the gold arrow: still at 164. The market was stalled. In *The Wagon Peddler's Triumph* he himself had figured out how to succeed. Later he had created that stirring drama called *The Patriot's Triumph* in which during the dangerous Civil War he had infiltrated the South to buy thousands of tons of cotton for

Father Abraham. A knot of arguing traders bumped into him, knocking him back against the fountain's iron railing. He clutched the dolphin's snout for support.

On Wall Street he had been the star of the cliff-hanger *The Broker's Triumph*, during which he had twice gone bust and twice come back. In *The Impresario's Triumph*, his constant vision had created the opera house. And now he was the star of *The Financier's Triumph*, in which he would in fact triumph only if he seized this hectic moment and *made* that triumph happen. The world was never yours until you *insisted* it was yours. While neither he nor Jay had planned anything like this madness, if Hannibal the Carthaginian didn't urge his troops over the crest of the world, he and Jay would never take Rome.

"Willie," he shouted, pulling the trader's lumpy face down to his mouth. With his other hand he pulled Flowers to him, indicating he was to bring Frisky and Bob in for a huddle on the top step, which wasn't easy, with all the knocks and thunks from careening bodies. Four pairs of ears bent down. "Let's start buying now, and get it up to over two hundred," he shouted. "Let's make history here today— the day we drove the Big Bear into the corner!" The five stood and cheered.

A dozen hefty, blue-coated policemen, with the easy power of cavalrymen pushing their horses through a storm-tangled wheat field, were using their billy sticks to cut a path through the howling mob. As if in a dream, Jim stared at them, wondering what the hell they were doing. A gent in a long black coat and a black silk topper stood in the middle of the policemen. His face was grim, his grizzled beard neatly trimmed, his bearing military. Behind him, also protected by policemen, followed six frightened, clerklike fellows clutching pads of paper and pencils to their chests. The bluecoats cleared a way so the militarylike gent could reach the top step. Jim grabbed a policeman's arm to ask what the hell was going on, but the copper rudely shoved him back.

The erect gent, ten feet from Jim, began to shout, but Jim heard nothing over the room's thunderous din. Despite the protection of the dozen policemen ringing the newcomers, the six clerks on the second and third steps were jostled about.

"Who the hell's that?" Jim shouted at Willie, who shrugged.

One of the policemen, a gray-haired captain, beat his billy stick on the iron railing, but the puny rapping attracted nobody's attention. To help out, Jim turned and beat his cane against the hollow side of the brass dolphin. *Claang! Claang! Claang!* Gonglike, the ringing penetrated the mob's roar.

The hysterical clamor dropped. The press of wild eyes and wet, beet-red faces stared up at the black-suited gent, who was clambering up on the topmost rail around the fountain like a giant black grasshopper. For support, one hand held onto the police captain's shoulder and the other grasped Cupid's head. The six clerks glanced around in terror, holding their pads before them like tiny white shields.

"I seen him before," said Jim to Willie. "Where was it?"

"I'm from the United States Treasury," shouted the black-suited gent. "My name is General Daniel Butterfield. I've come to announce the sale of 30,000 ounces of gold by the U.S. Treasury here and now. The Treasury wants the highest bid—"

The rest was lost in a explosive roar that had as its basis the single syllable *"SELL!"* With the snarling violence of a rabid leviathan, the beast of a crowd lunged forward. If the government was selling gold, so was every trader. Hands outstretched, billy sticks held before them to make a human fence, the dozen bluecoats struggled to protect the six clerks and Butterfield, who was wavering unsteadily on the iron piping five feet over the heads of the mob. Undaunted by the clubs, the hysterical beast leapt forward. The police dug in their heels, making their line rigid. The savage beast pushed harder, thousands of vicious traders intent on dumping their gold, all at the same time. Backward, step by step, the policemen were forced, till policemen and clerks, like peas under a giant's fork, were mashed against the fountain's iron railing.

Over their heads, Butterfield's mouth was shouting "Stop!" but no one heard. As if the ground were giving way beneath them, a dazed Jim and his crew were wrenched from their spot by the surge of the rioting mob. The five clung to the railing but were pushed around it to the other side. The railing under Butterfield's boots bent, bent, and finally under the pressure of so many rabid bodies it snapped backward with a loud crack. Arms flailing, Butterfield toppled rearward into the fountain's pond. The six clerks were quickly pushed in after, followed by the blue-coated policemen. On their hands and knees, in water up to their chins, they swam across the shallow pond with the frightened speed of beavers who had miscalculated a dam's strength. Seeing the need to drive up the market, Jim grabbed Willie by the arm and tugged.

"Buy, Willie, buy! Buy as if your life depended on it!"

"No, *sell!*" cried Willie. "Sell everything before it's too late!"

"Buy!" shouted Jim, pulling Willie's long frightened face within three inches of his. "We have to stop this panic!" The thunder around them was deafening, as if a hundred locomotives were roaring through the Gold Room.

"It's the U.S. Treasury!" shouted Willie, his teeth so close he was almost biting Jim's nose. "Nobody can fight it! We're ruined, Jim, ruined!" As if to prove it, Willie's fingers shoved Jim's face around and up toward the gilded arrow.

The arrow was falling, dropping from 161 to 156. Jim was stupefied. It had never dropped so far so fast. If this kept up, Willie would be right. He and Jay and the Erie were busted, bankrupt, ruined. When he turned back, Willie was gone. At the bottom of the steps in front of him was his old friend the middle-aged floor broker Albert Speyers—grizzled hair sprayed in all directions, gray eyes wild, blood on his shirt, vest half ripped off. Over his head, as if it were a sword, he waved a long-barreled pistol. "Where's Jim Fisk?" ranted Albert, wagging his pistol from side to side. Although he couldn't hear, Jim read his lips clearly enough. All the while Albert was staring Jim right in the face. "Somebody tell me where is that fat bastard."

Albert's bloodthirsty glare and the ugly pistol rooted Jim to the spot. Albert clambered up the stairs and put the pistol's cold snout against Jim's cheek. He shoved his nose almost against Jim's and shouted, "Hey, have you seen Jim Fisk anywhere?"

34

The Gold Room was a den of wild beasts.

—J. K. Medbery, *Men & Mysteries of Wall Street*, 1870

Jim considered running for it, but the iron pistol barrel jammed against his jaw paralyzed him. The hammer on the pistol was cocked, the lead cartridges in the cylinder fat and poised to fly. Albert's yellow-flecked, ash-gray eyes, only inches from his, were huge with craziness. Don't move a muscle, Jim cautioned himself. Even shivering might make Albert's trigger finger jerk and blow off the left side of his face.

"Who do you want?" Jim asked softly. Albert's grizzled head twitched as rabidly as a giant, hoary lobster whose enormous diseased claw was ready to tear off Jim's head.

"Jim Fisk," said Albert, his breath hot on Jim's cheek.

"I ain't seen him," said Jim in a slow, careful voice. "Lemme have that pistol." Albert's grim mug lit up with wild joy.

"Here!" he said, thrusting the pistol barrel-first at Jim, who took it. Albert stepped back to the bottom stair. He ripped open his shirt to expose dirty gray hairs on a fish-belly white chest. "Now shoot me!"

Pistol in his hand, Jim stared at him. Savage traders streamed by, collided into them, ignoring Albert's craziness and the cocked pistol in Jim's hand.

"Come on!" screamed Albert. "I'm ruined! Do an old gee a favor and shoot!" He pulled his shirt open wider to expose pale, drooping breasts.

He was mad. The plunge in gold had ruined him and driven the poor shake crazy.

"Come on, old fellow," said Jim. He lowered the hammer on the pistol, stuck it in his hip pocket, and grabbed Albert by the arm. Albert's dingy features collapsed in disappointment.

"You won't shoot me?" Guiding Albert up the five steps and through the crushed iron railing, Jim helped his stumbling friend into the knee-deep, tepid water of the fountain's pond. With his cupped hands, Jim splashed water into Albert's face and over his bowed head, then dried him off with his handkerchief. The water seemed to awaken the old fellow from a sleep, for he stared up and rapidly blinked his red-rimmed eyes.

"Jim! There you are!" Albert stretched his hands out, clasped Jim's arms, and shook him hard.

"Yeah," said Jim, fearful of him.

"Now, what did I want you for?" said Albert, his grizzled features vacant with hard thought. "It was important."

"Grant did us in, Albert," said Jim firmly. "He sold us out." Albert snapped to. Standing in the knee-high water, he turned to look out over the screaming mob of gold traders.

"We're all ruined, aren't we, Jim?"

"Busted," said Jim, watching Albert closely. "Just about every man jack that's on this floor."

Albert's hoary face twisted as if crushed by grief, as if a moment ago he had lost his entire family. His legs slowly gave way and he plopped into the filthy water like a toddler in a puddle. "What's Martha going to say, Jim? We've lost our house." Going behind him, Jim picked him up under the arms, carried him out, and set him on the dry steps. "We've lost our carriage, Martha. All our furniture." Spotting one of Albert's clerks, Jim called him over, explained, and left his boss in his hands. Jim's billy-goat cane lay on the steps, its polished shaft splintered in three places, the hollow goat's head half flattened by boot heels.

He pushed toward the exit, but an angry hand grabbed his shoulder. Alarmed, he spun around. Frisky's hands snatched Jim's lapels and shook him. He snarled, "You ruined me, Jim Fisk! You ruined me!"

"What?" shouted Jim, drawing back in surprise. Frisky was as good as they came, a solid professional. As the trade put it, he was "a big boy," a plunger who knew how to take the lumps of high-risk, high-profit trading. It took Jim five minutes to get across to the irate Frisky that it was Grant who had betrayed them, for the President had sent word last week that he wouldn't dump Treasury gold, that he was in it himself.

Outside the Exchange, the noon air of Broad Street was tired, tepid, as if this morning's brisk freshness had been stewed into a boiled pulp.

A ragged tribe of savages filled the street, their raw, screaming faces even wilder than the maddened traders back inside. Normally dozens of hacks for hire and fancy private carriages inched north and south along the wide thoroughfare; now only one was visible, and it a block away and heading north.

Jim plunged into the mob, eager to reach the sanctuary of Morris, Nathan three blocks downtown, but the harebrained crush in the street had a will stronger than his. Like a ship in a storm too strong for its screw, Jim was blown by a squall of rowdies to the other side of the street and a block farther away from his goal. Regaining his footing, he pressed against the gritty brick wall of a shop, gasping for breath and struggling to figure out what to do next. A bleary, red mug abruptly shoved itself into Jim's face, its rubbery lips spraying spit and whiskey.

"I've been robbed," shouted the fellow. Eager to slide away, Jim nodded sympathetically, and heading south, edged along the rough brick wall away from the ruddy-faced boozer.

In the street two tough brawlers, each with a broken whiskey bottle thrust forward as a knife, warily circled each other. Blood covered their heads and shirts as if they were in a fight to the death. A ring of pirates, grinning with delight, egged them on. Jim slid on downtown, wondering how the hell the mob had found out so quickly. He supposed it was the damn telegraph and the chalkboards outside brokers' offices.

He slid on past shop windows, each busted, many looted. At a haberdashery, a half-dozen fiends pranced about in the busted display window trying on hats.

"Get out of here!" screamed the shirtsleeved shopkeeper at them, hefting a large-bore, double-barreled shotgun. "Get out or I'll shoot!"

Fearful of getting shot, Jim hurried past. Seconds later, the booms of two shotgun blasts, followed by bloodchilling screams.

By edging along the busted shop fronts, he finally made four blocks of progress down Broad Street. The red brick building with the welcome, rich-looking gilt letters, *Morris, Nathan, Kincaid, & Co.*, stood across the way. Relief warmed Jim. As its iron safe held substantial amounts of bonds, gold, and securities for clients, the brokerage had been built like a small bank: foot-thick brick walls, barred and shuttered first-floor windows, and an iron front door. Behind those three curtained windows on the third floor lay safety, the secure conference room Jim had left Jay in this morning—had it been only hours ago? All he had to do was cross the street.

But scores of fierce, drunken rioters blocked his way, many with loot from busted shops. One ragged fellow wore three coats, one atop the other. Several carried two or three whiskey bottles. A tall, cruel-faced goat of a fellow paraded a dozen wallets in his belt like a Sioux displaying scalps. Jim drew back into a narrow alleyway to give the street a chance to clear. A rabble of these freebooters, like privateers plotting their next raid, milled around an enormous crackling bonfire that tossed sparks, smoke, and soot skyward. A powerful hand grabbed Jim's elbow.

"Jim!" came a shout. "Is that you?"

Startled, Jim spun. The broken nose and one good eye of Pat Lynch, the Hell's Kitchen tough he used as a bodyguard when he had to talk to angry strikers. Pat was walleyed, his misdirected eye glaring off in another direction while his good eye battened on you. Short and with the thick trunk of a boxer, Pat was the one gee Jim would rather have at his side in a fight than anybody else.

"Jesus, yes," said Jim. "What are you doing down here?"

"You told me to come."

Jim remembered nothing of that. "What?"

"Last night at Hanrahan's," said Pat. "I seen you this morning when you rode up with them two naked beauties, but I couldn't get through the crush to meet up with you. I got a bunch of the gang like you said."

"I forgot—I'm smarter than I thought." Jim reached into his left hip pocket and pulled out his thick wad. He split it and shoved half at Pat. "Here. Get me across the street, then get me and Mr. Gould up to Castle Erie."

"All right!" shouted Pat, eager to plunge into his work.

When he raised his arm, up lurched three of the brawlers who regularly worked with him—Yancy Boss, Hardhand Pick, and the one they just called Ear because years ago his right ear had been ripped off in Sleepy's Bar. Tough bruisers, each carried a heavy wooden cudgel. From their belts protruded the handles of large knives. Jim clapped all three solid backs.

With Jim in the center, the five pushed off the curb. As they were skirting the bonfire in the middle of the street, the yelping, milling freebooters spotted them.

"Fisk!" shouted a short, rough pirate, pointing his bit of plank at Jim. "There's the fat son of a bitch!" Jim jumped behind Pat.

Two dozen tattered, savage marauders surged forward, planks and stripped branches raised as clubs. Pat and his toughs, cudgels at the ready, closed ranks to protect Jim. The leader of the mob, a red-faced brute with a huge belly, stepped out in front of his band and waved his wide plank about with the ease of a pirate flourishing a four-foot cutlass.

"Give him to us," he shouted. The neck of a whiskey bottle stuck out of his belt. His jacket sleeve was torn off, and to judge by the bloody gash along the left side of his head, a large patch of his black hair had been ripped out by the roots. "He's ruined us, and we're going to ruin him." Jim stepped up beside Pat.

"I never ruint you," shouted Jim. "It was Grant. I'm ruint, too. He betrayed all of us." Jim recognized the big-bellied freebooter. Under the gash and soot he was a trader from the Gold Room, a gent for whom he had once or twice bought drinks at Delmonico's, but that was ages ago and in another lifetime. This red-faced savage with a four-foot plank looked ready to risk death to bust in Jim's head.

More wild-looking marauders gathered behind Big Belly. While they carried makeshift clubs of chair legs and planks rather than Pat and his crew's well-crafted cudgels, it was only five of them against two dozen vicious beasts.

Jim pulled out Speyers's pistol, stepped in front of Pat, and shouted, "I'll shoot dead the first man who gets within three feet of me!"

The mob's glazed, rabid eyes stared at the pistol, which Jim kept aimed just over the leader's scalped head.

"I'm going in that door there," Jim went on, pointing at the brokerage with the pistol. "Clear me a path, Pat."

With Pat and his boyos surrounding him, Jim edged across the street. Grudgingly, the raised staves and clubs drooped and allowed them to pass. Pat thumped on the door and shouted, and finally he was answered by shouts from within. A welcome series of clicks, a bolt was thrown, and they scrambled inside. Jim laughed; it was over!

In the empty conference room upstairs, Jay Gould, hunched over in his shirtsleeves, still sat in the same place in which Jim had left him this morning, writing in a large ledger with a clerk's twopenny steel-nibbed pen. The ticker-tape machine sat noiselessly at his side. At the window Dick Morris, the thirty-five-year-old, redheaded senior partner of the firm, stood delicately peeking through the drawn curtains. The muffled shouts of rioters, punctuated by distant gunshots, filled the air. Jay looked up.

"Jim!" he cried, jumping to his feet. His face was as white and beset as a haint's. "Are you all right? Look at you!"

"What?" asked Jim.

Jay came forward, his bony features vexed, one shaky hand tentatively extended. "Your coat, it's half ripped off," said Jay. "Where are your diamonds?"

Jim looked down. Only one of the three diamond studs he had stuck in this morning was left, and it was about to fall off. Jim plucked it and stuffed it in his pocket with Albert's gun. His best silk top hat, gray satin vest, and cane—all gone.

"Your trousers," said Jay, the spooky cast still stamped on his face. Jim leaned over. Below his large belly the bottom half of his right leg was ripped away. His right coat sleeve was gone, too, and the tail of his black coat was entirely torn off.

"How the hell did all this happen?" Jim asked. "They've gone crazy. That damn Grant has made monkeys of us all. I can't stand a skate that turns his back on his promises."

"Yes," said Morris, turning back to peer through the curtains, "before it stopped transmitting, the ticker said that the Governor won't send in troops. Although what is rumor and what is fact today, God himself only knows."

All afternoon Jay, Dick, and Jim waited in the conference room for the fever of riot to burn out so they could go home. His eyes vacant, Jim sat slackly in his chair, as empty and defeated as a giant, multicolored touring balloon punctured by the very mountain tip-top over which it was soaring. Hannibal's horrified eyes had witnessed every elephant, legion, and general tumble over the sheer drop of the Alps' highest cliff.

It wasn't fair, Jim told himself over and over. He had done right by all the others. Grant was too stupid to know which side of his bread the butter was on. Busted! For the third time in four years, he was squashed. Probably finished on Wall Street. Instead of leading more jolly charges against rascals like Vanderbilt, Jim would be ignored, snubbed, by every trader. God knew what line he could get into. Maybe Jay would think he was a jinx. He shot his partner a furtive, cautious look.

As if the day's fever had ravaged him too, Jay's features were yet more drawn and haunted than they had been earlier this morning. His cheekbones and eye sockets were more prominent, and he seemed to have lost weight and shrunk into the holes of his black suit, which appeared several sizes too big. Still, Jim saw that his usual spunk ran him. Except for the sporadic times he jumped up to peer out the window, Jay worked in his ledger books as steady as a clerk with his boss standing over him.

Every hour or so the mob's fever shot up to the boiling point. With a beam ripped out of an adjoining building, dozens of the screaming rioters battered the downstairs front door. In time to the thuds that rattled the tips of Jim's chair against the polished oak floor, the rioters chanted, "Fisk! Fisk! Fisk!" Under the blows the walls shook, the windows rattled, and the chandelier swayed. Hunched over his ledgers, Jay lifted his black, haunted eyes. Jim wasn't all that worried. To keep the battering ram from breaking in, Pat and his crew had piled a dozen desks between the front door and a support beam in such a clever way that the mob would have to push the whole building down in order to enter it.

Toward late afternoon Jim stirred and sat up. Jay was still scribbling in his red ledgers. "What you writing?" Jim asked. Startled, Jay made an ink blotch in the middle of the page.

"Figuring," he said, reaching for the sandwell.

"Well, damn it, *what* are you figuring?"

Whites showing, Jay's eyes glanced toward the curtained window. "Listen to those chants," he said. "What the hell did you do to stir them up like that?"

Jim snorted. "Me? Whose idea was it to bull up gold?"

"I told you this would get out of hand." Jay shook his head. "If troops were out there, we could go home."

"Hey," said Jim. "Let's not bicker. This is the time to stick together."

As night fell, the howls and yells of the savages grew as bold as the thunderous din back on the Exchange floor. Jay's pen froze; he was a phantom, little more than a pair of hollow black eyes and an empty suit of clothes. The bonfire rose higher, sending gusts of wild sparks that made Dick mutter that the building could catch fire. Staves and bottles raised like tomahawks, the rioters careened about the flames. Silk ties and ladies' scarves were tied around many rioters' heads, trailing ribbons of color like feathered headdresses. An unsettling drumbeat of distant booms and shots jerked the cavorting fiends in fitful rhythms.

As the gas didn't work, the remaining clerk brought in a lamp, which threw an eerie, flickering light. Dick and Jay cautiously pulled back the white broadcloth curtains from the three windows for a better view. Jim joined them.

"There they are!" shouted one of the street Injuns, pointing an accusing finger at Dick, Jim, and Jay in the third-floor windows.

"Fisk! Fisk! Fisk!" chanted the mob in deep angry booms.

"Gould! Gould! Gould!" came the echoing chant.

"This is only going to get worse," Jay said to Dick. "They might burn us out."

The gas globe of a single lamppost, framed by jagged shards of glass, stood tall above a boiling swarm of rioters at the end of the block. Jay edged against Jim, his eyes reflecting the orange flames of the bonfire. A rope with a noose at its end snaked over one of the lamplighter's pins. Jim's throat clamped, and he tasted bile and bit back the urge to throw up. Jay was staring in a fixed manner at the lamppost and the swinging noose. Jim squeezed his partner's slack shoulder.

"Will they attack my house?" asked Jay hoarsely.

"Why should they do that?" Jim countered.

Jay's grim face turned from the noose to Jim. "Why the hell should they attack us here?"

"Lies," said Jim. "All because of Grant's lies."

"As long as they don't attack Helen and the children," said Jay, turning back to the lamppost, on which swung two nooses.

"They're just stirred up," said Jim. "It'll all die down when they run out of whiskey."

"The real danger is fire," said Jay. "Here we're no better than rats in an oven. Call Pat, get us out the back. It's only a matter of time before they think of it." In the dark hallway Jim called downstairs for Pat, whose footsteps quickly clattered up.

"Are any of them punkers out back?" Jim asked.

Pat saw his plan at once. "You want to make a run for it?"

"What do you think?" asked Jim. In the gloom Pat considered.

"If we can get you to Castle Erie you'll be safe," he said. "You got them solid iron gates they can't break through, and ain't nobody going to batter down three-foot-thick stone walls."

"Let's do it," said Jim. "Send one of the boys to Johnny's Stable on Broadway. Tell Rufus to bring my victoria around to the entrance of the back alley. And be sure he draws the curtains."

Minutes later it was fully night.

In Broad Street four bonfires roared higher in mad dances. The mob's chants and shouts rose and fell with increasingly frenzied rhythms. The wooden fronts of half the stores along Broad Street had been ripped away to feed the bonfires. The chanting shouts of "Fisk! Fisk!" and "Gould! Gould!" were louder and more frequent. When Pat reported that the carriage was in place, Jim signaled Jay and Dick to follow him.

At the end of the damp, shadowy alley that opened onto Hanover Square stood the murky shape of the carriage and four horses against the faintest of bonfire orange. Pat leading, the four crept forward. The horses stamped impatiently, jingling their harnesses. Relieved to have reached the carriage, Jim opened the door and helped Jay up.

He had half pulled himself up into the carriage when the strange voice of the driver abruptly ordered him out. Jim looked up. In the nebulous orange glow, the silhouette of a large, cocked Navy Colt pistol was aimed at his head. It wasn't Rufus but a lost U.S. mail coach. No amount of money would tempt the driver to take them uptown to Castle Erie. Muttering under his breath, Jim helped Jay back down. With hard lashes of his whip, the driver pulled away.

The four huddled in the dark mouth of the alley waiting for Rufus. Without the screen of the coach, the two bonfires across the street in Hanover Square leapt high against the astounded fronts of tall office buildings. Wild figures with reckless torches, as filled with excitement as boys in a nighttime Fourth of July celebration, raced up and down the street. Their savage faces were bathed in a yellow-red fever, and their eyes gleamed like live coals.

"Let's go on foot," said Pat. "We can walk it in thirty minutes."

The other three agreed and set out, hugging the edge of the buildings, but before they had gone thirty feet, a voice cried, "Here they are! Over here, boys!"

A crackling torch blasted into Jim's face. He shrank back against Pat. Shouts, jostles. A half-dozen torches were held over their heads. Yellow-red masks of anger and delight surrounded them and yelled.

"You busted us, Fisk, now we're going to bust you!"

"That's his skinny little partner, Gould," yelled another. "String him up."

"No, damn it!" shouted Jim. "It was Grant!" He shoved back the torch jammed into his face with the powerful impatience of a cornered bear.

"String 'em up!" shouted a grinning face missing most of its teeth.

"Grant!" shouted Jim, sticking his muzzle into the nearest angry mug. "It was Grant!"

"String them! String them up!" echoed the circle of joyful, fever-yellow faces, deaf to Jim. He drew out the revolver he had taken off Albert and made a show of cocking it.

"I'll shoot the first man who touches me," he roared. The burning faces shrank back in fear, the torches popping sparks and dribbling tears of fire. Behind this inner circle of silent, fearful fiends, bolder demons were shouting and pushing forward.

"String them! String them up!"

The mob was gathering, thickening as the news of the capture spread along the street. Frightened, Jim looked around for a way to escape, but he only saw flames, nooses, smoke, yellow-red faces, a bloody scalp, and tomahawks, all racing by with the breakneck speed of nightmare. These were fellows whose faces Jim vaguely recognized from an earlier life, the one before everything went crazy. Their yellow eyes glinted as madly as demons from the hottest valley of Hell, threatening but surely harmless. He would shoot these savage animals, but he certainly didn't want to.

Jay edged close to his right arm. Jim glanced to his left to find Pat and engineer their getaway. His right arm was jostled. He fought to keep control of the pistol, but a giant's fingers squeezed his hand and his trigger finger was mashed. The pistol jerked, and though he didn't hear a shot, he felt the buck as a bullet was discharged into the crowd. The laughing, sneering face before him burst into a spasm of pain. The rioter's hand slapped his left shoulder, through the fingers of which abruptly spurted a fountain of blood. The crowd exploded in rage.

In seconds Jim—yelling "Stop it!"—was hoisted aloft and bouncing over the ocean of hands like an empty rowboat in a storm. Roaring torches were thrust toward him, and he closed his eyes against the hot sparks. Frantic, he scrabbled about in an effort to puncture the waves of buoyant hands, but his hands and feet couldn't gain a purchase on anything solid, as if he were being swept over a waterfall by a vicious current. The night sky glowed a faint orange. Cool air whipped his cheeks. The harder he kicked, the more eagerly the dozens of hands clutched his thighs, calves, and ankles. Jay swam by, arms wide and flailing, feet kicking, borne in the same direction.

Momentarily giving up the struggle, Jim looked through his feet to see where he was going. Twin nooses hung off the gas lamppost, its fiery grin the skeletal muzzle of death.

"String 'em up!" came a shout.

"Put them up here," came another, and the crack of a coach whip. "He'll run out from under them and snap their sorry necks."

A cheer rose on all sides. Terrified, Jim twisted his head. Four gray horses and the curves and shiny black exterior of a large victoria crept through the grinning crowd with the unrelenting grimness of a hearse come to express him to Hell. These idiots meant to use the victoria as a gallows drop. Jim lunged about, thrashing with his useless hands and feet in an effort to break through the buoying sea of hands. If only his feet could gain a purchase on the cobbles, he stood a chance of bulling through these liquored-up animals and running for it. But his hands were yanked behind him, and his efforts to escape were useless.

"Snap their sorry necks!" came a shout.

"Put 'em up and snap 'em off!"

Ropes were wrapped around his wrists and pulled tight. Hog-tied, he was lifted and dropped, lifted and dropped, then flung as easily as a sack of potatoes onto the victoria's rooftop luggage rack. With a thump Jay landed against him. Like landed fish in a boat, both wiggled and struggled to free themselves from the grass rope that bound their hands, but it was too tight.

Two rough silhouettes clambered over the top edge of the victoria, which was now backed hard against the lamppost's leering gas globe. With all his strength Jim struggled to free his hands, but the rope was too tight. One hulking pirate went to the rear and leaned out into space to grab the twin nooses, provoking a hurrah from the press of rioters. The other hoisted Jim up from the rear and shoved his protesting feet over the slippery iron luggage rails. The open noose stretched before him in the grinning hangman's hand. Fumbling for purchase, Jim's feet slid along the metal tracks of the rack. As in a nightmare Jim was abruptly enormously *large*, like a seven-story giant or a huge flying balloon, and at the same time ridiculously *small*, with the strength and size of a mouse.

"*Noooo*," he moaned. Torches lit the swaying mass of faces yellow and orange. The victoria lurched. His feet fought for a firm grip to stop the inexorable shove of the rogue at his back.

"Stuff this," said Jim as he neared the back of the victoria. He took a swift, sharp breath to calm himself. He had only one chance. He went slack. Aiming carefully with his booted foot, he kicked the pirate holding out the noose a hard, solid blow in the crotch. The hangman's rough face opened into a circle of pain and surprise. The shifting, roiling sea of yellow-orange faces gazed up with the rapt attention of stalls in the theater. Dropping the noose, the hangman reached for his injured part. Jim grinned. The hangman's legs slowly collapsed and he dropped rearward off the back of the victoria. As Jim spun to face the second pirate, he was grabbed from behind in a hard stranglehold.

For an eternity, the two danced and slid on the iron luggage rack. Jim tried to edge the fellow off the roof. The grip on his throat tightened.

"Swing him! Swing him!" chanted the mob.

Jim's throat was closed and he couldn't breathe. The strangler rocked Jim toward the driver of the victoria, who had half risen and

cried, "Bring him here!" Jim's foot mashed something soft that slithered, which must have been Jay. But no matter how hard he dug in
his feet, slowly, relentlessly he was dragged forward. The eager driver
brandished a coach whip in one hand and an upside-down whiskey
bottle in the other.

"Bring him over here!" the driver shouted. "I'll knock him out."

That voice! The glazed yellow mug of the driver! Rufus! Surely
Rufus hadn't brought the victoria up to help hang him—unless he,
too, had lost money today. Rufus raised the bottle over his head,
preparatory to striking.

With a mighty shove backward, like an awkward country waltzer
forcing his partner to the other side of the ballroom, Jim pushed the
strangler holding him toward the front of the victoria. In a calm,
deliberate manner, Rufus held the bottle poised for a few moments
over the two struggling forms, then brought it down in a loud crash
on the head of the bruiser strangling Jim. He dropped onto the roof
with a speed of a cow felled by the butcher's hammer.

"Down, Jim!" shouted Rufus, and he yanked Jim so hard his boss
slipped to the roof. The coach whip snaked out in the darkness over
the four grays in a loud, hard crack.

The grays lurched forward. Fearful of the horses, the mob parted.
The forward motion slid Jim backward along on the top of the victoria, bouncing his head and ears against the outer rails of the luggage
rack. Stunned, he stared rearward, his right cheek mashed against
the hand-high iron rail of the rack. The victoria was almost free of
the crowd. Two rough mugs appeared over the back of the victoria,
rioters who had jumped on it as it pulled away. With a groan of
despair, Jim hunched and scrabbled around to aim his feet rearward.
He kicked the snout of one so hard with his boot heel that the knuckles
gripping the luggage rack let go and he fell back. Meanwhile, the
other scrambled onto the roof past Jim and was crawling forward on
all fours toward Rufus. With the one-legged hump of a bound frog,
Jim inched after him.

Rufus glanced back, swung his coach whip, and lashed the at-
tacker across the head and back. The rogue's hands flew to his head
and he lurched upward into a kneeling position. Jay kicked him hard
in the stomach with both boots, which shoved the fellow half off the
side edge of the roof, but one hand of his still held on to the luggage
rail. Jim humped over and kicked him in the side with his one boot,
and off the fellow sailed into the night.

Lurching, rocking, clattering, the heavy victoria rushed northward through the cold September night, sweeping past the unlit city,

dark trees, and vacant buildings. The waving torches were now a block behind them. The shouts of the mob faded. Up Pearl they flew in darkness, for few gas lamps had been lit tonight.

Jim took great rasping lungfuls of air into his aching throat, and was grateful for the cool night that wrapped around them like a heavy winter cloak.

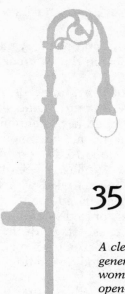

35

Josie Mansfield's Negro servant
Carter ushered Ned Stokes into her second-floor parlor at nine o'clock
that evening.

Behind the fox-head brass andirons, a small autumn fire flickered
in the hearth. She rose to greet him. The two gas globes on either
side of the mantel were turned low. The parlor's dozen potted ferns,
the dark wood of the chair rail, the heavy crimson-colored drapes
and valances mingled into a single hushed, mysterious effect. While
the room announced that Josie was a lady of taste and breeding, the
oriental throw rugs, piled on top of one another with bohemian care-
lessness, hinted that she was a bold and free artist.

"What's going on?" she asked. "I heard yelling in the street and
saw men running. Carter went up the back alley, but came back saying
there was trouble. I've been afraid to go out even for a paper."

An air of grimness had drawn Ned's lips into a hard line and
narrowed his gray eyes. " 'Black Friday,' they're calling it," said Ned,
and an elegant smirk warred with the stern line of his lips. "Our dear
Jim has cheated all of Wall Street."

"Cheated!" she said. She noticed that his eyes were fixed on her
dress of printed muslin, which demurely amplified her figure.

"The gold market's crashed," said Ned. "A mob has him holed up in his broker's office. If they catch the fat crook, I daresay they'll tear him limb from limb."

Josie started. "I should go to him. Jim needs me." He would see how much more there was to her than to Annabelle. Ned's gaze was hard and cocky, as if he saw through her intention.

"He saw *her* Wednesday afternoon," he announced.

Josie had spent every day since Ned's terrible news worrying what Jim's new liaison meant. "He hasn't been here," she said to Ned, her voice faltering. Her tone sounded whiny, speaking books about her lack of upper-class, beau monde poise. She slumped back onto the sofa. As the implications of Ned's news tumbled in, buzzing numbness spread through her chest. It would never end. Jim had always made a fool of her with other actresses and chambermaids, he was making a fool of her now, and he would always make a fool of her.

"And that little snippet Bridget tells me that Jim spent last night with Annabelle."

"Spent the night!" As if she had been slapped, Josie writhed against the sofa's cushion. Afternoon visits might be legitimate business; all night meant only one horrible thing. The last three nights Josie hadn't fallen asleep till past two o'clock, and then she slept fitfully, waking from dreams of suffocation.

If Jim abandoned her, she couldn't pay the mortgage on the town house. To give it up was to fall backward into cheap, cold rooms whose dirty hallways stank of boiled cabbage. She would have to sell the new, plushly upholstered chairs and sofas, Madame Rumplemeyer's beautifully fitting dresses. Another winter, perhaps a lifetime, in Hell.

Ned sat and his arm slid around her waist. She leaned against his warm male strength for a moment before she drew away.

"Are you all right?" he asked, his voice full of concern. "You looked as though you might faint."

"Did I?" Did Ned really care? She rose and he followed her.

"Sit down," he said, and his soft hands at her waist and elbow guided her back to the sofa. "Do you keep any spirits?"

"In the cabinet."

He pulled out a dark bottle, one of the many Jim kept there. "Port," he said. "A good one, too. Where are the glasses?"

She started to protest, but she said, "Ring for Carter."

Her servant had been at work since seven this morning, and his weary shuffle was more conspicuously put on than usual. After he banged down the tray with the cheddar, apples, French biscuits, and wineglasses, she told his startled brown face that he could go home. She carefully ignored Ned's glance. With Carter gone, Ned would be the only man in the house.

Port, new to her, turned out to be surprisingly savory—a thick, tart, and musty liquid fire, with a flavor that brought to mind antique, perfumed rubies. She breathed deep, appreciative sniffs, and the heady fumes dulled her loss. Ned poured them each another glass. She expected him to make an advance, but elegant gent that he was, he perched on the sofa opposite her and made witty, concerned chatter.

As the night deepened, in a well-bred, almost wounded tone, he said that she had never told him about her earlier life. The rich wine warming in her hand, Josie hesitated, wondering if she should lie. Finally, needing a friend tonight, she told him of her Boston birth and of life in the California mining camps with her mother. She made light of the rough life and left out the part about the coming and going of her mother's many so-called stepfathers. She put it that she had "lost" her father at an early age, careful not to say that it hadn't been from death, and that the truth was more that he had "lost" his wife and daughter.

He refilled their glasses. "You've had a hard life," Ned murmured. "How did you get east?"

Her toes tingled, and she felt relaxed. With gallows humor she described the actor husband she had married in San Francisco, his neglect of her, and their trip east in rattly stagecoaches and dusty, sooty trains over scorching deserts, icy mountains, and never-ending plains of scrub. Ned raised his glass in a toast.

"What pluck!" he said. "I wish I had been there to make it easier."

With a hurried, awkward movement, he rose and went around her back to the fire, where he fumbled with a poker. His face was turned away, as if he was hiding tears or a pained expression. Except for the crunch of the poker in the fire, the dark parlor was still. When she turned her head, his lips were there. His kiss tasted of port, cigar, and the male world outside. Of racetrack excitement, fashionable handmade wool, and privileged drawing rooms. Of the regal Hoffman House, august mansions along Fifth Avenue, and well-built, silver-appointed carriages.

She gasped and pulled back, exclaiming, "No!" He stood behind the sofa, caressing her neck and shoulders with his strong, soft fingers.

"Josie, Josie," he murmured, his gray, lustrous eyes pleading, "I'm not Jim." She pulled away, but the smooth hands on her neck and shoulders held her firmly in place.

He lowered his face to the top of her head. She felt pleasantly dizzy. His lips kissed the center part of her hair, and a luscious heat spread through her. His cologne, a resinous, woodsy essence, was intoxicating, and her neck tingled briskly. She shuddered and looked up at his soft, caring face.

"Ned, I don't want a man just now."

His delicate features recoiled in shock. His creamy cheek brushed hers, and his eyes, inches away, were bright and moist. "You think I'd hurt you?" His refined, sensual lips closed lightly on hers. She lost herself in the kiss, her neck leaning back over the sofa in a harsh strain that hurt yet added to the sense she was falling, unconscious, into bliss.

Several kisses later he joined her on the sofa. His delicate fingers stroked her arms, hands, and waist; he was more tender than Jim. Within the confines of a long kiss he eased her backward. Ned's body felt thin and hard, a rapier to Jim's blunt broadsword.

After a long, exquisite moment, she pulled free and rose. His shining eyes watched her light a stubby candle with a pine taper. She turned off the two gas globes, put her finger to her lips, and took him by the hand. Ned's lips nuzzled her palm. Holding the candle, she led him silently up the stairs in order not to awaken her visiting cousin.

In the fashionable mode of the day, she had decorated her bedroom to resemble a Turkish tent. Long bellies of Moorish cloth swung from the ceiling, and intricate Isfahan and Shiraz carpets hung from the walls. Muffled by thick fabric, the room was as silent as a forsaken oasis at midnight, and her candle's black-and-orange flutters made the bedchamber yet more wild and luxurious.

Ned's probing fingers took down her hair. Delicious shivers swam up and down her backbone. He unbuttoned her blouse, kissing and caressing her skin as he exposed it. As skillfully as a dressmaker, he helped her out of her skirt, from which she stepped as in a dream. She bent her face backward and kissed him. With the experienced fingers of a lady's maid, he unfastened the laces of her whalebone corset. Embarrassed that he might remove her chemise and ankle-length pantalets, she scampered into bed. Tilting his head, smiling in a bemused, adoring way, he undressed down to his shirt, blew out the candle, and joined her under the dark snugness of quilt.

His fingertips, soft as flower petals, caressed her face. She kissed his palms. He eased her out of her chemise, kissing her hardening nipples. She stroked his belly, and the curls of hair around his navel aroused her. Her pantalets came down, and his hands stroked her legs, thighs, buttocks. His lips grazed her body. Her nerves sang. He seemed to take forever, savoring her, for unlike Jim he was in no hurry. Jim plundered her with the piggy savagery of a child cramming a delicate pastry into his mouth. Ned used every part of his body—lips, fingertips, legs, hair, cheeks, thighs—to make hers sing, as if he had been waiting years to suck every drop of pleasure from tonight.

Once Ned had entered, her pleasure mounted and quickly exploded in wild joy. Left gasping, she held on to his hard back tightly. Tenderly he stroked her breasts. Her body, freed from long restraint, met his kind, loving energy and urged him on. He charged again. Encouraged, her passion mounted to a still higher peak before exploding in a second frenzy of fire and shuddering madness. Quiet. Peace. His eager lips. Again exhilaration, the mountain peak, explosion, frenzy, fire, wildness. Over and over she soared into excitement and fell back into exhaustion. She had been in bed with a dozen beaus, but none had ever given her so much. Her body contained more passion, more ecstasy, than she had ever suspected. That a man could give a woman so much joy—that she hadn't known it—shocked her. She kept her arms wrapped around his hard rib cage and clung on tightly.

At some timeless moment, he changed, charging more strongly against her. She met him. Without his saying so, she knew he was taking his long-delayed pleasure. She went beyond where he had taken her the previous times to another place, a silent motionless ice land where her soul entwined with his. Josie had no use for poetry, except when pretending to culture and practicing for the stage, but that was all she could call it, "entwining souls," as hers met his. Finally, she understood. This was marriage, two souls joined. With her head against the pillow, her eyes staring up at the dark ceiling, twin thick streams of tears scalded down her cheeks.

Ned rolled off and wiped away her tears with his soft fingertips. He murmured, "I've wanted you so much." With him no longer on top of her, she was chilled. She pulled up the warm quilt and snuggled against his hot body.

"I wanted you, too," she said, "but I was afraid."

Ned chuckled. "No need to be afraid."

"You don't think the less of me?"

"I think the more of you."

She ventured the largest obstacle. "You'll think I'm not good enough for you, being as you come from a family of class, whereas I'm only an actress."

His delicate kips kissed her cheek twice. "You're so exciting, Josie," he said, his voice low, serious. "Other women are buried by what they think they ought to be. You're fresh. You're alive to the world and who you really are. It makes all the difference." It was too good to be true, but she detected no false note.

"I'll give up seeing Jim," she said. "He was a mistake." Her belly felt different—warm, full, satisfied.

Maybe I'm pregnant, she thought, again holding on tightly to his bony chest. A little dizzy, afraid to say a word, she kissed his shoulder. Her fingers caressed his hard stomach and lean ribs. No fat on him. A rush of bliss shot through her. Tears of happiness again welled up. Pregnant! Ned's baby! She squeezed him. His snobbish family would come to be her family, the large, warm family she had never had, her staunchest defenders. She would be such a wonderful mother and such a poised lady that they would know the gossip about her stemmed from jealousy and envy. No more borrowing money from Sally Woods, no more begging money off Jim, and no more in and out of agents' dingy offices.

"Yes," he agreed, "Jim was a mistake."

She laughed and once more hugged his bare chest. The Stokeses of Philadelphia—what a trumpet's regal blare was in those words!—were a far finer family than Jim's. Almost American royalty, like the Tildens, Adamses, du Ponts, and Astors. Josie could breathe easily, live a peaceful life, and raise her children in a loving, secure house.

Josie became drenched by Ned's sensual adoration as they made love twice more.

36

The chief cause of this intense strain is the uncertainty attending the operations of Wall Street. The chances there are not dependent upon the skill or the exertions of the operator. Some powerful clique may almost destroy the securities upon which he relies upon for success, or make him wealthy by suddenly running up their value; so that no man who does not confine himself to a strictly legitimate or commission business—and but few do so—can say one week whether he will be a millionaire or a beggar the next. The chances are in favor of the latter result.

—James McCabe, *Lights & Shadows of New York Life*, 1872

Midnight in Jim's ornate, gilt office back on the third floor of Castle Erie. Rufus stood at the elaborate sideboard, spooning in hot turtle soup, brought over from Delmonico's.

Munching a lamb chop, Jim stood near the elaborately carved mahogany sideboard reading the morning edition of the *World*.

Jay sat on Jim's couch, surrounded by the papers, the *Times*, *Tribune*, and *Staats Zeitung*, the city's leading journals, as well as the more ragtag *Sun*, *Standard*, and *Star*.

"The papers should be quieting the public," said Jay with the sternness of a hanging judge, "not whipping them up to fresh panic."

Mouth full, Jim grunted and stepped to the window to peer out. In the hushed night of the city, the mobs had drunk up all the whiskey and let the bonfires burn out. Every man jack, his wife jill, and their jobbins were asleep, but like clocks whose springs were wound too tight, he and Jay and Rufus were too keyed up for rest. The past two days had been rough as a dried cob on Jim—so much trading, partying all night with Fanny and Daphne, breasting the mob on the floor yesterday and this morning, having the President betray him, and nearly getting hanged by a bunch of sore losers—but still, it was over. Folks would cool off. They would feel different when they saw that he was as broke as they. Maybe they would all march on Washington and string up Mr. Grant.

"Reckon the water's hot yet?" Jim asked his driver, who had half a lamb chop stuffed in his mouth.

"Sure!"

"Fill that big tub in Miss Audry's dressing room," Jim said, referring to the opera house's current prima donna. He winked at Rufus. "I maybe can't get in her pantaloons, but I can wallow in her tub!" Rufus cackled. "Hey," Jim said to Jay, "ain't you gonna come eat?"

Jay was hunched over the *Tribune*, and round the sofa leg was a snowdrift of newspaper bits. "I'm not hungry."

"This turtle soup here," said Jim. "It'll sit good on your stomach. These rolls, you can't get better rolls in New York."

Jay's battered face twisted about like a queasy sea. "Please, Jim."

"Hey, hey—I know you," said Jim. "When's the last time you et?"

Without looking up, Jay shook his head.

Jim turned to Rufus. "I seen the sum bitch eat a sandwich Wednesday night when we sat here celebrating! Could this dumb cuss have forgotten to eat since then?" Rufus shook his head in wonder at the idea.

Jim crossed the office to the built-in closet, from which he took a clean ruffled shirt and the striped formal trousers he kept for the rushed occasions when he couldn't get back to the Hoffman House before the seven-thirty curtain. From the wall he took down a dagger and his admiral's sword, an honest-to-God fighting piece with a sharp blade of German steel, a basket of carved gold, and a ruby-tipped pommel. Jay sat up, the *Times* crumpling noisily in his lap, and yelled.

"Will you get the hell out and go take your goddamn bath?"

"Will you eat something before you starve to death?" Jim yelled back, a grin lighting up his face now that he had provoked a spirited rise. Jay was going to be all right.

*   *   *

The hot water in Audry Pleasant's dressing room was as soothing to Jim's battered nerves as Frank Renhofer's turtle soup. He amused himself by waggling his rump around on what must have been the very spot Audry's good-sized butt wiggled on every day. Then he lay back and read the *Evening Post*'s account of this morning, which it called "Black Friday." Rufus toted iron bucket after bucket of steaming water, which he ladled into the porcelain tub so carefully that Jim was pleasantly heated without boiling.

"Beats having your neck stretched, don't it?" said Jim.

Rufus grimaced. "Don't joke about it, Jim. That was too close."

"Bring another pail of hot water," said Jim. Rufus cheerfully went and came with his iron bucket.

"You look as pretty-bright red as one of them lobsters," said Rufus. "I put on another kettle. I can bring you hot water all night if you want."

"Hey, listen to this!" said Jim. "It's that young stockbroker, Stedman, the one writes the poems in the paper:

> " *'Zounds! how the price went flashing through*
> *Wall Street, William, Broad Street, New!*
> *All the specie in the land*
> *Held in one ring by a giant hand—*
> *For millions more it was ready to pay,*
> *And throttle the Street on hangman's day.*
> *Up from the Gold Pit's nether hell,*
> *While the innocent fountain rose and fell.*
> *Loud and higher the bidding rose,*
> *And the bulls, triumphant, faced their foes.*
> *It seemed as if Satan himself were in it,*
> *Lifting it—one per cent a minute—*
>   *But listen! Hold!*
> *In screwing up the price of gold*
> *To that dangerous, last, particular peg,*
> *They had killed the Goose who laid the Golden Egg!*
> *Just then the metal came pouring out,*
> *All ways at once, like a water-spout,*
> *Or a rushing, gushing, yellow flood,*
> *That drenched the bulls wherever they stood!'* "

Eyes shining with delight, Rufus laughed and had Jim read parts of it again. "I wish I could learn me how to read," said Rufus.

"Don't Mr. Gould look awful?" Jim asked.

"He sure do. I ain't never seen him look so bad."

"We got to buck him up," said Jim. "I ain't never had as good a friend. You got to look out for your mates. If he don't snap out of it, I'm going to pour that terrapin soup down his throat myself, and then drag him down here and toss him in this hot tub. Put on two more kettles, Rufus. Ain't nothing like a hot bath to make a new man of you!"

"He's just down 'cause you two lost so much," said Rufus. "You keep on at him, Jim. You're the best thing for him."

After he had fetched four more buckets of hot water, Rufus said, "One thing don't make no sense to me." Jim had lain back, eyes shut, letting the heat soak into the cold marrow of his bones.

"Oh?" asked Jim, not opening his eyes.

"Wasn't you supposed to get word if the Treas'ry was gonna sell gold?"

"Yeah."

"Did you?"

"No."

"How come?"

Jim opened his eyes and stared at Rufus. "Hummm," said Jim, twisting his bulk and splashing a yard of water over the wide tub's edge. He settled back down and shut his eyes. "Don't know. I'll ask Jay."

When he had soaked much of the soreness out of his battered muscles, Jim dressed in his clean ruffled shirt and formal trousers.

"Fill up the tub for Mr. Gould," said Jim. "I'll send him down next." Jim picked up his sword and made a couple of vicious cuts in the air. "I'll take this, you keep the dagger. Some burnt trader might be lurking around the halls."

Favoring the bruised spot on his thigh, Jim limped up the wide marble stairs.

None of the opera house's dozens of crystal chandeliers was lit. On the landings' banisters the yellow flames of occasional lanterns threw sinister shadows, and in them grinning hangmen built rickety gibbets. On each landing Jim paused, stock-still, to listen.

The night was quiet, magnifying every creak and faraway thud, which he heard as frenzied gold traders busting in at distant side doors. The quiet chill gnawed at his heated bones. In every corner's shadow hellish demons jigged about, swinging open nooses. Jim shivered and advanced, his slippers making gritty, sliding echoes on the marble, the naked sword in his hand at the ready.

Jay lay on the couch, eyes open and staring at the ceiling. The lobster, lamb chops, rolls, *épinards au veloute*, soup, and slice of *bombe* lay untouched on the tray by the empty couch. The *Herald* lay across his chest, and along with the *Times* and the *Tribune*, the *Sun* and the *World* were spread on the floor. Jim shook his head in disgust.

"You didn't eat nothing," roared Jim.

Jay sat up. "I'm jumping like a telegraph key," he said wearily. "I may never sleep again. Every time I close my eyes I hear that damn ticker-tape machine and see thugs with nooses."

Jim poured himself a glass of champagne and gave a little roar in an attempt to inject some life into the room. "Say, did you ever hear from that bastard?"

"What? Who?"

"We paid him, did Butterfield deliver?" Jim asked.

Jay crossed the room to stand staring out the Twenty-third Street window. "Yes . . . I got word this morning."

"I never got word," said Jim. "Did you send somebody over?" The back of Jay's head nodded again. "I guess the feller you sent to the Exchange never found me," mused Jim. "Who'd you send?"

"One of Dick's clerks."

Jim pulled his sword out of his trousers band. It swished loudly as he sliced open an imaginary pirate standing in front of the velvet drapes. "I guess you started selling then?"

Jay turned back to the window. "Yeah," he said vaguely. "I wish I could sleep."

"I ain't going out there again tonight," said Jim. "I'm going to send Rufus over to get Josie."

"No," said Jay. "You agreed. No more women up here."

Jim's guffaw echoed hollowly. "Ain't tonight different? We ain't even going to be occupying these premises two weeks from now."

Jay shook his head in a baleful, weary way, as if to say Jim was too stupid to ever learn.

"I'll have him send for Annabelle," Jim pushed on. "The four of us will have a party." He grinned with the impish charm of a child deviling his parent.

"You have the judgment of a goat," said Jay in a flat tone. Jim beamed as if Jay had paid him a compliment.

"That damn Grant!" Jim shouted. "What a dumb mule *he* turned out to be. Didn't even have the sense not to dump Treasury gold on a market in which he owned a million dollars!" His sword cut back and forth in the yellow air, slicing the President from crotch to chin.

"Well, you had a little to do with all this," said Jay, facing him. His voice was stiff and brittle. "That was a near-riot yesterday and today."

"What!"

"You pushed things way too hard," said Jay. "You egged the crowd on too far. You spread around so many rumors, and bought so much for your own account—pyramiding up the way you did. I'm not sure Grant had any choice. He could have sent in the National Guard, but through Tweed you had blocked that at the state level. From his point of view, sending Butterfield in to sell gold was the easiest way to lance a dangerous boil."

Jim swished the German blade back and forth in a series of vicious cuts. "Who the hell's side are you on?" he asked.

"You know whose side I'm on," said Jay, voice crabby.

Like an expert fencer, Jim sword-hopped to the middle window, against the velvet drapes on which his sword delivered a dozen vicious body slashes. Panting from the exertion, he turned to Jay.

"Well, I *can't* see it from his side. Would you explain why an ass with a million in long gold would depress the market? Until that Treasury prong come marching in, the only things wrong was a little hullabaloo."

"Grant never had a million in gold."

"What? He did, too! I seen his statement at Annabelle's. She was holding the gold for him to keep his hands clean."

"That wasn't his. *I* financed that for her."

Jim blinked. "*You!*" With a dull clunk his sword fell to the carpet.

"Yeah, me. Like the whole world, she wanted to profit in gold."

Jim shook his head and stooped to retrieve his sword. "That wasn't the President's account?"

Jay stood resolute, his back straight, black beard firmly grasped by one hand. Above his set poker face, his bulbous brow seemed larger than usual. His eyes were as steady as needles.

"No," he said.

Jim scratched his head with the ruby button of his sword. "Damn! If he was never in it— When did you start selling?"

"I— Thursday. I lightened up on Thursday."

"I was buying Thursday," Jim mused. His blue eyes narrowed as if trying to see something on the horizon. His face grimaced into a crushed crosshatch of lines. "We were trying to push it over the top. How come you were selling?" There was a defiant, frozen cast to Jay's thin features.

"I told you as early as Thursday to take it easy, that I didn't like the look of things," said Jay in a hard tone. "I knew the President saw Jay Cooke, and there wasn't no telling what flea Cooke was sticking in his ear."

At that moment Jim's office shifted, growing both larger and smaller, lighter and darker, as if in some peculiar fashion Jim were two different people staring at the room. The walls and ceiling tilted as if he were on board the *Providence* and they were in a swelling, nasty sea. When had he felt this before? When he was standing on top of his victoria tonight, facing that grinning thunk with the noose. He had often had this divided sense, too, when dealing with Uncle Dan'l. You would discuss a strategy with him, and all of a sudden the old hoot got vague. A week or a month later you found out that the old rascal had gone off and done something on his own hook that might or might not be against his partner, but something that you damn sure didn't know anything about.

With a little clatter, Jim laid his sword on his chair, and he hunched his thick buttocks up on the desk's edge. From the humidor, he plucked up a cigar and lit it, taking his time.

"How'd you find that out?"

"Wednesday night. Remember the note I got? Annabelle got a letter from her sister that afternoon. Grant was at Cooke's place near Philadelphia."

"What? You didn't say nothing to me!"

"The very next morning I told you to take it easy," said Jay, voice testy.

Jim shouted, "The President tells his wife's sister to get out of gold—writing from the estate of the short pool's biggest hugamug—and it ain't worth telling me?"

"I told you to take it easy!"

"Hey, hey, damn it," said Jim, standing belligerently before Jay. "You didn't tell me the *whole* truth."

"I couldn't," said Jay, his voice rising into a shout. "Look what you did with the information about Grant—blabbermouthed it all over the place! Before that, you divulged precisely how we printed up extra shares for Vanderbilt. You can't keep your mouth shut about a goddamn thing."

Jim grinned sheepishly.

"If the Exchange plays fair," Jay said, "and if not too many brokerages fail, maybe we can salvage something from the wreckage."

"Maybe," said Jim. Jay was smart in financial matters, often found a way in the most obscure and difficult situations, but no way could he make a silk purse out of the sow's ear they were wrapped in now. "But I say you carried your secretness too far. You ain't supposed to keep things from your own partner." When Jay said nothing, Jim raised the tip of his sword to toy with a single chandelier leaf, making it tinkle.

"Partner?" cried Jay abruptly. "How much were we 'partners'

in this? I wanted a pool. Oh, nooo!—you had to have a free hand."

Jim whipped the sword's sharp tip down to Jay's nose. Jay pushed it away with an irritated shove, but Jim brought the tip back against his nose.

"You sold me out, Jay Gould," said Jim. "I see it now. You set me up. You set it up so I would keep buying gold."

Jay edged away from the sword's tip and backed across the Persian carpet. Jim followed, keeping the point aimed at Jay's nose. Jay pushed it away, but Jim brought it back. "You tricked me into thinking Grant was investing with Annabelle."

Jay knocked the tip away again. "If I'd told you," said Jay, "in five minutes it would've been the talk of every Broadway barbershop."

"Such a secret little bastard, aren't you?" said Jim, pressing him backward. Jay's spine hit the sideboard, and the sword's point pricked his Adam's apple. "Let your old buddy go to the gallows. The son of a bitch risks his own taters to snatch your chestnuts out the fire—so stuff him."

Jim smacked the flat edge of the sword hard against Jay's neck, raising a red welt. Holding his palm against the red mark, Jay slid around the corner of the sideboard. His right hand flopped around the sideboard for support, and found one of the silver platter covers, which he held up before him like a shield. The sword blade clanged against its edge. Jay ducked and scooted across the room, and he put Jim's fancy French desk between them. Jim chased him, and tried to stick him across the desk's broad reach.

"You're a coldhearted, godforsaken cow chip," Jim shouted. Jay kept the domed lid between his chest and the sword's sharp tip.

"You're a cheap bag of wind!" yelled Jay.

"You can't keep those things a secret, you know," said Jim. "Grant's probably too stupid to know that."

"But he never *bought* any gold, you big fat dummy!" said Jay. "After you swore you'd keep it a secret, you blabbed it to the whole world."

Damn! Jim had forgotten. "Blabbed?" said Jim. "*Blabbed?*" Jim lunged to the left and jabbed the sword at Jay, who caught the tip with a clang inside the curve of the silver dome. Jay was no different from all the other cheaters in Jim's life, the girls who said they would meet you and didn't, the bankers who would loan you all the money you wanted at midnight in Sally Woods's parlor, but changed their minds by noon the next day in their offices.

"I was a fool to ever have you for a partner!" shouted Jay.

"We ain't never been partners! You bitch about not having any chums—no wonder, with your sense of loyalty!"

"You're nothing but a jackass with a cock for a brain!" shouted Jay.

Jim rared back, swaggering. "Ha!—I just ain't scared of life, Jay Gould."

They glared at each other, both sweating, frazzled, and out of breath. Jay tossed the silver dome on the desk with a loud clatter.

"Go ahead," Jay said quietly, breath heaving. "I'm leaving. My back will be to you. Run me through." He turned and marched to the door.

"What's the use?" yelled Jim. "You're as bad as Daniel Drew. I don't know why God has cursed me with terrible partners, tricky bastards with hearts as cold as corpses'." Jim tossed his sword to the carpet. "I can't no more hurt you than I could Uncle Dan'l."

Jay opened the door and stalked out.

Rufus ran in, openmouthed, face stricken. "What's wrong?"

Jim silently pushed by Rufus into the hall. Jay disappeared into his office with a slam of his door, followed by the sharp snap of its lock.

Rufus whispered, "Is Mr. Gould ready for his bath?"

"Forget his fucking bath," said Jim, wiping the tears off his face with his sleeve. "I've been betrayed. Go get Josie."

"But you know what Mr. Gould said last time—"

"Stuff Mr. Gould!" Jim shouted. "I don't want to hear that name again!" He strode to his desk. "Here's a note. Run up the street, bang on the door, and get her out of bed. I want her pronto. I don't care if every reporter in the city sees her up here."

Two blocks away and a few minutes later, Josie Mansfield lay in bed, wide awake.

Ned snored lightly at her side. She wished she could sleep, but her mind raced and her feelings were a hot swirl of confusion. The first cock crowed. She would feel tired all day tomorrow, but there was no help for it. In a few hours her life had completely changed. No more Jim! A whole new life lay before her!

It had been stupid to be an actress. So little had ever come of it. With Jim, no matter how much he talked about their glorious future, a granite block stood between them made up of his wife, whom he wasn't going to divorce, and children.

She reached out in the dark to make sure Ned was really there, that it wasn't a dream. His hard, bony chest felt as real as the ridges on a silver dollar. Of course, she would have to cut back on what she spent; he didn't have near the money that Jim had. Out of pique Jim might cut off buying oil from Ned's refinery, but if necessary they could sell her house and rent rooms till he got on his feet. They could make a go of it. He would see how much of a help she could be.

Far away, dull thuds banged and thumped. She turned over to try again to sleep. More insistent thuds, this time rattling the walls and windows. She sat up. What was it? Outside, night had begun to gray. Virginia's slippers scraped by in the hall. Who could be banging at her front entrance?

A few moments later, Virginia's light knock at her door. Before her cousin could enter, Josie flew out of bed and tossed on a robe, not wanting Virginia to spy Ned. She opened the door a crack.

"It's a note for you," hissed Virginia. A robe thrown over her nightdress, her younger cousin held a candle that lit up her eager face.

"Note?" asked Josie. As Virginia passed it over, she stood on tiptoe to peer over Josie's shoulder.

"He's waiting for a reply," she hissed.

"Who?"

"The driver who brought it, silly."

"Thanks, I'll take care of it." She took the candle out of Virginia's hand.

Back inside her room, Josie ripped open the envelope.

Blossom—

What a terrible week! Come over right now—I've missed you something awful. I've got a bottle of champagne for the two of us!

All my love, from your Jim

Her bedroom was as silent as a tomb at midnight. The low-backed vanity seat creaked as she lowered herself onto it. She turned over the note and on its back wrote:

Dear Jim—

Go to hell. If I don't ever see you again it'll be long enough—

"What are you doing?" asked Ned from the bed.

Startled by his voice in the deep quiet, Josie whipped around. In the middle of her bed, shadowed by the swags of ceiling cloth and the single candle's flicker, Ned's pale upper body was half propped up by an elbow. She smiled. He looked like a fierce Arabian prince aroused by the distant bark of a jackal.

"He thinks he can pop his fingers and I'll come like a dog wagging its tail," she said.

Ned frowned. "Who?"

"Jim."

"What does that punch want?" he asked. In his alarmed voice she heard jealousy. With a saucy lilt, she teased him.

"He wants me to go over to see him."

"When?" came a low growl of protest.

"Now," she said pertly.

"What are you writing?" The jealous dear was suspicious. Josie delivered her triumphant stroke.

"That Jim Fisk can go straight to Hell!" She turned back to her table, and her pencil scratched against the silence.

"I don't know if I'd do that," said Ned. She spun to face him. He had got out of bed, and in the long flickering shadow that her body threw, he wrapped a sheet around his middle.

"Give it some thought," he said. Seldom had she been so sure of the rightness of what she was doing, and his doubt brought her up short.

"What do you mean?"

The sheet swathed around his middle, Ned crossed to her. A half smile played around his puffed lips, lips their kisses had swollen. She reached up and touched them. His lips pressed tightly, absently, against her fingertips.

"Well, you and I aren't exactly flush with money," he said.

"So?" she asked, putting a hand on her hip.

"So, I have to sell him oil," said Ned. "Let me see his note." Hesitantly, Josie passed it over. Brow furrowed, he studied it.

"Just as I thought," said Ned. "He still wants you." He grinned and his hand wormed under her night robe to rest on her bare shoulder. "He wants you tonight. Why don't you go over there?"

She wasn't hearing him right. "Ned!"

"What?" he asked blandly.

"I can't do that! Not after tonight—with you."

He considered the problem. "You're an actress. You'll have to act."

Josie floundered about for something to say. "But he's . . . goosing Annabelle, your wife!"

"I know," said Ned with a smile. "And I want to get him for that, but in our own good time."

393

"You don't understand Jim," she explained. "This time of night he's not asking me to come over to play charades. He expects . . . you know." She glanced at her bed's rumpled sheet.

His lean face weighed this. "Well . . . you might have to go along," he said. Her mouth opened but nothing came out. His firm hands rested on her shoulders. He couldn't—but his intense face meant it. When he saw that she wasn't buying it, he backtracked.

"It's only for a little while."

"Little while what?" she asked.

"Till we get him good."

"Get him? But, Ned—"

"Come on," he said. His hands massaged her shoulders. "You're a hell of a trouper, Josie. No 'buts.' "

She shuddered. His long delicate fingers left her neck and shoulders, slid under her robe, and lightly stroked her heavy breasts. She wanted to knock them away, she wanted it to be two hours ago when they had luxuriated on a cloud of love.

"But—you'll think I'm something that—that walks the streets."

From his position behind her, he raised her head. His lips kissed hers with a gentle, lingering touch.

"No, I'll think you're brave. I'll think that you're willing to do the courageous thing you've always done—to get what you need for yourself no matter what well-fed church matrons and deacons spout. I'll think you're true to us—and I'll love you for that."

"No!" she pleaded. "I've just found you. Please! It'll ruin it between us, my"—she couldn't say it—"*being* with him."

"No, no—I won't let it. It's *my* sacrifice—*my* sacrifice for *us*."

"Ned, I can't." She turned and threw her arms around his sheeted waist. "I want to be with you, be here with you." Her new life, new home and children, slithered away into the room's wavering shadows. He gently pushed her back. He cupped her chin with his hand and lifted it.

"Josie, I hate this, too, but we need time. I have to ship our weekly load of oil to the Erie tomorrow. Do you have any idea what'll happen if that's canceled?" His set features expected an answer, and his silence outlasted hers.

She barely whispered, "No."

"Ruin, that's what. The creditors will take over my business in a week. I'll be bankrupt."

"Our love will be bankrupt," she said. She had to make him see. "It'll never again be the same as it was tonight." He said nothing, but his hands went back under her robe and rubbed her neck and shoulders. "The house," she cried, throwing her most valuable asset

394

into the wreck of their love. "We can use the house." His fingers stopped kneading her neck.

"Sell this house?" he asked.

She nodded vigorously.

"Your home?" he asked.

"Yes!"

"Josie, you're sweet, but I can't." For several moments his soft fingers were motionless as he considered. "It wouldn't provide much," he went on. "It *is* mortgaged, isn't it?"

She nodded. "But I *can't* get in his bed," she said. "Not now. Not after tonight." He turned her head toward him, and again her chin was cupped by his soft palm. His smile was sad and bitter.

"Yes, you can," he said. "After all, you've done it hundreds of times, haven't you?" She didn't want to answer. Frozen, she just stared at him. Men didn't like you to say so. They wanted to pretend that even though you had been with other men you had miraculously remained a virgin. He smiled more broadly.

"Be reasonable. A few more times makes no difference. I'm not some narrow puritan. I'm a man of the world."

"I don't *want* to," she said, it coming out as a stutter.

"This is only for a little while," said Ned. "Only long enough for you to get a settlement from him."

"Settlement!"

"Hasn't he been with you for a long time?"

"Yes."

"Doesn't he owe you something?"

She snorted. "I've asked him for money a hundred times. He won't, Ned." She glanced at the rumpled bed. "Especially not after tonight."

"Maybe you haven't asked the right way."

He pointed toward the pencil. "Write that you're glad he wants to see you and that you'll fly to him in minutes. Then put on your most fetching outfit so that he can't resist you."

"Ned!" she wailed.

"It's the only way to buy a decent start for ourselves." he said sternly. She threw her arms around his waist. Under it his body was hard and unyielding.

"No," she pleaded. "Ned, no."

"Josie, you're allowing yourself to be tied to conventional shibboleths. Don't try my patience with shopgirl sentiments. Write the damn note and go!"

She wanted to protest more, but everything had been said. Ned was normally as pliable as a well-mannered clerk in Stewart's department store. On this he was as firm and sure of himself as a theatrical agent telling her he had no parts. She sensed that if she disappointed him in this, he would be through with her. She sighed. It really didn't matter two beans if she slept with Jim another week or two, as long as Ned didn't think it did.

Still it was with heavy reluctance that Josie pulled out a fresh sheet of notepaper, and as Ned dictated it, wrote Jim a note saying she would be right over.

37

*"I'll live to see the day, sir," said
Henry Smith, the broker, "when you
have to earn your living by going
around this street with a hand organ
and a monkey."*

*"Maybe you will, Henry," Jay
Gould cooed softly. "And when I want a
monkey, Henry, I'll send for you."*

—*The New York Times*, 1892

Not to risk throwing a shoe on the
slippery, deep ruts, George Gould dismounted from his horse Launcelot and led him up the lane. The narrow alley leading to his friend's
house was dusty, littered with trash heaps, broken chairs, and a three-legged table. It was still early enough to be cool, and sleepy dogs with
mangy sores lifted their heads and warily watched the tall boy walking the roan stallion.

The September air sparkled, clean against the cloudless blue sky.
It was Saturday, two whole days without school! As George passed
under the shadow of the witch's town house, he looked up at her dark
back windows. Flat-black eyes powdered with dust, they stared at
him, concealing the fiery, hellish secrets of Pa and his fiendlike coupling with the witch, white-skinned and evil as the egg sac of a widow
spider. A shudder passed over his thin shoulders.

It was a relief to enter his friend Stewart's warm stable, where
he was welcomed by the cozy smells of horse sweat, oats rolled in
molasses, and fresh straw. Stewart was brushing down Ginger, the
mare that their friends joked was more dear to him than his own ma
and pa.

"Hey, saddle up, slowpoke!" shouted George, lifting a thin hand in greeting. "I got to be home for lunch!" In nearby stalls, the family's half-dozen horses crunched their breakfast oats. His back half turned, Stewart continued brushing without looking up at George.

"I can't go," he said in a draggy, sullen tone. The steady strokes of the currycomb rasped against the mare.

"Can't go!" Irritated, George slapped the reins against his trousers. "But O'Malley is going to tear his head off!" Fourteen years old, George had grown an inch or so this summer but hadn't gained weight to compensate. Ma complained that like his pa, he didn't eat when he was worried, and demanded to know what was wrong. Now he hopped from foot to foot, a pale, awkward colt, unsure what to do with his gangly legs and arms.

Unknown to their parents, this morning the two friends were going to ride to Grable's farm above Seventy-second Street to watch Henderson and O'Malley, champion heavyweight wrestlers, settle a grudge match.

"Pa won't let me," said Stewart, still not looking up.

"He won't let you!" George scowled. "What'd you go and tell him for?"

"I didn't," said Stewart, straightening up. His face was twisted and marred by dirty tears. George's mouth fell open and he froze. He had never seen Stewart cry. "I can't go nowhere with you—can't be with you."

"What?" George wrapped the reins around his numb hand. "Why?" Stewart's lips trembled and his tears came faster.

"I got to sell Ginger," he wailed. George's mouth dropped open farther. Nobody loved his horse more than Stewart loved Ginger. "All because of your pa," said Stewart. "Your pa has ruint my pa. Something with gold. Pa says your pa stole from him—from everybody."

"My pa don't steal!" said George. "Take that back!" The clotted, sweet smell of molasses and the prickle of hay dust was sickening. Despite the warm stable, he was trembling. His face troubled, Stewart turned away to stare at the narrow stable door that led to his house.

"We've got to move, says Pa," Stewart said in a dull voice. "We got to sell the house. I got to sell Ginger. Ma has to sell her dresses, jewelry. Pa doesn't even know what business he's going to be in. He says the brokerage business won't never be the same. They almost hanged your pa last night, and he says if they catch him again they will, and by God he might be one of them to put the noose round his neck. He said he would cane me good if he caught me with you." Stewart turned to him. "Please go, George. Just go before he comes out and whips us both good."

---

*   *   *

George climbed the stairs as jerkily as one of his wooden puppet soldiers. Pa's evil was spreading. Pa was going to burn down the whole world so that only he and the spider-sac witch would be left. George's chest and arms were aflame with alarm, his mouth dry and salty. In his mind's eye, fire roared through the house, burnt Mr. Marks's School for Gentlemen, and left all Manhattan charred posts and rubble.

As usual, Pa's room, at the quiet back of the house, was clean and cool. The mahogany-framed mirror over the dresser watched him like a large silver eye. The bed's dark green coverlet lay as calm and still as a deep pond. In the closet Pa's black broadcloth suits stood like mute, outraged soldiers glaring at George's invasion. It wasn't forbidden, but George had no business in his father's bedroom.

He sat on the side of the bed next to the marble-topped table in which the pistol was kept. Feeling stiff and wooden, he wasn't sure what to do. The news that Pa had ruined Stewart's father and many others meant his father had begun his destruction of the world. George pulled open the pistol drawer.

There was no way out of it. It was up to him to protect Mama, Nellie, Edwin, and Howard. After the shooting, when Pa's evil spell was broken and he showed Mama what an evil king Pa had been, she would be grateful. Mama! Dear, kind Mama—an angel! He felt a little better, holding the heavy gun. Sweet to George, the soul of goodness to everyone. In every verbal exchange at dinner and breakfast her generous patience treated his evil father well, shushing the children and deferring to his wishes. The duty of a squire was to defend such goodness. With his father gone, George would become the head of the family. Mama would expect him to leave school and run the railroad. He would make sure that Stewart got back Ginger, and that his friend's parents regained their house.

But he had never fired the pistol, or any other gun. In a boastful, swaggering way, riders at the stables talked about a gun's kick, how it could knock the gun out of your hand and even break a finger.

He had to be ready. He stood up.

He would go to the stables and practice, preparing for Pa's return at lunch. He stuck the heavy, bulky pistol in his trousers band. With his coat buttoned, his father's full-length mirror said the bulge was scarcely noticeable.

Three long blocks across town, Jay Gould strode up the dark main aisle of the opera house. Limelights lit the broad stage into gaudy day.

"Can I see you a minute?" Jay called up to Jim Fisk. A large red ledger, Jay's personal financial records, was clutched in his hand like a shield. His face was fuller and more composed than it had been last night, as if he had slept for a week.

Across the brightly lit rehearsal stage were scattered fifty actors dressed in either peasants' rags or the elaborate wigs and ballroom dresses of pre-Revolutionary French nobility. The fetid, sweet odor of greasepaint mingled uneasily with the close, heavy air. Front and center stage stood Jim, resplendent in aristocratic red knee britches and black patent-leather boots. On his head sat a white silk wig and a black-and-gold cocked hat. Across the chest of his crimson frock coat a crossbelt held up his admiral's sword and scabbard. Although Jay thought Jim looked silly, he kept the disdain off his face.

"Zounds," cried Jim, cupping his hand to his ear and widening his eyes in exaggerated stage fear. His face was baggy, fatigued, and as off-white as dough. "Methinks I hear the rabble again." His stage whisper carried across the empty velvet seats into the farthest reaches of the vast, dark auditorium. Jay frowned and supposed this was an important moment in rehearsal.

The peasant girl who played opposite him, whose saucy beauty shone through her tattered costume, warned, "Be quiet, my lord. These new citizens have ears as keen as rats. They'll take us both in the next cart."

Jay knew about the upcoming production, called *The Broken Tumbrel*. It opened on a young, handsome French aristocrat, back in Paris after ten years in America, on his way to the guillotine for aristocratic crimes he had no hand in.

"Jim, please," Jay shouted up. "I only need you for a minute." Jim drew his admiral's broadsword from its scabbard.

"Hark! Yonder he is!" Jim's sword pointed at Jay, and his baritone thundered. Startled, Jay drew back.

"He's the one!" shouted Jim. "Shylock, sometimes called Midas! The usurer who sits at the center of his web piling up gold, clinking doubloon against guilder, sovereign against double eagle, watching his midnight tapers gleam against the brassy yellow." Sword slashing about as if engaged in a hot swordfight, Jim hopped forward. The raggley-tag cast of fifty stepped out of character to peer across the footlights' glare.

Jay's fist knocked three times against the ledger book's hard back. "Come off it!" he shouted up, but Jim only waved his sword in wider arcs.

"There stands the rake-renter who betrayed us all!" cried Jim. "The very Scrooge! I saw him yestereve, skulking across the ramparts, cloak over his head, cackling as he watched the mobs rage through the streets, hunchbacked, rubbing his hands together as buildings burned and the rabble boiled the avenues." Jim made an exaggerated stage shudder. "There he stands! Gould, the Jewish gold lover! Gould, the lickpenny weasel! The midnight vampire, flitting high and low where the sun's rays never shine. Sucking the blood of the innocent." Jim waved his sword in a great circle, as if to egg on the stunned, motionless troupe, who shaded their eyes with their hands and stared wordless at Jay. "I tell you, citizens, forget your gilded dukes, forsake hauling your horrified kings to the head chopper—seize that money-grubbing miser there, that skinflint Shylock, and rid yourselves of your chains forever!"

Jay hugged the ledger to his chest and considered turning on his heel and striding out. Give Jim a whiff of greasepaint and the worst came out.

"If you've had your fun," said Jay, "would you come down and talk?"

Jim dropped the mock-heroic pose and stepped forward so he could see over the footlights' glare. "I got to direct this rehearsal," said Jim in a more normal yet sulky tone. "The director come down with a bad case of gold fever last night."

Jay nodded, wondering why the new director was dressed in the lead actor's red costume. "Give me only ten minutes," he said.

Jim hacked the air twice with his sword. "Let me hear it with all these witnesses." He slapped the sword blade against the leather of his knee-high boot. "From now on I want plenty of ears when I deal with you."

"Belden didn't go broke," said Jay.

"What?"

"Belden's survived in fine shape, his company stronger than ever."

"So what?"

"So, he was my lead broker—both Thursday and Friday."

Jim's sword beat against his boot in a rapid tattoo. "Castle Erie stands?" he finally asked, his voice feeble.

"You could put it that way," said Jay. Jim turned and told a slight artistic sort to carry on the rehearsal. His boot heels clattered down the temporary pyramid of steps shoved against the stage. Jay turned and headed up the aisle.

"Hey, where're you going?" shouted Jim, waving his sword.

"In private," said Jay over his shoulder as he shot up the aisle.

He pushed through the padded swinging doors into the opera house's spacious lobby. On straight chairs, tipped against the plaster wall, sat walleyed Pat Lynch and a dozen of his unshaven Hell's Kitchen brawlers. The faint tang of whiskey floated on the air.

"Pat," said Jay, "would you and your fellows step outside for a few minutes? Please see that Mr. Fisk and I aren't disturbed." As if to show where his loyalty lay, Pat slowly turned his walleye to Jim, whose exaggerated nod of approval was as bold as a swagger.

"So?" asked Jim. "What now?" Above his head leered two gigantic masks of gilt paint, one grinning, one frowning. The crystal leaves of the tree-sized gold chandelier tinkled as Pat banged the outer double doors behind his ragged crew.

"Things are firming up," said Jay, his voice booming and echoing in the three-story dome over their heads. His finger tapped the red back of the ledger book for emphasis. "Not only is Belden going to survive, but so are four of the other brokers I used." Jim took off his three-cornered, cocked hat and wiped his brow with his coat sleeve.

"So?"

"So the Erie has made some money."

"And you? Have you made some money?"

"And me."

"And poor old Jim Fisk is busted, ain't he?" Jim stuck the cocked hat back on his head at a rakish angle. He lifted the blade of his sword to his face and stared at it with the tragic air of an actor about to fall on it. "Hanged by his partner. Sold out by the lickpenny he saved. Is there no justice under the blue vault of Heaven? Betrayed by a runty scoundrel with a silver dollar for a heart. Jim's bones left to be gnawed on by the jackals of Washington, and finally raked over by every court in the land." Jay heaved a great sigh and shook his head.

"Will you cut this out?" shouted Jay, his voice echoing off the lobby's plaster walls. "I came down here to talk about dealing with you fairly, but you're wearing down my patience. You had as big a hand in your bad luck as anybody. I begged you to make a pool. I told you what I thought last night—your blabbering about Grant, pyramiding all that gold, pulling in fellows who had no business in the market—I don't need to chew that again."

"I guess you don't! You ain't the one bankbusted!"

"I want to help you."

Jim's elephantine stage laugh scoffed. "No, thanks. You done helped me about all I can stand."

"We need to work together, Jim."

"What *did* you ever need me for, Jay Gould?" shouted Jim. "To be your clown? To sell your worthless paper to the Street?"

Jay pursed his lips. "You're still on the Erie executive committee," he said. "Unless you plan to resign, I need your vote." Jay glanced around the large lobby. "The Erie still owns this whorehouse. And I think you and I ought to work out how to handle the investigations. It doesn't make any sense for us to be at each other's throats."

"I'm the one going to be investigated, not you!" cried Jim. He leaned down and stuck his sweating face no more than a foot from Jay's. "You stayed behind the scenes, remember? You're a clever little shit, aren't you? Well, I'm going to tell everything! I'm not going to be your tongue-tied lightning rod!"

Jay stepped forward, his own anger pushing Jim's face back. "Who's asking you to lie? You tell them the truth, you tubby bag of wind. You can bet your last dollar I'll be subpoenaed, too. We'll both be under oath, and it would be stupid for either of us to lie, even if he had something to lie about." His face alarmed, Jim jerked upright and stepped back. His head whipped from side to side.

"Subpoena? Oath?" The tip of his sword scraped against the marble floor. "Like in court?"

"Sure," said Jay, "*exactly* like in court."

"What *is* a congressional investigation, Jay? We didn't break no laws. They can't put us in jail."

"No, we didn't break any laws," said Jay. "But this thing isn't limited to a few traders and some idiots running crazy in Broad Street."

Throughout the morning, when he wasn't listening to brokers' reports and issuing orders for Saturday's half-day stock market, Jay had read the papers' late-morning editions in a hectic attempt to sort fact from panic and bedrock from speculation. They all trumpeted a disaster that had crashed across the nation with the gale force of a continent-wide hurricane. From Chicago to New Orleans, from Boston to San Francisco, thousands of ordinary businesses—from tiny general stores to mighty railroads, from three-coach stage lines to multiplant steel corporations—had gone bankrupt from their owners' speculations in the gold market. Tens of thousands of employees were thrown out of work. Calm ordinary fellows, pillars of their communities, had sold their lifetime's accumulation of stocks and mortgages and shoved the proceeds into the Gold Room, causing the stock market to collapse. Banks were foreclosing on margin positions and bankrupting tens of thousands of their customers, and in the process, often themselves, too. Many more speculators, having successfully timed when to buy and when to sell gold, were being wiped out by the bankruptcy of their brokerage firms.

"Although after Congress hears a month's testimony from busted losers," Jay went on, "they'll decide to write a few more laws."

"Are you busted?" asked Jim.

"No, I think I made money."

"Think?" pushed Jim. "You don't never think. You always know."

"I made money."

"A lot?"

"If those brokers don't go broke, yes, a lot," admitted Jay. And he was now ready to make more. With his mountain of credit at these powerful brokerages, he had bought huge quantities of severely depressed rail stocks at this morning's session of the Stock Exchange. His broker spies told him Vanderbilt was doing the same thing. Both of them understood that the time to buy heavily was when Wall Street was being looted by mobs. "If all twelve brokers that I used come out whole, a hell of a lot." He shook the ledger in his hand at Jim. "When I picked them last Thursday, I picked the solidest houses on the Street so that the failure of the weak wouldn't carry us under." Jim shook his head in wonder.

"Smart, smart, smart! Jesus, you were always smart!" His mustaches waggled up and down with the exaggeration of a clown's arms. "I myself, now—I just couldn't cover myself in cowplop like you to make money." Jay's lips mashed in anger. "Old Jim broke. Too old for all this. Saw a bunch of reporters an hour ago. Almost knocked me over getting their story. You would have thought I lost their money, wounded them, the nasty questions they asked."

Jay opened the ledger and ripped out a page.

"I expect you to give me some money, Jay Gould, or I—"

Jay lightly punched Jim in the belly with the fist holding the ripped page.

"What's this?" asked Jim.

"Read it," said Jay. Jim lifted the ruled paper and read. His mouth dropped open in surprise, and his eyes widened as he stared at Jay.

"It's a promissory note. It says you're giving me a third of the profits from your trading!"

"A third for me, a third for the Erie, a third for you," said Jay. "I'm sorry I blew my top last night. I said a lot of things I shouldn't. I want to make a fair settlement. If you want to have nothing to do with me, I can understand that." He grinned and his free hand stroked the bottom third of his beard. His voice was softly gentle. "If I was in your shoes, I don't know if I would trust Jay Gould either, but still—the Erie needs your help." Jay's head bobbed. "Who else can make sure investors invest, passengers ride, reporters write well of us, and employees work?" Under the aristocrat's wig and three-cornered hat, a strange, elfin grin snuck across Jim's face. He shook the paper in Jay's face.

"You mean this?"

"I never meant anything more in my life."

Jim sheathed his sword. "You could keep it all," said Jim. "Old Jim would have nothing. He could go fiddle for it."

"No, you earned a third, you get a third."

"What strings are attached?"

"None," said Jay. "But I have been thinking."

Jim sighed and his blue eyes narrowed in suspicion. "Lord, Lord—when wasn't you thinking?" His rich, warm guffaw echoed off the plaster dome. "But no more gold purchases, okay?"

Jay grinned. "No more gold purchases."

Jim's eyes narrowed again. "Now, mark me, I don't want to give up the opera house."

Jay twisted his head about. The dome, chandelier, plaster, and gilt shone blue-white in the noon light. His smile was thin and ironic.

"I'm getting used to living in the middle of an *opéra bouffe*," said Jay. "Here's what we ought to do. Act this week before we're acted upon. It would be best if you took bankruptcy, probably took it fast. I'll set it up, handle the lawyers. You handle the press, you're best at that. Get them off this idea that we're to blame for the general craziness of the Gold Room." Jim lifted the promissory note ripped from Jay's ledger book and reread it. Ruddiness had blossomed again in his cheeks.

"How much is this worth?" asked Jim.

"I don't know exactly. It's going to take weeks to settle everything."

"Approximately how much?" asked Jim. "A few thousand or a hundred thousand?"

Jay's poker face smiled again. "Let's say several million."

"Ohhhh, Jay!" His blue eyes large and bright, Jim dropped his arm lightly over Jay's shoulders. "Do you mean it? Did you really do that well?" Jay nodded and a grin spread above his black beard. "All right, Mr. Wizard," said Jim, "you got yourself a deal!" He snickered, his head bobbing and shaking, his chest heaving in quick spasms. As if the humor of it was too much, he backed away from Jay and thrust a palm against the plaster wall for support. He raised his head.

A long bark of laughter burst from his plump lips and echoed crazily against the hard walls of the lobby, a series of high-pitched laughs as forceful as sneezes. Alarmed, Jay stared at him, wondering if he was having a fit. Jim's ribs rocked, his lungs drew in gulps of air, and tears streamed down his red cheeks. His large paunch shook, and he leaned his back against the smooth wall. Jay put a calming hand on Jim's heaving shoulder. As out of control as if in its final spasms, Jim's shaking form slid down the wall till it plopped on the marble floor, a laughing, heaving bowl of pudding in a crimson bag.

Jay dropped the ledger book and knelt. He lifted Jim's weak, jiggling chin. The blue of Jim's crazy eyes skittered about and Jim laughed.

Jay slapped his cheek. Jim's head went back and he laughed all the harder. Jay slapped him again.

Jim's head jerked up and his laugh abruptly stopped. He scowled and rubbed the scarlet welt on his cheek. "What'd you do that for?"

"You're hysterical," said Jay. "Pull yourself together."

"No, no, I'm fine." Another laugh heaved up, but he caught it. "It's just—yesterday morning I was as flush as any rascal in New York—at noon I was busted—last night nearly hanged—and noon today I'm a millionaire. Up, down, up, down! It's like being at the circus—you don't like it, wait a minute, another act's coming."

A series of loud thumps from the double doors leading to the street echoed through the lobby's cavernous vault. Jay started and spun on the black-and-white squares of marble to face the huge doors. Last night's experience of being tossed about by a lynch mob as handily as bricks in a blanket was still a raw wound.

Nostrils white and pinched, he slid next to Jim and whispered, "Could another mob be breaking in?"

With a slicing snick, Jim's sword came out of its scabbard. "I'm ready for them," he said, scrabbling to his feet. "But I don't see how it can be. Tweed sent over twenty police, and Pat Lynch has a dozen men out there."

One of the street doors opened and Pat's jagged, startled face peered in. His beefy arm shot up and unlatched the other door, and through the tall double doors marched six large policemen in blue uniforms and high, bell-shaped hats. In their center, struggling mightily against two policemen's restraining arms, was Jay's son George, his upper torso bare and smeared with rusty stains of blood.

"George!" shouted Jay, certain that his son was wounded. He rushed forward. "What's this?" George was crying and threw himself from side to side as the police struggled to approach Jay and Jim. Through the open doors, Pat Lynch and his rowdies crowded in behind and around the bluecoats.

"I didn't mean to!" the boy screamed. "She shouldn't have been there!"

Bewildered, Jay spoke to the police sergeant. "What's happened?"

"Don't let him kill me!" moaned George, writhing so hard that he almost twisted out of the policemen's grip.

"Son! Son!" said Jay, stepping forward to put a calming hand on the boy's rust-smeared shoulder. His son sprang back as if Jay's extended hand were the jaw of a rabid dog.

"No! No!" shouted the boy. "Don't let him touch me!"

"Your daughter Nellie, sir," the Sergeant said in a deep voice that seemed constrained. He doffed his bell-shaped helmet and lowered his eyes. "We've taken her to St. Luke's. The boy was playing with a pistol, and I'm afraid he's wounded her."

"Pistol?" Jay's eye went from one beefy, official face to the other. "Nellie?" George was still trying to wrestle out of the two hefty policemen's control, but their enormous Irish hands firmly gripped his upper arms. Legs unsteady, Jay stared at his son. The gilt ceiling, the blue-white plaster walls, and the black-and-white marble squares of the floor wavered.

"Nellie?" he breathed. "Hurt? Shot?"

The Sergeant nodded solemnly. To Jay, the world of marble, plaster, staring faces, blue uniforms, and George's yells slipped away. His whole being abruptly shrank from man size to the diameter of a small, hard, numb pea. He was falling. Jim's thick arms were around his waist and shoulders, supporting him, and he leaned against Jim's stout body.

As from far away, he heard his stiff mouth ask, "She's dead?"

"No, sir, not dead," said the red-faced policeman's hollow voice. Jay heard, She might not live.

"How bad?" He was in a long, dark burrow under the ground, and the daylight world was miles away. Light and the echo of voices came to him from the bright hole at the faraway end of the lengthy tunnel.

"She's hit badly, sir."

His vision swimming, Jay looked at George. As if his father's gaze were a whip, George jerked around in the policemen's arms. His cheeks and neck were splotched, blush-red and chalk-white, as if he had been slapped about. His hair was disheveled, his trousers filthy and torn. He wore no shirt, and across his bare chest, face, arms, and hands were cinnamon-hued smears and cakes of dried blood.

"Nellie's blood?" said Jay, swaying against Jim.

"Don't kill me, Pa!" George moaned, pleaded. His teeth were bared, and he struggled backward. "I'm sorry, I'm so sorry! Please don't kill me." He looked up. His frightened brown eyes begged the policemen gripping his arms. "Oh, please, sirs, don't leave me alone with him. Sirs, good sirs, sirs—*please* stay with me. Don't let him kill me." His voice was as hysterical as a wretch's being dragged to the gallows.

"Son, son," said Jay. "I'm not going to hurt you." His hand on Jim's arm for support, he again reached out to clasp George's bare shoulder, but despite the two stout policemen gripping his arms, his son broke away. With the frenzy of a crazed rabbit fleeing a wolf, George crashed face-first into the wall, making a sound like a large palm smacking against the hard plaster. Three policemen seized him.

"No!" shouted George, backing away through the crowd of on-lookers and dragging the policemen with him. "He'll kill me! He's the Devil!"

The Sergeant's arm stopped Jay's advance, and he explained, "He's a bit off his head."

Dazed, Jay stared at his son, his mind numb.

Jim stepped between Jay and the Sergeant. "Jay," he said, clasping Jay's arm firmly and shaking him roughly. "Go to the hospital right now." Jim turned and took the policeman's forearm. "Sergeant, take my victoria out front and race Mr. Gould here to St. Luke's. Pat, send half a dozen men with them. Don't let no rabble bother him."

Jim crossed the lobby to George, and hands up, half shielded the boy from Jay. "I'll stay here and take care of George." He nodded at the police. "A couple of these fine fellows will stay with us." Then to Jay, who still hadn't moved, "I'll send a dozen clerks and Pat's boys to get aholt of Stenson and Barnes. If surgeons can fix up Nellie, they can. God knows they had enough practice at Chattanooga and Gettysburg."

Motionless, the horde of police, Hell's Kitchen brawlers, Jay, and George stared at Jim. When nobody moved, Jim opened his hands wide, like a giant crimson bird about to jump off a cliff, and brought his meaty palms together in a thunderous crack. As if snapped out of a trance, the staring crowd jerked awake.

"Quick now!" he shouted. "Everybody get cracking!"

Part Five

THE STORM'S WAKE

Like an inspired fiend, Jay Gould had ridden out the storm to safety. . . . Opinion differed afterward as to whether he had gained nothing, lost all he possessed, or garnered eleven millions of dollars at one coup.
  —Matthew Josephson,
   The Robber Barons,
   1934

Regarding gold, we have seen the most gigantic swindling operation carried out on Wall Street that has as yet disgraced our financial centre. In addition, a great railway has been tossed around like a football, its real stockholders have seen their property abused by men to whom they have entrusted its interests, and who, in the betrayal of that trust, have committed crimes which in parallel cases on a smaller scale would have deservedly sent them to Sing Sing.
  —Editorial, *New York Tribune,* 1869

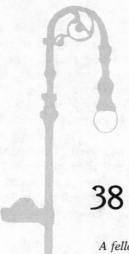

38

*A fellow can't have a little innocent fun
without everybody raising a hullabaloo
and going wild.*

—Jim Fisk, *New York World*, 1869

Annabelle Stokes couldn't avoid reporters the week after Black Friday.

The Monday morning *Tribune*'s lead editorial made much of her startled admission of having had a hand in the selection of General Butterfield for the New York Treasury office. It made even more of General Butterfield's having shorted 10,000 ounces of gold for his personal account only a half hour before he announced to the astounded Gold Room that the government was selling millions in gold. The paper called it "a serious breach of trust" that it had only learned from a brokerage employee ruined by the crash.

On Tuesday the *Times* editorialized that Annabelle's refusal to say what the President's attitude was toward investing "boded ill for the Republic." The paper supported congressional investigations into malfeasance, fraud, and market manipulation. It urged that sworn testimony be taken quickly. "If the public trust has been broken, the perpetrators ought to be speedily turned out of office. If theft is discovered, the stolen money ought to be swiftly prised out of stiff, crooked fingers and returned to its lawful owners. If criminal acts are uncovered, the miscreants ought to be rapidly sent to jail."

Stunned by the furor, Annabelle sent Bridget out to buy the rest of the papers. The story was on the front page of them all. On Wednesday, phrases such as "the President's family," "the In-Laws," and "the First Sister-in-Law" popped up in sneering articles and editorials in the major dailies. Even pro-Grant papers were saying that it looked as if "a good man" had been "led astray by greedy in-laws." As Annabelle went up and down stairs to do her daily chores, her chest and stomach felt filled with cold, wet sand, a leaden, glutinous grit that left her restless and edgy. The shrillness of the furor rattled her; its fury presaged some shameful, crushing punishment, a brutal retribution on her and the innocent Ulysses that she could not name. But surely, surely all this would evaporate in another week.

Twice she set out to talk to her friend Louise, and both times she was forced to turn back because of the reporters who lurked around her front stoop and trailed her wherever she went. Besides, she was ashamed to admit to Louise how often Jay came over, and how she had tricked Jim Fisk concerning Ulysses.

"It's time for you to go back home," said Jim in a gentle voice to George Gould. "I got to run up to Boston to see my family."

George's blanched face jerked, and his pale fingers picked at his trousers seam with the caution of a crab on a strange rock, a gesture that reminded Jim of Jay.

They sat over teacups and sweet English biscuits in the plush parlor of Jim's four-room suite at the Hoffman House, where George had been living since the Saturday after Black Friday. Jim's collection of canaries kept up a shrill chirping. Jim was squeezed into a high-backed armchair; George's thin form was perched on the edge of another, with enough room on the velvet cushion for a second boy.

Two days after the shooting, on the Monday after Black Friday, Jim had insisted that George accompany him to visit the hospital, where George, amid the powerful stench of carbolic acid and ether, fainted on entering the room where his sleeping sister lay swathed in white bandages.

Later, in an empty private room down the hall, George cried and told his father how sorry he was for playing with the pistol and for wounding Nellie. Jim wasn't sure why, but the boy kept his distance from his father, supposing, not without reason, that Jay might whale him for wounding his sister. Blinking back tears, Jim itched to say a few soothing words to make everything all right, but as long as the two talked—as fumbling as it was—he kept his big nose out of it. After George's stumbling apology, Jay said in a husky voice that he forgave George, but Jay's pale features were twisted in anger, his forgiveness as straight as a rope with a knot in it. George tearfully nodded and moaned that he wanted life to be as it was when he was younger. That was the one way, Jim reflected with a sigh, life never was.

Knowing Jay had his hands full with Helen, the doctors, and the other children, Jim insisted that George stay at the Hoffman with him. This last week the doctors cautiously gave Nellie a chance to live, having now survived three weeks.

George munched a sweet biscuit as if it were a cake of sawdust. "I don't ever want to go back to that house," he said. "I like it here."

Jim nodded again, for on top of distancing George from the scene of the shooting, he had gained the idea that the young man was bothered by more than the accidental shooting, terrible as that had been. To distract him, Jim had taken him on the town and sought to teach him a few things that a fourteen-year-old wasn't likely to learn from Jay Gould. How to pick out, trim, and smoke a cigar. How to get a decent bottle of madeira in a restaurant. How to pace your liquor. How to make sure Sally Woods gave you one of her best girls. Who the finest tailors were in the city, and how to order a suit that fit right. How to bluff at poker, and when to fold.

"You pa and me done talked," said Jim. "It's best if I go to Boston to see my family for a month or two, till things quiet down." Jim was still assaulted by swarms of reporters, hordes of angry gold traders, and gangs of process servers whenever he poked his mug out in public. "Your pa, now, he misses you something terrible. You got to be with him while I'm gone."

"He doesn't need me," said George, his face and voice retreating into bitterness. "He has the Erie, and he'll never get over what I did to Nellie."

"I didn't say it was easy," said Jim. "How many pas you got?" George's solemn brown eyes looked up, and he sighed.

"Just one."

"Do you want a pa, a good pa?"

"Yes."

"Well, you got a good one in Jay," said Jim. "The best. Remember what I told you about making sure things work, when you want them to?" George nodded numbly. "Sure, it's going to be hard," Jim went on, "but your pa ain't got but one George, and you ain't got but one pa. I know *he's* going to fight to make a new start with you, and if *you* want to have a pa, you better get in the ring and fight to have yourself a pa." George's head slumped forward. "Can you do it?"

"Yes," said George in a small, weak voice that didn't promise much.

"All right. Pack your trunk, and Rufus will drive you home before he takes me to the station tomorrow."

"Will you come with me, drive me home?"

413

Jim studied the question. "I would, but ain't no use in you getting shoved around by them damn reporters, too. You go on your own. You're gonna be all right."

However, from the sullen, resentful landscape of George's face, Jim wasn't so sure.

As Jim stepped out of his private car into the chilly air of Boston's late afternoon, a mob of two dozen reporters sprang on him with the force and claws of an angry bear.

"Where's Mrs. Mansfield?" shouted a reporter.

"Back in New York," said Jim, glaring at their eager, cruel faces.

"Did you bring Mrs. Stokes?" shouted another. Jim flinched. Was that story here in Boston? What would Lucy have heard?

"Is there any truth to the story that you're buying more gold?" shouted a third.

Dodging them, Jim backstepped up the metal stairs of the private car. Standing on the topmost car step, clinging to the brass handrails, he stared down in horror. On every raw face was the same keen leer. He considered locking himself in the car till they dispersed. An egg arced over the reporters' heads and thumped against his vest. The circle of squirming, pushing reporters laughed. Rufus edged around in the narrow door space and with a handkerchief wiped off most of the yellow mess.

"Let's get out of here," said Jim to Rufus. Jim stepped down and bulled his way through the clamoring horde. Trailing the questioning newshawks, Jim was halfway along the platform when a short man with a stumpy cigar stepped up, abruptly whipped thick legal papers from his baggy overcoat sleeve, and touched Jim's chest with them.

"Served, Mr. Fisk." As the summonses fluttered to the ground, a hatchet-faced woman in a purple hat and black veil pushed forward and shoved two other summonses, which also struck his chest and fell to the rail platform.

"Served," she sang, and she pulled out a long, thin notebook to record the time, date, and circumstances.

"Pick 'em up, Rufus," said Jim, shaking his head in despair. Around him two dozen grinning reporters scribbled away in their notebooks. "Boston don't act a damn bit nicer to a country boy than Broadway."

Four weeks after the shooting Jay left Nellie's hospital room at one in the morning. He watched Annabelle's house for a quarter of an hour to make sure no reporters were lurking behind nearby shrubbery. For the first time since the shooting and the crash of the gold market, desperate to talk to someone, feeling giddy, he tossed a quarter at her window.

"My God," she breathed in the darkened parlor, "how is she?"

"She lost a lot of blood the first day," said Jay. A single candle was lit, and they sat on the sofa, chastely holding hands. "For three days the doctors said we would lose her from shock. She survived that, but this past weekend the wound became infected." In the candle's raw light his eyes closed and his bleak face twisted in grief. "They put maggots in the wound."

Annabelle started. "Maggots!"

His shoulders quivered and he squirmed on the couch. "Experimental," he muttered, his lips stretched into a grimace. "Dr. Stenson noticed that a soldier at Gettysburg who lay unfound for five days with a terrible leg wound infested by the grubs didn't become gangrenous. He's tried it on a few dozen patients since with good results. His theory is that the worms eat the gangrene, the pus. Helen was against it. The fever kept rising, we were losing her. I could scarcely allow myself to give permission, but a man has to keep his head in these things. Finally I did. Her skin was as hot, dry, and hard as a carriage fender in August. All last Sunday night I rubbed her head with ice chips." He writhed on the couch as if it were a hard bench.

"During the hours after midnight I was sure I heard tiny white teeth grinding against her flesh," he went on. His shoulders shook again. "I couldn't go home, yet it was unbearable to stay. At dawn she was so hot I couldn't stand to touch her arm or face—but by midmorning it had broken. She's rallied, thrown off the fever completely. He's taken those damn white grubs out. She'll live!"

He began to sob, and she took him in her arms.

The crash of the gold market hit Wall Street like a dark, twisting tornado, leaving broken lives, broken businesses, and broken homes. Because of speculation, businesses as diverse as factories, banks, blacksmiths, haberdasheries, small railroads, and stagecoach lines went bankrupt. Like a tornado the crash roared away as quickly as it came, leaving the debris of depression in its wake.

Five weeks after Nellie entered the hospital, Jay and Helen drove her home. All the way he silently held Nellie's warm, limp hand, and in his other, Helen's. At his daughter's least movement and glance, he teared up. Clouds hung oppressively low, and ice-covered brownstones glared at the carriage's measured passage. Helen held Nellie's other hand and kept three quilts pulled over the small, thin body.

On a bitterly cold November day Jim Fisk returned from Boston with his tail between his legs. When he entered Jay's small office, his mustaches drooped, and on the tip of the left one hung a tiny icicle. He wasn't wearing his diamond studs or cuff links, as if their brilliant luster might make his gloom darker. As Jay listened to Jim's dull monotone describe his Boston trip, it was hard to believe this deflated balloon was the old Jim. Up there had been no haven from process servers, angry shareholders, and vicious reporters. Hounded for two weeks, he had given up and come back to his New York haunts.

Not only did the winter of 1869 come early, but as it deepened, it was more than usually severe. As November wore on, Jay fought to protect his gold profits in a perpetually dark Manhattan shrouded by low, blackish clouds pregnant with snow. His mood was as gloomy as the weather.

The first week of December dropped forty more inches of snow on Manhattan. Carriage and van traffic on Broadway came to a standstill. In such weather farmers didn't send crops to depots. So few workers came in that manufacturers closed their factories. Railroad crews, confronted by scores of snowslides, stayed in their train barns and played cards. As no one paid rail charges on goods that couldn't be shipped, in the last part of November and during December Jay and Jim watched in despair as the Erie's income and profits fell further than normal during the winter slump.

Much of the misery he had prophesied to Grant came to pass, and the economic depression hit the Erie, too. Much as he hated to, right before Christmas Jay was forced to cut the wages of all Erie employees by a fifth, himself and Jim included, so that he wouldn't be forced to fire a fifth of the men. Most other rail lines and businesses had made similar cuts weeks before. Many doctors, dentists, and lawyers had halved their fees. In New Jersey, starving tramps swarmed across the frozen landscape, sometimes forming outlaw bands that terrorized farmers. Even the stream of European immigrants, who had come over since the War in such a flood, dried up; indeed, many returned to their native land.

As the depression spread and winter deepened, debtors cried for easier money, a transfusion of hot blood for a freezing, weakened accident victim. Grant and his new secretary of the Treasury cautiously consulted with bankers, railway men, manufacturers, and merchants about the best tonic to invigorate the country's frail health. Many advocated a gigantic infusion of newly printed greenbacks, but with the conservatism of a country doctor ordering the patient bled, Grant decided to administer the stern treatment of gold convertibility, claiming in a speech to Congress that the first step in restoring the country's strength was "to secure a currency of fixed stable value." Jay angrily described this to Jim as making as much sense as reviving a drowned man by wrapping him in shaved ice and draining his blood.

Throughout the decline in business conditions, the newspapers continued to ravage Jay, an easy, convenient target. Whether he was buying and selling, or sitting out, he was blamed when the stock market went up, and he was blamed when it went down. He was said to be "as furtive and deadly as a spider." He "fed on the betrayal of friends and fattened on the ruin of stockholders." He had "lied and bribed his way to a power that has raised him above the law." He had "a genius for trickery and thimblerigging, a boldness in corruption and subornation, and a talent for strategic betrayal." He became invested with "a sinister distinction as the most cold-blooded corruptionist, spoliator, and financial pirate." He was compared to a deadly vampire bat and a venomous spider, the reporters' overripe prose suggesting that he was in fact not human but a creature who lived in dark, moldy places and relished the rich juices of innocent victims.

Christmas was a peaceful holiday, reserved for religious reflection and a quiet time with the family. Jay, Helen, and the children opened their presents at ten o'clock, went to church at noon, and ate dinner at four. Jim was invited, but he went to Boston to be with Lucy and his children.

New Year's Day was different, public and exciting, a merry occasion of warm, bustling visits between families. As usual, Helen sent two hundred invitations to their traditional at home. Jay had argued against having it this year, but Helen insisted, saying the whole family needed livening up. As often when Helen felt strongly about a family matter, Jay went along.

On New Year's Day half of New York enjoyed the other half's hospitality from noon to three o'clock, while from three to six these roles were reversed. New Year's night was reserved for the young folks' chaperoned supper dances. As usual, the Goulds' at home was called for the first shift, noon to three, as Helen liked to get the work over with before she went calling. Midday this New Year's was cold yet bright, a welcome change from the gloomy days of November and December, and a promise of a better year than '69.

At a quarter to noon, dressed in his best three-piece suit of blue wool, Jay entered the second-floor parlor. To accommodate the expected crowd, the parlor furniture—the marble-topped center table, the little groupings of plush chairs and felt-covered tables—was pushed back to the walls. The double doors leading to the dining room were thrown open, and Helen and the three maids fluttered about the crowded dining room table with final preparations.

Jay stood about awkwardly. The vicious edge was off the press articles and editorials, and he was hopeful that with spring, a pickup in business, and the congressional hearings—which were sure to exonerate his and Jim's role in the crash—life would settle back to normal.

He was hounded by thoughts of Annabelle. He always wanted her, yet he only allowed himself a midnight visit once every week or two. Sex had created his children, mysteriously brought them into the world, and it was sex that was destroying them. Nellie shot, George mad. Jay wasn't sure how Nellie and George were connected to the crash of gold. Perhaps only by time—all three incidents happened on the same weekend—but they felt bound together. As a result, his desires were edged with terror. What kind of monster was he? Of what was he capable—the secret mysterious part of himself that he couldn't see—that was dark and unknowable and that had caused such destruction?

Howard came up. Jay gladly abandoned these disturbing thoughts, dropped to a knee, and gave his son's small warm body a hug. It had been a terrible autumn, a crushing past six months, but surely brighter days lay ahead.

A merry fire crackled in the parlor and the dining room, and the house was filled with the minty smell of pine. On the sideboard stood crystal decanters of brandy for the men, and rich, amber plum wine to fortify the elderly who would shyly be pressed into "taking a drop." Helen called out for him to carve the hams. He gave her a hurried kiss and hunted up his knife and steel. As he cut, the spicy odor of cloves, cinnamon, raisins, and mustard wafted off the juicy slices. He and Helen had been closer over the past two months than in years. With a husband's instinct, he sensed she knew nothing about Annabelle. For some curious reason, rumor had it that Jim had been involved with her.

As she set the last platter of hot tarts on the packed table, Helen placed a friendly hand on his shoulder. Jay looked up from his carving and smiled. She kissed his cheek.

"Everything done?" he asked.

"Yes, thank God."

"Let's relax and enjoy ourselves."

Her anxious face smoothed into a smile and she nodded eagerly.

Jim Fisk came by early, his arms fumbling with presents for the whole family and full of stories about the opera house's new production, *Dido and Aeneas*. Josie Mansfield was to star as the founder and queen of Carthage, who when the Trojan Aeneas left her to found Rome, sang a magnificent aria and destroyed herself by jumping onto a burning pyre. Jay sighed and said he hoped like hell this production was profitable, that he hadn't realized how hard the theater business was.

With Jim's entrance, George's sullen face lit up. As he talked to Jay, Jim shot George, who stood off to the side, little winks and nods of intimacy. Jay was suddenly angry at both, partner and son, for the light that shone in George's eyes was the warmth that once had gleamed for him.

Surprisingly, from noon to one o'clock, only a half dozen of Helen's female friends came by, all without husbands and children, along with two of Nellie's schoolfriends.

By two-thirty the verdict was in. Except for a few diehard friends and dozen meek Erie employees, not one of last year's scores of New Year's guests was coming to this year's at home. What had been happening in dribs and drabs since Black Friday had happened collectively on this public holiday. Jay felt ashamed and embarrassed, a pariah, but not so much distressed for himself as he was for Helen and Nellie, George and Howard, and four-year-old Edwin, who peered around the empty parlor with bewildered eyes, gravely aware that something was wrong but too frightened to ask what. The part that hurt the most about the gold crash was what it had done to his family. How could their "friends" hurt a four-year-old child?

Jay squatted and held the boy. For himself, it didn't really matter. He had always been shy and reserved, no public person. He could force himself to live with what the newspapers mistakenly printed. But Helen and the children were different. That George wanted to be away this afternoon, that Nellie sat in a chair in the middle of a row of empty ones, striving to act as if the bare parlor didn't matter, that Helen bustled about, carrying untouched platters of tarts and ham back to the kitchen and yet more hot platters out, as if any minute last year's horde would descend—it was too much. He wanted to tell them he was sorry, that he had never meant for them to be hurt, but the words were frozen in his mouth. He couldn't think how to put it without making it worse. After all, a man had to maintain a calm, steady front. Edwin's warm arms were wrapped around Jay's neck, and he gave the boy another squeeze. Jay had done nothing wrong, had only done the same things that every businessman he knew did daily, certainly nothing illegal. To be tarred a pariah by a shrill, howling pack of hyenas, and to have it stick, was the grossest of injustices. That Helen, George, Nellie, Howard, and Edwin were splattered by the same tar was the hardest blow yet.

At three o'clock, as quick and furtive as thieves, the servants hustled the two dozen platters from the dining room down the back stairs to the kitchen, for custom allowed them the rest of the day off. By three-fifteen the six Goulds were alone, huddled together in the parlor's gaping space. Jay was silent and morose, Helen nervous, Nellie and George drawn, Howard merry, and Edwin a pale goblin with his father's staring black eyes. As yet nobody had said a word about the lack of guests.

He had brought this misery on them himself. For all of his so-called brilliance, for all of his keen awareness of markets and brokers, he had been a fool, ignorant of the immense power of public opinion. He had been blinded by his need to make himself into some sort of great man. The need to think he could outwit everyone else, beat them at their own game. He had ignored how much the opinions of others could sting and lash, and now those others were torturing his family.

"I don't think it would be wise to go visiting this year," said Helen, looking out the front window as if this wisdom were written in the icy branches of Fifth Avenue's few trees. "We didn't in fact receive many invitations."

"Mama's right," said Jay. "Folks have been riled up over business problems. Next year it'll be different."

"It's all right, Papa!" whispered Nellie, reaching for his hand. She squeezed it tightly. "No matter what, you have us. It's those awful reporters, who want to sell more papers."

Jay drew her to him and nodded, allowing her the comfort of having a scapegoat. Her warmth chased away some of his chill. But she was wrong, he knew; it wasn't the newspapers who had done this to his family, but him.

Dido and Aeneas was due to open February first. The billboards announcing the production trumpeted the debut of Madame Josephine Francesca, Josie's freshly minted stage name.

By mid-January the opera had been in rehearsal for four weeks. One frosty morning Teddy Corsi, the production's plump, middle-aged director, cornered Jim Fisk in his large office. He hesitantly opened the conversation by saying that Josie was no better now than she had been when rehearsals started.

"No better!" said Jim. "Come on." Jim waved Teddy into a seat and shoved forward the gold humidor. While Teddy perched on the edge of the visitor's chair, Jim leaned back against his leather-padded cushions.

"She can't sing, Jim," said the short, fussy director. His bald, waxy head was circled by a ring of short gray curls that sprang up with artistic friskiness. "She thinks fine acting is putting on a new dress between scenes. She doesn't remember her lines, which I can't decide is a blessing or a catastrophe. On top of which, this 'manager' of hers—"

"Ned Stokes?" Manager, indeed! Jim had stomached about all of Ned that he could stand. "Tell him to stay out of the theater."

"I have," said Teddy, "but it doesn't do any good."

"Call the cops."

"She won't rehearse if he's not there."

"Who's the director down there—him or you?"

"That's why I'm talking to you," said Teddy. "He bellyaches constantly that I don't know my job. The lights on her aren't strong enough. The pyre isn't big enough. She doesn't have enough lines or songs. My God! She's got the lead. You told me from the first it would be hard, but like a fool I thought about the money and didn't listen. I said that if I had to, I could get a performance out of a cow. But I've changed my mind, Jim. Cows are not cut out for the stage, not even young, comely heifers. When she sings, it's like a hanging." Jim had negotiated a hundred disputes like this over the last year. He had learned to proceed with caution. It wasn't wise to change directors or stars two weeks before the opening.

"A hanging?" asked Jim with forced softness. With impatience he tapped his manicured nails on his rosewood desk. He hated a man who didn't seize his job by the horns and wrestle it to the ground.

"A hanging," said Teddy. "She sings only to hang herself, and high. In every song she makes straight for the most inaccessible notes, without a springboard, and when she reaches them she hangs on in despair, wavering between two or three high notes. She stays there crying, suffering, an object of pity, ready to be cut in pieces. I stand there, wincing."

Jim rolled up his copy of the *World* and lightly beat it against the edge of his desk.

"The whole cast stands around, suffering too," Teddy went on. "She stops short, leaving the mortal terror hanging above her in the air, frantically gesturing me and everybody back for a minute of silence with a wave that says this time she'll get it right or bust. Up she climbs again, or to be more exact, suddenly there the notes are again, more unhappy than ever."

Jim rapped the rolled-up newspaper in a louder drumbeat against his desk.

"This goes on for an hour," Teddy plunged on, "then in an injured voice Mr. Stokes says it's enough, that she has to rest her voice— which she certainly does." Teddy's plump face was grim. "I don't think I'm a temperamental man—"

Jim silenced him with a wave and an overpowering slap of the newspaper against his desk.

"It was one of the reasons I hired you," he shouted.

Teddy jumped. "Damn it," the director shouted back, "it's me or her! In twenty years in the business, I've never said that, but I can't go on. I've got leg kickers in the chorus who could do better."

Even though it was before noon, Jim rose and stepped to the sideboard. He poured a brandy and shoved it into the director's small, fat hand. Teddy nodded thanks and gulped it down, rubbing his lips with the back of his hand.

"Not a *good* job, mind you," Teddy went on, "but better than her. Every one of those girls sees this show as the laughingstock of the season. I haven't bothered you with my problems, but a dozen girls have left for other productions."

Jim scowled. Something must be wrong. Teddy had never before taken a stand on anything. It was one of the reasons he had hired him.

"But you have contracts with them," said Jim. Teddy stood and drew himself to his full height, nearly five feet.

"If you open this production with Mrs. Mansfield, it will so damage your reputation as an impresario that you'll never attract a crowd back into this theater. Is that what you want?" Shocked, Jim closed his teeth and opened his lips in a grimace of pain.

"It's that bad, Teddy?" Jim asked softly, earnestly.

The director nodded wearily. "I've tried hard, Jim, really I have. I know how important she is to you. But the truth is—yes, yes, it's that bad."

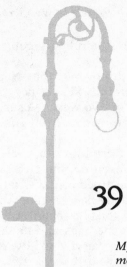

39

My dear Dolly: Will you see me this morning?
If so, what hour?
                    Yours truly, ever, James.

—Jim Fisk, letter to Josie
Mansfield, 1870

Sharp needles of March rain blew against Josie Mansfield's face and throat as she opened the front door of her town house. Amid a night-dark flurry of cape, rain, and wind, Ned Stokes scrambled into the front hall. The storm's wet breath blew out the candle in her hand. Ned's cold fingers fumbled inside her robe for her waist and breasts.

Angrily she pushed them away. "No, you're all wet," she hissed. "Virginia might hear. Come upstairs."

To make her bedroom resemble an oriental tent even more, she turned down the gas lamps and lit two soft kerosene lanterns. Ned stripped to his wet, baggy underdrawers and rummaged in her closet. His handsome face triumphant in the orange glow of the lamps, he held up Jim's midnight-blue robe with the black velvet collar. He slipped it on, then turned his back to strip off his wet drawers. His wearing Jim's robe didn't sit quite right with her, but saying so would ignite his scorn toward Jim.

Dwarfed by Jim's elephantine blue robe, Ned threw himself across her bed. "Well?" he asked. She said nothing, hoping to dodge the familiar questioning about her success in obtaining a cash settlement from Jim, but instead drew the open edges of her flannel robe to her neck and settled demurely onto the foot of the bed. Ned sighed.

"Now, Josie, you know very well the refinery gets more than half its income from the Erie."

In other words, once Jim discovered that Ned was also in her bed, he would stop buying oil from Ned's refinery, and as Ned never tired of telling her, bankrupt it in two weeks. A surge of anger nearly made her snap that *all* her income came from Jim, but she held her tongue.

The fire loudly cracked the fresh lumps of coal, eating them with eager, orange tongues. The first evening that Ned sent her to Jim, the night of Black Friday, she had assumed Ned was talking about a week or two of jollying Jim along, a week or two at the *most*. Over the following weeks she discovered that he meant a week or two at the *least*. For months now she had gone back and forth between her two lovers. While Ned paid diligent lip service to how much the arrangement bothered him, that he allowed it to continue for so long told her what he really thought.

"He just won't," she said finally. She hated going through this. Still, another five minutes and they would blow out the candle, the horrible necessity of money forgotten.

"You have to hold it firmly in your mind when you deal with him," said Ned. She was in an impossible situation. It was as if Jim held one leg, pulling at her, and Ned the other. If this tug-of-war kept on she would be ripped from crotch to gullet.

"He's just not going to give it to me," she said.

"He will if you want him to," Ned said, his voice turning harsh. "You have to press harder."

"I don't think he's got any ready money," she said. As if these words bumped open a catch holding down an inner spring, Ned jerked upright.

"Not got any!" In the dim light, framed by the maroon, gold, and beige cloth that draped her headboard, he appeared as fierce and bold as a Turkish prince giving orders to his thousands of desert followers. Even though she sat at the foot of the bed, she edged back till she was almost falling off. "Didn't he clean up in the gold bust? Doesn't he own the opera house? What about his steamship line? Doesn't he keep a big house in Boston? Isn't he a director of the Erie?"

She had to make him see how impossible it was. "He's being sued by a thousand lawyers," she said, gripping the carved bedpost for support. "He has a dozen attorneys working full-time on his cases. He's strapped. And he *lost* money in the gold bust. The opera house is losing buckets of money. After all, he had to fold *Dido*."

Ned pursed his lips and shook his head in disgust. "How can you defend him when he did *that* to you? After all, your name was on posters all over town." She hated arguing with him. She wasn't sure how he accomplished it, but she rarely beat him in a disagreement.

The familiar argument went back and forth. To her protests that she didn't want to see Jim again, Ned had his usual clever answers. Surely Jim owed her something for the years she had given him, and surely Josie wasn't going to abandon such a claim. She and Ned had no money, did they? Mashed down by his scorn, she shook her head no.

Certainly Ned did all he could for them, didn't he, spending all his waking hours making contacts so that he could get more business, often spending whole days at the track, in the bar at Delmonico's, and in bawdy houses where oil buyers were found. She nodded. With the $50,000 that they had decided Jim owed her they could live for two or three years while they got on their feet. She kept nodding. Somewhere in the distance a loose shutter driven by the storm hammered against the house.

"Maybe it's time for the letters," said Ned.

Her head jerked up. "No," she said hotly. "We talked about it. That's blackmail." She wanted to step into the cool hall, go find that damn loose shutter, and fasten it. The word *blackmail* didn't disturb the urbane, sophisticated glaze on Ned's face.

"He's got to see that you're serious."

"No, Ned, please. Not yet." The shutter's loud knocks were hammering again. Hammer—shutter—*Jim!*

"It's him!" said Josie, half rising in fright. "He said he might come over. Quick! Out the back door."

"Jim—here now?" said Ned, eyes wide in alarm.

"Do you want him to see you?" she asked. It delighted her to rub his face in it. "You want me to 'entertain' him, don't you? I'd be just as happy to bring him in, let him see us together, and call it quits."

Ned's haste ignored her fresh answer. He shot off the bed, tossed off Jim's robe, and drew on his wet underclothes, shirt, and dark suit. While he buttoned his trousers, she hurriedly hung the blue robe in her closet and flew around the room, straightening. She lit the candle and waited by the open door, and in seconds they were racing down the stairs.

"Josie!" came Jim's voice over the rain's furious lashing against the hall windows. Ned gave her a hurried good-bye kiss in the downstairs hall, his wet cloak chilling her hands and neck.

"All right, all right," she promised Ned in a whisper, "I'll try again." She pulled away. Jim's blows against the front door sounded strong enough to bust it open.

"Josie, open up! It's me, Jim!"

425

"Good," Ned whispered back. "But if it doesn't work this time, we use the letters." Another series of hammer blows.

"Josie!" shouted Jim. She nodded and gave Ned a hard shove toward the kitchen. Giving him a half minute to escape through the back, she leaned against the front door. Through it came the forceful vibrations of the storm and Jim's fists.

She gritted her teeth and opened the door. The wind and rain whipped against her face. Jim's bulk slid in and the candle blew out. As she pushed the door closed, his cold, wet fingers found their way under her robe. She untangled herself, grabbed his hand, and led him up the stairs. In her bedroom, he reached into the closet for his blue robe. She started. Suppose it was still warm from Ned's body? To distract him, she moved around the room and began to turn out the lamps, leaving only the bedside candle.

Grinning impishly, however, Jim noticed nothing. In contrast with Ned, he had nothing on his mind but her. In seconds his stout arms swept her off her feet and onto the bed. In the dim light his childish good humor quickly loosened the knot in her stomach. After all this time, knowing him as well as she did, being in bed with him was as carefree as being five years old and playing dolls with your best friend. To stop the shivering that abruptly came over her, she held on to him tightly, and his big, warm body rocked against her. She asked him to blow out the candle, and after he did, she hugged him more tightly and wished the dark innocent hours would never end.

By one in the morning, the spring storm had spent itself. Outside it was silent. Inside, with the fire out, Josie's bedroom had a damp, earthy feel, as if the storm had stalked through it while she and Jim were lost in lovemaking and a half hour's sleep.

Jim lit the candle. As he pulled on his large trousers, Josie wiggled off the wet spot under her. Naked and cold, she pulled the smooth sheets and the silk quilt around her. She watched him dress by the candle's flickering light. He poured water out of his huge boots onto the hearth before pulling them on.

"What a man goes through for a woman!" he said. The white shirt he pulled over his head was large enough to be her nightgown.

Jim said he had seen a lilac silk shawl in Stewart's window that was her to a tee, and here was fifty dollars if she decided she wanted it. Despite its dampness, the bill's paper crinkled against her palm. The greenback was blackened with use, and a moldiness rose off its cold surface as if it had been folded and tucked into the secret pockets of a thousand people.

426

She extended the crumpled bill back to him. "I don't want this."

In the candle's orange glow his face assumed a roguish expression of mock delight. With a dainty gesture, his fingers plucked the bill from her hand. "I certainly can find another home for this little bird."

She grasped his other hand, wiggled herself back to her side of the bed, onto the cold wet spot, and drew him down next to her.

"Jim, you promised me more than just dribs and drabs," she said.

His pleased, roguish expression fell away. "Aw, not again. I've told you what's going on. I'm having a hard time. I've never seen money disappear so fast." Her stomach heaved about with the violence of a banging shutter in a storm. It was impossible. Ned on one leg, pulling, Jim on the other. All she was left with was the rip in the middle torn open by their tugging—a rip, a hole, a nothing into which each jumped whenever he wanted. Her rib cage shook, her shoulders twisted, sobs jerked savagely against her lungs. Overpowered by the awfulness of the situation, she threw herself onto the pillows. Out tumbled more sobs and tears. As she calmed down, she became aware that his broad hands were massaging her back.

"There, there," he said. She couldn't stand the touch of his soft hands, as if they were sucking something away rather than giving to her. She sat up and knocked them away.

"It's not fair," she yelled. "How would you like to ask for every little thing you wanted—a dress, a piece of furniture, a few dollars to buy groceries?"

He recoiled. His voice driven by anger, he ticked off on his fat fingers how much he had given her. "I pay for Carter. I bought you your first carriage and a fine mare. You've got three fur coats, a box full of more jewels than you can wear, and a closet full of clothes that I've footed the bills for. Damn it, you've done fine by me."

"Haven't I entertained all your big-shot friends that you wanted to have quiet little talks with?" she asked. "Haven't I served them their suppers, poured them their whiskeys, listened to their schoolboy jokes, and clucked over their problems with wives and girlfriends? I was promised a career on the stage, which I never got."

His plump lips curved into an impish grin. "You got your chance," he said, "but I'm not a magician."

While she studied this remark to see if it was an insult, he stood up. He attached the diamond cuff link to his damp shirt with the speed of a fellow about to bolt. Naked, only half under the quilt, she wanted the protection of her gown and robe, but they were somewhere on the floor. She certainly wasn't going to scramble around, naked, to find them. She pulled the cover higher up on her chest.

"I ought to have a settlement so I'm not your puppet," she said.

"Puppet!" he said. "You come and go as you please."

"When you dole out money in dribs and drabs, I damn sure am."

"Aw, Josie!" His voice was thick with weariness over this stale argument. She was sick of it, too, tiresome scenes from a depressing play. She had to get the $50,000 Ned said they were due or give up asking.

She took the plunge. "Then you're forcing me to do something I don't want to." She pulled the silk quilt more tightly around her neck.

"I am what?" he asked, puzzled.

Josie was standing on a steep cliff, poised to dive, buffeted by cold winds that threatened to knock her over. She could still backtrack. Hundreds of feet below her beckoned angry ocean waves. She heard Ned say, "Jump," but hitting the cold water would be a shock. Yet the woman who swam in those raw, stormy waters would become strong, would gather what she needed to live for herself. She took a deep breath and leaped.

"I want what's due me," she said. "You're forcing me to sell my letters." His face became painted over with amusement.

Jim shook his head and laughed. "Who the hell wants them?"

"The *Tribune* and the *Mirror*."

This time his laugh died from lack of mirth. "The *Trib* and the *Mirror* want to buy the letters I wrote you?"

"You're a public figure, Jim."

Amusement dropped from his face, leaving the hollow, grayish slackness of someone given bad news coming to realize that it wasn't a tasteless joke. "This isn't like you, Josie. They're personal."

"Of course they are," she said. "So is my livelihood."

He frowned and shook his head as if to clear it. "You won't hurt just me. You'll hurt Lucy and the children."

"Haven't I begged you to settle something on me?" she demanded.

He heaved a great sigh, as if only with reluctance was he finally accepting this new and bitter element. Josie wanted to take it back, put the candle out, and again snuggle up with him under the quilt. He glanced about the cloth-shrouded bedroom as if bewildered.

"Is this blackmail, Josie?" he asked in a voice made hoarse by hurt and contempt. The terrible knocking in her chest had to be her heart. She stalled by rearranging the quilt around her torso.

"What?" she asked in a voice that even to her ears sounded full of stupidity. His neck had reddened, a flush that had half risen into his cheeks.

"I suppose if I settle that $50,000 on you, I get the letters back, is that it?"

Her throat, as stiff as dried mud, was too rigid to answer. She nodded. Jim strode to her vanity and snatched open the little side drawer where she used to keep them.

"Where are they?" he bellowed. He dropped the drawer. Jars, vials, and hairpins flew over the carpet. She pushed back against the cloth-covered headboard. He yanked out the drawer from the other side of the table, glanced in it, and threw it to the floor. "Where are they?" he demanded again. He strode to her, his boots cracking and splintering the flimsy wooden drawers as he stomped across them. As strong as a bull, he might pull her fingers off, one by one.

She drew back and knotted her hands into fists. "They're not here." She wouldn't tell him that Ned had put them in a bank vault. If he heard that, he would rip off her arms and legs. He stood at the foot of the bed.

"Where are they, Josie?" he shouted. To better protect herself, she sat up and drew her feet under her, as far from him as possible.

"In a safe place till this is settled," she said.

He strode to the side of the bed. She scooted to the other side.

"Maybe you better go," she said.

He reached over and with a single yank whipped off the quilt and sheet. A rush of frigid air raked her naked flesh. She slid off the bed, away from him, one hand over her lower parts, the other across her breasts. His boots walked across the bed, but she was already fleeing the room.

In the hall she pulled the door shut behind her and held on to the glass doorknob. The knob turned as he tried to open the door. Bent over in concentration, her naked rump stuck out toward the stairs, Josie squeezed the cut glass so tightly that her palms hurt, but on the other side, Jim was stronger. The knob heated as it twisted in her hands. Her naked breasts trembled in the freezing hall air, and cold drafts blew against her backside and around her exposed legs. Any minute the shouting and the slamming doors would wake Virginia, who would daintily trip down the stairs, stare naïvely at Josie's shocking state of undress, and ask in a sweet, innocent voice what the commotion was.

Against all her force, the bedroom door was slowly pulled inward by Jim's superior strength. Abruptly Josie was wrenched halfway into the room. He grabbed her wrists, yanked her completely inside, and kicked the door shut. Still bent over, straining backward, she kept her vulnerable naked flesh as far from him as she could.

"You can beat me," she yelled, "you can tear the house down, but you won't find those letters." His chest was heaving in large, gulping rasps. He said nothing, stood stock-still, only squeezed her wrists and stared into her eyes with the uncertainty of a maddened bull confronted by a yapping terrier. "If you hurt me," she went on, "I'm warning you, I won't wait for money. I'll walk them down to the *Trib* or *Mirror*'s office and *give* them to the editor."

"Okay," he said, his voice a croak, wavering and cracking as if he could barely keep his outrage under control. "Okay." Her wrists were clamped so hard by his hands that a boot might have been mashing them against the floor. He pulled her face close to his. "You ain't got 'em here. You get 'em and give 'em back."

"They're mine," she said. "You gave them to me."

"Or I'll tear this house down plank by plank. As for you printing them, ain't nothing in 'em but fribble-frabble 'tween you and me. No newspaper is going to publish such tittle-tattle."

"Then you shouldn't care if they are sold."

"Didn't you hear?" His voice rose dangerously. "You give them back!"

Aware how naked and defenseless she was, she nodded. He yanked her wrists. Pain and a wave of dizziness passed over her. He yanked again, and again she nodded. He seemed satisfied by her nodding grimace of pain. He cast two or three more wild glances around the room and dragged her to the bedroom door. He dropped her wrists and stalked out, slamming the bedroom door behind him.

She sank, the rough Persian carpet scratching her naked haunches. His heavy bootsteps receded down her hallway stairs.

She buried her face in her hands, where she cried and snuffled, her sobs coming in long, uncontrollable spasms.

When his heavy footsteps reached the downstairs hall, he slammed the front door, too. She jumped as if he had slapped her.

40

*If I denied all the lies told about me, I
should have no time to do business.*

—Jay Gould to a reporter, 1879

Toward the end of April, spring
blew such a sweet, light breath on New York that Jay found it hard
to believe there had been a winter.

The linden and mulberry trees blossoming along the side streets
of Manhattan's Twenties and Thirties were lush and green. Bringing
a fresh, exhilarating atmosphere, a crisp breeze swooped down from
Canada and blew away the brownish-gray haze and foul stench of
Hunts Point.

Wanting to give his family a treat to make up for the harsh winter,
Jay leased the estate at Irvington-on-Hudson from the widow of
George Merritt. Keeping the reason a secret, he announced a special
one-day outing with the family for the last Sunday in April.

Overdressed in a multitude of rich, multicolored silk and lace
gowns, spring danced around the posh railcar on the ride up. No
matter how many questions Helen and the children asked about the
outing, Jay put on a mysterious smile and would only say that they
were "going to the country for a surprise tea." With spring he was
less tense, more relaxed. Surely his family's "exile" would soon be over.

Nellie's eyes shone, and Edwin and Howard's faces were bright
with glee. Helen, finally beginning to show her fifth pregnancy, appeared serene. Only George, still sullen and withdrawn since the
pistol accident, had an uneasy, furtive expression. Jay frowned, but
didn't dare say anything. As usual for him these days, George had
asked to stay home today, but Jay had insisted he come, hoping the
new place would delight the boy in spite of his adolescent resentment.

He longed for George to drop his standoffish sullenness and join the rest of the family; he desperately wanted back the son he had so mysteriously lost.

The wind ruffling his beard, Jay forced himself to relax further. Nothing written about him in newspapers was particularly good, but there was less of it. He was learning to live with the occasional vicious article that still depicted him as a sinister spider. Restlessly turning over the past, he often looked back on the gold episode as a crowded nightmare, one full of devils in a burning, shifting landscape, but containing valuable lessons. While money still flowed from the opera house's accounts as fast as blood from a war wound, Jim swore that his new production, *Loki and the Nymphs*, would turn its red ink into a gusher of black. Jay's health had improved, and his winter cough and chest pains had completely dropped away. No longer having to fill two jobs—run the Erie and fend off so many gold suits stemming from Black Friday—he was less tense and slept better. Indeed, Friday and Saturday nights he sometimes slept a full eight hours.

Again he saw Annabelle regularly, midnight visits once or twice a week. Visits more furtive than ever, full of passion fit for an opera, followed by days of anguish and self-recriminations. He was secretly investing in the Fifth Avenue dress shop she was opening under her maiden name, Gantry. They both hoped the new business would make her financially independent. He kept promising himself he would stop the visits, but he saw himself as like a drinker putting off abstinence week by week.

At the Irvington station a four-horse open buckboard met them. It was driven by a bent-over, aged seafaring duffer with an enormous wart at the side of his nose. With a mysterious smile Jay instructed his family to climb in the buckboard, and as they pulled away, he chatted with the old sailor, Silas, as if he had known him a long time. From the rearmost bench, George said they were going to a horse race. Buoyed by the sprightliness in his son's voice, Jay turned and smiled. One look at his father's pleasure was enough to shove George back into sulkiness.

A large-bowled, filthy pipe clutched in his stained teeth, Silas drove them down a shaded, rutted lane, at the end of which stood a massive granite gatehouse. They passed through it and up an orange gravel road that wound through spacious carpets of lawn. Intoxicated by his own excitement, Jay breathed in the lush fragrance of new grass and spring flowers. The winding lane led up a long, gentle hill to a large white house, which as the open carriage drew closer, was seen to be a mansion of white marble with a great tower. Around the mansion and its many white outbuildings were ancient, huge trees, linden, elm, beech, and pine. From Helen to Howard, the Goulds stared at it, awestruck.

"Papa," whispered Nellie finally, "it's beautiful!"

"It's Camelot," murmured George as they swung around the final curve. This time Jay didn't look at or respond to the boy, but he remembered the King Arthur books George read so avidly. This place might work yet. Helen, Nellie, and Edwin were speechless. Turrets, bays, finials, buttresses, trefoils, stone traceries, and crenellations flung themselves in every direction. The green carpet of grass sloped down to the wide, quiet Hudson. As the carriage pulled up to the massive front porch, Nellie asked softly, "Who lives here, Papa?"

A large smile made his dark beard rise at the corners of his face. "*We* live here. I've leased it." They oohed and aahed.

Silas the driver was the mansion's caretaker. With a warm smile making his wart wiggle, he helped them down, opened the front door, and introduced them to his stout wife. Hobbling before them, Silas led them into a wide, spacious central hallway. Jay felt immensely gratified and pleased that he could give his family such a retreat. It was little enough for what he had put them through. Silas led them into a huge parlor on the left, filled with large furniture, then back across the hall to an elegant dining room. Nellie ran forward to peer at the long table set for tea. Helen slipped her hand into Jay's, and he gave it a squeeze.

From the Hudson, Lyndhurst might look like a castle, but inside it resembled a Mediterranean villa. It was light and airy, spacious, and its large pieces of furniture opened up the interior space rather than making it gloomy like so many town dwellings. They passed through a billiards room, gymnasium, bowling alley, and finally a two-room library, its shelves three-quarters empty. His family's further cries of pleasure made him chuckle. Even George seemed to like it, except when Jay glanced his way.

"Outside there's twenty acres for you boys to run around on," said Jay in an exuberant tone. "Show us the stables and greenhouse, Silas."

"Yes, sir," said the caretaker. "And afterwards my missus would take it wrong if you didn't drink her tea."

"Tea would revive us greatly," said Helen, pressing her hand on Silas's arm. "I'm sure she and I will get along fine. The greenhouse, Jay." By the warm smile on her plump face, Jay saw that she liked it. Lyndhurst would not only be a haven for him, but for every Gould, a place to shield his family from the harsh, intrusive world.

The large carriage house held twenty carriages, from light gigs to heavy barges, and had stalls for fifty horses. Out back of the stable was the greenhouse, a towering coliseum of thin steel struts and countless panes of glass, two city blocks long, with a giant wing at either end. Gazing up at it in awe and pride, Jay told Nellie and Howard that it was the largest greenhouse in America. In Moorish style, a dazzling onion dome pushed a hundred feet above it into the sky.

They entered, and its warm, humid air was as hushed as a cathedral's. It was empty of plants, its ground torn and filled with the stubble of roots and dead shoots. Jay proposed climbing to the observation platform at the top of the onion dome.

Silas demurred, saying his days of climbing to the crow's nest were over, but George said he wasn't afraid to go. Jay leading, the two trooped up the slatted iron steps toward the platform, which hung like a sky-going raft against the curved glass wall of the dome. It felt good to be doing something alone with George. It reminded him of the wonderful days they had spent together at the office before—the crash. The climbing was warm going. The higher Jay climbed, the hotter and more humid became the air. On the ground Helen and the children grew as small as mice. Finally they climbed onto the iron-slatted sky raft. Jay pushed open one of the vent frames. The peaceful Hudson Valley was spread before them, a nubby green carpet that stretched from the Palisades to the northern highlands.

"It's . . . beautiful, Pa," said George.

"It is," said Jay cautiously. George's face didn't close up. They were so high that he had the sensation that they were floating, ballooning over the Hudson Valley, soaring fifty feet above the treetops, master of all below. "I took an option on the place," Jay said in a neutral voice. "If everybody enjoys it, and the business does well enough, I'll buy it."

Up next to the thousands of panes of glass, as if they were near the sun, the heat was yet more humid and intense. Sweat broke out across Jay's back and chest, and ran in streams down George's flushed face. For a few moments Jay silently gazed at the fluffy clouds and the Hudson Valley's luxuriant greenery. Despite the heat, he hadn't felt so at peace in months. George, his face soft and open, also appeared at ease, as if his standoffishness had fallen away. Jay touched his son's arm, but George gave him a sullen glance and pulled back.

"Son, son," whispered Jay, "can't . . . bygones be bygones?" George's deep brown eyes were morose with suffering, as if contracted by pain. Jay winced, and sweat prickled him under his arms and across his face.

The silence was broken by the drone of old Silas and the other

Goulds far below, as well as by dozens of tiny knocks and thumps against nearby panes of glass. Jay's eyes narrowed as he peered about. A bee was knocking against one of the nearest panes, struggling to escape through the clear glass to the faultless blue. Jay looked behind him. Glass panels stretched away in every direction, and from them also came faint bumps and knocks. Scores, hundreds of insects were thunking against the glass in futile attempts to escape the elephantine greenhouse. His shoulders hunched. These few must be but a fraction of the thousands, tens of thousands of insects snared by this gigantic glass mansion, their fate to bang their brains against the transparent walls of this huge glass trap till they fell, battered, exhausted, and weakened unto death, to the ground.

"I wish . . ." said George softly. Jay turned to him. The boy's eyes—no, he was a man now, if a young one—were filled with tears. Jay's own eyes prickled with tears. Around them the air was a hot, moist cloud trapped against the thousands of panes of heated glass.

"Things are—" said Jay. "We—" his voice faltered. George's face was sweaty and teary. Blinking back his own tears, Jay guessed that as usual his son had forgotten to bring a handkerchief. He wondered if it would embarrass George if he offered his. Jay tentatively held it out. George hesitated, then took it. Jay smiled. George blew his nose.

"I've been . . . thinking," whispered George. "Uncle Jim talked to me . . . a whole bunch. Oh, Pa! Why can't things be like they were?" Jay nodded, casting around inwardly for the right words. According to Jim, somehow George had found out about him and Annabelle. The boy felt Jay had betrayed the family, especially Helen. Jay's dark broadcloth suit was as uncomfortable as a hair shirt, and the heat up here had soaked his socks and feet with sweat. Sweat streamed down George's red face as if he were wax and melting.

"Things happen, son," he said, hoping these neutral words would help. Returning the handkerchief, George nodded, appearing less belligerent, more understanding than he had been in months. Jay's chest was tight, as if the heat were shrinking a wide belt of thick leather around his upper torso. He had probably pushed George as far as possible for one day. The last thing he wanted was to have a disagreement up here. He thought they had better start back down, but his legs wouldn't move.

"Why did you do it?" George asked.

The heat scratched Jay. "What?" he breathed, alarmed.

George was crying again. "Stewart's dad is busted, so is Moss's. They say—you stole from them. That you're a crook, a thief."

"No, I didn't steal," said Jay. Glad his son hadn't mentioned Annabelle, he handed back the handkerchief. "I only . . . bought and sold."

George blew his nose and wiped his face, taking a long time at it. After a long silence, George's red face looked up and nodded.

"I'm—sorry, the gun and all," said George. "Uncle Jim says . . . everybody makes mistakes." The boy handed him the damp handkerchief.

Jay put his hand on his son's shoulder and squeezed. "Nothing would make me happier than to wipe all that out of my life," Jay said. "But it happened. Can't wash it away. Nothing will do that." The heat continued to assault him with the force of a blast furnace. George snuffled and nodded. "I was wrong—driven crazy by gold madness," Jay stumbled on. "As if the Devil had got hold of me. It won't happen again. Nellie's pain. The Hell you went through. Every time I think of what I caused, it's awful."

Depleted, he fell silent. George was staring at him, eyes filled with as much misery as hope. Jay tried to come up with more to say. The knocks and thumps of trapped insects beat against the panes with the fury of thousands of tiny mad drums. They should go back down.

"I want—nothing would please me more," Jay fumbled on, "us to forgive each other, go on as before. I want you to come in the business, soon as you're finished at Mr. Marks's."

His face pale, contorted, and sweaty, George twisted about as if acutely uncomfortable. "You still . . . want me?"

"Yes—of course."

"I didn't mean to," George whispered, his eyes teary and dark with urgency. "Please."

"Accident," whispered Jay, and he touched his son's arm. "Forgive me, the Hell I put you through."

"It's all right," said George. His tears ran again, and he started sobbing. Jay's own tears mingled with his sweat. He again passed his handkerchief to George. The band around his chest squeezed tighter. From a hundred feet below came Helen's tiny shout.

"Will you two come down so we can have our tea?"

Jay pulled George to him and hugged his son. The young man's hot, sweaty body wriggled against his as if struggling to escape the embrace. An emotion as raw and fierce as a hot savage wind blew out of Jay's chest. He sobbed and clasped George harder.

For several moments his son's arms fluttered at his sides, as useless as a butterfly's broken wings, then wrapped around his father's back and squeezed tightly. The leather band around Jay's chest contracted in a sudden fierce pain, then burst.

He had his son back!

41

If homicide is regularly indulged in, it leads to immorality.

—John William De Forest, *A Union Captain's Record*, 1860s

Balancing to keep his weight off his painful right big toe, Cornelius Vanderbilt stood in the office behind his house. In the open doorway to the stable yard, the one-legged man clambered up the three stone steps.

For a fellow with only one leg and a wooden crutch, General Dan Sickles hoisted himself easily, even gracefully, up the steps and into the room. Cornelius restrained himself from taking the half-dozen strides forward to shake his visitor's hand. Wanting to see how much of a handicap having one leg was, he forced the newcomer to cross to him. He damn sure wasn't hiring a cripple who couldn't manage himself.

A graying man of forty-five with a thin, bland face that would be useful to a diplomat, Sickles thumped easily over the wide boards and shook Cornelius's hand. His grip was dry, hard, and smooth, reminding Cornelius of the texture of one of those palm-sized, sea-worn pebbles that covered the beach on Montauk. Sickles murmured a few well-turned words of greeting. The ex-general's suit was far better tailored than Cornelius's black frock coat, an elegant three-piece getup of blue wool set off by a white shirt, breast handkerchief like a bold white blossom, and a maroon necktie with small white checks. Cornelius waved his hand around the rough wood walls of the former tackle room.

"I asked you to my private office for the sake of confidentiality," he said. "Sit on that chair there." The pain in Cornelius's right toe merely throbbed this morning. It had been his back teeth yesterday, when he had carried around peppermint and cloves to press against his gums.

Sickles casually dropped himself on a straight chair and leaned the oak crutch against a box of bridles. The rich blue wool of his empty pant leg was neatly sewn against itself. Cornelius was as impressed as he was when a hunting dog with just three legs didn't let his loss stop him from doing that which he loved most, running down rabbits.

"You handle yourself pretty good," said Cornelius.

"I've never let it get the best of me," said Sickles with a self-satisfied smile that said no real man let such a trifle as a missing leg slow him down.

Through the wavery windowpanes appeared a patch of dark, angry cloud. Against the far wall the potbellied stove softly burned, its cozy heat pushing back the chill of the rainy April morning. On the stove's hot surface sat the cracked and stained pot of peppermint tea whose spicy odor flooded the room. Cornelius gave his visitor a smile.

"The fellow that recommended you said you got up the day after you lost it."

"I was with McClellan, the Young Napoleon," said Sickles derisively. "A cannonball shattered my knee. I had to destroy the horse."

"He said that you got up the next morning and shaved yourself."

Sickles's handsome smile was smug, as if he got a lot of mileage out of his loss. "That story has got around, hasn't it? I did, and I did it to keep up my spirits. The afternoon I lost it I made up my mind not to let it get me down. Carrying on my usual routine kept that from happening."

Scrutinizing the other, Cornelius nodded in a calm, sage way. He found Sickles handsome, too handsome. Eyes like clear gray glass. A nose as sculpted as that on a department-store dummy. Manicured fingernails. The sweet, ripe odor of his visitor's apple hair pomade fought with his office's fresher, cleaner scent of peppermint. Cornelius reckoned that such looks and grooming were attractive to women; certainly womanizing was part of this fellow's reputation. Cornelius didn't trust handsome men.

Sickles's history was mixed. Before the war he had been a congressman often mentioned as a man who would one day be president. But in '59 he killed his wife's lover in a notorious duel four blocks from the White House that everybody agreed was actually murder.

After a few weeks in jail, he got off with some slick lawyering, but his presidential hopes as well as any further elective career were over. To every gossip's surprise, Sickles even took the strayed wife back. One of the first to enlist, like so many other bright, eager lads—like Cornelius's dead son, George Washington Vanderbilt—Captain Sickles made brevet general within a year and a half. During the last part of the War he was one of Grant's best generals, a real scrapper, till the loss of his leg sent him back to Philadelphia. Still one of Grant's favorites, since the War he had been ambassador to Spain, but the rumor was that he now wanted to make money, big money, something his army and diplomatic ties couldn't help him with.

Cornelius leaned back, unsure how far to proceed with this slick piece of work, and said, "I need a fighter, a scrapper."

As if carefully considering Cornelius's need, Sickles pursed his well-molded lips and slowly nodded. "Well, I'm a pretty good scrapper."

"That's what I hear. I been in a war of my own the past two years with a couple of upstart pups."

Sickles's smile glowed with amused contempt. "Ahh! Gould and Fisk."

"The same," said Cornelius. He was irked by Sickles's smugness, but he hid it. "I beat them when they tried to smuggle my money into New Jersey. I lost a fair amount of money in the Cattle Car War, but I drew even with them on Black Friday."

"I thought you lost money."

"No, I got out nearly even. I was on the short side, which ultimately was the right side to be on."

Pain flared in Cornelius's right toe, and he stretched out his leg. Something was always reminding him how few years he had left. He had finally learned how to live—that is, how to acquire and use "the power"—but the more he found out how to do it, the less health he had to use that knowledge. It was manifestly unfair of whoever designed this world.

"And how can I help you, Commodore?" asked Sickles.

"The Erie has no room to grow," said Cornelius. "Here recently Gould has had to almost live in Washington, and Fisk goes down there every week to testify. Those damn congressional idiots—they can't hold on to a runt of a rabbit even when he is thrust into their hands!"

"The congressional committees found they had done nothing illegal?"

"Yes," Cornelius said, "but I'm sure you see that Fisk's former bosom companions, the daily newspapers, condemn them." Sickles narrowed his gray eyes as if he thought Cornelius was trying to put something over on him.

"Mr. Tweed is on their board," said Sickles, "and certainly no one knows better how to keep the fires of politics from scorching his friends." Sickles was shrewder and better informed than his slick, handsome face led Cornelius to believe. Nowadays even his former crony Judge Barnard was more beholden to Gould than to Cornelius.

"I need the right man to lead the Erie shareholders," said Cornelius.

"The right man?" said Sickles. "In a takeover? Aren't you the mightiest railroad man in America? Why not you? Or your son?"

"If you and I get together, we're going to have to keep things quiet where my son's concerned. William didn't think I should oppose them in the gold market." A gust of April rain rattled the window. Troubled at how the interview was going—it felt as if he was being interviewed—Cornelius paused. He considered going into his strategic plans, how necessary it was to monopolize rail traffic into New York if the Central was to last for years, possibly hundreds of years, after his death. But Sickles had already pulled out of him more than he had wanted to say. The small fire in the iron stove popped pleasantly, and the room was spiced by the odors of crushed apples and peppermint. Cornelius sighed, for he needed help. If he was an aged hound who still thrilled to his thousandth rabbit as much as he had to his first, Sickles appeared to be a three-legged hound whose loss had not dulled his teeth or killed his eagerness to hunt. They might be right for each other. Cornelius pushed on. "I think things would work smoother if someone other than myself organized the dissident Erie shareholders."

Sickles leaned forward, bright eyes following Cornelius, and nodded. "I've heard talk that the English shareholders aren't happy with the present officers."

"Not to speak of the Boston lot," said Cornelius, pleased that Sickles was getting his drift. "I myself secretly own nearly ten percent of the Erie. The right man, a fighting leader, could gather proxies, call a board of directors' meeting, and kick those rascals out."

Quickly, easily, Sickles said, "Such a man would have your support."

"All my support."

"To become president of the Erie?" Sickles mused in a smarmy tone.

Cornelius started. Some operator! Not half an hour, after only a little fencing about, and this one expected the top job. Cornelius considered casually drawing the interview to a halt and saying he would think about it, and letting the fellow dangle a few weeks before dropping him. But maybe this eagerness was exactly what he needed.

"President of the Erie," repeated Cornelius, drawing out the moment so he could reflect on the idea. "Yes, I would back that man to be president. However, I would also expect him to cooperate fully with the Central."

"Naturally." For a few moments Sickles was silent as if turning all this over in his mind. Finally he said, "These two have survived a dozen attacks over the past two years."

"Up to now they've led charmed lives," said Cornelius. "But even a cat's lives come to an end."

"How much do you know about me, Commodore?"

"Not too much."

Sickles leaned forward so far that if his single leg slipped he would topple off the straight chair. Again his ripe hairdressing, an odor as sweet as crushed apples, hit Cornelius. His big nose wrinkled. He had never put anything on his hair in his life.

"I've worked as a lawyer," said Sickles, "been a congressman, fought for my country in the War, and now represent my country to the Spanish court. But I've never had any money. I'm nearing fifty. I don't want to enter my old age penniless. I'm a man of tastes, Commodore, and to be honest"—here he laughed nervously, for the first time twisting about as if ill at ease—"I've always indulged them whether I could afford them or not. I came when you wrote because I hoped you might have a proposition that would enable me to get what I need. I think with your backing I can certainly get you what you want."

"You said 'certainly,'" said Cornelius. "You're awful damn sure of yourself."

"I do say 'certainly,'" said Sickles with a cocksure toss of his elegant chin. He leaned back as if snatching the Erie from that damnable Gould were easy. However, the greed and the relish for the scrap itself that shone in his gray eyes—these were the very qualities his son William lacked.

"Good," said Cornelius, eyeing the other warily. "How soon can you start?"

As gracefully as a stork rising on one leg, Sickles rose on his single foot. As the General laughed, Cornelius held his breath: such a strong roar of laughter must knock him over. But Sickles stood rock steady.

"Let's say this morning, right now."

Cornelius decided he liked this one-legged general, despite his bland, slick face, his too-easy smile, and his apple-scented hair. Standing up, his gout stabbed the joint of his right toe, but he scarcely noticed it.

He clasped Sickles's smooth, firm hand and they shook on their deal. In General Sickles, Cornelius decided, Major Gould and Admiral Fisk would finally meet their match.

Part Six

THE
FINAL
BATTLE

*The Erie record of Mr.
Jay Gould should have
sufficed to banish him
from decent business
society. The perpetrators
of these frauds should
have no place among
reputable people.
Whatever they touch, they
defile.*
    —*The New York Times,*
    1877

42

If these informative letters from Mr. Fisk indeed exist in the handscript of one of the gold crisis's perpetrators— and we have every reason to believe they do—the public's best interest, not to speak of the interests of the republic, demand that they be published, and published speedily. A source who has read them states unequivocally that they delineate the precise relationship of the Grant administration to the Great Gold Conspiracy that rocked the republic not many months ago. The presidency is a public trust, and the public interest must be served by those entrusted with it. These letters should be brought forth now so that the involvement—or the lack of it—of the present administration can be settled once and for all.

—New York Herald, 1870

Over the next few months much of the righteous anger directed by newspapers at Jim Fisk and Jay Gould for their role in Black Friday cooled off.

In late spring the congressional hearings in Washington stoked up the fires, leading some editorial writers to call the linkage between the Grant administration and Black Friday "The Crime of the Century," but Gould's calm testimony in Washington proved as inflammatory as paving stones. Still, against his assertion that the economy's subsequent collapse proved him right, other witnesses to the conflagration charged that he had likely been the cause of the market's turmoil. "I had to buy," Jay insisted, "or else to back down and show the white feather."

Like many other ambitious reporters, Eric Harris, the political reporter from the *Tribune* who had dogged the steps of Jim Fisk, Jay Gould, and Annabelle Stokes the closest, suspected that there was a stronger connection between the Grant administration and the Erie than the testimony showed, and that not only had the President's sister-in-law profited from gold trading but that Grant and possibly his wife had, too. If Eric could show that the President had fried his fish in Fisk and Gould's pan, he would indeed have the Story of the Century, not to speak of a shot at an editor's job.

One sunny afternoon in the late spring of 1870, Eric tried to entice Ned Stokes into giving him the notorious letters by plying the man-about-town with madeira at a bar behind the Belmont racetrack.

"I notice that what I gave the *Herald*," said Ned, responding to this morning's scathing editorial, "they put to good use."

Seeing his opening, Eric jumped in. "There are a couple things my editor has to know," he said. "Who were the letters written to and just *exactly* what's in them?"

Ned leaned forward. "Remember, Fisk has a big mouth." Ned twisted his head conspiratorially to the left and right, and then whispered, "I could arrange for the *sale* of the letters."

Oh God, thought Eric. A whale of a story thrashed up to him, opened its mouth, begged to be taken, and all his editor had given him to fish with was the red-white-and-blue cotton worm of patriotism on a bent pin.

"I went over this with Mr. Greeley," said Eric. "He won't *buy* news. Says it's not right. He appeals to your public spirit."

Ned sat back, laughing. "I'm as yankee doodle as Mr. Greeley," said Ned, "but I got to eat, too."

"How much is in them about the President?" Eric asked.

"Let me put it this way," said Ned. "The fat fellow didn't hold much back from his inamorata."

"Greeley just won't pay," said Eric, struggling to stay calm.

"He ought to learn how," Ned said, "or in a few weeks you and him'll be out the biggest story that's hit this town since the War."

Over the next two weeks Eric mingled often with his fellow reporters in the loud, crowded grogshops off Printing House Square. He appeared to join in the hearty, bragging give-and-take, but he kept his mouth shut and his ears open. He learned that these letters of Fisk's were probably written to Josie Mansfield, in whose house Fisk had privately entertained many big-shot financiers and politicians, that Ned Stokes was an uncommonly close friend of Josie's, if not her paramour, that Ned had surely read the correspondence, and that if the price was high enough, these two would sell them, good manners and good taste be damned.

In the middle of May, Eric mounted the short, narrow flight of stairs to the small loft over the city room where the bald head of Horace Greeley was bent over his wobbly desk. He didn't relish what he had to do, prize money out of his editor in chief for a story.

Once over the doorsill, Eric stood quietly and patiently watched his boss. The quire of foolscap, occupying the only clear space on the desk, melted rapidly underneath Greeley's racing steel nib. The air was clotted with the reek of moldy, drying paper. Heaped on the desk were confusions of clippings, old newspapers, battered books, and stories held together by rusting pins. At his left a pair of scissors was catching a hurried nap, while at his right a pastepot and a half-broken box of wafers appeared to have had a rough-and-tumble fight. With a flourish at the bottom of the sheet, Greeley noted where and when the article was to run and looked up.

"I can see it in your face," said Greeley. "You're here because of Stokes. I told you to drop it."

"Sir, we've never had such corruption in an administration."

"What about your Tweed story?" The sun winked off Greeley's gold spectacles in a flash as bright as the old man's intelligence.

"I can't get anybody to talk," said Eric. "There are no loose threads to pull. He's got the city government in his pocket, as well as the state, and he has plenty of friends in Washington." Greeley sighed, took off the spindly spectacles, and rubbed the bridge of his nose.

"President Grant is one of our country's greatest heroes."

"He's the president who allowed that pair of rascals to nearly bankrupt the country," said Eric, referring to Fisk and Gould. Greeley groaned, and his gold spectacles waved Eric off.

"That's claptrap and you know it. Nobody got hurt unless he stuck his foot in the fire. I won't have sensation-mongering around here." The story Eric wanted to uncover, but which was too farfetched to broach to Greeley's down-to-earth questioning, was that Fisk, Gould, Tweed, and Grant all conspired to make millions in the gold market. Having uncovered and published such a story, Eric could found his own newspaper.

"Suppose Grant profited?" asked Eric. "Suppose Grant promised to do something for Fisk and Gould and it's in those letters?" A discussion of the paper's duty to the public always got Greeley's attention. "Don't we have a duty then to get them and expose them to the public?" The argument tugged at Greeley's mild features, and he meditatively tapped the gold spectacles against his battered desk.

"But, Eric—a man's letters to his mistress! Come on!"

"Sir, if we don't, the *Mirror* or the *Sun* will."

"If the *Mirror* wants to buy them, fine and good," said Greeley. "If there's real news in them, we'll copy it the next day and add our voice to the chorus." As if in thought, Greeley leaned back in his squeaky chair and mused. "The danger is that *Fisk* will buy them." Greeley spread apart the earpieces of the spectacles, glared at the lenses, and then shook his head. "Wake up, Eric. That's what this is all about. We're no more than a stalking horse for Stokes in his game against Fisk." Several of Eric's shrewder drinking chums had mouthed precisely this theory.

"That's certainly possible," said Eric. More reflective, Greeley rocked back and forth in his swivel chair.

"The danger is that Fisk will buy the letters back and burn them. The republic will never know whether its war hero is a crook—or not. Grant will never clear his name." He tapped his glasses on the desk. "Find out from Stokes what's actually in them, will you? And find out how much he wants." He sighed and gave a shudder of disgust. "This really is the most sordid business, Eric. I'm not sure we should be in it at all."

"Right, sir," said Eric, backing out the door before his boss changed his mind. "I understand perfectly."

Midnight again in Josie's Turkish bedroom. The windows facing the street were open to admit the May night's fresh breeze, which carried the clean briskness of linden trees, open sea, and the street cleaner's fresh water. Josie sat at her vanity brushing out her long black hair. Ned sat in the room's single armchair, his lean face a drawn slab of gloom and self-pity.

"How dare he cut off my oil sales!" he said. "I'll lose the refinery." He threw himself to his feet and paced around the room.

Josie eyed him in the mirror. "Ned, please. Let's call it off."

"Call it off!" he said, stopping in his tracks. "Now it's all we have. He'll pay. He doesn't know it yet, but he will."

"Ned, no," she said.

To her it was all getting worse. Next week Ned's refinery would be in a receiver's hands. Over the last few months she had sold half her dresses and every piece of jewelry, much of the proceeds going to Ned. And they had nothing to show for it, because now Jim sent the notes that Ned dictated back to her unopened. It was the lack of money that had changed Ned. When he had a few dollars he was fine, but when he was without, he became nasty. She would have burned the letters and ended the whole mess herself, except that three months ago Ned had taken them out of the house "for safekeeping," and now he said they were in a bank vault, the location of which he kept a secret so that "you don't inadvertently spill it to Jim. He's powerful, you know. He might have the vault opened or buy the bank."

"I'm afraid of him," she said. The wind blew the curtains, their lace folds billowing in with the fullness of plump cheeks. Strange, she thought, how often I see Jim's face in them. "He was almost violent twice now."

"You've got that gun I bought you, don't you?" he asked. She nodded. In her drawer, minus the bullets, which she had hidden under the flour sack in the pantry. She put her hand on his arm.

"Ned, let's just go away together." The two of them on a train, leaving the sticky web of New York. Boston would be nice, but Lucy was there. Philadelphia was a sprightly town, but Ned's family was angry with him. She never wanted to see San Francisco again. "Maybe Chicago or New Orleans—even Europe."

"We'll go away," said Ned, "but in time, and in style. We owe it to ourselves. Hang on another couple of weeks. We're not done. By the time the papers finish roasting him, Jim Fisk will beg us to take fifty thousand dollars."

"But, Jay," protested Jim, "there ain't nothing in them damn letters!"

Jay gave Jim a sharp look. "Nothing?"

His coat off, Jim faced Jay in the side aisle of the orchestra section. He felt harried, needing to deal with Jay and with the new production. On the stage behind him, under the glare of a few limelights, the director guided the shirtsleeved actors and actresses through the steps of his newest production, *The Pharaoh's Pyramid*. Because it had actually opened and run for three nights, *Loki and the Nymphs*—despite the glitter of Nully Pieris—had suffered worse losses than *Dido and Aeneas*.

"Not a thing," said Jim, his powerful arms opening in a wide gesture of innocence. "This fribble-frabble is the work of that mangy-feathered peacock Ned Stokes."

"Then clear the air," said Jay. "Give the letters to the newspapers yourself." From under his arm Jay took a copy of *Harper's Weekly*, seemed about to say something, and stuck it back.

"But I don't have copies of them," said Jim. "I writ them on the spur. All they are is notes saying I'm coming to see her, or let's have dinner, or come to the Hoffman House, with the other kissy-kissy women want to read." Behind Jim the actors droned their lines.

"Well, tell the damn newspapers that," said Jay.

Jim sighed a stale hot wind of exasperation. He didn't like the role that Ned and Josie had cast him in, the villain in a drama that Ned had crafted called *The Mistress's Revenge*. Still and all, he couldn't believe that Josie had had much of a hand in it.

"I've told them and told them, but they just think I'm covering up," he said. "How can reporters be so dumb as to think that *I'd* be so dumb as to say in a note that me and Grant was rigging the gold market—and that *I've* just told Mr. Grant to give Mrs. Stokes whatever money he wants to place on gold?"

Jay's mouth pursed as he considered this. "How much does Josie want?"

Jim leaned close to prevent the words from floating up to the actors on stage. "Fifty thousand dollars," he whispered. Jay's response was a rifle shot of urgency.

"Pay her." As frugal as Jay was, the response rattled Jim. True, paying Josie, ending it, would be a welcome relief. He would start a bonfire with those damn letters. But if he bought the letters back he would have to endure a lifetime of Ned's gloating every time he entered the bar at Delmonico's. Ned would lean over to whisper to his chums, who would all gawk at Jim and roar with laughter. Damned if he would give Ned that satisfaction.

"I can't do that to Lucy," said Jim.

"Now's the best time, with Lucy and the children in Europe," said Jay. Jim's family had been in Paris for the past month, ever since stories about the love letters first flared in the papers. Despite his apologetic letters, his wife's in return never mentioned the headlines. In a way that he couldn't fathom, her not mentioning them was worse than if she had excoriated him.

"Don't you see?" said Jim. "There's nothing wicked in them to suppress." His face was twisted by his plea. "It's their *not* being published that makes them so damn scandalous."

"Do something," Jay said. "I've had over a hundred letters from angry shareholders. I've had visits from four outraged directors. Passengers are beginning to ride the Central instead of the Erie." Jay's voice softened. "The Erie could go under because of these damn letters."

"Naw, it won't."

"Yes, I'm telling you."

"It's that damn gold fiasco," said Jim, grimacing and twisting about. "I'm not blaming you, but our luck changed with that." The stiletto of a soprano's high note made Jay glance at the lighted stage. Jim turned and cast his arms wide enough to take in the whole stage. "But things are going to change—we got something here! Egypt!" Pleasure swelled his chest. If they loved this new show and its songs, the public would forget those stupid *billets-doux*. "Everybody loves Egypt! We're going to build both the Sphinx and the Great Pyramid right here onstage. Everybody will come."

"We can't stand any more notoriety," said Jay. "Look at this." He pulled out the magazine, the latest *Harper's Weekly*, and opened it. On the editorial page the caricaturist Thomas Nast had drawn Jim as a combination bloated Puck and preening hog with hat-pin long mustaches, dressed in a loudly checked suit.

"He's really vicious, ain't he?" said Jim in an awed voice. Nast's pen had endowed him with as much evil as the worst slavemaster in *Uncle Tom's Cabin*. "You know that's not who I am."

"Will you do something about those letters?" said Jay, urgency scraping his voice. Jim's shoulders slumped. He wanted to forget the damn letters and let the scandal die a natural death. But with Ned fanning the flames, the sticky mess stayed at a boil.

"All right," said Jim. "I don't know how, but I'll settle it."

Jay walked off, back straight, boot heels clacking on the floorboards. Jim sighed and turned to the stage. Somehow he had to turn the name of this play in which he had been thrust from *The Mistress's Revenge*—in which he starred as the villain—into *The Mistress's Triumph*—in which it came out all right for him in the end.

He threw his shoulders back as he approached the footlights. He wasn't sure how, but he would do it. He had made every play in which he was cast into a *Triumph* of some sort, and it was only a matter of seizing this thing by its horns to make it come out his way.

43

Over the next few weeks, the storm in Manhattan's press over Jim's love letters mounted, but with nothing to print except the promise of something to print, the hard wind began to blow itself out. As the storm abated, Jim felt he had triumphed over the editors, Ned Stokes, and Josie. Another few weeks and it would all be forgotten.

Aiding him was *The Pharaoh's Pyramid*, a success from its first night. Within a week the brassy drive of its music, the saucy, rhyming joy of its songs, and the daring curves of its actresses' yellow tights made it New York's most popular stage show. Every evening a proud Jim stood at the main floor's mobbed back doors as the crowd exited. There he received warm compliments as well as brotherly digs in the ribs from thirsty theatergoers elbowing their way toward Delmonico's, Hanrahan's, and other stylish restaurants for champagne and oysters.

One balmy night in early June, Jim was approached by a tall, distinguished-looking colonel in a uniform of scarlet gabardine and yellow piping. Over cognac and cigars in the tiny bar of the opera house, Colonel Charles H. Braine diffidently offered Jim the post of colonel of the Ninth Regiment of the National Guard. As aromatic blue smoke of their Cuban cigars curled around them, Jim recalled what he knew of the Ninth. He frowned, for the regiment was supposed to be dying. Its membership was below two hundred, and its uniforms, horses, and equipment were in sorry shape. Its marching band was sour, and its morale so low that in bars around town the outfit's own officers groused openly that they would soon disband it.

To prevent this, Colonel Braine manfully offered Jim his own post of colonel of the Ninth because the outfit "desperately needed new blood."

Jim blinked, and even blushed. "Me—Colonel?"

"Colonel, the number one spot," said Braine. Jim laughed. The offer, the aged, perfumed cognac, the evening's wonderful performance, and the blue cigar fumes stimulated him, lifting his spirits.

"I don't know," he said, the pony glass of cognac tiny in his hand. "I'm like one of our Erie locomotives—I always have a tender behind." Jim laughed at his own joke. As the Colonel's stern, earnest face looked puzzled, Jim explained. "I never rode on horseback in my life without having to take my meals off a mantelpiece for three days afterwards."

Colonel Braine said he would demote himself and take the post of lieutenant colonel. "The Ninth is in a slump," he went on, "but with a public figure like you at its head, we might have more glorious days."

Glorious days! Jim's mask of flattered amusement hid more interest than he let show. As Braine droned on, military pictures, enhanced by cigar smoke and cognac, paraded across Jim's mind. He was riding a prancing stallion at the head of a gaily uniformed troop. With a fierce, metallic clatter he drew his cavalry sword and pointed it forward. With the crowd along the sidewalk goggling, his white stallion rose on its hind legs; his troops' brave faces lifted and eagerly charged a fearsome enemy.

Best of all, Jim could present himself to New York's citizens unmasked by the interpretations of newspaper reporters and editorial writers. He would make himself into such a popular commander that the shrill twaddle about love letters and the corruption of Grant would fade away.

Sticking out his hand to cement the bargain, Jim said, "It's a deal."

Within a week Jim signed up one hundred Erie and opera-house employees. It was his long-standing regret that he had never served in the army, for his skills in organization and morale boosting were what made a campaign successful. He promoted his driver Rufus to sergeant, and he sprang for uniforms for the two of them.

One warm morning two weeks after Jim had taken over the regiment, he and Henry Page, leather heels clacking on the marble, were walking arm in arm along Castle Erie's third-floor corridor. While the birdlike Henry was the house manager of the opera house, he was also a newly commissioned captain of the Ninth. Jim was deep in a conversation about ballroom decorations, champagne vintages, the merits of bands, and the menu for a "bang-up midnight supper" for the Ninth's first military ball.

As abruptly as a robin settling on a branch, Jay Gould was at Jim's elbow. "What's this about you as a colonel?" Jay asked. These days Jay was bristling with confidence over having brought off his coup of taking over the Pennsylvania Railroad, in which he not only captured the board but negotiated a contract that opened a route to Chicago for the Erie, breaking the stranglehold the Commodore had about their line's neck. On Jay's face was a half frown, half smile, as if he didn't know whether to disapprove or find Jim's new enthusiasm a joke. After all, in peacetime there was little for the National Guard to do except drill, march in Fourth of July parades, and give fancy balls. Jay went on, "Isn't it enough that you're a railroad magnate, an opera impresario, and admiral of the Sound?"

In his element, Jim guffawed and nudged the meek Henry with his elbow. "If we get attacked again by the Commodore," he bellowed, "we'll not only have a navy but also our own army!"

Jay's smile was as sweet as tart lemonade. "You must be the first person in history to simultaneously hold the titles of colonel and admiral."

Jim cocked his head, for this hadn't struck him. "Do you think so?"

"Am I supposed to address you as Colonel-Admirable Fisk or Great Admirable–Colonel Fisk?"

Jim's booming laugh echoed against the long hallway's marble floor and plaster walls. "We got a position open as major. You want it?"

With a smile as fine as a needle, Jay shook his head.

Jim reared back and said in a loud, amused baritone, "You'll regret it. We're going to have our first outing next week—a moonlit parade down Fifth to the best midnight ball ever held by a New York troop."

"Good," said Jay. "Just be quiet when you pass my house so you don't wake me up."

When General Dan Sickles swung himself into Cornelius Vanderbilt's private New York Central car on the Saturday before the Fourth of July, Cornelius was too irritated with his one-legged general to bother shaking hands.

"You're late," said Cornelius. Outside the conductor signaled the flagman, whose red flag told the engineer to pull out.

"I wanted to make sure the platform was clear," said Sickles, adjusting his blond crutch under the arm of his well-tailored, gray plaid suit. "I wrote you on the need for secrecy." He hobbled over to Cornelius's wide picture window to peer out at the deserted platform. "This isn't a good place to meet."

With a yank, the train lurched forward and almost threw the one-legged general to the thick Chinese carpet. Grasping the backs of the plush armchairs and the surface of the table as handholds, Sickles pulled himself along to drop into the chair across from Cornelius. The rail owner's nose wrinkled. The tang of lemony hair pomade was sharp, a scent more piquant and rich than the odor of crushed apples at their first meeting. Cornelius sourly supposed that the fellow could now afford a better grade of hair grease.

"If I hadn't learned it from the society column of the *Herald*," said Cornelius, "I wouldn't know you were going to Saratoga. I felt maybe giving you a ride to the racetrack might give me a chance to hear of your 'progress.'" From the hard cast of Sickles's smooth features, none of Cornelius's tone was lost on him.

"Why are you attacking me?" asked Sickles. The Central's round-house, dozens of parallel tracks, and the train yard slowly rumbled by.

"Let's see now," said Cornelius, his voice still bristling with anger. "Here's a bill for twenty-two hundred dollars for a stupid trip to England." He snorted and glared at Sickles with mock surprise. "Why not the south of France or Italy? They're even more expensive!" He studied the next bill. "Six hundred and fifty dollars to go to Boston—what did you do, stay there or buy a hotel room?" He picked up the whole batch and shook them in Sickles's face. "Flower bills, wine bills, clothes bills, restaurant bills. Bills from racetracks, from Long Branch, from Washington. I hired a fighter. Someone who would take Gould by the horns and bring me the Erie. If I wanted a high-living gadabout, I'd have hired my namesake son and saved myself his allowance."

Sickles's narrowed eyes acknowledged the insult. "Nobody talks to me this way. If this train weren't moving, I would leave now."

Cornelius waved to the shacks that rapidly flipped by. "Leave anyway."

"Tell me what to do with these first," said Sickles, opening the leather-and-brass dispatch case by the side of his armchair. He drew out a wad of papers, rummaged through them, and handed over one. "This is Bedlow's proxy for 5,000 Erie shares." He flipped on through the stack. "Here's Roxy's for 11,000. Slocum's for 4,000. Fairchild's for 40,000."

"Forty thousand!" exclaimed Cornelius, eyeing the papers in Sickles's fine, manicured hands. "Fairchild owns that much?"

"My 'stupid' trip to England," said Sickles, a cold sneer twisting his voice. "He's only the broker who controls most of the English shareholders."

Cornelius snatched the proxies, staring at each with pop eyes and an open mouth. He tossed the papers on the white tablecloth and struggled out of his coat, scratchy in the July heat.

"We've got almost half of the proxies we need for a real fight!"

Sickles gave him a bland, level gaze and said, "A leaf from Mr. Gould's own copybook—and Fisk and Gould know nothing."

"What!" shouted Cornelius. He thumped the proxies. "These are what keep Gould in office. Surely these fellows have told him."

"Not necessarily," said Sickles. "Not if they were approached the right way. By someone they had come to trust."

"You?"

"A gent who takes them to restaurants and the track, feeds them well, shakes his head over their losses, discusses railroad business with them, and commiserates with their dismay at ever getting a dividend out of our mutual friend Mr. Gould."

Cornelius muttered, "Hell will become an ice cake the day that happens. He keeps every penny for the road."

"The other shareholders see their directors as more interested in gold and opera than railroads."

"Let's call a board meeting and throw the rascals out."

"We—you—are not ready," said Sickles firmly. An empty water glass had crept across the table and was rattling against the carafe. Irritated by the rattle, Cornelius picked up the glass and set it to the side with a smart rap.

"Who are you? One of those Union generals who almost cost Mr. Lincoln the War? Study, study, plan, plan, never attack—as if the war can be won sitting on your bum and thinking?"

Sickles snorted. "You forget that my mentor was General Grant. His rule—marshal overwhelming force and only then crush the enemy with a not-to-be-denied attack. When I move, I will *win*. If I move now, I might *not* win."

Cornelius squirmed about on his chair's velvet cushion. "I'm getting on, Sickles. I don't have many years. I want to beat those pups."

"I've spent three months studying Mr. Gould and Mr. Fisk, and reviewing your previous attempts," said Sickles. His smooth features were veiled, hooded, closed, yet he spoke with passion, as if giving a sermon. "You failed before because you weren't used to such shrewd fighters. Prior to Fisk and Gould, you had poor opponents. You could afford to prepare poorly, use inept strategy, and fumble details." Cornelius crossed his arms as if to ward off the blows from this line of reasoning. "When Gould entered the picture you weren't in readiness. Your intelligence was weak—look how long it took you to learn what Gould was up to in the Cattle Car War. But if you'll hold your horses I'll beat those two."

Few people spoke to Cornelius with such firm bluntness. Yet he ground his teeth and heard the smooth fellow out, for he wanted such a shrewd, tough fighter on his side. "You really think you can beat them?"

"First I'm going to undo his Pennsy deal," said Sickles, "without its appearing that you or I had a hand in it."

"Ah! Keep the Erie bottled up!" said Cornelius with delight. The train had reached top speed. Its wheels clicked along in a merry rhythm, and the broad Hudson sparkled to their left. The other nodded.

"As for the Erie itself," Sickles went on, "I've spent three months getting to know every shareholder who owns more than a thousand shares. I've wined and dined every director. I only mention the Erie in passing, saying that I'm a shareholder who wouldn't mind collecting dividends. I let them tell *me* they're displeased with Gould. I'm careful not to reveal our purpose to those who are delighted with him and think the press is treating him and his fat sidekick unfairly."

Warming to the conversation, Cornelius leaned forward and asked, "What do they say?"

"Not many are happy with his participation in the gold fiasco, nor with Fisk's in that opera house," said Sickles. "Most would like to see them out. But all of them know what a tough fighter Gould is. I wait till the time is ripe to tell my new friend our plan, assure him that I'll do all the dirty work, and ask for his proxy and a pledge of silence. So far it's worked." Sickles's well-tailored shoulders shrugged. "Frankly, clever and bold as he is, and with his hands on the levers and throttle of the Erie, if Gould gets wind of it before we strike, we're lost."

"Lost?" As the speeding train went around a curve the water in the carafe sloshed about. Cornelius braced to keep from sliding off his chair. Sickles leaned forward, as at ease with the motion as a sailor on a ship.

"Every time he's discovered one of your strategies, he's come up with a better plan. When I strike, I want a series of surprises to crowd him so hard *nothing* his clever brain devises will work as a defense."

"Crowd him," mused Cornelius. That was good. "Press him so hard he can't defend himself—yes." This fellow knew strategy. Cornelius would gladly give up one of his legs—preferably the right one attached to his gouty toe—for Sickles's guts, energy, and youth. "It all sounds fine," he stammered, "but it's taking so long."

"Relax, sir," said Sickles, leaning forward yet farther, braced by his blond crutch, to peer out the window. "I'll bring you the Erie, and it'll be in this world, not the next." Using the crutch as a pole, he pulled himself to his foot. Cornelius's back teeth hurt as he craned his head upward.

"Where are you going?"

"We're five miles out of Poughkeepsie," said Sickles, drawing the crutch under his arm. "I'm going to tell the conductor to stop there. I'll take the next train up. The last place in the world I want to be seen is getting out of your private car in Saratoga. Fisk is likely to be there, and I'm sure a lot of men curry favor with him by telling him your movements."

Cornelius smiled at this cunning. "Maybe you're the right man to defeat Gould after all."

Sickles gave him a hard expression of contempt, one that said openly that Cornelius was a fool to have misjudged him. His voice was frigid with sarcasm. "Yes, indeedy, maybe I am."

"Am I rich, Oakey?" demanded Bill Tweed of the Mayor of New York.

"No, not that I can see," said Mayor Oakey Hall, squirming about on his hard seat. Bill, his mentor and good friend, shoved a forkful of lamb shoulder, lavishly spiced with cracked pepper and garlic, into his mouth. It was muggy and hot, the evening of July fifth, and Oakey was dining with Bill in a private room on the second floor of Fraunces Tavern at Broad and Pearl. Making Oakey even hotter, the sporadic popping of firecrackers, left over from the fourth, burst through the open window, while from the street came the irritating mutter of drunks and the grunts of a pig and a goat battling over a foul head of cabbage.

"Hell, no, I'm not rich," said Bill. "I get income from my directorships—them I'm able to hang on to—but I ain't rich, not by a long shot." Over the past few months, Bill, nearing fifty, had suddenly gone to seed. Oakey didn't even like to look directly at his friend's weathered face. Everything about the once-vigorous fellow was bulging, protruding, distending. His paunch had swelled till he must weigh three hundred pounds. His short beard was all gray. Even his nose seemed to have grown, lengthening like a reddish fall squash aching to be plucked. His checkered vest was more encrusted with food than usual, as if he didn't pay attention to where gravy splattered. His massive shoulders slumped, and when he had entered the room, it was with a loose shuffle instead of his former big man's bounding step.

"No, you're not rich," said Oakey. Hoping now to capture the other's attention, he asked, "What are we going to do about the Oranges' parade this year? I thought of banning the march, but it's not only the Orangemen. Every Protestant in the city will resent my caving in to the bastard Irish."

Bill nodded soberly. Once his attention was fixed on it, he didn't have to be told twice how serious the problem was. Every year the Protestant Irish Orangemen marched down Eighth Avenue on July 12 in commemoration of the Battle of the Boyne in 1690, when Protestant King William of Nassau had beat the hell out of Catholic James II of England.

However, as they had for 180 years in Ireland, the city's Catholic Irish hated everything about this celebration of a prominent Catholic's defeat, from the bold orange banners to their own priests' annual bleating about the importance of free assembly and obedience to the law. Oakey wanted to satisfy both sides, the first tactic when you mediated between factions.

And as sure as the Oranges paraded down Eighth Avenue every year, the Catholic Irish riffraff, constitutional right of free assembly or not, demonstrated against them. Last year, 1869, they went further than a mere demonstration; they assaulted the Orange burghers in a pitched battle with sticks, pipes, bricks, and fists that left five dead and scores wounded. That battle brought a simmering feud to a rolling boil, and this year the bubbling mess threatened to surge out of the pot. All through May and June the Greenmen had openly boasted in bars, tenements, and up and down Eighth, Ninth, and Tenth avenues, that if the parade were held this July twelfth, they would exterminate every vile Orangeman.

Thoughtfully Bill Tweed reminded him, "The Orangeman has damn few votes."

A pained expression on his face, the Mayor refilled their glasses with wine. "But if I cancel the parade," he said, "every Protestant in the city will come down on me."

"If the dumb Oranges insist on marching," said Bill, "let them take care of themselves."

"The papers will crucify us," said Oakey. "We won't be—"

Bill smiled in a crafty way. "Have Kelso ban it," he said, referring to the Police Superintendent, "on the grounds that the public has the right to 'quiet enjoyment of the public thoroughfare.' "

"Kelso!" cried Oakey. "A great idea! I can deny having anything to do with it. I knew you'd come up with something. Thanks, Boss!"

During the next week, not only a dozen newspapers but many of the city's clergy demanded to know what had become of the constitutional right of free assembly. The *Tribune* asked whether New York was being dictated to by an Irish mob. The *Mirror* hinted that the Police Superintendent was taking orders from Dublin.

Like a sleeping bear angrily awakening, the entire city was aroused by the issue. Catholic Archbishop John McCloskey did a back-step and bravely defended the Orangemen's right to march. In every bar in which they congregated, the Catholic Irish chortled, bought each other drinks, slapped one another's backs, and boasted that in showing the Orangemen what was what last year they had destroyed the outrage of that damn parade forever.

In Albany the tumult was clearly heard by the dapper Protestant governor, John "Toots" Hoffman, who arrived in New York City on July 10, two days before the Orangemen's parade, to discuss the matter with Bill Tweed and other political allies. He entered Delmonico's, the one across from city hall that was the second home of city politicians, at one o'clock, erect with the knowledge that in his glen plaid he looked every inch a gentleman of culture, suavity, and polish.

The Governor found State Senator Bill Tweed in an upstairs private room, pacing about. A glass was in his hand, and a bottle of whiskey sat amid the crystalware on the white tablecloth. The sight of Bill so bloated and seedy shocked Toots, but he hid it under his smoothest bonhomie.

Bill was agitated, so much so that he wouldn't sit. He paced about the bright room with the shambling, jerky gait of an aging circus bear on a chain. Toots sat at the table. From the waiter who stuck his head in the doorway, he ordered jellied consommé and a river trout, while Bill ordered a large steak and a platter of fried potatoes.

"You can't let 'em ban this parade," said Toots to Bill, poking his soup spoon at Bill's moving form. "We'll get killed in this fall's elections." Still on his feet despite the arrival of the food, Bill hunched over the table and sawed off a hunk of meat. A third of the steak in his hand, Bill stalked off toward the window, tearing off bites as he paced.

"You ever get heartburn?" Bill asked.

The Governor almost laughed, but stifled it. "Sure. Lay down, that's the best thing for it." Toots could commiserate with Bill, for the papers were giving him undeserved hell.

When the articles had begun, they said he was the "engineer" of the corruption in city government, then its "Dictator," and finally the "King." A few now used the jocular term for Bill around Tammany, "the Boss," as if it were another name for the Devil. The theme was the same, almost word for word, in every editorial—"Tweed and Company," his "hirelings and dupes," and his "vast fortune" made through municipal fraud. Under the guise of reform, "the Boss" had deceived honest citizens. Only the most corrupt days of Rome and Venice rivaled present-day New York. How much longer would honest Democrats and other citizens tolerate the "incumbus" of Tweed and his "minions"? The *Times* demanded to know, How did "the Boss," a chairmaker by birth and trade, manage to put away ten million dollars in the course of the last six or seven years, if not by "dishonest means and centralism"?

Bill paused before Toots and thumped his chest with his fist to bring up gas. "I thought maybe water would put the fire out, but it don't help," said Bill. "I got this burning all the time, Toots, night and day. It wakes me several times a night, when I ain't getting up for the fifth time to pee." Bill stopped at the table and gulped down a deep swallow of whiskey.

Toots started to say something about the effect of whiskey on the digestion, but thought better. Bill looked awful, an aging, gray, bloated fly caught in a sticky web spun by the crafty newspapers out of his own many-handed deal making, his inability to say no to almost everybody, and his many enemies' innuendos and lies. Despite the damage it did the party, Toots read with an amused eye such crap as the *Times* printed. If Bill could find an entire $100,000 in one lump, Toots would be the state's most surprised citizen. The real surprises were, one, that the *Times* had so far conducted its campaign of vilification without proof, and, two, that despite the barrage, Bill hadn't replied. The grapevine said that the Tammany leader thought any reply would only dignify the charges. For all of Bill's vaunted political savvy, Toots thought keeping mum was a giant mistake.

"How the hell could you have let Kelso ban the parade?" Toots pressed him again. Bill turned from the window to face him.

"You're thinking nationally?" asked Bill. Toots knew the way Bill had it figured, if he managed to fend off the press's vicious attacks. It was him, Toots, to take Grant's place in '72; Bill himself to the U.S. Senate; and Mayor Oakey Hall on to the Governor's slot. Bill gave him a hard, beady stare.

"We have to think nationally," said Toots. "The Constitution says the Oranges have the right to free assembly. Do you want the opposition hollering in two years that we don't know the meaning of the Constitution?"

From the volcano of Bill's large paunch rose a rumble that erupted in a rolling belch. He fished a matchstick out of his dirty coat's pocket, dropped into the chair across from Toots, and jabbed it at his back teeth.

"The Irish will howl like banshees if we reverse ourselves now."

"Here," said Toots, handing over a slip of paper with the tentative gesture of a waiter offering a cigar to a caged but dangerous bear, "I wrote this coming down on the train. Doesn't it answer all questions and keep the Greens in their place?"

ORDER OF THE GOVERNOR
OF THE SOVEREIGN STATE OF NEW YORK

I hereby give notice that any and all bodies of men desiring to march in peaceable procession in this city today, the 12th instant, will be permitted to do so. They will be protected to the fullest extent possible by the military and police authorities.

Toots went on. "We'll surround the Oranges by the National Guard, all five companies."

Slumped in his chair, Bill closed his eyes and pictured it out loud. "Everybody gets something. The Oranges get to march without getting hurt. The Greens get to protest, which they love. The clergy and papers are satisfied that democracy is safe, and no voter's been denied his rights. I like it." He opened his bloodshot eyes and beamed at his dapper ally. "Toots, you *are* ready for national office. I believe you have the seeds of greatness in you." Toots squirmed as awkwardly as a schoolboy basking in a teacher's unexpectedly warm praise.

"Thanks, Bill. I'll write out the orders for those National Guard units tonight."

44

*It is almost impossible to estimate the
number of dresses a very fashionable
woman will have. Most women in
society can afford to dress as it pleases
them, since they have unlimited
amounts of money at their disposal.
Among females dress is the principal
part of society. What would Madam
Mountain be without her laces and
diamonds, or Madam Blanche without
her silks and satins? Simply
commonplace old women, past their
prime, destined to be wall-flowers.*

—Anonymous New York society
  critic, 1872

"Oh, God, let it be a customer,"
prayed Annabelle Stokes as the front bell of her Fifth Avenue dress
shop tinkled.

She came around the counter with her most welcoming smile.
Since Black Friday last year she had lost weight, and the lack of flesh
in her bust and hips wasn't flattering. Despite her youth, wrinkles—
small but definite—appeared around her eyes and mouth. Her new
thinness made her neck too long and her eyes a little too big. Last
year she had worn her glossy black hair loose; this year in her role
as a shopkeeper she wore it parted in the center and pulled back
severely into a tight bun at the nape of her neck.

Annabelle's spirits drooped, for it looked as if her visitor was
another person selling newspaper space. The young woman's face

was unfashionably tanned as if she spent hours trooping from shop to shop without the protection of a bonnet or parasol. Unlike Annabelle, she wasn't wearing a hoop under her skirt, without which most ladies would not be seen on the street. Her expression was open and eager, too, not closed and wary like a browsing customer's.

"Yes," said Annabelle, "how may I help you?" Except for newspaper-space salesmen, a city health inspector who had hinted about for a bribe, and two lace salesmen come to collect overdue invoices, Annabelle had not had a visitor in her dress shop, much less a cash customer, all week. She was well aware how much ladies liked to finger items and browse through fancy shops, even if they didn't buy, and hers was on Fifth Avenue near Thirty-sixth, in the midst of fashionable town houses and other smart shops. Her shop was being avoided.

"I'm Phoebe Cary," said the woman, the triangular slant of whose head reminded Annabelle of a fox's. Annabelle studied her visitor with a professional eye. Probably a widow selling lace. "You're in business for yourself," went on the visitor, her smile tentative. "I heard about your new shop yesterday—up the street, but it was so late—I came to see if you wanted to join Sorosis. I'm on the nominating committee, and we need more members." Annabelle frowned, unsure what the woman was selling but certain that she couldn't afford it. Though initially financed by her gold profits and cash from Jay, the shop was now nearly broke.

"I'm afraid not," she said.

"Oh, you think we're political or something!" said Phoebe, edging near Annabelle. "It's nothing like that. It's social. No, not that, either. We have speakers on medical subjects, household, legal, scientific, literary, artistic—anything in fact except politics. I said that when we started, *no politics*. Whenever we get a speaker who brings up the suffragette movement—why, we simply shout her down. Won't have it, I tell you, and anybody who says we do is a liar." Annabelle was confused and her face said so.

"But you don't know what I'm talking about, do you?" Phoebe went on, her fingers lightly touching Annabelle's long cotton sleeve. "I'm talking about Sorosis, the women's club that meets at Delmonico's." A bell rang faintly in Annabelle's memory, but she couldn't place the name.

"What would I have heard?" Annabelle asked. It was ten months since Black Friday, and for the past six months she hadn't paid much attention to anything but her new dress shop, the way any owner did when the new business was all outgo. From her gold profits she had paid back Papa much of the money that Ned had cheated him of, and she bought back the huge mortgage on her house.

Her four-month-old dress shop was everything she wanted it to be: a wide front window with three elegantly draped dummies, walls papered and painted in light, bright yellows and whites, and bolts of maline, silk, crenoline, tulle, and lace hidden behind modest cabinet doors. All that was missing were customers. She supposed they kept away because it was widely rumored that she had engaged in an affair with Jim Fisk and served as the conduit for Ulysses to invest in gold. A month ago, despite Jay's investment in the shop, she had been forced to make a small new mortgage against her house to keep the shop open—an ominous sign.

"You heard about the Dickens dinner put on by the Press Club?" asked Phoebe. Annabelle's dim memory stirred again.

"The Press Club held a dinner," said Annabelle. "Women weren't invited—or didn't go. There was some flap over it."

"Yes, yes," said Phoebe, her eyes sparkling. "That's when we started. Jennie June Croly's husband is editor—actually editor *in chief*—of the *World*, and she writes for the paper, too, not because she's his wife, but because she's good, you know?" Although the mention of a newspaper made her stiffen, Annabelle nodded.

"Through her husband she applied to go to the dinner," Phoebe rushed on, breathlessly, heedlessly. "The committee didn't answer. I applied, too—I write books, and my husband works for *Harper's Weekly*—children's books, maybe you've head of Sophie Alice Lanford, who is the little girl in my stories?" Annabelle shook her head.

"Then you don't have children—they all know about her," said Phoebe, her rush of words continuing. "The committee didn't answer either of us, as if our being in the same room with Mr. Dickens would be inviting field mules to hear the great man. A few other ladies applied, and still nothing happened. Then I met Mr. Greeley at a St. Paul's picnic—that's Horace Greeley, the editor of the *Tribune* and a wonderful man—and he said he wouldn't preside over the dinner unless the Press Club committee treated us fairly. Of course, you know how embarrassing it would have been if *he* wasn't on the dais. Three days before the dinner the committee sent Jennie Croly and me word that if enough of us would apply, we could come. They were going to put us at special tables—like children at a Christmas dinner—just outside the doors of the hall. Not quite in, you see, but not quite out, either. So Jennie said we wouldn't go under those circumstances; we would 'tip over the teapot' and have our own luncheon two days later. Which we did. We invited Mr. Dickens, but he's a man, you know, and he found it convenient to be elsewhere while we were having our meeting."

The picture Phoebe Cary described had a bracing effect on Annabelle. The gumption of these women, their confidence, against male powers-that-be contrasted vividly with her own sodden, beaten-down spirits. Sometimes for weeks she didn't see Jay, so fearful was he of discovery by the press. Over the past month she had become afraid, too, sometimes needing a tablespoon of laudanum to enable her to sleep. If her dress shop stumbled on for another two or three months as it had over the past four, she would have to close it. All the money she had earned on gold would have been spent, and she would be back where she had been before she walked into Jay Gould's bedroom office in New Jersey—on the verge of bankruptcy.

She was even more strongly affected, however, by the mention of *Harper's Weekly*, the *World*, and the *Tribune*. During her testimony at the two congressional hearings in Washington this spring, reporters had badgered her with scores of insulting questions. It was best for her and Jay's sakes to keep away from the press. Best to push this fast-talking, breathy little creature who was so well connected to the papers right out the door.

"Thank you for the interest," said Annabelle in a voice she forced herself not to make cold, "but I don't have time for more social activities."

"But you own your own business!" said Phoebe, undaunted. Annabelle grimaced. Her shop was more like a leaky skiff on the rough Atlantic than the seaworthy craft this writer made it sound like. "You're exactly the type that enjoys Sorosis."

"Thank you, but no."

Phoebe gave her an artful look of coy understanding. "Maybe there's someone you think it will displease."

Annabelle lied. "I have too much work. I'm really quite busy." The summer stillness of the shop mocked her.

"You're not busy now," said Phoebe.

"Hardly."

"Then come have lunch and we'll talk."

To Annabelle's surprise, her hands were trembling. For months she had been alone with her shop except for lace and cloth salesmen, a few customers, and trips to the concierges of the grand hotels who condescended, in return for tips, to send her out-of-town ladies requiring an expert dressmaker. There was something soothing about Phoebe's chatter, a part of life that Annabelle missed. With her friend Louise away at the seashore for the summer, she could hardly remember when she had eaten a meal with someone other than the children and Bridget. The few midnight visits with Jay were all whispers in the dark, even more furtive and desperate than before the crash. While Phoebe's chatter revealed that she herself was in some ways a child, at least she promised better company than Annabelle had enjoyed in months.

"You're wavering," said Phoebe with a big grin. "I can see it."

Annabelle smiled. "Lunch, then," she said. "Where shall we go?"

"Why don't we go to Del's?"

"*Del's?* We can't go there." As the finest restaurants in New York, the four Delmonicos didn't serve women without a male escort, particularly the one nearby at Twenty-third, which catered to the society crowd.

"Didn't I tell you?" said Phoebe. "That's where Sorosis meets. I'm on the luncheon committee. I make the arrangements myself with Lorenzo Delmonico. He won't be stuffy if you and I nip in for a little bite."

The world was changing. Annabelle hadn't been in the hushed, churchlike atmosphere of the uptown Delmonico's since—since Ned, really. Three years ago. She pictured fresh flowers sprouting from starched linen, gleaming plates, and a smooth respectful waiter pampering her. A rigid part of her relaxed. She would go. If it meant her last two dollars, today she would have a lunch and a chat she fully enjoyed.

The two women set off south along Fifth Avenue, Annabelle under a lacy parasol, Phoebe under a summer bonnet. The heat, rising up from the pavement under Annabelle's skirt, roasted her legs. Pointing out the green ribbons fluttering on so many coachmen's top hats and upper arms, Phoebe chattered on about the Orangemen's parade tomorrow and the possible riots by the Catholic Irish. As wilted and thirsty as a cut flower, Annabelle arrived at Twenty-third Street eager for Delmonico's magical resuscitation.

The restaurant was four dignified stories. Twenty stone steps led up to the arched entrance, before which stood two jowly doormen in long forest-green coats, white gloves, and black-and-white-striped vests, as somber and aristocratic as a king's footmen. Annabelle hesitated at the bottom of the steps, the hot paving stones burning her feet. Along the curb a dozen private carriages, their silver trim elegant against black paint, rested with the air of giant awkward insects taking a noontime snooze. In knots under the leafy ailanthus trees, the carriages' ragged, hunkered drivers, their hands cupping cigar butts, talked in soft mutters. As she and Phoebe paused, the red-eyed drivers gave them the surreptitious, inquiring glances that unaccompanied women could expect.

Inside, the vestibule was dim and cool. A tall white-jacketed waiter, his face as grave as a priest's, escorted them into the cathedrallike room. As quiet and stately as a convocation of bishops, a hundred of the richest, the most powerful, and the most aristocratic of the city sat over the best lunch Manhattan could provide. With sober gallantry the waiter sat them at a table set for four. Bearing water and bread, a blond, German-looking boy with the face of an angel politely inquired, "Three or four, madame?"

"Two," said Phoebe, turning back to finish her anecdote about the man who had tried hard to join Sorosis but who had been refused entry, to the great hilarity of other members of his sex. "*They* can have a club for horses, medicine, politics, eating, drinking, books— anything—" The tall waiter with the minister's face interrupted her.

"Excuse me, madam. Will anyone else be coming?"

"No," said Phoebe, "only the two of us." The eyes of Annabelle's new friend glittered strangely. Annabelle wondered if this was the first time that Phoebe had eaten here by herself, without a male escort.

With an expression as awkward as a priest's refusing a supplicant communion, the waiter glanced around the room before he whispered, "I can't do it. I can't serve you." Their hands unmoving on their punch glasses, two elderly businessmen at a nearby table were staring.

Phoebe lifted her eyebrows and gave Annabelle a smile that said, "What silliness!" As if not to embarrass the waiter, Phoebe whispered to him, "Ask Lorenzo Delmonico to come over." Annabelle opened her mouth to say they should leave, but Phoebe silenced her with a stare and a firm pat on the back of her hand.

Lorenzo Delmonico arrived, dressed in a black morning coat and gray silk vest that a lord might wear to marry off his daughter. His face wore the humor and dignity of a well-entrenched archbishop.

"Mrs. Cary," he said in a low, hearty bass to Phoebe. "What a pleasure! But the club meeting isn't for two weeks."

"My friend and I here just want a quick bite of luncheon," said Phoebe, sitting straight and assuming a simple dignity that Annabelle had not yet seen.

"Hello, Mrs. Stokes," said Lorenzo with a courtly bow in her direction. "It's been too long since you brightened our room." Annabelle inclined her head and briefly lowered her eyes. Phoebe didn't seem to take note of the name. "I'm afraid not," said Lorenzo to Phoebe with an amused smile and a firm shake of his head. "It's not that *I* care so much, and I certainly know both you ladies, but we have our rules. It would displease many of our customers." Indeed his customers, mostly male but some ladies, too, were peering at them with frowns.

"Well, I don't think it's right," said Phoebe, her dignity breaking down. In her voice was injury, the whine of a toddler, and a little girl's petulance. "I come here all the time with Phillip. I've eaten in this room since I was a little girl. You brought me a chocolate bear when I was eight years old, Lorenzo—remember? I had my coming-out party upstairs, and it was I who arranged for Sorosis to eat here. We certainly don't have a male escort for it." This assault made Lorenzo's smile grim and tentative. His bass was a whisper.

"I can't."

Annabelle put her hand on Phoebe's sleeve. "We can eat elsewhere."

"I'm sorry," said Phoebe, turning to her. "I haven't been thinking. Have I embarrassed you?"

"I'm not embarrassed," said Annabelle, realizing with surprise that she wasn't. "No need for a fuss. All I want is a decent meal." That was true. She wanted a quiet, well-served lunch, a meal like the gray-faced pig a table away was having, pan-fried oysters in milk and butter with crusty bread. His large spoon suspended, wattles lifted, Gray Pig stared over with an outraged sneer that they had dared to mar his noontime pleasure.

"I'm hungry," declared Phoebe, her shrill, childlike tone carrying to every paneled corner. "I don't know where else we can get in, if I can't get in a place where I'm known." For a few moments the three were frozen in a silent impasse.

"Just because a man's not with us?" asked Annabelle.

Lorenzo nodded gravely.

"It's not right," Phoebe loudly complained to Annabelle. "They know who we are. It's not as if we're ladies of the evening."

Every diner was watching now. Annabelle wanted to become small, slide under the table, and crawl, unseen, back out into the noon sun. Being stared at here was the last thing she needed. It brought up too many of this crowd's memories of her role in the gold crash, not to speak of gossip about what she was doing now, which would produce remarks that no lady should be "caught dead" patronizing a shop run by "such a scandalous creature." The smart thing to do was slink out, buy bread and cheese, and have a rough tea in her shop.

Lorenzo cocked his head askance. They could sit here and demand service like suffragettes, of course; yet while Lorenzo wouldn't toss ladies out bodily, he might order the waiters not to serve them. He was well known for not serving those who didn't pay their monthly bills promptly.

"I'll get us an escort," said Annabelle, giving Phoebe's arm a hard squeeze. "Don't move."

Annabelle rose and walked through the dining room, past the curious stares of half the diners, and out into the July blaze of sunlight. From the top step she surveyed the street. Blinded by the fierce sun, she marched down the gritty steps and up to the first knot of filthy, ragged coachmen. She asked if one of them would like to eat inside. The drivers, unwashed and red-eyed, many with smudged green ribbons on their shirts and hats, glanced at each other in silent, bewhiskered astonishment.

"Go in there to eat?" asked one dirty fellow in his midthirties.

"Yes, they tell me I can't eat without a man at my table."

"Ain't never been farther than the front hall," he said. His flinty gray eyes gazed upward at the jowly, aristocratic doormen in their black-and-white-striped vests. Wistfully he added, "I am hungry."

"I'll pay for the lunch," she said.

"Here's your chance!" shouted his mate, who clapped the tall, thin driver on the back. The others egged him on.

She offered her clean cotton sleeve to his filthy hand. "Come on."

To the hoarse cheers of the other drivers, Annabelle and the grinning driver marched up the stairs. Through the cool vestibule, into the main dining room. The august diners stared at her as she entered, and Lorenzo still hovered over their rear table like a lordly question mark. Phoebe had half pulled back from the table as if to leave. The diners' heads swiveled in unison to watch Annabelle glide across the restaurant, the driver on her arm.

With a flourish, she seated him in the chair between hers and Phoebe's. Wanting to rush the moment so that they didn't get into an argument, in a strong, clear alto that carried to every corner of the room, Annabelle gave Lorenzo their order: "A pan roast for three, Mr. Delmonico." Across the restaurant came laughter and a few scattered rounds of applause. A politician of the first rank, and appearing a little amused by his own defeat, the magisterial owner grinned and gave a small bow before padding off.

Phoebe grabbed Annabelle's arm and gushed, "That was wonderful!"

On their way back to Annabelle's dress shop, Phoebe bubbled with enthusiasm, replaying the episode over and over. Suddenly she asked, "What was it Lorenzo called you?"

Annabelle's heart thumped. "When?"

"Some other name."

"Stokes," Annabelle said feebly. "It was my married name."

"Annabelle—Stokes!" Phoebe's hand flew to her mouth. "That's where I heard it before—in the paper!"

The early afternoon glare of the July sun was so strong that it had melted away every shadow on the gray pavement, and yet a cold shiver passed over Annabelle.

"Now you know why I can't join your club," Annabelle whispered.

Phoebe looked bewildered. "No, no, more than ever, you must join," Phoebe said. "You're brave. I read the testimony. You didn't do anything wrong. A woman with your pluck is exactly the sort of person we need." There was no wind in Annabelle's sails. Despite Phoebe's youthful enthusiasm, this could go nowhere.

"Phoebe, I would love to join." She placed her fingers on Phoebe's sleeve, where they trembled slightly. "Since the gold crash I've been lonely. Having lunch with you—I—I didn't mean to take advantage of your ignorance to embarrass you. I only wanted a bit of normal company—for a change. I'm a pariah, no one wants to be with me. I can't even get work for my dress shop. You've been sweet. Let's forget it now, and if my presence today has caused you any embarrassment, I apologize."

"Embarrassment?" said Phoebe, her pointed features shocked and bewildered. "No! You'd be perfect for the club."

"I won't be accepted," Annabelle said.

"After today? Suppose we let the members vote on it."

"Fine," Annabelle answered, but no sooner was the word past her lips than she regretted targeting herself for another rejection. Yet standing here in the white glare of the July sun, she couldn't spoil Phoebe's childlike grin of triumph by taking it back.

45

*Processions of all kinds and
nationalities are allowed on the streets,
and to forbid only one, and that because
it is* Protestant, *is an insult to every
American citizen.*

—*The New York Times* on the
Orange Day Parade, 1870

"Charles!" said Jim from the door
of his suite at the Hoffman House. "What is it?"

Colonel Charles Braine, his face contorted by anger, stepped inside. "Stupid, stupid orders!" he said, waving a paper. "We're expected to guard this damn-fool promenade tomorrow. Ten thousand drunken Irish in the streets are so many lit sticks of dynamite!"

"The day New York City allows a mob to dictate to her," said Jim gravely, echoing the views he had heard many times this past week, "is the day her prosperity and greatness ends."

Jim ordered up supper. Excited, he considered cracking a bottle of champagne, but sparkling wine didn't seem soldierly. Rufus opened a bottle of red and set the table by the window with a lace cloth and Jim's best silver.

"I hate to take the men out," said Charles, frowning. "They're not ready. Knowing how to wield a heavy stick or a sword will be more useful than knowing how to pencil in a dance program."

Jim's blue eyes narrowed. "Despite so many troops—you think there'll be trouble?"

"Why not prepare for it?"

They joined the other units at ten o'clock that night. The Forty-first Street Armory was a vast cathedral space, torch-lit, in which hundreds of uniformed, nervous civilians milled about with their edgy Sunday horses. Shouts and whinnies competed with each other. The cool night air was shot with the reek of burning kerosene, cleaning oil, cigars, gunpowder, horses, fear, and excitement. Jim chatted with the troops, boosting their spirits.

Along with the first sunlight of Orange Day, rumors as black and raucous as crows flapped into the armory. Jim became alarmed, although he hid his shakiness beneath a soldierly mien. One rumor screeched that a mob had stormed the armory on Avenue A, intent on seizing its muskets and powder, and was only turned back by the stoutest clubbing from the police. An hour later another shrieked that four hundred Irish stevedores from piers nine through thirty-four had stalked off the job. Jim heard that on Spring Street an orange-clad dummy had been hanged in front of Owen Finney's saloon. When he worriedly repeated these to Charles, the latter told him to pay no attention, that troop movements were always accompanied by groundless rumors.

Late that morning, as they were mounting, Charles asked Jim to address the troops. "The new fellows are from the opera house and the Erie," said Charles. "It could be rough today, and a word from you may stiffen them up."

Thoughts of the rousing speech that would buck up the fellows drove away the worries flapping in Jim's head. "I'd be happy to bully up the boys," he said. "They're probably as nervous as I am."

Jim and Charles sat on their horses before the Ninth's five hundred soldiers, who like their senior officers had turned out in their smart scarlet-and-yellow uniforms. Half had arms, although many were muskets not fired since the Revolution nearly a hundred years ago. The band members carried only their musical instruments. Taking turns, Jim and Charles told them that stones and tools might be thrown at them, but that they were expected to stand firm. They weren't to fire their rifles unless their senior officers ordered them to. The soldiers—many of whom had done no more military duty than blowing a French horn in a parade or carrying a spear behind an opera star's soprano—glanced uneasily at their chums.

"The Ninth will show itself today as the finest unit in the city!" concluded Jim, and he thrust his shiny sword over his head. The applause that followed, swallowed by the clanking of other units moving out, died as quickly as it would have in a church.

They emerged from the vast armory near noon. Although the sky was half covered by low clouds, the July sun shone through, white and savage with tropical heat, and the midday air was sweltering. At first there were few pedestrians about, but as Jim and his men neared Thirty-third Street, many ragged men in workclothes passed, sporting bright green ribbons, ties, armbands, and hats, and carrying bottles and sticks.

By the time the troop reached Lamartine Hall at Eighth and Twenty-ninth, the six-story building that contained the Orangemen's clubhouse, sweat had made large dark circles under the arms of Jim's scarlet tunic. The parade was scheduled to begin at two o'clock, but by two-thirty, instead of the thousand marchers that the police expected, less than a hundred Orangemen had gathered to exercise their constitutional right of assembly.

Jim was glad to see J. J. Kelso, the thick, florid, no-nonsense police superintendent with a curly shock of red hair, arrive on his brown gelding and organize the procession. Kelso put a force of 250 foot policemen in front, and he followed them with the crack Seventh Regiment, bayonets fixed, and then the Orangemen. The apprehensive marchers were flanked on the left by the Eighty-fourth, and on the right by the Twenty-second and the Sixth regiments. The Ninth, Jim's unit, was ordered behind the Orangemen. Behind Jim's troops, another battalion of 250 policemen closed the rear. Jim felt relieved. Three thousand soldiers and policemen surrounded 100 marchers, 30 protectors for each Orangeman. Surely, thought Jim, with so many protectors even Irishmen wouldn't start trouble.

With Jim and Charles at the head of the Ninth, the parade, nearly an hour late, finally set out. Jim leaned over to Charles and shouted, "This is the reverse of a parade. We're hiding the marchers instead of showing them off!"

Charles smiled weakly, not taking his blue eyes off the shabby, four-story tenements that lined Eighth Avenue. Jim's eyes apprehensively followed his. In the windows and on the roofs were perched ragged, screaming creatures wearing green, more like frenzied beasts than people. In an effort to calm them, Jim forced a smile and waved cheerily. Overhead the sun was a white, angry fire. He was glad when, from the bowels of the procession, the Ninth's band struck up the jaunty tune "The Teton Donkey Walk."

At the corner of Twenty-seventh Street, a group of desperate-looking Irish fellows were assembled on a wooden shed that projected over the sidewalk. Warned by the Seventh's commander to go away, they hesitated. The soldiers leveled their rifles at them. Uttering defiant threats, the youths hurried down and disappeared. Jim grinned at Charles and winked. The soldiers were carrying the day! He hoped the newspaper reporters had seen that. In the next block several tomatoes arced toward the Ninth from an upstairs window. Jim ducked. One splattered against the head of the foot soldier in front of Jim, who turned out to be Captain Henry Page, the birdlike manager of the opera house. Jim suppressed a grin as Henry picked tomato out of his ear. In the next block more garbage rained down. Cursing the dumb Irish, Jim plucked rotten stumps of cabbage, damp tea leaves, and greenish driblets of putrid meat off his uniform's scarlet field.

A decade of heat crawled by over the next hour. Straining forward as much as he could from his perch on Claremont, Jim couldn't see what the prow of the massive parade encountered that made it stop and go in cantankerous, maddeningly slow jerks. This was a march through Hell. Although an amused grin was plastered on his face, he only wanted this horrible afternoon over. There were forty more blocks to go.

They passed Twenty-fifth Street, where the Irish on the roofs hurled down dismantled chimney bricks. Fearing he would be hit on the back of the head, Jim twisted about, dodging and keeping an eye on the rooftops on both sides of the street. A whole brick smashed into the head of the red-uniformed trooper in front of Henry Page, and the fellow collapsed as abruptly as an ox felled by a butcher's sledgehammer.

Charles shouted, "Keep 'em moving!" and ordered the trooper carried.

Gripping the reins tightly, Jim urged his nervous stallion through the marching soldiers to the injured trooper, who was being carried by Henry Page and three other soldiers. His unshaven face was thrown back, mouth gaping, and his red-rimmed, open eyes stared upward at the rude, white sun. Henry's pale face turned up. "Jim, he's dead!"

Dead! A wave of numbness crashed across Jim's sweaty body. *No!* Dead—from a stupid parade? Sick and nauseous, he wanted to buck up the men, and opened his mouth to say something, but nothing came out. Whiter and with stronger, more vicious heat, the sun's fire battered his skull.

Nearby a loud shot rang out, and Jim struggled to hold Claremont still. By the solid crack of the echo the rifle was powerful, maybe a Sharps buffalo gun. A soldier of the Eighty-fourth moaned and crumpled. Along with the soldiers of the Ninth, Jim looked up. A cloud of white gunsmoke drifted from the third-story window of the dilapidated tenement to their right. Word of the Ninth's death was passing through the ranks. The Eighty-fourth was in no mood to take chances, and fifty of its soldiers thrust their rifles and muskets toward the window, ready for the order to fire. Abruptly one gun went off, and then without orders, an unexpected volley rolled down the line of the Sixth, Ninth, and Eighty-fourth regiments. Jim and the other officers twisted about in their saddles, the barrage taking them by surprise.

Like an echo, a rattle of gunfire answered them from several houses up the street. Charles, along with the other officers, shouted, "Cease fire! Cease fire!" More weakly, Jim copied this cry.

The street was full of clouds of smoke, which slowly cleared to reveal confusion running wild. Screaming in terror, men, women, and children fled in every direction, the strong trampling the weak. Eleven bodies lay stretched on the western sidewalk, some piled across each other. Unsure what to do, Jim twisted in his saddle and stared. Scarlet-tunicked soldiers, as if wounded, clutched their shoulders and stomachs and sank to their knees. As if expecting another attack, the troops didn't stoop to help their mates but reloaded their muskets and rifles. A man streaming with blood crawled painfully up a doorstep, while on both sides of the street staggered crouched bleeding forms. Jim goggled speechless as one, then three, four of his troops slid to the cobbles. He was looking in the direction of Henry Page, who was gaping upward at the fired-upon house, when the top of Henry's skull exploded, splattering bits of bone, gristle, and blood over Jim's leg and his horse's sweaty gray side.

"Henry!" Jim screamed, and jumped off his horse.

He dropped to his knees and bent to his friend. Above Henry's mustache, his head was a horror of insane, malevolent snakes writhing in a bubbling swamp of blood.

Jim leaned back on his haunches. He was in a forest of red trousers. The bitter stench of burnt gunpowder. His stomach was rebelling. Gray cobblestones cut into his knees. With a loud thump, another scarlet soldier fell two yards away, a writhing animal clutching its stomach, groaning and twisting in pain. Jim hobbled over on his knees. With horror he recognized the soldier's rough red face—Sergeant Rufus Jones.

"Rufus!" Jim shook him by the arm, but his friend and driver was lost in a strained grimace, his eyes crazed with pain and shock. Out of a hole in the stomach of his scarlet tunic spread a yet darker red stain. "No!" shouted Jim, knowing from the War how serious were stomach wounds. "Doctor! Got to get you a doctor!"

Jim sat back amid the forest of shifting legs. He opened his mouth and shouted, but nothing came out. No, not Rufus and Henry! The play would soon be over—they would stand up and take bows before thunderous applause. No, Henry was dead—really dead—and Rufus badly hit. But when you dreamed awful nightmares, you always woke up.

He pulled himself to his feet, as wobbly as a new wren. Soldiers from the Ninth and the Eighty-fourth dashed about in a frenzy. Rifles were pointed in the air and fired. As if from a great distance came screams and yells, squealing and flapping. He turned, and a mass of flesh, hair, and skirt slammed against him, knocking him backward. As he hit the ground something twisted and snapped. He sat there, hands on the cobbles for support, numb and dazed, breathing hard, sweat pouring off his face. He tried to stand, but pain in his ankle stabbed him and he sat back.

"My ankle!" he cried. "Nurse! Nurse! It's broken!"

Charles was suddenly leaning over him. "What's wrong?"

"Broke my ankle," said Jim. "My God, Charles—war! Awful! Rufus—Henry!"

"Let's get you a doctor," said Charles. "Parade's pulling out."

"Pulling out!"

"No good staying here," said Braine. He pointed at a doctor's shingle on the house to the right. "We'll leave you with the doctor."

On horseback, captains, lieutenants, and majors dashed up and down alongside the troops and shouted the scattered infantry back into ranks. Soldiers lined up. Four fellows from Company E picked up Jim in a sitting carry.

"Rufus!" he shouted and pointed. "Bring Rufus!"

"Jim!" said Rufus weakly.

"Rufus!"

Under Charles's order to hurry, Rufus was picked up by three scarlet tunics, his head dangling as loose as a piece of cheese on a string. He and Jim were carried into the yard and up the dark, narrow stairs of the house.

The doctor's small, low-ceilinged surgery was cool and calm after the heat and angry turmoil of the street.

Jim was deposited in a chair and Rufus in the middle of a heap of flies on a grime-covered wooden table. Amid the whine of angry insects, the clump of boots, and the jingle of spurs, the soldiers left.

The smiling, gray-faced doctor turned to Jim and rubbed his long fingers as if impatient to work. "Where are you hit, sir?"

"Not me, him. Take care of him first."

"He's a sergeant. Officers first."

"Do him, damn it!"

The lanky doctor threw up his hands in exasperation. With a rusty pair of tailor's scissors he cut open Rufus's red coat. Rufus's stomach was soaked with bright red blood. His pale chest heaved violently. His rapid animal groans came faster. "Bullet in there," the doctor said.

He reached behind him and picked up a blood-encrusted knife from a filthy tray. Quickly he cut a slit eight inches long across Rufus's stomach. He ripped back the skin with his left hand. He savagely stuck in the fingers of the other. This invasion made Rufus stir only a little, but with gale force it drove Jim against the surgery wall. For a moment the doctor's gray features strained in concentration, then brightened. His bloody fingers emerged from the hole. His face blossomed into a smile. Jim peered forward, eager for the good news. While his left hand held open the wound, the fingers of the doctor's right hand triumphantly flaunted a black bullet.

"The offending party," said the grinning doctor.

Jim shouted, "Rufus! It's out!"

Rufus's face was glazed with sweat, and a pale, ugly cast clouded his rugged country skin. Jim hobbled to the table.

"Rufus, talk to me!" Jim thrust his ear to Rufus's lips.

The doctor pushed Jim back and bent to Rufus's face. "I'm afraid the patient is dead, sir."

Jim leaned back against the wall and closed his eyes. A kaleidoscope assaulted him, dazzling lights, mad colors, bubbling blood. Frenzied shouts, a skittish horse under him, and the hellish pain of his ankle. The coppery, suffocating stench of blood, writhing scarlet snakes, and Rufus's heaving chest. The doctor's hands fumbled with Jim's leg. He felt his boot being cut away.

"It's not broken, sir," said the doctor in a cheerful voice. "Just dislocated. Hold still." A spasm of intense pain shot through the length of his leg. Jim roared. The doctor's face beamed.

"All done!" the doctor said. "A bandage, a cane, and good as new in a couple weeks." A six-inch-wide strip of dirty cotton shirt was wound around Jim's foot, and a dirty cane appeared. "There! Five dollars for you, twenty for the operation, and you're all set to fight again."

Dazed, Jim pulled out his wallet, but the doctor had to extract the money. Using the cane, he hobbled to the window. In the street, soldiers in the red-and-yellow uniforms of the Ninth stood guard over the dead and wounded. Good, he thought, I'll join them and get them to come for Rufus.

At that moment a group of Irish protestors, milling around the doctor's front gate, spotted Jim. The largest, a hulking lout, pointed up and shouted, "There's the piggy colonel! Kill the villain! Hang him!"

Startled, Jim stepped back, away from the window. Ten or twelve Irish—all large, rough-looking galoots, unshaven, their clothes a collection of rags—surged through the gate, cutting off Jim's way to his men.

Using the cane to ease his ankle's awful pain, Jim bumped down the stairs to the kitchen, while loud bangs and shouts came through the doctor's flimsy front door. As he reached the bottom step, the door made a splintering sound. As he turned into the kitchen, there was a crash as the door burst open.

The thugs saw his red uniform and shouted. His one boot and cane bumped through the kitchen, and he slammed the back door behind him. He was standing on a tiny porch that extended into a narrow alley bounded by high wooden walls. He hobbled forward, despairing of reaching the street before they caught him. An overturned barrel stopped him. He righted it, and with painful difficulty hauled himself on top of the wobbling surface. An empty backyard!

He threw his cane over the wall, then hurriedly pulled himself on top of the fence's narrow plank. For a moment he teetered there, then crashed onto the other side. The force of landing knocked the breath out of him. A spasm of intense pain was thrust up his leg from his ankle. From the other side of the fence, the fast stamp of running boots.

For a time that might have been hours but was probably minutes, he clamped his teeth against the pain and lay still, trying not to breathe noisily, for any sound might give him away. The sticky, gritty muck in his mouth was sand and mud, but he didn't dare spit. He cocked his head.

Silence, not an earthworm stirring. He fearfully drew himself to a sitting position. He looked around for the cane, and with it pulled himself to his feet. The pain in his ankle stabbed as if a nail were driven in it. He hobbled toward the next yard and ran into a clothesline as if he were blind. Weaving like a drunk, he backed off and slunk across the neighboring rear yard. A succession of alleys, deadly clotheslines, angry ash cans, squeaking gates, stinking privies. Breathing hard, dripping with sweat, desperate, his torn red tunic mostly disguised by a seedy frock coat, Jim limped out onto Sixth Avenue a half hour later. The street had a stripped, denuded air. The windows of shops across the avenue were broken. North and south, no people and no carriages, except for a black barouche a long way downtown. Leaning heavily on his cane, disguised by the old coat he had stolen, Jim hobbled down Sixth Avenue toward his hotel. The barouche rattled toward him, moving at a fast clip that said it wanted nothing to do with the neighborhood through which it passed.

Exhausted, desperate for help, he scrambled into the middle of the street. He raised his cane and shouted at the barouche to stop. Its driver cracked his whip over the horses' backs and swerved to the right to give this fat beggar the widest possible berth. The passenger put his head out the window. Jim recognized him!

"Jay!" shouted Jim. "It's me!" Jay Gould stared blankly, his dark eyes looking through the disguised Jim as if he weren't there. "Me! Jim!"

Jay's pale face opened in surprise. "Jim! You're alive!" His fist beat on the roof of the carriage and he shouted to his driver. "Stop, John, it's Mr. Fisk!" Jay hurriedly pulled him into the carriage.

"I went to Cooper Square!" cried Jay, holding Jim's hands tightly. "They said you and Rufus were dead!" Jay started laughing and crying at the same time, tears and an insane giggle mingling.

Jim blurted out his story. Jay winced and gasped at the numbers of deaths, and he was hit hard by those of Rufus and Henry.

Finally Jay asked, "Do you want to go to the hotel?"

"Take me to the wharf," said Jim. "I need the vacation I canceled. I'll spend the rest of the weekend in Jersey."

Jay squeezed his arm. "That sounds sensible."

Taking the local train, Jim reached Long Branch by late afternoon. He hired a carriage to take him to Borrows' Hotel Continental. The rippling, multicolored pennants atop the hotel and the flutters of ladies' pastel dresses on its white veranda brought tears to his eyes. But for luck, he could be lying in the city morgue with Henry and Rufus.

After a cool bath, Jim hobbled onto the white veranda to join the vacationers from the city. It was early evening, tranquil and radiant. Somber and numb, he settled into a rocker at the corner where he could view both the ocean and the dunes of sea grass.

He propped his bum leg on pillows and gazed in a stupefied fashion at the sunset. The wide sunset—bands of saffron, fringed with turquoise—blended into pink and stretched like scarves around the horizon, except in the west, where the sinking sun turned half the heaven into an orange forge of fire. But none of it meant anything to him. Businessmen down for the weekend, eyeing his bandage with grave expressions, inquired how the parade had gone. Their thin, sober sons and coquettish daughters stood at a respectful distance and listened.

Dazed with shock and grief, often in tears, Jim shook his head and filled them in. As his tremulous voice described the day, the two dozen faces ringing him gaped with horror. A doctor knelt before him, unwound the dirty rag, and declared that his ankle was indeed badly sprained. He rebandaged it and told Jim to keep off it for a week. Although invited by a dozen tables, Jim declined to face the well-lit dining room. Hit by a raging thirst, Jim asked for hot tea, and two gauzily dressed nymphs raced to fetch it.

Four times over the next hour, he was forced to retell his story. Day began to pass through its death throes, and the enchantment of the sunset faded. The waves washed the pebbles onto the beach, rolling gravel in, rolling it out. Rufus, gone. Henry, gone. For nothing. For nothing, for nothing. An undulating vapor curled upward from the shore, and a gray mist enveloped the evening. The day was dead.

The next morning, back in the rocking chair, Jim drank coffee, read the papers' reports, saw again the screaming crush of Irish, and sniffed again coppery blood and the acrid bite of gunpowder. The scene at Bellevue Hospital had been a sad and painful one, the *Sun* reported; the ambulances kept discharging bloody loads, and groans of distress and shrieks of pain filled the air. The dead were carried to the morgue, around which, as night came on, a clamorous multitude gathered to look for slain friends. Tears streamed down Jim's cheeks at the stupidity of it all. To Jim's dismay, the Ninth, with four dead, one dying, and eight wounded, had suffered the worst losses.

The hotel's guests insisted on helping him in a thousand small errands. A competition broke out among the youthful nymphs over who should share the honors of nursing the hero and fetching the only drink that soothed his raging thirst—well-sugared lemonade.

By late morning these gauzy angels, bored with their ministry, had either gone for a turn on the boardwalk or to change for lunch. For a half hour Jim was left alone. In this quiet moment Rufus's and Henry's deaths once more dragged his mood under as forcefully as a riptide pulling a swimmer into its mad depths. Jim missed his driver's cheery face and rude quip as he might his own hand or eye. Worse than grief was his guilt; he had led Rufus and Henry as brazenly as a Judas goat led bleating lambs to slaughter. He was no more than a buffoon, a fumbling clown, crashing through others' lives, ruining them. He was not only responsible for Rufus's and Henry's deaths, but for the anguish that had forced his wife Lucy to abandon Boston for a months-long vacation in Europe with the children, to escape the damaging articles about the phantom letters and the scandals kicked up by the fact that the letters had not been published. Several times a black iris closed around the edges of his vision to darken the sparkling, white-capped ocean and gleaming sand.

Hearing a laugh, Jim looked up. Around the corner of the breezy, white veranda came Rufus and Henry Page in their spangling scarlet uniforms—whole and unwounded, arm in arm, their boots clattering merrily against the hollow floorboards. As they strode forward, they were laughing, grinning, and pointing antic fingers at Jim's bewilderment over the capital joke they had played on him.

As suddenly they disappeared. Jim blinked. The sun beat down. The sand glared. They weren't there. A shiver iced up his back. His mind had played a trick. Grains of sand, driven by the wind, whipped against his cheek. He shivered again and stared for the longest time at the empty veranda, framed by the bright sky, sand, and ocean, but no one came around it. Life would never be the same.

A *Sun* reporter found him there after lunch, his bandaged leg propped up, drinking lemonade poured by five pastel-frocked nurses crowding around the hero's rocker. The reporter asked how he had arrived in Long Branch. As sober as a hanging judge, Jim described the horrors of his escape. The reporter nodded gravely and said that the police blamed the troops for starting the riot with wild shooting. Rumor had it that an officer of the Eighty-fourth was blind drunk. Jim declared such stories to be "horse hockey."

The reporter led off his front-page account in the next morning's *Sun* by describing Jim in his seaside rocker. He elaborated on "the bevy of females that surrounded Colonel Fisk. A beautiful girl was fanning the hero's brow." The rest of the story was taken up by an account of Jim's escape, one that comically expanded on the difficulties of finding enough disguise for a person of his bulk, and further garnished with speculations on the outcome of historical battles if generals such as Alexander the Great, Wellington, and Sherman had used similar military tactics. The afternoon papers embellished the comic aspect of the escape still more.

Newly arrived friends announced that back in town these stories were drawing contemptuous comments about Jim. Rumors flew about as to the time of his departure from Manhattan, the exact status of his ankle, and the nature of his disguise—wags said that he arrived at the parade masquerading as a buffalo and fled it in the costume of a three-legged field mouse. Some held that he had been too frightened to appear at the parade at all; others that he had been in the parade but fled at the first shot; still others that his ankle was no more injured than that of Mayor Hall, who sat out the riot in City Hall. The most prominent rumor was that he had escaped to Jersey in an old woman's Mother Hubbard bonnet.

The next morning Jim's eggs and grits were spoiled by the lead editorial in the *Times*. "The Colonel's valor is equal to his piety. He has shown that he can fight and pray, and when needful, run away in a manner surpassed by few soldiers of any age."

JIM FISK'S WONDERFUL WOUND, read the *Herald*'s headline. The *Tribune* called it "his wounded (?) ankle." The *Sun* called him the "Mushroom Mars."

In a fresh scarlet tunic, Lieutenant Colonel Braine arrived at Long Branch for lunch.

A table had been set up on the breezy porch so that Jim didn't have to leave his rocker. After this morning's newspaper stories every one of his nurses discovered more pressing missions of mercy.

"My God, Charles," said Jim. "Sit down and have some of this veal."

Charles brought up a chair with earnest-faced stiffness.

"They're saying I'm a coward," Jim went on, waving his fork indignantly. "You know I was in the thick of things." Still, his heart wasn't in his protest. He felt too guilty.

"I know that, sir," said Charles. "Suppose we issue some sort of communiqué."

"Splendid idea," said Jim in a meek voice. "Give me a piece of paper. I'll write out something." Charles's long military face looked thoughtful.

"It might not have been a good idea to leave the city."

"They weren't chasing you with a rope, were they?" asked Jim.

"No," admitted Charles.

"Suppose we give this to the reporters," Jim said, reading the announcement: "Lieutenant Colonel Braine takes occasion to deny that Colonel Fisk did not properly command the regiment, and asserts that Colonel Fisk did his full duty to preserve the public peace and was foremost in the fray. Colonel Fisk did not leave New York until he was informed that his command was on the march to the armory and that the mob had been checked. Colonel Fisk is confined to his room on account of injuries received, and will not be able to leave before a week."

As did every New York paper, the *Times* printed the communiqué in full, but its word at the end of the week was typical of the attitude the papers took toward anything Jim did these days: "Perhaps of Colonel Fisk it may one day be said of him that he was first in war, first in peace, and first in the pockets of his countrymen."

Jim supposed this, too, would blow over. That afternoon a note from Jay was brought to his rocker which said it was urgent for Jim to return to town.

He was needed! Carefully easing his bum foot to the floor, he planted his cane on the floorboards and leaned forward to rise from his rocker.

"Rufus!" he shouted, then slumped back in the creaking chair as he tearfully remembered that he would never again hear that rough voice. With only his cane for support, he tottered to his feet.

46

Many women look jaded, have an anxious, half-startled expression, and seem weary. They are living in a state of dread lest their secrets be discovered and the inevitable ruin overtake them.

—James McCabe, *New York by Gaslight*, 1882

At noon on a rainy Thursday in late September 1870, Annabelle Stokes paid the fifteen-cent fare and boarded the Fort Lee ferry at the west end of Houston Street.

An unseasonal fog shrouded the North River. Once she was aboard the swaying ferry, the slippery, dew-covered gray planks of the Houston Street docks appeared insubstantial, ghostly. Despite her calm appearance, inside she was fearful and jumpy. Collisions were frequent during such rough or thick weather, and at least once every winter, ice swept a ferry miles off its course. She ignored the other passengers herding forward and walked toward the rear of the long, wide deck. Her bonnet, pulled forward over her brow, matched her coat, and a double black veil of mourning concealed her face. At this midday hour, the ferry, built to carry hundreds, was nearly deserted. Its prow drove through a restless, scummy waste of offal, horse droppings, white-bellied fish, and tannery scraps, a muck that threw off a stench that made the clammy air doubly hard to breathe.

At Twenty-third Street three passengers came on board, one of them the short form of Jay Gould, encased in a raglan overcoat of dark gray. Her heart jumped. She had not seen him in broad daylight in months. So as not to be recognized, Jay's black felt hat and long blue scarf covered much of his face, giving him a sinister, furtive appearance. To hide her excitement, she lowered her eyes.

As agreed in their unsigned, emotionless notes, she followed at a safe distance. Even though she forced herself to walk evenly, smoothly, her gait was as restless and jerky as a puppet's. She felt breathy and displaced. This ferry seemed to exist out of time, out of place, as if it were a crude celestial barge plowing uneasily through wet, steamy clouds. Jay completely circled the deck, pausing to peer into every public room and sailors' passageway, doubtless looking for reporters. After he nodded in her direction, she walked into the forward passenger lounge, a windowed room facing the front of the ferry with long rows of benches much like those in a schoolroom.

Tense, she took a seat on the scarred empty bench against the back wall, facing forward toward the window that looked over the crowded prow. Off to the left a fat woman in a Mother Hubbard bonnet shepherded three children of grammar school age. Closer, fifteen feet to the right, a wrinkled-faced old farmer sat on a side bench and spread out on brown paper a long loaf of crusty bread and a stick of Italian salami. The ferry swayed, and her stomach felt queasy. The kindly old man nodded at Annabelle's interest in his lunch. With a smile, thick Italian speech, and a universal pantomime with his plump hands, he offered her bread and sausage. Relieved by the innocuous passengers, she returned his smile and shook her head no.

A newspaper folded under his arm, Jay stepped over the door saddle as cautiously as a cat entering a stable of stamping horses. Not to give the game away, she turned her eyes to the front window, against which the fog crowded like a ghost anxious to spy on them.

Jay sat down casually next to her, leaving a foot and a half of space between them that he filled with the folded *Tribune*. Her heart beat more strongly. His black felt hat dropped into his lap. When he pulled his blue scarf down, his black eyes had a haunted aspect, yellow and diseased, and were sunk into their sockets as if in retreat. She winced. He scrutinized her veiled face with intense concern.

"How have you been?" he asked. It had been more than a month since they had seen each other.

"I think I'm fine," she said, smiling. Her white-gloved hand briefly touched his arm to make sure he was really here. She suddenly felt much better. "How about you? Are you all right?"

"Just barely," he said with a weak, self-mocking smile, for as she knew, he hated self-pity. His dark eyes, his strongest feature, became more focused, intense, and steady. He pulled apart the folds of his blue scarf. To her surprise, his blue bow tie was carelessly knotted, hair and beard untrimmed, and normally smooth shirt rumpled. Against the black felt of his hat, his pale, delicate hands didn't stop fidgeting. The lines in his thin face looked stretched to the point of exhaustion. Again she itched to touch him.

"I haven't seen you in daylight in so long," he said. He blinked, as if the sight was making his eyes tear, or was painful. "Remember those evenings, how we talked and talked?"

She remembered the kisses in the kitchen, the feverish, secret walks up her stairs, the feel of his flesh, their nights of excited talk. She relaxed and grew more open to him. How strange to be here, outside, with him in the daylight. Before the crash they had talked for hours by candlelight about their interests—finance, German music, city politics, English poetry, and Italian opera and painting. His passion for orchids and books, hers for banking, fabric, and clothes. A woman, if she was lucky, had one great love in her life. Never another like it. Here sat hers, his ragged features appearing to waste into death, and she couldn't comfort him.

She removed her white gloves. "What's the matter?"

"I told Helen about us," he said.

She gasped. It meant he would break with Helen—or with her. Her heart was beating in an irregular rhythm. She trusted herself only to nod.

"My boy . . . Nellie's getting shot," he went on. "I've thought and thought about it. I blame myself." His pale hands twisted the brim of his hat. His lips moved nervously, his eyes weren't as fixed as usual, and what little color his cheeks had was gone.

"You! What did you have to do with that?"

"Things got so out of hand," he said.

It alarmed her that after the news about telling Helen, he hadn't followed it up by saying he would break with his wife. That meant — To give herself time to sort this out, Annabelle asked. "How *is* Nellie now?"

"Fully healed, but the doctor says she'll never have children."

"My God, the poor thing!" she said. The deck lurched sideways. Annabelle felt as if she were floating through a swaying white void.

"Yes," he said. "And my son, George." He shook his head and blinked back tears. "I think he . . . found out, knows about us, you and me." As if their low voices had aroused him, the thick-waisted old Italian man, crumbs spilled over his blue workshirt, stared at them with a large-eyed, solemn expression.

"Your son knows!" she said.

"I think so," he whispered, the words almost lost in the throb of engines. "I think knowing drove *him* mad," he went on, his voice

487

urgent. "God knows what he was doing with that pistol behind the stable, he wouldn't talk much when Jim or I asked him. I almost lost Nellie, and I almost lost him. I wish it had been me he shot! I've been doing penance—for buying gold, hanging on to the Erie against Vanderbilt, being Jim's partner—having you." Penance? Her hand pressed his arm. He pulled back.

For a few moments they sat in silence, her torso twisted slightly toward him. The rush of filthy river water washed against the ferry's bow and sides. Her thoughts picked feebly through the bleak, nightmarish wreckage he presented. Slumped against the hard back of the bench, Jay stared resolutely forward, the brow of his hat crumpled in his hands.

"Thank God for Jim after the crash," he went on. She sensed he was avoiding any talk of the two of them. "George was hysterical. Jim took him under his wing, calmed him down. While Helen and I were at the hospital, Jim kept him in his suite, took him about town, looked after him like an uncle." His cracked lips parted, and he shot her a weak glance. "I was so furious I was afraid I might kill the boy." A ripple of pain crossed his face. "Then I would have killed myself." Once more she rested her hand on his arm. He started as if she had brushed him with a hot poker.

"Sorry," he whispered. "I can't see you anymore. You see that, don't you? It's cost too much."

She could say yes, and let him go. That was the right thing to do. It was wrong to see him again, wrong to take him from his family, and wrong to have any more to do with the man who had helped her heap muck on Ulysses. But in the whole world there wasn't another intense pair of eyes like his, nor another person like the one whose restless delicate hands moved over his hat, nor another whose brain had his fire. She would never be happy if she wasn't with him. Despite the power of her feelings, she only lifted an eyebrow.

"Can't see me?"

"Want to, but can't, can't, can't."

"Jay, we still love each other," she said with all the force she could muster. "That hasn't changed, that won't change." As if this time a hot poker were held against his ribs, he winced.

"Yes," he said. The old Italian man, now finishing up his bread and hard sausage, leaned back, legs casually extended, entire thick body in a relaxed, loose aspect, and gazed in their direction. A touch alarmed, Annabelle glanced at him and wondered why he took such an interest in them. Could he be a reporter—in disguise?

"No, that won't change," he said. With a glance at the Italian farmer, whose blue eyes were still fixed on them, Jay took both her hands in his and pressed them. The Italian smiled as if he understood. "I've loved you too much. Everything in my body burns to be with you, to return every midnight to your house, but I can't. I've hurt enough people. I won't again." He took a deep, gasping breath and released it. "I—oh, what's the use?" He dropped her hands. "I can't be around you. You just—inflame me. You make me crazy." Her hands wanted to run under his shirt, she wanted to feel his chest against hers, his legs between hers, his naked back inside the circle of her arms.

"I was crazy to think I could have you without causing damage," he went on. "I've been half mad all these months. Mad to possess what I have no right to possess. I'm paying. I almost destroyed my son and daughter."

Her chest churning with emotion, she turned away from his rejection to stare through the ferry's wide window. Pressed against the panes was the fog's thick gray shroud. From atop the ferry came the sharp shriek of a whistle. The splashing of the paddle wheels abruptly stopped. Mother Hubbard fearfully snatched to her the two nearest children. An ominous silence. The Italian man cocked his head forward, one wild eye on the front window as if a monster might crash through it. Jay abruptly sat up.

"What's happening?" he asked. A ship's prow appeared fifteen feet in front of their ferry. A long hull dashed by, half hidden by the mist. A horn blew and the paddle wheels started up again. The Italian waved his loaf and smiled in their direction.

"A little too close," Jay murmured as he dropped back against the bench. Her heart was hammering. The ferry ground on. She stared at him, unable to decide what tack to take. She wanted him, she sensed he wanted her, but as it had been for months, the situation was impossible. "Here," he said, "this is for you." Out of an inner pocket he drew a stiff sheet of folded paper and passed it to her. It was her promissory note on his investment in the shop, marked "paid in full."

"What's this?" she asked.

He gave her a hard, cold stare, one that turned his ragged, sad face into a stranger's. "It's no payoff, if that's what you mean," he said. She nodded and held the paper before her, unsure whether to accept it. For a long moment he gazed at her, his face filled with pain and longing. "How I love you!" he breathed. "I can't see you again, but how I'll miss you!"

Her throat tightened and she felt herself sinking, as if the ferry were sliding down a sloping river into the center of the earth. The rush of the side paddle wheel slowed.

"I understand," she said, forcing out the words. "I don't like it, but I understand. You, your responsibilities. It's one of the things I most admire about you." She stood, swaying, her legs wobbly. She didn't want to go, but she didn't want to stay. She felt numb with shock and dismay, although the pain of distress was beginning to prickle. He looked up, startled. She folded the stiff paper, unsnapped her handbag, and stuck it in. As if in a dream, from a distance she was watching herself move and talk.

"We're pulling into the upper part of Manhattan," she said. "I'm going to get off here and take the train back down. It would be wise for you to stay on the ferry." She glanced around at the nearly empty lounge.

"I'll be waiting," she said, backstepping and struggling to smile. "For a little while, anyway." As he stood, her laugh, clumsy and forced, struggled to push away the moment's clotted, strangled oppression. She pushed her left hand into a white glove. "I'll listen for an acorn rattling against my bedroom window." She threw her head back. "For a scratch at the back door. For an unsigned note saying some mysterious person will visit at midnight." His lips bared his teeth, and he shook his head.

"I can't," he whispered.

"You won't . . . you may."

"I may, but I won't."

"Good-bye, Jay." She held out her bare right hand.

As if afraid, he hesitated before touching it. His fingers were tentative and moist, a clasp nothing like the dry, firm hand that had been so bold with the hidden crevices of her body. She gripped his fingers firmly, shook them twice in a mannish way, and dropped them. When she looked up, the old Italian man was standing close by, his brown-paper parcel under his arm, and a broad, wistful smile on his thick lips.

"*Amore!*" he said with deep, liquid feeling and a swagger of his thick head. She fingered her veils, turned, and strode out to the gangplank.

Half an hour later she was in the sooty, rattly car of a public train on her way down Manhattan. The narrow car rocked from side to side. Her head swam. She was in a swaying dream, a sooty, rattly nightmare. An arid dry wind blew about within her, an intensification of the same sweet, painful shock that assaulted her whenever she visited the small bank and farm back in Gantry. Her heart was a large waste of parched desert, one that hadn't felt rain for months and had been dry too long to expect any for years, if not forever.

She took out her linen handkerchief and held it in readiness to go up under her double black veil, but when she reached Fourteenth Street the square of white linen was still dry.

On an unseasonably brisk day in early October the bell over the shop door tinkled—and tinkled and tinkled. Alone as usual, Annabelle peered around the back partition.

Grunting loudly, a large matron was shoving her wide, elaborate arrangement of hoopskirt and bustle through the shop's front door. Annabelle came around to greet her. The fat matron tottered forward, a harried, wattled cow whose lower half was encased in a six-foot-wide bluebell of a dress. Her paunchy bear of a husband, in frock coat and spats, gold-headed cane tucked under his arm, held the door for a thin, blond calf in pale blue chintz who was very likely their daughter. At the curb of Fifth Avenue stood a brass-trimmed brown carriage, a liveried driver, and a footman.

In a bellow that carried up the length of the shop, Momma announced that the dressmaker Madame Rumplemeyer had died the day before, "the victim of a horrid stroke." Her husband and daughter trailed her advance. The floor shook and the crystal jars of fresh sachets trembled against the glass countertop. The height of the season was upon her, the cowlike woman trumpeted, and no dressmakers were free. Eloise here was to be married in five weeks to the "most promising" of the Harriman boys, the ones whose father was "so big" in railroads and banks. At that, Poppa puffed up as if it were he who was "so big." Momma Bolton needed a "really grand" wedding gown for Eloise.

Taking over, Poppa Bolton's bassoon announced that he was in the clothing business the same as Annabelle, the manufacture of buttons, and that even though he was known in the trade as the King of Buttons, he had made his money "one button at a time." Quiet, pale-cheeked, and to Annabelle's taste washed-out, Eloise hung off to the side, shoulders slumped, hands folded together, as indifferent to the antics of her parents as a wild goose to a squall of summer rain. Would Annabelle take on the commission of the wedding dress for Eloise, the trousseau for her European honeymoon, and of course matched dresses for the bridesmaids?

For form's sake, Annabelle frowned as if her schedule were crowded and asked the date of the wedding. At the answer, she frowned more deeply, consulted a nearly empty notebook, then smiled and said that while it was a large commission, she could squeeze it in.

"Oh, *good!*" said Mrs. Bolton with warmth. "At a ball last spring I saw the 'look' I"—she glanced at Eloise, who was staring at the front door, before she gushed on—"*we*—want. A rich blue satin skirt, *en train*. Of course, for Eloise here everything *has* to be in white. Over the skirt was looped up a perfectly magnificent brocaded silk—white, with bouquets of flowers woven in. This overskirt was flounced with white lace—you could tell it certainly wasn't cheap!—and caught up with bunches of feathers in bright colors. I think a little color might be nice, don't you? She wore a shawl, but we can do without that. She had the most beautiful headdress—white ostrich feathers, white lace, gold pendants, and purple velvet, but purple isn't right for a young girl's wedding, is it? She carried a darling *small* fan, don't you know?—a bouquet of rarest blossoms, a teensy-weensy lace handkerchief, and the most exquisite jewelry."

The crisp air of the shop still rang with her shrill notes after she stopped. Caught off guard by this deluge, Annabelle stared at her. A faint smile played around Papa Button's clean-shaven cheeks, a smile grown used to such geysers. Eloise studied the pattern stamped into the ceiling's tin panels as if none of it concerned her. The barbaric, overstuffed outfit in which Momma Button wanted to marry off her daughter would make Annabelle the laughingstock of Fifth Avenue. She had to change Momma's mind or forego the job.

Treading cautiously, over the next half hour Annabelle showed the heavy matron pictures from *Harper's Weekly* and other fashion magazines in an attempt to put her weighty, cumbersome notion of fashion on a diet.

"See, Momma," said Eloise finally, rolling her eyes toward the tin, "it's the same thing Madame Rumplemeyer told you." Poppa Button nodded solemnly.

"Let me sketch out some styles the young people enjoy," suggested Annabelle. As she spread out drawings on the counter, the Button Queen muttered to His Majesty, "Where have I seen her before?"

Poppa Button answered by asking how much longer this would take, and saying that he was hungry. Her heart thumping strongly, Annabelle hoped the woman had a short memory. A commission to do such an important wedding would remove some of the stigma attached to her, and if she did a splendid job, she stood a chance to take over a portion of the late Madame Rumplemeyer's profitable trade.

As soon as possible, Annabelle packed off Poppa and Momma Button to Delmonico's for lunch. She quickly had Eloise's slouched form out of her dress and up on the box for first measurements. The hitch in the girl's gait, as well as the sour odor on her breath, made Annabelle decide that this pale calf was three months pregnant. To further secure the commission, she drew out Eloise, whose nasal whine confided that she had set her heart on marrying a duke, one in England or France, but that she had settled on Andrew Harriman after Poppa announced that he had spent enough on her. "After all," Eloise concluded, "you can't get everything you want in life."

At her feet, the cloth tape in her teeth, Annabelle hummed agreement. Eloise was the antithesis of the ladies she met at Sorosis. The girl would spend her days changing dresses and visiting department stores in a constant, failing effort to keep her husband's eyes on her and to outdo other ladies' displays of fashion. Books and drawings spread over the counter, Annabelle went over "looks" with Eloise, conspiratorially giving her to understand that her new dressmaker was on her and not her mother's side in the planning of the trousseau.

Then Poppa and Momma returned, reeking of wine, steak, and onions. Annabelle had sketched six possible dresses, giving the three a wide choice of design. Well acquainted with the soft afternoon light of Trinity Church, she pointed out how each dress would show. Using a basic design of the Parisian designer Charles Worth, she emphasized how a body of white silk overlaid with Brussels lace would pick up the light. A veil fixed to Eloise's hair with white silk roses and orange blossoms, she went on, that modestly covered the bride's face as she walked down the aisle and during the ceremony, would make a stunning effect.

"Cover her face!" said Momma. "I never heard of such a thing!"

"She will lift it for the first time when the ceremony is over," said Annabelle. "Your daughter will *set* fashion, madam, not be a slave to it." Eloise's lips parted and her eyes glittered. Momma buttoned her lips and silently, shrewdly examined the social possibilities.

Showing himself shrewd in his own sphere, Poppa's bassoon worried over the expense of so much Brussels lace. Still chewing over the cud of the veil, Momma's sharp violin overrode him. Flutelike, Eloise's high notes danced lightly in and around her parents', agreeing here, disagreeing there, often obtaining her way in decisions that surprised Annabelle. She wondered which of the three was dominant.

Late afternoon shadows had gathered, important first decisions had been reached, and the button royalty had drawn on their gloves when Momma stopped in her tracks. She pointed a quivering white-gloved finger at Annabelle. *"Stokes!"* came her frenzied shout. "This is that horrid Stokes woman!"

Poppa Button asked who, and Momma's injured tone explained Annabelle's connection to the corrupt White House. Poppa's soothing bass said it didn't matter, all that counted was whether she could sew a good-looking dress. Momma shook her wattles firmly. Eloise piped up. She liked Mrs. Gantry. There weren't any other dressmakers free, and not only were they in the middle of the season, but Madame Rumplemeyer's death had heaped her work on all the others.

"No, no, no," said Momma Bolton. "What will Mrs. Harriman say when she finds out that Eloise's wedding dress was made by a— a saboteur!"

Annabelle wanted to laugh but said politely, "I'm only a dress-maker."

"Awful as it will be," responded Mrs. Bolton's wounded tone, "we'll find someone else." Papa Bolton's bassoon tone was low and mournful.

"But there's nobody else this side of Boston or Philadelphia," he said, "and they have seasons there, too."

"Then we shall go to Philadelphia or Boston," announced Momma in a heroic tremolo. In the silent stare that Eloise and Poppa exchanged was the weary prospect of a dozen trips for fittings. Annabelle would lose this enormous job if she didn't do something. The Button Queen was now halfway to the door, beckoning imperiously for her two subjects to follow.

"Mr. Bolton," said Annabelle, "may I have a private word?"

"Come, Edward!" commanded his wife.

The Button King looked from her to Annabelle and back again. "Just a moment, Marie."

Whispering, Annabelle told him that she wanted this job so much that she would do it for one-half her normal price. He fixed his ob-durate blue eye on her.

"Half?" he said.

"Half."

"Why?" he asked, and by the blunt power of his single-word question, as well as his stubborn wait for an answer, he showed Annabelle what crafty qualities had enabled him to crown himself the King of Buttons.

She told him that she expected to do the twenty bridesmaids' dressed at her regular prices.

His smile recognized another, if lesser, member of royalty. "All I have to do is convince Mrs. Bolton," he mused, and glanced over his shoulder at his wife's fleshy face. Annabelle nodded. He stared Annabelle in the eye and his smile deepened. He said, "Two-thirds off."

Annabelle flinched. At that rate she would lose two thousand dollars, but then she might make it up, eke out a small profit even, on the bridesmaids' dresses. "All right," she said.

In royal waters now, the Button King broadened his smile and went on, "Provided you toss in four more evening gowns at the same rate." Annabelle gasped.

"Four more!"

He nodded vigorously. Over his shoulder his fleshy, wrinkled queen, as if she heard the negotiations, sternly shook her wattles from side to side, *No*. Annabelle had to make it worth his while to battle her. She nodded her assent. Bearing a triumphant grin, Mr. Bolton left Eloise with Annabelle, took his wife's arm, and escorted her outside the shop and down Fifth Avenue.

"She'll never let him do it," said Eloise in a nasal, philosophical whine. "Momma would rather die than have Mrs. Harriman think she bought anything for this wedding that wasn't first-class."

But the deal was struck. From the amount of supervision and cautionary advice she gave over the next four weeks, Mrs. Bolton was far from dead. Annabelle smiled and fitted, hired back her seamstress Mrs. Grumby and four more besides, and during the last week worked three nights through to make sure the sixty dresses were perfect.

The wedding took place on a gorgeous Sunday afternoon. Inside the bride's dressing room, Annabelle did her part to make Eloise look radiant. She sent the bride up the aisle of Trinity Church in a white cloud of rustling silk and gauzy maline that caused appreciative gasps and rich murmurs to float from the crowded pews. Eloise was launched into the world, and so in a sense was Annabelle.

47

My dear Josie,
All the differences could have been
settled by a kiss in the right spirits, and
in after days I should feel very kindly
toward you out of memory of the great
love I have borne you.

—Jim Fisk, letter to Josie
Mansfield, 1870

"You want me to resign?" Jim Fisk whispered to Jay.

His eyes averted, Jay bobbed his head.

"Resign from the Erie!" Jim whispered. The weeks of inactivity forced by his badly sprained ankle had put weight on him, and his trousers pressed against his middle and his starched collar bit into his fleshy neck. Resign! No more board meetings. No more working with Jay. No more fat checks. No more planning Erie strategy, no more reassuring flocks of nervous shareholders about the future—no more being a man to reckon with on the Street. Jim twisted about on his swivel chair, ducking and swaying.

"No, Jay—no, no, no," said Jim.

Jay jumped to his feet and paced about with the restless grace of a cat. Some of his tension was due to Helen, Jim figured; overdue by weeks, she was supposed to give birth to their fifth child any hour.

"We're under a lot of pressure," said Jay. "The newspapers keep leaning on us. You're a corrupt clown, I'm the corrupt villain of the Street, and those letters will prove it." Jay sighed and shook his head violently. "That Pennsylvania deal fell through. We needed that western outlet badly. The opera house is barely breaking even." He came

---

496

to stand behind the desk, next to Jim's chair. "You know I want you with me." Jay patted Jim comfortingly on the shoulder. "I feel about you the way I would a brother." Jim, eyes prickly with tears, nodded and gazed up at Jay.

"Thanks," he said huskily. Jay *was* like a brother to him, despite the other's inability to show much warmth. Jim sighed.

"If you don't resign, we'll both be kicked out of the Erie."

Jim's legs abruptly felt as numb as two sticks. "Kicked out?" said Jim. "You, too?"

"Both," said Jay firmly. He glided around the desk and dropped back into the chair. "I've been visited by six directors, including your chum Bill Tweed. I've received letters from hundreds of irate stock-holders and passengers. Bill says he's even heard whispers that board members are plotting to gang up against us."

"But resign?" asked Jim, his face aghast.

"I'm afraid so," said Jay. "Or at the next board meeting, Hart-man's going to bring a resolution calling for your ouster."

"Hartman!"

"It'll never die down till you get rid of those damn letters," Jay announced, his voice strengthening. "If I were in your shoes, I'd go see Howe and Hummel."

Jim winced but didn't answer. Several times over the summer Jay had recommended the two lawyers, but Jim had put off seeing them. Famous, notorious even, Abe Hummel and William Howe were the two best criminal lawyers in the city, a young, slick-haired dandy in spats, and a fat, older shyster who sometimes dressed in outra-geously colored suits. They were often able to save the most vicious ax murderer from the rope, the clumsiest thief from a cell, and the most careless embezzler from restitution.

"I don't know what law Josie and Ned are breaking," said Jay, "but I do know they're extorting money or blackmailing you."

"I should see them," Jim said, yet his voice lacked conviction. Whenever Jay brought up Howe and Hummel, his spirit became as enfeebled as an exhausted bear's mired in quicksand.

Good as Howe and Hummel were, they and Jim were natural enemies, as breach-of-promise actions were the firm's specialty. For years Howe & Hummel affidavits alleging "seduction under promise of marriage" had troubled the morning-after brainwork of playboys and stagestruck businessmen. Deep terror smote the hearts of gents-about-town who found Howe & Hummel stationery in their morning mail. The invitation to call at the firm's offices brought the recipient running at full speed and bathed in perspiration, for through their legal offices youthful actresses and chorines were able to magically transmute last spring's iced-over infatuation into this winter's snug wrap of silver fox. Hummel would set down the details in an exhaustive affidavit, the truth of which the scorned show girl swore to. The named gent, panicked and sweaty, was given his choice of a breach-of-promise suit with wide publicity or a quick, businesslike settlement. It cost anywhere from five to ten thousand dollars to redeem a Howe & Hummel affidavit; this heart balm was split fifty-fifty between the injured lady and her attorneys. If he paid, the affidavit was burnt on the spot, and true to Howe and Hummel's promise, they made sure that this was the last heard of the girl.

"Prosecute those two as criminals," said Jay. "Get rid of them, and when things quiet down—I don't see why you can't come back on board the Erie." The oxygen of hope fanned the flame of Jim's spirit.

"As managing director and vice-president," said Jim, "like I am now?" For the first time since Jay had brought up the subject, Jim's voice carried strength and resolve.

Jay smiled. "Of course," he said. "I need you. What do the papers say? We go together like ham and eggs—a horse and wagon—a hand and glove." Gratitude prickled Jim's nose and eyes. He pulled out his handkerchief and gave his nose a loud honk.

"Thanks, Jay," said Jim. "You've stuck with me through this whole thing. I'm lucky to have a partner like you."

That afternoon, with a letter to the board of directors, copies of which were circulated to the newspapers, Jim resigned from the Erie's staff and its board "for reasons of a personal nature."

In the great flapping of editorials that followed, the newspapers applauded, but sniffing the exhilarating whiff of blood, they called in yet stronger language for the publication of the telltale love letters.

Jim didn't abandon his elaborate office on the third floor of Castle Erie, and he announced that of course he would continue to operate the Grand Opera House. Over the brisk fall days that followed, he gave himself several stern talkings-to. He saw himself as the trounced villain in a play written by Ned Stokes entitled *The Mistress's Triumph*. Jim needed the starring role in a play called *The Cuckold's Triumph*—or better, *The Cuckold's Revenge*—but the shameful demands of the role of cuckold made him reluctant to accept the part.

Jay's fifth child and second daughter, Edith, was born, and his strained face became a composition of pride and pleasure. Happy for him, Jim took him to lunch at Hanrahan's, Jay's favorite spot. His own pleasure was only marred by his distance from his own family.

With the advent of the school year, Lucy and the children had returned to Boston. To gain some perspective, Jim tootled up for a visit, one that, because Lucy was icily frigid toward him, turned out to be awkward, silent, and full of pain. Even his girls seemed distant, as if he had hurt them. Back in the city, in his purposeful mood of straightening out his life, he wrote Lucy in a letter what he hadn't been able to say in person. He promised to put these awful problems behind him, and he went on to say that he desperately wanted his entire family together again.

He was a man now. He had been through his twenties and early thirties with a light heart and fast footwork. It was time to put his boyhood playthings away and become a pillar of the community—wear suits as sober as a banker's, give opinions to newspapers as grave as a judge's, and be seen about in public with other earnest pillars of the city.

As part of this fresh start, on a nippy morning in early October Jim pulled on a sealskin coat and marched to Jay's office.

"Yes?" asked Jay, glancing up from an enormous red-and-black ledger. Jim stepped up to Jay's desk.

"I'm taking your advice," said Jim. "I'm on my way to see Abe Hummel."

"Well, congratulations!" said Jay, jumping to his feet and thrusting out his pale hand to be shaken. "Give both your troubles a swift kick in the rear end for me, too."

While the state bar association forbade advertising legal services, Howe & Hummel ignored it.

Over their shabby but roomy offices on the ground floor of a three-story, red-brick, mansard-roofed building at the southwest corner of Leonard and Centre streets, across the way from the notorious Tombs, hung not the modest shingle of a firm of counselors-at-law, but a sign forty feet long and four feet high with enormous block letters spelling out HOWE & HUMMEL'S LAW OFFICES. It caught the eye of anyone in the vicinity. Illuminated by night, it shone as a beacon of hope and a portent of rescue to prisoners in the Tombs, the six-story, grimy city prison. Those who could not afford to retain Howe & Hummel kept their families and friends on the hop to round up the necessary cash. Few prisoners peering between the bars of the Tombs failed to read the bold red headline on the yellow background as shouting anything less than OVER HERE IS A WAY OUT.

Jim entered the storefront waiting room, a low-ceilinged, crowded space with sticky, knife-scarred benches and seven waiting clients—four painted prostitutes, two sharp-eyed grifters, and a fellow who lounged about with the darting eyes of a pickpocket. The prissy clerk behind the desk took his card, told him to take a seat, and nanced away behind a partition. Larding the air was the sweet scent of rosewater and cheap rouge and the sour reek of mud and horse dung. Jim seated himself well away from the others. Fourteen eyes assessed him as if calculating how much his clothes would bring in a pawnshop. According to an article in yesterday's *Herald*, so pervasive was Howe and Hummel's practice in the city's criminal circles that they represented twenty-three of the twenty-five men waiting in the Tombs on murder charges.

The clerk came out and whispered to Jim that he would be next. After a sullen-faced prostitute and a silkily dressed pimp strutted out of the inner office, Jim was called in.

Abe Hummel was a man in his midthirties. A bit nervous here in the den of his natural enemy, Jim daintily shook the lawyer's small, cool hand. To his relief the lawyer didn't laugh at his initial statement of his problem but gestured him into a much-used leather armchair near a tiny coal fire. "Of course, I've read the newspapers," said Hummel, "but I'd like to hear your version."

As Jim began, Hummel inched onto the smudged leather armchair across from him. He was so short that his shiny black shoes didn't touch the floor. Hummel was elegantly dressed in a dark blue suit and diamond studs and links. His impersonal, neat features said that Jim's story would likely turn out to be an interesting problem in a subject as intricate as boiler mechanics. Jim wondered if the tiny coal fire at his knees was where Hummel burnt the girls' affidavits.

Under the lawyer's questions, Jim gave Josie's and Ned's background, as well as the particulars of his own alliance with the actress. Occasionally a bellow came from the other side of the partition, and the floor rattled and the wall shook, as if a dangerous rhinoceros were being penned in a hog sty. Jim supposed Howe's office was next door.

It took Jim an hour to lay out the facts, but finally he had presented the entire tawdry mess. When he asked what Abe thought— they had quickly gotten to first names—the lawyer held up his smooth diminutive palm.

"I want to consult with Mr. Howe," said Abe, glancing at the partition, "but I believe we can shut up her and her paramour. We'll charge them both with blackmail."

"Blackmail?"

"Yes, sir," said Abe, nodding firmly. "My experience has been to knock these things in the head. Kill 'em off at once."

"That's a bit strong," said Jim. "I don't want to damage her reputation that much." Abe's eyes stared with the superior gaze of an owl unsure how to answer a wren's childish question. His voice was gentle.

"Do you want to be nice to her, Jim, or do you want to stop her?"

Jim wanted both, but he reckoned it would sound foolish to say so. "Stop her, of course," he said, "but not ruin her."

"These things can't be done with half measures," said Abe. "If you want to put this matter to rest, I'm your man. If you want to really yourself with her . . ." Here Abe shrugged and smiled.

Jim squirmed on the leather cushions, for this was taking an ominous turn. Being in court on blackmail charges would ruin any chances Josie still had for a stage career and a respectable life in New York. Still, Ned was tenacious and tricky and might escape, yet nobody in the New York bar was more tenacious and foxier than Abe Hummel and William Howe.

"Can't we just go after Stokes?" asked Jim in a small voice. Those dark steady eyes gave Jim an appraising look.

"You have to make up your mind," said Abe. A brush of kindness crept into his voice. "It's either mercy—or it's no quarter given and none received. Yes, it'll be nasty, but we can bring you out of it looking much better than you do now, and possibly with them in jail. I'm certain I can get them to stop badgering you."

"All right, then," said Jim with all the eagerness of his eight-year-old son for school. "Whatever you think best."

When news of the suit reached them, the *Sun*, *World*, *Times*, *Herald*, and *Tribune* rolled out their largest type in screaming headlines. The *World* called it "The Trial of the Century." The *Times* expected to finally get to the bottom of this "scandal-ridden administration." Five days after the news hit, the circulation manager of the *Herald* treated his staff to dollar Havana cigars.

On a frosty October morning a week after the prosecutor had served Ned and Josie with papers, Jim was entering his carriage in front of the Hoffman House when a series of pecks tapped his shoulder. He turned, and a tangle of legal papers fell to the cold paving stone. The tall, hunched form of Frogface the process server was hurrying away.

"Served, Mr. Fisk!" he sang out gaily.

Cursing, Jim picked them up. Mrs. Helen Josephine Mansfield was suing him for libel. Shaking with anger, he rushed downtown to Abe Hummel's office, where he marched in without waiting.

"Damn it all!" Jim shouted, and he shook the papers at the calm face of the lawyer. "Looky here what you've done! Now they're even with us!"

With infuriating calm, Abe held up his small hand. At his gesture, the rouge-cheeked show girl sitting in the visitor's chair continued, in a small, quavering voice, to describe an evening with a gent-about-town. Abe nodded as he inked her words on foolscap. As she talked, her large blue eyes blinked upward in Jim's direction, and her spirited bosom thrust forward. Ignoring the invitation, Jim only glared at her. When Abe finished blotting the paragraph, he gave Jim's red, steaming face a glance, then he asked the girl to wait outside for a few minutes.

Abe picked up the papers that Frogface had served and waved Jim into the worn leather armchair. The dapper lawyer dropped into its companion on the other side of the small grate. Using his manicured index finger as a guide, he read through the dense legal copperplate. When he put the papers into his tiny lap, he gazed at Jim with a smile as merry as a street urchin with a dozen roast potatoes.

"We've got them now," Abe said. Jim started. A rich chuckle followed from the small lawyer, a burble as cheerful as a miser's on scalping a street vendor. "Oh, depend on it," Abe babbled on. "Better—far, *far* better—than I'd hoped."

Jim's face screwed up into a puzzled knot. "How's that?"

"You see, when we complained that Mrs. Mansfield and Mr. Stokes blackmailed you, we were relying on the public prosecutor to do our work for us. He might have done it well, and he might not have." He picked up Josie's papers. "Now *I* get to do it."

"What do you mean?"

"As the accused, the bawd would not be put on the stand to testify against herself, nor could her flesh peddler." Jim shrank from the harsh words. It made Josie sound like a—whore, and Ned like a pimp.

"So what?"

Abe's slim hand rattled the papers. "She's made herself the plaintiff, not the defendant! She'll have to get up on the stand and complain." Abe leaned forward. "I get to cross-examine her!" Jim peered at the lawyer's excited face.

"Why are you so happy about that?"

"Oh, what a dumb lawyer she's hired!" said Abe. He sat back and cackled. "She's trying to save money with this cheap little trickster." Suddenly the lawyer was stone-sober. He pointed his short finger at Jim. "Don't ever try to save money when you hire a lawyer, Jim. Let this be a lesson to you." Grinning, Abe rose and rattled a generous amount of coal into the grate, as if the occasion called for a celebration. Jim tried to puzzle it out, but he couldn't see the advantage they had gained and said so.

"When I get finished with her," Abe said, "she won't have enough reputation left to get a job as a scrubwoman in New York—maybe not in the whole country."

Jim's mouth dropped open. The picture of Josie, brown eyes brimming with tears, saucy mouth twisted in hatred of him, was alarming.

"Why don't we just do all this to Ned Stokes?" he said brightly. "He's the brains behind this." Abe turned Josie's legal paper to face Jim.

"Your Mr. Stokes is smart enough not to allow *his* name on this. *He* hasn't complained that you've libeled him." Jim thought he saw it.

"You mean he's putting *her* forward to do *his* dirty work?"

"Right in one," said Abe, and from his black eyes, thick lips, and expensive gray suit an exuberant joke seemed to bubble forth. "But I shall have a few surprises for him, too."

"Abie," said Jim. "Please. Get her off my back, don't destroy her." Abruptly all jokes were aside. Abe faced him with a cold stare.

"Jim, do you still love this woman?" Jim's hands twisted together, two large restless pups unsure what to grab. He saw it, all right. If he loved her, now was the time to say so. This feud was hotting up to such a sizzle that somebody was going to get fried. If he wasn't careful, there wasn't going to be much in the way of feathers left on Josie when this was over.

"Please, just soft-pedal it," said Jim, skipping the question of whether he loved her. "It wouldn't be hard to make her look pretty bad."

Abe raised Josie's legal paper and tapped his finger against it as if to knock loose an answer. "We must win this libel case."

"Why 'must'?"

"If she wins, she may well turn around and sue you for damages. Then heaven help your pocketbook *and* your reputation."

Jim sighed the weary air of defeat. The way Abe painted it, there was only one thing to do, and Jim summed it up. "Attack and attack hard."

"I'm afraid so."

To escape the fire's heat, Jim stood. If only Josie had seen through Ned from the beginning. On the other side of the wall of legal books, beyond the footlights, the audience now peered at Jim intently to see what he would do. They weren't sure what the name of the play was that they were watching, whether it was *The Cuckold's Defeat* or *The Mistress's Revenge*. It was up to him to decide. He turned to the lawyer.

"Do what you have to, Abie," he said. "I don't know that I can watch you do it, but do what you have to."

As if eager for battle Abe sprang to his feet and stuck out his small, smooth hand for Jim to shake.

"We'll have them in court in a month or so," he said. "And I'm very much afraid you'll have to be there."

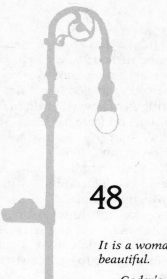

48

It is a woman's business to be beautiful.

—*Godey's Lady's Book*, 1852

A week later, on a brisk fall afternoon near closing time, the front bell tinkled in Annabelle's shop. Stephen Whitney, the cloth and lace wholesaler, dropped in for the third time this week.

Nervously pushing his gold spectacles back onto his nose, he explained his visit with a sheepish male grin and the lame "I was just in the neighborhood." His brown broadcloth suit brought in the dusty scent of street, horses, and tannery sulfur.

When Annabelle first opened the shop, the graying wholesaler had called on her once a month, but now, although she had even less business for him, he came by every week. Strapped for cash, she hadn't paid him for even a tenth of what she had purchased since she opened, credit no other wholesaler allowed her.

As he often did, he helped her close the sticky back shutters. Although he was a tall, ruddy, strong man, there nevertheless hung around his blue-gray eyes an air of gentle melancholy. It wasn't illness, for his quick smile, sure movements, and slim figure for a man in his forties argued that he was in robust health, but he seemed detached and removed, as if he were preoccupied by another world.

As he helped her drop the heavy iron bar across the back door, the male odors of leather, cigar, and horse prickled her nose and stirred her. She sensed, with the instinct of a salesgirl alone with a sweaty shopkeeper, what she was in for and her heart began thudding. After she pulled down the shades on the front window, his hand on the door firmly prevented her from opening it. An uneasy smile dodged about his mouth.

"Will you have dinner with me?" he asked. She stepped back.

"Mr. Whitney!" she exclaimed. "What's this all about?" Annabelle liked him, badly needed the credit he extended, but didn't think of him romantically. She hadn't thought of anyone romantically since Jay broke with her, so intensely had she flung herself into making the dress shop work. In the orange sunlight of the waning fall evening his ruddy face became flustered and he nervously poked the bridge of his gold-rimmed, octagonal specs with his index finger.

"I thought—you're a customer—a consideration—all the business you've given . . ." His voice trailed off and inwardly she groaned. Nothing between a gentleman and a lady was ever simple and straightforward.

"I hardly know what to say," she said. That sounded like a schoolgirl's ingenuous nonsense. His smile brightened and he ran a hand through his salt-and-pepper hair.

"Would you *like* to have dinner with me?" he whispered. So the credit he had extended her didn't have to do with her business prospects.

"What does Madame Brossard pay for Brussels pigeon?" Annabelle asked suddenly. Ablaze in the orange light, his head jerked.

"What?"

She pressed again, "What does Chez Etoile pay for that German layeresque you sold me last week? I saw it in their window." His eyes darted everywhere but on her face as his index finger again poked up his gold specs.

"I can't discuss other shops' business."

"They pay more than I, don't they?" she demanded. "Mr. Whitney, have you been subsidizing me?"

"Subsidizing? No."

"I suppose that's why I haven't been buying lace from other salesmen," she said. "You've cut your prices to your cost."

"I—" He twisted about with the anguish of a schoolboy caught in a lie. He turned away. "I have shaved my prices."

"And now I'm invited to dinner," she said in weary conclusion. His face appeared as guilty as her son Richard's the time she caught him playing in the drawer that held her undergarments.

"My intentions are strictly correct, Mrs. Gantry," he said.

"What *are* your intentions, Mr. Whitney?"

He leaned forward, parted his dry lips, but no words came.

She helped him. "To get to know me better?"

505

"Yes," he said, nodding with relief.

"I've heard you speak of your son and daughter," she said coolly. "What will your wife think of your having dinner with me in a public place?"

His eyes glassed over. "My Marie—died," he said. "Last year. I thought you knew."

Annabelle went numb with shock. The light of the fading sun made his anguished face appear orange and diseased. She had been toying with him the way a cat cruelly knocked about a mouse before she ate it.

She bowed her head. "I'm sometimes a clod of earth." She put her hand on the rough broadcloth of his arm. "Forgive me. I didn't know." His Adam's apple bobbed, and he nodded several times.

"When she went, I thought I would die, too," he said. "I knew I loved her, but I didn't know how much till she died."

They went to dinner at Hanrahan's. The bottle of ruby claret he ordered was the merriest wine she had ever tasted, and the restaurant itself had never sparkled more with life and gaiety. Over the next two weeks he came by almost every day. Annabelle noticed how her mood had brightened. Whenever he called at the house, he brought little gifts for Richard and Matilda and spent a few minutes with each. Still, she took care to keep herself a bit distant, turning aside two more offers for dinner before she accepted again. She liked him as a business friend, she needed his credit, but she couldn't successfully imagine any closer bond.

On a cloudy fall day Annabelle arrived home to find several large black carriages, which possessed an ominous official appearance, parked in front of her house. Half a dozen stiff men in black coats stood about with the vacant, self-important air of policemen on duty. She entered her front door fearfully, certain that a warrant had finally been issued for her role in Black Friday. In the parlor, however, she found her sister Jenny and Ulysses, who rose upon her entrance.

"I was going to write," explained Jenny, her face as set and hard as those of the officers outside, "but I tore up every letter."

"Did Bridget get you tea?" asked Annabelle. "My God, there's not even a fire in here. It's freezing."

"I told her not to bother," said Jenny, her tone chilly. "We won't be long." At her side Ulysses, appearing as presidential as a henpecked husband at a quilting party, nodded and gave Annabelle the tightest of smiles. He couldn't have been more restrained if he were tied up with rope. She asked them to sit and said she hoped they would stay to supper.

"I thought when you first wrote me," said Jenny, continuing to stand, "that in sisterly fashion you wanted to make up, that as our prospects had improved so had your family feeling towards us. You were quite superior when we married, sure that you had made a much better match. It was clear that you didn't want to see your country in-laws again. If you didn't talk or write to them, she and her stupid husband weren't likely to visit and embarrass you, were they?"

"Jenny!" Annabelle exclaimed.

Ulysses had also opened his mouth to protest, but when Jenny shook her head at him vigorously, he stepped back half a pace. "I need you to support me, Ulys, not to stop me." She turned to Annabelle. "I see now that you were up to your usual selfish, cruel pursuits. You deceived me, and worse, hurt Ulysses, who's as trusting as a child in family matters. Like so many decent men he can't see as clearly as I what you have done."

"Done!" cried Annabelle. "That's just it. I have done nothing."

"Before and after the election, weren't you after us all the time to visit?" asked Jenny. "You always had this little dinner, or that little at home, where your friends Mr. Gould and Mr. Fisk were present. At them, didn't I hear an awful lot about gold? And weren't the tones pious! How much it would help the country! Then it was Mr. Fisk's boat on which we were taken to the Jubilee. Who arranged all this, Annabelle? Who made it seem as if poor Ulysses was involved? You know as well as I that we have nothing—"

"And so I've said!" Annabelle declared. "Before the committees, and to the papers, but I'm not believed. Sure, I bought gold—but is that a crime?"

"The President's family should be above such things," said Jenny. "Certainly you know that no matter what lies are slung around in the newspapers, Ulysses and I have gained nothing from these disgraceful events."

"President's family!" said Annabelle. "How am I a member of the family? How am I to eat? I bought gold because it looked as if it would go up, and you've no right to tell me I shouldn't have."

"I've come here to say in person what I couldn't write," said Jenny with venomous force. "It will be best if from now on you separate yourself from me and my family. Ulysses won't say it for himself"—here she threw him a glance of contempt—"but he doesn't want to see you, either. And stay away from Papa and Mama."

"Papa! Papa—how is he? I haven't heard a word—" Since she sent him part of her gold profits to help him back on his feet.

"No thanks to you, doing much better," said Jenny. "I speak

frankly for your entire family when I say that none of us wants to have anything to do with you again."

"But—you're my sister."

"Exactly," said Jenny. "That's what has made all this so hard to believe, that a family member would work to destroy a man's career more powerfully than even his political enemies."

With that she shepherded Ulys out, and the front door closed with a firm crash. Annabelle sank onto the sofa and took several deep breaths. My God, she thought, what next?

On the Tuesday morning after the Bolton-Harriman wedding, Annabelle Stokes arrived at her Fifth Avenue dress shop feeling particularly low. The chilly fall air brushed against her cheeks as she stood before the elegant shop window, the unused brass key in her hand.

Framed by the window's velvet curtains and swags were her four mannequins, each dressed in a bustle, wide hoopskirted dress, and yards of Shephen Whitney's imported laces, the elaborate, cluttered style that tasteful Fifth Avenue ladies wore to endless lunches, teas, receptions, dinners, and theater parties. In this sharp, invigorating air, these showy costumes appeared oppressive, heavy bundles of cloth designed for long hours of pampered idleness, a mode of life that, even when she had indulged herself in it during her marriage to Ned, Annabelle found maddening. Over the past weeks, the whining, demanding bridesmaids of the Button King's daughter had given her a bellyful of females who coddled themselves in dreary idleness, and so had the steady trickle of fashionable clients that accompanied them.

Despite her modest good luck of establishing any clientele at all, Annabelle was abruptly sick of Frenchifications, sick of the gauze on lace on silk designs of Worth, Herbault, Boivin, and Trouvère, and sick of fabrics, satin flowers, and furs that were *distingué, recherché,* and *nouveau,* the adjectives that appeared in every department-store and specialty shop advertisement. Complex as was the hand-sewn construction of Eloise's wedding gown, many ladies wore at least one like it every day. Annabelle was caught, stuck, in a nightmarish spider's web of frilly lace embroidered with rows of pearls and needle-toothed gossip. Not the least of it was that she didn't relish a life of manipulating clients through the standard Parisian mixture of imperiousness and flattery.

She unlocked the front door and was greeted by musty staleness. Leaving the blinds down so she wouldn't be disturbed, she dragged two of the plaster mannequins out of the window. Behind the rear partition she slipped out of her dress, removed her hoops and bustle, and put back on her skirt. The lack of so many layers of cloth made her lighter, more buoyant. To blow away the fetid night air, she threw open the six back shutters.

When the mannequins were denuded of hoopskirts and bustles, their blunt breasts and smooth, flesh-covered plaster crotches mutely pleaded for cover. She spread three large pads of rough art paper on the long work counter. Charcoal gripped tightly in her fingers, she sketched a dress for the active sort of lady who wrote for a newspaper. She ripped that sheet off the pad and drew another for a lady who sold advertising space, then an outfit for riding a bicycle in Central Park, then one for running a restaurant near Union Square, another for supervising children in Murray Hill, one for managing a stable, and one for operating a bakery—sensible outfits for sensible ladies working at sensible occupations.

Careful not to smudge the cloth with the flaking, gritty charcoal, she used her left hand to drape it over the mannequins. She stood back and studied the effect. Back to the pads of paper, the edges of which fluttered in the crisp breeze. A dress for walking she decided to call the Fifth Avenue Walking Dress. Back in the War Dorothea Dix had insisted her nurses work without bustles or hoops; based on her memories of those simple lines, Annabelle sketched another four styles. Ready-goods manufacturers who hired girls for their whirring machines forbade them to wear dresses with voluminous slips or frilly petticoats, any sort of hoop or furbelows; for the fun of it Annabelle designed three outfits for such tasks.

Polite taps came twice at the front door; both times she ignored them. The horrid lime-green bloomer-dress that the plump speaker at Sorosis wore—it wasn't a garment that Annabelle would wear, but maybe if she used a fawn brown velveteen, cut the tunic like this, added a sash, got rid of those bloomers, and put on a jacket—she sketched rapidly. She stood back. Not bad, she thought, not half bad.

By noon the wastebasket was full of failures, and a score of charcoal sketches covered the long countertop. Her hands were smeared with grainy black dust, streaks of which smudged her cheeks and lace blouse. She stared at the drawings. While the upper crust looked down on any garment not handcrafted, the newest machines made stitches as small and fine as did any hand. If she contracted out the work, most of these simple designs wouldn't be expensive to cut and sew. Surely some ladies would buy sensible, comfortable-to-wear garments that cost a fifth of elaborate, hand-sewn ensembles.

That afternoon she raised the blinds and opened the shop. Her only caller was the wholesaler Stephen Whitney, who dropped by with a sample of Dieppe lace. She took him into the back room, on the walls of which were pinned two dozen of the charcoal sketches. He peered at them owlishly. She followed him around as he stepped from one to the other.

"Tell me honestly what you think," she said. The windows were still unshuttered, and the fall breeze revived her flagging energy.

He paced around silently, his face screwed up, glancing uneasily from the drawings to her. "What are they for?" he finally asked.

"Well—for the shop," she answered, her voice a bit waspish.

He waved toward the front. "Out there?" he asked in disbelief. Taken aback, still she nodded vigorously. He shook his graying head. "Nooo," he said, "you'll throw away all the goodwill you earned from the Harriman wedding."

"I can sell them."

His boots shuffled on the floor. "And to whom, pray tell?"

"To anybody," she answered. Again he shook his head. "Everybody," she went on. "The ladies in Sorosis—they'll buy them."

"A handful of customers." He was agitated, his head bobbing from side to side and his hands waving north and south. "Up and down Fifth Avenue—*there* are your customers. Ladies with money who buy layered getups." Annabelle shook her head and pointed to the drawings.

"These are outfits *I* want to wear," she said. "I'm sick and tired of cinched waists, of not being able to draw a full breath. Here, look." Her voice rushing on, she pointed to the Fifth Avenue Walking Dress. "This line here—it flatters with*out* requiring a corset. The skirt is *three* inches off the ground. Do you have any idea how distracting it is to worry constantly about muddying a skirt?" Stephen paced nervously about the small room, then turned, his swarthy face stricken.

"I don't understand you," he said. "You risked your money— your last dollars—on this shop. I understood that, a businessman's risk. You patiently waited months for the right moment. You finally get it—I was afraid you'd go broke first—and no sooner do you have a shot at this highfalutin crowd than you throw it away."

"Will you help me?" she asked. "I have to buy fabric, find a manufacturer. Line up credit. Take out advertising. A lot of things."

"I won't allow you a nickel to make clothes for—suffragettes." He made the name sound worse than "whore."

"Not for suffragettes," she said patiently, "merely for women to do things in."

He sighed. "Aw, Annabelle. I can't refuse you anything, but for this it's cash on the barrelhead. I won't advance you a single dollar, so don't ask."

While the wind in her sails was diminished, Annabelle plowed ahead. Using her slim profits from the Bolton wedding, she bought fabric through Stephen's wholesale business, and accompanied by him, she plunged into the crowded, noisy world of the Lower East Side, where they found a grimy factory that did first-class cutting and sewing at a reasonable price. Despite his objections, Stephen helped in a score of other ways, from the purchase of thread to the color of the final trim. He cautioned her not to have many dresses made up, but because the factory owner gave her a large discount for quality, she ordered a dozen copies of her best eight designs. Using half of her remaining bank account, she bought quarter-page ads in three weeklies, including the ultrafashionable *Harper's*.

During the first week, however, the newly restyled mannequins drew only one customer inside the shop, although many Fifth Avenue ladies, a puzzled frown wrinkling their faces, paused to peer fixedly at the four outfits labeled *The New American Style*. Annabelle wore the new dresses herself. Pretending not to notice, she hoped the stares she gathered in the street were of admiration, not condemnation. Phoebe gushed over the new outfits, promptly buying three and wearing them several times a week. Annabelle mailed copies of the ads to the ladies of Sorosis. To each she attached a personal note saying lengthy fitting sessions weren't necessary and that she would allow credit if they wished to try the garments at home.

Over the next two weeks the shop was as deserted as ever. Stephen said little, but across his lowered blue-gray eyes and swarthy cheeks was a glaze of distress. He had been right. Without telling him, she went to a Worth Street moneylender, mortgaged her house to the full extent, and used the money to place ads in *Harper's* for three more weeks.

But they drew no one into the shop. This time she had no Jay Gould to bail her out, for even if Stephen was willing to, he didn't have this kind of money. Another few weeks and she would again be hanging over a cliff by her fingernails. The dress shop would be another failure to add to her marriage, Ned's bankruptcy, and the foolishness with Jay. She supposed she could go back to Gantry, but the life she left when she was twenty was long, long extinguished. Several mornings she could scarcely bring herself to put on one of the new styles, but it proved impossible to talk to the few ladies who came in to ask about them when she herself wore a bustle and hoopskirt.

The next week six of the new outfits were bought, mostly by supportive members of Sorosis. The President, Jennie June Croly, came in with Phoebe and bought one of the Fifth Avenue Walking Dresses. Along with the new styles, Annabelle sold health corsets, which didn't cinch so tightly, and suspenders instead of the waspwaisters that pinched every lady's middle, no matter what her size, into an eighteen-inch tube.

While her new customers admired the cut of the garments, and particularly their comfort, almost every one complained about their overall bagginess. Over a cool November night, the three gas lamps turned up full and hissing like split steam pipes, damning herself for not following Stephen's advice and for initially buying so many dresses, she sat at the rear counter and redesigned the garments and sketched new patterns for the cutters.

Phoebe took the eight styles, copies of the ads, and Annabelle's drawings to Boston and Philadelphia to show department stores. Annabelle received tiny orders from a store in Boston and two in Philadelphia, as well as a favorable write-up in the *World* under Phoebe's name, and one in the *Sun*, which touted walking as excellent exercise for ladies. The fashion editors of the *Trib*, the *Times*, and the *Herald* only noticed the outfits to dismiss them as examples of the worst sort of modern barbarity. Jennie June Croly wore the Walker to the November Sorosis luncheon, where it was greatly admired.

The next week Annabelle sold nearly a dozen. In late November, to her delight Annabelle had to go back to the manufacturer for another two dozen dresses, which she persuaded him to cut and sew on a month's credit. What sold particularly well was the Fifth Avenue Walking Dress, with its hunting jacket cut deep in back and square in front, and its wide-bottomed skirt. Several ladies remarked that it was the first time in their lives they had worn a skirt that cleared the ground. Not worrying about snagging your skirt on roots or dragging it through the filth was as giddy as flying. Besides, wire hoopskirts and whalebone bustles were so heavy! Many wanted a second such outfit, something in a different fabric and cut. Keeping the basic design, Annabelle fashioned another style and displayed it, too, in the window.

Each week that winter the number of Walkers that the shop sold and the shipments billed to department stores were larger than the week before. Annabelle hired an assistant to help with sales and fittings. Her checkbook went up and down erratically as she juggled income, accounts receivable, and the increasing payments for advertising, fabric, freight, wages, and manufacturing. The back room became so crammed with cardboard boxes and makeshift wooden dress racks that there was scarcely room for Mrs. Grumby the fitter to sew. Stephen shook his head with the amused delight of a father admiring his daughter's success in a church bake sale.

In late December Annabelle realized with a start that to keep up with the demand she must open a larger shop.

*   *   *

The day before Christmas Eve was a cloudy, cold Friday that promised snow. Almost crowded out by cardboard boxes, Annabelle sat at her rolltop desk in the cozy rear of the shop working at her accounts. The potbellied stove roared happily.

Over the winter season she had sold nearly 200 of the new outfits, 150 of them the Walker, which now came in five styles, corduroy and wool, and half a dozen colors. To prevent other dress shops and manufacturers from copying the designs, she had acted quickly, spending money she really didn't have. One version of the Walker was sold at a low price, while another was designed for ladies who wanted to pay more and wear a more exclusive style. When she had presented Stephen a check for her last fabric bill, she thought his furrowed brow and smile appeared as disappointed as it was pleased. Annabelle supposed that a man didn't like to see a woman financially independent.

She looked up as her new assistant scurried behind the partition for the broom and dustpan. "Enough, June," she said. "Go home early. Do a little Christmas shopping."

"Are you sure, ma'am?"

"We won't see many customers tonight. Ladies are in no mood to buy Walkers, and at this time of year wise husbands buy lace and jewelry."

In minutes Annabelle was alone. This was a time of day she loved, the quiet moments when the potbellied stove gave off its thin, efficient odor of burning coal, when warmth had finally penetrated into the shop's every nook, and when the heat had drawn into the air the wispy essence of lace, the shimmering lightness of silk, and the nubby rub of wool. Distantly she heard carolers singing "Jingle Bells." She sat back, the ledger weighing heavily in her lap. It had been a hard three years, but the flame of a real business burned here. If she nurtured it, this small fire could flourish into a blaze that for years to come would keep her and the children warm. Humming "Jingle Bells," she pulled down the blinds, locked the front door, banked the coals in the stove's orange-red belly, and was shuttering the rear windows when Stephen's exuberant coin rapped against the front glass.

She flew forward, a smile welcoming him. Stephen's cold face was as red and excited as a child's looking forward to Santa Claus.

Inside, he unwound his maroon scarf, unbuttoned his massive gray overcoat, and fumbled with his specs. A small blue-velvet box appeared in his hand from nowhere. Her heart sank. She hadn't bought him a present.

"I'm very fond of you," he said. His hands awkwardly maneuvered, and in them the tiny blue box opened. Against the midnight-blue velvet shone a circle of emeralds against a gold band—a betrothal ring. "I want—I love you. Will you marry me?" Stunned, she stared from the emerald ring to his dancing, hopeful face and back to the winking green stones.

"Marry—" She should have seen this coming, but she had been so swept up by the shop. "How—" She started to say "sweet," but that was too patronizing, as if he were shoving a box of candy at her. He took her hand, but instead of allowing him to put the ring on her, she took the box with her other hand. Tears prickled her eyes and nose. "I'm touched," she said.

His index finger shoved his spectacles back on his nose and his hopeful smile fell. "It's—no?" he whispered, face gray in despair.

The companionable, sisterly feelings she felt toward Stephen were nothing like what she had felt toward Ned and Jay. She considered putting off her answer, but delay wouldn't make it easier. She put the velvet box back in his palm and held his hand.

"It's no," she whispered. His lips parted and his eyes blinked as if pushing back tears. It was like denying a child Christmas. She felt stuffy and numb. He snapped shut the box's lid.

"Will you—think it over?" he asked in a plaintive voice.

In her gentlest tone, she said, "I'm sorry. It will still be no."

Over the fifteen months since Black Friday, she had been her own person and free, and no matter how small it was, she reveled in her newfound success. Having made her own judgments and mistakes, she had engineered her own triumph, this successful shop, which made her independent. She had no wish to be second fiddle to Papa, Ned, Jay Gould—any man. The velvet box slid into the side pocket of Stephen's overcoat, where it made an ungraceful lump.

"Please," Stephen whispered, his face in pain, "don't dismiss me so quickly." Despite her wish to cut this off, she nodded.

His pocket bulging with the ring box, he walked her home in a restless, awkward silence. His eyes darted at the door of her brownstone as if he wanted to be invited in, but she couldn't stand any more of this clumsy fumbling. She couldn't think of a word to say that didn't sound banal. His gloved fingers affectionately squeezed her arm through her wool coat and he was off.

That night after the children and Bridget had gone to bed, Annabelle sat in the parlor before a cheerful fire. The glass of rich sherry that she sipped warmed her. It had started to snow as she put Matilda to bed, large, powdery flakes, and every time she looked out the front window, snow still drifted down. Harness bells jingled by.

Now was when she ought to be lonely, when everyone was off to bed and she was by herself, but she wasn't lonely, not a bit. Stephen was a companion she enjoyed, a seasoned businessman wiser about business affairs and daily life than Phoebe with her wild-eyed enthusiasm, a settled friend with whom Annabelle could share triumphs and failures. Over the past few months he had become "Uncle Stephen" to Matilda and Richard. She sighed. With his two children grown, he clearly ached for the ups and downs of a second family life.

The house gave one of its loud, popping cracks that sounded as if the roof were splitting. He was someone, too, against whom to snuggle up on a raw evening like tonight. She sighed again. If she persisted in saying no, it would be the end of their friendship. Despite her misgivings, that night she slept soundly.

The next morning rapidly clanging church bells announced Christmas Eve. After the two-inch snowfall, Manhattan glistened as white and festive as an icy wedding cake.

Annabelle strode to the shop through crisp air colored by the resinous tang of woodsmoke. Boys' excited shouts echoed in the cold as they belly flopped on sleds and scraps of planks. Annabelle's boots crunched loudly against the fresh snow. The harnesses of horses lingle-lingled as their hooves clopped by, breath steamy white against the freezing air. Rarely had Annabelle felt so exhilarated, so excited, so glad to be alive. The cold bit her nose and cheeks, but under her heavy coat her limbs moved warmly. The combination of brisk air and warm, fluid movements drove her zestful thoughts faster.

When she compared Stephen with her first months with Jay, he sank in the balance. With Jay everything had been dramatic, important. Before Jay there was Ned, who made her into half of a glittering couple, the toast of New York. She had forged a hot, strong bond with those two knights, one black, one white, a bond she would never feel with Stephen. She sighed, and the deep intake of frigid air braced her. Maybe Ned and Jay had ruined her for a tie with a levelheaded man. Those two had been going places fast, influencing people, while Stephen was possessed by no strong ambition. Over forty, wherever he was going he had already arrived. She was fond of him and trusted him, but she didn't *love* him. She didn't feel toward Stephen an ounce of the desperate need that she had felt for Ned and Jay. On the other hand, she wasn't desperate or needy now.

The exertion of tramping through the snow was pleasantly warming. The chilled air in her lungs was as fresh as icy water on a roaringly hot July day. She turned onto Fifth Avenue. She must stick to her no. Near the curb a Civil War veteran, his blue uniform ragged and filthy, winked a cheerful eye in her direction and shouted, "Hot corn, get your hot corn mush!" She smiled at him and hurried on. Maintaining her no to Stephen would cost her his friendship. He would tamely swallow his disappointment, profess undying amity, and gradually stop coming 'round.

She sighed a cloudy breath into the frigid air. She didn't want to lose his genial companionship. In a way it was a pity to tell him no only because she wasn't *mad* about him. With powerful clarity Annabelle saw it unlikely—impossible, actually—that she would ever again be insane with love.

Never again. *Never again!*

A sumptuous bouquet of baking loaves wafted across the sidewalk from Haas's Bakery, a summery sweetness as intoxicating as the nectared fragrance of a buzzing May garden. Abruptly Annabelle broke into an exuberant peal of laughter that turned several black derby hats and snug bonnets in her direction. Being *mad* for a man was no reason to marry him! *Mad* meant you were too *insane* to know what you were doing!

At that moment a new and clear vision of marriage was driven into her, one different from all her prior ties with men: the tie to her father, the tie to Ned, and the tie to Jay, around each of whom, to a varying degree and distance, she had revolved like a moon. Unlike those three, Stephen was a man she could live *without*, a man around whom she did not revolve. Her marriage to Ned had been a product of her youth and exuberance. Her affair with Jay had been one of passion, an impossible mad passion. With Stephen it might be something vastly different—mellow love.

Her biting step quickened on the powdery snow. Her brain whirled. Marriage could be a partnership of equals, two suns circling each other, a sustaining union nothing like the master-chattel shackles into which most marital hopes atrophied. With icy clarity she recognized that any such newfangled alliance was likely to fail, but that it was the only one that gave her a chance at happiness. This time her unfettered exuberance came out as such a rich chuckle that several men threw sharp glances her way.

She would tell Stephen *yes*, provided he understood that she was to possess her own business and manage her own life. Nothing could ever again draw her into being the functionary, the handmaiden, the hireling of another person's goals—man or woman.

She slowed, her boots chewing loudly on the crust of snow. Stephen might understand. He was older, in his forties, certainly mellow. He might have the wisdom. If he didn't, she didn't want the marriage.

Her steps crunched faster. She could hardly wait to see him.

516

49

MAGNIFICENT MANSFIELD
The Falstaffian Fisk Routed
Horse, Foot, & Dragoons
by the Late Partner of his Joys

The Dirty Linen of a Lifetime Washed
Publicly in a Police Court

—New York Herald headline, 1871

On Saturday morning, January 6, 1871, Josie Mansfield, nervous and jumpy, was driven by her Negro servant Carter through the slushy, snow-covered streets to the Yorkville Police Court for the second session in the trial of *Mansfield v. Fisk.*

As yesterday, fashionable carriages were parked helter-skelter against the courthouse curb. The grimy hallway inside was crammed with the same fashionably dressed ladies and gentlemen come to witness "The Trial of the Century." Despite the rumbles in her middle and her tripping heart at being the center of so much scrutiny, Josie held her head high, pressed forward, and a way miraculously opened. In her wake flared a roar of speculation.

As her lawyer had instructed, she was dressed soberly in a severe dress of black silk, demure velvet jacket, jockey hat, and illusion veil that both hoped would conceal what the *Sun* and the *Mirror* constantly described as her "voluptuous charms." She came alone, for Ned and Mr. Wickers, their lawyer, had agreed that it would be better for Ned and Josie not to sit together in court or even act as if they knew each other. Her cousin, Virginia Williams, had agreed to accompany her for the ordeal, but this morning Virginia pleaded severe cramps and "a perfectly horrid headache."

With prim movements, Josie eased onto the hard straight chair at the table with Mr. Wickers, the tall, beaky lawyer, who resembled a goose with a perpetual head cold. The wood-paneled courtroom possessed a stark quality, as if its plaster walls, polished wood rails, high windows, and hard chairs, like a brightly lit bare stage, allowed no shadows or concealment.

Mr. Wickers glanced up from an elaborate doodle on a pad of foolscap. Josie smiled, and his goosey grin cut his face like a beak.

"Put your veil up," he instructed. She lifted the folds of her veils onto her jockey hat's brim. Yesterday afternoon he had examined her, bringing out the wrongs that Jim had done. This morning was the opposition's turn at her.

"Remember now," the lawyer said, "take your time answering. If you come through this as I think, we'll be well on our way to teaching Mr. Fisk a lesson he won't soon forget." He had spent hours coaching her how to fend off Jim's lawyer, and he promised to intervene against any of Hummel's well-known vicious attacks. After all, she reminded herself, I'm an actress. On the stand I'm playing the most important role of my career—a wronged woman.

Her gaze stealthily crept toward the opposing lawyers' table. As yesterday, Jim, dressed in his maroon admiral's uniform, resplendent in gold braid, sat between his two lawyers. He wore it to gain an edge on the jury's sympathy by making them think he had fought in the War. Well, she would sneak into her testimony that he had never served a day in Mr. Lincoln's army.

After that, the jury was brought back in, twelve men as ordinary as clerks, who shuffled along the two benches to their seats. When they had finally settled, their eyes stared at Josie with hot, speculative gleams. Josie recognized these male fires. Each was asking himself how far he could get with her. As Lawyer Wickers had instructed, she didn't return the glances, but dropped her gaze as demurely as a virgin. A clerk's shout sang out and all rose. Thin and stooped as an aged hound, the gray-haired, black-robed judge rustled in and took his place behind the high bench.

With loud thumps everybody sat. Josie was called to the stand. Her heart beat rapidly as she stood. Mr. Wickers had warned that Howe and Hummel would have investigated her thoroughly, and that she must be prepared to answer questions from the first day of her life in New York. A furious scratching rose from the pencils of the dozen artists to her right. With deliberate slowness, putting off the ordeal, she approached the oak witness chair. Over and over Ned and Wickers had assured her that Jim would settle before the trial—"on the courthouse steps," Wickers kept saying, as if the phrase itself would call forth Jim—but inexplicably, he hadn't yesterday, and he hadn't this morning.

As she seated herself she took care to move in a dignified way. A waving field of pale faces peered at her with the curiosity of a crowd at a circus. During the cross-examination she would be asked every manner of question about her private life. Hummel was going to hold up her drawers to the entire gallery and shout, "Behold, ladies and gentlemen, how she has soiled them! This woman is not fit to be in your company, much less for you to associate with!" No amount of cash was worth this.

She spotted Ned in a pink waistcoat and solemn face seated in the first row, his trim figure glorious in a new Alexis jacket colored mocha cream. She wanted to smile at him, and she wanted a supporting smile in return, but neither dared acknowledge the other. His gold-headed black cane swung casually to and fro between his manly legs as if these goings-on were paltry fare to such a worldly fellow as he. She mustn't look at him, and yet his confident face was the only one she wanted to look at.

Abe Hummel rose and approached her. He was dressed in a dapper, navy-blue suit with an ivory death's-head suspended from the gold watch chain that crossed his vest. His slick, dark hair and swarthy features were as handsome as an actor's, but Josie saw that his diminutive frame would never succeed onstage. The little lawyer smiled and tipped an imaginary hat toward her, yet all the while his black eyes bored into hers, as if searching for the precise caliber of her soul. Josie blanched and hurriedly looked away.

His questions were posed with respectful politeness. For the first half hour they were innocent enough, asking her how she had first met Jim, how often she saw him, and establishing that she had arrived in New York with little and now possessed a house, several furs, a servant, a carriage, and closets of expensive clothes. Hummel appeared too tiny to harm her, as puny as a six-year-old boy. Her grip on the chair's twin arms relaxed, and her feet pressed less tightly against the floor.

Hummel cocked his head in a perplexed fashion, and posed another soft-voiced question that yet carried to the rear of the packed courtroom. "Isn't it true that you induced Sally Woods, who runs a bawdy house, to introduce you to Mr. Fisk?" A loud rumble swelled from the well-dressed horde on the benches.

The elderly judge banged his gavel and wordlessly glared about for quiet. Josie's heart hammered and her mouth was so thick that she didn't know if she could answer at all. To steady herself she pressed her feet against the hard floor, pushed her bustle against the chair back, and reminded herself to sit up straight.

"No." It came out as a croak. She cleared her throat and said in a stronger voice, "No." Hummel's dapper shoes danced toward the jury, and he smiled in their direction, his crafty expression saying, "Watch this." His black pumps spun back to Josie.

"I can call Miss Woods and any number of the young 'ladies' in her employ," cooed Hummel. "Would you care to reconsider your answer?" Josie took a deep breath.

"I don't remember asking her," she said in a low voice. "The meeting was accidental." Hummel smiled and nodded in a nasty way.

"But at her West Twenty-seventh Street house?"

"Yes."

Hummel bobbed his head in several more damning nods. His black, mocking eyes seemed to know everything.

"Can you not tell me," he asked, "whether in a town near San Francisco a pistol was pointed at a man's head in your presence?" Her slippery fingers grasped the chair's arms. How much did he know? She hadn't discussed her life in California with Mr. Wickers because it had nothing to do with the case.

"There was a circumstance of that kind happened," Josie cautiously admitted. The owlish Hummel beamed as if she were a promising fledging.

"Was the gun pointed at a man by the name of D. W. Perley?" he asked. The sound of that old name made her start. How did he know about Perley? She didn't want Ned and Virginia to know about him, much less the flock of reporters to her left, half grins looping below cynical eyes. She wanted to deny it, but if Hummel knew Perley's name, he must know more.

"Yes, sir," she said in a small voice. Hummel's tiny fingers began to toy with the ivory death's-head that he wore as a watch charm.

"Was it pointed at him by a person with the name of Warren?"

Josie glanced at Wickers, whose pencil sketched an elaborate doodle on his foolscap as if it were more important than her distress. Again Josie longed to deny the accusation, but Hummel had stung her so hard with the Sally Woods question that she was afraid. He glared with the confident eagerness of an owl expecting a mouse to break and run, to provide sport. Either "yes" or "no" would be meat to him. She forced the answer through her unwilling lips.

"Yes, sir."

"And Warren was your stepfather?" he asked.

No harm in this one. "Yes, sir."

520

Hummel smiled in an encouraging way, and Josie relaxed her grip. Maybe this wouldn't be so bad.

"And Warren cooked up a scheme with you whereby you were to be 'intimate' with Perley—an elderly lawyer, I believe, and married—so that Warren would 'catch' the two of you and blackmail Perley, didn't he?"

"No!" shouted Josie. The crowd's stir and buzz rose louder than before. Reporters scribbled and artists sketched rapidly.

Lawyer Wickers was on his feet, outrage on his face. "Objection! Your Honor, he's leading my client and badgering her."

"What!" Hummel shouted at Josie, causing her to shrink in the chair. "*No?*" His small face was torn in disbelief. "*No*, he didn't blackmail Perley?—or *no*, he didn't catch you and Perley and put a gun to Perley's head?" She wanted to smash that doll's face. She half raised herself by pressing down on the arms of the chair.

"*No* to none of it!" she shouted. Next to the purple jacket of Howe, Jim's teeth were bared in a painful wince.

"Objection sustained," said the thin, elderly judge in a low growl. "Counsel will ask one question at a time." A flood of relief swept over Josie. She lowered herself, turned, and thanked the judge's hawkish profile in a soft voice, but he ignored her.

"Yes, Your Honor," said Hummel in a respectful tone that further buoyed Josie, but her tormentor's expression didn't seem bothered by the judge's scolding. He turned to Josie. "You admit that Warren pointed a gun to Perley's head. Didn't that come about because you and Perley were caught half dressed?" He made her sound so tawdry. She had been a foolish sixteen-year-old. She must brazen out the rest of this. She again tightened her grip on the chair, and then noticed the sharp-eyed lawyer was watching her fingers.

"No," she answered. Let him prove all this.

His right hand crept along his blue vest to the ivory death's-head, which he rolled between his thumb and forefinger. He pierced her with his dark, merciless eyes and asked, "Didn't Perley write a check to your stepfather?"

The wooden arms of the witness chair were so slippery with sweat they were hard to grip. Deny it all, she told herself.

"No."

"Mrs. Mansfield," he continued, his tone so bright and winning that it surprised her, "I have subpoenaed the bank's records." The pleasant tone and the ugly threat jarred her.

"Well—he may have."

"He *may* have," Hummel roared in an abrupt switch of tone. "And he *may* have been blackmailed, *may* he not?"

The crowd gasped collectively at the shouted words. Above its rumble rose her lawyer's cry. "Objection! Objection!" In Josie's heart the damage was done. Once the afternoon's papers hit the street, Ned, her cousin Virginia, and all of New York—if not the whole country from Boston to Atlanta—would conclude that she was in league with the whorehouse madam Sally Woods. And if she had blackmailed in California, she had likely blackmailed in New York.

A few moments later Hummel read from an earlier interview with the *Herald* in which she had been quoted as saying, "While acquainted with Mr. Fisk, I was always supplied with silks, wines, food, and everything that I could desire."

"That is not so," she said. She had practiced this point with Lawyer Wickers a dozen times, and it was a relief to fall back onto the well-rehearsed words. "Mr. Fisk was only my friend, and he never paid me a penny. My money came from profitable speculations on my behalf conducted by a broker named Marston, another friend. Right from the start in New York, I have paid my own way."

At the defendant's table a disgusted Jim wagged his head from side to side. Hummel nodded soberly, while his eyes, out of the judge's sight and directed at the jury, lifted toward the ceiling. Several jurors grinned and nudged their neighbors.

What had she admitted to? She felt dazed. It was hard to think. She wasn't sure what she was doing here or how all this had happened. Wickers had said Jim would be on trial for libeling her, but it felt as if she were on trial. She drew a deep breath. This was dangerous ground, but on the other hand they had practiced and practiced her answers.

Then his adroit, well-informed questions forced her to admit— for all of New York to snicker at—that as an unmarried woman she had lived with a married man in his Jersey City hotel suite. Josie wanted to sink through the floor in shame. After this morning no respectable household in the city would allow her to enter. As the morning wore on he further forced her to admit that her stock winnings were paid to her personally by Jim, that Jim had aided her in buying the Twenty-third Street house, that Jim had paid for the furnishings, and that they had cost about $65,000. Her wire bustle pressed against the oak back of the witness chair, her whalebone stays dug into her flesh, and hours, years seemed to pass. Hummel then dragged out of her that she no longer possessed the notorious letters that Jim had written her, and that she had given them to "Ned Stokes for safekeeping because it would keep Mr. Fisk from stealing from me what was rightfully mine."

Among the gauzy veils Ned's head was wobbling from side to

side. With a start she remembered that he and Lawyer Wickers had been adamant that she wasn't to mention Ned's name on the stand. As he shook his head to and fro, his mouth formed the silent word *Noooo*. He was accustomed to deferential treatment in the society columns, and the several news articles over the last few weeks that connected him with Josie had upset him horribly. But she was exhausted, utterly wrung out. Too many faces had stared at her too long. It was no use hiding. This Hummel knew everything, and Ned wasn't up here and didn't understand how hard it was.

"No further questions, Your Honor," said Hummel. "Call Mr. Edward Stokes."

"No!" said Josie, leaning forward. "You can't!"

"Why not, Mrs. Mansfield?" asked Hummel, smiling at her. "You yourself have introduced his name and sworn in open court that he possesses these letters." He turned to the judge. "Your Honor, Mr. Stokes, please?" As smooth as an actor in a well-rehearsed bit of stage business, he pivoted, arm and finger outstretched, to the rear doors. "Who I believe is lurking in the back of the courtroom, attempting to slink out of this hall of justice." With a vast stir and rustle, the audience swiveled backward. Before Ned could escape, the bailiff ushered him forward.

"You may step down, Mrs. Mansfield," ordered the judge. "Call Edward Stokes." A little giddy that her interrogation was over, Josie wavered as she stood.

On the way to her seat she passed Ned. His lips were bared with fury, eyes yellow with hatred, while his face struggled to maintain a contemptuous urbanity. She kept her eyes on a spot on the back wall. She would never again be able to look a soul in the eye.

Josie sat next to her lawyer, who grazed her sleeve with two fingertips and gave her one of his weak, goosey smiles. She found a handkerchief and savored the cotton's dryness against her wet palms. She shifted in an agitated way, for she knew what was going on within Ned—a volcano of hatred. It was bad enough for her up there, but she had precious little reputation to lose. Although half busted most of the time, Ned was really someone in society. If Hummel humiliated him, Ned would be even more furious. Still, Ned was stronger and more resourceful, as hard to get ahold of as a well-greased pig. He was cunning enough to embarrass even such a slick lawyer. With any luck he would figure out a way to save them both.

She prayed that this would be so. Since they first attacked Jim six months ago, they had laid out a few thousand here, a few thousand there, borrowed everything they could, till their legal fees alone—which they had spent to revenge themselves on Jim and to collect the $50,000 that they reckoned Jim owed her—added up to nearly $30,000. They had counted on a handsome settlement out of court, but as the months slipped by, it hadn't come to pass.

The short, dapper Hummel took his seat next to Jim, while William Howe, the lion-headed, pudding-bodied lawyer in an outrageous purple coat, diamonds, and checked trousers rose like a festooned mountain climbing to its feet. He was far larger than Jim or Bill Tweed, well over 300 pounds, possibly 350. The floor shook as he crossed to Ned, who glared at him. When eating with Jim, Josie had often seen Howe, dining alone, in the Broad Street Delmonico's, where he typically consumed two of every course—two bottles of wine, a pumpkin and a fish chowder, a whole trout and a filet of Dover sole, roast beef as well as pork chops, and a cherry tart along with a bowl of Delmonico's famous coffee ice cream. This morning he was outlandishly dressed in trousers with checks of black and white, a white doeskin waistcoat, and a suitcoat of royal purple, which was normal for him. In place of a tie Howe wore a clover leaf of gold set with white, pink, and black pearls that held a diamond dewdrop suspended between the points of his collar. The crowd strained forward, for the newspapers covered the trial performances of William Howe as routinely, and for much the same reasons, as they covered the theater.

Yet, surprisingly for such a gross man, Howe began as Hummel had with Josie, soft and gentle as a summer breeze. Josie relaxed, for the tone of his gravel-voiced questions was that of one urbane gentleman discussing the innocent affairs of another. Howe nodded his shaggy gray head as if he well understood that a gent of Ned's breeding and background would have little in the way of a personal bond with "a largely unemployed actress," as Ned described her. Not a cough or murmur was heard from the packed benches, as if the audience didn't want to miss a word of the master's performance.

After a quarter of an hour, in response to Howe's summary of his testimony, Ned ostentatiously concluded, "Yes, my friendship with Mrs. Mansfield was entirely an innocent one. Whenever I visited, Miss Williams, Mrs. Mansfield's cousin, invariably sat between us." Josie smiled, for Ned had cleverly wiggled right through Howe's ham-sized hands.

"Ummmm," said Howe with a crafty roll of his eyes in the direction of the jury that caused them to squirm and grin in foolish delight, "like a duenna?"

"Yes, I should think that's it exactly," said Ned, triumphantly crossing one elegant leg over the other. His straight back, his fashionable pink satin waistcoat cut on the diagonal, and his careless expression displayed him as a model of composed urbanity, a well-bred gentleman who would hardly count a tawdry actress among his friends.

Yet a half hour's questions and testimony later, both of Ned's elegant pumps were firmly pressed against the wooden court floor and he was leaning forward, almost lunging out of the witness chair.

"No," shouted Ned, his face mottled, "I did not manage Mrs. Mansfield's household!"

He answered the next question with, "Yes, I accepted loans from Mrs. Mansfield, but only for investment purposes."

To the next question he said, "No, I did not comport myself as if I were married to Mrs. Mansfield!" Howe's bullhorn voice asked if he was aware that he was under oath.

"Yes."

"Are you aware that I intend to call Miss Williams to the stand?" Her cousin! Josie's heart began to hammer. This wasn't fair.

Ned started. "No," he said in a doubtful tone.

Howe stepped closer to the witness chair. "Are you aware that I intend to call Mrs. Mansfield's servant Carter to the stand?"

Carter! What could he say? And he was a Negro! But she remembered that they were people, too, now that Mr. Lincoln had won his war. Carter had seen Ned leave through the back door many a morning. Ned's lips bared before he answered.

"No."

"And that I have sequestered him so that there's no chance he may be suborned?"

Ned lunged about in the chair like a fancy trout floundering on the ribs of a skiff.

"Please answer," Howe insisted in a sweet voice. Ned shook his head.

"Please indicate your answer for the stenographer," ordered the judge.

"No," Ned spat out. Howe smiled and nodded his shaggy head in the direction of the judge as if to say that now he was getting somewhere.

"Do you know the penalties for perjury in New York State?" Howe asked.

"Not exactly."

"Substantial, sir," said Howe. "Perhaps in light of this testimony that I shall introduce you would like to restate your answers?"

Ned then admitted that he had slept over at Josie's house, yet maintained, "But I only stayed overnight when it was very stormy."

"Only when it was stormy?" said Howe in a loud comic voice that rang from the high ceiling and back walls.

"Yes."

"*Only* when it was stormy?" said Howe in a tone of utter disbelief.

"Yes," insisted Ned. This was crucial, for if the jury believed that Josie had slept with both men during the same period, her reputation would be so besmirched that nothing Jim charged her with in his blackmail suit would be construed as libel. Howe's pudding face made a clown's mug toward the jury as he puffed himself up like an immensely fierce purple tomcat.

"I put it to you, sir," he shouted, arms raised as high as a preacher's, "that the weather this past winter, spring, and fall must have been fiercely inclement every night of the week!" Like a master actor holding his audience spellbound, he dropped his arms and turned to the jury to growl, "Indeed, I put it to you, sir, that we have suffered a series of the most inhospitable squalls these parts have known since my granddad was a pup!"

Laughter bent over the twelve members of the jury and came as a roar from the crowd. Even Josie's protectors, the elderly, hawk-faced judge and Goosey Wickers, smiled.

The judge said it was noon. Howe said he had more questions for the witness, as he intended to show that this "gentleman" had controlled the plaintiff through a combination of trickery and sinister influence. He would take it as a great favor if the court would instruct the witness to be on hand Monday for further questions, as the witness was bound by few ties to the community. He possessed a history of evading his responsibilities, including the support of his own children, in evidence of which the shaggy lawyer would like to present an affidavit from the children's mother. He handed up a paper. Josie cringed. Ned must be even more furious at this last round of insults to his standing as a gentleman.

The hawk-faced judge faced Ned and sternly asked if he understood what was being said. His teeth bared, Ned nodded and promised to be in court at nine o'clock Monday morning.

The court recessed for the weekend. When Ned stepped down from the stand Josie wanted to reach out a hand to soothe the naked rage that twisted his mouth and brow, but she didn't dare make matters worse by showing the crowd how close they were. He stalked past her. She rose to leave. From the buzz, the titters, and the searching looks directed Josie's way by departing ladies and gents, no one in the courtroom—spectators, newspaper reporters, or jury—believed that on his overnight visits she and Ned had enjoyed only the delights of conversation. There he was, scurrying out the back door.

Indeed, the ladies who peered at her sideways through their dark veils undoubtedly thought that Josie was no better than a prostitute, and that Ned had played the role of "fancy man" in all this, planning her moves like a street pimp and sharing the luxuries she wheedled out of Jim with her sexual favors. Howe and Hummel's questions had made Jim appear the victim of Ned and Josie's criminal scheming.

Ignoring the shouts for comments from reporters shoving against her, Josie lowered her veils and pushed through the crowd. She maneuvered through stiff backs, blind elbows, and bustles toward the exit, her eyes searching for Ned. At a little lunch at her house maybe he would rage about and discharge his venom. She wanted to throw herself into his arms and for the two of them to leave New York for who-cared-where and start their lives over.

Ned wasn't in the crowded anteroom just outside the courtroom, but in the wide hallway. Here she didn't have to push her way through. When the crowd realized she was headed toward him, a path was hastily cleared, and as she drew near, a hush fell. Ned stood talking to a portly fellow, his back straight, gray eyes as arrogant as ever, although his pink silk waistcoat was crumpled. He hadn't seen her, but the hush of the mob's gabble alerted him that something was up, and his arrogant gaze swung on her.

His head snapped back and his eyes recoiled. In his narrowed gaze she saw it plain. He didn't want her. He didn't want anything to do with her. From his self-centered point of view, she had brought all this down on him. She wanted to walk by, head high, but she wasn't able to.

"Ned," she implored in an urgent whisper.

"What?" His head was reared back, nose lifted, as if she stank, his eyes coldly forbidding. She wanted to plead that this public world had nothing to do with the private world they made together, but the words wouldn't come. She wanted to place her hand on his sleeve, yet she didn't dare. From all sides eyes peered at them. She wanted to touch him, to hold him, to comfort him and be comforted by him, yet he regarded her with the warmth he would give a snivelly, muddy rat whose tail had streaked his gray trousers.

For the longest time they stared at each other. "Mrs. Mansfield," he said finally in a tone of utmost aristocratic weariness, "I think it best you go your way and cease badgering me." His eyes lifted to the crowd, and he raised his voice so they could hear him. "I have gone out of my way to befriend a person in the arts, and little but trouble has it gotten me." Speechless, she stared at him. "Good-bye," he said, and turned back to the portly gentleman.

Keeping her back straight, she walked to the front door. Her thighs and feet felt thick and numb, yet she forced herself to put one foot in front of the other as she stepped into the cold street and peered about in vain for Carter and her carriage.

Flecks of snow stung her cheeks. Where was Carter? What did "sequester" mean, anyway? With faces half hidden by fans and veils, malicious female eyes stared and whispers eddied about her. It didn't matter. Nothing did. All she wanted was to get away from these hideous people, get away anywhere, just get away.

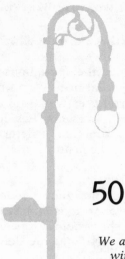

50

*We all know he loved both women and
   wine,
But his heart it was right I am sure.
He lived like a prince in his palace so
   fine,
Yet he never went back on the poor.*

   —"The Ballad of Jim Fisk," 1871

On the windy sidewalk, dressed only in his maroon admiral's uniform, Jim waited for his carriage. He smiled and nodded and chatted with the warm crowd—once again he was the old Jim Fisk whose star shone in the sky's zenith— although he was scarcely aware of a word he uttered. These court sessions had thrown a lot of mud on his trousers, but at least the world now saw that he had been hoodwinked by a pair of greedy adventurers.

At the rear of the dozens of reporters and spectators ringing Jim, a face glared, one as vicious as a rabid ferret's. It was Ned Stokes, eyes overflowing with scalding venom. Jim started and drew himself up, expecting Ned to lunge through the crowd in an attack. The less he was in that man's presence, the better. Jim looked away, but his mind's eye still saw Ned's yellow eyes—*yellow?*—Ned's eyes weren't yellow, but gray. Jim's carriage edged to the curb. The cold silver of the carriage door's handle reassured him, as did the tiny metal step under his boot. As he swung up, he stole another look over his shoulder. Ned still glared with venomous loathing, eyes twin suns set in a bilious, jaundiced face.

Ned's yellow eyes floated in front of him all the way to the office.

My, he had been furious! Maybe this morning's drubbing would teach the spoiled dandy a lesson.

Back at Castle Erie Jim signed the opera house's payroll checks, gave the new house manager several orders, and made sure the advertising for next week's performances was properly ordered. After that, he was too restless to do any more work. Besides it was Saturday afternoon, the opera house was practically deserted, and Jim had promised Lucy he would look in on cousins at the hotel visiting from Brattleboro. He grabbed a hack.

A quarter hour later the Hoffman House's white marble and copper-covered cupola rose out of the January gloom. Home, at last! Never had the mansard roof, the enormous American flag, the granite balustrades, and warm, elegant shops below appeared more welcoming. His carriage swung to the curb, and the doorman opened the door.

Forcing heartiness, Jim shouted, "How's your old tin oven, Charlie?"

His face bright with a smile, the doorman took Jim's elbow to steady his descent from the carriage. "I hear you come out good this morning."

"The right side's winning for a change," Jim said with relief. A wave of exhaustion passed over him. Thank God the worst was over!

Inside the warm, paneled foyer he was greeted jovially by the bell captain. As he passed through the brass and mahogany lobby, alive with the yellow glitter of scores of hissing gas globes, he raised his cane to a couple of corn traders. He headed across the deep cream-and-maroon carpeting for his second-floor suite. He would take a nap and freshen up before sending a bellman to the cousins announcing his intention to visit.

As usual he didn't bother taking the elevator, but veered leftward toward the showy grand staircase. Relishing the strength in his legs, he scarcely used the cane and took the red-and-maroon carpeted stairs two at a time. The glare of the lobby didn't penetrate far up the paneled staircase, and the second-floor hallway appeared as dark and gloomy as early evening. They ought to turn on the gas up here on days as dark as this. After all, the Hoffman House was supposed to serve the city's finest four hundred.

Something—someone—moved there. He neared the top stairs. Yes, someone was behind the elephant-leaf potted plant to the right of the elaborately carved newel post. Very likely it was Malloy, the house detective, set to catch a knob rattler sneaking up from the lobby. In the half gloom the man, yellow eyes aglow, stepped out from behind the dark, broad leaves and raised his arm, at the end of which was a little shiny rod—a pistol.

A pistol!

In the murky light a long pale face floated above a pink satin vest. *Ned!*

"Ned!" shouted Jim. He threw up his left arm to protect himself.

A flash blinded him. A crack like a mule skinner's whip. A blow hit his arm, which flew back against his face. The brass buttons of his maroon sleeve clacked against his teeth.

"No!" shouted Jim. He was trapped. If he turned and ran down the stairs, his back would be a broad target. Better advance the half-dozen steps and knock the pistol out of Ned's hand.

Jim raised the cane in his right hand, bellowed, and charged Ned.

Another flash, another roar. A blow hit him so hard in the chest that it knocked him backward.

Jim hit the carpeted stairs with a jar that further stunned him. The carpet's rough fabric dug into his cheek. For a moment he was suspended on the top step, then he turned backward. The step below thumped against his broad bottom and he rotated again, his nose mashing into the carpet's scratchy pile. He stretched out his arm to stop his bumpy rolling, reaching for the balusters, but the polished spokes twisted out of his fingers. As he rolled, his head banged against the carpeted stair treads. More and more rapidly, with the thudding momentum of a giant, heavy beer keg, he turned over and bounced down the staircase. Several times he lifted his head to prevent it from being whacked, but the next stair caught it as he was twirled about, and no matter how he held it, the stairs cracked his noggin every time he spun over.

The parlor of Jim's second-floor suite was transformed by the mournful, hangdog air of the dozen frock-coated men gathered there.

As he entered, Jay Gould recognized Bill Tweed, Mayor Oakey Hall, Judge George Barnard, and a dozen other friends of Jim's. The canaries in the half-dozen gold cages were chirping in high merry screeches. The heavy, ripe odor of ether assaulted Jay, making him abruptly woozy, that same inner rockiness that had enervated him when Nellie lay near death at St. Luke's. The liver and onions of lunch rose in his gorge, which he forced back down. He nodded at Bill Tweed, who inclined his head and made woeful eyes toward the bedroom door.

Jay crossed and cautiously opened it. Inside were more doctors in white aprons, seven of them, standing over the large, stretched-

out form of Jim, which lay naked on the wide bed in the middle of
the room. Two bearded, aproned doctors looked up. Their white
aprons and shirtsleeves were smeared crimson as if they were butch-
ering cattle. The coppery stench of blood, the putrid stink of ether
sucked at Jay with the force of a riptide. He gripped the cold doorknob
for support. The white sheets and wet blood wavered and swam. The
doctors became white shadows; their voices, hollow echoes. His legs
wouldn't hold, and he slid down a long, slippery tunnel.

The next thing Jay knew, he was sitting on a straight chair in
Jim's parlor, something cold in his mouth. Those damn canaries were
still raising a racket. With one arm draped around Jay's shoulders
to support him, Bill Tweed held a glass of cool water to his lips. The
other men eyed him bleakly. Jay focused on the clear taste of the water.

When he spoke his voice came out as half croak, half whisper.
"How is he?"

"Stokes shot him," said Bill. "Point-blank." He pulled out a white
handkerchief and blew his nose.

"Yes," whispered Jay, "but how is he?"

"Don't nobody know," said Bill. "When I got here there was two
doctors come. I sent Pisket around to get Stone, Steel, and Enos
Foster." Bill honked his nose into his handkerchief. "They got Stokes
locked up in the Ludlow Street Jail."

Russell Sage came in then and clasped Jay's hand. "God, I'm
sorry," he said. Russell's face was drawn and strained. "What an
awful thing!"

It wasn't till late afternoon that Dr. Stone came out. Jay stood
up immediately. The bloody apron was gone, and the white-bearded
doctor was dressed in an everyday frock coat and black satin vest.
The room now held several dozen of Jim's friends, who formed a loose
circle around the door.

"Mr. Gould," Dr. Stone said as he stood in front of Jay. Eyes
downcast, the tall doctor shook his head. "I'm afraid it's hopeless."

"Hopeless!" cried Jay.

"We've spent an hour and a half digging for the bullet." The
doctor shook his head again.

"Where's he hit?" asked Jay.

"He received a small wound in his arm," said Dr. Stone, pointing
to a spot below his left elbow. "It's not important. But one bullet
caught him in the gut"—he pointed to the left side of his satin-covered
paunch—"and has torn his liver and kidneys." He gazed down at his
upturned palms as if they offended him. "If that wasn't bad enough,
we can't even find it."

"You've operated?" said Jay. The putrid whiff of ether wafted off the doctor's clothes.

"Oh, yes," said the doctor. "But he's so fleshy it's hard to work inside him. I don't dare look any further. He can't stand the shock." Jay put his hand on Russell's shoulder for support.

"You don't think he'll live?" asked Bill Tweed.

From days of consultation with Dr. Stone at St. Luke's, Jay knew that deathlike pause. "I'm afraid not another twenty-four hours," said the doctor. "He'd be dead now if he didn't have the constitution of an ox."

Dead? thought Jay. No, he's too full of energy. With my weak chest, I might die, but not Jim. The tall doctor placed his hand lightly on Jay's shoulder.

"You can see him now if you like. He's been asking for you." He spoke to the circle of bearded faces. "Afterwards the rest of you may visit. A brief visit, you understand."

Jay pushed away Russell's offer to come in with him. Several deep breaths steadied him.

Jim's peaceful face lay above a wide field of clean blue blanket. He might have been sleeping. Wrapped in white gauze, his left arm lay on top of the blanket. The bedroom appeared scrubbed and tidied, no traces of blood. Cautiously Jay sniffed the air, on which lingered only the trace of ether. In the far corner near the hallway door two younger doctors stood discreetly out of earshot. A dull, gloomy light was thrown through the curtained windows by the overcast January afternoon. Jay hesitantly approached. His partner's face had a pale, yellowish hue. His mustaches had been hastily brushed to the sides, not waxed and twisted into their usual points. His eyes were closed, and he lay so still that Jay wondered if he was still alive.

"Jim?" he shyly called.

With the jerkiness of a wounded butterfly, Jim's blue eyes fluttered open. His face weakly beamed with pleasure. "Jay," he whispered. "I was afraid I wouldn't see you."

"Not see me!" Jay said, blinking back the sting of tears. "Of course I came. How would I run the Erie without you?" Jay pulled up a chair and laid his fingers lightly on Jim's limp hand. Its warmth flooded through him. For long moments Jim said nothing, as if Jay's words had to work their way through several locked doors before they reached his mind.

"Ah, you'll have to get along without me," said Jim. Jay's heart jumped, and he wondered if Jim knew he was dying.

"You're going to be fine," said Jay.

"Naw, I ain't," said Jim with another pause and a weak frown. "Didn't they tell you? I'm a goner."

Jay forced a flaccid smile and searched for encouraging words. "Don't say that."

"I seen them in the War," said Jim. "A fellow don't survive these gut wounds." Jim squeezed Jay's hand, and his touch was slack and weak, like Nellie's feeble strength that September. Jay put his other hand on top of Jim's. Jim smiled weakly. "I was hoping you'd come," said Jim, voice more breath than sound. "I didn't want to leave without saying good-bye."

Jay wanted to grip Jim's weak hand so tightly that he couldn't get away, but afraid he would hurt him, he stopped himself. He looked at the window and blinked to hold back hot tears.

"Aw, it's all right," said Jim, his fingers giving Jay's hand a little squeeze. "How do the preachers say it? I'm going before you to clear a path through the woodbine." The sly cast on Jim's face said this was all somehow a joke. Tears ran openly down Jay's cheeks. He felt embarrassed and childish, and at the same time smiled at Jim's jest. "Hey, that's better!" whispered Jim at Jay's smile. "Sun through the rain."

Jay removed his hands from Jim's and drew out a handkerchief. The stiff, dry cotton under his sweaty fingers was a welcome diversion. He blew his nose with several loud blasts. He was sitting so far forward on the straight chair that he was almost falling off it. He edged backward.

"We've had our differences," said Jim. "But we're ham and eggs, aren't we? Flapjacks and molasses."

Jay smiled. "Hand and glove. Rapier and broadsword. The best."

"We shook 'em up good," said Jim. "We gave 'em as good as we got."

There was a scuffle and thud at the door, which was flung open. The two young doctors stepped forward. A police captain in a blue uniform entered first, with a coatless Ned Stokes drawn behind by two hefty sergeants. Iron manacles held Ned's delicate hands to his chained waist, and at his feet clanked chains. The buttons of his satin vest were ripped off, and it hung loosely from his starched white shirt like two broken pink wings.

"Colonel Fisk?" said the police officer. "I'm Captain Byrnes. Is this the man who shot you?" He grabbed Ned by the shoulder and thrust him forward. Ned's smudged face was twisted, the manic grin of a savage who didn't care what civilization did to him now that he had scalped his enemy.

"Yes, that's the man who shot me," said Jim firmly. "That's Ned Stokes."

"Take him back to prison," ordered Captain Byrnes. The two sergeants shoved Ned before them and went out the door. His blue cap in both hands, Byrnes stood in the still-open doorway, staring awkwardly at Jim. He was embarrassed about something. Jay rose to face him.

"What's the matter, Captain?" said Jay. "You have your evidence."

"Yes, sir, but there's one thing more," said the Captain in a gruff, apologetic tone. His voice lowered yet more into a growl. "I need to ask Colonel Fisk to swear to what he just said."

"I'm sure he'll do that." The Captain's hands fidgeted with his broad blue cap. His rough voice became softer.

"And I have to ask him if he believes he's dying."

Jay stepped toward the man. "What!"

"Of course I am!" whispered Jim behind him. "I swear I'm dying. And I swear Ned Stokes is the man who shot me."

"Thank you, sir," said the Captain, his hand now on the doorknob. "Mr. Gould, I'll mark down you and these two doctors as witnesses."

After he had left, Jay asked, "What was that about?"

"I want to hang that bastard," said Jim. "Too bad for Ned Stokes—he made me study a lot of law recently. A dead man's deposition can only come in court if he's certain when he gives it that he's dying. That ought to pluck Ned's goose. The law presumes the dying don't lie." Jim gave Jay a broken, diseased wink. "Course, the Captain didn't ask if I felt I might make a miraculous recovery." A frown crossed Jim's face. "Would you wire Lucy?" he asked. "I want to see her."

"I've already sent a telegram. I set up an express from Boston."

Jim's eyes widened. "An express? Just for Lucy?"

"It's the least the Erie can do."

"I'm not going to die till I've seen her," said Jim. Jay nodded and squeezed his hand. Jim closed his eyes and seemed to sleep peacefully. Releasing his pent-up breath, Jay eased back against the straight chair's hard back. He again wiped his face and hands with his cotton handkerchief. The room was quiet, the doctors at the far end motionless, the silence oppressive. An hour stalked by before Jim's eyes fluttered opened.

"My only brother died when I was fourteen," said Jim.

Jay leaned forward and took Jim's hand again. "Yes," he said. The room was too hot, and Jim's hand was slick with sweat.

"You've been like a brother," Jim went on, his blue eyes fixed on Jay. "Closer at times than a brother." A tear rolled out of his eye.

Jay whispered, "Thanks," blinking back his tears. He did love Jim, the most unlikely brother he could imagine. Jim's weak grip squeezed back. "I hate to pull out, but be sure that wherever I go, I'll keep an eye out for you."

Swept up on a surge of tenderness, Jay put his other hand on Jim's and squeezed it in the rush of feeling.

"It ain't going to be Heaven," said Jim, gravel and fun in his low voice. "But then neither are you. We're both goin' to Hell, sure as shootin', but I'm going first. I'm going to set me up another theater—the Mephistopheles Opera House!"

"Suppose the Devil has other plans for you?" asked Jay.

"My next production," Jim announced in a rough whisper. "*The Fall and Rise of Lucifer!* Starring the greatest archangel of all time. The story of Heaven's rebel, told for the first time from his point of view! How he crossed his old dad—and won! Down in the fires of Hell, collecting sinners, forging his new strength—it'll play forever down there. And don't say we'll be given other things to do—the Devil won't be able to resist it. Might even let him take the lead a couple nights. Everybody's a ham, you know." He coughed several times, and the two doctors came forward anxiously.

"You'll be needed, too, bo," said Jim. He waved the doctors back with his gauze-wrapped arm, seemed to concentrate his will on his breathing, swallowed, and went on. "Some way to get sinners to the playhouse. Hell ought to have all the iron and coal we need. Lots of heat for the furnaces and forges. Hire a couple hundred smithies and hammer out—the Fire and Brimstone Line! From the pits of China to the ranges of Tennessee—the line to ride when you're going to the Boss's Grand Opera House! Somebody's got to organize the line, Jay—float stock, keep the books, sell tickets, collect sins or whatever passes for money down there—" He started coughing, red spots rose in his cheeks, and it seemed as if the cough would never stop, as if it would rip out his lungs. The two young doctors were at Jay's side.

"Mr. Fisk," one said, "please don't excite yourself. Not if you want to see Mrs. Fisk." Jim's blue eyes appeared wild, mad, angry. He squeezed Jay's hand, and his head jerked in short, quick nods. Jay turned his head, and his expression and free hand silently asked the doctors if he should leave. The older of the two gazed heavenward and made a face that said it didn't matter. Jim's eyes were closed.

The ormolu clock on the mantel ticked. The fire in the grate popped, and a mound of exhausted coals gave way and collapsed.

Jay pulled out his watch. An hour and twenty minutes had passed since he had entered. Jim's eyelids fluttered.

Jay whispered, "How do you feel?" Jim's blue eyes opened and his face broke into a grin with so much of its former power that it was as if the sun had emerged into the gloomy room.

"Dying ain't so bad," he said weakly. "When you were a boy did you ever run away from school and fill yourself with green apples?" Jay shook his head. Jim smiled faintly.

"I did," Jim went on, "all the time. Me and my gang used to play hookey and apple-raid up and down the hills around Brattleboro. If we went too early in the year, we got our apple feast all right, but we made ourselves sick. I feel just like I used to feel when I et too many green apples. I've got the most awful bellyache."

Under the grayest of dawns Jay watched Jim's breaths, more labored and irregular than ever, and forced himself to breathe in a different rhythm.

Lucy Fisk, her face haggard, felt Jim's hot forehead and rapid pulse, and gave Jay a look of helplessness.

"I must see to the children," she said. "Will you stay?"

"Of course," said Jay.

Jim's breathing became more ragged. Jay moistened Jim's lips with a cloth wrapped around ice. Toward eight o'clock Jim's chest rose with difficulty and then collapsed. He passed into a period of shallow, easier breathing, as if he had given up fighting for deep breaths. Feeling numb, slack, leaden, Jay wondered if he should send for Lucy.

Another nurse came on duty, her white uniform looking crisp and fresh. Jay's shirt now felt stitched out of damp dishrags. As the cloudy winter light increased, he clung to Jim's sweaty hand. Whenever he wiped his palm, he held Jim's wrist with his left hand as if afraid Jim's life would fly away if he didn't hold on to him.

Jay wondered if the doctor should change the bandage. He turned to the nurse— With a start, he saw Jim wasn't breathing. His own breath caught, he leaned forward. With a rustle of starched uniform, the nurse stood up, hands clasped in front of her.

"Quick," Jay said, "ask Mrs. Fisk to come in." She went out.

No, the blue blanket gently lifted and fell. Relieved, Jay released his breath and sat back, watching the blanket's blue field attentively. It took forever for the blanket to rise between breaths.

Clutching Jim's hand, he watched closely. Again Jim wasn't breathing. Jay sat forward.

537

But the blanket lifted, fell. Jay sat back.

Lifted.

Fell.

It didn't move.

Again his breath caught and he leaned forward. For the longest time the blanket didn't lift. Jay released his breath—he *was* gone. Unseen, Jim had crept away. The door opened and Lucy and the nurse stood there. Unable to speak, Jay stood and gave them several quick nods. Lucy's shoulders sagged and she began crying. A pair of strong male arms circled her shoulders, and she surrendered to them. She looked up into her minister's tear-streaked face.

"Oh, Henry, Henry—he's gone!"

The next day, to pay tribute to Jim, New York went to as much effort and expense as it had on any of its heroes. The manner of his death created sympathy even among those who viewed him with revulsion. Although Colonel Fisk had appeared less than glorious during the Orange riot, everyone agreed that he met his death with admirable courage. The *Times*, which had hated Jim more than any other paper, called the shooting "brutal and cowardly," and went on: "There was a grandeur of conception about Colonel Fisk's rascalities which helps to lift him above the vulgar herd of scoundrels."

Horace Greeley on the editorial page of the *Tribune* put it: "What a scamp he was, but what a curious and scientifically interesting scamp!"

Their readers felt they had lost a friend. On this freezing morning the whole of New York went a little wild with grief. Talk of lynching Ned Stokes became so common among Erie employees and members of the Colonel's Ninth that Police Superintendent Kelso rushed 250 police to guard Stokes at the city prison. A force of ten men was stationed in front of Josie's house because of threats against her. The Erie board of directors met and passed a resolution of regret, as did the Erie employees in Buffalo. The Delavan House in Albany, the Hoffman House in Manhattan, and the Revere House in Brattleboro lowered their flags to half mast.

There were other opinions. The Burlington, Vermont, *Free Press* suggested that the safest thing that could be said of him was "that he made a nice, quiet corpse." Remembering Black Friday, members of the New York Stock Exchange shed no tears. Horace Greeley's *Tribune* went on to say, "Undoubtedly the present management of the Erie will endeavor to hide all their crimes in his grave."

Clergymen across America found ample material for their sermons the day of his death. The heights that Henry Ward Beecher's sermon reached were typical.

"And that supreme mountebank of fortune—the astounding event of his age," he preached, "that a man of some smartness in business, but absolutely without moral sense, and as absolutely devoid of shame as the desert of Sahara is of grass—that this man, with one leap, should have vaulted to the very summit of power in New York, and for five years should have held the courts in his hand, and the Legislature, and the most consummate invested interest in the land in his hand, and laughed at Washington, and laughed at New York, and matched himself against the financial skill of the whole city, and outwitted the whole, and rode out to this hour in glaring and magnificent prosperity—shameless, vicious, criminal, abominable in his lusts, and flagrant in his violation of public decency—that this man should have been the supremest there; and yet in an instant, by the hand of a fellow-culprit, God's providence struck him to the ground! Yet I say to every young man who has looked upon this glaring meteor and thought that perhaps integrity was not necessary, 'Mark the end of this wicked man, and turn back again to the ways of integrity!' "

Jay sat before the coal fire in his library and stared at the flames, struggling to make sense of what had happened. A damp handkerchief was squeezed in his hand, two more stuffed in his coat pocket. Jim had liked to say they were brothers, hyperbole that Jay often ignored, but the loss felt as great. God, he missed the big fellow, his ready laughter! Jim had swum into his life, enlarging it, warming it, bringing the world in on his coattails. With him about, the office was full of laughter, merriment, jokes, shouts. Normally Jay didn't think laughter and shouts had a place in business, but this morning he saw how much he would miss them. He knew himself, his own grim sobriety, his own dismal earnestness, and right now he hated his nature. Such jolly warmth would never invade his life again. No matter how much he might appreciate such qualities, Jay knew his own forbidding nature would allow damn little of it. That warmth had flashed once, like a giant, jolly sun, and was now extinguished, blown out like a candle. The rest of his days would have a quiet, subdued—bleak—quality to them, one no amount of his soul's earnest application of hard work would ever bring back.

In his broad-planked, peppermint-scented den in the stables behind his Washington Place house, Cornelius Vanderbilt read the papers and reflected that now that half of that pair was gone, General Sickles could no longer hesitate to strike the Erie. He sent a message to the New Fifth Avenue Hotel, where his general resided in the royal style befitting a commander in chief, that ordered the fellow to come around for a strategy session.

At the Tombs Ned Stokes made himself as comfortable as his cold, fetid cell permitted. Most of his toiletries and wardrobe had been sent over from Josie's and his rooms. He was allowed a carpet on the floor, and although Saturday night the bedbugs had pricked his flesh in a dozen tender spots, his meals were good, being delivered from Delmonico's. His rose-scented toilet water partially kept at bay the jailhouse stench of mud, open sewers, and rank privy buckets.

He gave several interviews, in none of which did he pretend repentance. A *Sun* reporter found him wearing a handsome frilled shirt with three magnificent diamond studs. "On the little finger of his left hand sat a large and costly solitaire diamond ring. He wore a pair of lavender-colored trousers and a silk velvet dressing jacket, whose sleeves, pockets, collar, and lapels were trimmed with pink silk, heavily quilted. His feet were encased in silk stockings, and he wore a pair of slippers richly embroidered with gold lace." In the bars on Printers Row the reporters who had interviewed him raised schooners of beer to a great story and agreed that the most fit words you could write about Ned Stokes always opened with, "He wore . . ."

Sunday night and most of Monday Jim's body lay in an open gold-handled, rosewood coffin in the great lobby of the opera house. The marble lobby as well as the entire stone front facing Eighth Avenue and Twenty-third Street was festooned with black crepe. As visitors entered on Monday morning, a life-sized portrait of Jim in his colonel's uniform stared down at them.

A long line of citizens shuffled inside from the terrible January cold to view their late friend in his open coffin. Clad in his scarlet-and-yellow uniform, white kid gloves on his hands, gold sword at his side, mustaches waxed to fine points, Jim looked as if he might wake up at any moment to lead some further antic.

When Andrew, Jim's barber for years, reached the coffin, he took the ends of the mustaches in his fingers, stifled a sob, and gave them an expert twist, saying, "One more twirl, dearest of friends, for the last time!"

Outside the freezing wind gusted. A crowd of 25,000 surged toward the entrance, blocking all traffic on Twenty-third Street and Eighth Avenue. Policemen were forced to brandish clubs to make room for the funeral procession to form in front of the opera house.

At the funeral in the packed First Baptist Church late Monday afternoon, Bill Tweed spoke.

"Jim was a man of broad soul and kindly heart," he said, his voice thick with emotion. "In his business transactions he was governed by principles which seemed peculiar, without being insincere. He did more good turns for worthy but embarrassed men than all the clergymen in New York."

Josie Mansfield didn't visit Jim before or after he died, for as she put it to Virginia Williams, "I have to think of my reputation." She didn't visit Ned, either. Instead, on Monday morning she called on real-estate brokers, with whom she discussed how much her furnished town house would fetch over its mortgage. She had decided to live in Paris for a few years, and she wanted what she could scrape together for a new start. She planned to spend the next few days carefully packing her wardrobe into twenty trunks. She reckoned she had learned a few mistakes to avoid when she started over.

The newspaper reporters pressed Jay to say something. "We have been working together for five or six years," he said, stiff with grief, "and during that time not the slightest unpleasantness has ever arisen between us." He laid Jim's troubles to "an excess of youthful spirits," and said that of late he had achieved a new dignity of conduct. "Since the dissolution of whatever ties existed between him and Mrs. Mansfield, he has been a changed man. He had ceased to practice many of the old habits of which he has been accused, and was in every way becoming what all who loved him desired he should be."

Late Monday afternoon, the slow cortege that wound its way through the bitter January cold across Manhattan to the New Haven Railway station at Fourth and Twenty-sixth Street was just what Jim would have liked—huge, magnificent, and military. The shot-torn Civil War flag of the Ninth was draped over the coffin. No sun showed through the heavy clouds, which threatened more snow. On the sidewalks, despite the windy cold, stood thousands of mourners.

Wrapped in a heavy buffalo coat, Jay Gould led the cortege. Since the shooting he had been spiritless. Jim's energy had been too exuberant for him to accept that it had been snuffed out by two cents' worth of pot metal. Over the past two days he had struggled to assess his loss, but he was only poorly and numbly coming to grips with it; a great furnace warming his life had been extinguished, a bonfire that he only dimly realized would, very likely, never again be ignited.

Led by his groom, Jim's riderless horse followed his coffin, the stirrup hoods reversed, his colonel's boots and spurs attached. Six colonels of other New York regiments rode alongside and General Varian brought up its rear. Drums muffled, the band of the Ninth over and over thumped and trumpeted "Dead March" from *Saul*. Among the many marchers were the entire Ninth, the officers of Jim's steamship line, the Narragansett Steamship Company, a horde of Erie employees, six platoons of commissioned officers of the National Guard wearing crepe on their left arms and sword hilts, and a large German band. Behind a ragged mob of walking marchers followed a quarter mile of carriages.

The day of his funeral the *Herald* forgot its criticisms of him to write, "His vivacity, his incessant, effervescing good humor, his bands of music and flocks of canary birds, his boyish love of show, of colors and gems and golden braid; that reckless frankness, which made the world the confidant of his business, his dreams and affections; his insatiable thirst for applause; the world to him was a stage, and his whole life, even those phrases of life which decorum veils, an acted comedy—no more striking phenomenon of human nature has been seen in our time."

The *World* summed up the day: "Never since the martyred Lincoln was borne through New York's streets was so impressive a spectacle witnessed. His influence on the community might or might not have been bad, but it is certain that many people, more or less wise and more or less honest, sorrowed heartily at his funeral."

That night Jay, numb and drained, rode on the Erie special with Lucy, Jim's children, a hundred friends, and her minister as it rolled at a decorous speed toward Brattleboro, Jim's birthplace and final resting place. On Tuesday, January 9, 1871, a jam-packed noon service was held in the Baptist church in Brattleboro, the town's biggest.

The aged Chaplain Edward Flagg of the Ninth, who had risen from his sickbed to do this duty, preached the sermon.

"He who lies before you was no common man," quavered his infirm voice. "He was not like the mass of men. As to his faults, I will not speak of them. A censorious world will do them ample justice. When his good qualities are balanced against his bad, I venture to say we will have at least an equipoise. He was magnanimous by nature, and never consulted his means when he wished to do a good deed. Colonel Fisk was generous to a fault."

Jim was to be buried on a hill near his mother. Only thirty people ventured out the half mile on the afternoon of this bitterly cold day to witness Jim being laid to rest, dressed in his colonel's uniform and with his gold sword by his side. Jay Gould was one.

After the short graveside service was intoned and the rosewood coffin was lowered, only Jay and Lucy remained.

As if the two of them wanted to accompany Jim as far as possible on his last journey, they stood in the stinging cold the entire thirty minutes it took the two struggling gravediggers to throw the frozen clods onto the coffin and fill up the grave.

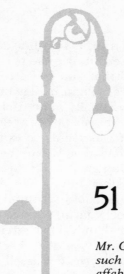

51

*Mr. Gould was the ideal president and
such a one never existed before. He was
affable to every employee from the head
of the department to the humblest
tracklayer on the road.*

—G. P. Morosini, unpublished
memoir, 1890s

Over the last days of January and
into February 1871, a damp torpor settled over the granite walls and
marble corridors of the Grand Opera House. The twenty-six-hundred-
seat, red-velvet theater was eerily dark every night, while the third-
floor offices of the Erie Railroad, as fully staffed and busy as ever,
nonetheless felt empty and hollow to Jay Gould.

Unable to sleep past four-thirty in the morning, Jay, step as
steady as ever, poker face as expressionless, rose and tramped across
town through dark, frigid dawns, while about his eyes lay a haunted
expression.

In late January, he read about Annabelle's impending marriage
in the *Tribune*. The announcement called up a dark freight of grief,
weighing the skiff of himself with almost more than it could bear.

Jim, lost. Annabelle, lost.

The past three years, since that midnight rowboat ride to Jersey,
had been the most tumultuous of his life, and not the least exhilarating part was having Jim and Annabelle to share it. As he would
never have a partner like Jim again, neither would he have another
lover, much less one to match Annabelle. Jay felt disillusioned now,
sober and slack. His wanting to be a great man, to do great things,
to be the fellow who had first sent trains from the east to the west

coast of the continent, was a trap, a snare, a delusion, one more dangerous than a hundred Vanderbilts. He had to put partners, lovers, and delusions behind him. All that you could count on was sober reality. If you assessed it correctly, and made your plans in accord with its nature, you were far less likely to be tricked.

Equally damaging to him was his father's legacy of hard work, he reckoned, the notion that it was manly to exhaust yourself into your plot of ground. His father had always expected more of Jay than as a boy he could do, and as Jay grew older, his father always demanded more. Not that his father didn't live the same way, demanding of himself more than he could accomplish. And now as an adult, like his father on their rocky farm, Jay always worked for the Erie, his farm, at a pace greater than his own strength could handle. Difficult as it would be for him, he would cut back.

As he strode across town, his friend Russell Sage often joined him, but gone were excited plans and shrewd conversations about the future of railroads. Alternately ballooned up and punctured by grief, Jay wanted someone willing to tramp along without demands; the graying financier seemed to sense this and acquiesced.

On several dreary February mornings, Jay paused at the top step of the Erie's sweeping staircase and cocked his ear as if to catch Jim's high, strutting laugh or the soft slide of a chorus girl's slipper on the corridor's marble. All that sounded in the quiet building were the echoing clack of his own shoe leather and the rasp of his winded breath in air as thick and damp as a cold swamp's. Afternoons he left before three-thirty, hurrying down the winding stairs as if fleeing the fall of night. For two years the Empire-style offices on the third floor had been the cab of a crack express train. He had been the engineer, Jim the fireman shoveling coal into a roaring boiler, the two of them determined to break some speed record. Now the stone building felt as cold, damp, and lifeless as a broken locomotive in a scrap dump.

The headquarters staff was afflicted the same way. No matter how often Jay told Morosini and the other employees to speak up, they still whispered as if Jim had been shot yesterday. Jim's ornate office at the head of the sweeping staircase remained untouched and empty, for Jay couldn't bring himself to install someone else in it or dismantle it. With Helen he discussed the need for a rest and a change of climate. In late February he made plans for a month of sunshine in southern Italy and France. Such cheerful medicine might put this cold, lifeless winter behind them.

Late one drizzly March afternoon two months after Jim was buried, Jay stood in muffler and topcoat at Morosini's desk giving last instructions before he tramped home, his voice as crisp as ever, but flat.

Beyond them were the desks of the clerks' bull pen, where forty steel nibs scratched along the black lines of green-shaded ledger pages. The late-afternoon, dry essences of ink, sweat, glue, and the day's fatigue wafted through the large space. Abruptly the wooden floor shook under Jay's feet and a loud boom rocked the building. Morosini's small, white face, as startled as a wren's at a hunter's first shot, darted up from his pad. Clerks' heads snapped up across the bull pen. A hullabaloo of shouts surged through the open double doors.

"My God," said Morosini, "the boiler's burst." Jay, thinking the same thing, broke for the hallway. From every door pale clerks' faces above white shirts peered out fearfully, for loud shouts and the clatter of boots echoed up the main stairwell at the hall's north end.

At the stairhead Jay paused, his hand on the cold granite of the balustrade, and looked down. Boiling up the first flight of marble steps, like a baying pack of hounds, were a score of men. Leading the intruders was a one-legged fellow with a blond crutch. Behind him were four blue-helmeted policemen, one of whom Jay recognized as Sergeant McKenna, head of Twenty-third Street's police team, and another dozen stout men.

"That's a general!" said Morosini, pointing at the one-legged man. Indeed the dark blue campaign hat, yellow sash, and thigh-length blue coat were those of a Union general, many of whom still wore their uniforms about town. Twenty feet below Jay, One-Leg, a handsome fellow with gray eyes set in a flushed, swaggering face, grabbed the marble banister with one hand and with the other lifted the blond crutch and pointed it at Jay like a rifle.

"You must leave these premises, Gould!" he shouted.

"Is the building on fire?" asked Jay.

From the inner pocket of his campaign coat, the General drew a mass of papers backed by a legal-looking blue jacket.

"Your own mismanagement is the only thing on fire," shouted the General, his voice overloud for the single flight of stairs separating them. "You are forthwith dismissed as president of the Erie. Please leave the premises at once." The General drew himself up as if he expected Jay to obey. For a confused moment Jay goggled at the fool's smooth, hostile face, then he conferred with Morosini.

"Does an addled general have a suit against us?" he whispered.

"Not that I know of," Morosini whispered back.

"What do you want?" Jay called down. "Who *are* you?" Erie

clerks crowded around him at the granite balustrade with the eagerness of bored schoolboys excited by a quarrel between teachers.

"I am General Daniel E. Sickles," shouted the General. "I represent a large coalition of stockholders who intend to install new management of this road." Sickles thrust the legal papers over his head and rattled them. "This is the Federal Southern District's signed warrant of entry allowing me full access to these premises." Face mottled with red splotches of excitement, Sickles turned to the stout men surrounding him, each of whom carried a billy stick. "These are Pinkerton agents, my troops to see that justice is done. They are to secure the building and all books and records that you might destroy to hide your malfeasance." Wild lights danced in the General's eyes, and he clapped Sergeant McKenna on the shoulder. "The Sergeant here is going to present service to you." He handed a blue-backed paper to Sergeant McKenna.

"Sergeant McKenna," said Jay to the city police officer. "You know that I am the legal head of the Erie. Please arrest this man. You may be sure that I will file charges for criminal trespass." Sergeant McKenna's beefy Irish mouth gaped, and in a long uncertain moment he turned first to Jay, down to the legal paper, back to Sickles, and again to Jay.

"Beggin' your pardon, Mr. Gould," said the Sergeant, "but he come up to me with a paper with what looks like a federal judge's seal, sir."

At his side General Sickles ended the argument by waving his arm to the stout, bearded Pinkertons. "No need for debate," he shouted. "Up the stairs. Carry out your orders." With his surprisingly fast hop and a jangling of the silver chains against his gold scabbard, he led them past Jay, Morosini, and the dozen Erie clerks. With a clatter of boot heels on marble, the intruders, as if fully knowledgeable of what was where, headed toward Jim's office at the head of the stairs.

When Captain Crandel arrived with six patrolmen an hour later, Jay squeezed through the crack in the bull pen's barricaded doors into the hallway.

"We're very glad to see you," said Jay to the familiar face. He had already sent clerks to three Wall Street law firms in order to file petitions in every federal court that would accept one.

"What is this, sir?" asked the tall police officer.

"A lunatic general," said Jay, although the half-dozen burly, sullen Pinkerton agents standing around the hall took much of the thrust out of his assertion. With the Captain and his patrolmen at his heels, Jay found Sickles sitting behind Jim's inlaid rosewood desk, the crutch leaning against its edge, riffling through papers in the drawers.

"What the hell do you think you're doing?" demanded Jay. The crystal leaves of the chandelier, stirred by the entrance of so many people, swayed and tinkled. Jay caught a whiff of Jim's old scents, bay rum, talc, and Macassar oil.

"Looking into the company's business," announced Sickles in a bold voice, his audacious gray eyes on the tall captain and the six policemen. Using his blond crutch for a pole, he pulled himself to his foot. "Looking into the company's records for malfeasance, misman-agement, and neglect, not to speak of misbehavior, impropriety, and general wrongdoing." Strutting across the blue parade ground of his chest were a corps of shiny medals and a platoon of red, green, purple, and yellow campaign ribbons, a pageant of military bravery that Jay couldn't read. Captain Crandel hurriedly doffed his hat as if military generals outranked captains of police.

With a flourish, Sickles again drew a mass of blue-backed papers from his inner pocket. He hobbled forward to present them to the Captain.

"Gould here is the trespasser," announced Sickles, "illegally bar-ricaded in the east side of the building. I demand you remove him and his men from the premises before they destroy evidence of their crimes."

"Captain," said Jay, "you've known me for two years, ever since Mr. Fisk and I moved into the neighborhood." Half a head taller than either, Captain Crandel looked from one to the other in bewilderment.

"Mr. Fisk, God rest his soul," said the Captain, "give me brother money when he was out of work and then found him a job with the Erie." He shook his head. "But this is a Union general, Mr. Gould," he said in a respectful, almost awed, voice. "These here is federal court orders."

This felt like a dream to Jay, a nightmare. A mad general and insane police. "Meanwhile, he's attacked my staff and driven them out of their offices," said Jay, his voice rising. "Our jobs are to run the line for the safety of the public. These—criminals—are interfer-ring."

"Criminals!" Sickles objected. "I have the votes of six directors and the fresh proxies of the majority of the line's shareholders. I intend to call a board of directors' meeting tomorrow morning. At it, this thief and his crooked cronies will be booted out of the Erie."

The man's audacity and knowledge of corporate procedure rattled Jay. "I want *him* arrested for criminal trespass, breaking and entering, and disturbing the peace," he said. "I will damn sure press charges."

"Arrest me, sir," said Sickles to the Captain as he plucked the blue-jacketed legal papers from his hand and waved them about, "and I shall have you in federal court for obstructing a federal order." He thrust the crutch under his arm and hobbled back to the desk. "I want Mr. Gould and his henchmen off the premises by nightfall."

They continued to argue heatedly. Finally Captain Crandel stepped between them and raised his large hands, which he held up till the two of them were silent. "Hold on," he said, directing his words to Sickles. "I've known Mr. Gould a long time. I don't know a more decent man. If he says he belongs here, he does." As if he thought better of his statement, he glanced uneasily at Jay. "I'm going to find the Inspector."

Captain Crandel assigned his six patrolmen to Sergeant Mc-Kenna, ordered him to keep the peace, and left. Jay retreated to the bull pen's barricaded doors. He slipped through and had a desk jammed against it. He shouted for Morosini to join him and stalked into his private office.

He threw himself into his swivel chair. His heart was pounding, his mouth dry. Lips pinched, face grim, Morosini glided in, notebook at the ready. The glass of water that Jay poured trembled in his hand. He needed the kind of help Jim had rounded up during the gold market crash.

"I'm not going home tonight," said Jay. "Send a messenger to O'Malley's and Harry Hill's for Pat Lynch. I want my own army. You stay, and pick out the roughest of our fellows. It's double wages this week if they stay the night."

"Right, sir."

For a moment Jay was lapsed in thought. Finally he said, "There's only one person who would prepare and finance an attack like this—Vanderbilt."

"The old man!" said Morosini. "Still?"

"Who else?" said Jay. "The Erie is still his key to dominating the country's rail system. With Jim gone, he figures we're weakened and demoralized. He's hired this one-legged general as his cat's-paw. He's wormed his way into our board. We won't know who we can count on till we call a meeting—although tonight we must send wires to everyone who owns a large block of shares—put forth our views."

"What are we going to do with Pat Lynch?" asked Morosini. Jay grinned, showing more confidence than he felt.

"We're going to use the same tactic on the General that he used on us—force and surprise," Jay said. "We're going to throw that one-legged grasshopper into the street—at midnight, when he least expects it—and toss his crutch out the door on top of him."

Spooky midnight shadows hovered over Jay and Morosini. The two small men stood in the middle of the opera house's vast stage, carbide railroad lanterns held high over their heads. Muscles tense with the strain, Jay kept raising himself on tiptoes to peer through the inky gloom. Their whispers echoed in the hollow space, which magnified the gritty slide of their boots. The towering flats of Egyptian scenery, the guy wires holding up the stage sky, and the ropes and suspended sandbags appeared as threatening as giant insects, otherworldly nightcrawlers.

"Who's there?" called Jay nervously, thrusting forward the fizzing lantern to illuminate the space alongside the snarling dog-god of the Nile. Out of the utter blackness came a clatter. Morosini crowded Jay's back.

"It's me, Pat," hissed a tough voice, and around the towering Sphinx's head came the hunched form of Pat Lynch. "I got 'em like you said."

On Pat's heels followed a half-dozen other hunched toughs, arms up to shield their eyes from the lanterns' harsh glare. Night creatures these were, members of the rough gangs that scuttled around Hell's Kitchen, or Satan's Circus, as do-gooders and preachers called the West Side. Wary, Jay shrank back. This hulking, tough-faced crew circled Jay and Morosini.

With a forced grin, Jay asked, "How's your old tin oven?" Jim's old catchphrase.

Pat, his good eye on Jay while his walleye was battened on the others' rough mugs, smiled ruefully. "He was a wonderful man, sir."

Jay nodded and eyed the toughs. "We'll need more men."

"I got twenty coming, maybe more," said Pat. "These fellows, see, come wit' me from the Hell Hole and the Billy Goat, the last two joints I was in." He pointed to two plump, unshaven faces above seamen's jackets. "Here's Bill and Jack Bowe of the Gophers, me own gang."

Jay saluted, and the pair grinned savagely. Over the next half hour, more of Hell's Kitchen silently arrived. Crazy Button of the Gas Housers. Black Jake, Pickles, Cyclone Louie, and Snatchem of the Dock Rats. Hop Along Peter, Dutch Heinrich, and Red Rocks of the Dutch Mob.

Armed with clubs, they were on the third floor, halfway down the corridor, before the snoozing policemen knew what was what.

Jay boldly opened his lantern door, and the frightened half-dozen cops bolted and were swept down the hallway in front of him and his ragged army.

"Who's there?" demanded Sergeant McKenna, backing away toward the far window. One hand shielded his eyes from the white glare, the other held his billy stick upraised. Jay waved his men forward.

"Me, Jay Gould."

"Oh, Mr. Gould, you scared me half out of my mind," said the Sergeant still backing, but more slowly. "What is it?"

"Repossession," said Jay in a loud, exultant shout.

"Now, Mr. Gould!" said the Sergeant, glancing behind to see what he was backing into. "You know I got me orders. I can't let you do it."

Big Nose and Pat Lynch stepped from behind Jay into the circle of light and lunged forward.

"Pat!" cried the Sergeant. "Nosey! What are you boys doing here?"

"You ain't got no say in this," said Pat. "You blues leave now or get tossed out with this hoppin' general." For a few seconds, terror was stamped upon the half-dozen policemen's faces.

"Who's all that wit' you?" the Sergeant asked. The tiny force of police were backed against the window at the far end of the corridor. Pat rattled off half a dozen names. A bug-eyed patrolman tugged McKenna's sleeve and hissed that they should leave. Jay stifled a chuckle. A way through the thugs opened for the policemen, which they scurried through.

With the boots of the police echoing down the stairs, Jay silently and dramatically pointed at the double mahogany doors to the conference room. Big Nose and Mike McGloin charged them, shoulders forward. The splintering crash resounded throughout the opera house.

"Let's go in!" shouted Jay. His lantern swinging frantically, Morosini grabbed Jay's arm and pulled him back. Jay snatched the lantern out of Morosini's hand and held it up so his Hell's Kitchen army could see to push through the splintered doors. Fired by excitement, he followed them in.

At the far end of the room the long conference table had been turned on its side to serve as a barricade, which Jay's gang was ferociously attacking. Behind it Pinkertons held up billy sticks, truncheons, and the broken legs of chairs, with which they whacked any tough who came within reach. The battle was at a standoff, for the table was an effective shield.

Like a general directing his army on a wild battlefield, Jay stood in the middle of the room and shouted instructions at Pat and his men. All that counted was grabbing Sickles. He pulled on an arm, that of Red Rocks, leader of the Dutch Mob, and directed him to attack the east flank of the conference table. Four of the Dutch Mob went at the slit between the table and the wall, which had been plugged with two straight chairs, and overpowering the resistance of three Pinkertons there, they pushed their way in. They were met by more clubs, and driven back, backing around the table holding bruised shoulders and heads. Disappointed, Jay pulled Yakey Yake, Ike, and Happy Jack off their struggle to pound the center of the conference table into a bag of splinters and sent them through the hole, and he followed up this attack with two Dock Rats. The space behind the table was a dark pit of swinging elbows, loud cries, and vicious oaths.

"Watch the table!" came a shout, and its large mahogany surface moved toward Jay, who jumped back, as did his guerrilla force. The conference table tipped forward and hit the floor with a terrific clash, its legs in the air with the defeated stiffness of a slain dragon.

In the momentary quiet, Jay held up his lantern. To his delight, the Pinkertons and General Sickles were revealed, backed against the plaster wall, arms shielding their eyes from the harsh glare, busted chair legs and billy sticks raised, like insects exposed when a rock is turned over. Sickles had backed himself into the far corner, propping himself upright with the help of the two walls, and he held his blond crutch by its foot like a two-handed broadsword of old.

"Grab 'em!" shouted Jay. Pat led the charge. Clubs were raised, a cheer went up, thuds and oofs sounded, and howls and curses flew around the dark room like terrified bats.

Quickly Sickles and the fifteen Pinkertons were tied together in a chain. Like a captured centipede, Sickles and his agents were marched out of the conference room into the hallway, where the Erie clerks were lined up, clapping, faces beaming. Once Sickles was in the street, Jay decided, he would post Pat and his men to make damn sure he didn't get back in.

"March 'em!" shouted Pat.

"Halt!" came a shout from the far end of the hall. With a clatter of boots, three large lanterns advanced down the hall toward Jay, Pat's crew, and their captives. When they neared, Jay recognized J. J. Kelso, the redheaded Police Superintendent.

"Mr. Kelso!" shouted Jay in surprise. "What are you doing here?"

Kelso stopped a dozen feet in front of Jay. By his side Sergeant McKenna held up a large rugged police lantern. Behind Kelso were two dozen bell-shaped helmets, and the silhouettes of police rifles were stark against the lanterns' bright glare.

"I might ask you what you are doing, sir?" said Superintendent Kelso.

"Escorting trespassers off my property," said Jay, his voice rock solid.

"I have here a federal court order that says General Sickles has a right to occupy these premises, Mr. Gould."

"That's all very well," said Jay, drawing the blue-jacketed legal papers from his pocket that his lawyers had obtained this evening, "but I have orders from two federal judges that say this is a state, not a federal matter, and that these men are trespassers."

Superintendent Kelso's wide brow wrinkled. "Sir?"

"The Erie corporation is chartered in New York State," said Jay. "It's regulated by New York State law and its courts." He passed the legal orders over. "These federal judges agree that the federal government has no jurisdiction over it."

"Mr. Gould is wrong," said Sickles, leaning on his crutch and poking his stump in Jay's direction. "I gave this leg at Gettysburg to prove the primacy of the federal government in disputes."

Heated arguments over the next quarter hour failed to clarify the issue. Kelso declared that he was a simple policeman, no judge, and that he had no idea whose claim was right. His Solomonlike judgment was for each of them to occupy half the third floor, after which he extracted a promise from both that they would not attempt to physically toss out the other, but leave the matter to the courts. He would post twenty men in the upper hall, day and night, to enforce the agreement—Jay and his men were to keep to the eastern half of the floor, Sickles and his to the western.

"And any man—including the generals and presidents present—who interferes with the other's men gets clapped in jail," shouted Kelso, "where I'll personally see he is stuck for as long as it takes him to cool off."

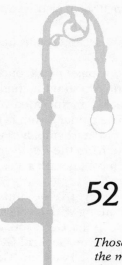

52

Those who have looked most closely into the matter feel sure the hour has come that will severely test the most accomplished of all modern criminals, Jay Gould.

—Editorial, *New York Tribune*, 1871

At nine-fifteen the next morning Morosini called Jay to come out to the bull pen. Stomach knotted, Jay peered through the cracked double doors into the corridor.

Broken glass, bits of brass, scraps of paper, mud from the street, and sticks of furniture littered the marble floor, the laying of which Jim had supervised two years ago. Eight high-ranking military officers, generals and colonels, in full Union army dress—yellow epaulettes, parade swords, red-and-yellow sashes, spurs, and dress hats—stood patiently as the barricade at the entrance of the conference room was dismantled. Hanging over the mess was the stench of an unlimed privy, as if the police and Pinkertons hadn't bothered to search out the water closets in the fire stairwells.

"What the hell now?" asked Jay.

Their swords and spurs jangling, the officers disappeared into the conference room. At eleven they jingled back out. Jay had to do something. "Where's that damn Judge Barnard?" he thundered.

"I now have four men out looking for him." said Morosini.

Lanky, graying, Russell Sage, the Erie's newest director, came in at noon with the afternoon newspapers and a lunch pail from Hanrahan's. Russell's calm, horsey face soothed Jay's frayed nerves somewhat. After he brought Russell up to date, Jay leafed through the papers, whose headlines were set in type as large as that used for Jim's death.

Once more the Erie was front-page news, once more the Scarlet Woman of Wall Street. Any sympathy the line had garnered over the tragedy of Jim's death was quickly incinerated in the rabid fury of anger at Jay. The *Times* said, "The spider's web is rent asunder." The *World* alerted its readers to "a battle royale, a clash of titans."

"Modern criminal," Jay read from the *Tribune* in a sarcastic voice to Russell. "Doesn't the public have enough sense to know that they make up this stuff to sell papers?"

"Nope," said Russell with a wry grin of amusement.

The *Tribune* announced that along with General Daniel E. Sickles, well known for his brave exploits at Gettysburg, a new board of directors had been elected for the Erie: General George B. McClellan, former commander of the Army of the Potomac; General John A. Dix, who had served briefly as president of the Union Pacific before the war; and generals A. G. Barlow and A. S. Diven, as well as Colonel Henry G. Stebbins and three other officers prominently connected to railroads.

"It reads like the top echelon of a Union order of battle," said Russell.

"For a few dollars in director's fees these dumb generals will do whatever Vanderbilt tells them," said Jay, his voice cracking with outrage. "The public thinks that a man who charged up Malvern Hill is the soul of integrity and a guarantor of straight dealing."

When Judge Barnard arrived at five that afternoon, he was outraged. "It's clear that this man is a pirate, a buccaneer with scurrilous federal protection. First, I shall issue a mandamus voiding the federal court's order. A federal court cannot decide a local matter that has not passed through local courts. It's usurpation of jurisdiction." He looked around. "Is there a glass of something about? Something strong?" This gush of legal phrases was as soothing to Jay as hot water on sore bruises. He jiggled a finger at Morosini, who pulled out a bottle of whiskey and poured the Judge three fingers. After a big swig of fuel, the Judge's outrage flared up anew.

"Then I think something for our local policemen to use as authority," he said, "a temporary restraining order that demands the interlopers leave the premises forthwith."

Jay nodded with satisfaction. "I'd like warrants for the arrest of this lunatic general for trespassing," he said, "breaking and entering, disturbing the peace, and the misuse of police officers."

"And I damn well think you should have them," said the Judge.

Shortly thereafter Jay presented these new orders to Captain

Crandel. "They look okay," said the Captain, "but the Inspector told me plain as dog not to do nothing without the Commissioner's approval. It's all these Union generals. It's hard for folks to be tough on general officers they served under in the War." Jay gave Russell a look of pained exasperation. Everything they tried seemed to have been prepared for in advance by Sickles.

That night both sides dug in, each making privy arrangements in separate stairwells and establishing supply lines for provisions, the Erie to Hanrahan's, the occupying force to Delmonico's.

By the third and fourth days the putrid stench from the stairwells and the overburdened water closets was so much worse that during their tours the policemen held wet handkerchiefs over their mouths and noses. The trash in the hallway—scraps of wood, old sheets of newspapers, broken chairs, mud, shards of glass, bits of brass chandelier, and odd pieces of clothing—rose so high that only a narrow passage wound through it, like a wild animals' path through dense bramblebush. Sick over what was happening to his Erie, Jay paced about and seethed. There had to be some way out of this mess.

As Jay was unable to have a good wash, his chest and back began to itch. Some of the same gritty tension settled over him as when he sat with Nellie in the hospital, when he sat in Jim's room the night he was shot, and when he watched his sister Polly die—the sense of desperate helplessness as the life of someone he cared for dribbled away before his eyes.

Banks, worried about their Erie loans, sent senior vice-presidents to confer with both sides. From his cell in the Tombs, still waiting trial for murder, Ned Stokes declared Gould unfit to run the Erie. On the stock exchange the Erie's stock fell to a new panic low.

For five days and nights Jay did not leave the opera house. His beard and skin itched constantly and his body felt oily, for he couldn't obtain even a good sponge bath. Tossing about on the slick leather couch in his office, Jay slept no more than three hours a night. Like a crab picking at a dead man's face, his painful cough fastened again to his lungs. Twice he had his old recurring nightmare: He was in the confining hull of a ship with Helen and the children; it was punctured and seawater rushed into it, quickly rising to their chins. When Jay grasped Helen's and George's hands, they were so greased he couldn't hold on, and the current tore them away from him, out the black hole in the hull, away to death.

In the small, dark hours of the morning Jay often rose and stared out the window at the gaslit, bare cobblestones of Twenty-third Street and numbly struggled to understand how he had led himself into such an unholy mess. The situation seemed hopeless. He gripped one leg of his child, the Erie, and Sickles and Vanderbilt held the other, and the two teams would rip the line apart before they finished.

On the sixth morning of the siege, Russell came over early. He found Jay alone in his small office, standing by one of the two floor-length windows.

"What's the matter with you?" asked Russell.

Jay wiped his face with a balled-up, filthy handkerchief. "Nothing."

"You look like you've seen a ghost."

Jay shot him a hard glance. "Do you believe in ghosts, Russell?"

"Not 'specially," said Russell.

Jay turned back to the window and looked down at the workmen trudging to work. "I saw one last night," he said, his voice hollow and a little shaky. "I woke up sometime after midnight." With his face averted from Russell's, he spoke into the window. "It was quiet in here, out in the bull pen. I was wide awake, the way you are at four in the morning and you know you won't get back to sleep. So not to light a match, I got up and came over here to read my watch by the window, the light was so bright."

"Light?" asked Russell in a puzzled voice.

"Moonlight," said Jay. "As bright as noon. The moon was perfectly full, hanging over the roofs like a child's balloon. I could see every building for blocks around, each slate on the roofs, every mullion in the windows, the chimneys, every brick. A voice said, 'Jay.'"

Jay whipped back around to Russell, his face aglow. "Russell, it was him! I jerked around. He was—"

Russell frowned. "Who?"

"Jim!" said Jay. "In his silly colonel's uniform. He was standing right there." Jay pointed an excited finger at the other window. "The moon was so bright, its beams spilled through that window like sunlight. His tunic wasn't gray, the way colors are in moonlight, but blood-red. His face was ruddy, the way it was when he was alive, the yellow piping on his tunic as vivid as the first day I saw it."

" 'Jim,' I said, "you're all right!'

" 'Never better,' he said, giving me a smug smile.

" 'I'm ruining it,' I told him. 'They're tearing apart our company.'

" 'Hey, slack off the sheets,' he said. " 'You're doing everything you can.'

" 'No, no—it's my fault. I pushed too hard. It's the gold thing again.' "

His eyes huge, Jay approached Russell. "Then he was standing right next to me. His big, meaty hand patted me on the shoulder. He clasped me, embraced me, and *I felt him*. Russell, I felt his wool tunic against my palms, on my cheek. He was *warm*, and I smelled talc and bay rum, the way you did in the morning when Andrew got through shaving him. Ghosts aren't warm, are they, Russell? They don't smell, do they?"

Russell looked at him queerly and smiled gently. "No, don't think so."

"I told him I'd always pushed too hard, at the tannery, in the brokerage, as a surveyor, with the Erie—I got us in the gold mess, pushing too hard." Jay bowed his head and turned toward the window. "Then he says, 'Jay, Jay—go easy on yourself. It all works out.'"

"Well," Russell went on, "you ought to listen. He's right enough."

Jay stood stone-still for several more silent moments, face glazed as if back in the moonlight watching Jim's ghost.

Russell stirred and put a question. "Well, what else?"

"Nothing. I woke up at dawn, lying back on the couch."

"It was a dream," said Russell.

"No, it was real!" said Jay excitedly. "I'm telling you bright and red as noon in August. As warm as you." Jay clasped Russell's hand and held it in both of his. Pulling gently on his friend's arm, he looked anxiously in the other's face and asked, "You're real, aren't you?"

Appearing a little nervous at having surrendered his hand, Russell laughed queerly, as if laughing were a strain. He drew his hand back and regarded Jay with a fixed, uneasy stare. "Yep, real enough, I guess. Except for one thing."

"What?"

"It's the wrong time of the month—there wasn't no moon last night. It was black as a bat. There won't be a moon for days."

The seventh morning of the siege found Jay pacing in his small office with Russell Sage on the couch.

"We've got to do something," said Jay. "The line is crippled, and this fight could go on for years."

The court battles would provide careers for platoons of voracious lawyers. Jay's dream of throwing a set of tracks across the continent was shuddering dangerously. Over the last four years he had done everything he could think of to bring it off—allied himself with Daniel Drew and Jim Fisk in order to come to command a great railroad; battled the hardiest railroad magnate in the country; and gained for a while absolute control of the Erie. Now this Sickles had tossed large iron crowbars into the Erie's cogs and gears, and like a giant loco-motive whose very progress destroyed it, the engine that drove Jay's dreams was tearing itself apart as it shook to a halt. If he snatched out any one iron bar that Sickles thrust into the works, the one-legged general was adept and resolute enough to thrust in another. Like the female thief before Solomon, Sickles was willing to kill the baby in order to prevent his losing the contested prize.

"I can't do it," said Jay. "I can't let the Erie be dismembered."

"What, then?" asked Russell.

"Morosini!" shouted Jay.

The head clerk hurried in. "Sir?"

"I'm going to pen a note for you to carry to the General," said Jay. "I want to talk to him personally, only the two of us."

Morosini's mustache twitched eagerly. "Do you have a plan?"

"A little bit of magic?" said Russell with a wry, impish grin.

"No plan, no magic," said Jay, his poker face grim. "I only want to talk, see what can be worked out."

"I'll come with you," said Russell, rising.

"No," said Jay firmly, "let me talk to this grasshopper alone, without his having an opportunity to bluster and posture for someone else."

The next morning at ten o'clock Jay squeezed through the barricaded double doors into the corridor.

The hallway itself dismayed him. The stench of sour piss, sweat, and shit was as rank as a foul pigsty. Heaps of paper, broken file cabinets and worktables, costumes and props from the theater, and scraps of clothing rose against the sides of the corridor with the anarchic barbarity of a wild gorge. It was March 18, and he had been battling Sickles for more than a week. He had lost weight, and his black beard was unkempt. His face was paler than usual, his eyes more sunken, his brow more bulbous, as if his skull were drawing into a living death's-head.

Jay pushed open the makeshift conference room door, a dozen raw planks nailed together by Pinkerton carpenters. Sickles, dressed in a fresh blue uniform, gold braid, and shiny medals, sat at the head of the battered conference table as if to show Jay who would dominate the meeting. His lips were twisted into a victor's cocky, mock-gracious smile.

The first quarter hour went slowly, in wary small talk. That Sickles was an experienced negotiator was apparent at once. He was in no hurry to get down to business, willing to feel Jay out through seemingly casual chatter about the lack of privies, his need for a bath, and how much he wanted a hot meal on a clean tablecloth, much as if this siege were a jolly field exercise during peacetime.

"It seems silly for the two of us to keep banging our heads together," said Jay. Sickles picked up his blond crutch and, as if he needed more room to maneuver, edged his chair back.

"Give me a proposition," said Sickles, a speculative light flaring in his gray eyes.

"I can hang on a long time," said Jay. "The rebels were outnumbered three to one, but it took four years for the Union to bring them to heel. You could be camped out in this privy for a year." Seeming unperturbed by the prospect, Sickles tapped the crutch against the table's rim and smiled with cutting menace.

"I learned how to fight from General Grant," he said. "The only way to win a fight is to inflict *damage*."

Jay nodded to cover another surge of anger. With Sickles swelled up by cleverness, it might be an opportune time to discover if Vanderbilt was truly behind this raid. "Is the Commodore pressing you hard?"

Sickles gave a snort of humor and tossed his head. "What makes you think he's got anything to do with this?"

"He's a difficult man to work for," Jay remarked casually. "My late partner did a few jobs for him in the brokerage business," he lied. "Jim said the Old Walrus—that's what he called him—was impossible to please." While Sickles's cocky smile said he could handle Vanderbilt better than Jim Fisk, from the way his butt squirmed on the chair, Jay reckoned that his barb had struck the quick. At least one card was faceup on the table. Here was one hound none too fond of his huntmaster.

"Let me do some thinking," Sickles said, abruptly ending the meeting. "Shall we sit again tomorrow?"

Jay nodded. He had gotten nowhere, but maybe the wound from his barb would fester.

The next day's meeting went much the same. At the third morning's meeting, Jay dangled a ploy before the General. "Of course, after you have beaten me, your fight has only begun. There's only one president of a line that Mr. Vanderbilt has faith in—himself." Sickles tapped his crutch against the underside of the table, toying with it absently.

And at noon, Jay tossed out the hastily formed plan he had put together to keep the Erie from being dismembered. "You've got proxies of nearly half the shares, I've got nearly half. Suppose I were to resign and vote for you as president?"

"I don't need your votes," said Sickles with sneering pride. "I have my own board."

"While the share price has been falling, don't you think Vanderbilt has been buying?" said Jay in a deceptively mild and questioning tone. "Many of the proxies that you think still back you have been sold to him by the rabbits who signed them." He paused to allow his next sentence its full importance. "The new owner can withdraw his proxy. Do you really think Vanderbilt wants anyone but himself and his son to run this line?" Sickles's gray eyes stared fixedly as if the notion of Vanderbilt's double-crossing him had caused him plenty of thought. His lips pursed. He pulled his crutch to his side and poked the floor with its rubber tip.

"I'll take my chances."

"You don't have to take that risk," said Jay in a tone of friendly reasonableness. "Not if we vote together."

"How's that?"

By the intense interest in his face, Jay judged Sickles well hooked. "According to the Erie bylaws," he said, "once the majority of shareholders vote in a president, who sits for a five-year term, it takes a three-quarters vote to recall him."

"Five years," mused Sickles. "Three-quarters." The crutch swung about absently, a gesture Jay was learning meant that the General was thinking hard. "Vanderbilt's not likely to ever obtain that many votes."

"Right."

Sickles shifted uneasily. "And what do *you* get?"

"The opera house and a promise to time the announcement myself."

"To make a few bucks on the stock. It'll go up when this trouble's resolved." He pressed the top of the crutch against his cheek and gave Jay an intent stare. "And the Commodore won't be able to remove me?"

Jay gave him the thinnest of smiles. "I wrote that bylaw myself," he said, "so I couldn't be thrown out of office. It's worked so far— till you crashed in here. I'd say it's not likely."

Sickles leaned back and mused, "I could run the line to suit myself. Pay myself whatever I wanted to."

"I'll draw up the papers and meet you here this afternoon," said Jay, "when you and I—since to all intents and purposes we are now the Erie—shall pass board resolutions to please ourselves."

After he and Sickles met that afternoon, Jay explained the arrangement to Russell Sage, who immediately wanted to buy Erie shares, too. They sent a messenger to Dick Morris, Jay's lead broker, and gave him instructions on their purchases.

After he had left, Russell asked, "Well, is this the end of the Erie for you?"

Jay replied with a grin, "The General may well run the line into the ground. Nothing was said that I couldn't buy Erie shares in the future."

Russell laughed.

Three mornings later, after he and Russell had bought all the Erie shares they could finance, Jay once more sat across the conference table from a puffed-up Sickles. In front of him was his unsigned resignation from the Erie, the last paper to sign to make the deal final. Sickles dipped the pen in the inkpot and held it out, but Jay sat back, only staring at it.

This was not only the end of a chapter of his life, but the end of an entire part of the book. Sad, he glanced around the battered conference room, wondering what Jim, wherever he was, was thinking about this deal. Certainly Jim's ghost was furious over the destruction of the opera house, that much was sure. That long-ago foggy night, Jim and Jay had scrambled over the Hudson together, fighting and scrapping. A few nights later on the pier at Taylor's Inn Jim had given the Commodore's thugs a good thrashing.

Sickles's hand silently urged forward the pen, but Jay only smiled thinly. A more intense feeling of regret and sadness came over him. Together Jim and he had made the Erie sing. They had shoved gold back down Mr. Vanderbilt's throat, and saved themselves in the midst of the century's worst crash. To throw off the intense feeling, Jay shook his head at Sickles, who frowned in bewilderment, as if fearful that he was about to be tricked out of his victory. Then those damn love notes of Jim's to Josie, the trials, the shooting.

It was all over, all gone, and it would never be the same. Jay shot the worried Sickles a smile, daintily accepted the pen from his opponent, and scribbled his signature with a flourish. He shoved the document back to the General. Appearing relieved, Sickles insisted on a glass of sweet sherry to celebrate the brittle occasion.

"You're not a bad fellow, Gould," he said, large in victory. "Too bad we weren't on the same side."

Having no similar feeling, Jay stood up and said, "My only regret is that neither Jim nor I will see the Commodore's face when he finds out that, after all, he won't get the Erie."

"I won't see it, either," said Sickles with a smirk, "but you can be sure that his roar will be heard from one end of Manhattan to the other." A gloating wave drove his chuckle. "But then, he's a man can use some disappointment. Heaven itself won't be large enough for him." Although it was distasteful, Jay shook hands with Sickles.

"I'm off to Delmonico's," Jay said. "I promised to buy a dozen reporters oysters and champagne." With a glass of champagne raised to Jim, he would announce his resignation before the opening of the afternoon stock market session.

"A dozen!" snorted Sickles. "Wherever the Sphinx of the Street deigns to speak, there will be a hundred of the thirsty swine."

Sphinx, indeed. Announcing his own relinquishing of the Erie was no occasion for champagne. Behind his poker face Jay felt like a goat being driven down Wall Street to slaughter.

After Jay announced to the reporters that he was resigning in favor of General Sickles, Erie shares climbed five dollars within an hour.

Over the next few days they jumped twenty dollars. Before the week was out Jay and Russell judged the market to be at its peak and sold out their entire position, new and old shares, to thousands of buyers eager for the new military board of directors to carry their investment on to riches.

Combined with his profits from Black Friday, Jay came away with millions in profits from his four years with the Erie. If the death of Jim and the loss of Annabelle had rung down the curtain on the most intoxicating part of his life, the loss of the Erie brought to a close all his dreams of making himself into a great man. He was rich now, but that was all. A smart rich man, true, but more accurately, a smart, sickly, hated rich man. His youthful dreams—of regaining the paradise he had before Ma died—all that was ashes. Only a fool would blow into those ashes and attempt to raise a phoenix. He would in fact be lucky in his lifetime to overcome the scorn and hatred of most others toward him. Last week a columnist in the *Tribune* had called him "the most hated man in America," and Jay had no reason to believe the statement was wrong.

The *Times* summed up the attitude of much of New York: "There is but one man in Wall Street today whom men watch, and whose name, built upon ruins, carries with it the whisper of ruin. He is one whose nature is best described by the record of what he has done, and by the burden of hatred and dread that, loaded upon him for two and one-half years, has not turned him one hair from any place that promised him gain and the most bitter ruin for his chance opponents. They that curse him do not do it blindly, but as cursing one who massacres after victory."

All this hatred, much of which puzzled Jay, had come about because of his unrealistic dreams—the gossamer stuff in his head.

When he thought this, as he often did on his midnight walks, his mind recoiled in horror from what others commonly thought of him. It seemed incredible that bright dreams—mere nerves dancing in his head—could have the destructive power of a runaway locomotive. This vision of what he had done to himself frightened him, and as much as he might want more of the "jolly warmth" that his life with Jim had held, he was now fearful of any life not based on reality and highly sober assessments of it.

He could continue in the rail business. After all, it was the field about which he knew the most. But he would make sure that his dreams never again got the better of him. He saw no way a man could live without dreams, but they would have to serve his more prosaic side, lest they further destroy himself and his family.

"Well, Pa," asked William Vanderbilt four days later as he drove his father downtown to the Central's offices, "what nonsense now? Attack General Sickles and his battery of generals?"

Outside the carriage a nasty March rain was blowing. Cornelius, ignoring the rain that whipped into his face, was hunched in his corner of the carriage, a buffalo robe spread over his knees. He peered out of the window at Broadway's immense river of carriages and vans, stovepipe hats and bonnets, shopgirls and urchins.

"No," the old man growled.

"No," William said, mimicking his father's growl. "Good! I only wish I believed you. I totaled up what this last adventure of yours cost us."

"Enough, William."

"No, not enough!" insisted William. "You want your empire to live on after you, right? You want me to carry it on. Adventures like this, in which we overextend ourselves in order to triple our size at a stroke, must succeed or cripple us. No firm can take these chances over and over without eventually failing. I can take the Central, make it grow naturally, and it will last another *ten* generations. Another 'coup' like this last and it's us who will be mangled by the Street." Cornelius turned to glare at William. His white hair flew about his head, his cheeks were rosy from rain and anger, and he bared his rotten teeth.

"Gould!" he shouted. "Gould! Gould! Gould!"

"Sir?" Without his anger, William wondered, how would his father find the energy to stay alive?

"He's me!" roared Cornelius. "I've met myself of fifty years ago in battle. Now—if I had a partner like him, or a *son*—" He glared accusingly at William, whose eyes broke away from his father's.

563

William ground his teeth to hold his tongue. He had never pleased his father, but then nobody ever had. Only his dead brother George Washington Vanderbilt had been the ideal son, but William was completely certain that if either Jay Gould or his late brother endured twenty years as Cornelius's son, it would all come down to the same in the end, for no grown man could develop, grow, and flourish under twenty years of a powerful father's heavy-handed, autocratic rule. William sighed. Power—the large, raw, cunningly directed energy that managed good-sized chunks of the world—was not passed easily from father to son. Maybe that was a good thing, or an all-powerful dynasty would have come to rule the earth centuries ago and precluded William or his father from owning so much as a clod of it.

"Henceforth," said Cornelius, nodding vigorously, "I shall have nothing more to do with Jay Gould, except to defend myself."

Within a week General Sickles moved the Erie offices out of the opera house back to the company's former mundane quarters on West Street.

Left in the muddy offices on the third floor with Morosini and a dozen clerks, Jay had the opera house disinfected and put it up for sale for the benefit of Jim's estate, money for Lucy and Jim's children.

The following week Jay announced to Morosini that the opera house had a buyer and that he was taking a two-month vacation in Greece, France, and Italy.

"Am I out of a job?" asked Morosini.

Jay grinned and shook his head. "On the contrary, you'll be quite busy."

Morosini's thin face bobbed like a robin's at the sight of the morning's first worm. "Doing what?"

"While I am gone you will open offices for a new firm called Gould and Company," said Jay. "Of which I want to give you some shares in appreciation of your years of loyalty. This country still needs transcontinental railroads, and I still think I am the man to build them. Although at a somewhat less hectic pace than in the past. So does Mr. Sage, who's prepared to add his capital to mine. The management of the Union Pacific are in a three-way squabble that by fall will boil over and cripple all sides. We'll open a new brokerage account with Dick Morris, and while I'm gone, I want you to assist Mr. Sage in quietly building up a position in Union Pacific stock. Very quietly, if you follow me."

Morosini's Italian eyes glowed with excited pleasure. "Yes, yes—indeed, I follow you!"

Jay's hand toyed with a fragment of his beard. "I'll keep in touch by wire," he said, smiling.

"Yes, sir." His face was suffused with pleasure.

"Without Jim," Jay went on, "it'll never be the same, but maybe in two or three years the three of us will send a Union Pacific train from New York to San Francisco without a single stop."

A NOTE
TO THE READER

The historical canvas on which are painted the Erie wars, the scandals of the Grant administration, and the crash of the gold market is vast and richly peopled, and it is too large and complex a canvas for a novel to completely depict. To create this story I have bent history and freely mixed fact, speculation, and fiction. Names have been changed, characters created, and incidents altered or devised so that despite having historical counterparts, all the characters are fictional. As an example, Annabelle Stokes is a compilation of several historical figures, not all young and female. Jay Gould's children are here born earlier than in historical fact. The Cornelius Vanderbilt of history was not as involved in the gold crash as he is in this story. Ulysses S. Grant's wife was actually Julia T. Dent before she married, not Jenny Gantry; however, her relatives did take advantage of their sister's position at the White House to attempt to enrich themselves.

This is fiction suggested by history—that is, the novel, the drama, that these historical accounts, newspaper stories, myths, ghosts, and legends inspired.

—D. P.

ACKNOWLEDGMENTS

Jubilee Jim and the Wizard of Wall Street was written with the help of many people. Fellow writers Richard Strong, Katie Anders, Carolyn Wheat, Donna Meyer, Roy Sorrels, and Elizabeth Powers listened to most of the book and offered numerous suggestions, without which the novel would be a poorer story. The book collections at the New-York Historical Society and the New York Public Library were invaluable, and their staffs were always generous with their time. My literary agent, Milly Marmur, made suggestions that showed how well she understands the literary as well as the commercial portion of her business. The novel was aided immensely by the enthusiastic, sure editorial hand of Meg Blackstone at Dutton. Copy editors save writers and readers untold vexation. *Jubilee Jim*'s Bill Reynolds had his work cut out for him, and he did a wonderful job of helping me make the fuzzy more clear, the awkward more graceful, and the grammatically lame able to walk.

And most of all, thanks to Diane, my wife, for putting up with my writing *Jubilee Jim*. God knows how spouses put up with writers, but a special corner of heaven should be reserved for them.
